GEARS OF WAR 3

COALITION'S END

KAREN TRAVISS

Based on the Xbox 360 video game series
from Epic Games / Microsoft

orbit

www.orbitbooks.net

ORBIT

First published in the United States in 2011 by Galley Books,
a division of Simon & Schuster, Inc.
First published in Great Britain in 2011 by Orbit

A CIP catalogue record for this book
is available from the British Library.

ISBN 978-0-356-50104-8

Typeset in Electra by Palimpsest Book Production Limited,
Falkirk Stirlingshire
Printed and bound in Great Britain by
CPI Mackays, Chatham ME5 8TD

Orbit
An imprint of
Little, Brown Book Group
100 Victoria Embankment
London EC4Y 0DY

An Hachette UK Company
www.hachette.co.uk

www.orbitbooks.net

To the memory of the British Merchant Navy seamen of the Arctic Convoys (1941–1945) who gave their lives to ensure that vital war supplies reached Russia, and for all 35,000 British merchant crew—men and women—who died during World War II to keep the "Red Duster" flying.

ACKNOWLEDGMENTS

My thanks go to Mike Capps, Rod Fergusson, and Cliff Bleszinski at Epic Games, for letting me loose in their wonderful universe; Epic Games cinematics director Greg Mitchell, DC Comics editor Jim Chadwick, and the outrageously talented voice cast of *Gears of War 3*, for striking sparks off me; and Ed Schlesinger (senior editor, Gallery Books/Pocket Books) and Anthony Ziccardi (VP, Deputy Publisher, Gallery Books/Pocket Books), for making it happen. The whole is indeed greater than the sum of the parts—and a hell of a lot of fun.

GEARS OF WAR TIMELINE

(ALL DATES ARE SHOWN IN THE MODERN SERAN
CALENDAR—BEFORE EMERGENCE OR AFTER
EMERGENCE.)

80 B.E. (APPROXIMATE)—A long-running global conflict begins to sweep the world of Sera as the Coalition of Ordered Governments (COG) and the Union of Independent Republics (UIR) fight over imulsion energy resources. This becomes known as the Pendulum Wars.

17 B.E.—Infantry lieutenant Victor Hoffman holds the besieged Anvil Gate garrison against UIR forces and makes his name. Adam Fenix—a weapons physicist—leaves the army to work on his dream of the ultimate deterrent, an orbital laser weapon to end the Pendulum Wars.

9 B.E.—Adam's wife, Elain, a biologist, goes missing in the underground caves of Jacinto, leaving him with a young son to care for—Marcus.

4 B.E.—Marcus Fenix enlists in the COG army against his father Adam's wishes, serving alongside his boyhood friend Carlos Santiago.

3. B.E.—Carlos's younger brother Dominic—"Dom"—enlists.

2 B.E.—Intelligence reveals the UIR is close to building its own satellite weapons system. A commando raid headed by Hoffman is staged to sabotage the UIR research station at Aspho and seize its data. Carlos Santiago and Major Helena Stroud (Anya Stroud's mother) are killed in the battle. Hoffman, Marcus and Dom are decorated for gallantry. The seized data enables Adam Fenix to perfect his Hammer of Dawn orbital laser, which eventually brings the UIR to the negotiating table.

SIX WEEKS BEFORE EMERGENCE DAY—The UIR surrenders and the Pendulum Wars are finally at an end, although a handful of small UIR states, including Gorasnaya, refuse to accept the armistice and vow to fight on.

EMERGENCE DAY—With no apparent warning or motive, an unknown species of sentient creatures—the Locust Horde—erupts from underground caverns and attacks cities across Sera simultaneously. A quarter of Sera's population is slaughtered in the initial attack. E-Day, as it becomes known, is the start of a fifteen-year war for survival.

1 A.E.—The COG, fighting a losing rearguard action against the Locust, is driven back to Ephyra, the granite plateau where the Locust can't tunnel. In a desperate bid to stop the Locust advance, new COG Chairman Richard Prescott orders the destruction of all Sera's major cities using the Hammer of Dawn. Although civilians are urged to take refuge in Ephyra, few can reach the plateau in time and many millions die in the Hammer strikes.

2 A.E.—The Locust, slowed but not stopped by the global destruction, are back in even greater numbers. The few civilians outside Ephyra who survived the Hammer strikes band together in gangs, living hand to mouth in the ruins. The Stranded, as they call themselves, see the COG as an enemy.

10 A.E.—The Locust attack Ephyra. Sergeant Marcus Fenix disobeys Colonel Hoffman's orders and tries to rescue his father, a decision that leads to the fall of Ephyra. Adam Fenix is buried in the rubble of the Fenix mansion when the Locust attack, and Marcus faces a court martial. His death sentence is commuted to forty years in Jacinto's notoriously brutal prison, nicknamed the Slab.

14 A.E.—The Locust overrun the prison, and the inmates are set free—except Marcus. Dom Santiago rescues him and Marcus rejoins the COG army. Using Adam Fenix's research notes on the Locust tunnels, the COG detonates a Lightmass bomb underground, but the "grubs" are back in force a few weeks later. The human population of Sera has been reduced from billions to a handful, and the last COG bastion— Jacinto—is now under threat.

14 A.E.—Chairman Prescott plans a final all-out assault on the Locust warrens by tunneling into their strongholds around Jacinto. The Locust in turn begin their push to take the city. The COG finds that the Locust have been waging an underground war with another aggressive species known as the Lambent, and were forced to the surface by them.

Marcus and his fellow Gears find recordings by Adam Fenix in the Locust command center, describing how to flood the tunnels, and the COG makes a final, desperate decision to wipe out the advancing Locust. Evacuating the city, they deploy the Hammer of Dawn to sink Jacinto and drown the Locust forces.

14 A.E.—The column of refugees moves from place to place evading the few surviving Locust, eventually settling on a remote volcanic island that the Locust never reached— Vectes, a former COG naval base. The local population has never seen a "grub," but is plagued by Stranded pirate gangs. Forming an unexpected alliance with the last of the UIR's Gorasnayans, the COG newcomers and the islanders drive off Stranded pirate gangs and begin to rebuild civilization.

15 A.E.—The brief peace is shattered when Lambent life-forms appear in the seas around Vectes, destroying ships and sinking a Gorasnayan imulsion drilling platform, the last remaining source of imulsion fuel. Chairman Prescott is found to have an encrypted data disk, the contents of which he refuses to reveal to Colonel Hoffman. The remnant of the COG is now effectively besieged on Vectes, fending off Lambent attacks from the sea.

PROLOGUE

TRANSMISSION BEGINS.

LAMBENCY DETECTED IN INCREASING RANGE
OF EXISTING LIFE-FORMS INCLUDING
LEVIATHANS AND SMALLER MARINE
CREATURES. TWO PREVIOUSLY UNKNOWN
SPECIES NOW SPREADING: AMBULANT POLYPS
APPEAR TO PARASITIZE FAST-GROWING
ORGANIC STRUCTURES NICKNAMED "STALKS."
POLYPS SELF-DETONATE. PLEASE ADVISE. DATA
AND IMAGES TO FOLLOW. COG PERSONNEL
FENIX, SANTIAGO, STROUD UNHARMED.

TRANSMISSION ENDS.

(TRANSMISSION SOURCE: UNKNOWN. RECEIVING
STATION: UNKNOWN.)

**BOATHOUSE 7 WORKSHOP, NAVAL BASE, NEW
JACINTO: LATE STORM, 15 A.E.**

Sam's laughing her ass off.

She's been fixing her bike and giggling to herself for a

while now, and then she just busts out laughing like someone invisible told her a joke. Now, I get moments like that too. But it's the hooch. You understand, don't ya? It's been a long, long war. We all cope the best way we can.

So I ask her. "You gonna share?"

She's almost crying. She has to set down the wrench while she gets her breath back. "Dizzy, have you seen Baird?"

"Yeah, plenty. But he ain't *that* funny."

"I mean his new workshop. His *private* workshop."

"Can't say I have."

"He's . . ." She takes a deep breath and tries again. "It's . . ." Finally, she screws her eyes shut and takes a run at it, 'cos it's the only way she's gonna get it out, I reckon. "It's in the old lavatory block. He's set up his kit in one of the stalls and he's using the crapper for a seat. I *saw* him."

That does it. She's bent right over and I can't hear anything now except wheezy gulps of air, but eventually she straightens up and there's tears running down her face. Damn, it's a nice thing to see someone laugh like that. However bad things get—and shit, they're bad right now—some folks can still see the funny side of life.

See, if you don't concentrate on the good stuff, you go crazy. You gotta laugh, or you gotta love, or you gotta drink; that's how you get through the day when you've been at war for as long as anyone can remember. The one thing you just can't do is look it in the eye and see just what a goddamn mess we're in, or else you end up like Hoffman. Or Marcus. Both of 'em with the weight of the world on their shoulders, and a lot older than either of 'em needs to be.

But . . . lord-almighty know-it-all Corporal Damon S. Baird sitting on the john, all full of piss and importance? This I gotta see. "I better go take a look."

"He's out on patrol this morning," Sam says. "I'll take you

over there tonight. We'll grab a camera from Barber and stalk him. Record the moment for posterity." She starts giggling again. "Caption contest. Baird, full of shit . . . ah, so many jokes, so little time."

"What's he doing, then? What's so secret?"

"No idea. I think Hoffman's given him something to fix." She winks. "But he spends a lot of time tinkering with that bot, too. I think they want to be alone."

She's laughed herself out now, so she carries on working on her bike. But I can see she's still thinking about Baird sat on his porcelain throne, because every so often I catch her grinning to herself.

"Sometimes I'm glad he's such a tosser," she says. "I need an outlet, you know? A focus for my negative side. Like that thing they have on ships' hulls." She gestures with the wrench, frowning like she's forgotten the word. "Come on, Diz, what's it called? You were in the merchant navy. You know what I mean."

"A sacrifice block?"

"That's it."

"It takes the hit and stops the other metal getting corroded."

"Exactly. That's it. Baird's my sacrifice block."

She laughs and gets back to work. The world ain't funny at all, truth to tell. We've run and run for fifteen years, and now we've painted our asses into a corner. This island's just about the last nice place left on Sera because the Locust couldn't tunnel this far out into the Serrano Ocean. But the Lambent—those assholes found us. They're worse than those goddamn grubs, believe me, and now they're here, right on our coast, blowing up our boats. They *detonate*, see. Walking bombs. They come in all shapes and sizes—crab things called polyps, tree things called stalks, even whale-sized things and butt-ugly eels—and they got this weird glow about 'em kinda like jellyfish. That was why the grubs came out of their tunnels and started killing us. The glowies was down there killing *them*.

Well, that's one mystery solved, anyhow, even if we still don't know squat about the glowies. And now we got nowhere left to run.

Damn shame. It's a real pretty island. I thought it'd be a good place for my girls to grow up safe, but all I done was drag 'em somewhere else even more dangerous. Maybe we shoulda stayed Stranded. You can hide better. You're just a little rat in a sewer. Nobody knows you're there.

Anyway, it's all quiet again—for the moment. I'm changing Betty's gearbox fluid. The old girl's showing her age. It's tough to find parts for grindlift rigs, so Baird helps me make 'em. He ain't so bad really. As long as I keep his mind on the nuts and bolts, he forgets that he thinks I'm a bum.

So anyway—I'm under Betty, draining her reservoir, and I hear the doors open. I see boots walk by and I hear Colonel Hoffman say, "Sam, you got five minutes?"

"Yes, sir," she says, and the two of them wander outside. She's gone for some time, maybe half an hour. By the time she comes back, I'm working on Betty's electrics, so I can see Sam's face as soon as she walks in. She don't look so happy now.

"What did Hoffman want?" I ask. The colonel's real strung out at the moment. It's the latest polyp attack. It's started him fretting over Anvil Gate again, just when he oughta be forgetting it. "Everything okay?"

"He finally told me how my dad got killed." Sam sort of shakes her head. "He thought it was time I knew. All this polyp siege shit's brought it back to him."

The siege of Anvil Gate was more than thirty years ago—way back in the Pendulum Wars, when we didn't even know what a grub or a glowie was. Hoffman's taken his own sweet time with that. It ain't like him to be so squeamish. Sam's named after her old man. He never lived to see her born. Damn, that just breaks my heart.

"You wanna talk about it, Sam?"

"It was quick." I can see she's hurting. "But Dad decided to stay." And then she just stops.

I got daughters. I can handle this. "Sorry, sweetie. I don't understand."

"He stayed to defend the fort," she says, picking up the wrench again like she needs something to take her mind off the news. "Hoffman said Dad had the chance to leave Anvil Gate when they evacuated the civvies. He could have left with my mother. But Hoffman said he wouldn't leave his platoon behind."

Now most folks would call that a hero. Damn right: a man who stands his ground for his buddies, *that's* a hero. The best man you can be. But I can tell Sam don't agree with that. Gear or not, she's still a little girl who never knew her daddy. I gotta pick my words real careful now.

"Must have been a tough call for him, Sam."

She nods and starts working on the bike again. But her mind ain't on it. She's just going through the motions, working a plug this way and that without really moving it.

"I hate myself," she says at last. "All I could think at first was that he left me and Mum to stay with his mates. But I'm a Gear. I *know* it's not that simple."

No, it ain't, and it ain't simple being a dad, neither. I didn't exactly choose to join the army, see. I got drafted— Operation Lifeboat, Prescott's smartass idea to turn Stranded bums like me into Gears. You do your bit, and the government gives your family food and medicine. I let the COG press-gang me to save my little girls.

You'd be amazed what a fella will do for his kids.

"Your dad must've been real scared that you and your

mom wouldn't make it if he let the Indies win," I say at last. "Like I was real scared my girls would die if I didn't join the COG. Hardest goddamn thing I ever did."

I didn't know Sergeant Samuel Byrne, but Colonel Hoffman says he was a good man. That's word enough for me. I'm just telling Sam—Samantha Byrne—the truth as I see it.

She looks up at me, eyes kinda glassy. You know what I like about her? She ain't afraid to admit what she's feeling. Tough don't mean keeping it all bottled up. I hope she's getting somewhere with Dom—poor bastard, still grieving—because they'd fit real well together. It'd do 'em both the power of good.

"Thanks, Diz," she says. "I'll be okay."

You can look at it a couple of ways. Either Sam's dad stayed at his post, or else he abandoned his family. I don't know why Sam's dad chose to stay and die. He had a whole lot of reasons, I reckon. Some of them wouldn't make a speck of sense to anyone who wasn't there, so they can just shut their mouths until they're in the same shit and have to make the call. But I know Gears will die for their buddies. And I know that I'd do anything to make sure my girls grow up, even if I'm not there to see it.

Because that's what good fathers do. And your kids might not always love you for doing what's best for 'em, but that goes with the territory.

The right thing ain't always the *popular* thing for a fella to do.

You just gotta hope that one day they all understand what we had to do to survive.

CHAPTER 1

*So how many different varieties do those frigging glowies
come in?*

(Major Gill Gettner, Raven pilot,
seeing the first Lambent stalks emerge on Vectes)

**KING RAVEN KR-80 ON PATROL OVER NORTHERN
VECTES; TEN DAYS AFTER THE INITIAL LAMBENT
LANDING, STORM, 15 A.E.**

Damon Baird tried to recall exactly how he'd felt on E-Day
when he saw his first grub.

He remembered the detail but not much of the emotion
that went with it. But he guessed it had been pretty much
like he felt now; a churning gut, a tight scalp, and a hardwired animal reflex to run or fight. He didn't know why
these stalks looked different from the others, or what those
big red blisters were doing on their trunks, but he knew at an
instinctive level that he either had to blow the shit out of
them or run like hell.

Being twenty meters off the ground in a hovering Raven
ruled out making a run for it. He sighted up on the nearest
blister instead.

"Control, this is KR-Eight-Zero, contact in grid echo-five,"

Gettner repeated, like she was explaining it to the thickest kid in the class. "*Major stalk incursion.* Three of the bastards have just erupted. I know Delta Squad's a regular mini-army, but we could still do with some help."

Mathieson's voice never rose above flat calm, no matter how much shit hit the fan. "I heard you, Eight-Zero, but echo-five is inland. Please confirm your position."

"I know it's damn well *inland,* Mathieson. That's why it's significant and why we'd like a little backup. They shouldn't be *here.*"

"How many polyps?"

"None. *Yet.*"

"Understood, Major. Stand by."

Baird adjusted his aim again. Gettner was a charmlessly acid bitch, but she was right. The stalks, the monstrous tree-like growths they'd first encountered only weeks ago, should have been a long way out to sea.

No. We got that wrong. They're here, and that means they've found a way to come up through granite. This place was supposed to be safe.

Yeah, like Ephyra. Like Jacinto. Why do I always believe that crap?

The stalks had already sunk a warship, an imulsion drilling platform, and any number of small boats. Maybe busting up through igneous rock was all in a day's work for them.

"Fenix, I can't hold this bird here all day," Gettner said. "Those things had better shit or get off the pot."

"Yeah, I'll pass that on, Major." Marcus stared down the sights of the door gun while Nat Barber, Gettner's crew chief, took recon images. "How long has it been now?"

"Two minutes," she said.

"Give 'em ten."

"Okay, talk among yourselves, kids. I'll just waste some more of our extremely limited fuel."

This wasn't the way it was supposed to be. Stalks erupted in seconds, and then the polyps—evil little shits, all legs and fangs—poured off them like giant homicidal crabs and blew up in your damn face. But there was no sign of them. The stalks just stood there, glowing and waiting.

I've never seen blisters on stalks before.

The more Baird looked, the more he could see a cross on the membrane, almost dividing it into quadrants.

"Okay, what the fuck *are* those things?" he asked, more for the comfort of hearing his own voice than to get an answer. "The blisters, I mean. Answers on a postcard, please."

Dom Santiago shrugged. "Seed pods."

"That makes me feel so much better."

"Well, you asked." Dom looked over his shoulder. "Hey, Cole Train? That remind you of anything?"

"Yeah," Cole said. Everyone—six Gears and a dog—was jostling for position on the edge of the crew bay, trying to get a clear shot for when the inevitable polyp spatterfest kicked off. "Those weeds you get on old construction sites. The ones with those big seed heads that go off with a bang. Man, I used to laugh my ass off playing with those as a kid."

"Me too," Dom said. "Don't tell me you never popped them to see how far the seeds would shoot, Baird."

Baird was reminded of his solitary, miserable childhood again. He was a rich kid from a founding family. He didn't have adventures in forbidden places. He had extra lessons.

"I never played on construction sites," he said, feigning disdain but wishing he'd climbed over a KEEP OUT sign just once in his youth. "Dear Mama would send the butler to do that shit for me. The bitch . . ."

Dom turned to Bernie Mataki. "What about you, Sarge?"

"We didn't have them on the South Islands."

"Construction sites?"

"No, that kind of plant."

Marcus was hunched over the door gun, scowling at the stalks. "Ephyran balsam," he said. Oh, so he knew what Dom meant, too. "Gunweed. *Glandulifera ephyrica*."

Marcus Fenix had never played on any damn building site, Baird was sure of that. His family—no, his *dynasty*—was even richer than Baird's. The Bairds had a few nice paintings and a gated mansion: the Fenixes had a walled estate and more priceless art treasures than the frigging National Museum of Ephyra.

And now nobody had anything. The grubs believed in equality, at least.

"Oh, yeah, I forgot," Baird said. "You and Dom, carefree childhood buddies, yadda yadda yadda . . ."

"My *mom*," Marcus growled, "used to take me for walks around the Hollow. My mom the *biologist*."

Dom gave Baird a discreet jab with his elbow. "Just zip it, Baird."

He said it in a weary voice, barely audible over the noise of the Raven even on the radio link. So Marcus had lost his folks; big deal. Everyone else had, too, and Baird didn't think the how and the when of it made much difference now. But he shut up anyway. He kept his eyes on the blisters as the Raven hovered level with the tops of the branches, feeling the air buffeting and drying his eyes. He didn't dare look away to put on his goggles. Mac the asshole-hound squeezed his head between Baird's leg and Dom as if he was keeping an eye on the stalks too.

Five minutes . . . six . . . and still nobody said a word.

Then the blister that Baird was focused on suddenly stopped throbbing.

"Whoa, heads up. Here it comes." Baird's finger tightened on the Lancer's trigger. "Any second now."

"Steady, people," Marcus said. "Make every round count."

Then the blisters stopped pulsing, all of them, all at once. The red glowing patches dimmed like cooling embers and turned a dull gray. It was hard to define, but Baird felt he was watching something set hard like concrete, all the life draining out of it.

"I think the show's over, baby," Cole said. "Hell, I want my money back. I paid to see glowie crabs."

Gettner backed the Raven away from the stalks, climbing ten meters to do a slow loop above the branches.

"Okay, I'm setting down," she said. "They look dead to me."

"You sure?" Baird asked.

"You're the glowie expert. You've sawed up a dead stalk. Can't you tell?"

Baird shrugged. Nobody knew enough about the Lambent yet, not even him. "I have trust issues. Especially when it comes to glowies."

So where were the polyps? His best guess was that they didn't emerge *from* stalks but *with* them, just like they turned up with Lambent leviathans. It wasn't a comforting thought either way. It was just a missing piece of a jigsaw puzzle, and Baird didn't like uncertainty.

Gettner landed in the open field a good fifty meters away from the stalks, so maybe she was having second thoughts. "Okay. Let's get this over with."

Mac rumbled deep in his throat, eyes fixed on the gnarled trunks. Bernie bent down to talk to him. The mutt was nearly hip-height, a leggy, scruffy deerhound thing with a gray wiry coat and a mournful thousand-yard stare. He was still peppered with small burns from his last skirmish with the polyps.

"No glowies, sweetie," Bernie said. "It's okay. No nasty polyps."

"He's got some scores to settle," Baird said.

"Haven't we all." She jumped down and wound Mac's leash tight around her hand. "Well, at least we get to examine the things properly now."

Marcus led the slow walk across to the stalks with the caution usually reserved for an unexploded bomb.

"I'm counting on the dog," he said. "Animals sense all this shit long before we do."

Baird gave Mac a wide berth. He might have looked lovable and slobbery now, but Baird had seen him nearly rip a guy's scalp off. The locals trained their dogs to run loose and attack Stranded raiding parties. Baird didn't have a problem with that, seeing as most of the Stranded gangs were vermin who only came to Vectes for a spot of rape and pillage. He just didn't want to test how good the dog's asshole recognition skills were.

Dom walked up to the first stalk and rapped his knuckles against the rock-hard trunk. "They look like weathered stone."

"Yeah." If Baird hadn't seen the stalks erupt from the soil he'd have been willing to believe they'd been there for centuries. There was no sign that they'd ever been alive. "Or petrified wood."

Marcus looked down the trunk. "Wonder what it uses for roots?"

"Look, this is a volcanic island," Baird said. "We should be safe here. If this place is grub-proof, why isn't it glowie-proof?"

"Yeah, good point." To Baird's ears, that was as good as a medal. Marcus wasn't big on praise. "At least we can find out more about these things now they're not growing in a hundred meters of water."

Marcus paused and pressed his finger to his earpiece, listening to some incoming message. He shut his eyes for a couple of seconds, a sure sign that the news pissed him off.

"Yeah, I hear you, Colonel," he said. "No, we found the dog . . . yeah, Bernie's fine . . . what is he now, a goddamn geologist? Okay, we'll secure the area and wait until you show. Fenix out."

Bernie looked at Marcus, jaw clenched, doing that sergeant-to-sergeant telepathy thing. Baird watched, fascinated.

"Oh," she said ominously.

Marcus pulled off his do-rag for a moment and scratched his scalp, showing a lot more gray in his black hair than Baird remembered. It was rare—and weird—to see him bareheaded. Somehow just removing a scrap of faded black cloth made him look human and vulnerable, not a hairy-assed war hero at all.

"Hoffman's bitching that you didn't tell him you were off-camp," Marcus said, retying the do-rag. "And the Chairman's coming to take a look for himself."

That was all they needed—a royal visit from Prescott. "Is he bored or something?" Baird said. "'Cause if he is, there's got to be some latrine that needs digging."

"Just humor him, Baird." Marcus might have meant Hoffman, come to that. "He's sending Dizzy to uproot one of these things for analysis, wherever the hell he thinks we're going to get *that*."

Bernie slipped off Mac's leash and let him sniff around. "That'll be you, Blondie. You're the nearest thing we've got to a scientist these days." She tapped Baird's chest plate. "Just don't lose that bloody disc. It's all Hoffman goes on about."

Baird never forgot about the data disc. He kept it tucked inside his armor. He slept with it under his mattress. He even kept it within arm's reach when he took a shower. Hoffman was counting on him to decrypt the thing and his technical honor depended on it.

"Wow, you two have some really boring pillow talk,

Granny," he said, pulling it out to waft it under her nose. "But it's kind of hard to look Prescott in the eye. I think he knows I've got it."

Mac barked a couple of times. Bernie turned to see where he was. "And what's he going to do about it? Wrestle you to the ground and take it off you?" She set off to see what the dog was yapping about. "Actually, I'd pay good money to see that."

Cole ambled over to Baird and gave the stalk an experimental prod with his boot. "Weird shit, baby."

"Yeah, the whole frigging world's made of weird these days."

Mac kept barking. Cole looked past Baird and frowned into the distance. "I ain't a dog expert," he said, "but Mac's the silent and deadly kind of puppy. He don't usually bark."

Marcus and Dom turned around at the same time. Bernie had caught up with Mac and was watching him cast around with his nose buried in the grass as if he was picking up a scent. Bernie slipped her rifle off her back and gestured to Marcus to come over.

"I don't think he's found a bone," Baird said.

A herd of cows was watching from the next field, heads poking over the low hedge. Then they all wheeled around and cantered away as if something had spooked them. Mac started growling, eyes fixed on a spot on the ground.

Baird braced for the worst. Mac pawed the grass, still growling, then began digging frantically, but Bernie yanked him back by his collar.

"I think we should get airborne again," Marcus said.

But Baird couldn't feel any vibration under his boots. Back in old Jacinto, that was the first warning of a grub emergence hole opening up. He was about to point that out to Marcus when Mac broke free of Bernie's grip, the pasture around them heaved and cracked open like an earthquake, and Baird realized they were further from the waiting Raven than he'd first thought.

A huge charcoal-gray trunk erupted ten meters away, speckled with red luminescence. Baird caught a faceful of wet soil flung out by the sheer force of the emergence. He ducked his head, pure reflex, and that was when he saw the flurry of legs coming up over the edge of a crater like a spider crawling out of a plughole.

"Polyps!" Dom yelled.

Yeah, the little assholes had finally decided to show up. But at least Baird had answered one question now.

They came *with* the stalks. Not out of them.

POLYP EMERGENCE HOLE, NORTHERN VECTES.

It was tough to say which kind of Lambent or Locust was the worst. But Dom had his personal freak-out league table, and polyps had taken the top slot from Locust tickers.

They were landmines—walking, running, hunting landmines.

They were small fry compared to a Berserker, but they swarmed. They *scuttled*. And that hit a primal nerve deep within him. All those fast-moving legs and the sea of fanged mouths were an unstoppable tide of destruction sweeping in to devour him. It was hard to hold his ground and fight the urge to run.

But if he turned, they'd overwhelm him, and he'd be dead. Some days he wasn't sure if that mattered, not now that Maria and the kids were gone, but today it felt like it mattered a lot.

The creatures surged up from the gaping pit around the stalk, rushing out in all directions like milk boiling over the sides of a pan. All Dom could take in was the mass of dark gray legs. The first polyp he hit detonated in a spray of greasy guts and took out a couple of its buddies as well, but the others kept coming as if nothing had happened. Maybe they were buoyed up on adrenaline and instinct, just like him. The only thing he could focus on was a ninety-degree cone of the wave coming straight at him so that was where he emptied his clip, sweeping left to right and back again, ears ringing from explosions and automatic fire. Then the deafening noise of a Raven drowned out everything. Its downdraft threw leaves and grit in his face.

Gettner yelled over the radio even though she didn't need to. "Get out of there! *Delta*! Just get the hell out and let Barber hose them!"

"Can't," Marcus panted. "Try not to hit us."

"Shit, Marcus, there's maybe a hundred of—" Gettner's voice was silenced for a moment by the rattle of the Raven's door gun right over Dom's head. Polyp spatter and mud rained on him, peppering his face with sharp fragments. "They're splitting up. They're breaking away."

"Track them," Marcus snapped. "Go on, get after them."

Gettner ignored him. "You sergeant. Me major. I'm staying."

Dom reloaded without looking. If he glanced away from the front rank of polyps, they'd be on him and he'd lose his legs or worse. He just had to keep firing. He was aware of Baird and Cole just in front of him to the right, but beyond that everything was a blur with only the jagged legs and fanged mouths of the polyps in ultrasharp focus. So he aimed, and he fired, and kept firing until he emptied the clip. He could hear his own ragged breaths. It felt like the oncoming wave was never going to end. Every time he hit a polyp, two more popped up.

"How many?" he yelled to Baird. "How many did she say?"

"I estimate a metric fuck-ton." Baird swapped out an ammo clip. "Stop me if I'm getting too technical."

"From one stalk?"

"Don't worry about the math, Dom." Cole pulled out a grenade and drew back his arm, ready to swing it. "Just frag the bitches."

Dom saw the grenade arc out into the polyps and sink in the sea of thrashing legs. There was no sound, just a blinding white light that engulfed him and left a neon afterimage on the sky. It took him a few seconds to realize he was flat on his back under a rain of mud, winded and gasping, still firing his Lancer into the air.

Gotta get up. Polyps. Gotta get up. *Once I'm down, I'm dead. Oh shit . . .*

Dom scrambled to his knees and spat out soil. For a moment there was nothing—no noise, no movement, no pain, just an awareness that he was caked in mud and not able to stand. *Is it over? Is it?* Then someone grabbed the back of his collar and hauled him up.

"Whoa, maybe I didn't judge that right," Cole said in his ear. He sounded like he was underwater. "Sorry, baby. You okay? 'Cause the crab-fuckers ain't."

Baird appeared from nowhere and stared into Dom's face, frowning. "Yeah, Cole throws like a girl these days. How many geniuses can you see?"

"None," Dom said. It wasn't the first blast he'd been too close to. Now he knew it wasn't going to be his last, a kind of shaky anger took over. "Just one asshole."

"That's terrific. Two would mean concussion. Which would be bad."

Dom managed to look up and make some sense of what was happening. He couldn't see any polyps now, and judging by the way Marcus was searching from side to side in the grass, he'd lost sight of them too. The field was churned up. A trail of craters led into the long grass.

"Did we get them all?" Dom called.

"You okay, Dom?"

"Yeah, fine. I said, did we get them all?"

"No. Two packs split off." Marcus turned around, covered in polyp spatter. He wiped his face with the back of his hand before pressing his earpiece. "Eight-Zero, we're clear here. Can you see the rest?"

"I'm following one," Gettner said. "Hard to tell what's downdraft and what's actual movement in the grass."

"I'll take the other pack on foot. Fenix out."

"Where's Boomer Lady?" Cole asked.

"Wherever the dog is. He's gone after the polyps." Marcus turned to jog away. "I'll catch up with her. You stay here and wait for Hoffman."

Cole spread his arms in exasperation. He felt obliged to keep an eye on Bernie, even though she really didn't need it.

Baird slapped him on the back. "Come on, Granny's indestructible," he said. "Look what she's survived. Two wars. God knows how many fights with grubs and Stranded. Roadside bombs. Oh, and she eats *cats*, for fuck's sake. If *that* hasn't killed her, nothing will."

"She's *sixty*," Cole said defensively. "And it's startin' to show, even if she don't accept it."

Baird put on his couldn't-give-a-damn face, which Dom knew was an act, and knelt on the edge of a crater to inspect it. Dom could hear Gettner's Raven circling the fields on a search pattern, fading in and out as she changed direction. At least he knew his hearing wasn't permanently damaged. But if he had a few more close calls like that, he'd be the one they'd scrape up in a bucket, not Bernie.

"What can you see?" Dom called.

"Sweet FA." Baird had his head down the crater. "I can't tell if this is a hole they came out of, or a hole we made frag-ging them."

Cole ruffled Dom's hair apologetically with a huge hand. "You sure you're okay? You look pretty spacey."

"I'm all right."

"I see that nobody's asking how *I* am," Baird said.

"Oh, sure. You turned glowie yet, Baird?" Cole had a knack of bursting Baird's anxiety bubble. "One of those bitches skewered your leg and you ain't griped about it for *days*. That ain't normal for you."

Baird was convinced glowies had some kind of infection and that he might have caught it. They'd seen glowie grubs, Brumaks, and leviathans, so the idea of a glowie Baird wasn't unreasonable, just disturbing. Baird knelt back on his heels and prodded his ankle as if he was testing it.

"I *check*, Cole," he said. "Trust me, I check. Every day. In the dark."

Cole chuckled. "Yeah, I *wondered* what you was doin' in the closet, all on your own . . . hey, I can hear another Raven. Now everybody smile and play nice for Prescott, okay?"

Mel Sorotki's voice broke into the comms channel. "This is KR-Two-Three-Nine—we have a visual on you. Interesting crop you've grown there. Can't wait to see your roses."

"Ooh, thanks for joining us, Lieutenant." Baird made his usual *pfft* of contempt. "Did you stop for directions?"

"All complaints in writing to the Chairman, Baird. And gosh, here he is!"

A couple of fields away, the sound of a machine gun followed by a firecracker sequence of detonations was loud enough to get Dom's attention.

"Gettner's found her glowies," Cole said. "See, Dom, there's always a silver linin'. When you hit those bitches, you know they ain't gonna come back and fight another day."

"And you can see the assholes in the dark."

"Didn't help the Locust much though, did it?" Baird said.

Sorotki's Raven dipped low over the pasture and circled the first batch of stalks before setting down. Hoffman jumped out of the Raven and headed Dom's way with a determined stride.

Victor Hoffman had been Dom's CO in his commando days, way back in the Pendulum Wars. Dom still found it hard to think of the old man as the Chief of the Defense Staff. Cities had burned and sunk, most of the world's population was dead, and the mighty COG was now just a town of refugees with a fancy flag and a few ships, but Colonel Hoffman still remained, the last senior officer left standing. He was a rare fixed point in Dom's life.

"Anyone injured?" Hoffman asked. "Goddamn, Dom, you look like hell."

"I look better than the polyps do now, sir."

"Where's everyone?"

"They went after Mac to get the stragglers," Dom said. "Don't worry. Bernie's okay."

Hoffman made an unconvincing attempt to look more interested in the stalks. "She damn well better be."

"If you want to go find her, sir, I can stall Prescott."

Dom had always been fond of Hoffman, but he really felt for the poor old bastard these days. He was widowed and he blamed himself for it. Dom knew that pain all too well. But Hoffman had eventually taken the risk of another relationship, and Dom knew that was something he'd never do.

"Thanks, Dom," Hoffman said at last. "But it's easier for all of us if I keep an eye on the Chairman." He clambered over the churned soil to inspect one of the blisters, now just a rock-hard gray bulge with a mark on it like crosswires. "How the hell did these bastards get inland?"

Dom could still hear the occasional crack of an exploding polyp in the distance as he watched Prescott amble across the field, stopping to prod at the grass around the stalks. In his oilcloth jacket and muddy boots, he looked more like a country squire inspecting his crops.

It wasn't a casual inspection, though. Dom felt he knew Prescott well enough by now to spot the difference between Prescott going through the motions and Prescott on a mission, and this was a very focused Prescott indeed. He squatted to pick something up and examine it in his palm. Then he pulled out a scrap of paper and carefully wrapped it.

"What's he doing?" Baird asked.

"You still think he'd tell *me?*" Hoffman muttered, giving Prescott the *hairy eyeball*, as Sam called it. It was a look of pure suspicious venom, eyes narrowed and lips pressed into a tight and unforgiving line. "Don't get me started, Corporal."

This was the war within the war—Prescott versus Hoffman. Dom had taken sides and there was never any question that he would stick by his old boss until the bitter end. What kind of head of state still kept secrets from his right-hand man, from the head of his armed forces, when the whole world was going to rat-shit around them?

Prescott did. And whatever his last remaining secrets were, they were on the data disc that Baird was incubating in his shirt like a demented hen. It was hard to have any conversation with Prescott these days without wanting to grab the asshole's collar and shake the truth out of him—whatever it was. Only the prospect of more Lambent stalks finding their way ashore distracted Dom from doing exactly that.

Prescott walked up to them with that look that said he expected their undivided attention. He was clutching something else in his hand now, and he held it up to the light between his thumb and forefinger like a diamond. It looked like a finger-length thorn attached to a chunk of polyp shell.

"Gentlemen," he said, but when he looked away from his prize he was staring straight at Baird. "Have you noticed anything new about the polyps?"

"We're still cataloging all the nifty new features on the stalks, Chairman," Baird said. "But stick it on our list and we'll get around to it."

"*Spines*. The things have grown spines, Corporal." Prescott handed it to him as if he hadn't even heard the backchat. Dom peered over Baird's shoulder and saw it was a sharp spur made of the same stuff as a polyp carapace, thick green-gray shell. "I think they might be *evolving*."

THREE KILOMETERS FROM THE STALK SITE.

Bernie caught up with Marcus in a field of oilseed and tried not to look old and out of breath.

The crop was in flower, a hazy carpet of brilliant saffron with a sickly perfume that hung over it like incense. Marcus waded through it waist-deep, calling for Mac.

"He's in there somewhere," Bernie panted. Her head was starting to ache from the intensity of the smell. "He'll let us know when he finds something."

"Maybe they self-destruct if they don't find a target in time."

"Maybe they don't," she said. "Maybe they pair off and start making more bloody polyp babies."

Marcus turned around and caught her staring at him. "Okay. We'll assume the worst." He searched between the rows of plants, pushing the foliage aside with his Lancer. "Mac? *Mac!*"

Bernie took advantage of the brief respite to get her breath back and listened for sounds of movement. "You never had a dog when you were a kid, did you?"

"No." Marcus, effortlessly competent in most things, seemed a little put out by failing to master dog training in minutes. "So he's not too traumatized to chase polyps."

"You've seen him in action," she said. "He's trained to

inflict damage. If something hurts him, it just makes him more aggressive."

The distant rumble of a tractor made her look around but she couldn't tell if it was in the field or not. It could have been a farmer completely oblivious of the morning's drama and just going about his business, or someone out on the road, heading to find out what all the helicopters and explosions were about. She picked her way between the rows of oilseed, trying not to trample the crop.

"Mac!" She put her fingers between her lips and whistled. "Mac! Come!"

Marcus started moving again, taking slow, deliberate paces. The polyps hadn't run away before. If they'd learned to stalk their prey . . . no, it didn't bear thinking about.

We don't even know if the bloody stalks are coming up in places where we can't even see them.

And nobody knew if this was just an infestation they could live with, or the beginning of the end. It was hard to know how much panic to invest in all this. Bernie could hear Marcus's breathing in her earpiece, getting more shallow and rapid as he moved deeper into the scented yellow sea. She kept him in her peripheral vision just in case the radio went down.

The tractor noise was growing louder as if it was heading in their direction, but Bernie still couldn't see it. The dips in the field were deep enough to hide an approaching vehicle. That meant she probably wouldn't spot a bunch of polyps until they were right underneath her.

It was like crossing a minefield. She moved her gaze up and down from the horizon to the ground a few meters ahead of her as she walked, looking for movement in the crops. The best she could do was listen for rustling and hope she got a few seconds' warning.

Suddenly Marcus stopped. "Hold it!"

He aimed his rifle into the oilseed, stepping back out of the crop onto the strip of bare ground at the end of the furrows. The only thing Bernie could hear now was the puttering of the tractor.

Then the plants shivered. She aimed automatically. A polyp scuttled out of the oilseed and Marcus opened fire, detonating the thing so close to his boots that he almost lost his balance. Bernie swung around to cover him, expecting more polyps to follow. If there was one, the others wouldn't be far away.

"We're going to be doing this every frigging day," Marcus said, wiping a gobbet of polyp flesh off his chest plate. "That's going to suck up a lot of resources."

The tractor noise sounded like it was heading toward them now, but Bernie was too busy listening for polyp movement to worry about it. There was more rustling. She moved into position to face it head-on.

You don't scare me, you little bastards. I've killed plenty of your mates. Come on. Come and get it. Come and get it for all the Gears you've crippled.

Marcus spun around. "Goddamn!"

Bernie almost opened fire. But the gray shape that shot out of cover wasn't a polyp. Marcus lowered his rifle and stepped back. It was just Mac, panting and excited. He cowered as if he was expecting a good hiding, but Marcus looked as wary of the dog as the dog did of him.

"You naughty little bugger. Don't you scare your mum like that again." Bernie grabbed Mac's collar with relief and put the leash on, letting him lead her back into the crops. "You don't like dogs much, do you, Marcus?"

"Not a matter of liking or not liking," Marcus said. "Habit."

"You going to tell me?"

Marcus was a few meters ahead with his back to her now.

She saw the slight roll of his head as if he was debating whether to answer or not.

"Prison," he said at last.

Bernie didn't need him to say any more. He was never going to talk about his four years in the Slab, but maybe that was just as well. She had a pretty good imagination when it came to human excesses. She wasn't sure if she wanted to find that the bottom of the barrel went a lot deeper than she'd thought.

The tractor sounded close now. "He's coming to find out what the hell we're doing to his crop," she said.

"I thought they all stayed in touch by radio."

"Can't expect them to monitor all the channels."

"Better warn him off before he hits a polyp, then. He won't know they're on the loose."

Mac was still pulling like a train, following what Bernie hoped was a polyp trail. Marcus jogged toward the crest of the slope to get a better vantage point. He seemed to have forgotten that he could run into a polyp any time, but that was Marcus all over: once he realized someone was in the shit, that reflex to save the world kicked in and he lost all sense of his own vulnerability.

Just like Mac. Head first, defend the pack, bugger the risk.

"Marcus, slow down a bit, will you?" Bernie called.

"It's okay. I see him."

"What, the tractor? *Marcus!*"

He reached the top of the slope and raised both arms as if he was flagging someone down. Bernie broke into a trot and tried to steer Mac the same way.

"Hey! Stay in the cab!" Marcus was yelling to get the driver's attention. "No, *stay in the cab*! Polyps!"

Bernie drew level with him and looked down the slope. A small tractor with a disk harrow had come to a halt on a track through the center of the field. Maybe the driver couldn't hear, because he leaned out of the cab and shouted a reply that was lost on the breeze. Marcus motioned him to stay put again, holding both palms up.

"Stay there—we're coming over." Marcus started jogging down the slope. The tractor driver settled back in his seat and waited. "Good. He's got it."

Bernie was wondering if the man even knew what a polyp looked like when she saw him look down from the tractor's high cab. He stared at the ground for a moment. Then he jumped up, or at least he stood up as far as he could inside the vehicle's plastic canopy. Mac started barking.

"*Polyps!*" Marcus took off at a sprint. Bernie followed without thinking. She could see the things now, four or five of them clambering up the tires and onto the hood. "They're all over the goddamn tractor."

The look on the farmer's face said it all. The poor bastard couldn't even run for it. He'd stayed put like he'd been told and now he was trapped. He screamed and tried to bat off the polyps with his bare hands, and Bernie couldn't do a bloody thing for him.

Marcus squeezed off a burst as he ran and took out two polyps, crazing the windshield, but it was too late. The cab lit up with the blast, rocking the tractor on its suspension. The driver stopped screaming.

"*Shit.*" Bernie ran down the slope. Mac pulled free and raced ahead of her, heading for the remaining polyp. "Mac, *no*! Leave it! *Leave!*"

She expected to see him blown to pieces. But he cannoned into the polyp at full speed, head down like a charging bull, and sent it tumbling down the track for a couple of meters before it detonated. It took Bernie twenty long seconds to reach the vehicle. Marcus was already on the radio to Gettner.

"Fenix to KR-Eight-Zero—we've got a fatality."

"Eight-Zero here. Mataki's down?"

"Negative. She's okay. It's a civilian."

Bernie climbed up on the tractor to check the driver. He was a mess. His legs were so badly shredded she couldn't actually see their outline, and he wasn't breathing. But when she touched his shoulder he slumped back and blood spurted over her.

Arterial blood, under pressure. Oh fuck . . .

"He's still alive," she called. "Marcus, give me a hand. Quick."

"Did you get that, Eight-Zero?" Marcus climbed into the cab from the other side. "We need a casevac. Move it."

When Bernie saw that much blood then drill kicked in unbidden, an autopilot that didn't care how scared or nauseated she was. It simply took control of her hands because she'd done this too many times before. Upper leg wounds were a bastard to deal with. She had a minute to stop the bleeding, maybe only seconds by now because the man was already unconscious. Marcus pressed his fist hard into the driver's groin to pinch the artery closed, but it didn't make much difference. The blood seemed to be coming from everywhere at once. The two of them worked in desperate silence, fighting a losing battle against the pumping blood.

"I can't stop it," Marcus said at last. Bernie wondered if he saw Carlos every time he dealt with terrible injuries. "He's bleeding from too many places."

"I've seen Gears survive worse."

But that was when there'd been field hospitals with proper drugs and the best equipment, and that time was long gone. Bernie was just going through the motions because drill told her not to stop until it was really, completely *over*. Marcus still had his fist pressed into the artery when the Raven landed. Bernie couldn't feel a pulse. Barber ran up to them hauling a gurney.

"I think we've lost him." She looked at Marcus and they seemed to reach a silent agreement to let go. She found she was clutching a bunch of rags heavy with blood. "The locals are going to have our guts for garters."

Barber peered into the tractor, then looked away for a second. "Just as well. Even Doc Hayman couldn't fix *that*." He took a breath. "Come on, let's move him. I bet he didn't imagine his working day would end like this. Have we got an ID?"

"Not yet."

"Okay, I'll just give Lieutenant Stroud the location and leave her to do the NOK."

Sometimes death was so universally present, so all-pervading, that it didn't need mentioning by name. It was as invisible and taken for granted as oxygen. Bernie only noticed it when it wasn't there. But when it was spoken about, it had two faces—one that was familiar to the point of being casual, the other just embarrassed dread. Today she felt the dread. It would pass.

Mac trotted around, nosing through the grass on the track and seeming none the worse for his run-in with the polyp. When Bernie got his attention by snapping her fingers, he looked up at her with a disturbingly human frown. He was a sad-looking dog at the best of times, but now he looked as depressed as she felt. He knew things were going badly wrong.

"Is he done?" Marcus asked, pressing his earpiece with a bloodstained finger. "I'll let Hoffman know we're bringing in a body."

Bernie picked up Mac's leash. He gazed at her expectantly for new orders. "Yeah, I think we found them all," she said, slipping him a piece of jerky by way of reward. Her hands were trembling from the effort. "The ones from the last stalk, anyway."

She could never shake the feeling that all this was her fault, or at least the COG's. Vectes had escaped the Locust invasion, one of a handful of isolated, tiny islands protected by volcanic ridges. Now Jacinto and its refugees had landed on the doorstep unannounced and uninvited, bringing disaster with them.

"What are we going to do with the tractor?" she asked. "We can't just leave it covered in all that shit for his family to clean up."

It was going to be bad enough when they had to drive the thing again. And they would, she was sure; they didn't have a choice. Sera had been burned and bombed and poisoned back to a pre-industrial world. There were no new tractors rolling off assembly lines anymore.

We've all done it. We've all climbed back in a 'Dill or a Packhorse and tried not to notice someone's blood. But not these people. The war's just begun for them.

Combat was haunted by small, painful aftermaths that most people never thought about. Marcus caught her staring back at the vehicle and nodded, as if he was mindful of those small things too. Yet again, she saw him as a twenty-year-old Gear waiting for extraction on a beach in Ostri, kneeling over the remains of Carlos Santiago, ready to take his friend home for the last time.

"Yeah," Marcus said. "We better take care of that."

CHAPTER 2

*When are you going to listen to me? You've got four weeks'
flying time left before you start eating into the fuel reserve
that'll guarantee getting back to the mainland. There's no
more imulsion. We can't even go foraging around
abandoned depots like the old days, and you can't convert
aircraft or warships to run on cooking oil. We're stuck on an
island in the middle of nowhere. And whether it's this year,
or the next, or a century's time—we'll need to leave here
one day.*

(Royston Sharle, Head of Emergency Management,
to Colonel Hoffman)

STALK EMERGENCE SITE, NORTHERN VECTES.

Hoffman wished he'd taken a leak before he left base. Dr.
Hayman's grim prediction about his aging prostate was coming true like a curse.

But it would have to wait. There were at least three problems ahead of his bladder in the queue, and the most urgent
one was coming over the radio right now.

"Colonel, we've got a dead farmer," said Marcus. Hoffman's gut knotted. "Polyps."

"Got an ID?"

"Not yet." Marcus paused. "He bled out over Mataki. Try not to yell at her."

Hoffman hesitated. "Understood, Fenix." Sometimes it was as if there had never been any feud between them, no punches swung or court martial or jail. Marcus was selfless, twice the man his damn father had been. "Can you recover the body?"

"That's taken care of. We're heading for Pelruan in a few minutes."

"Okay, I'd better get up there and make some reassuring noises as soon as Prescott's finished his nature trail. Hoffman out."

Prescott was still ordering Baird around, getting him to collect samples for some goddamn reason. What did the man expect to do with them? There were no more labs and no more scientists. Hoffman seized the brief lull to slip into the bushes and relieve himself.

Yeah, don't yell at Bernie. Be grateful she forgives and forgets. Or forgives, anyway.

He wasn't sure the locals in Pelruan would be that tolerant. They'd want to know what he was going to do to protect them now that the hellish outside world had come to their island. He didn't have any answers.

So why are the stalks coming up here? And how?

He was zipping up when he heard twigs crack behind him. He turned, expecting to see Prescott, but it was Mel Sorotki.

"Sorry to interrupt your pee break, sir, but there's a real mess in the field over there."

"Say again, Lieutenant?"

"Dead cattle. The polyps fragged them. It's all barbecue-sized chunks."

Hoffman sighed. "Here we go. We're going to be tear-assing all over the island keeping a lid on these little shits."

"Baird's got a theory."

"Good. I'll take it. Let me go talk to him."

Baird always had a theory. He was an engineer, a man who was happier with machines than with people, but in that logical engineer way he could also break most things down to basic principles and come up with insights. Sometimes Hoffman worried that he expected Baird to do the job of entire universities full of experts.

But Baird basked in it. Hoffman was happy to pat him on the head for being a clever boy as often as he wanted.

"Take a look at this." Baird thrust a folded chart under Hoffman's nose. It was a survey map of Vectes, heavily penciled over with flight paths. Sorotki's crew chief had scribbled PROPERTY OF MITCHELL K—RETURN TO KR-239 on the margin. "This island's volcanic, but there's always a network of fissures. So you get underground rivers or seams of softer rock. Simple answer—the stalk finds a way through a gap from the ocean. All we have to do is stay away from the fissures."

"Depends where they are. And how far the stalks and the polyps can spread from those points. Which we don't know yet."

"So we find out. We plot where they come up."

"I never had you down for an optimist, Baird."

"I'm not. If I'm wrong, they can be up our asses anytime, anywhere, anyhow."

"Okay, so we start plotting the emergence sites." Hoffman studied the chart. Vectes was about seventy kilometers north to south, only five thousand square kilometers, but it was a lot of ground to keep an eye on with a small Raven fleet and a worsening fuel shortage. "If there's a pattern, then we have a containment strategy."

"Yeah, but remember all those busy little polyp legs. They get around."

"So we can keep them out," Hoffman said. He'd dug defensive ditches to trap and kill the recent polyp invasion from the sea. "We've done it once. We can do it again."

Hoffman pressed his earpiece to call Control, gesturing to Sorotki to get the Raven started. "Mathieson, we've got a dead civilian. I'm going to be tied up explaining that to Pelruan. You better brief Trescu. I don't want him bitching that we don't keep him in the loop."

"The Gorasni probably know already, sir," Mathieson said. "They monitor our voice traffic."

"All the more reason to come clean, then." Miran Trescu had played straight with him so far—straight enough, anyway—so he'd play straight in return. Whether Gorasnaya regarded itself as part of the happy COG family or hankered after its Indie past, they were all in the same shit together now. "Tell him I'll talk to him as soon as I get back."

Richard Prescott was walking around the field, stopping occasionally to study the stalks. Hoffman didn't know what he was up to, but the man never did anything without a good reason. Every action, every gesture—every *word*—was calculated and controlled, designed to achieve a result that Hoffman couldn't guess at. He resented Prescott for even making him *want* to guess. Like the goddamn data disc and whatever was on it, it ate at him when he needed to keep his mind on the immediate problem.

"Let's move, Chairman," he said. "We need to get to Pelruan before the corpse does. Hearts and minds time. Baird, Cole—with me."

Hoffman ducked under the Raven's rotors and settled in his seat, staring out of the crew bay so he wasn't tempted to look at Prescott and start festering again. Cole buckled himself in on the opposite bench, effectively putting a wall between the two men. He winked when Hoffman glanced at him. The man was a natural diplomat.

"Don't worry, I ain't gonna puke on you, sir," he said cheerfully. "I emptied my tanks on the ride up here."

"That's decent of you, Cole." Hoffman gave him a conspiratorial nod and radioed Anya Stroud. She'd be waiting for the Raven at Pelruan. "Lieutenant? Do we have a name yet?"

"We think it's Leon Whellan, sir. It's on his land. Married with two kids." Anya sounded as if she'd taken a deep breath. "Lewis Gavriel's gone to find his wife."

Hoffman wasn't sure why dead family men were somehow more tragic than single ones. He felt worse about those who hadn't left any family to grieve for them. They'd been erased, past, present, and future. And after the COG had lost millions of civilians in Tyrus alone, he wondered if he was making too much of a single fatality here.

But Pelruan was a small town, just a few thousand people. Every death hit them hard. They needed reassurance that they weren't a forgotten irrelevance to the newcomers in the south of the island.

Their island. Their farms. We can't make this work without them.

Sorotki cut into the comms circuit. "Sir, Eight-Zero's a few minutes out. And Control says the grindlift rig's going to be in position in half an hour."

"Good. The sooner we know what kind of rock those stalks can get through, the better."

Anya was already waiting at the landing area by the harbor when the Raven set down, pacing an imaginary line in front of the Packhorse and swamped by armor that didn't quite fit her. But she was growing into it in other ways. Pelruan was her responsibility now.

Hoffman had wondered if he'd dumped too much on her by giving her command of the small garrison here. She'd been a desk-bound ops officer until a few short months ago, and that was a tough transition for a woman in her thirties.

But she's Helena Stroud's daughter. That's a warfighting pedigree. I just hope she doesn't have her mother's penchant for suicide missions.

Hoffman jumped down from the crew bay and inhaled the scent of wood smoke wafting on the air. It was the morning's snakefish catch being processed in the smokehouse down by the slipway. The Lambent threat out at sea—leviathans, stalks, even smaller glowies trawled up in nets—had forced the trawler fleet to make the most of shallow water species. The prospect of a few meaty, smoky fillets distracted Hoffman for a moment before duty crashed in on him again.

Goddamn. How is all this going to impact the food supplies?

If stalks were coming ashore, then areas of farmland would have to be off-limits. Crisis begat crisis. The farms were already struggling to catch up with the influx of refugees.

So add food rationing to the list. Well, we've had plenty of practice at that.

"Hello, sir . . . Chairman." Anya glanced past Hoffman to acknowledge Prescott, doing it by the book. "I've set up a temporary morgue in one of the fishery stores. It's got refrigeration."

"Let's hope we don't end up filling it," Prescott said. "What's the mood like?"

"Cooperative. They always are. Model COG citizens."

"Is Lewis Gavriel back yet?"

"I'll radio him, sir."

Prescott wandered off to corner Baird. For a moment Hoffman wondered if Prescott knew Baird had his disc, and his insistence on coming along for the ride had nothing to do with the stalks at all. That was the problem with a devious son of a bitch like the Chairman. You could waste your life trying to second-guess him. Hoffman resisted the temptation and focused on Anya.

"You'd better draw up an evacuation plan, just in case," he said. "I'll get Sharle to work out where we can put a few thousand extra people if we need to."

"Already done, sir. I've had a few spare evenings to kill since the last polyp attack." Anya was the kind of junior officer every CO needed: organized, efficient, loyal, uncomplaining, and always two steps ahead of the clusterfuck in question. Hoffman had never known her to have one fallible human lapse of temper or judgment. "Sergeant Rossi's organizing lookouts. We're going to be reliant on civilians to raise the alarm."

"They know the land better than us anyway, Lieutenant. Good plan."

She shielded her eyes to look up into the sky, scanning for the inbound Raven. "How are we going to monitor the whole island, sir? Most of it's uninhabited."

"We can't. We'll just recon what we can for as long as we've got fuel."

Goddamn. We're relying on farmers and fishermen waving flags and calling us on their walkie-talkies now. Some army.

In just fifteen years, the Coalition had collapsed from a global superpower with satellite early-warning systems to a threadbare city of refugees using hand tools. For a moment it wasn't the fruitless war against grubs and glowies that ground Hoffman's spirit into the dirt, but the thought of rebuilding afterward.

Even if they wiped out the Lambent, he'd never live to see Sera get back to normal. It would take generations.

Anya turned around and looked south-east. "Here it comes, sir."

Gettner's Raven above the trees and circled overhead

before landing in a whirlwind of dust and grit. When the rotors slowed to a stop, Marcus emerged with Dom and Barber to unload a body-bag strapped to a gurney. Hoffman kept watching that door until he saw Bernie step down with the dog.

Hoffman could only stare and heed Marcus's advice.

Don't yell at her.

She was covered in dried blood. Her pants and cuffs were black with it, and there was a big smear on her forehead as if she'd wiped her hand across it. He knew it wasn't hers— damn, he hoped it wasn't, anyway—but it still made his stomach lurch. He'd lost Margaret because he hadn't stopped her taking a crazy risk. His history repeated itself on a daily basis, but this was one thing he knew he couldn't cope with if it happened again.

One day, it's going to be Bernie. It'll be her zipped up in one of those bags, and I just won't be able to go on.

"That better not be your blood, Mataki." He said it to silence the inner voice. Maybe if he said it often enough, it would never have to happen. "Or I'll—"

"I'm fine." She certainly didn't look fine. "I'm just not Doc Hayman."

"So what kind of shape is he in?" Now Hoffman had to make an effort not to fuss over her. "The widow's going to want to take a look."

Marcus loaded the gurney into the back of the waiting Packhorse. He stared at Hoffman with just the faintest moment of defocus in that unsettling pale blue stare. Bernie wasn't the only one who'd had to pick up the pieces once too often.

"He's intact from the waist up, Colonel," he said. "Better clean him up before she sees him, though."

Anya jerked her head in the direction of the town. It was five minutes' walk away at most. "I'll drive. I've set up a morgue."

"Expecting a crowd?" Marcus got into the passenger seat as Anya opened the driver's door.

"Might as well plan for it," she said.

The Packhorse set off down the track to the harbor road. Dom, Baird, and Cole followed on foot with Prescott. Hoffman hung back with Bernie, keeping one eye on Mac while Mac kept one accusing eye on him. The animal belonged to Will Berenz, Pelruan's deputy mayor, but he'd latched on to Bernie to the point of being a pain in the ass, gazing up at her with such besotted devotion that Hoffman felt he was competing with a four-legged rival. Mac was a jealous dog. Hoffman found it painful to realize that he was a jealous man.

"You been poisoning that dog's mind against me?" Hoffman asked, trying hard to jolly things along. "Is he okay?"

Bernie nodded. "He's a regular polyp hound. Whatever happened to him when he was missing just made him want to kill more glowies."

"You better clean up before the civvies see you." Hoffman took off his kerchief, unscrewed his water bottle, and soaked the cloth as he walked. "Here. Let me do it."

"Vic, not in front of Baird. Please. He'll only take the piss."

"Goddamn it, woman, we're not exactly a secret." He grabbed her arm to bring her to a halt and wiped her face and hands like a grubby kid. There wasn't much he could do about the blood that had soaked into her pants. "Just snarl at him and put him in his place. Like you do with me."

"Okay, I disobeyed your orders. But I had to find the dog." She pulled free of him and walked off. "Now I'll do as I'm told and stay on base."

"Well, that's big of you, Mataki." No, that wasn't fair. She'd just had a man die in her lap. Even for a veteran sergeant, things like that never got any easier. "Sorry. I'm just worried that I'll damn well end up burying you."

Bernie managed a smile. "As long as you don't dump me on the compost heap. I'd prefer to be turned into jerky."

Hoffman reached in his pocket to pull out the rabbit's foot she'd given him, taken from an unlucky animal she'd hunted for the pot. "And this goddamn thing isn't working." The stew had been pretty good, though. He was slowly getting used to life with a survival expert. "Maybe I need all four to change my luck."

"It's going to take a lot more than luck," Bernie said. "Just remember that the people here aren't used to living with monsters under the bed. They might overreact."

"I'm damned if I can think what constitutes an *overreaction* at the moment, babe." Hoffman shook his head, suddenly feeling very old. That was happening too often lately. "Because this shit just isn't showing any signs of bottoming out."

Vectes—unspoiled, fertile, picturesque—had waited out the war, cut off from the horror on the mainland since before the global Hammer strike. The small population carried on and kept the mothballed naval base ticking over. But they'd never seen a grub, never had to run for their lives, and never had to fear the vibrations under their feet that warned a Locust attack was coming. Hoffman decided that if they lobbed bricks at him and Prescott now that the glowies had invaded then he couldn't really blame them.

The harbor was a horseshoe shape, framed by a gravel road that ran down to the slipway. Hoffman could see a small crowd waiting by a pickup truck. A woman in overalls got out of it and stood blocking the Packhorse's path, forcing it to slow and stop.

"Looks like the missus," Bernie said, speeding up as if she was going to intervene.

"Anya can handle it." They'd almost caught up with Prescott now. "The civvies trust her."

"I promised her mother that I'd look out for her."

"And you have. That's why she's in command of the garrison now. Back off, Bernie."

Prescott reached the Packhorse before them, but he had the sense to stand back and let Anya deal with the widow. Hoffman could see Anya talking to her, making calming hand gestures while Marcus blocked the Packhorse's tailgate. More locals began coming out of the waterfront workshops and houses to see what was happening.

Anya was doing her best in a situation where there could be no right words to sort things out, ever.

"I want to see him," the woman kept saying. "I want to see my husband." She was dry-eyed but she had that over-controlled, slightly shaky voice that said she was about to lose it completely. "I want to see Leon. I've got a right."

She went to open the Packhorse's rear door. Anya put a careful hand on her arm.

"Let's do this inside, Mrs. Whellan," she said quietly. "Not out here."

"No, I want to see him *now!*" the woman snapped. "Not laid out in some damned warehouse. It's nothing to you, is it? *Nothing*. You see it every day. It's just another slab of meat to you."

Marcus did one of his slow head turns and faced the onlookers. "Okay, time to give Mrs. Whellan some privacy, people."

Maybe there *were* some right words after all. The crowd—about seventy locals now, a single animal with one reaction—seemed to hold a communal breath for a second and then turned away and dispersed in silence. Marcus had an effortless, reasonable authority that made people listen.

He put his hand on the door latch. "Are you ready, ma'am?"

Mrs. Whellan nodded. Bernie moved in and helped Marcus pull the body-bag out on the tailgate as gently as

possible, but it still looked as dignified as hauling a sack of
potatoes. It was what the widow wanted, though. Marcus was
right. You didn't argue with someone in that state.

"Ma'am," Bernie said, "there's some blood. Only fair to
warn you." She looked into the woman's face but didn't get a
reaction. "You can say stop, any time you want."

Marcus pulled the zip open. Mrs. Whellan turned her
head away and took a few moments to force herself to look.

"Oh." She put her hands to her mouth. "Oh God."

Prescott picked his moment to be statesmanlike. "I'm
very sorry for your loss, ma'am. We'll do everything we can
to—"

"No, it's not him," the woman interrupted. "That's not
Leon. It's not my husband."

Hoffman cringed.

"But he was working on your land," Anya said.

"Yes, but that's *Daniel*. Leon's cousin. Where's Leon?"

Mrs. Whellan was all blank confusion for a second or
two. Then she burst into tears, knees sagging as if she was
going to collapse. Anya caught her arm and steered her away
to a nearby house to sit down on the porch. Hoffman tried to
imagine what it felt like to be told a loved one was dead and
then find it was another member of the family instead.
Relief never really got a look in.

"Yeah, that went really well," Baird said, sighing. "Now
we've got to find another housewife to traumatize."

Hoffman had had enough of hearts and minds for the
day. He still had a field of stalks to examine. "Anya, call me
back when Gavriel gets a town meeting set up," he said.
"The rest of you—with me. Dizzy should have that rig in
place by now."

They trudged back to the Ravens. Sorotki, Gettner,
Mitchell and Barber were playing cards in KR-80's crew bay,
unfazed in that seen-it-all way of Raven crews.

Sorotki looked up as they approached. "How are they taking it?"

"Wrong stiff," Baird said.

"You're just too sentimental." Sorotki got to his feet and collected the cards from the rest of the crew. "I don't want to make your day plummet downhill any faster, Colonel, but there's another farmer going ballistic. The one whose cows got fragged."

"I'll talk to him," Prescott said. "The colonel's got his hands full right now."

Hoffman's reflex reaction was to wonder if it was another maneuver, but a helpful gesture was sometimes just that, nothing more. *He's got me. He's made me doubt every damn thing I see, and he doesn't have to lift a finger now to do it.* Bernie must have seen him twitch, because she gave him a warning nudge in the back.

"Thanks, Chairman," Hoffman said, deciding he was getting too tangled up in this. "I'm not good with farmers."

His working relationship with Prescott had hit rock bottom when he'd stolen the data disk, and now it was scraping along in a kind of frosty neutral gear. Prescott knew he had it. He also seemed to know that Hoffman hadn't cracked it yet. Maybe that amused him.

"Just walk away, Vic," Bernie whispered. She knew him far too well. "Okay? Just *focus.*"

As Sorotki came in to land at the stalk site, Hoffman spotted Dizzy's grindlift derrick making her way down the narrow two-lane approach road. Prescott leaned past Cole and Bernie to get Hoffman's attention.

"That brown patch around the stalks," he said. "What's that?"

Hoffman turned to look down. Prescott didn't mean the churned soil. The pasture around the stalks looked as if it had been scorched by weed killer. The grass was brown and limp, a pool of dead vegetation that extended out from the stalks by a couple of meters. It hadn't been like that when they left.

"Maybe it's from the polyp spatter," Hoffman said.

Prescott shook his head. "Then we'd see patches, not a radial pattern. Corporal Mitchell? Let's get some pictures of that."

Mitchell took the recon images in silence and nobody said anything for a while. The Raven landed and Sorotki had shut down the engines before anyone even moved.

Marcus leaned back in his seat and stared out in the direction of the stalks. For once, even Prescott looked visibly troubled. In a world that had lost the science and technology it had taken for granted, inexplicable things now scared Hoffman more than he was willing to let on. There were no more Adam Fenixes left to step in and invent a solution.

"So the stalks kill pasture," Hoffman said. "That could be an even bigger problem than the goddamn polyps."

CHAPTER 3

*Would Prescott do it? If the Hammer of Dawn could still
incinerate every city on the planet, would he target Vectes
to get rid of the Lambent? He wiped out most of Sera to
try to stop the Locust—and I hear he took that decision
with Hoffman. Men who can see millions of lives as
collateral damage aren't really worried what happens to a
handful of farmers.*

(Pelruan resident, expressing doubts to Mayor Lewis Gavriel)

**THE JACKSEN FARM, ONE HOUR AFTER THE
STALK INCURSION.**

It was a damn small gate, just tractor-sized, and Betty was
broad in the beam. Something had to give. And it wasn't
going to be Betty.

Dizzy Wallin slowed his beloved grindlift rig to a crawl
and sized up the terrain before bringing her to a halt. A
small, miserable-looking guy was sitting on the tailgate of a
pickup parked in the field. When Betty's shadow fell across
him he glanced up, looking like a depressed weasel.

Dizzy opened the side window and leaned out as far as he
could. He loomed two meters above the man. There was no
way to look nice and reassuring while driving Betty.

"Reckon I'm gonna have to roll right over the fence, sir."

The miserable guy stood up with his hands thrust deep in his pockets. "Go ahead," he said. "It's not like things can get any worse."

"I'll give you a hand repairin' it later."

"That's nice." His face didn't change. "Thanks."

Dizzy released the brake and rolled forward. He didn't even feel a bump as Betty crushed the flimsy wooden gate and the hedge to either side of it. Now he was face-to-face with the first complete stalks he'd seen. Goddamn, those things were *big*. They didn't look much like the chunks that Dom and Marcus had brought back from a wrecked ship a few weeks ago.

He'd heard all the stories about the ones that sank the Indie imulsion rig, though. Where the hell did they stow all those polyps? He'd served on imulsion tankers. It still twanged a nerve in him.

Prescott stood with his back to the stalks, talking to Hoffman and Lennard Parry as if they were all just doing a nice spot of sightseeing at a monument. Bernie stood a few meters away with that scruffy hound of hers on a tight leash.

The Chairman was wearing what Bernie called his lord of the manor rig—rubber boots, oilcloth jacket, and woolly jumper—and Dizzy caught her eye for a moment. She winked at him and did a subtle nod in Prescott's direction. *Just look at him*. Yeah, folks' breeding always showed on their faces, no matter how much cow dung they had on their boots. Prescott had *pedigree*.

There'd been a time when Dizzy had been sure he'd shoot Prescott if he ever met the asshole. This was the man who'd told the world it had three days to get to Jacinto before he vaporized the rest of Sera. This was the man who'd caused the deaths of millions and made Dizzy and his family into Stranded.

Not Hoffman. I know he was top brass when it happened, but I don't blame that man, no sir.

Dizzy found he could stomach Prescott because his girls needed him to. A man really could endure anything for his kids.

"Hey, Diz!" Parry signaled to indicate where he wanted Dizzy to pull up, and walked across to meet him. "Feeling adventurous?"

Dizzy gave him a thumbs-up. "You point me to the spot, Staff, and I'll make a damn big hole in it."

"Okay, we need to see how far down these stalks go." Parry was clutching a small monitor and a coil of cable in his arms. "Whether they have roots. What kind of rock they've come through. That sort of thing."

"You got it. Let's drill."

"See if we can uproot one of 'em first so we can do a test bore underneath. Help me get some chains on the one on the left."

"Oughta be like pullin' up daisies."

"I wish."

Dizzy climbed down out of the cab. The grass beneath him was brown and dead. "So the weed killer didn't work, huh, Len?"

"Not guilty." Parry took another look at the dead grass. "Maybe we ought to hose down our boots when we're done. I don't like the look of that."

Marcus wandered over to them with a bundle of thick twigs tucked under his left arm. He was whittling one to a point with his knife.

"Just an experiment." He stabbed the twigs into the ground at regular intervals around the edge of the brown patch. "Check these markers later and see if it's still spreading."

"Whatever it is, it's toxic," Parry said. "But lots of plants pump out poison that kills other species around them. Walnut trees, for a start. Can't plant clover or tomatoes within twenty meters of 'em."

"Fucking Lambent walnuts," Marcus muttered. "That's all we need."

He walked away and stood guard with his Lancer cradled in his arms like he was expecting more polyps. Prescott joined him, which was kind of odd; they were never social. They just stood there a meter apart, avoiding looking at each other.

"You think that piece o' pantie elastic's gonna hold, Len?" Dizzy asked.

Parry winked. "You sure that oversized junker of yours can handle that chain?"

"Don't you let Betty hear you say that. She's real sensitive about her weight."

"I don't know how heavy that stalk's going to be. You might need to weld her back together again."

"Only one way to find out. Hitch her up and see what breaks first."

Dizzy trusted Parry's common sense. The man was a Logistics Corps staff sergeant, and that meant he was one of a special breed. His ragbag crew of engineers and tradesmen, cobbled together from the survivors of three support regiments, had kept Jacinto powered, watered, fed, and housed for fifteen years. They rebuilt the city every day after the grub attacks and never bitched about it—well, not often. No, uprooting a few stalks wasn't going to bother Parry, not one damn bit.

And he always treated me right. Yeah, he remembers way back. And so do I.

Parry shackled the chains to the rig's winch and Dizzy climbed back up to the cab. Once he shut the door with that satisfying clunk, he was in another world. No goddamn thing could touch him. He sat behind a steering wheel meters off the ground and far from the chaos beneath his wheels, the master of all he surveyed thanks to Betty. He probably wasn't half as safe as he liked to think, but it still made him feel *good*.

Ah, Betty. We've been together a damn long time too. Ain't gonna damage you if I can help it, sweetheart.

He loved this rig. Folks said it was downright unhealthy to love a machine, but she'd never let him down, she'd never lied to him, and she'd saved his ass more than once. That was a lot more than he could say for flesh and blood.

"It's okay, darlin'." He patted the dashboard. "This might sting a bit, but all you gotta do is pull. Then we can see what's under that grass. You ready? Okay. Easy does it, sweetie . . ."

He started the engine. Betty rumbled into life with a steady vibrating pulse as good as a heartbeat. Up here, he wasn't a Stranded bum or a drunk. He was a derrick driver, a combat engineer, the man who literally dug you out of the shit. Gears depended on him.

Dizzy hadn't seen his life working out like this, but he reckoned nobody was where they planned to be these days. Being alive was the only measure of success worth a rat's ass. He jiggled his shirt pocket to feel the reassuring slop of liquor in his flask and reminded himself to start brewing another batch that evening. *Potatoes*. Damn, those made some real fine hooch.

Dizzy gave Parry a thumbs-up and waited for him to get clear. The winch mechanism whined. Then he felt a jolt as the cable took up the slack. Metal groaned. He held his forefinger on the motor control as Betty began dragging the stalk out like a weed, swiveling on his seat to try to catch a glimpse in the wing mirrors.

"How we doin', Len?" he called.

"It's starting to give." Parry was looking to one side of the field, getting hand signals from one of his team. He raised his arm and beckoned Dizzy forward. "Just a couple of meters, Diz . . . that's it . . . come on . . . steady."

Dizzy slipped the clutch and Betty crept forward, creaking and rumbling. Things were going fine, but then he felt the engine start to struggle. He put his foot down. Betty was starting to churn soil now. He could feel the tires losing purchase. On the dashboard, the winch warning light lit up red.

"Diz, slacken off!"

"Whoa—goddamn!" Dizzy didn't drop the revs fast enough and for a second he felt he was treading air. Then there was a crack loud enough to hear over the engine noise, and Betty lurched forward. Something smashed against the rig's tail panel like a hail of bricks. The chain had broken.

"Hang on, Diz—the stalk's snapped at the base," Parry yelled. "Shut her down."

Dizzy scrambled down from the cab to inspect the damage. The stalk had broken clean off just below ground level, but most of it was still rooted firmly in the soil. Betty's winch assembly dangled from its mounting, held in place by a couple of bolts. Apart from that she was in one piece.

"Sorry, honey." He patted her as the others clustered around the stump to examine it. Marcus bent to pick up a fist-sized chunk of stalk. The broken surface was gray and honeycombed with holes, a lot like pumice but much harder and heavier.

"Now *that's* different." Baird took it off him and turned it over in his palm. "The internal structure, I mean. Last one we chopped up was more like a tree trunk. Yeah, my money's on them evolving."

Prescott looked at Baird as if he'd discovered gravity or something. "Or perhaps it's a mature one."

"Then why do they look different as soon as they come out of the ground?"

Prescott nodded as if that made sense somehow. "See if you can cut some sections out of it."

"You want a souvenir paperweight?" Baird asked. Damn, he was a rude asshole, even to the Chairman. "Because that's all it's good for. We don't have any way of analyzing except to look at it under Doc Hayman's microscope. She'll love that. Not."

For some reason Prescott didn't give Baird an earful. He didn't look down his nose at him, either. There was something going on, something weird, and when Dizzy looked in Hoffman's direction, the Colonel was watching the pair of them like an impatient buzzard who thought his dinner was taking too long about dying.

"You never know, Corporal," Prescott said. "Our Gorasni friends might have hidden talents when it comes to analytical skills. I'd still like some specimens. And some of the dead grass, too."

"If you're ready, sir, I'm gonna start drilling," Dizzy said. "Give Betty some elbow room. Might be a lot of grit flying around."

Betty could drill a vertical shaft wide enough to drop a two-man grindlift. A little bit of granite wouldn't bother her. Dizzy lined up the telescoping drill over the stump, hit the starter, and felt a kick as the bit engaged with the ground.

It was like drilling through the Ephyran bedrock to break into the grub tunnels under Landown. *Poor old Tai. Damn, we lost a lot of good Gears that day.* Sometimes the past interrupted the present so often that Dizzy wondered if he was getting those *traumatic flashbacks* that Doc Hayman kept talking about.

The drill bit flung out gobs of turf, mud, and stalk, then slowed as it went deep and started hitting denser rock. Betty shuddered. All Dizzy could do was watch the depth indicator and wait.

Twenty meters . . . come on, girl.

Betty twitched a couple of times. Now the drill note changed. Whatever was beneath the stalks wasn't solid and the bit was finding voids.

Dizzy powered down, hoisted the drill clear, and reversed Betty clear of the shaft.

When he clambered down from the cab again, he made sure he brought his rifle with him this time. Parry and Marcus were kneeling to peer down the hole. Betty had sunk a shaft clean through the stalk and the ground next to it, giving Parry a good cross section to examine.

"Spot on, Diz," Parry said. "Now let's take a shufti at what's down there."

Dizzy checked the hole and marveled that he could still be that accurate with a few drinks inside him. He wasn't sure he could have done it sober. Parry plugged the cable into the monitor and lowered into the hole, but Baird did a double take at what was on the business end of the cable.

"Hey, that's a bot camera!" he said, none too happy. "Have you been stealing my spares? Aww, come on!"

"Keep your wig on." Parry winked at him. "We've got fifteen bot cams and one damn bot. How many does that teddy-bear substitute of yours need?"

"I've got to keep Jack operational."

"And I've got to look down holes. But I can drop you down there for a personal inspection if you prefer."

Baird humphed and sulked. Dizzy edged around so he could see the portable monitor.

"Yeah, it's a fissure. That fits the survey map." Parry knelt back on his heels. "Stalks follow the path of least resistance. Like everyone does."

Dizzy kept looking. Bernie's dog suddenly lunged for the hole and she had to hang on to his lead to hold him back.

"I'm going to defer to Mac's risk assessment skills," she

said, sliding her rifle off her shoulder one-handed. "He can hear something. Be careful, Diz."

Stones and loose soil trickled down the borehole. Dizzy heard them tinkle on something hard so he stuck his head in the hole just to check if he could see the bottom of the shaft.

It looked real weird. "I can see water down there." There was a faint shimmer deep down as it caught the light. "Goddamn, I sunk a well! Shame I don't drink that stuff . . ."

Parry peered in and frowned. Then he lowered the bot cam again and paid out the cable to near its maximum. Dizzy looked back at the monitor.

Shit, that *really* didn't look good. Now he could see something glittering, and knowing his luck it sure as shit wasn't diamonds.

"Len, I don't reckon that's water." Dizzy had to carry a Lancer like an infantry Gear, but reaching for it wasn't second nature. This time he found himself clutching it like a lifebelt. "Len, we got *lights*. And it ain't miners down there."

Everyone reacted at once. The goddamn dog went crazy and nearly knocked Dizzy into the hole. Marcus pitched in and hauled Parry back by his shoulder. Dizzy scrambled upright and took a few steps back just so he could aim down into the shaft, and then polyps boiled out of the hole like cockroaches out of a drain. Everyone was firing. Some of the damn things escaped and went racing across the grass with Mac in hot pursuit.

"Dom—with me!" Marcus yelled, pulling a grenade from his belt. "Everyone else—give us some room!"

"Marcus—"

"Get clear, Diz! Grenade—*out!*"

Marcus slipped the pin and dropped the frag down the hole. The explosion threw a shower of polyps and gravel high into the air, then it all rained back down again. Dom moved in and emptied a couple of clips down into the smoke.

Everywhere fell silent except for cawing birds disturbed by the racket. Bernie jogged after Mac but there was a loud echoing crack like a grenade going off and she started running. Hoffman looked like he was getting ready to haul her back, but he caught Marcus giving him a look—that don't-do-it look—and turned his back on her.

"Okay, now we know where these things are going to come up, we can avoid them," Hoffman said. "That's something. Len, I want a full plot of the island showing where the fissures are, and we make those no-go areas. It'll mean moving anyone living near them. We'll monitor a corridor either side of the fissures daily for stalks."

Dizzy kept an eye on Bernie. She was on her way back with Mac on the leash, but he didn't look too good. He was limping this time. He really had a thing about polyps. Dizzy expected him to be scared of them by now, but he just seemed to chase them like they were rabbits with extra legs.

"Silly little sod," Bernie said, rubbing the dog's ears. Mac started licking a singed patch on his leg. "I'd better get Hayman to take a look at him. He's been through a lot these last few days."

"Yeah, and *you* have, too, so stop chasing after him, Sergeant," Hoffman snapped. Marcus looked embarrassed by the old married spat the two of them were having and took a sudden interest in the dead grass. "I need you fighting Lambent, not nursemaiding that goddamn *poodle*. If he ends up as ground chuck, it's too frigging bad."

Bernie suddenly got a real cold, mean look on her face. Marcus interrupted just at the right time. "Anyone want to take a look at the dead area?"

He tapped his boot against one of the wooden stakes he'd stuck in the ground. They weren't on the edge of the brown patch anymore.

Hoffman let out a long breath. "Goddamn it . . ."

"It's still spreading."

"We better start measuring this shit properly."

Baird sneaked up behind Parry and tried to take the bot cam, but Parry snatched it clear. "And then what do we do about it?" Baird asked.

"No idea," Hoffman said.

The Gears could shoot polyps until Hell built a ski resort, but this creeping shit wasn't going to be that simple to stop.

Dizzy decided that he was long overdue for that drink.

DISUSED LAVATORY BLOCK, VECTES NAVAL BASE, NEW JACINTO: LATER THAT DAY.

Baird wished he'd reminded Hoffman that engineering was his forte, not software.

The data disc definitely wasn't Prescott's shopping list or vacation snaps. It wasn't going to give up its secrets without a fight. But he couldn't resist a challenge, Hoffman was counting on him, and—ah, screw false modesty—he was probably the most technically able guy the COG had left.

Sometimes he wondered what had happened to all the real scientists and engineers over the years. He supposed it was inevitable that academics weren't built for survival, but even so, one of the assholes could at least have had the decency to stick around and answer a few questions.

So it's down to the likes of me, Parry, and Doc Hayman to fly the flag for rational analysis. Wow, we are so screwed.

At least the lavatory now had a makeshift door. Royston Sharle would never miss that wooden pallet. Baird kept one eye on it as he ran the decryption program just in case some jerk decided to drop in uninvited, and there was a high chance it was going to be Prescott judging by the way the guy had been looking at him today. Prescott wasn't stupid. Who else was Hoffman going to ask to crack the security on the stolen disc? Prescott knew he had it and was just jerking them around by smiling sweetly and letting them sweat.

Of course, Prescott—being a devious shit like all politicians—might have *lured* Hoffman into breaking open his desk drawer and then done the outrage act just to make sure that Hoffman didn't go looking for something else that was *much* more interesting. Yeah, that was the Chairman all over. He was the sole survivor of a brutal jungle of twenty-four carat backstabbing bastards. Poor old Hoffman was just an honest Gear with a bit of gold braid, a colonel trying to do a general's job.

No contest. He'll tear you up for ass-paper, Colonel.

But why would he want to put you off the scent unless you were getting too close to something dodgy anyway?

While the program was running, Baird rested his boots on his ammo crate desk and tried to imagine what secrets Prescott could possibly think were worth hanging on to at this late stage of the game.

The COG was deeper in the shit than it had ever been. They'd sunk Jacinto. Okay, they'd drowned the grub army and their snotty bitch of a queen too, but now they were stuck on an island in the middle of nowhere. The Gorasni imulsion rig was a pile of rusting steel somewhere on the seabed and they were running out of fuel fast. The Lambent freak show had taken over from the grubs as resident pain in the ass. Now if *that* didn't mean it was time to fess up and tell everyone the truth, Baird didn't know what was. And anyway—who the hell was left to keep secrets *from*? What would Prescott think was worth keeping to himself?

Maybe the slimeball had just flipped. Perhaps he'd finally lost the plot after years of trying to save the unsavable. Everyone had their breaking point.

Do I really believe that? That we're all fucked and there's nothing we can do about it? So why am I sitting in a lavatory like a total moron trying to decode this stuff?

Jack the bot was propped on a crate in the corner with a dust sheet draped across his open inspection plate, the last autonomous robotic drone left in the COG. Baird was determined to keep him running even if it meant ripping out some old lady's pacemaker for parts. Jack was *special*. He was a prototype with a cloaking system.

Everyone bitched about the COG never developing cloaking for Gears, but how much use would it have been against a Berserker's sense of smell, or a metal detector, or even this frigging glowie contamination? Sweet FA, that was how much.

Baird still wanted it, though.

"Okay, Jack," he said. "If you were the most powerful leader in the world, not that *that's* saying much these days, what would you hide? Top secret technology? A crate of gold bullion? A stash of chocolate and some interesting Ostrian porn?"

Jack didn't seem to have a view on the matter. With his arms folded back and the sheet draped over him, he looked like a forlorn armored nun at prayer. Baird went back to his decryption.

The computer pinged and he sat up to check it. As he swiveled, something snapped under him and sent the plastic lid lurching off to one side. He grabbed the edge of the desk to stop his fall, relieved there was nobody there to see him topple off a frigging *toilet*, and checked underneath the porcelain rim at the back. One of the rusty bolts holding the lid had sheared off. He rummaged in his toolbox for another one and crouched down to screw it into place.

"So this is your state-of-the-art facility," said a voice from the doorway. "Very minimalist."

Baird looked up as Marcus wandered in. This was definitely *not* routine. Marcus wasn't the gregarious kind and he didn't drop by for chats. The most social thing he did was show up at the sergeants' mess and have a drink, usually on his own and in total silence.

Marcus tweaked Jack's dust cloth. "So . . . new low-tech cloaking system?"

"Hey, he'll be as good as new when I'm done with him," Baird said defensively. "What do you want fixed now?"

"Nothing. Just seeing if you've had any luck with the disc."

It was the first time Marcus had acknowledged that it even existed. As far as Baird knew, Hoffman had told just five people that he had it: Baird, Cole, Marcus, Dom and Bernie. He wasn't sure if the old man had even told his buddy Michaelson about it. So it didn't get mentioned, just in case. Baird wondered how long they could keep a lid on it. The careful silence had lasted about two weeks so far.

"Zip," Baird said. "I tell you, Prescott's pulled out all the stops to protect whatever's on *this*. No wonder he's so fucking relaxed about Hoffman yoinking it."

Baird waited uneasily to see if Marcus was going to say anything else, because the man rationed words like there was only one box of them left in the world. Baird had served with him for eighteen months yet never really had a serious private conversation with him. It was a lot more scary than he expected. He wasn't sure why.

"If it's that sensitive," Marcus said, "why wouldn't he memorize the information instead?"

Damn, we're talking. We're actually talking. "You think it's a decoy, don't you?"

Marcus shrugged. "Wouldn't put it past him."

"I get the feeling you don't approve. How else are we going to get the information? Beat it out of him?"

"He's still the legitimate head of government. I don't like playing games with him."

Baird had expected a pat on the back for being resourceful. He was slightly miffed not to get it, but then Marcus always

played it straight, even when he was dealing with utter bastards.

"*You're* not," Baird said. "It's me and Hoffman who'll get
it in the neck if anything goes wrong. You only *know* about
it. But I suppose that's just as bad as far as you're concerned."

Marcus turned around and leaned on the door frame,
looking out into the dusk. "Yeah."

"It's either complexity or volume."

"What is?"

"The disc. If there's anything on it at all and he isn't just
jerking our chain, then it'll either be too much data or it's
too complicated to keep in his head. Or both."

Marcus grunted. It was the longest conversation Baird
had ever had with him, really *with* him rather than *at* him.

*Shit, just tell me he's not going to spill his guts about Anya
next . . .*

No, this was still Marcus. He probably didn't even make
small talk with her. Every word was measured and ground
out for a pressing reason.

"Okay, try another tack," Marcus said. "Not *what*. Why.
Why would he need to keep anything to himself now?"

Baird wasn't sure if Marcus wanted the question answered
or if he was just thinking aloud for a change. "Because it'll
piss us off so much that we'll shoot him," Baird said. "Or it'll
put something at risk. It's not personal stuff. I can't see the
guy giving a damn what we think about his bank deposit box
or weird sexual kinks—if he's got any."

"Yeah." Marcus looked back over his shoulder like something had suddenly occurred to him, tilting his head to
check out the toilet bowl. "Are the sewers still connected to
this block?"

"No idea. Why?"

"You're sitting on an ingress point," Marcus said, and
walked off.

Baird stood thinking that over for a few moments and suddenly felt uneasy. But he finished tightening the bolts on the seat and sat down to check the screen. The program had quit again. It made him forget his worries about getting a stalk up the ass.

"Shit," he said. "Shit, shit, *shit*."

Now he'd reached the limits of his competence. He'd never hit that wall before and it scared him. He needed someone with better computer skills, but he couldn't think of anyone with that expertise, let alone someone he would trust.

Whatever it is . . . it's not magic. It can be cracked. Everything *can be cracked.*

Baird took his mind off the problem for a while by tinkering with Jack's main servo, hoping a sudden idea would bubble up from his subconscious, but it didn't work. He shut down the computer and tucked the disc inside his shirt. This time he put a padlock on the lavatory door, but that was only to keep that thieving asshole Parry away from his personal stash of spare parts. He rattled the lock and chain just to make sure, and went in search of Hoffman.

Looking for Hoffman meant entering Admiralty House, the main admin block. It was all a bit obvious. And Prescott hung out there too.

He knows I've got it. He damn well knows. He's just biding his time working out how to make my life a total misery.

The easiest excuse to hang around was a visit to CIC. Sooner or later, everyone passed through it. Baird walked into the ops room and found Lieutenant Mathieson at his desk listening to the radio net, arms folded on his chest and his eyes shut. Baird thought he was taking a nap, but he gestured to Baird to wait—still with his eyes shut—and seemed to be listening to something riveting on his headset.

Baird cringed when he saw that the windows on one side

of the room were still patched up with boards and plastic sheeting. That exploding leviathan really had done a lot of damage to the base. Yeah, maybe he'd left that detonation a little too late after all.

"Two secs," Mathieson said, opening his eyes. "I'm trying to pin down a signal."

Baird pulled up a chair to get in Mathieson's eyeline. The guy was in a wheelchair because he'd lost his legs to a mine, and Cole kept telling Baird that it was rude to loom over him. Baird couldn't see why it was different from any man sitting on his ass in a regular seat, but there was no point pissing off a lynchpin like Mathieson. He'd taken over from Anya as the control room boss, and that meant he was a person of tactical importance when it came to asking favors and watching backs.

"Hoffman?" Baird mouthed.

Mathieson shook his head. So Baird waited. A couple of other Gears walked past the open door—Rivera and Lowe, Prescott's personal protection team—and glanced at him as they disappeared down the passage.

Eventually Mathieson slipped off his headset. "Sorry," he said. "If you're looking for the Colonel, he's gone back to Pelruan to address the restless natives."

"Stranded?"

"What?"

"The signal."

Mathieson shook his head. "No idea. I've heard it a few times before." He put the headset on again. "I just caught a blip on a weird frequency, that's all. Like a satellite data-burst."

"Sure it's not another Hammer satellite on the fritz?"

"No, it was on the old meteorology sat frequency. And it's the wrong sound. Sats all sound different. You want me to get Hoffman for you?"

"It's okay." Baird didn't want to make it look too urgent and draw attention. "I'll catch him later."

"Baird, can I ask you something?"

Here we go. The whole damn base knows.

"Knock yourself out, Lieutenant."

"You any good at making socket joints?"

That was a relief. "Might be. Okay, yeah. I am."

"One of the Gorasni guys says he's got someone who can make prosthetic legs if he can get the metal components."

Poor bastard. Mathieson was determined to get back to the front line. Baird couldn't say no. There was a time when he wouldn't have seen it as his problem and not lost a second's sleep over it, but not anymore. All he could think of was how Cole—or Bernie—would react if they found out he hadn't done his bit for Mathieson.

"Yeah," Baird said. "Can do. I'll go talk to them."

"Thanks," said Mathieson. "I'm going to walk again if it kills me." Suddenly he stopped and adjusted his headset, frowning as if he'd heard something that bothered him. "Damn, there it goes again."

"You spend too much time at that desk," Baird said. "You need to get out more."

"That's how I hear things nobody else does. I can spend time wandering around frequencies." Mathieson gave him a knowing look. "But if you come up with the socket joints, then I'll be *able* to get out of here. Won't I?"

For once, Baird felt like the asshole everyone told him he was. There was a difference between being aware that he said crass things—people expected him to—and that horrible involuntary surge in his chest that warned him he'd feel like utter shit whenever he remembered what he'd just said.

"I'll make you into a champion *sprinter*, Mathieson," he said. "Leave it to me."

Mathieson smiled and went back to the radio net. Now

that Baird had taken up the challenge, he *had* to do it. And it was going to be a lot easier than cracking that disc. His technical morale needed a boost.

Rivera and Lowe were lounging around outside as Baird left the building. They gave him an up-and-down look as if they were deciding whether to piss on him. He'd never known them all that well, Gears or not, but it was the first time he'd noticed them acting as if he wasn't on the same team. Maybe they thought they were in the fucking Onyx Guard or something.

Too grand now, are you? Or maybe Prescott's told you I've got his precious disc.

"Isn't it time you went back to doing a real job?" Baird said, slowing his pace but not stopping. "Who's going to throw stones at Prescott now the Stranded are gone?"

Okay, there was always the chance that Hoffman would finally lose it and deck Prescott, but most of Jacinto's refugees thought the sun shone out of the Chairman's ass. They were still alive against all expectations, and oddly grateful for that.

"He's the Chairman," Rivera said. He and Lowe had stopped mixing with the rest of the grunts. "You might want to remember that sometime."

Baird had to hand it to Prescott. He'd incinerated most of Sera with the Hammer of Dawn, killing millions—maybe even billions—and his grand plan to wipe out the grubs in their tunnels had ended with having to sink Jacinto and run for it. He might have been responsible for more dead humans than the Locust had. But still the idiots followed him.

Would the last chairman have done a better job? Baird would never know. What else could anyone do in a world bombed and burned back to the last century, except find somewhere to hide?

For once, Baird knew he didn't have a better plan than that. And whatever great ideas and theories he'd come up with over the years, the world had simply stopped making sense to him roughly fifteen years ago, and now it had stopped making sense all over again.

And he was starting to remember *exactly* what E-Day had felt like.

CHAPTER 4

At 1000 hours this morning, the Union of Independent Republics signed a formal surrender to the Coalition of Ordered Governments and concluded a peace treaty. It is with profound relief that I tell you the Pendulum Wars are now at an end, and that the COG and the UIR will embark on a program of reconciliation and rebuilding to heal the terrible scars—individual and national—that this long, terrible conflict has left upon Sera. We hope that the state of Gorasnaya will come to accept our offer of reconciliation and formally agree to the cease-fire in line with other UIR states.

(Chairman Tomas Dalyell's official announcement to the citizens of the COG, six weeks before E-Day, fifteen years earlier)

HANOVER, SOUTHERN TYRUS: SIX WEEKS AFTER THE END OF THE PENDULUM WARS.

It was late morning, but the street cleaning vehicles were still pushing a tidal wave of ribbons and paper flags along the gutter.

Hanover had welcomed home more troops last night, and Hanover knew how to party. Cole glanced out the limo's side window and grinned to himself. That was definitely an item of ladies' underwear hanging from the lamppost that he'd just passed.

But what else were folks going to do at the end of a eighty-year war, except celebrate like crazy for a few weeks?

Damn, it was hard to believe the Pendulum Wars were over—really, finally, definitely *over*. Cole didn't have to have any more fights with his agent about enlisting. The man didn't *understand*. Cole felt he had to do his time in the army like every other citizen, and he didn't want to pull that *reserved occupation* shit any longer. Thrashball wasn't like mining or farming or crewing freighters. It wasn't *essential*.

Now I ain't gonna get the chance to serve. Might make Momma happy, but I still didn't do my duty.

The limo slowed to a stop in the heavy traffic and he went back to reading the contract. In half an hour, he'd be in his agent's office, upsetting the man all over again and telling him he wasn't leaving the Cougars. This nice contract from the Sharks wasn't going to change a thing. It wasn't about the money.

This is home. Tried leaving once, didn't like it. Home's worth any amount of money.

"So did you get to see it, Mr. Cole?" the driver asked. "Are you going to buy it?"

Cole looked up and realized the car was still south of Centennial Bridge. Damn, the traffic was slow today.

"The apartment?" Cole leaned forward and pushed the sliding partition fully open. Josef—Joe—always drove him around town, a real nice guy. It didn't feel right having this dumb glass barrier between them like Cole was from a different world. "Hell, I thought it was gonna be simple. Nice apartment, easy for my folks to get around town, close enough for me to keep an eye on 'em." He checked his watch. He still had plenty of time. "Now, Dad likes the ocean view, but Momma don't like seagulls. Says they shit on the windows. You ever tried to clean seagull shit off glass? She says it's like needles set in concrete."

"It's the fish bones." Josef checked over his shoulder before pulling out into the next lane. To the traffic around him, Cole was just a big silver limo with tinted windows, an anonymous guy with a lot of money and somewhere important to go. "But your mom doesn't have to clean her own windows anymore, does she?"

"You don't know my momma. She don't want other folks keeping her house clean. Or me paying for *anything*."

"That's moms for you."

"Ain't that the truth."

The whole wealth and stardom thing still made Cole uneasy. It was something he put up with to play thrashball, not his reason for playing. The hardest thing to handle was people treating him like he was better than they were. When he reminded them he was a regular guy, just like them, his agent would sigh and tell him not to spoil it for them because they needed someone to look up to. That was the whole point, he said; they could ask Cole to sign a shirt or something and feel *elevated* by it. The last thing they wanted to hear was that Cole was ordinary, because that took the shine off everything.

Elevated. What the hell does that mean, that they're lower than me or somethin'? That just ain't healthy.

Cole settled for the thrill of winning and the fun of seeing people excited and happy when the Cougars won. Did life need to be any more complicated than that? No, it didn't. He already had all he wanted and then some. He put the contract back in the envelope.

The limo wasn't moving. They were now stuck in a sea of gridlocked cars.

"Traffic's worse than ever," Josef said. "I bet someone's broken down on the bridge and blocked a lane. People just don't know how to *merge* in this city. Mind if I put the radio on in case there's a traffic bulletin?"

"Feel free, baby," Cole said. "No rush. My agent can wait. It's not like he does it for free."

Cole was still thinking about how he'd get his parents to accept the penthouse apartment as a gift. He wasn't really listening to the radio; he was staring out the window, struck by how blue the sky was, and wondering why there were no seabirds wheeling over the water. Maybe they'd all been partying too. He could see the pillars of Centennial Bridge. There were always birds perched along the cables like a string of beads, but not today.

Then, in the way that words you weren't really listening to suddenly got your attention, he heard someone say *evacuate*.

"Holy shit!" Josef leaned forward and turned up the volume. "Mr. Cole, did you hear *that*?"

Cole leaned forward, straining to hear. "I just heard *evacuate*."

"Jannermont's under attack—they're trying to ship people out." Josef fiddled with the radio again. "What the hell's going on?"

Jannermont.

Cole felt suddenly sick. His folks lived there. Who would want to attack Jannermont? "Man, you tellin' me the Indies have started their shit again?"

"They're not saying Indies."

"What *are* they sayin', then?"

"They're saying that . . . things are coming out of the ground."

Cole happened to look at the cars either side of him and saw the drivers staring down at their dashboards, not taking much notice of the traffic jam. They were glued to their radios too. He didn't know which station he was listening to.

It was just a breathless reporter talking to even more breathless people. It sounded like the guy was on a street somewhere, grabbing people and asking them what they'd seen. It was hard to hear what he was saying over the noise of artillery fire and yelling.

"So what did you see?"

"They came up out of the ground. They just burst out of holes, right through the pavement."

"Were they armed? What did they look like?"

"They had guns. They were big and scaly. Gray. I've got to go—please, I've got to get home."

Cole sat back in his seat, bewildered. Maybe this wasn't the news. Maybe this was some dumb-ass stunt or a drama trailer, some stupid shit like that. But he knew it wasn't. The live report just cut off mid-sentence and he was now listening to an announcer in a quiet studio, but that didn't make what she said any more real or help him understand it any better.

"I'm sorry, we seem to have lost that link. I'll try to recap on this morning's developments—we're getting reports of attacks on cities across Tyrus, attacks by some kind of alien or animal species that's emerged from underground. So far we have no idea of casualties, but eyewitness accounts suggest that the loss of life is . . . substantial. We're getting reports of similar attacks right across Sera. The Chairman's due to make a statement soon, but in the meantime police are advising everyone to stay indoors and to keep the roads clear for the army and emergency services."

Cole's mind was racing. How close was all this shit to his folks? He had to check they were all right.

"I gotta get to a phone, Joe," he said, turning to look out of the rear window. The traffic behind was at a standstill as far as he could see. "I gotta check on my folks."

"Fucking *aliens*? Animals with guns?" Josef was all high-pitched and disbelieving. "Sorry, Mr. Cole. But what the hell *is* this?"

Before Cole could answer, Josef looked to his left, seemed to spot something, and hit the gas hard. The car's wheels spun for a second and then it shot out into a gap in the traffic to tear across three lanes. Horns blared angrily. Josef didn't stop until he was clear of the bridge approach road. He pulled over by a garage and turned to Cole.

"You wanted to make a call, Mr. Cole."

"You're the man, Joe," Cole said. He jumped out of the car and headed for the phone booth. When he picked up the handset, all he got was a rhythmic *peep peep peep* with a recorded message telling him the service was unavailable and that he should try again later.

"Goddamn." He jogged back to the car and bent over to talk to Josef through the side window. "The phone's out. I'm gonna see what I can find out."

"Mr. Cole, I better get you home. Things are going to get crazy and dangerous."

Home was the last place Cole planned to go. "Take the car, Joe. Go find your family. I gotta get hold of my folks. I gotta work out what's happening."

He waved Josef on to stop him arguing and broke into a jog. There were stores on the next block. One of them would have a phone that might be working, or at least a TV or something. He didn't do his own shopping now, but he remembered the store from when he didn't have people running all his errands and trying to organize his life for him. He found himself jogging past a line of cars waiting to get onto the bridge. There didn't seem to be many pedestrians walking about, but when he crossed the next intersection he could see why. There was a big crowd at the row of shops up ahead.

Everybody had the same idea. They were drawn to anywhere that had a TV or radio. They were spilling out of the coffee shop and packed tight in front of the electrical store. They didn't even take any notice of Cole when he ran up to them. Usually, he'd collect his own crowd in seconds, all jostling for an autograph, but today he stood at the back, towering over them and staring at the rows of TVs lined up in the window.

It was like watching a mosaic made from bits of hell.

The news had taken over every channel. The TV folk must have gotten the images from a traffic camera or something because they were just grainy black-and-white pictures, and the time code at the bottom of the screen showed they were an hour old. But they were clear enough for Cole to see things he wouldn't have believed even in a movie.

The footage showed a highway that looked like the main road into Jannermont, with cars and trucks generally getting on with their business. One moment they were moving along; the next the road ripped up from one end to the other like someone pulling the backbone out of a fish. Vehicles were hurled everywhere. Bodies were thrown from them. For a couple of seconds it looked like an earthquake, weird and unreal, and then things started coming out of a big hole in the pavement.

They weren't human, but they had two legs and two arms. And most of them were carrying rifles.

Then they used them. They opened up at something out of the range of the camera. Someone ran past the bottom of the frame and fell.

Cole couldn't so much as breathe for a few seconds. The footage stopped abruptly and the studio anchor appeared, looking as shocked as Cole felt. At the bottom of the screen, captions kept flashing up names of cities—former Indie cities, too, not just COG ones—that had been attacked or that had lost all communications.

The watching crowd was completely silent. Folks were used to seeing bad shit from the war on TV, but nobody had ever seen anything like this.

Eventually someone spoke.

"They're everywhere." It was a man standing a couple of rows in front of Cole. "What in the name of God are they?"

"Yeah," said a woman. "And why now, why that the war just ended? What's the government doing?"

For once, nobody took any notice of Augustus Cole, the Cole Train, the Cougars' star player. He was just another shocked, bewildered, scared guy—oh yeah, he was scared all right, because that was the only sane thing to be—and his world had changed forever.

But whatever the government was planning, Cole— scared or not—knew what he had to do.

He was going to find his folks and get them somewhere safe. He'd move them into his house, whether they liked it or not. Dumb as it was, he wondered if his agent would still be waiting for him, but the man had to know by now that Sera was under attack. That contract could wait.

But Cole had a feeling none of that shit was going to matter ever again.

MATAKI FARM, GALANGI, SOUTH ISLANDS: SIX WEEKS AFTER THE ARMISTICE.

On a bad day, Bernie Mataki was sure she could feel the steel pins that held her leg together.

Each time she put her boot down on the pickup's clutch, it nagged at her. It wasn't so much a pain as a vague awareness that the leg was *different*. The civilian doctor had said that it was something like the phantom sensations amputees felt, itching limbs that just weren't there anymore, but he told her she still had her leg and she had to settle for being grateful for that. A lot of Gears didn't have that luxury, he said.

Like I need to be told that, you soft civvie bastard. What do you *know about it? Sod all. You spent the war delivering babies and examining piles.*

Bernie drove slowly down the track and stopped to take a look at the finisher calves. That had been Neal's idea in her absence. She preferred rearing beef herself, but he was the one stuck here doing the work while she was away, so she couldn't complain.

The dog jumped down from the flatbed as she opened the door, expecting some work. She snapped her fingers at him to turn him back.

"Not today, Mossie," she said. "They're settling in. We'll go and move the ewes after lunch, okay? That'll keep you busy."

The dog was always pleased to see her, no matter how long she was away. She got the feeling Moss was happier to have her home than Neal was.

My fault. He really thought we could make a go of this once I left the army. I'm the problem. Not him.

The Pendulum Wars were now over and she would have been demobbed at fifty-five anyway. She knew there would always have been a day when she had to leave the army, if she didn't get herself killed first. It was just the way the shutters came down so suddenly and completely. One day she was elite infantry, a specialist, a platoon sniper, someone with status in a tight-knit clan, and the next moment she wasn't anybody at all. She was wounded, given a medical discharge, and turned out of the regimental family forever.

Maybe I could have stayed on in a support job. Maybe I still could . . .

Neal was on the roof messing around with the TV aerial when she got back. She wondered if he'd seen her. She made a point never to startle anyone balanced precariously on a chimney stack, so she waited for him to finish and notice her.

Eventually he looked down. "Bloody telly's gone on the blink," he said. "Can't get any channels at all."

"What is it?"

"I dunno. The aerial looks okay. I'll have to phone some overpriced tosser from Noroa to fix it. That's going to take a week."

"Well, we'll just have to stare balefully at each other across the table instead." That was the problem with living on a small island. If you wanted anything more than the basics, it meant a ferry trip to Noroa. "Or we can listen to the radio."

"You finished, then?"

Bernie peeled off her gloves. "Yeah. How do you feel about sheep?"

"I think I'll stick with you, love. Sheep can't cook."

"Seriously. I think we should cut back on beef and run more sheep. Better price. Easier to manage, too."

Neal climbed down the ladder and frowned at his skinned knuckles. He sucked them briefly to stop the bleeding. "It's your farm, Bern," he said. "I'm easy."

Yes, it *was* Bernie's farm. It was also her curse. There were days when she hated it, not just because hill farming was tough work for two people with only occasional hired labor, but because the place was 500 hectares of resentment, anger, and guilt. She'd fallen out with her brother over it. She'd also never been sure whether Neal had married her to get a share of it.

Well, he'd kept the place from going to ruin while she was deployed, so if he wanted it, he was welcome to it. Right then she'd have traded it all for transport to Ephyra, half a world away, and a few more years with the regiment.

Come on, the war's over. Really over. Not just over for me—over for everybody. I've got to deal with it sooner or later.

"You want to go to Noroa?" Neal asked. "Change of scenery. Do some shopping. Cheer you up a bit."

"That'd take a lobotomy," she said, and went into the house.

Neal called after her. "I picked up the mail while I was off-camp. There's a letter with a Lake Station postmark."

Bernie stood in the narrow flagstone passage, looking into the bright yellow kitchen. She'd been born in this house. This was her childhood home, her family's farm and land. But even after eighteen months back in civvie street, she couldn't get used to it again, neither its old familiarity nor its unmilitary scruffiness. Neal, poor sod, had never learned to put anything away. He thought harnesses were okay hanging on coat hooks and that boots didn't have to be wiped on doormats.

He's a farmer. Like Dad.

Bernie was used to spit-and-polish and Sovereign's Regs. The 26th Royal Tyran Infantry had been her life since she was eighteen—nearly twenty-seven years' service, twenty of them frontline—and she wasn't going to turn back into a civilian that easily.

Unless I want to. But I don't. I really don't. I want to feel the way I used to. I want to belong. I want to matter. I want that comradeship again.

She hung her oilcloth coat on the hook and ran a finger across the old writing bureau that doubled as a hall table. Dust: not thick enough to write her name in, but enough to make the sergeant in her order that the whole damn hall be scrubbed down, preferably with a toothbrush. She'd have to clean the place or it would nag at her. Neal was okay with dust and washing-up left overnight in the bowl, but she wasn't.

She sorted through the mail—feed bills, the vet's invoice, her monthly war disability pension—and found the envelope with the Lake Station postmark.

"So you've remembered I'm still alive, eh, Mick?" Bernie

debated whether to open it or not. Blood wasn't thicker than
water when it came to money, not by a long chalk. Her
brother never lost a chance to remind her he'd been robbed
of his inheritance when their father died. "You want the
fucking farm? Have it, mate. And the dust."

"What does that bloody waster want now?" Neal asked,
walking up behind her. "Tell him to piss off. I'm fed up busting my gut so that he can cadge money off you." He paused
for breath. "Come on. It's time for dinner."

Bernie opened the letter anyway, ripping the envelope
open with a callused thumb. "Lunch."

"Ooh, la-di-bloody-da. *Lunch*, then."

But it wasn't what she expected. Something fell out onto
the flagstones and she bent to pick it up. It was a photo of a
newborn baby trussed up tightly in a pink blanket, looking
none too happy about it, and she already knew what was
going to be written on the back.

It was Mick's handwriting.

Thought you'd like to know you've got a new great-niece.
Philippa Jane, three kilos.

There was nothing else in the envelope. Bernie studied
the picture for a moment, wondering if Mum and Dad
would have been angry with her for not rushing over to
Noroa to see Mick and make peace. She handed the photo
to Neal. He glanced at both sides and wedged it in the frame
of the mirror hanging by the door.

"A grandfather at his age, and all. Well, at least that's
something he's good at. Breeding." He disappeared into the
kitchen and she caught a delicious whiff of roast poultry as
the door swung open. "Chicken. Should be done to a turn
by now. Come on, you lay the table and I'll carve."

Lunch was one of their own chickens with homegrown
vegetables. The big wooden table felt solid and comforting
beneath her elbows, the food was good in the way that only

fresh homegrown stuff could be, and the view from the kitchen window was a peaceful one of a wintry gray sea in the distance. For a moment, she felt that she might eventually learn to appreciate this kind of life again. Neal laid down his knife and fork on the edge of his plate and got up to switch on the radio. He didn't like silence.

"Ah, bugger it," he said. "Listen to that. What's going on today? Maybe they've had a transmitter failure on the mainland."

The radio was normally tuned to the Ephyra World Service for its weather and shipping forecasts, but all Bernie could hear now was the random crackle of static.

"Leave it," she said. "We can retune it later. Your food's getting cold."

Neal sat down again and they went on eating. She hadn't run out of things to say to him so much as forgotten where to begin saying them, so she said nothing. He kept fidgeting in his seat as if he was building up to something. She braced for incoming.

"Bern," he said at last. "I'm trying. I really am. I read all that stuff from the veterans' association. I know it's a big change for you, but the war's over for *everyone* now."

"Yeah." *But they didn't suddenly disband the army.* "I know."

"Look, I added it all up," he said. "I counted all the days we've actually spent here together as man and wife. One thousand three hundred and seventy-two. About three years in all. Out of seventeen."

"Okay. But I'm home now."

Neal slammed down his fork. "No, you're *not* home. You're *not* home at all. You want to go back to the bloody army."

"Look, I've gone from a busy regiment to a place where I don't even see the neighbors for weeks at a time. It's hard."

"Okay. I know I can't really understand what it was like, but I've always been there for you. Just tell me how to handle a wife who wants to be on the frontline in a war that isn't there anymore."

"I didn't know it would take me this long to adjust."

"Bern, the world's changed. We've got to make this work here. Otherwise what were you fighting for?"

Bernie wished she knew. Sometimes she asked herself why she'd enlisted. It had to be more than some old bastard of a recruiting sergeant telling her that women made bad snipers, but it was all so long ago that she couldn't remember the feelings that had driven her.

I think I wanted to get away from Galangi. I thought Mick would take over the farm. I should have let him.

"I was fighting for my mates," she said. She had no other words for it. "It's hard to feel like I belong here again."

As soon as she said it, she realized she'd told him he wasn't one of her mates and that he'd never understand her world.

Shit, that's not fair on him. "Sorry, love," she said. "That came out all wrong."

Neal was a pretty mild bloke. When he lost his temper, which wasn't often, he just slammed things around a little. Nothing got smashed and there was no yelling. He just stopped eating, got up, and scraped what was left of his meal into the compost bin. But she could see he was seething. He spun around.

"Your mates," he said. "Your bloody *mates*. Where have they been since you got discharged, eh? Do they call? Where's that dickhead you were shagging who left you high and dry? The one who made officer and ran off with the rich lawyer? *That's* your mates. *I'm* the one who married you and kept the bloody farm going while you were away."

That hurt. Neal knew how to do that, just as she did, with

that unerring aim that long-married couples always had. She decided to keep her mouth shut because there was no point rehashing all this crap.

It was true. But she couldn't explain why he was also wrong, not in a way that wouldn't escalate the recriminations. She was too tired and pissed off for that.

And she hadn't thought about Vic Hoffman in a long time. Not as an ex, anyway.

"I'll fix the radio," she said.

Neal did the washing-up in silence while she fiddled with the dial and tried to get a clear signal. Reception wasn't good on Galangi at the best of times; that was why the radio was tuned to the EWS. But she couldn't get the South Islands station, either.

It had to be the relay. The chances of the TV and the radio both developing faults at the same time were remote. She switched the set off and shrugged.

"We're cut off again," she said. "I'll test the walkie-talkies. I might pop over and see if Dale's having the same problems."

But there was no rush. There was still a fruit pie to finish. She'd just cut a slice and was transferring it to a plate when the phone rang. Neal put down the dishes and went into the hall to answer it. It struck Bernie that he was as stuck in his role of house-husband every bit as much as she was still trying to be Sergeant Mataki.

There was a buzz of conversation but she couldn't hear what was being said, only the tone and the long silences. Whatever it was, Neal was upset. When he came back into the kitchen, his face was chalk-white and he looked bewildered, as if he'd had very bad news and didn't know what to do next.

Oh shit. That's not like him.

"That was Dale." His voice was shaky. "It's started again."

"What has, sweetheart?"

"The war. The bloody war."

"What?" Bernie's immediate thought was that she was thousands of miles from base with no fast way back. She was already calculating when the next ferry could get her to Noroa's military airport when her common sense kicked in and started asking questions. "How the hell can *that* happen? How does Dale know?"

"They've attacked Ephyra. And nobody can get a line through to Noroa."

"Who's *they*? The Indies?" Dale was just the bloke who grew cereals a few klicks south of them. He didn't exactly have a hotline to the Chairman. "Where's he getting this information? Come on, Neal, wars don't just start up again."

"He's on the harbormaster's frequency. Someone got an emergency broadcast out before the TV went off the air. These things have come up out of the ground."

"For fuck's sake, *what things*?" Bernie was getting annoyed. She hated it when people couldn't just get to the point and spit it out. "Where?"

Neal swallowed. He was looking right past her, shocked, confused, and running out of words.

"Everywhere," he said. "Every-bloody-where. Right across Sera. And these things—they're not human. They're *really* not human."

IMULSION TANKER *BETANCOURT STAR*, SOMEWHERE IN THE SOUTH-WESTERN APPROACH TO THE SERROGAR PENINSULA, ONE HOUR LATER.

It was time for a drink. A coffee, mind you; zero-crack-sparrow-fart was way too early to take strong liquor, even for Dizzy.

And he'd given up all that stuff. He really *had* this time.

He walked along the deck, picking his way carefully around hatches and cleats in the predawn darkness. When he reached the bows, he took out his hip flask and threw it over the side as far as he could. He almost kissed the flask goodbye, but he wanted this over and done with, and you didn't kiss an enemy.

He didn't see where the flask sank. He just heard the splash, and then the tanker swept past and the damn thing was gone forever.

"That's the last of it," he said aloud. "I'm done with you. No more hooch."

It had taken him a real long time to reach that stage. But he was going home to Lena and the boy, and this time he was going home sober.

Back in the galley, he made a couple of mugs of coffee, then climbed the ladder to the bridge, balancing the scalding liquid in one hand. It had always seemed easier when he was drunk. He found the skipper leaning on the radar screen with his arms folded, staring out over the tanker's deck. It didn't take a lot of men to run a modern tanker. The crew rattled around in a ship this size.

Dizzy put the mug on the console out of elbow range and joined in the silent staring. Ahead of them, the *Star*'s deck stretched nearly 200 meters into unusually flat and calm water. Even the sea had caught a dose of this new peace.

"Kinda lonely out there, Robb," Dizzy said. The horizon was still a deep violet band speckled with the distant navigation lights of other vessels. He could see the three distinctive green lights on the mast of a minehunter a few klicks north as she swept one of the main channels into the port. "I'm gonna miss convoys."

Robb picked up the mug and slurped. "Yeah. It's going to take some getting used to."

For the first time since he'd joined the merchant navy,

Dizzy couldn't see the familiar neat formation of other cargo vessels and the NCOG destroyer escorts around the *Star*. There were no UIR submarines stalking them now. The *Star* could sail safely on her own. It felt strange not to be under constant threat of attack. A man could get used to anything and miss it—even a war. Dizzy took a pull of coffee and wondered how long it would be before he stopped sleeping with his life jacket under his pillow.

"I was about to say we could get back to normal," Robb said. "But peace isn't normal. Not for any of us. It's goddamn *ab*-normal."

"No torpedoes. No shells." Dizzy said it to convince himself rather than the skipper. "We can go any damn where we want, and nobody's gonna try and sink us. Ain't that somethin'?"

Robb pushed himself back from the console and studied the sweep on the screen. The radar plot was dotted with vessels clustered around a fringe of coastline, the approach to Porta Ogari.

"We're going to be running into mines for the next fifty years, armistice or no armistice," he said, nodding at the view from the bridge. A second minehunter was crossing from starboard. "But yeah, no more torpedoes up the ass, at least. When's your boy being demobbed?"

"Already is," Dizzy said. "His unit got back to North Sherrith last week. First thing I'm gonna do when I get home is buy him a beer. If he's old enough to fight, he's old enough to get a man's drink inside him now."

"Not going to introduce him to your finest special reserve, then?"

"Hell, no." If he told Robb he'd given up the sauce, the guy would never believe him. Dizzy had said it too many times before. "His momma would strangle me with a dead snake."

Robb laughed his head off. "Yeah, it's tough being a step-father. Tell me about it."

"Richie's a good boy." Dizzy liked to think he'd been a better dad to the kid than the deadbeat who'd fathered him. He'd tried damned hard. "Never been any trouble. But now he's gotta find a job. They don't always teach Gears a trade, see."

"Always room for a trainee engineer in the Merch, Diz. You tell him that."

Once the *Star*'s imulsion was offloaded to the refinery, Dizzy was done for this trip. He checked his watch. They'd be alongside and discharging in an hour or so, and he could hand over to the relief engineer to take the tanker back to New Temperance. Then it would take maybe another hour to get his papers checked and stamped and all that official bullshit, and he could be on the transcontinental train to Ephyra and across the Tyran border by late afternoon.

Usually, he'd stop by his favorite bar in Ogari for a little liquid refreshment. What was the place called? Hell, all he could remember was the street. It didn't matter. He was never going to visit the place again. *I swear.*

"I'm gonna take a stroll around the deck," he said. "Oughta be a pretty sunrise."

"Diz, you sound like a man making a fresh start."

Robb verged on being a mind reader sometimes. They knew each other too well. "Reckon I am, Robb. The whole world's doin' it."

The tanker was nearly 220 meters from bow to stern, a big rusty metal maze of a place to walk around and—when a fella was in need of some quiet time—with lots of little places to waste a few hours. Dizzy leaned on the rail to watch the sun come up.

Goddamn, it *was* peaceful. There was just the background throb of the engines and the quiet rush of water past the bows.

Even the gulls weren't up and about yet. Normally, he'd see them wheeling in the gloom before the sun came up, silent white ghosts that sometimes squawked as they loomed out of the darkness and scared the shit out of him.

Ogari was getting closer, changing into constellations of lights. Dizzy could pick out the towers and storage tanks of the refinery.

I'm going home.

Yeah. Hope Lena likes the necklace. 'Cos it's a damn long way to take it back to get a refund . . .

A flash of light caught his eye and he looked up. He could have sworn it was a burst of flame, but he couldn't tell from the faint afterglow if it was the refinery flaring off gas or just the first rays of the sunrise catching something he couldn't see. He went back to contemplating the horizon and tried to remember the name of that damn bar.

Cantari? Coroneta? It'll come to me . . .

He raised his binoculars and had another look at the refinery, still a few klicks away. A long trail of vapor drifted lazily from one of the cooling towers. As he scanned the coastline, he picked up movement and saw a small port authority boat heading out at high speed. It was the harbor pilot. A big, awkward girl like the *Star* had to be guided into a busy port because some folks didn't seem to understand a tanker couldn't swerve to avoid them.

But the pilot was on a different course. Dizzy watched the boat peel away and head up the coastline.

It was just routine, something that Dizzy saw every day of his working life. He thought nothing of it until the ship's collision alarm went off at ass-clenching volume and he almost dropped the binoculars.

The siren switched immediately to the muster alarm—two short blasts, repeating—and Dizzy decided that Robb was either jerking his chain or he'd accidentally hit the controls.

That was hard to do, though, and Robb wasn't the jerking-around kind. But Dizzy was damned if he could see anything worth alerting all hands for. It wasn't the fire alarm, for sure.

"Goddamn it, Robb, you nearly made me shit myself!" Dizzy moved toward the center of the deck so he could be seen from the bridge. He gestured to indicate what-the-hell. "There ain't nothin' out here!"

Robb couldn't hear him, of course. But he was gesturing back at Dizzy to come up top, and he didn't look as if he was joking. Something was wrong.

"Goddamn." Dizzy listened for changes in the engine noise as he made his way back up the deck in a hurry. That was all it could be, an engineering problem. That was shitty timing. He'd be stuck in port fixing it now and he could kiss goodbye a week of his leave. "What the hell is it now?"

He ran up the exterior metal stairway to the bridge wing and opened the door to find a dozen of the *Star's* crew clustered around the radio. Robb had the mike handset to his mouth, his thumb hovering over the trans-mit button. His gaze was fixed on the speaker suspended above the helm position.

Everyone was listening intently to a crackling transmission, and that was the moment when Dizzy realized the crisis wasn't a leaking valve or anything else he could fix with a wrench.

He just caught a few words. Someone behind at the door shoved him impatiently, but he couldn't look over his shoulder. The voice traffic froze him to the spot.

"I repeat, we're under attack. We're shutting the port. Any vessels alongside—we're getting them out fast as we can."

"PHM, roger that, we'll assist. Estimate fifteen minutes. Audacious out."

Audacious was an NCOG warship. "What the hell's happening?" Dizzy asked.

"They've started it again, the Indie fuckers." Dolland, one of the cooks, raked his fingers through his hair. His apron was covered in some kind of brown sauce. "We can't dock."

Dizzy was crushed. All he could think of was Richie being recalled and how short the peace had been. He should have known it wouldn't last. The war had been going on too long for folks to break the habit.

"What have they done?" he asked.

Robb pressed the transmit button. "PHM, this is crude tanker *Betancourt Star*. We picked up your transmission to En-COG. Please advise, over."

"Harbor Pilot to *Betancourt Star*, we've got a situation here. You're going to have to divert to the military port at Cape Aelis, over."

"Understood. *Betancourt Star* out." Robb slipped back into the cockpit chair. "All stop. Let's wait for the pilot." He leaned across the console and switched on the long-wave radio. "Okay, it'll be on the news. I bet we'll hear more than we'll get from the harbor master."

"But we can see the refinery from here," Dizzy said. "We can see the goddamn town, too."

"Yeah, but why can't we see anything else?" Dolland craned his neck to get a better look. "Where's the helicopters? I don't hear any gunfire, either."

"Maybe they just strolled in with rifles," Robb said.

"But Ogari's the best part of a thousand klicks from any UIR border. How did they get here?"

Robb was getting impatient. "I'm not the Indie chief of staff, kid. I don't know how they did it. But they did."

Dizzy squeezed out of the packed bridge and made his way down to the deck again, followed by Dolland and one of the other engineers, Welson. They stood on the port side and stared at Ogari's skyline. Eventually, most of the crew who weren't on watch came out on the deck to look.

Dizzy hadn't imagined those flames. The city was under attack.

An explosion lit up the sky and sent thick clouds rolling high into the air. A heartbeat later, Dizzy heard the distant boom.

"Well, shit," Welson said. "The assholes must be targeting all the refineries."

The crew watched helplessly, saying nothing. The silence was broken by a tinny voice. Dizzy turned to see where the sound was coming from. Dolland was holding a small radio to his ear, listening to the news.

"Turn it up, buddy," someone said.

Dolland obliged. "It's a bad signal. Maybe they took out a transmitter too."

So the Pendulum Wars weren't over. The surrender was all a double cross, a goddamn bluff to get the COG to drop its guard. Dizzy felt almost choked by anger and betrayal.

"You rot in hell, you Indie bastards!" It was dumb cursing an enemy that didn't even know he was out here, let alone hear him, but what kinds of assholes broke ceasefires like that? "Fuck *you*! We should have finished you *all* off with the Hammer of Dawn, not just a couple of goddamn ships!"

"Amen to that, buddy," said Welson.

Dizzy didn't know he had that much venom in him. He didn't even get that mean when he was drunk. He'd just finally gotten used to the idea that the war was over, and now he had to start all over again.

Indies were rotten to the core. That was all there was to it.

Maybe it'll all be over again in a couple of days. The Chairman won't take this shit lying down. Not now he's got the Hammer. They'll wind their necks in once he fries a few cities like he promised.

More explosions ripped along the skyline. Dizzy could definitely see the fierce yellow glow of flames in the refinery now. Dolland retuned the radio and held it closer to his ear; his expression changed.

"Listen, it's *not them*," Dolland said. "It's not the Indies. It's something else."

Welson turned around. "What do you mean, *something*?"

"The news says they're *not human*."

"Whoa, so they're fucking performing seals or something?"

Dizzy had to repeat it to himself before the words sank in. "Aw, goddamn it, make sense, buddy. Come on, what are they, Gorasnayans? Those assholes never accepted the cease-fire."

"I don't know what the hell they are. And neither does anyone else from the sound of it. But it's not the Indies."

Robb leaned out of the bridge door and yelled down at the crew.

"Get up here!" he called. "Quick! Dalyell's on the radio!"

When Dizzy followed Welson onto the bridge, the atmosphere was different—not just tense, but scared into silence, and the merchant navy didn't scare easy. Just about the whole crew was crammed in there now, twenty men, even though they could have listened in their cabins. Dizzy felt they were all clinging together out of fear and disbelief. Everyone had that same lost stare. Dizzy perched his backside on the edge of the chart table and listened.

The voice of Chairman Dalyell was crystal clear. It was pretty steady, too, considering the news he was breaking to the world.

"*Citizens, we don't know what these creatures are, other than the fact that they're not human. We don't know where they come from. We don't know what they want. But they're tunneling under our cities and emerging to slaughter our people. Our combined forces throughout Sera have been mobilized to deal with them. I ask you all to remain calm, as*

*you have done through so many years of war. Stay in your
homes unless ordered to evacuate, and listen for emergency
information on all broadcast stations. That, my fellow citizens, is all I can tell you until the situation becomes clearer."*

Nobody said a word for a few moments. Then Welson
broke the silence.

"This is crazy," he said. "It can't be true. It's some exer-
cise. Some shit like that."

Dizzy could only think of Lena and Richie back in North
Sherrith. What was happening to them? He had to find a
way to call them. "Where else have these things come up?"
he asked. "Do we know yet?"

"The news said Jannermont, for sure. It also said *all
across Sera."* Robb held up the maritime satellite handset.
Dizzy could hear the faint voice of a recorded message
repeating that the service was temporarily unavailable. Every
damn ship out there had probably decided to call in at the
same time and overloaded the sat network. "Everyone pick
one number to call, because we're all going to want to ring
someone to see if they're okay when the sat's back in service.
It'll probably be the only chance you'll get."

It was funny how the body didn't really need any help
from the mind to carry on doing what it needed to do. Dizzy,
unable to think straight beyond how he was going to get in
touch with Lena, found himself putting on his ear defenders
and heading for the engine room to check the generators. It
was like a reflex. The second engineer, Milos, was already
down there, wiping his hands on a rag.

"Diz, are they aliens or something?" Dizzy read his lips.
"How did they get here? Did they land? I mean, I know
everyone's saying they came out of holes in the ground—
but how come we've never seen them before? You don't just
get a whole new breed of things come out of nowhere like
that."

Dizzy couldn't think beyond the moment. The creatures were here. His family was somewhere else, without him and probably shit-scared, and he had to get to them. He just had to.

Canopus.

He remembered it now, just when he didn't need to—the name of the bar.

It was the *Canopus.* He wondered if it was on fire, burning with the rest of Port Ogari as creatures nobody could fight off or explain away destroyed Sera one city at a time.

CHAPTER 5

*They think we're paranoid. They wonder why we still keep
them at arm's length. Five centuries ago, we won and lost an
empire of four hundred million citizens. During the
Pendulum Wars, Gorasnaya's population fell from twenty
million to ten. After E-Day, it was two million. After the COG
deployed the Hammer of Dawn, we were reduced to fifty
thousand. Now, after the Stranded massacres and the
famines and the disease and the cold, there are only four
thousand of us. And they wonder why we always have one
eye on the exit.*

(Commander Miran Trescu, on the cultural gulf
between Gorasni and the COG, 15 A.E.)

NEW JACINTO, VECTES: THE PRESENT DAY, 15 A.E.

Miran Trescu tried not to break into a run as he headed for
the helicopters. That smacked of desperation, and he
refused to look needy in front of the COG. It had been hard
enough crawling to the old enemy for help. Now he had to
rely on their air assets.

But he had no intention of sitting on his backside waiting
for crumbs of information from Prescott—or Hoffman. He
hoped the assault rifle slung across his back made that clear.

The COG troops stood around in small groups, poring over maps. Hoffman was deep in conversation with Marcus Fenix, Santiago, and the big thrashball player, Cole. Baird wasn't there; nor were the female Gears who occasionally patrolled with them, but this was the core of Delta Squad, and that meant this was a crisis.

Trescu was struck by how much Hoffman relied on Delta when he still had a couple of brigades at his disposal, as well as some apparently competent if unlikable majors and an assortment of lieutenants. Yanik said it was a regimental thing. They shared a common tribal bond, that death's-head emblem of the 26th Royal Tyran Infantry bearing the motto *Unvanquished.* Trescu understood tradition and heritage all too well.

But we're the vanquished. What do I have to show for throwing my lot in with the COG? We've lost our flagship and our imulsion platform. We're marooned here. And I have to beg for a ride in a COG helicopter.

But Gorasnaya still existed. His people still survived, after a fashion. And that was all that mattered.

Trescu slowed down as he approached Hoffman, imagining his father's reaction if he'd lived to see his son finally agree peace terms with the COG. General Egar Trescu would have backhanded him across the face before disowning him. He'd made his son promise never to surrender. It was a terrible thing to break a promise to a dying man.

But it's a different war now, Papa. The old enemy is irrelevant. We're fighting extinction. And that is something I shall never bow to.

Hoffman stopped talking and turned as Trescu came up to him. He never looked a happy man at the best of times, but today was clearly not one of his better days. The thuggish shaven head and abrupt manner weren't a veneer for some misunderstood poetic soul. Sometimes, though, they seemed to be a shield held up against the terror of failure.

*I know that feeling, Hoffman. I know what it's like to be
afraid that your mistakes could mean the end of your people.*

"Commander," Hoffman grunted.

"Colonel," Trescu said. "Are you flying reconnaissance
today?"

"Yes."

"Then I'd like to join you." Hoffman always responded
best to plain language. "If I go back to my people with a first-
hand report rather than relaying yours, it will be far easier to
manage their expectations."

"They won't swallow my imperialist COG bullshit, you
mean."

"Exactly."

Hoffman pointed to one of the Ravens without blinking,
as if the comment had bounced straight off him. In another
world, Trescu decided he might have grown to like the man.
"KR-Two-Three-Nine," he said. "Make yourself comfortable,
Commander."

The Raven crew chief greeted Trescu at the door with a
casual salute and handed him a radio headset. The tab on
his armor said MITCHELL K. and he looked to be in his early
twenties. The Pendulum Wars were probably only a vague
memory from his childhood if he recalled them at all, and
that brought home to Trescu how few years separated the
seasoned vets like Fenix from the men they now served with.
The word *Indie* didn't evoke quite the same emotion in the
likes of Mitchell as it did in the others. The monsters he'd
grown up dreading were Locust, not other humans.

*And my son . . . he doesn't remember any other kind of war.
Or a Gorasnaya with an army and an empire.*

"We're going to recce the interior, sir," Mitchell said, fiddling around with a battered camera. He indicated the lens.
"Don't tell Baird, but I liberated one of the bot video feeds."

"Won't he realize that when he sees the images?"

"Too late then, sir. Possession's nine-tenths of the law."

The camera had a distinctive logo—the stylized ever-watching eye of the Ephyran TV station that Trescu had once despised for being a tame propaganda mouthpiece for the COG.

"Did you liberate that, too?"

"There's only bad news these days," Mitchell said. "The hacks are much happier now they're doing something productive."

"Productive?"

"Crops need growing. Homes need building." Mitchell stuck his head out of the bay door and tested the camera's focus. "It's not as if there's any real news to cover, is there?"

The COG hadn't changed much, then. *And they had the audacity to call us an oppressive regime.*

Fenix and Dom Santiago jumped into the helicopter followed by Hoffman. He sat down facing Trescu and didn't wait for the Raven to get airborne before refolding a map and slapping it on Trescu's knees. The two men were a meter apart, no more, but Trescu had to listen on the radio to hear him.

"Here's the geology." Hoffman ran his forefinger along curving penciled lines on the map, his hands surprisingly well manicured despite a lot of cuts and bruises. "Big rifts in the bedrock here, here, and here. Basically, they cut off the northwest of the island, slice through the central uplands, and fork south around here. They're mostly at the center around the volcano."

Trescu studied the map. The single north-south fissure on the survey map stopped forty kilometers north of the naval base. "The stalks might not be able to reach the settlement, then."

"But we don't know how many small fissures and lava tunnels there are. We'll see."

Trescu was aware of Fenix studying him, just an

occasional passing glance, but whenever Fenix was looking, Trescu knew he was *analyzing*. Trescu didn't attempt to carry on the conversation as the helicopter headed north over farmland and into the island's interior. Ravens seemed much noisier than the UIR's Khimeras. But perhaps he was just letting the filter of nostalgia deceive him. There were no Khimeras left for comparison.

Dom didn't meet his eyes. He was staring out of the bay door, his rifle on his lap, but it was hard to tell if his mind was on something else or if he simply didn't like the company of an *Indie*. Yanik—always gossiping with the unfortunate Donneld Mathieson—said Dom's brother had been killed in the Pendulum Wars, like Lieutenant Stroud's mother. The years that had passed hadn't healed or erased the pain, but had simply been crossed off in calendars. Trescu understood that too.

The radio crackled. "I'm following the line of the rift now," the pilot said. "Can't see anything yet."

Beneath them was thick virgin forest. The heart of the island was an extinct volcano. There were probably fascinating creatures down there that had developed in isolation from the rest of Sera, but they were an uncurious lot, the COG. They must have had a presence here for centuries, and yet they'd left this place untouched and remained satisfied with an existence on the fertile coast and lowlands.

And this was where they developed chemical and biological weapons to use against us. Hard to imagine I'm helping them defend it now.

Fenix turned his head suddenly and pressed his finger to his earpiece. "Sorotki, look due east. Can you see a light patch in the trees?"

"Got it." The Raven turned. "Come on, Mitchell. Turn over, rolling—action. Did I get that in the right order?"

Mitchell's shoulders shook as if he was laughing. Trescu

couldn't hear him, but he saw him say something as he attached his safety line to the rail and braced himself against the frame to steady the camera.

The Raven dropped to twenty meters above the tree canopy, sending a flock of black-and-white birds wheeling from the branches. Trescu craned his neck as far as he could to catch a glimpse of whatever Fenix had spotted.

"It's okay—it's only a couple of dead trees. Normal ones." Mitchell lowered his camera. "Keep going, Mel."

"Okay, back on course," Sorotki said. "So what's Professor Baird's theory, then? I do miss his informative yet abrasive commentary, don't you?"

"Ingress via cave systems." Marcus unbuckled and moved to the door gun. "Makes sense. We've seen them come up from the seabed."

"So are they like fungi or something? You know, all the real activity goes on underground and all you see above the ground are the fruiting bodies and the spores."

Dom stirred. "Wow, it's just like having Baird right here with us."

"He's got a point," said Fenix.

Sorotki sounded amused rather than offended. "Yes, chopper pukes have active intellects too, Dom. I still don't see where the polyps fit in, though. One minute they're on leviathans, then they're on stalks."

"Maybe they're like ants." Fenix had never seemed the kind for small talk. "They get everywhere."

"What triggers them to detonate?" Trescu asked. "Do they wander around looking for a victim? Or do they combust anyway?"

"No idea," Dom said.

"But *why* do they combust? Why does any organism self-destruct as a matter of routine? I can think of only one thing. Reproduction."

Fenix made a noise that might have been a laugh if he'd given it a chance. "Goddamn. We never asked that."

"I'm Gorasni," Trescu said. "We're a very pessimistic people. It saves time."

"Doesn't take us much further, though." Hoffman adjusted his binoculars. "It probably doesn't matter if that's how the Lambent spread if the only way we know how to stop them is to blow them up. I think that's known as lose-lose."

Trescu had no answer to that. He spent the rest of the flight watching the body language of the Gears around him. It was as educational as interrogating them, even if it didn't fill in the detail. Fenix looked at Hoffman as if he were a distant father he wished he could understand; Hoffman occasionally glanced at Fenix as if searching for the right moment to say something and never finding it. His interaction with Dom seemed much more relaxed and born of an old familiarity. Hoffman made direct eye contact with him, and when he wanted to get his attention to point out some feature in the landscape, he didn't rely on the radio. He leaned across and tapped his knee. Those two knew each other well. There was genuine affection. Hoffman's set jaw relaxed for a few moments before returning to grim contemplation of whatever haunted him.

And there was a strong bond between Fenix and Dom. Fenix kept looking at him, just a second's pause in his regular sweep of the cabin, but dwelling on him long enough to show concern. When their eyes met, Dom nodded almost imperceptibly as if to reassure him he was okay.

Ah, yes. This is the man who had to put his wife down like a dog. This is the man who searched for her for ten years and found her far too late. But still he goes on. We all refuse to accept the inevitable end.

Trescu thought of all the species that had become extinct

on Sera over the eons and wondered if any of them had been convinced that they would survive because they were somehow too special to die. He doubted it. Only humans could believe the world couldn't exist if they weren't around to validate it with their presence.

"Goddamn it," Hoffman muttered. He pressed his field glasses to his face. "Sorotki, I don't like what I'm seeing. Forty-five degrees to your port side, range about two klicks."

"Roger that." The Raven looped left. "Yeah . . . I see it now."

Trescu turned in his seat to look. In the ocean of green, he could see a dark patch. For a moment he thought it was another variety of stalk and slipped his rifle off his lap, ready to open fire if the branches turned out to be swarming with polyps, but it was clear when the Raven got within a few hundred meters that it was a stand of dead trees. These weren't bleached ash-gray with age. The trunks were covered in normal bark, but every leaf was brown and withered.

"Test a theory for me," Fenix said. "See what's in the center of that."

"I can guess," Sorotki said. "Come on, Mitchell, it's photo opportunity time."

Sorotki brought the Raven down to fifty meters above the dead area. It was wider than Trescu had first thought, a good hundred meters across. And at the heart of the destruction were a couple of stalks, now just spent husks like some abstract piece of sculpture.

Everyone looked down as the Raven circled. Trescu caught the expressions, the same tight-lipped realization that wherever the stalks emerged, the vegetation around them died. Hoffman glanced at Marcus as if he wanted confirmation of something that Trescu could only guess at.

"*That's* what's going to kill us if the glowies don't get us first," Marcus said. "Loss of workable land. Crop shortages."

"Mitchell, get me a picture with some scale in it." Hoffman marked something on his map. "Then we come back and check the spread every twenty-six hours."

Mitchell leaned out and ran the camera in short bursts. "Maybe we'll work out a formula. Like one stalk puts out enough shit to kill however many square meters of land."

It was fascinating to watch a communal theory form. Trescu agreed with their unspoken assessment, but he didn't join in.

This was an island, and an island that relied wholly on its agriculture. There was nowhere left to import food from. Vectes might as well have been the entire world.

And this island used to be the COG's biological research center before they decommissioned it. Such elegant irony. They keep forgetting that. We don't.

"Okay, Sorotki, move on." Hoffman sat back and took off his cap to run his hand over his shaven scalp. "If we're lucky, the stalks won't spread far beyond the fissures, and the contaminated zones will have a limit. We can work around that."

"And if we're not lucky?" Trescu asked, knowing the answer. He just wanted to hear Hoffman's strategy for survival.

"Then we might end up teetering on the ledge," Hoffman said. "And we'll have to decide when to jump."

CNV *SOVEREIGN*, DEEPWATER BERTH, VECTES NAVAL BASE: ONE WEEK LATER.

"I hope you brought a mop," said Michaelson.

The captain stood with his back to Hoffman, shuffling irritably through piles of papers on his desk. The day cabin looked like a grenade had hit it. Paper was stacked on every surface and inspection hatches hung open with their wiring looms spilling out like entrails. Hoffman could have sworn his boots squelched as he trod on the rug. The warship, the last Raven's Nest carrier still operational, was starting to show her age.

"Spring cleaning, Quentin?"

"Damn leak," Michaelson said. "They're still trying to track it. You know how leaks are—they can show up a long way from where they started. I'm rescuing my paperwork."

Hoffman checked out the big blue leather chair on the far side of the cabin before he risked planting his ass in it. He picked up the sheaf of papers stacked on the cushion before he sat down, and tidied them into a pile on his lap.

"Beats a leak that starts from the bottom up, I suppose," he said, glancing up at the deckhand for telltale droplets.

"Ah, Victor, you're getting the hang of the navy at last."

"What are you looking for?"

"A list of Pendulum War fuel caches."

"Damn, you keep filing that far back?" Hoffman looked through the papers on his lap. They were detailed logs, at least on the side he was looking at. When he flipped one over he found the reverse had been used for something else entirely, a penciled diagram of some collision damage. Some of the pages had that velvety texture that came from being repeatedly erased and reused. "I never realized how many records you saved. We jettisoned decades' worth at HQ when we banged out of Jacinto."

"I saved some rum, too. Help yourself. Under the bridge repeater. But I need that list."

"Proper rum? Not moonshine?" Hoffman ducked down and rummaged in the cubbyhole. He pulled out a five-liter steel canister that could have held anything from acid to fuel. "I'll take a rain check. Thought you'd run out of the good stuff."

"The day we run out of rum is the day En-COG ceases to

exist, Victor. *Rum*. Not distilled beet alcohol with caramel, or however Dizzy makes his brew. No disrespect to Private Wallin, but I like my paralyzing agents to have a little subtlety. Ah—got it!" Michaelson flicked through a dog-eared manual with a brown cloth cover. "There *must* be some caches nobody's found."

"Optimist."

"Not necessarily. When you reduce the population of a planet by ninety-nine percent in the space of a few years, fuel reserves don't get used."

"New fuel doesn't get refined, either."

"It's still worth investigating. We don't yet know how Ollivar's damned pirate fleet stays fueled, do we? And they're still out there, Victor. We pick up the odd radio transmission."

Hoffman shrugged. "Good luck to 'em. If the assholes try to come back, we can commandeer their vessels and drain the tanks."

"Royston's been bending my ear about the rate we're using fuel."

"And mine. But I need to keep my birds in the air right now."

"You diverted all the way down here to say that?"

"No, I just wanted a word with you in private before the meeting."

Hoffman wanted to clear his yardarm, as Michaelson was fond of saying, before he got down to discussing encroaching stalks or fuel crises. He hadn't told Michaelson that he'd stolen Prescott's encrypted data. It wasn't that he didn't trust him; he did. But he was an old friend, an ally, and a decent man didn't burden his friends with information that would compromise them.

And how would I feel if he'd had the disk and didn't tell me?

Hoffman would have felt betrayed. So he had to level with Michaelson. If he didn't, he was as bad as Prescott, withholding information from his own people when it might actually make a difference.

If we even knew what the hell it was.

He put the pile of papers on the nearest dry surface. The cabin smelled of disinfectant and damp wool. Every sound including his heartbeat became unnaturally magnified.

"Quentin, you know I told you there's something you'd be better off not knowing?"

"Oh dear . . ." Michaelson raised his finger for silence and dogged the door shut. "Go ahead. I'm all grown up now. I can take it."

"I've got a data disc that troubles me."

Michaelson raised an eyebrow. He put his hand flat on the steel door as if he was monitoring vibrations. Maybe he was. "What's on it?"

"No goddamn idea. I've got Baird trying to decrypt it. I stole it."

"Good grief . . . from Prescott?"

So much for my discretion. "That's quite an inspired guess."

Michaelson shrugged. "Well, who else is likely to be clinging to classified information when we're going to hell in a handbasket? He's done it before. Do you think he knows it's missing yet?"

Hoffman sometimes had out-of-body moments when he could see and hear himself as a stranger might. The stranger who studied him at that moment found it faintly ludicrous that a veteran Gear whose decisions had shaped an entire war could be reduced to playing stupid motherfucking *games* with the head of state while the world was circling the drain.

"Oh, he knows I took it." Maybe Prescott *wanted* him to take it. No, this was getting too layered and complicated. He

could hear Bernie scolding him for wasting energy on endless what-ifs. "We had harsh words about it."

Michaelson, still leaning on the door, blinked a few times
as if he was busy thinking. "It's chaff," he said flatly. "A diver-
sionary tactic. You think he'd keep anything that sensitive on
a disk?"

"Yeah, I've had that discussion with Baird. But even
Prescott can't retain high volumes of complicated data in his
brain."

"He can wind you up like a clockwork toy, Victor. It's a
decoy."

"But what would he try to divert me *from*?" Hoffman
wasn't offended by the observation. Prescott was manipula-
tive; that was part of the job description for a politician, and
Hoffman knew his own buttons were obvious and easy to
press. *Yeah, but he's still got to deal with me.* "I'm damned if
I can think of anything a sane person would need to conceal
at this stage of the game."

"Sane," Michaelson said. "That raises a question we
haven't really factored into the equation yet."

"Goddamn, don't even *start* me thinking that he might
be mentally unfit for office. Where the hell would *that* leave
us?"

"Without a deputy to replace him, or a court system to
challenge his fitness."

Hoffman didn't like where this was going. There was an
inevitability to it. The last thing he'd ever thought would go
wrong was Prescott's mind. No, the crafty bastard wasn't
crazy. This was business as usual for him. He'd held back
crucial information so many times before that it was a reli-
able sign of normality—for Prescott.

"Look, if I see him talking to any trees," Hoffman said, "I
promise I'll take him out back and shoot him myself. Out of
kindness."

Michaelson pocketed the radio handbook. "You'll let me know if I can do anything on the encryption front, won't you?"

"You got anything better than Baird?"

"On software? Alas, no, but the offer stands. Who else knows about this?"

"Delta Squad. Bernie."

"Naturally."

"But I haven't told Anya yet."

"Does she need to know?"

"I've never kept anything from her. I need my inner circle."

"Okay. Put on your loyal face and let's go see the boss fella."

Bernie had taken to calling Hoffman, Michaelson and Trescu the Triumvirate, as if they were a power bloc of some kind. She had a point, because that was how things were starting to shake out. They met Prescott a couple of times a week in Admiralty House for a sitrep, sometimes with civilian representatives present, sometimes not. Today was a *not* day. Hoffman had never been a meetings kind of man, but these sessions mattered. It was more than a chance to pool information and plan. It was an opportunity to sniff the pheromones and work out who was up to what.

And Prescott had to look him in the eye. He had to sit across the table from Hoffman knowing that his most senior officer had his precious disc and was working on cracking it.

And don't think I'm not looking at every other damn thing you're doing, asshole.

When Hoffman opened the door, Prescott was studying some charts pinned on the wall, a pencil in one hand. Trescu, arms folded across his chest, sat at the far end of the table watching him in silence as if he was working out the best angle for a head shot. At least there wasn't much chance of him ganging up with the Chairman. But then Trescu always looked like an utter bastard. It was the combination of the immaculately trimmed black beard and that dark, dead, intense stare that did it.

And the fact that he blew a prisoner's brains out in front of me. That as well. But at least you know where you stand with him.

"Sorotki just dropped off the latest aerial recon images, gentlemen," Prescott said, not looking away from the wall. The chart was a map of Vectes peppered with flagged pins. He marked something on it. "Main item on today's agenda—the contaminated zones are still spreading. So far, we appear to have lost fifty hectares of crops and pasture. Worst scenario plan, please."

Trescu looked at Hoffman and nodded toward the other end of the table. The reconnaisance images were fanned out in a sequence. Hoffman and Michaelson sat down to leaf through them.

"Royston's already got that in hand," Hoffman said. "He's our end-of-the-world guy. Where is he, by the way?"

Prescott still didn't look at Hoffman. "He's gone to revise his worst-case scenario."

"Up or down?" Sharle normally told Hoffman everything. "Is this about fuel?"

"Well, the less fuel we have, the more creative we'll need to be about where to relocate."

Ah, screw him. I'll ask Sharle myself. Hoffman dropped the subject and noted the time between images. He was looking down almost vertically on the suddenly familiar crown of a stalk with a patch spreading out from its trunk like a shadow. The dead area wasn't uniform—more a ragged ink blot in most shots—but he could still see that the zones were expanding more slowly as the hours and days went on.

Maybe it'll stop. Maybe things can improve.

"The math would take me hours," Michaelson said. "So, broad brushstrokes. Five thousand square kilometers of island, mostly virgin forest or mountain, and we can't see much of what's going on in there. We live on the cultivated margins and depend wholly on what we can grow and graze. How many stalks is it going to take to destroy enough arable land to starve us out?"

That was about the size of it. Nobody mentioned polyps. They had suddenly become a temporary problem compared to what the stalks could do in the longer term. Polyps could be detonated. The toxin—or whatever it was—couldn't.

Hoffman took a breath. "We still can't tell if there's a limit to how far these things can extend beyond the fissures. The gamble is how long we wait before we start relocating people."

"All I'm seeing," Prescott said, still not meeting Hoffman's eyes, "is that there's a fissure running more or less east-west and cutting off Pelruan from the rest of Vectes. Are we going to wake up to a stalk hedge across the north of the island?"

"We have an evacuation plan in place, Chairman. I don't want to implement it until we have to. We've got some serious work to do before we shift three or four thousand people down here."

"Is your Hammer of Dawn satellite network still working?" Trescu asked. "All of it, I mean."

Answering a question like that from a UIR officer would once have been unthinkable. *Ex-UIR*, Hoffman reminded himself. *He's one of us now.*

"We had a hell of a job even hitting that leviathan with it," Hoffman said. "The sats are starting to fail. And we can't incinerate stalks every time they pop up."

"I wasn't thinking of its destructive capacity." Trescu got up and walked over to the chart as if Prescott wasn't even there. "Can it relay images? I understood it could."

Prescott didn't move out of his way. "Oh, did you?"

"That's the weather sat system," Michaelson said. "It's almost inoperable. The long-range comms network will go down next."

"If you could acquire images from low orbit, you wouldn't need your Ravens to fly reconnaissance." Trescu took his knife from his belt, then stepped aside to open the sash window. He started sharpening his pencil, sending shavings floating away on the breeze. "But I imagine you've already considered that."

Hoffman hadn't, because the weather sats weren't that good to start with. The resolution was fine for big weather systems. Anything as small as a stalk on the ground was beyond them. "We'll look into it," he said.

Trescu inspected the tip of his pencil and sat down again. "When do you plan to start rationing?"

"Fuel or food?" Michaelson asked.

"Either. Both."

Prescott was tossing a pin in his palm while he studied the map. Then he looked Hoffman in the eye for the first time since he'd walked in, and pressed the pin slowly into the board with his thumb.

"Food's effectively controlled by central distribution, anyway," he said. "People don't have grocery stores to plunder. We're old hands at calculating how many calories any given human needs to survive, aren't we, Colonel?"

"We're pretty good at stretching imulsion supplies, too, but that doesn't mean we'll never run out."

"I've got the latest minimum figures, if anyone's interested." Michaelson opened his notebook. "The chief engineer's drawn up his best estimate of how much of each fuel we need to set aside to guarantee getting the fleet back to the mainland."

Trescu tilted his head. "A one-way trip."

"Yes. Using the minimum number of hulls required to move the existing population. Not cruise-level comfort, and no margin for error. This is the last-resort scenario."

The window was still open. Hoffman could hear the puttering sound of a distant outboard and the rhythmic whoosh and thud of waves hitting the granite cliff beneath the naval base. There were no Centaurs rumbling along the roads, no distant pounding of artillery shells, no city noises at all. This time, though, the quietness wasn't blissfully peaceful, but a reminder of how impossibly distant from the mainland this island was.

"We always planned to resettle the mainland one day," Prescott said. "Let's not paint this as the start of a panicky retreat, shall we? The intention to return has been public from day one." He gathered up the images and put them in a battered folder. "By the way, I want squads to gather samples from each stalk site, especially if there's anything unusual."

"Twenty-meter-tall instant trees and killer crabs not unusual enough, Chairman?" Michaelson said.

"I mean anything that shows change." Prescott flapped one hand vaguely. It wasn't a gesture he used often. "Different features on the stalks. Other life-forms that are affected. We were getting quite a Lambent menagerie trawled up in the fishing nets, remember. Now, any other business?"

"Did we decide anything?" Trescu asked irritably.

"Very well, I'll see you all later."

Prescott swept out. As he opened the door, Hoffman caught sight of his personal protection Gears—Rivera and Lowe—waiting outside. They vanished down the stairs with him. What was it Baird called them? *The Onyx Guard rejects*. It was acidly cruel, as Baird usually was, but they did behave more like the security elite these days then regular Gears. The Onyx Guard was long gone, though like so many other units.

Trescu sat staring at the open door for a few moments.

"What *is* he afraid of?" he asked.

It was a good question. Hoffman got up to leave. "Never seen him afraid of anything. Not even when he was face-to-face with a grub. In any other man, that'd make me admire him."

"That man is *afraid*." Trescu stood up and pointed in the direction of the stairs with the pencil. "Can't you see it?"

"We're all investing in brown underwear now, Miran," Michaelson said. *Miran?* So they were *that* chummy. "Maybe the Chairman's finally got the picture too."

Hoffman jumped to one conclusion. It was about the disc. Trescu had some kind of radar for detecting weakness in others, much like Prescott's, and Hoffman was inclined to trust it. If Trescu said the man was rattled, then maybe Hoffman was getting too close to something.

He almost—*almost*—started telling Trescu about the disc. Old habit from another war shut him up before he parted his lips.

"I'm going to crunch some fuel numbers with Royston," he said, and left Trescu with Michaelson.

GORASNI CAMP, NEW JACINTO: 15 A.E.

Trescu paused on the edge of the camp and scanned the rows of tents.

It was just as well that the warm season was coming, and Vectes had a mild climate anyway. At least he didn't have to worry about losing more people to hypothermia like last winter. But that was little comfort when he considered that he could take in what was left of the entire Gorasnayan nation with one slow glance across a refugee camp.

This was all they had: tents, the possessions they could carry, and the few animals and vehicles they could load onto

ships for the voyage. They'd arrived on Vectes with an imulsion platform still operating out at sea, but now they didn't
even have that. They were . . . stranded. The word alone
almost choked him.

As in marooned. Not as in filthy savages. Never that.

Irony was inventively sadistic. The Gorasni now had less to
their names than those gangs of Stranded vermin. Trescu's
instinct for survival—a communal thing, not his individual
welfare—insisted he never stop thinking about how far Gorasnaya had fallen in the world order of Sera since his
great-grandfather's day. It was all that kept him from going
under.

We were an empire. This should never have happened.

He walked on. He made a point of having lunch with his
wife and son every day, however brief that meal might be.
Three rows into the tent village, new wooden huts had
already sprung up to replace those burned down when the
polyps had swarmed through the naval base. A couple of
men—Jorgi and Emanu—were nailing oilcloth onto the roof
of one of the huts and paused to acknowledge him. A small
tabby cat lay curled in the doorway, basking in the sun.

*I know my entire nation by name. Every last man, woman,
and child. Even that damn cat. That's something only a dying
people can manage.*

"How's it going, sir?" Jorgi called. "We heard the Raven
pilots on the radio. The stalks are poisoning more farmland."

"I wouldn't worry too much yet," Trescu called back. It
was hard to keep anything quiet in a community this size
and he'd given up trying. He wasn't sure he even *wanted* any
secrets these days, and he didn't care if Hoffman knew his
comms were monitored. He knew Hoffman monitored his.
"Chairman Prescott has a map on his wall with pins stuck in
it. So everything is under control, thanks to the might of the
COG's little *pins.*"

"Shouldn't we be thinking about our own evacuation plan?"

"The stalks are a long way from here. And where do you plan to run? Vectes is still safer than the mainland."

"We won't have enough fuel to leave."

"I promised the COG that we would join them if they protected us," Trescu said. *And I should be planning to save my own people, not drowning hand-in-hand with the COG.* "Until they break their word, that's the way it stays." He looked down at the cat. "And you, Sosca—stay clear of Sergeant Mataki. She's on the prowl for fur linings."

Trescu continued his walk through the camp, taking the long route home so that he was *seen.* It mattered. It was how he maintained command. There were many here who thought he was a traitor for agreeing a formal peace with the old enemy, let alone joining the COG and allowing them access to the imulsion—men like Ianku Nareci.

Just muttering. Just idle noise.

None of them had made a move against him; none of them had the balls to dare. He was a Trescu, for God's sake. His father had defeated superior COG forces at Branascu, and his grandfather had driven them back from the border. He had *pedigree.* Gorasnaya had never signed the surrender because it had never been defeated, however weak it had become over the centuries, and that was because men of Trescu lineage had been in command.

I handed over our fuel and our future to Prescott and Hoffman. But they're not the enemy. They're not the ones killing us now.

When he reached his own tent—nothing fancy, nothing better than his people had—he could see that Ilina had company. Stefan Gradin, a man at a loose end now that his imulsion platform had been destroyed, and Teodor Marisc—Trescu's senior warrant officer, just *Teo* to just about everyone—were sitting outside passing a smoke back and forth between them. They got up slowly as if they were stiff from sitting down too long.

"Your missus booted us out, Commander," Teo said. "We have to smoke outside now, she says."

"Good for her." Trescu took the roll-up out of Teo's hand and ground it under his heel. "Filthy habit. And a dangerous one in a flammable environment. Remind me to ban it. Come on, let's eat."

Ilina gave him a wink as he ducked into a tent fragrant with the aroma of lamb and garlic. It was amazing what a smart woman could cook on a camping stove. Piotr, ten years old and already a good shot, was cleaning his rifle in the corner with a frown of intense concentration.

"So is this a command meeting or lunch?" Ilina asked pointedly. Trescu walked up behind her and kissed the top of her head. "Because lunch gets you fed and a meeting *doesn't*. And don't try sweet-talking me."

"I wouldn't dare, beloved. Can the boys stay? They've been waiting to see me. Hungry work, waiting."

"Okay. But you'll have to fill yourselves up on bread. I only made enough for three servings."

"They can have mine," Piotr said. "I don't mind."

"No, you've got a lot of growing to do." Trescu pulled a chair back from the table and motioned to his son to sit down. The meeting would take place with the boy there, joining in if he had something to say, not conducted over his head as if he were incapable of understanding what faced his people. It was essential that he learned what it took to hold a nation together. The duty might well fall to him one day. "So eat everything your mother puts in front of you. Understand?"

"Yes, Dad."

"Good." Trescu reached for the bread basket and tossed a

couple of knot-shaped rolls to Teo and Stefan. "Now, what's so important that it can't wait until after lunch?"

"*Weird shit*, Commander," Stefan said, using the Tyran phrase. "We were testing the engines in *Amirale Enka* and we picked up a stray transmission. It broke in on the old maritime control frequency."

"What was it?"

"I don't know. It was a databurst. Like satellite noise, you know?"

"Not a scrambled COG channel?"

"I know what their scrambled channels sound like. This wasn't it. And they're not bothering to encrypt now anyway."

Trescu's first thought was that Hoffman was testing the Hammer of Dawn uplink. He could simply ask the man, of course, and he was pretty sure he'd get a straight answer.

Well, they did admit the Hammer net was failing.

Perhaps he thinks the Hammer generally is too touchy a subject. At least that means he doesn't want to alienate us.

"Dad, are they going to bomb us again?" Piotr asked.

History was a live beast for Gorasni. Piotr hadn't even been born when the COG had launched the Hammer of Dawn strike, let alone the Pendulum Wars. Ilina gave Trescu a weary look, passed around the bowl of lamb casserole, and said nothing. He knew she disapproved. She didn't want her son taught to hate strangers. He had to find a good reason of his own, she said.

I don't want him to have one. Because then it'll be too late. And maybe the COG won't kill us deliberately. Maybe they'll just make another lethal mistake. I have to be able to trust their competence.

"Don't worry, they don't have any more bombs," Trescu said. "Only the Hammer. And if they used it on us . . ." He looked at Ilina. "It would be out of carelessness. Like they vaporized their own people to save them. So that's all right. Isn't it?"

"You're doing that tight voice, Daddy. The one where it's a joke but it isn't actually funny."

"I'm sorry, Piotr." There was nothing like a perceptive child to put a man in his place. "You're old enough to understand this. It's too early to completely trust the COG without question after so many years of war, and they seem to feel the same about us. We have to earn one another's trust."

"But they killed everyone. They burned all the cities."

"They burned their own, too. I know that's hard to understand." Trescu tried to be neutral to appease Ilina. "But the Locust were so dangerous that the COG thought it was worth doing anything to try to stop them."

"But they didn't burn Jacinto." Piotr seemed to be following the logic pretty competently. "And the Lambent are even worse, everyone says. So . . . why don't they use the Hammer again?"

"It doesn't work properly now." Trescu began to worry that Piotr was storing up a few nightmares for later. He had to distract him. "And Hoffman's okay. He wouldn't do it again. His wife died when the COG burned its cities, you see."

Teo cocked his head. "Where did you hear that?"

"Yanik," Trescu said. "He chats with Lieutenant Mathieson. Not much hard intel, but lots of interesting gossip."

"So what do we do about the databurst?" Teo asked.

Trescu went on eating. "Nothing. And I don't want everyone thinking we're about to be incinerated, Teo—be sensible. Tell me if it happens again. But leave me to raise the matter with Hoffman."

Piotr fished a chunk of leg bone out of his casserole and peered into the hole. He loved the marrow. It was his special

treat and Ilina made sure he always got it now that meat was
back on the menu. Trescu watched him scrape it out with
the tip of his knife, frowning with concentration, and spread
it on a crust. Vectes could have been a pleasant, well-fed
exile. But it wasn't Gorasnaya, and he had to remember that.

"Dad, am I allowed to speak to the Cogs?" Piotr asked.
He took a child's delight in using the word. It brushed close
to a Gorasni profanity. "Is it true they eat cats?"

Stefan chuckled. "Only the sniper woman with the dog.
Have you seen her boots? Tabby fur."

"They've got a real thrashball star, Piotr," Ilina said,
shooting Stefan her narrow-eyed *shut up* look. "Maybe it's
better if you talk to him."

Everybody loved thrashball. Piotr's face lit up. "Can I,
Dad? Please?"

"I'll see what I can do," Trescu said, winking. He cleared
his plate and got up, beckoning to Teo to follow him. "Sorry
to run, Ilina, but we have to check a few things."

Once they were at a safe distance from the tent, Stefan lit
up another messily rolled cheroot. He looked sheepish when
Trescu glared at him, but he lit it anyway.

"Aww, I couldn't smoke on the rig, Commander," he
said. "Don't be too hard on me."

"Very well, enjoy it while you can." Trescu checked his
watch, the gold one his father had given him. It had been his
grandfather's, too. Both men would have had a fallback plan
ready to roll out, even with their most trusted allies. They
would have expected no less of him. "I want a contingency
plan. I want to know how much fuel we could lay our hands
on and how many people we could evacuate to the nearest
land if we reach a point where we think the COG is unwise
to stay here."

Teo gave him a thumbs-up gesture and slapped Stefan on
the back, making him cough up smoke. Even if the plan was

never put into action, just knowing it was there would reassure people.

"But I *like* the Cogs, Teo," Stefan said, wiping his mouth on the back of his hand. "You weren't on Emerald Spar when the polyps attacked. You didn't see how the Gears fought to save us. Not the drilling platform. *Us.*"

"I *was* there," Trescu said. "And you're right. They risked their lives for us. But this isn't about friendship or gratitude. It's about being prepared."

Stefan gave him a wary look. "You wouldn't return the favor? You wouldn't go to their aid if they needed us?"

Trescu felt his scalp tighten a little. He felt suddenly *dishonorable*. He was doing his sworn duty, putting the defense of the Gorasni nation first, but the thought that he might abandon Gears to their fate after fighting alongside them suddenly stuck in his throat.

The psychological bonds forged in combat didn't take much notice of flags, borders, or promises made to dying fathers. That came as a surprise to him.

"We'll have to keep them out of trouble, then," Trescu said. However justified his prejudices were, the world wasn't a clear-cut place. "Just so they don't drag us down with them."

"Of course, sir," Teo said. "Very wise."

CHAPTER 6

*My father warned me that a politician couldn't be a hero
until he was dead and history put him in context. I have no
ambition to be a hero, but I would like to be understood one
day. Our job is the necessary dirty work that nobody else
wants. Hoffman would understand that. A soldier's job is
much the same. But would Marcus Fenix believe my reasons
for acting as I did? And does it matter as long as Serans
survive to have the luxury of debating whether I was a
coward or a traitor? Part of me thinks it does. This is why
politicians write memoirs—it's our plea in mitigation.*

(Chairman Richard Prescott, son of former
Chairman David Prescott, from his unpublished memoirs)

KR-239, ON PATROL OVER NORTH VECTES.

"My mom used to do this," Sorotki said.

Dom had his gaze fixed on the landscape beneath, scanning the woods for trees that didn't belong there. "What, she strafed armored columns?"

Marcus watched from the other door. It was oddly quiet without Baird and Cole. Even Mitchell, manning the door gun, hadn't said much that morning.

"I mean on long car journeys," Sorotki said. "Count the

red trucks. Or cows. Or twenty-meter-high invasive life-forms."

Dom recalled doing much the same with his kids, Bennie and Sylvie. His breath jammed in his throat for a second. "What keeps you cheerful, Lieutenant?"

"Okay, I'll shut up."

"No, I mean it. I've never seen you in a shitty mood. Ever."

There was a sudden silence, or at least the radio conversation stalled. It was turning into one of those accidentally serious conversations that Dom tried to avoid in case he found himself talking about Maria or the kids and making everyone squirm. He caught himself thinking about them a lot less now. He wasn't sure if that meant he was successfully shutting out the pain, or just coming to terms with his loss.

Acceptance.

Maybe you do get there in the end somehow, just like the bereavement counselor said.

"I just program myself," Sorotki said at last.

"What?"

"Go through the physical motions often enough and the feeling becomes real. It's a feedback thing. I read it somewhere. Force a smile often enough and eventually your brain registers *happy.* Signal in becomes signal out."

This was the point at which Baird would have bitched about crackpot pseudo-science and popped the bubble of a promising discussion. Dom glanced across the crew cabin and caught Marcus's eye. For a moment, he seemed distracted from the job in hand and looked as if he was listening intently for the next tip. Everybody wanted to know how to make the pain go away, even Marcus.

"I'll try it," Dom said.

"Gettner's switch got stuck the other way, I think."

"Yeah, is she all right? She's not herself lately."

"Fatigue, I reckon. Can't talk yourself out of that."

By the time Dom looked around, Marcus was focused on the terrain again. They hadn't clocked any new stalks today. Dom caught himself falling into a familiar bargaining loop; if he suppressed any hopeful thoughts that the stalks might be thinning out, then he wouldn't have to face the plummeting disappointment when they popped up again. Like all persistent things, though, trying to unthink them just made them impossible to shut out.

He understood all too well now why Dizzy relied on alcohol. It was a tool. It was no different from Sorotki's feedback trick, just tougher on the liver and less respectable in a society that prided itself on stoic discipline and clean living.

"Contact," Marcus said. "Port side, range about five hundred meters. Just above the top of the trees."

Sorotki turned the Raven. "Oh . . . yes. Nice healthy crop."

Dom had to lean out of the crew bay to see the stalks. Twisted charcoal-gray branches poked above the tops of the trees. There was still plenty of green foliage around them, so these had only just erupted.

He caught a strong whiff of fuel on the air. "Shit, have you serviced this bird recently, Sorotki?" he asked. "Smells like you're leaking juice."

"Preflight checks. We do them, Dom."

"It still stinks."

The Raven was about a hundred meters from the stalks now. Dom couldn't see any movement, but that didn't mean there weren't any polyps.

"Don't waste ammo," Marcus said. "Shoot 'em if they're a direct threat, but we can't pick them all off every damn time."

"Is there *anything* we're not running out of?"

Marcus grunted. "Yeah. We've got hydroelectricity."

"Great, we can run this bird on batteries, then," Sorotki said. "I'm going in to get a closer look. Mitchell? Time to get snapping. Prescott wants to see every poxy freckle on these things."

"Yeah, shame he hasn't got a PhD in biology," Dom said. "Why the sudden interest? Is he a stalk spotter now or something?"

"No idea. Desperation, maybe."

The Raven tracked slowly along the line of the stalks. Dom studied his map—hand-drawn by Mathieson—and it looked like the stalks were behaving as expected. They were following the fissure, pushing up through the softer bedrock and soil that filled the gap in the granite.

"Whoa, hold position for a moment, Mel," Mitchell said. "I've got to line up the images with the grids."

"Any particular height, your majesty?"

"No, I can adjust for that, thanks."

"Oh good."

Marcus gripped the safety rail above his head and leaned out of the door as far as he could. It looked so risky that Dom was about to step across and grab him, or at least snap a line on his belt. He was staring at something. His whole body suddenly tensed.

"Sorotki, come around again." Whatever he'd spotted had rattled him. That wasn't like Marcus at all. "There's something on the ground."

"How many legs?"

"Not a glowie. I just saw a flash when the downdraft hit the leaves."

"A flash of *what*? You want to winch down? I don't recommend that."

Dom cut in. "Land somewhere sensible and we'll track back on foot," he said. "Mitchell's got a fix on it, right?"

"I saw a reflection," Marcus said. "And there's no watercourse on the map."

"Ponds come and go without ever being mapped," Mitchell said. "One of the thrills of navigating visually."

"Oh, I *loved* exploring ponds when I was a kid." Sorotki was in full nostalgia mode today. "Frog spawn. Diving beetles. Dragonflies. Haven't seen any of them for years, though. Everything's disappearing."

"I'm glad Baird's not here," Mitchell murmured.

The Raven looped away and headed for the nearest open ground. Dom knew he had to be Marcus's common sense when it came to personal safety. It was Marcus's only routine lapse of sanity. He was as rational and smart as his father, but when he ran into a risk, he had to be the first one to take it. Dom had worked out over the years that it wasn't the dumb ignorance of underestimating danger, or even that it-can't-happen-to-me cockiness he saw in the youngest Gears, but a compulsion to save, to rescue, to put himself in harm's way for others.

Sacrificial. That's the word. Sacrifices appease. Who's he appeasing now?

Plenty of things could make a kid grow up into a man who needed to be the one who took care of everyone else; fear of losing them, guilt at having lost them, or even to make up for not being looked after himself. Dom watched Marcus's jaw twitching as he waited for Sorotki to fly low enough for him to jump out. Maybe it was all three.

"What's so important about water?" Dom asked. "The one thing we've got plenty of here is rivers."

"Liquid," Marcus said. "Reflections off *liquid*."

He jumped down through the whirling storm of dust and leaves and ran clear of the rotors. Dom was still chewing on the word *liquid* as the Raven lifted and left them standing in the clearing. They had two hundred meters to walk to find the target.

The stench of fuel was still overwhelming. Now that

Dom was used to clean country air, he noticed the background urban smells that his nose had learned to ignore in the city. Everything in the army had reeked of imulsion or lube oil, and so had Jacinto.

"He's got a leaking fuel line, for sure." Dom was annoyed that Sorotki wasn't taking his warning seriously. "I tell you, we're not getting back in that death-trap until I've checked it *myself*."

"Liquid," Marcus said again. "Come on."

"What?" Dom could see the tops of the stalks anyway. He didn't need the compass. "If this is a quiz, you win."

Marcus strode ahead through the undergrowth. Dom followed, scanning from side to side for polyps. He wouldn't be able to hear them rustling in the bushes with the noise that Marcus was making. It was only when he noticed that the fuel smell was stronger than ever that realization dawned on him.

"Marcus, are we talking about *imulsion*? Is that it? Goddamn *imulsion*?"

Marcus glanced over his shoulder. He was as near to pleased as Dom had seen him in a long time—pleased for Marcus, anyway. The frown had vanished for a while.

"Yeah, and how was it first discovered?" he asked.

"Oozing out of the ground. Pooling on the surface."

"Yeah. Exactly."

Dom wasn't too breathless about the prospect of a new fuel supply to keep his mind on the forest around him. He looked for damage to tree trunks and charred vegetation, straining to tune into the background clicks and rustles. Polyps would be hard to spot with all this cover. They could be up your ass before you knew it.

Now I know why Bernie prefers to patrol with a dog.

Marcus was fifty meters away from him by now, zigzagging from one side of their path to the other with his eyes on the ground.

"Remember that stuff's combustible," Dom called. "Did you hear me, Marcus? *Combustible!*"

That was what made imulsion such a valuable fuel. It didn't need much refining and it released a lot of energy. If push came to shove, the crude could even be pumped straight into a vehicle as long as you didn't mind replacing the cylinder heads five times a year. Dom tried not to get his hopes up.

How do I know all that?

Dom remembered with another pang of loss that caught him off guard. His dad had told him. Eduardo Santiago had been a mechanic. He'd taught Dom how to strip down an engine before he was ten. Dom had forgotten most of it, but he hadn't forgotten how much he cherished those weekends spent tinkering with wrecks in the workshop with his father and his brother Carlos, while his mother kept fetching trays of snacks.

We were happy. It was easy to be happy.

God . . . what I wouldn't give for one more hour with them all.

"Marcus?" Dom couldn't see him. *Shit.* He was gone. "Hey, Marcus? *Marcus!* Where the hell are you?"

He whipped around but all he could see was a palisade of tree trunks. His stomach knotted. He pressed his earpiece to try the radio, pulse pounding and his mouth suddenly dry.

"Marcus, come in—"

Something moved. Marcus suddenly rose from the undergrowth as if he'd stood up from a squat. He had his arms at his sides, Lancer slung across his shoulder, and his head was tilted back as if he was looking up at the sky. But his eyes were shut. He didn't move a muscle. Dom wasn't sure what he was doing but he decided not to interrupt.

Eventually Marcus opened his eyes and turned to look at Dom. He did that little triumphant nod that he reserved for special occasions.

"Imulsion." He pointed down at his boots. Dom could only see him from knees up. "The stalks are growing through a pool of goddamn imulsion. Sorotki, did you get that? No frogs. *Imulsion*."

Sorotki's whoop over the radio nearly deafened Dom.

"Fuck the frogs, Marcus. Fill her up!"

Yes, he'd definitely got it.

VECTES NAVAL BASE, NEW JACINTO.

Gossip spread fast in a community like the naval base. It was a strange creature known as *buzz*, and on a good day it could overtake radio comms faster than a greased weasel.

Baird realized today was a good day when Royston Sharle caught him rummaging through the waste metal skip behind the workshops again and didn't threaten to shoot him. It was an act of unashamed theft of precious recyclables, but for once Sharle just laughed his ass off.

Baird straightened up indignantly and peered at Sharle over the skip's side.

"It's for Mathieson." He blurted out his excuse before Sharle could open his mouth. Nobody would dare bust him for helping a Gear in a wheelchair. "Me and some Gorasni guys. We're making prosthetic legs for him. We need some metal blocks to machine."

"Y'know, I really ought to put down rat poison for you," Sharle said. He was a big, cheerful guy who'd somehow stayed that way despite years of doing a job that was all about misery, death, and shortages. Maybe you had to be unhealthily optimistic to be an emergency manager. "Go on, take it and sod off. You're worse than the Stranded. And I'm going to change the lock on the gate this time."

"Gee, thanks. You're all heart."

"Beat it before I spread a rumor that you're not a

completely selfish dick." Sharle grinned. "You heard, then? You monitor the comms net. I know you do."

"What?"

Sharle's grin spread further. "Imulsion."

"Yeah, we're going to run out soon, and you want me to convert the Ravens to run on Dizzy's moonshine. Or coal. I'm all over it. Really, I am."

"No, Fenix *found* some."

Baird's first thought was that the locals at Pelruan had been hoarding a few hundred liters in a cowshed, but then he decided it had to be something the Stranded had left behind. Those assholes had caches of stuff laid up everywhere. But every little helped.

"Wow, so we can run *Sovereign* for a few hundred meters?" Baird stuffed his belt pouches full of scrap and started to clamber out of the skip. "That's just *terrific.*"

"Baird, you're out of the loop. Fenix landed slap bang in an *imulsion field.* Parry's on his way up there with the Indie rig guys to check it out."

Baird paused with one knee on the steel ledge. No, that couldn't be right. Vectes didn't have imulsion reserves. The geological survey didn't say *anything* about imulsion. The naval base had been built in the days of sailing ships, long before imulsion had even been discovered, so it wasn't as if the place was chosen because it had its own supply. And once everyone started using the stuff, the COG would have searched damned hard for a local source rather than ship it by tanker halfway across Sera.

He hoped nobody remembered his confident prediction that there was no fuel to drill for here. Barber would never let him forget it.

"Okay." There had to be an explanation for this. Baird's world just wasn't that randomly lucky. The natural progression of things in life was to get worse, and the last fifteen years were living proof. "I know Marcus is Mr. Perfect and everything he touches shits candy, but how the hell did he happen to find imulsion in the middle of nowhere?"

"Stalk patrol," said Sharle. "The stuff's oozing up all around the damn stalks."

"Whoa, I heard the S-word there." A theory was crystallizing. "What are the odds of that?"

"Look, I don't care if the stuff has to be pumped out of Prescott's ass. We're going to extract as much as we can and be thankful."

Sharle disappeared into the workshops, whistling happily as if a new source of fuel made everything all right. Well, it meant they could fly more sorties, watch the stalks popping up everywhere, and maybe set fire to some more polyps. They'd have a stockpile to leave the island if they needed to. But it didn't change much else as far as Baird was concerned.

He remembered what the world they'd fled looked like. It wasn't worth going back anytime soon.

He scrambled out of the skip and set off for his workshop to unload his haul, jangling and rattling as he walked. He'd take it over to Yanik the Disemboweler after he finished his recon duty. It was handy to have something else to keep him occupied when he needed a break from that frigging computer screen telling him DECRYPTION FAILED or FOLDER CONTAINS NO DATA. It contained data, all right. He could see that much.

Cole, waiting at the helicopter pad, looked him up and down as he approached. "Hey baby, you been rootin' in the trash again?"

Baird looked down at his armor. "Why?"

"You're covered in all kinds of shit."

"Yeah, I needed some parts." He mimed a hinge action with his wrist. "Mathieson."

"That's a real nice thing to do," Cole said, climbing into the Raven. Barber stuck his head out of the cockpit door and nodded at them. "And we got *juice* again! You heard what Marcus found?"

"Yeah, I heard."

"You ain't exactly thrilled, are ya?"

"I hide my giddy excitement well, don't I?"

The Raven lifted off. Baird belted himself in and Barber leaned over him, smirking.

"Imulsion," Barber said slowly. Yeah, he remembered, all right. And he was never going to shut up about it. "What was it you said? If there *was* imulsion here, you'd devote your life to charitable work, if it was okay with the tooth fairy. Yeah, you did say that. You *so* did."

"Well, he's doin' somethin' kind for Mathieson," Cole said. "Don't that count?"

Baird heard Gettner laughing over the radio. That meant she'd hit the transmit button just to let him hear how hilarious she thought it was. She wasn't the laughing kind, so that *hurt*.

"Glad I could inject some happiness into your empty life, Major," Baird said. "Now, I hate to be a killjoy . . ."

"No, you *don't*," she said. "You fucking *love* it. It's your mission in life."

". . . but I've got a theory."

"Oh God. Here we go again."

"Yeah, I've said it before. The glowies seem to be attracted by imulsion. They ended up at the drilling platform, and they ended up here. Both places are so far off the chart that it can't be a coincidence. Oh, and the boats. They found teensy-weensy boats in the middle of a frigging big empty ocean."

"Maybe the imulsion's bubbled up to the surface because the stalks opened a channel," Barber said. "And the boats the glowies blew up weren't all running on imulsion."

"Yeah, yeah . . . look, I never said I had all the answers. But it's *still* too much of a pattern."

Gettner interrupted. "I just want fuel. I don't care if I've got to arm-wrestle polyps personally to get it. As long as we can keep an eye on those things, we can survive."

"And the brown patches? It's not like a dog pissing on your lawn. They're *killing the crops*. Am I the only one who stayed conscious in math class or something?"

Cole swiveled in his seat so that the wind was in his face. He was probably going to throw up, but he always had the sense to check the slipstream first. "Seems a bit *premature* to even be thinkin' about runnin' away yet. It's a big island. We ain't seen that many stalks so far."

"I'm up for going home." Gettner said it in a weird confessional kind of way. "I really am."

But there was no home left. Jacinto—the proper one, not this shack city—was just an interesting reef now, submerged by fifty meters of ocean. Well, *that* killed conversation stone dead. It was a bit of a shock. Baird hadn't realized that Gettner felt that bad about life.

"Come on, folks." Cole stepped in to try to jolly them up. "Watch me puke-bomb the next swarm of polyps. Hey, anyone interested in settin' up a thrashball session for the kids? Like we did back in Port Farrall, remember?"

"Yeah, and I froze my nuts off," Barber muttered. "Okay, I'm in. Nothing too violent, though."

"That's more like it." Cole gave Baird a don't-start-it look, eyebrows raised and chin down. "So are we doin' Pelruan again today, ma'am?"

"We'll do a sweep of the fissure zone, and then I'll land and pick up some admin stuff from Anya." Gettner sounded back to normal again after that gut-spill about going home. "Then we'll swing back via the existing stalks at the farm and grab

some more images. Unless anyone wants to do a foot patrol,
Baird."

"I can see just fine from here, thanks, *Major.*"

Baird had made up his mind. The glowies probably followed the imulsion. It didn't account for everything, but it
did explain why they were here.

But why now? *Why didn't they show up in imulsion fields
before?*

Every day was like E-Day now. Everyone had asked the
same questions about the grubs. But there was never an
answer about where the Locust had come from. The question was forgotten in the end, because an answer didn't seem
to have much bearing on staying alive. Baird propped his
Lancer on his knee and kept his eyes on the countryside
below.

*And what frigging use were our scientists? No damn
answers.*

Well, none of the assholes were around now. At least
there was some poetic justice in that. He watched the tops of
the trees blur beneath him and felt discreetly for Prescott's
data disc under his chest plate.

What kind of encryption do the Indies use?

No, that was one favor he couldn't ask Yanik. He shook
off the idea and kept his mind on the trees. The fissure ran
for forty kilometers roughly east-west to the south of the
town, a five-kilometer corridor mostly covered by woodland.
Gettner took the Raven up the northern edge to the northeast coast and then looped back toward Pelruan. They were
about ten kilometers east of the town when Barber spotted
something.

"Heads up, Gill," he said. "Bear zero-four-five."

"Stalk?"

"Brown. A *lot* of brown. Can't see any stalks yet."

"Okay, let's take a look."

Some trees had naturally copper foliage, but not these. Baird knew they were dead as soon as the Raven came within fifty meters of them. Gettner circled in a big arc while Barber took photographs.

"I don't see any stalks," Cole said.

Baird reached for the field glasses. There were no telltale twisted gray branches protruding through the leaves below. The dense foliage looked like a carpet of bark chippings, and there wasn't a hint of anything green in the small gaps that gave a glimpse of the woodland floor.

"Maybe it's *short* stalks," Barber said. "That would mean they've changed again. That'll get Prescott excited."

Baird lowered the glasses. "Yeah, that's what worries me."

"You want us to take a look on the ground?" Cole asked. "We can rope down."

Baird was up for that. "Come on, Barber, give me the camera. We'll grab some images."

"I'm going to hover," Gettner said. "No messing around. You have a look and come straight back, okay?"

"You care really, don't you?"

"Just do it, Baird."

Cole swung out on the winch and vanished beneath a mat of dead foliage. Baird watched his head disappear before following him. The branches snagged his pants and he held his breath, half expecting something unseen to sink its fangs into his leg, but his boots hit the ground. He was still in one piece, standing next to Cole in the deep shade.

Woods were full of sound and movement. Baird wasn't the outdoor type, but he knew that much, if only from hanging around with Bernie. They were quiet places; they weren't *silent*. This one was.

It was completely dead.

There wasn't anything green and alive anywhere—not on the bushes, not on the ground, not in the trees. There was no birdsong, and there were no insects. Baird was surprised just how obvious that complete absence of life now seemed to him.

He did a slow 360 turn, scanning the ranks of tree trunks to look for stalks. They should have been visible—a different color, a distinctly different shape—but there was nothing.

"Man," Cole whispered. "I'm gonna have nightmares about this one day."

"It's all fucking *dead*."

"Yeah."

"What the hell's killed it if there's no stalks?"

"Damned if I know." Cole pressed his earpiece. "Eight-zero, this is Cole. We're gonna grab a few pictures for the album. Kinda hard to describe, ma'am."

There was a crackling pause. Then Gettner's voice came over the radio. "What's down there?"

"Nothing," Cole said. "Absolutely goddamn *nothing*."

PELRUAN, NORTHERN VECTES.

There were fresh flowers on the town's war memorial, a small bunch of something yellow and cultivated that Bernie couldn't name. The blooms reminded her of pea flowers.

But these weren't edible and they weren't medicinal. If a plant wasn't in her bushcraft database, it didn't make an impression on her.

Old age. Or too long on the farm. Or no soul left. Never mind.

She paused out of respect as she passed the modest granite pillar and noted that the flowers were tied with the same handmade ribbon as the dried-out wreath that had been placed there some weeks ago. It was navy blue with a narrow scarlet stripe, the colors of the Duke of Tollen's Regiment.

That was who she'd come to see. She had some fences to mend.

Mac trotted ahead of her. This time he didn't race off in search of familiar places or Will Berenz, so he seemed to have made his own choice about which human was going to get custody of him. He paused to pee up a dry stone wall and waited for her to catch up.

"The bar," she said. "Go on. Pub. Drinkies."

Mac looked as if he nodded in agreement, then headed toward Pelruan's main bar. Will had trained him well. It was just a single-story wooden house like the rest of the homes, and Bernie was sure there were other informal places where the locals gathered for social liver destruction, but the bar— did it even have a name?—was one of the four main places where people tended to congregate to gossip. If they weren't in the bar, then the next place to try was the town hall, or the green outside, or the small crescent of cobbled road at the top of the harbor.

The six Tollen veterans were in the bar as she expected, playing cards by the window. The youngest was in his late seventies but they could still handle firearms. They'd even done their bit in defending the town from the last polyp invasion. But Bernie wished she hadn't made them fight alongside the Gorasni.

The Duke of Tollen's Regiment had the worst possible memories of Gorasnaya.

Frederic Benten—still effectively the NCO after all these years—looked up as she came in. They acknowledged her as if she hadn't yelled at them about duty when they objected to serving with Indies who'd beaten and worked their mates to death in the last war.

"Anyone drinking?" she said. Mac flopped onto the rush mat in front of the empty fireplace and stretched out as if he was a regular. "I'll get them in."

Benten laid down his cards. "We haven't seen you around for a while, Sergeant. How are you?"

"Contrite." She went behind the bar and poured the beer herself. The woman who ran the place was out, so patrons were expected to help themselves and leave payment. The coins and fragile, dog-eared banknotes in a wooden tray under the counter were just barter tokens for odd jobs, clothing, or preserves. Bernie paid with a bag of brass screws. Baird wouldn't miss them. "We haven't had a chance to talk since the leviathan came ashore. I thought it was time I showed my face."

"How's the lad with the leg injury?"

"Oh, he's improving, thanks." Benten meant Anton Silber. A polyp had detonated under him during the battle and shredded him from the left knee down. "Doc Hayman saved his leg. Natural healing. She just glares at bacteria until they commit suicide."

It got a laugh and the old men took their beer. There didn't seem to be any hard feelings.

"This is by way of apology," she said. "I'm sorry I made you fight alongside the Gorasni. I've got no right to lecture you about duty. I'll never know what you went through in their prison camps."

Benten contemplated the foam on his beer. The man sitting next to him, Chalky, reached out and patted her hand.

"You got us to fight, Sarge, and we all survived," he said. "And you were right. It's not like you're some civilian talking through your ass about forgiveness and how we ought to put history behind us. It was your war too."

"Is it true what you did to those Stranded?" Benten asked. He looked down as if he was embarrassed to ask a woman that kind of question. The Stranded were loathed and feared on Vectes, so dispensing very rough justice had made Bernie into something of a celebrity here. "Did you really chop off their . . . ?"

Bernie nodded. "Yeah. And I shoved 'em down their throats. But I couldn't tell if they bled to death or choked." She waited for the reaction. She wasn't ashamed, not in the least, but she wasn't sure if they'd already heard all the grisly detail. Judging by their expressions, they hadn't. "There are some scores you've got to settle before you can move on with your life."

"We never settled ours," Chalky said.

"I know. I'm sorry."

"The Colonel told us to think of the Indie imulsion as war reparation. Now we haven't even got that."

Bernie had to ask. "How are you going to handle it if we need to move everyone south to the base?"

"Can we keep away from them?"

"Yes. They generally stick to their own camp."

"Then we'll stick to ours, too," Benten said. "If it comes to that."

Bernie joined in their card game and kept them topped up with beer for a while, reminding herself that she was only twenty years or so behind them, and this was how the younger Gears saw *her*: old, full of wild stories they'd never hear, but not completely useless yet. She treated the old boys as she hoped the youngsters would treat her.

But she couldn't sit here all day, even though her joints told her she was due a nice long rest. She'd give it a couple of hours and then find Anya. Life felt like a round of honoring old promises. She had her duty to veterans, and her duty to the dead, to Major Helena Stroud—her old CO—in particular. The Major had planned to prepare her daughter for a frontline role but she got herself killed too soon, so now it fell to Bernie to make sure Anya didn't die too young like her mother had.

I promised, Major. Anya's shaping up fine. I really wish you could see her now.

Bernie had just laid down a disastrous hand when her radio buzzed. It was Anya.

"Pelruan Control to Mataki, come in."

Bernie pressed her earpiece. "Mataki here, ma'am. Go ahead."

"Bernie, have you heard? We've found imulsion."

"Say again, ma'am?"

"Imulsion. I've only got sketchy details at the moment. They're waiting for the Gorasni rig team to assess it."

The old boys couldn't hear the other side of the conversation. "Glad to hear they're being useful, ma'am," she said, not quite taking it all in. "I'm on my way to the signals office. Five minutes. Mataki out."

She stood up. Mac snapped to attention from an apparently dead sleep. "You'll have to excuse me. Looks like we've found an imulsion supply. I'm going to check in with Lieutenant Stroud."

Benten raised his beer glass. "Well, that'll please the Chairman, but how does it change things?" he asked. "The stalks and the polyps are still here. The land's still dying off."

Bernie had to agree. "But it's probably better to be in the shit *with* fuel than without it. At least we've got the option of making a run for it."

"Where are you going to run? You only ended up here as a last resort."

"We'll think of somewhere," she said. "Even if it's bloody Galangi."

Bernie drained her beer and shook the old boys' hands before washing up the glass behind the bar. It was very much a make-yourself-at-home place. *Galangi.* Would the island still be okay? Would any of her neighbors still be there? She thought that over as she made her way up the path to the signals office. Anya was outside with Drew Rossi, poring over a map spread on the hood of the Packhorse.

"Would you believe it?" Rossi said. He tapped the map. "Great timing. A damn lake of juice right here."

Bernie could hear a Raven engine droning somewhere in the distance. She peered at the map over Anya's shoulder. "Were we drilling for it? Hoffman never said a word."

"It was a lucky accident. Marcus fell over it."

"How lucky?"

Anya didn't look as pleased as Rossi. "He found more stalks. Then he found the imulsion they were standing in. *That* kind of lucky."

"Well, we just pump it out, then," Bernie said. The Raven noise was getting louder. It was coming in to land. "Once the stalks are up and we've cleared out the polyps, they're dead, and—"

"KR-Eight-Zero to Pelruan, we've got a situation twenty klicks east of you." It was Gettner. Raven pilots never seemed to break a sweat but there was definitely a hint of tension in her voice. "Stand by to transmit recon images back to VNB."

"She's in a hell of a hurry," Rossi said. "Landing here only saves her fifteen or twenty minutes, tops."

The helicopter swept overhead, low enough for Bernie to see the scuffs and repairs to its underside before it dipped out of sight behind the houses. Gettner wasn't heading for the usual landing area a kilometer away, either.

Anya refolded the map. "Okay, let's go see what the problem is."

They didn't wait. Running to meet the Raven didn't make things happen any faster, but somehow standing there while the crew rushed to find them felt wrong. They jogged down the alley between the houses and intercepted Barber and Cole running toward them. Barber had the recon camera clutched under his arm. Mac loped around, tail thrashing as if he expected a chase.

"Ma'am, we've got a contaminated zone without stalks,"

Barber said. "Just dead land. I don't know what help the images are going to be, but I'm transmitting then back to base anyway."

"But it's still centered on the fissures, isn't it?" Anya said.

"Looks like it. But if this stuff is happening randomly, then we've got another new problem."

Rossi shook his head slowly. "It never rains but it fucks. When are we going to get a break?"

Nobody had an answer, least of all Bernie, although she realized she must have thought one was possible to even bother carrying on. Barber rushed into the signals office with Anya. Cole hung back with Baird and put his hand on Bernie's shoulder.

"Boomer Lady, you *never* seen anything like this," he said. "It's all dead. Everything. No polyps. No stalks. Just *dead.*"

"So how the hell are we supposed to track it if we can't see the stalks?"

"It's a small island until you try to patrol every square meter," Rossi said. "Then it's big."

Cole shook his head. "Patrollin' ain't gonna stop this. You want to take a look for yourself?"

Bernie didn't think she had any more answers than Cole did, but she wanted to see it anyway. Then Anya came back out of the signals office in a hurry.

"Prescott wants soil samples," she said. "Let's go check this out."

"What's *wrong* with that tosser?" Bernie stopped herself. Voicing dissent wasn't good for morale. "Sorry, ma'am. But we don't have the technology or the experts to analyze this stuff anymore."

"Never mind me," Baird said.

"Yeah, okay, Blondie, you work miracles. But you've said it yourself—you're not a biologist. Anyway, why's he so obsessed with samples?"

Anya shrugged. "Well, there's Doc Hayman, I suppose."

"She's a doctor," Rossi said. "A scab lifter. She's not a biologist either."

"Okay, so we all know what we *can't* do." Anya suddenly snapped into officer mode. "Now let's concentrate on what we *can* do. Rossi, plot the contaminated zones on the map and work out who we need to evacuate first if it keeps expanding at the same rate. I'm going back with Gettner to take a look. Come on, Bernie. Bring the dog. He's our radar."

The Raven seemed to reach the edge of the dead area far too soon. Bernie could see the dead treetops from a couple of kilometers away and that brought it home just how close it was to the town. She looked at Baird for a reaction, but he had his goggles pulled down over his eyes.

"I hate a threat I can't shoot," she said.

Cole murmured. "Amen, baby. I miss those ugly grub motherfuckers."

Gettner set down on the edge of the woodland and Barber showed Anya the compass bearing to walk into the contaminated area. Bernie picked her way through straggly thornbushes—springy and alive when she tested them with her boot—and into the cover of the trees.

The silence really was striking, like nothing she'd ever experienced before. Mac sniffed the air but stopped short of rooting around in the leaves like he usually did. He looked up at her with an accusing gaze that asked why the hell she'd brought him here.

Clumps of wildflowers with straplike leaves and long stalks of mauve flowers nodded in the dappled sunlight. Then, as if someone had sprayed weed killer around, the woodland floor became a carpet of brown vegetation with a clear boundary between the live growth and the dead stuff. Bernie looked up at the branches. The trees looked dead too.

"Tell me this isn't anything to do with the shit we used to develop here," Baird muttered. "I mean, this was Toxin Town. Chemical and biological weapons research. We keep conveniently forgetting that."

"We'd have seen something before now," Anya said. "That was all twenty years ago, at the very least."

Cole wandered back to Baird's side. There was no cracking of dry, dead twigs underfoot. The dieback had been sudden and nothing had dried out yet. "Goddamn . . ."

"I'm going to ask Prescott to his *face*." Baird seemed more pissed off than usual. "Asshole. Maybe *that's* his precious secret. I mean, suddenly he's extra-interested in this shit."

"What secret?" Anya asked.

Baird winced. Anya didn't know about the disk, then. Well, it was Hoffman's decision to decide who he told, Bernie thought, but he could at least have warned her he hadn't told Anya.

"He's always got one," Bernie said. *You're going to have to tell her, Vic.* "Just when we think he's told us everything, something else crops up. Like those Sire things Marcus found at New Hope."

She walked up behind Baird out of Anya's field of vision and shoved him hard in the back with her elbow. *Shut your trap, Blondie.* He jerked his head around and glared at her.

"Okay, I'm sorry," he whispered. "It's *zipped*. Okay?"

The further they walked into the woods, the more profoundly dead the place looked. And there were still no signs of stalks or polyps. Eventually they walked back to the edge of the dead area and stood staring at it for a few moments. The line between dead and alive was unnaturally stark. Bernie stood on the precise edge of the brown foliage like a kid stepping on cracks in paving to see the sky fall in. She scraped it with the tip of her Lancer's chainsaw.

Mac stuck right by her legs, so close that she almost

tripped over him. He really didn't want to explore, and that was a worrying sign. He'd hunt polyps that could blow him apart, but he didn't like what he could sense now. She rubbed his ear with her free hand.

"No worms. No beetles. Nothing." Disturbing the leaf mold under trees usually turned up all kinds of small crawling things. "No flies, either."

Anya bent down to scoop some of the soil and dead leaves into a plastic bag. "I don't know how much more of this stuff he wants."

"What's he doing with it?"

"Oh, it's probably for his nature table," Baird said. "He's had a breakdown. Or he wants us to think he has. Crafty asshole."

Bernie glanced down at the ground just to see if there was anything else worth retrieving, and that was when it struck her. She was standing inside the dead area—a good fifteen meters or so inside it.

See, there's the scrape in the ground I just made.

"It's really moving," she said. "Blondie, look how far it's spread since we've been here. Look. *Look.*"

Baird did a good impression of a surly teenager reluctantly forcing himself to look at something that couldn't possibly be of interest to him. "You sure?"

"Yes. That's a meter a minute, more or less."

Anya came over to look. She actually measured it with her boot, marking out heel-to-toe from the scrape to the edge.

"Then we'd better hope it slows down." She looked past Bernie in defocus for a few moments, lips moving silently as if she was working something out. "Because unless my math is wrong, it'll be south of Pelruan in about fifteen days."

Bernie rarely felt helpless about anything. There was always something that could be done, said, built, found, destroyed, or shot to improve the situation. Gears were trained to be self-reliant and tenacious, and self-reliant, tenacious people tended to become and remain Gears. But she felt helpless now. When she looked at Baird—the ultimate I-can-fix-it kind of bloke—she could see it in his face, too. She could wage war on grubs. But it was hard to think of what damage could be inflicted on a brown patch spreading under your feet. She didn't even know what this enemy was.

"You remember the first weeks after E-Day, Granny?" Baird asked. E-Day seemed to be preoccupying everyone lately. "Total clusterfuck. Chaos. But we got the idea pretty fast."

He was trying to be upbeat in his own way. Bernie's E-Day memories were of being cut off from civilization, desperate to pick up a rifle and deal with the bastards, but not knowing where to start.

Yeah. That was pretty much the way she felt right now.

CHAPTER 7

*Just go. Get home any way you can. I don't know if this
ship's going to be commandeered, confined to port, or sent
back to sea. It's chaos out there.*

(Robb Arden, skipper of imulsion tanker *Betancourt Star*,
to his crew, after the emergence of the Locust Horde on E-Day)

**NEW SHERRITH, TYRUS: THREE DAYS AFTER
E-DAY, FIFTEEN YEARS EARLIER.**

The trains weren't running, the phone lines were down, and
almost all civilian air traffic had been grounded. Dizzy
hitched a ride from the docks on a chemical tanker going to
Andius and counted himself lucky.

Those ugly gray things that had burst out of the ground
three days ago were spreading further across Sera. And the
chaos was spreading right along with them.

The traffic was mostly trucks, police cruisers and ambu-
lances. And the army was everywhere. Dizzy had never seen
so many military vehicles. APCs and troop transports
streamed past in convoys and he craned his neck, half
expecting to see Richie, but he knew that was a slim chance.

"Where are all the cars?" he asked.

"Everyone's been told to stay put and leave the roads clear

for essential traffic." The tanker driver was listening to the radio, now a constant stream of confused casualty figures and official warnings about roads being closed and cities being off-limits. "That's all the northbound routes closed. They're turning freight off at the next exit. Gonna have to drop you off, buddy."

Dizzy clutched his canvas holdall, stomach knotted as he strained to catch reports of what was happening in other towns. The name he was dreading was Mattino Junction. But the reports were talking about cities across the whole damn world, in Ostri, Pelles, and Vasgar, not just in Tyrus. He didn't want to know about them. He needed to hear what was happening back home.

The reporter had started calling the invaders *locusts*. Whatever these things were, they were coming up out of the ground and just killing everyone in their path. They weren't taking prisoners and they didn't seem to be heading for anywhere in particular. They didn't seem to have a plan.

The driver turned up the volume at the mention of Jannermont.

"*. . . and casualties there are estimated at a hundred thousand so far. We're getting reports of fresh fighting around Nordesca . . .*"

Dizzy stared out of the window. Things didn't look normal, but he couldn't see any of the burned-out buildings, bomb craters or the other signs of war that he was expecting.

What are they? How did they get here? What do they want? What did we ever do to them to deserve this?

APCs and tanks lined the side of the road and the bridge across the highway. Gears, anonymous in full-face helmets for the most part, were marshaling traffic while a few cops looked on.

"They're picking off the cities one by one," the driver said quietly. "But they haven't reached Ephyra yet. When that happens, we won't even have the news to rely on."

Dizzy's stomach was rumbling from two days of missed meals, but what he wanted most was a drink. His hip flask was somewhere on the seabed off Ogari.

"You heard *anything* about Mattino Junction?" he asked. "My wife and boy are there."

"Yeah, you said."

"I can't get a call through. I can't raise the neighbors. I can't get through to the government emergency line. I ain't seen a news broadcast for two days, and the radio's just streaming out useless shit. Yeah, I know we got trouble, and I know we got a lot of folks dead and missing, but goddamn, how can a town just *not matter* like that?"

The driver made a small noise as if he was going to say something but decided it wasn't a good idea. He stared ahead at the tail of the truck in front for a while.

"There's just too many places been hit," he said at last. "I'm trying to get home too."

Up ahead, orange lights flashed on the gantry over the highway. A warning was picked out in white lights: ROAD CLOSED—DIVERSION AT NEXT EXIT. A roadblock of armored vehicles was spread across all six lanes. The tanker driver slowed and followed the truck in front of him down the ramp.

They were crawling through a residential area now, and heading west—away from Mattino. Eventually the traffic ground to a halt.

Dizzy was fifteen kilometers from home and going in the wrong direction. But fifteen klicks wasn't far. He could walk that in a few hours if he had to.

"Mind dropping me off at the fuel station?" Dizzy asked. "I'm gonna take my chances. Might find out more if I move through the towns."

"If that's what you want, buddy, but you're gonna get stopped at a checkpoint before then. Good luck."

The fuel station was closed when Dizzy jumped down from the cab. He peered in the window, hoping to buy something to eat and try the phone again, but there was only a single security light on and no sign of anyone inside. When he walked back across the forecourt, he saw the hand-scrawled sign taped to the pump next to the exit.

CLOSED FOR FUEL. COG OFFICIAL PERMIT HOLDERS ONLY.

Dizzy decided to try further down the road. He could hear the distant rumble of vehicles from the highway, but nothing else seemed to be moving. From time to time he'd look up at a window and see a worried face staring out. Maybe it was worth knocking on the nearest door and asking to use the phone, but he didn't know just how spooked folks were and how they'd react. All the rules he was used to had vanished. This wasn't the regular war and he was in central Tyrus now, a place where people didn't expect to wake up and find the enemy in their front yard. The Pendulum Wars had mostly been fought well away from the COG heartland.

Lena, you'd have the sense to stay put, wouldn't you? You'd listen to the Chairman on the radio and do what you were told. And Richie would—

Richie would have gone straight back to his unit, whether he'd been recalled or not. Any Gear would. The thought of Lena on her own in the middle of all this shit terrified Dizzy and left his stomach churning.

Maybe the locust things ain't reached Mattino yet. Don't panic. Just keep walking.

Up ahead he could see a man nailing boards over his windows like there was a storm coming. From what Dizzy had heard over the last fifty-two hours, it didn't seem like a few wooden planks would stop one of these locust assholes.

They'd just come up through the floor. He started walking faster, trying not to break into a run.

"Hey, can you help me?" he called. Anyone who saw him would know that he was merchant navy from his kit bag and his seaman's gray duffel coat. "I'm trying to get to Mattino."

The man paused in mid-swing and looked around. "It's cut off," he said. "They tried to evacuate everybody."

"Whaddya mean—tried?"

"It was on the TV news. They shipped the survivors out."

Goddamn it. *Goddamn it.* "Where?"

"Hey, I wasn't taking notes. All we know is what's on the news. The government can't find its ass with an atlas right now."

If anything brought Dizzy crashing to the ground, it was hearing that. The COG was organized. The COG always had things under control. The guys in charge had been fighting a war for decades, so they knew what they were doing. They weren't fazed by attacks or any of that shit.

But they were now. He could see it all around him. Tyrus was paralyzed. Nothing was working.

"I gotta get home," he said, knowing full well that this guy couldn't help. He just felt better for saying it, reminding himself what he had to do to stop himself panicking. "Where did they take the survivors?"

"Sorry, I don't know. Look, these things could come up anywhere—you shouldn't be wandering around." The man banged another nail into place and looked down at Dizzy. "You're welcome to come in if you want."

"Thanks, but I need to get to my family."

Dizzy carried on walking. He'd crossed the next main road before he realized that he should have asked the man for something to eat. He was too upset to feel hungry, but he knew he was going to feel like shit before too long if he didn't eat something.

And something to drink. Water. Yeah, just for once—god-damn water.

He'd forgotten about everything else except getting home. He hadn't even stopped to take a leak for thirteen hours; that made him realize how dehydrated he was. *And that ain't smart. Won't be able to think straight if I don't get some fluids in me.* Even the realization that one of these locust things could bust up out of the ground beneath him didn't matter, because the biggest fear tying his guts in knots was losing Lena and Richie. He walked as fast as he could, still fighting the urge to start running no matter how much his legs insisted. He knew he couldn't run that distance. He had to pace himself.

And it wasn't the slope of the road making his heart pound. It was sheer animal panic. He *had* to keep his head.

Goddamn it, ain't there even a patrol out here? How can everyone just run and hide like that?

He spotted a public phone box and tried dialing the usual numbers again—home, the Fiorellis next door, and then the COG casualty information bureau. His fingers moved automatically after so many tries. Each time he dialed, he got the same single continuous tone interrupted by a message that the exchanges were down.

Well, the bureau's still gotta be in one piece. It's a Jacinto number. So that means Lena and Richie are okay too.

Part of him knew that reasoning didn't make any sense at all and that he was just bargaining with himself. He could hear the low booming of artillery fire a long way off. By the time he reached the top of the hill, the sound was louder, and he was looking at low gray cloud that somehow didn't seem right on such a sunny day.

It was smoke. He could tell because the clouds had tails that led down to the ground. A jungle of towers jutted out of the haze. It looked like hell even at this distance, with fresh palls of smoke billowing up through the layer that had already settled over the place like a shroud.

That was Mattino Junction.

Down there, that was his home. It was his last fragile link with Lena and Richie. He thought he was going to puke with fear, but there was nothing inside to fetch up, and it left him nursing a terrible burning pain just under his ribs. He heard someone say "Oh God . . ." and then he realized it was him.

Get a grip. Do something. Just get in there and find out where they've gone.

Dizzy started to jog down the road. He just couldn't hold himself back now. He heard an engine—a bus, maybe, or even a utility vehicle—but he couldn't tell where it was coming from and he didn't plan to stop. If he kept going, he'd reach the intersection with the eastbound highway and he'd be on the final leg to Mattino.

Damn, I'm not even making sense to myself. But what am I going to do, turn around and go back? Where do I go if I don't check out the town? How the hell am I gonna find Lena and Richie?

A horn honked behind him. That was enough to snap him out of the whirling panic and make him look around. An army Packhorse in COG polar camo, all black, white, and gray patches, was bearing down on him. It was a strange paint job to see in Tyrus. The brass must have drafted in everything with wheels that they could lay their hands on.

The Packhorse drew level with Dizzy and a Gear stuck his head out of the side window. "Hey, sir, where the hell are you going? We've got a movement restriction in place. Turn back."

Damn it, they could see the town, couldn't they? Where the hell did they *think* he was going?

"I gotta get to Mattino Junction. I don't know what's

happened to my family. My boy's a Gear, see. He was home on leave. I ain't heard from my old lady either."

The Gear put his hand to the side of his helmet for a second or two as if he was listening to his radio.

"What's his name and unit?"

"Private Richie Wallin, Two-Five Sherrith Cav. My name's Dizzy Wallin." Pretty well every COG citizen had a military connection of some kind, so Dizzy didn't expect any special treatment. He just thought these guys might know something. "I gotta get home."

"I think you'd better forget that, sailor." The Packhorse stopped just ahead of him and the Gear got out. "Any civvies who made it got shipped down to Corren. We've still got guys in Mattino fighting the grubs."

Grubs. Dizzy hadn't heard the name before. So that was what they were calling these locust things. "How do I find out? How do I find out if they're there?"

"Come on, get in."

"No, I gotta go look for my family!"

"Dizzy—is it okay if I call you Dizzy? Look, Dizzy, even if you make it into Mattino without getting your head blown off, what are you going to do?" The Gear took his arm. "Find the house? What if they're not there? What if the *house* isn't there? The hospital's been burned out, so they're not going to be there, either. You might as well come back to Andius and sign in at the refugee center. If there's any information, they'll be the first to have it."

There was a man inside that full-face helmet, a guy probably a lot like Richie, but it was hard to listen to someone when you couldn't look him in the eye. Dizzy went to shrug him off but the Gear still had hold of his arm. His grip said he wasn't joking.

"Sir, you've got to come with us."

Dizzy must have been in worse shape than he thought.

Not only did he do as he was told, but when he managed to climb into the back of the Packhorse—which was a lot harder than he expected—someone handed him a bottle of Record Breaker soda. There was a picture of that thrashball guy Cole on the label. A couple of young Gears were sitting on the bench seats, helmets on their laps, and from the expressions on their faces Dizzy guessed that he looked pretty bad.

He was dehydrated, starving, and he hadn't slept in days. He knew that. But he wasn't hurt or dead, so it was no excuse, and that made him feel guilty.

"They'll find them," one of the lads said. "But it's pretty fucking chaotic right now, sir."

Dizzy had to admit that the sugary soda tasted better than any hooch. He could actually feel it flooding his body, a kind of slow warm relief spreading through him from the stomach out. One of the Gears passed him a candy bar. They were good boys, just like Richie. He could hear the buzz and crackle of their radios as the Gear who'd stopped him chatted to Control.

Eventually the guy turned around and leaned over the back of the passenger seat. It took him a few seconds to speak. Dizzy knew what he was going to say and he felt his face go numb, like someone had opened a door and let in a freezing wind.

"I'm sorry," said the Gear. "Richie Wallin. They've logged his COG tag."

It was real hard to lose a COG tag when it was under your armor.

Someone had taken it off Richie's body. The world was falling apart, and Dizzy was starting to crumble with it. He couldn't manage a reply, not yet. It wasn't real. It couldn't be.

"Shit," said one of the guys in the back. "How are we ever going to stop these things?"

Dizzy sat in silence as they drove to the refugee reception center in Andius. It was a big modern sports center packed to bursting with confused, scared people just like him, and staff who couldn't tell him anything. The place smelled of sweat and vomit. Kids were crying. He waited four hours to be recorded and tagged, then fell asleep on the tiled floor with his kit bag for a pillow long before they could find him somewhere to bed down.

Someone shook him awake. For those first blissful, blank seconds, none of this had ever happened, and he wasn't sure if he was back on board *Betancourt Star*. Then his memory kicked in and he remembered where he was and why he was here. A uniformed police auxiliary who looked like she hadn't slept for a month turned over the tag on his jacket and checked his name.

"Mr. Wallin?" she said. "I'm sorry. I'm afraid we've found your wife."

COUGARS STADIUM, HANOVER: FIVE DAYS AFTER E-DAY.

Cole had never had much trouble making up his mind about anything. Today wasn't going to be any different.

He sat in the directors' box high in the stands, watching the seats below. They were already starting to fill up. He should have gone down to the dressing room to make his peace with the rest of the team first, but he couldn't face that yet. He'd see them later.

Five years. That's all. Didn't know where I'd be today. Don't know where I'm gonna be five years from now.

He had no idea why anyone wanted to come and watch a thrashball game when the world was going to rat-shit, but maybe that was the whole point. You carried on as normal for as long as you could, living life as fully as you could, or else the assholes trying to kill you had already won without lifting a finger because you'd already done the dying for them.

I shoulda gone out and played one last time.

Hell, I'll be back one day. When I've settled some scores.

Suddenly he could smell that wonderful match-day stadium smell, all fried onions and smoky meat and cinnamon. Someone had opened the doors. He turned around.

"Mr. Cole?" It was Gaynor, the boss's assistant. He always sent her to do the awkward personal stuff. "We didn't expect to see you back yet." She took a little breath. "I'm really sorry about your parents."

Cole tried to find something to say that wouldn't make her feel any worse or start him off again. "There's a lot of people grievin' now," he said. "Gonna be a lot more before this is over. Is the boss man here yet?"

"Yes, Mr. Mortensen's on his way up."

"Did he say if my agent called him?"

Gaynor frowned a little. "He didn't mention it."

"Okay." Cole hoped Mortensen had been given some warning, but if he hadn't, it was too bad. It wasn't going to change a thing. "Thanks, Gaynor. You've been real kind. You always have."

She gave him a puzzled look, half smiled, and shut the glass door behind her. He turned back to the stadium and tried to take in as much detail as he could so he'd always remember it. There were the snack vendors loading their trays, the groundsmen doing last-minute stuff to the pitch, and fans already in the touchline seats chatting or reading newspapers. Life went on.

But the atmosphere had changed. He could feel it.

Better make sure I keep my shit together. Gotta give 'em the full Cole Train act today, baby.

Eventually he heard Mortensen coming up the steps two

at a time. The manager's playing days were long over, but he liked to prove to himself that he hadn't gone to seed yet. Cole looked him in the eye as he walked in.

"Hey, good to see you back, son." Mortensen dragged up a chair and sat down next to him. "Don't feel you've got to rush back to playing, though. Give yourself time. How are you feeling?"

Cole decided to cut to the chase. He couldn't bear dragging this out any longer than he had to, and there was no easy way to work up to the bad news. *Better out than in . . .*

"Boss, I ain't coming back," Cole said. "I've enlisted."

Mortensen just stared at him for a while and didn't say anything. He didn't seem angry. He just looked like he didn't understand and was waiting for Cole to go on and explain.

"Did you hear me, Boss?" Cole tapped his knee. "I'm joinin' the army. I'm gonna be a Gear. Passed my medical and everything. I'm waiting for my papers."

Mortensen was still staring into his face, blinking. Cole decided to wait for it all to sink in. Maybe he shouldn't have just dumped it on the guy like that. But he couldn't explain the situation any better if he took all day doing it.

"No, no, you can't," Mortensen said at last. He wasn't so much shaking his head as moving it slowly from side to side. "Are you crazy? Cole, do you know what you're *doing*?"

"Yeah. I can't sit on my ass while those things are killin' us. It's real simple. I love playin' ball, but it's a game, and what's out there ain't."

He almost expected an argument about letting the side down and breaching his contract and all that shit that didn't actually matter when there were already millions of dead in cities all over Sera. Hanover hadn't been hit yet. It hadn't even seen refugees pouring into town, like the cities to the north had.

But Mortensen's eyes filled with tears instead. It was a

hell of a shock. Cole felt terrible for upsetting him. A smack in the mouth would have been easier to take.

"Cole . . . you understand what you are?"

"Yeah. I think so."

"No, you don't. You're a phenomenon. You've only been playing pro for five years and you've broken all the records. There's a statue of you out front. There's maybe half a dozen players in the league who ever got that recognition—and that was after they *retired*."

"Yeah, I've already had it all and I've still got a whole career in front of me." For a moment, Cole felt a pang of something awful that he didn't even have a name for. It almost stopped him breathing. If he looked at it for one more second, he'd see what it was and start to regret things that hadn't even happened yet. So he just shut it out. "I'm lucky. I know I am. But there's a *war* on."

"Yeah, but the government's letting us carry on. They could have shut all the stadiums on safety grounds, and God knows they need the space for refugees, but they're letting us carry on as long we can—for *morale*. To keep people going. To help 'em stick together."

"Look, it's done, Boss. It's gonna happen. I'm sorry."

"Fuck it, Cole," Mortensen snapped. "It's not about being a great player. You're someone people *believe* in. Yeah, thrashball's only a game, but it makes people feel good. We *need* that right now."

Cole could have done all this shit by phone, talked to the media, and just slipped out the back door to boot camp. It wouldn't have hurt half as much. But he knew the influence he had on folks. And the fans who paid his wages deserved an explanation.

"Yeah, Boss," he said at last. "That's why I want to go out there and tell them myself. Will you let me do that? Before the game starts?"

Mortensen got to his feet and wandered around the box. It took him a few minutes to settle himself, but then he finally picked up the phone. Cole didn't want to listen. He was focused on the stadium now, on the crowd that was filling the seats and waiting for the whistle. They knew he wasn't in the lineup today and they knew why. Walking out there was still going to be hard.

Am I gonna be any use as a Gear?

Well, at least nobody's left to fret about me. Momma would have gone nuts. Dad would have had the news on all day.

Mortensen put the phone down. "The chairman's gone ape-shit. He's going to have the press office all over us." He gestured to the door. "I'll deal with him. You get out there ten minutes before the whistle and do what you need to do."

"Thanks, Boss. I'm sorry it had to be like this."

Mortensen pinched the tip of his nose for a moment, blinking. "You're going to come back when it's over. Yeah? Because you *are* going to come back."

"You know it. My agent and my lawyer are gonna be on my ass until I do." *I can do this. I can get out there and face 'em. And I can pick up a rifle and fight, once someone tells me how the hell to use it.* Cole forced a big grin. "Shit, I'm more afraid of the sponsors than the grubs, baby."

Getting onto the pitch meant a long walk down the back stairs and cutting through one of the fire exits. Mortensen walked down to the touchline with him, still shaking his head as if he was arguing with himself.

"Go on," he said. Cole could hear the stadium announcer introducing him. "They're listening."

The crowd always started the Cole Train chant when they saw him, but when he stepped onto the pitch this time there was just polite applause. Everyone knew his folks had been killed. Maybe they weren't going to be shocked to hear what he had to say.

Whatever that's gonna be.

Cole didn't know what he was going to say until he took the public address mike in one hand and the applause stopped. For once, it wasn't a capacity crowd. He wondered if the missing fans were just staying away or if they were among the dead. It put him off his stride for a moment. He tried to focus again.

"I'm gonna keep this short, people. I came to say good-bye. See, I just enlisted. I'm a Gear now." He paused for the reaction. He didn't know what he expected them to do, but he didn't expect what he got, which was a murmur that went around the stadium like one big gasp. His Cole Train act kicked in automatically whether he wanted it to or not. "We're in big trouble and the Cole Train's gotta go kick some grub ass. Yeah, that's right! We all gotta do our bit and fight these things, 'cos they ain't gonna listen to reason! Are *you* gonna enlist? Are ya? Are ya gonna help me put 'em back down the hole they came from?"

Nobody said a word for a couple of seconds.

"I ain't hearin' you, folks! I said, are you gonna help me?"

Finally some guys in the front row seats to his right started yelling. "Yeah, Cole Train! We're with you!"

"Are ya? And are we gonna win?"

"Yeah!"

"I said, *are we gonna win?*"

"*Yeaaahhh!*"

The yelling and cheering picked up, one section at a time. It was weird. It wasn't a bunch of beer-fueled crazies making a noise for the hell of it. The only way he could describe it was that they *meant* it.

Then it began. The crowd started chanting the way they did at every game—"Cole *Train*! Cole *Train*! Cole *Train*!"— and getting faster and faster until it sounded like a speeding locomotive. He couldn't make himself heard now. It felt like the right point to walk away. If he stayed a second longer, he'd burst out crying, and that wasn't going to inspire anybody.

His folks had been real proud the first time they saw a game. They didn't care if he scored or not. They were just proud.

I ain't even started missin' 'em yet. Hurts so much I can't feel things right.

It felt like a damn long walk back to the exit. He saw the news cameramen heading his way from the touchline and decided to duck out until he got his shit together again. Hell, the press people could fend that off for a while. It'd keep 'em busy. He had nothing more to say anyway.

Mortensen covered him as he broke into a jog and vanished into the tunnel behind the security barrier.

"Are you staying for the game, Cole?" he asked. "I've got the car out front for you. It'll wait."

"Tell the guys I'll stop by in the morning when it's all calmed down some."

"You make sure you do."

"Promise."

Cole just wanted to get out as fast as he could, even though he knew he couldn't—wouldn't—change his mind. There was no way he could carry on playing as long as those grub motherfuckers were still out there.

The lobby was almost deserted except for the folks at the concession counters. They smiled at him and he waved back, but they probably hadn't heard what he'd just done, so he didn't need to get involved in any depressing conversations and goodbyes.

He swung open the main doors and paused by the statue outside. He always joked about it, but it made him squirm to see himself up there larger than life, and he was pretty large to start with. No, it wasn't *him*. It was something else with the same name, something people wanted to believe in, but it wasn't the Augustus Cole that was *him*.

There was no point looking back.

"Take care of the place for me, hear?" he said to the statue, and got into the waiting car.

GALANGI, SOUTH ISLANDS: ONE WEEK AFTER E-DAY.

"What are you doing?" Neal asked. The house smelled of bacon and burned toast. "Your breakfast's getting cold."

Bernie straightened up and tested the rucksack for weight. "Getting ready for recall. They'll be mobilizing everyone."

"Oh, for God's sake. Are you serious?"

She pointed to the rifles laid out on the bench in the back room. She had her own Longshot—perfectly legal, COG army surplus—and the Indie sniper rifle that Major Stroud had looted for her personally. If the COG wanted *that* back, they could come and try taking it. Yes, she was serious.

Neal's shoulders sagged. "The governor told us to stay put and conserve supplies. Don't be so bloody stupid, woman."

"Just watch the news," she said. The TV transmitter was working again, and now even the most remote South Islands could see what was happening to the rest of Sera. "They're going to need every Gear who can hold a rifle."

"Bern, get real. You're forty-eight."

"Forty-*seven*. I could have served frontline until *fifty-five*. And I'm fit enough to work a farm, but not fight?"

"So you're just going to hop on the bus and head for the front."

"Don't take the piss." Bernie knew how the row would go. "It's about duty."

"You already did that. It's time to worry about *us*, Bern."

"Yeah, but you're going to want some other Gear to put his duty first and save our arses when those grubs show up down here, aren't you?"

"Grubs *tunnel*. How are they going to tunnel to the islands? They'd have to dig under the seabed. And there's an abyssal trench between us and Noroa that's deeper than the height of Mount Chen." Neal grabbed his drover's coat off the hook in the hallway. "But maybe they've got bloody yachts, eh?"

From what she'd seen of the Locust on the news, they were smart enough to operate a ship. "If they have, then I'm not waiting for them to get here."

"You know what? I've got to give the weaners their lung-worm shots." Neal gestured with a big veterinary hypodermic that looked like a caulk gun. The gadget made injecting cattle a one-man job, another reminder of how long he'd run the farm single-handed while she was away. "They still need looking after and they don't stop for grubs."

He slammed the door behind him. Moss started barking as the utility's engine coughed into life and roared away. Neal would come back in a couple of hours as if nothing had happened, like he always did, so Bernie went to see what he'd left for breakfast and assembled it into a bacon sandwich.

There were no garrisons anywhere near Galangi. Who was going to pull troops back from the mainland cities to defend a speck on the map with fifteen hundred inhabitants on the opposite side of the world? Galangi was going to have to look after itself.

Well, most of us have rifles. That's more than the average civvie in Tyrus has got.

She went to switch on the radio but stopped herself. Hanging on every news bulletin was just making things

worse. *Not strangers. My mates. My bloody regiment.* This
was a global crisis, and as long as she was capable of fighting,
she had a duty. But she couldn't do a thing about it unless
she could get to Jacinto, and all flights from Noroa to the
mainland—once a month at the best of times—had been
grounded.

Her daily phone call to 26 RTI headquarters got the
recorded message from the phone company about suspension of service again. While she dialed, she noted that the
paint on the wall was peeling and added it to the mental list
of things to sort out. *Repair the fence, paint the hall, kill the
grubs.* The recorded message repeated.

*Sod it, I can't sit around waiting for permission. Let's do
some resource investigation.*

Bernie grabbed her coat and went to get the quad bike
out of the barn, wondering if she could persuade Dale to sell
her a couple of horses for when the fuel ran out. The islands
depended on imported imulsion. When she checked the
gauge on the storage tank it showed three-quarters full, and
that was the way it was going to stay. She rummaged in the
tool locker for a padlock.

Nobody on Galangi locked their houses or outbuildings.
It was an old-fashioned Islander society based on handshakes
and knowing every bloody cough and spit about your neighbor's business, but this invasion wasn't predictable and
orderly like the Pendulum Wars. She had a feeling that people would change. She padlocked the fuel store and set off
for the town.

The route was a couple of kilometers over open country
before the track joined the paved road down to the coast,
and it was fifteen klicks before she saw another human
being. Jim Kilikano had a dairy herd and traded cheese,
milk, and the occasional duck for Mataki steak and mutton.
He waved at her from his tractor as he hauled feed across the

field, not looking particularly worried about grubs or anything else. She waved back and carried on.

This was why people liked the remote end of the South Islands. It was another world. Noroa occasionally got tourists who were willing to spend weeks getting there to see the wild coasts and breathe crystal-clear air. They didn't visit Galangi often, though. Maybe it had something to do with the island's only town being called Port Slaughterhouse.

It didn't look as bad as it sounded. It was just the place where they slaughtered export livestock before shipping the frozen carcasses to Noroa. Nobody could accuse the white settlers who colonized the islands of being coy.

Bernie rounded the last headland and saw the ferry still alongside at the jetty, where it had been for four days. She parked the bike outside the post office and walked up to the fuel station. One of its two pumps was already draped with a sign saying SORRY NO LIGHT GRADE.

"How's tricks, Dan?" The owner was bent over an outboard motor, ratcheting away with a socket spanner. "Heard anything from Government House?"

"I'm only the council delegate," he said, not looking up. "We're just below the postman on the governor's priority list."

"No fuel rationing yet, then."

"Well, the ferry office on Noroa says there's a tanker due in a few days. It left port before the grubs invaded. So when we see how much fuel we get after Noroa's had its share, then we'll know if we're being rationed, won't we?"

"When's the ferry heading out again?"

"When the fuel gets to Noroa, so we know it can get back."

It was a four-hundred-kilometer trip. Bernie found herself wondering whether a fishing vessel might be heading that way. But that could mean getting stuck on Noroa for weeks, and she couldn't face turning up on Mick's doorstep right now.

"Can I use your radio, Dan? I need to call Government House. Bloody phone's down."

He straightened up and gestured out back. "Yeah, but the governor's staff are getting really shitty if you use the emergency channel."

"I've had worse than snotty clerks."

"Tell 'em you're a war hero."

It made her cringe. He never let her forget that medal for Aspho Fields, and she knew from the way he said it—no matter how genuinely or kindly—that he didn't know what drove her.

"Don't take the piss," she said, "or I won't vote for you next time."

She walked through to the back of the workshop and picked up the radio mike. "Galangi Protectorate to GHN, over." It was only when she heard the crackle of someone starting to respond that she realized just how pathetic she was going to sound. *A middle-aged farmer's wife with a dodgy leg and rusting sniper skills.* "GP to GHN, over."

"GH Noroa here, go ahead."

"My name's Mataki." Okay, she was going to lie. Nobody was going to care about discharge technicalities when every country on the mainland was being invaded. "I'm a reserve Gear. I need to rejoin my unit in Jacinto and I can't make contact. Is there any way I can reach a garrison?"

Bernie braced for an earful and had already worked out just where she'd tell this pen-pusher to shove his next comment. But all she got was a long pause, the sound of someone putting their hand over the mike, and then a strangely relieved and different voice.

"Mataki, this is the duty incident controller—Constable Thomas. You haven't had recall orders, have you?"

"No, of course not." Well, that was true. "How are they going to contact me?"

"Then stay put. We need you where you are." The copper went off-mike for a few seconds. "Look, we didn't know we had any Gears on Galangi. We're not going to get any help from Ephyra if the Locust attack. None of the islands will. We're on our own. Can you organize a militia?"

Part of her brain nodded and said that was exactly what she should do and where she'd be most use. The other part whimpered that she wanted to be with her old mates in 26 RTI again, and this wasn't quite what she'd had in mind.

But it's my bloody duty. And that's what I want to do, isn't it?

"Yes, I was an infantry sergeant." It was automatic. The man didn't seem to notice the past tense. *No, no, I want to get to Jacinto. I don't want to organize a bunch of civvies.* "I can do that. Most of the adults here are competent with shotguns."

"Right, now we know you're there, we'll want you to stay in contact, okay? We'll need a list of contact numbers and radio callsigns."

Bernie was suddenly aware of Dan standing in the open doorway. She shut her eyes, cringing at the glimpse into her own selfish subconscious. "Will do," she said. "Thanks. Mataki out."

She put the handset back in the cradle, crushed. Dan wiped his hands on an oily rag and shook his head ruefully.

"Bugger me," he said. "This is all getting a bit serious, isn't it?"

"You'll have to call a meeting." *No, no, no. This isn't going to stop the grubs. I need to get back to the regiment.* "Give me a day to work out how I'm going to do this."

"And placate your old man." He slapped her on the shoulder. "Good on you, girl. Count me in."

Bernie picked up some groceries from the food store next door and put her money on the counter, still numb. *Is money going to mean anything now?* The bags of sugar and flour she'd just bought would probably become currency pretty soon. *We're going to be cut off for a long time.* Would she end up holding back grub attacks, or keeping order among her own neighbors when essentials started running really short?

Well, serves me right.

"Where have you been?" Neal asked when she opened the front door. "We didn't need any groceries."

"I've been talking to Government House." There was no point pissing around and making excuses. "They want me to set up a local militia. We're not going to get any help from the mainland if the shit hits the fan."

He looked at her for a while, head slightly on one side. Moss came bounding down the hall and thudded into her legs, tail wagging furiously.

"Shit, I really thought you'd gone until I saw your Longshot was still here." Neal let out a breath and took the groceries from her one-handed, pulling her to him for a hug as if she'd just come back from the front. Moss jumped up for a pat on the head too. "You'd never make it to Ephyra, love. I know how bad you feel, but we need you here. Don't we, Mossie? You're the only Gear in town."

"So I am," she said, wondering how much worse she would have felt leaving the poor sod on his own again and maybe never coming back. He'd always been there. He might have bitched and griped about it, but she could count on him. "Just like old times."

CHAPTER 8

We don't have tents for an extra three thousand people. Until we've built more accommodation, we'll have to do what we did in Jacinto—everyone has to share their space. Take a lodger. I think we should brace for some social friction.

(Royston Sharle, Head of Emergency Planning, New Jacinto)

IMULSION SITE, EIGHTEEN KILOMETERS SOUTH OF PELRUAN: PRESENT DAY, 15 A.E.

"Jackpot," said Staff Sergeant Parry. "Now all we have to do is pump this stuff out."

The forest floor was dotted with bright pools of glowing imulsion. Dom looked around at the dense screen of dead trees and equally dead stalks.

"You going to put a road through here?"

"Nothing fancy." Parry picked his way between the luminous puddles. "This is a job for Betty. Once she's flattened the trees, we can lay some trackway and get a rig set up. Stefan? What do you think?"

The dour Gorasni rig workers looked unusually excited. Stefan Gradin kept shaking a small glob of imulsion in a glass jar and peering at it as it ran down the sides. Borusc Eugen nodded approvingly and gave Parry a thumbs-up.

It didn't strike Dom as very scientific, but this was the best anyone could do these days. Equipment had broken down, worn out, been destroyed, or had just been left behind because it couldn't be moved when they abandoned the cities one by one. None of it could be replaced.

It's like being back in the Silver Age. Printing by hand. Distilling fuel in boilers. Making ammunition with lead shot. And it's just going to get worse.

That made the Gorasni who'd run the Emerald Spar platform the world experts in imulsion technology. Dom respected their guts, but he wanted to see bespectacled guys in lab coats again.

"It's very *liquid*," Stefan said, shaking the jar like a cocktail bartender. "Not much refining needed. Very good. Very *volatile*."

"Great." Dom looked down at his armor and noted that he was spattered with the stuff. The ground felt like a swamp under his boots. "Just great."

He backed off a few meters and went to stand with Marcus, who was engrossed in a three-way radio conversation.

"Yeah . . . yeah, I get it, Baird." Marcus listened with his eyes shut and a frown of intense concentration. "Colonel, did you hear all that? . . . Okay . . . Baird? Just stay with it. Hoffman's talking to Rossi. Fenix out."

"What's Baird bitching about now?" Dom asked.

"They've found a contaminated zone east of Pelruan with no visible stalks. It's spreading fast. Hoffman wants the farms in its path evacuated and cleared of food supplies."

"Saving cabbages. Yeah, that's what I signed up for." It made sense, but it didn't thrill Dom. "Okay."

Parry must have heard the conversation. "How fast?"

"They're watching it happen," Marcus said. "Baird says it could get close to Pelruan in fifteen days."

"Shit, does this thing have any pattern at all?"

"Well, it's still following the geological fissures."

"That's damn awkward timing, Marcus. We better hope it runs out of steam before then."

Poor bastard; Parry and his sappers were spread pretty thinly at the best of times, even with the majority of Gears tasked on construction and food distribution. Dom gave him a sympathetic pat on the back.

"At least we'll have the fuel to move everyone, Staff," he said.

"We've got to recover whatever supplies and materials we can. That's the time-consuming bit." Parry beckoned to one of his construction people, a slight woman who didn't look much like a bricklayer. "Rena, see if you can commandeer some tractors to haul the lumber away. Dizzy can be here and clearing a path inside an hour."

"I hope he's sober," Rena said. "It's his day off."

"No, much better if he's drunk." Stefan held the jar at arm's length and walked away from the contaminated area to a clearing fifty meters away. He placed the jar carefully on the ground and jogged back. "*Much* better. Everybody stay clear. Welcome to chemistry class."

He slipped his rifle off his shoulder and took a shot at the jar. It went up like a mortar. Everyone flinched except Marcus, who stared at the smoke and dying flames around it with a look that said he was waiting for the punch line.

"See?" Stefan spread his arms. "You need a *good* drink before you drive into imulsion seepage like this. A *man's* drink. Possibly the last that will ever touch your lips . . ."

Sorotki's voice broke in on the radio net. Dom had forgotten about the waiting Raven for a moment. "Good show!" he said. "Fill her up. Marcus, you want to finish the recon?"

Parry paced out distances and scribbled notes on a scrap of cardboard. "Prescott's wetting his boxers about this. He wants a sample. Can you take one back to base with you?"

"I think I liked him better when he didn't give a shit," Dom said. "Yeah, we'll do it as a kiss-o-gram. Hand it over."

It was just another glass jar with a screw top, and if the stuff hadn't been faintly luminous it could easily have passed for a urine sample from someone with a hell of a lot of health problems. Dom shook it gingerly and held it up to the light as he and Marcus walked back to the Raven.

"That's a goddamn incendiary device," Marcus grunted.

"I know. Just looking. Why's Prescott interested in this?"

"Maybe he doesn't trust the Gorasni."

"It's probably mutual." Dom climbed into the Raven and sat with the jar cradled in both hands. "Well, there's always that retired chemistry teacher to take a look at it, for all the good that'll do."

Mitchell held out his hand for the jar as the Raven lifted clear. He did the shake-it-and-watch thing too. "Dom, you should go see Doc Hayman about this, pronto."

"I thought it was yours, Kev."

"Ha. Yeah, that'll teach me to drink the local brew."

Sorotki cut in. "I'm going to check out the whole length of this fissure." He sounded even more cheerful than usual. "There might be some more seepage along it."

Mitchell settled down by the open door and tucked one edge of his folded map into the leg pocket on his pants, pencil in one hand. "If this was normal Sera, you'd be a rich man now, Marcus. A fuel tycoon."

"Money's overrated," Marcus said. "It never bought me what I needed."

It was as near as Marcus ever got to a personal revelation. Dom had stopped thinking of him as the rich kid a long time ago. Money hadn't done much for Cole and Baird, either, but nobody ever seemed to gripe about it. There was a lot to be said for shared hardship.

The sweep back and forth along the fissure took half an hour, but they couldn't see any more pools of imulsion.

"Well, perhaps I was being optimistic," Sorotki said. "Damned if I can work out what the connection is, though. Leviathans with polyps. Stalks with polyps. Stalks *without* polyps. Stalks with dead patch. Dead patch without stalks."

"Stalks with imulsion," Marcus added.

The dead brown patch extended about five klicks northeast. Dom watched Mitchell penciling the new boundaries on his chart.

"Okay, we have a pattern," Mitchell said, holding up the battered map. "All the contamination's in the top third of the island. Nothing south of this line here."

Dom shrugged. "That's assuming we've spotted everything. And we haven't even scratched the surface of whatever's in the center of the island."

"Got to go with the best information you've got at the time, Dom."

Marcus seemed to have his mind on something else. Dom could tell. Marcus didn't move his head, but his gaze shifted back and forth between what was beneath the Raven and a point on the metal deck. Sorotki looped back west to overfly the new dead area near Pelruan. Dom reached across and prodded Marcus.

"What's up?"

Dom had learned to lip-read pretty well after years in noisy helicopters. Marcus just mouthed one word: *disc*.

Dom nodded and said nothing. All Prescott's little bomb-shells, all the details he let drop when he felt like it, probably ate at Marcus on a personal level. There had been a time when his father had worked closely with Prescott. Marcus came from the decision-making classes.

But his father had never told him much about the Hammer of Dawn until the thing was finally tested on the UIR fleet. Dom still couldn't imagine how a father could keep anything that big from his son, even if he thought it was the kindest thing to do.

"Wow," Mitchell said. "That's getting a lot closer than I thought."

Beneath them, a wide brown strip of dead trees pointed toward Pelruan in the distance, like a ragged highway under construction. Mitchell pulled out the camera and started recording again. Sorotki took the Raven down lower and circled above the western boundary of the contamination.

"Well, the sooner we move everyone to New Jacinto, the easier it's going to be to keep an eye on them," he said. "Round 'em up and move 'em out."

Mitchell laughed. "You've been hanging out with Mataki and her sheepdog too long."

Sorotki turned west on his usual loop over Pelruan before returning to base. Marcus nudged Dom and held out his hand for the imulsion sample. He stared at it as if he'd never seen the stuff before.

"You think he's going to mix it with gunpowder and set fire to it, like they did in the old days?" Dom asked. "Because that's about the only analysis he can do now."

"Prescott?"

"Yeah."

"Maybe." Marcus was getting worried about all this, because Dom rarely heard him speculate, regardless of what was going on in his head. "I can usually work out what he's up to. But not this time."

"Maybe he's finally panicking."

"Wouldn't be good for people to see the Chairman lose his shit."

"Hey, we function without him pretty well. Where's the

strategy coming from? Hoffman, Michaelson, and Sharle. Not him."

"Everybody needs a figurehead," Marcus said, handing back the jar. "If only to have an ass to kick."

Dom had to admit that Prescott was good at holding people together. He'd never realized just what a messy job that was until he saw civilians with every reason to squabble suddenly *not* squabbling. The Gorasni were getting docile and the Pelruan locals had gone from a certain amount of resentment of the Jacinto newcomers to accepting that everyone's fate was linked. The army had well-honed methods for doing that and the structure to enforce it, but not civvies. Even in the COG, they still had to be more persuaded to do the sensible thing than ordered.

"Yeah," Dom said. "I'm not sure what the COG would look like now without him."

VECTES NAVAL BASE, VEHICLE COMPOUND.

"Dad, can we come along?" Maralin asked. "Please? We haven't been out of the camp for weeks."

Dizzy climbed up to Betty's cab and balanced on the step with one hand on the open door. "Ain't nothin' much to see out there except trees, sweetie. I'll be back in a few hours."

Teresa pitched in to back up her sister. They were twins, fourteen going on forty like all teenage girls, and Dizzy found that trying to be mom as well as dad to his daughters was stretching his parenting skills these days. They needed a woman's guiding hand. They were good girls, no trouble at all, but having to spend so much time without their dad had made them clingy. They were scared to let him out of their sight now.

"*Sam's* going," Teresa said pointedly.

Dizzy stood his ground, trying to let common sense

wrestle his guilt into submission. "Sam's a Gear, and she's ridin' shotgun."

Sam wandered up behind the twins with her Lancer and revved the chainsaw for a second.

"When you can handle one of these, you can go off-camp. You don't want to run into glowies without one." She ambled around to the other side of Betty and swung up onto the step in one movement. She made it look easy. "Here's the deal. You go help out in the school, and I'll give you firearms lessons. I'll check with Mrs. Lewelin, mind."

Teresa nudged Maralin. "Okay, Sam. See you later, Dad."

Dizzy didn't dare argue. Yeah, every kid needed to learn about rifles in this world, and Sam was the right one to teach them. He waited for the twins to walk away and slammed the driver's door shut. Sam settled into the passenger seat and rested the Lancer on the open window.

She patted his arm. "Diz, we're so busy staying alive that we've got kids now who can barely read and write. If your girls teach the little kids, everyone gets something out of it, right?"

"I ain't complainin'. You got a way with 'em. They look up to you."

"Teenagers, see. I look like a rebel to them."

"Goddamn," Dizzy said, starting the engine. "I always thought I was doin' the right thing."

"Bringing up two kids on your own is tough enough without doing it outside the wire." She didn't use the word *Stranded,* but it wouldn't have offended him. It was what he used to be. Maybe he still was. "You did fine, Diz. They're good kids."

Dizzy drove out of the compound and took the perimeter road to the main gates. He'd been driving this rig for six years, the price of keeping his kids fed. *Operation Lifeboat. Lifeboat for who, goddamn it? Wasn't for the good of our health, Chairman, was it?* It was an honest job and he took pride in it. But he still wondered if the girls would have been happier if he'd stayed Stranded and been a full-time dad.

Maralin probably wouldn't have survived, though. Maybe he'd have been dead by now, too.

"I left my girls alone with strangers for weeks at a time," he said. "That ain't right."

"Diz, the Lifeboat camp was organized." Sam always went out of her way to make him feel better. "Qualified people, taking care of *everyone's* kids. Not exactly strangers. How else were you going to feed them properly and get medical treatment?" She adjusted the wing mirror as Betty rumbled north. "My mother raised me alone too. So did Anya's mother. We didn't turn out so bad."

"Ah, maybe this is 'cause I got girls," Dizzy said. "They're that age, y'know? They're going to be dating soon, and that's when it all goes to rat-shit. I dunno where the hell to start."

"Jacinto's a small community now. It's not like they're alone in the big city."

"You know what's funny?"

"What?"

"We ain't worryin' about grubs or glowies bein' the dangers, either of us. We're worryin' about other humans."

Sam checked the charge on her Lancer. "Oh, I think we'd better start worrying about the glowies again, then. They can ruin your entire day."

Dizzy was nowhere near the fissure zones yet, not that he was worried about polyps. Betty had shoveled them up like rubble when they attacked the naval base. Hell, she could even roll right over mines; just a few weeks ago she'd been sweeping the main road with a chain flail, detonating devices planted by the Stranded gangs. She could take a hell of a pounding and keep right on going. He felt safe in her.

"So you're just going to drive in and knock the trees down with the scoop," Sam said.

"That's the plan. Open up a gap so we can roll out some trackway and the tankers can get in to pump off the juice."

"I hope it's a big deposit. Or whatever you call it. Funny that the stalks came up through it."

"Maybe they're the way it got to the surface."

"Baird's bound to have a theory on that."

"We never did get that picture of him on his throne."

Sam burst out laughing. "It's still on my to-do list. I want it framed and hung in the mess."

It was a nice day and Dizzy decided to enjoy the drive. He'd learned to live in the moment, not because he was happy to find himself alive for one more day like some of the folks he knew, but because he'd found a way to unplug himself from his memories. He didn't look back because it hurt too much. He just looked forward. That meant his girls' futures.

"You readin' the map?" Dizzy asked. "I don't want to uproot the wrong wood."

"Keep going," Sam said. "I'll tell you when to turn off the road."

"Goddamn, I'm gonna piss off another farmer by churnin' up his fields, ain't I?"

"Stick to the edge of the field wherever you can." Sam checked the map against her compass. "Can't rely on the satellite positioning anymore, but you're never alone with basic fieldcraft. Okay—another eight hundred meters, then go right."

Dizzy glanced at the dials on Betty's dashboard, calculating the distance, then dropped a gear to approach the turnoff. "Hang on to your hat!" Betty lurched off the road, bouncing a little as her sheer weight ironed out the bumps in the grass. He picked up the radio handset. "Len, we're headin' your way. You got all your folks clear?"

The channel clicked. "We can hear you coming, Dizzy. You knock them down and we'll clear them away."

"Bear left," Sam said.

"Okay, I'm heading for that hill."

"Stay on this course." She sighed. "I feel bad about this. Felling healthy trees, I mean."

"Just shut your eyes and don't look, sweetie," Dizzy said. "It ain't like we're gonna waste the wood, after all."

"Well . . . it's all going to end up dead anyway from whatever toxin those stalks crap out everywhere."

Dizzy checked his bearings with Parry. The forest was a wall of trunks with a thick dark roof of leaves, nothing complicated or delicate. This was what Betty was built for: drilling, dragging, digging, and generally creating paths through battlefields in any plane or direction. Dizzy slowed and slipped the clutch.

"Okay, Diz, whenever you're ready," Parry said. "Go for it."

Dizzy whooped. "Whoo-*hooo!* Brace for impact, Sam!"

Betty rumbled into the first rank of trees and a slight shudder ran through her chassis. The noise of creaking wood rose up the scale. Then the trunks fell in slow motion, crashing onto the undergrowth and sending up clouds of leaves, insects, and twigs. When Dizzy reversed to take another run at it, he could see the ragged root balls exposed to the air, still shivering.

"I'm gonna keep goin' until I can't drive forward anymore," Dizzy said. "Then I'll back off while they drag the trunks clear."

"You mind that you don't get bogged down," Sam said. "We don't know what's under the soil. There could be pockets of imulsion. Voids. Whatever."

"Betty's too big to fall down a hole."

Sam had her elbow resting on top of the open side window. "She's not too big to get stuck, though, and who's going to tow her out?"

Dizzy moved in again, using the scoop as a battering ram. There was a satisfying creak and crunch, followed by two more trees collapsing in front of him.

Then something thudded onto the top of Betty's cab.

"Keep your arm inside, Sam." Dizzy backed up a few meters. "Gonna be a few branches fallin'."

He glanced at her. She was holding her Lancer upright, two-handed, watching behind Betty in the wing mirror. "Okay, Diz."

Thud. Another branch hit the cab roof, but he wasn't sure where it had come from. Maybe it had just been caught up in the roof rails and slipped down.

Sam looked up at the cab's head lining. "Diz . . ."

"What?"

She leaned forward to take a closer look in the wing mirror. "Oh shit, here we go," she said. "*Polyps.*"

She reached for the handle to close the window, but dark gray legs scrabbled over the edge of the glass. That was all Dizzy saw before Sam shoved the Lancer out the window and opened fire. A loud bang made his ears ring and warm, sticky fluid splashed over his arm. Sam wound up the window as fast as she could.

"They're all over the rig," she said. "Back up and try to shake them off. Or I'll have to get out and shoot the bloody things before they find a way in."

"We're okay. Betty's built like a tank. They can't even put a dent in her." Dizzy could hear polyps scuttling all over the roof, legs tapping on the metal. Had he left a ventilation scuttle open? He couldn't remember. He got on the radio. "Len? We got polyps all over us. You better look out."

Polyps were bad enough on their own. But polyps on the loose with flammable imulsion everywhere were much, much worse.

"We don't see them," Parry said. "Where are they coming from?"

Sam pressed her face to the windshield to look up as far as she could. She flinched as a couple of polyps thudded onto the hood right in front of her, scrabbling at the glass. The damn things were now swarming all over Betty, prodding and poking to find a way in.

"Can't sit here all day until they get bored, Diz," she said. "Either I get out and pop them all, or we get Parry to do it."

"With all this juice around? Sam, it's gettin' real *lethal* out there."

"So let's back away and find somewhere safer to do it. They'll detonate anyway."

Dizzy looked ahead, trying to work out where the things were coming from. It was only then that he saw the spots of greenish-yellow light in the dark canopy of leaves, right up in the branches, and they sure as shit weren't carnival illuminations.

The polyps were sitting up the trees like goddamn vultures.

"Holy shit!" He grabbed the radio handset from the dash. "Len, they can *climb!* Up in the trees! They're right above you!"

"Okay, everyone clear the area," Parry said. "Everyone, get clear of the imulsion. *Now!*"

Sam started scooping ammo out of the dash and stuffing it in every available space in her pouches. "Change of plan, Diz," she said. "Come on—I've got to get out of here and give the engineers some cover."

"You damn well stay put," he snapped. "You ain't goin' outside, Sam. Hear?"

There was suddenly a lot of chatter on the radio circuit.

Parry was calling Marcus. "Parry to Fenix, we've got polyps at the imulsion site. We could do with some backup, over."

"Diz, this is my job," Sam said, reaching for the door handle. "I'm not Maralin, okay? I'm a bloody Gear."

Dizzy hit the internal door lock on the dash and started backing up as fast as he could. "Yeah, but you ain't fireproof. Sit tight."

A cascade of polyps tumbled off the roof and landed in a heap on Betty's scoop. Some of them detonated, spattering gunk everywhere, and now he couldn't see through the windshield. He changed gear and lurched forward a few meters to try to shake the things off, then slammed Betty into reverse again and put his foot hard down. She wasn't moving like he expected her to. Some of her wheels were spinning in wet ground.

"Fenix to Parry, on our way," Marcus said. "Forget the imulsion. Get out of there."

"There, we got the big boys comin' to help out." Dizzy wasn't thinking too mathematically but it would be at least eight to ten minutes before Sorotki reached them. "Just gotta get these assholes off Betty before they mess up her paint job."

"Diz, if that imulsion ignites—"

Betty was a big, heavy, tin box with a lot of places for polyps to cling to. Dizzy pressed his face to the side window to try to see what Betty's wheels were bogged down in, because he was sure the ground had been solid when he drove in.

He hit the gas again. Yellowish pearly liquid spattered the glass. Now he knew what Betty was stuck in.

"Sam, I don't want to scare you none, but there's another shitload of imulsion right under us."

Sam stared straight ahead at trees full of polyps biding their time. Then she twisted around in her seat and peered at the mesh that separated the cab from the compartment behind.

"Hear that?"

Dizzy could. It was a kind of tapping, scratching sound, like a cat trying to get out of a garbage can.

"I don't want to scare you, either," Sam said. "But I think those little bastards have found a way into Betty."

KR-239, INBOUND FOR THE IMULSION FIELD.

Marcus leaned out of the crew bay and pressed his earpiece. "Len, have you cleared everybody out yet?"

"No," Parry said. "The grindlift rig's stuck in a seep and Dizzy and Sam are pinned down by polyps. Take a look."

"Nearly at your position." Sorotki was flying low and flat out. Dom watched the tops of the trees streak by way too close beneath him. "I suppose strafing's out of the question."

"Yeah, unless you want deep-fried Dizzy. The imulsion's going to go up like a blast furnace if it ignites. Betty's built like a Centaur's big sister, but she's not fireproof."

"Okay," Marcus said. "You drop us and we go in on the ground."

"That still doesn't solve our glowie problem," Mitchell said. "We'll need to throw them a decoy of some kind."

Dom moved from side to side in the center of the crew bay to try to keep both flanks in view as best he could. On his left, he caught a quick glimpse of the imulsion pools. A few seconds later, he looked right and saw the trail of churned turf leading to the trees.

"Got him." Mitchell pointed. "Mel, loop around right and follow the tire tracks . . . *oh shit*. Visual on Betty, your port side, Mel. Not looking good."

As the Raven banked, Dom could see Betty was sitting in what looked like a marsh of imulsion, but that wasn't her biggest problem. She was covered with polyps. They were clustered on every flat surface and even hanging on the side rails. Their lights looked more yellow now. These damn things changed every time he saw them.

"Either we get them off, or we get Betty out." Marcus swung back inside the crew bay and pulled a couple of foam extinguishers off the bulkhead. "Dom, grab one of these."

The units were ten years past their expiration date and designed for small onboard fires. Dom raised an eyebrow. "That's a bit optimistic, Marcus."

"Remember what Tai used to say."

Dom hadn't thought about Tai Kaliso in a while. *We must be creative.* He always said that when he grabbed the nearest and strangest tool to use as a weapon. It hadn't saved the poor bastard from the grubs, though. Dom took one of the extinguishers and wondered if polyps would explode if he sprayed them.

"Okay. I'll improvise." The Raven was so close to the tree-tops below that Dom could see movement in the branches. "Those assholes are up in the trees, Marcus. But they couldn't climb a few weeks ago."

Marcus hefted the fire extinguisher. "So they're a quick study. I'll note it for the Chairman."

"Ready to rope down?" Sorotki asked.

"I've got a better idea," Marcus said. "Drop to a meter or so and we'll jump. If we take a long run at them, it might draw them off."

Dom wasn't sure if Sorotki had heard what he said about the polyps in the trees and tried to interrupt. The next second, something large and gray with a lot of legs landed with a thud in the crew bay and Dom's brain didn't even pause to find a word for it.

"Whoa!" He booted the polyp over the side and it exploded in midair like a grenade cooking off. Debris peppered the Raven and rattled across the deck. "Shit, Sorotki, did you frigging hear me? They're right beneath us!"

"Nice dropkick," Mitchell said.

"Sorry, Dom, did I miss that?" Sorotki might have been oblivious of the close call or just at normal chill level for a Raven pilot. "Okay, stand by—forty meters—twenty—ten.—okay, go!"

Dom jumped out a heartbeat behind Marcus and steadied himself for a moment. The ground felt firm but he could smell imulsion again. Sixty or seventy meters ahead, Betty stood looking like she was tiled with polyps.

"What's that noise?"

He heard the muffled buzz of a chainsaw, then a really loud bang, as if a tin can had blown up on a bonfire. Betty shook. A couple of polyps lost their footing and plopped to the ground, but didn't blow up.

"Shit, that's coming from the rig." Marcus started running toward Betty, finger pressed to his earpiece. "Diz? What's happening in there?"

"Ah—that was Sam." Dizzy sounded shaky. But at least he was alive. "We got polyps in Betty's drill housing. Sam's crawled through to the back to hold them off."

"Goddamn, Dizzy, you're setting off explosions *inside* the fucking rig?" Marcus's voice suddenly got the polyps' attention and they started to move. "Are you out of your goddamned mind?"

Marcus speeded up but Dom grabbed his arm to slow him. They had to let the polyps come to them, or Betty was going to be engulfed in flames. The creatures turned like a wave and jumped off the vehicle, scuttling through the puddle of imulsion to rush at Marcus and Dom.

Dom let them get clear of the imulsion before he opened up with his Lancer and detonated the first wave. Marcus sidestepped three of the things and shot them as they overshot their target.

"Dozens," Dom said. "Shit, *dozens*."

It was all he could manage. There was just no time to think when polyps attacked in a wave. It was just *bang, bang, bang*, trying to pick them off from second to second before they got close enough to take your legs off. His focus became a tunnel again. Marcus kept firing, falling back a meter at a time to lure the polyps further away, but Dom could hear yelling on the far side of Betty. It was the Gorasni.

"Little shits! *Garayazki!* Over here!" Stefan and Eugen tried to draw off the rest of the polyps. "Yeah, *pashenki*, you come and get some!"

Dom glanced up for a second to see more polyps dropping out of the trees like bunches of ugly gray fruit. At the same time, Betty shuddered and something exploded, but he couldn't tell if one was connected to the other. The Gorasni guys were yelling, further away now. Explosions lit up the forest. Dom kept firing and reloading. It was chaos, blinding and smoke-filled, and right then it was all he could do to pick off the polyps and try to keep Marcus in sight. It was only when he drew breath to reload again that he spotted Parry and his engineers taking potshots at stray polyps too.

But nobody could keep shooting things that detonated without igniting some of the imulsion vapor. The trees were now on fire. A huge explosion lifted Betty a meter off the ground before she crashed back down on her suspension. Marcus—typical, goddamn *typical*—just broke off from the polyps and sprinted through them. Dom froze in horror for a moment as Marcus cannoned through the things, kicking one clear then treading right on another to leap up on Betty's mudguard and rip the driver's door open.

Dom charged after him. It was pure instinct. Smoke and flame rolled from underneath Betty but he knew he had to be right there with Marcus.

"Dizzy! Get out!" Marcus hauled Dizzy bodily from the

cab. Dom half-caught him and the two of them staggered backward. "Sam! *Sam!*"

Marcus vanished into the cab and Dom had no choice but to drag Dizzy clear and then try to go back. Before he could climb back up the vehicle, Parry and his crew appeared to fend off the next wave of polyps. No sane man turned his back on a charging mass like that, but Dom had reached the point where they'd become part of the background noise and his bigger fear was what would happen to Marcus.

Dom scrabbled halfway into the cab. The bulkhead panel behind the seats was hanging open and he could hear loud hissing sounds. He was about to squeeze through the gap when Sam, her face blackened and smeared, burst out through it like a cork from a bottle.

"Ah, shit—"

"Come on, *out!*" Marcus yelled. "Out, *now!*"

Dom stepped back blindly to crash hard to the ground and Sam fell on top, winding him. By the time he got to his feet, he could see Marcus hosing down the interior of the cab with the fire extinguisher.

Someone slapped Dom hard across the back. His legs almost buckled.

"Dom, we get them, eh? Now we save the crude." It was Eugen. He led Dom and Sam away. "Get your Ravens. Get them to drop soil, or else we lose all this. You understand? Parry! Parry, call your Ravens in!"

"I'm on it!" Parry yelled. "They're coming. Just get clear, will you?"

Marcus dropped down from Betty's cab and it was only then that Dom realized he was gripping Sam's arm. He let go, embarrassed.

"You okay, Sam?"

"My eyebrows didn't make it."

"You chainsawed polyps inside the goddamn rig?"

"No, I *shot* them. I *chainsawed* holes in the bulkhead to get a clear shot into the rear compartment before they got to us." Sam looked shaken. Flames were licking the trees behind her. "Confined space. Remember? We'd have been dead otherwise."

Dom realized he was scolding Sam because he wanted to yell at Marcus. "Okay. I'm sorry. Look, go and wait with Dizzy and we'll casevac you." He saw Marcus walk away, finger pressed to his ear, and broke off. "Give me a minute."

Dom walked up behind Marcus and waited for him to finish on the radio. Fear for his welfare had dissolved into the usual shaky anger, just like scolding a kid who'd run into the path of traffic.

"You're going to get yourself fucking killed, Marcus," he said. "What's up with you?"

"Couldn't let them cook," Marcus said, matter-of-fact. "And we need that rig."

"Don't you ever stop and think before you get into a burning vehicle?"

"No. And neither would you." Marcus rolled his head as if his neck was stiff. It was his get-off-my-case gesture. "Nobody died. Baird or Parry can fix Betty. Now all we have to do is stop the imulsion field—ah, *goddamn it!*"

A snowstorm of grit hit them seconds before they heard the Raven pass overhead. It swept on over the trees and hovered a hundred meters in to drop a load of soil on the burning imulsion. Dom could hear more helicopters approaching.

"Two-Three-Nine here." Sorotki's voice popped in Dom's ear. "If you two want a ride back to VNB, move it. Dizzy's a bit chargrilled. He really needs to see Doc Hayman."

"Okay." Marcus looked around, dusting dirt off his armor one-handed. "We'll need a hand hauling Betty out."

"She'll have to wait. That's a two-bird job."

Sam didn't say a word on the flight back. Dom took a first-aid pack and wiped her face. She didn't even protest. She just looked him in the eye and managed a smile, and there was something in it that unnerved him. He caught Marcus looking their way and giving him that *go on* look.

No, this isn't going anywhere. It can't.

If things had been different, if his whole life had been different, he would have jumped at that chance. But he'd never feel that way again after Maria, and if he did—shit, he'd never be able to live with himself for giving in to it. It wasn't about betraying Maria's memory. She'd have told him so. It was about knowing he didn't deserve to be happy again when he couldn't save his kids, and when the only way he could save his wife in the end was to shoot her.

Sacrifice was clean and easy. Surviving your loved ones wasn't. Dom tried not to meet Sam's eyes and carried on cleaning her up.

Dizzy took a swig from his hip flask and held it out to Sam. She took a mouthful and coughed her guts up.

"I feel better already," she said hoarsely. "Thanks."

But she wasn't looking at Dizzy. Dom slammed shut that door in his mind and made sure he would never let it open again.

CHAPTER 9

SITREP #18A

Extent of contaminated zones and stalk ingress at 0001/G/01/15

CURRENT WESTERN BOUNDARY OF CZ: 16 km approx. from Pelruan.

RATE OF SPREAD: 15cm approx. per minute as measured at 2345/B/38/15 to 2445/B/38/15. (Variable.) Spread has slowed but appears irregular in shape and rate.

FORECAST: If the rate of spread continues, two farms west of Pelruan will fall within the CZ within eight days, and Pelruan itself will be cut off with only coastal/sea access.

ACTION: Four-hour monitoring to continue. Evacuation contingency team to remain on one-hour alert.

(Prepared by: Major G. Gettner and R. Sharle)

VECTES NAVAL BASE, NEW JACINTO: TWO DAYS LATER, GALE, 15 A.E.

"Colonel? Colonel!"

Hoffman carried on walking across the parade ground while he tried to place that voice. It took four more strides before the name clicked in his head.

Ingram. Keir Ingram.

Whatever the man wanted, it was guaranteed to make Hoffman late for his meeting with Prescott. He was one of the civilian neighborhood representatives from old Jacinto, a *real* civvie—not civilian support staff, who were very nearly Gears. Regular civvies were a species that Hoffman rarely had much contact with these days.

And he's been waiting for me. There's no way he'd run into me here and now by accident.

Hoffman stopped and turned. "What can I do for you, Mr. Ingram?"

"Is it true that you're moving everyone out of Pelruan?"

"Maybe." Hoffman didn't ask why Ingram was bothered about it because he didn't want to hear the answer, not right now. "The decision hasn't been made yet."

"Is there ever going to be any consultation with us on this?"

Ingram did routine, necessary things like organizing his neighbors for cleaning duties and kitchen rosters. Hoffman didn't think of him as a troublemaker. He was a thin, balding, schoolmasterly kind of guy in his fifties who looked as mild as he was. Jacinto civilians had lived under siege for so many years that they'd developed an almost military sense of a chain of command and an ability to suck it up. But hearing Ingram talk about *consultation* in a tight, scared voice unsettled Hoffman at a primal level.

"What's to consult about?" Hoffman asked. "It's my duty to protect them, and it's easier for me to do that if I've got all the civilians in one area."

"This camp's bursting at the seams already," Ingram said. "We're still trying to catch up with rebuilding the houses the last polyp attack burned down. Eighty percent of families are still living in tents or barracks."

"I know that, Mr. Ingram." Hoffman checked his watch to prepare for making his escape. The gesture alone was usually enough to shut anyone up. "But Pelruan's our people and they keep us fed. We'll make room."

Ingram's jaw sagged a little, disappointed. "I asked you instead of the Chairman because I thought you wouldn't give me a mealy-mouthed answer."

Ingram didn't want mealy-mouthed, and he didn't get it. Dealing with emergencies didn't require a goddamn referendum every time. It never had. Hoffman saw no reason for things to be any different on Vectes.

"If you want to talk about representation, that's above my pay grade." He turned to make it clear that he was moving on. "Look, you're a councilman and you talk direct to the head of state. How much more representation do you want?"

"More than *this*," Ingram said, looking more crestfallen than offended. "But thank you for your candor, Colonel."

Hoffman carried on to Admiralty House. Michaelson stood on the steps outside the main doors, sipping from a white tin mug and chatting with Sharle and Trescu. It still disturbed Hoffman to see a COG uniform and a UIR one side by side without close-quarters combat being involved. Some reflexes never went away.

"Ah, the natives are restless," Michaelson said, raising his mug like a toast. "Did you park in his space, Victor?"

"He just wants a frigging vote on where we put displaced persons. I hinted we'd do things the Gorasni way."

Trescu didn't blink. "I'm glad you've seen sense."

"I told you they'd get pissy about it sooner or later," Sharle said. "Thank God we're not trying to do this at minus twenty degrees."

Michaelson tipped the slops from his mug under the short hedge beside the doors. It was the first time Hoffman had noticed that the bushes were dotted with white blossom. He could actually smell them now, a sweetly spicy scent like cloves.

"Prescott hasn't shown up yet," Michaelson said. "Does anyone have any bad news they don't want to share with him?"

"Me," Sharle said. "I know he doesn't want to hear this, but I went ahead and did a dispersal scenario plan. As in the circumstances under which we'd have a better survival rate if we broke up into smaller groups."

Hoffman didn't like it any more than Prescott would, but he wanted to hear. "Why?"

"Why did I do it, or why is it better?"

"Both."

"Well, if we can't reach the mainland, we'll have to island-hop, and there's nowhere big enough to take thousands of refugees."

"We've thrashed this out before. The more widely people are spread, the less able I am to defend them."

"I'm looking at the Stranded and learning lessons," Sharle said. "Assholes or not, an awful lot of them have survived without any of our infrastructure, troop numbers, or weapons."

Trescu reached out and picked a sprig of scented blossoms from the bush. "Speaking as a small community, I can tell you that it makes you neither invisible nor more resilient." He stripped the leaves with his thumbnail and tucked the sprig into his buttonhole. "Which is why we asked to join you."

"I'm not advocating we do it," Sharle said. "But I'm obliged to investigate every option. We might need to rethink the big city model we've been clinging too all these years."

Hoffman didn't want to say it in front of Trescu, but dispersal would mean the end of the COG. Either it was one community with structure and purpose, or it was . . . nothing.

Trescu knew that anyway. Gorasnaya was in the same position.

"Damn it, I'm going to see where Prescott's gotten to." Hoffman pressed his earpiece to summon Lowe and Rivera. They'd be with the Chairman, wherever he was. They did damn all else now except provide his close protection, God only knew from what. "Hoffman to Rivera, over." He waited. "Hoffman to Lowe, over."

There was no response. Prescott didn't carry a radio, so that option was out. Michaelson held the doors open and gestured like a butler.

"Let's see if we can bumble along somehow until the divine presence decides to grace us," he said. "After you, gentlemen."

On the way in, they passed the open doors of CIC. Mathieson looked up from his desk and craned his neck.

"Colonel, may I talk to you when you've finished your meeting?"

"I'm free now, Lieutenant."

Mathieson's gaze flickered past Hoffman. He was a tactful lad. This obviously wasn't meant for other ears. "Oh, later will do, sir. Thanks."

In the meeting room, Trescu spread his maps and lists out on the table. "We can accommodate five to six hundred extra people," he said, not looking up. "If you can find that many in Pelruan who don't want to shoot us on sight, that is."

Sharle was still all smiles, Mr. Nice Guy. "Don't worry, we'll remember not to put the Tollen vets with you."

Hoffman was surprised that Trescu even offered. The Gorasni still kept to themselves. It was time for a conciliatory gesture. "I appreciate the work your rig team's doing at the imulsion site," Hoffman said. "Dirty, dangerous job."

"If we need imulsion, then it must be done."

"So when will we have some usable fuel?" Michaelson asked.

Trescu penciled some cross-hatching on his map to the east of the Gorasni camp. "Three days. Slow, but there'll be a steady supply for as long as we can enter the dead zones. Once your grindlift rig is repaired, we can install more derricks."

The sound of boots on the stairs distracted them. Prescott was talking to someone, probably Rivera, and Hoffman caught the word *Hayman*. Prescott must have been wearing the doctor's patience thin. Hoffman could imagine the old battleaxe's reaction when the Chairman showed up asking her to find out why the grass had died.

"My apologies, gentlemen." Prescott closed the door behind him and joined in the ritual of staring at the maps. "I'm afraid Dr. Hayman can tell us nothing about the site samples, and the weather satellite's unable to give us images of the island—as we expected. I'd hoped to have something more concrete for you."

"Oh, as long as you're here, Chairman, that's all that matters," Michaelson said sweetly.

Prescott's jaw tightened but he slipped straight back behind the mask of reassuring, unflappable omniscience again. Something other than Michaelson was getting to him. Things were bad, but no worse than they'd been many times before over the years.

"So where are we this morning?" he asked. "Good news, bad news?"

Hoffman slid the latest sitrep across the table to him, even though he was damn sure Prescott must have seen it already. "Bad news—still touch-and-go on Pelruan. Good news—Wallin's grindlift rig will be back in action tomorrow, and the drilling team estimates they'll be extracting up to ten thousand liters of crude a day when they begin pumping."

"Which we will be conserving until the storage reserve is fifty percent above minimum and every vessel is full to capacity," Sharle said, smiling in that avuncular way that said he'd chop their goddamn fingers off if they so much as siphoned off a teaspoon of it. "After which, we will still *economize.*"

"So we have options again." Prescott's mouth was making positive sounds but he'd definitely lost some of that polished smugness. "We can move. We can monitor. We can, to some extent, manufacture. Our most pressing short-term problem is still housing and food production. So, no need to evacuate the town yet?"

"I'm going to ask for volunteers to relocate," Hoffman said. "Then when we need to move them—*if* we need to— we won't have as many to ship out in a hurry."

Hoffman's ifs and maybes were starting to creep back in again. He knew he was kidding himself. Prescott still seemed distracted by the reports on the table and pored through them, not even looking up. "Excellent idea. Anything else, gentlemen?"

For once there *was* an extra item, the political kind that Prescott could toss and gore for hours. It might keep him occupied. Hoffman shoved it into the arena and stepped back.

"Yes, Chairman," he said. "We have some disgruntled civilians griping about not being consulted. Keir Ingram waylaid me to bend my ear about it."

"He's keen to start local elections again," Prescott said, completely unabashed. "I'm aware. He brings it up once a year, regular as clockwork."

"Good, then I can leave the civil unrest and coup suppression to you." *Job done. His problem.* "Adjourned?"

"Adjourned," Prescott said. "Good day, gentlemen."

He vanished again with Rivera and Lowe. Hoffman had no idea what he did when he wasn't in his office, but he'd never been the kind of man to want to chew the fat over a coffee even when coffee still existed. There were just very few private diversions on Vectes and no gentlemen's clubs in which to do dodgy deals over port.

As long as he's not in my face, fine. I don't care where he goes.

Sharle steered Trescu away to discuss the imulsion situation. It was a handy moment for Hoffman to peel off to CIC and find out what Mathieson wanted.

"Wait for me, Quentin, will you?" Hoffman said. "I've just got to see what the kid wants."

Donneld Mathieson was sitting at his desk, headset in place and fidgeting with a gadget Hoffman couldn't recognize, opening and closing it one-handed like someone absent-mindedly clicking a pen.

"Everything okay, son?" Hoffman asked.

Mathieson jerked out of his trance. "Something's bothering me, sir." He put the gadget down and beckoned. "I recorded it this time. Do you want to listen?"

"Listen to what?"

"A radio signal. A databurst." Mathieson pushed back his wheelchair and grabbed a headset from a desk nearby. "Listen to this."

He plugged in the headset and indicated the button to press. Hoffman shut his eyes, one hand cupped over his right ear, and listened. It was just electronic noise—two or three seconds at most—like any satellite transmitting or receiving data. It repeated a few times.

"I looped the recording so you could get a better idea of it," Mathieson said. "It's just one burst."

"Mind if we share this with Captain Michaelson?" Hoffman asked. Mathieson half shrugged. Hoffman stepped into the hall. "Quentin? Something you might want to hear."

Hoffman handed the headset to Michaelson and watched his face while he listened with a deepening frown.

"How the hell did you catch it?" Hoffman asked. "It's just a couple of seconds."

"It got too regular," Mathieson said. The gadget on his desk caught Hoffman's eye and he realized it was a metal ball joint. "It's always the same time—not every day, but when it happens, you can set your watch by it. No idea what the data is. That'll be decoded by the receiving station."

"One of our former Stranded visitors pinging pirate friends?" Michaelson asked. "A trifle high-tech for them, though."

"I don't think so, sir." Mathieson tapped the receiver on his desk as if it would make sense to them. "I'll show you my calculations if you like, but the transmission source is probably on Vectes."

Michaelson picked up the metal socket joint from the desk and bent it back and forth. "Is this Baird's handiwork?"

"Yes, sir," Mathieson said. "He's working on prosthetic legs with some of the Gorasni guys."

"Splendid." Michaelson smiled. "Could that burst be an uplink to the met sat?"

"Possibly, sir. No idea why anyone would want to do that, though."

"You said it *got regular*." Hoffman realized he was almost whispering. "When did it start?"

"I've been picking it up on and off for six weeks. But it's become more frequent."

"Just log it," Hoffman said. No, six weeks didn't fit known satellite activity at all. "Thanks, Lieutenant. Good work."

The long walk across the parade ground gave Hoffman and Michaelson a chance to talk unheard. "If it's been going on for some weeks, then it's not Prescott uplinking to the weather sat without telling Mathieson," Hoffman said. "Who made the transmission for him, anyway, and who's got the kit to do it? Damn, I should have asked, but if I look paranoid he knows he's got me."

"It's not who's calling that intrigues me so much as *who* they're calling." Michaelson looked up at the sky rather than out to sea. It was a reflex when it came to satellites. "Who else is still out there?"

"If it's not Stranded, and not us, then it's got to be the Gorasni. I'd be mightily pissed off if Trescu's precious frigate was still lurking somewhere."

"*Nezark*'s gone. We found her wreck, remember."

"Yeah, you're right." Hoffman shook his head. "But it wouldn't be the first time the Gorasni have gone off and done their own thing. Look, you're very buddy-buddy with Trescu. Any ideas?"

"Ah, the fellowship of the sea," Michaelson said. "I think he's worried about Prescott. You know, I do detect the first whiff of desperation about the Chairman. All that *busy* work, trying to analyze the Lambent."

Hoffman's strategic vision was condensing into a modest plan to make it through the next week in one piece. If Prescott was starting to feel out of his depth, that was worrying. Anything that could rattle that man's sense of divine omnipotence was serious shit.

Hoffman found himself hoping that the asshole really was just cracking up like a normal man after all. The alternative was too terrible to contemplate.

"Yeah," he said. "Go sweet-talk your nautical buddy sometime, Quentin. We need to know."

GORASNI CAMP, NEW JACINTO.

There was an art to being the alpha male, and Trescu had learned it at his father's knee. He forgot he'd even had to acquire the skill. But there were times lately when it became a conscious thing, something he had to concentrate on using because what he was asking himself and his people to do was so . . . *unnatural*, so un-Gorasnayan.

As he walked down the main track through the camp—he made sure he was seen at least once a day—he spotted a knot of people gathered around one of the water standpipes. There was nothing unusual about that; people had to collect water, and when people paused, they gossiped. But his instincts were still those of a fighting man. He got that whiff of trouble, the signs that the Gears called *combat indicators*, normal things that were now not quite normal. And he knew the mood of his community like he knew Ilina's.

There was no point sidestepping it. Boils had to be lanced. He squared his shoulders and headed for the gathering at a steady pace. They all nodded at him politely as he approached.

"Where are we going to put all these extra people, Commander?" one of the women asked.

"It's temporary," Trescu said. "And the choice is either taking them into your homes, or erecting more shelters."

"But if we have imulsion," the woman asked, "why don't we just go home now? Why stay now that the stalks are invading the island?"

It was the old debate; better to fight and die in Gorasnaya than live an uncertain existence as refugees, especially with an old enemy's charity. The decision to come to Vectes hadn't been universally popular. Trescu hadn't exactly taken a vote on it.

"Because we stand a better chance of surviving with the COG than without them." Trescu's father had always told him never to explain his orders, but this wasn't the battlefield. "We would have lost Emerald Spar with or without the COG. Now we have fuel and food again. It's not my first choice either, but the threat we face now has changed and we can't take it on alone. This isn't like the Locust or the *garayaz* Stranded, believe me."

He carried on walking, looking for the next sullen group of citizens to challenge to defy him. The camp was like a miniature city, with neighborhoods that supported him and others that were less enamored of his policy. But there was no open revolt. They had the right to carp, but they didn't have the right to threaten the precarious existence of the Gorasni people.

Combat indicators. Hah.

The COG did love its jargon. He found himself strolling now, chewing over the last encounter with Prescott. Something was very wrong there. Something about the man had shifted focus. There were issues that seemed to concern him more than the stalk incursions.

He wants samples of this contamination. We all know what this base used to be. Am I getting naive?

Trescu was a naval officer who'd had to become a soldier because his country needed him to be one. He could see that the path ahead of him was suddenly empty—no children playing, no women hanging out washing between the tents, no men hammering planks in the endless repair of the camp. It was unusual, and on the mainland that almost always meant something bad was about to happen.

I'm in my own territory. This is insane.

But he was in a part of the camp that wouldn't have elected him if they'd had a vote, which they didn't. He kept walking, expecting to be intercepted by an angry delegation.

Then a loud crack rang out and the ground five meters in front of him threw up a plume of dust.

It was a long second before he realized it was a rifle round. Some bastard was shooting at him.

It was the most obvious thing in the world, a sound that would have sent him diving for cover out of pure reflex if he'd been anywhere else but this camp, but he was so stunned that he just paused where he stood for a moment. He didn't even look up to see where the shot had come from.

And the shooter *meant* to miss. Any Gorasni with a rifle was a marksman by necessity.

So this is a show of some kind. Well, I can put on a show too.

Trescu carried on walking, hating himself for feeling slightly shaken. Nobody would dare assassinate him, not with Teo or Yanik always ready to settle the score and nowhere to hide from them. By now, he could hear the buzz of voices rising around the camp and the sound of people running to see what was happening.

Crack. A second round struck the path at a shallow angle, once again a safe five or six meters ahead of him. This time there were shouts and cries as people ducked.

One more shot, *just one more*, and he would stop and do something *educational* about it. He had an audience now. He had to show his people what happened to those who tried his patience.

He had a pretty good idea who it was, anyway.

"Get down!" a woman yelled. "Commander! Are you crazy?"

Trescu carried on, not changing his path or his pace. There would be a third shot, he knew. Where were they coming from? It wasn't from the naval base walls behind him, and there were only a few structures inside the camp with enough height to allow a sniper shot like that—the bathroom blocks. There was one to his right.

"Commander, what the fuck are you *doing*?" That was Yanik Laas. Trescu could hear him running down the path after him. "Get down! What if he's drunk and hits you by accident?"

Crack.

The third round struck a little further ahead of Trescu than the last. Now it was time to stop and turn around — deliberate, expressionless, to make it clear that he was angry rather than in fear of his life. He could see the water tanks of the bathroom block set on a wooden platform above the rows of shower stalls. He set off for it at a steady pace, fists balled.

Everyone had come out of their tents now. If there was anyone taking a shower then it would be unfortunate, but he had an example to set. He ran up the rickety maintenance stairway to the top of the structure and drew his pistol.

Ianku Nareci was standing there with his rifle broken under one arm, completely relaxed, looking like he needed a smack in the face to teach him a lesson.

"Well, Commander," Nareci said. "What are you going to do about it? Get your COG friends to spank me?"

Trescu glanced over the side at the gathering crowd to make sure what he did next would be seen. Nareci had to learn, but so did everyone else. He walked up to the man, pistol still in one hand, and punched him hard in the face. It hurt: he hoped the pain didn't show. It probably hurt Nareci a lot more, though, because he fell against the safety rail and took a few moments getting up. Trescu holstered his pistol and grabbed him by the collar before he could regain his balance. He had the crowd's full attention now.

"That's right, save your strength to beat your own people." Nareci hissed through a mouthful of blood. "Not our enemies."

"Shut your mouth, *garayaz.*"

It was a struggle to shift a man of Nareci's weight. But Trescu forced him over the rail headfirst with a tight hold on his belt, keeping him off-balance so that there was a real chance of letting him fall. He took out his pistol again and tapped it against Nareci's temple.

"You know why I don't kill you, Ianku? Do you?" Trescu shook the man and almost let him fall. "Because I can't afford to lose a single Gorasni citizen. Not even a turd like you. Do you hear me? I'd love to blow your brains out for pure amusement, but we need all the breeding stock we can get."

"You're a fucking *traitor*." Nareci's voice was just a strangled grunt, but he wasn't giving in. "Now we're pumping imulsion for those COG bastards and they're handing a few cans of fuel back to us like *charity*. Your father—"

"Don't you *dare* use my father's name, you worthless shit." Trescu let him slip a little further. That stung. He didn't need Nareci to remind him how he'd betrayed his father's dying wish. "He'd have cut your throat as soon as look at you. Yes, I let you live. I let you whine. I do that because if this community splits into factions, we'll all die. But if you piss me off one more time, I'll kill you and give your wife to Yanik. Understand?"

Nareci squirmed around to face him. "Yeah, why don't you bend over and take it up the ass from the COG again? That's all you're good for."

That did it. Trescu almost pulled the trigger. But that was something he would only ever do when he was in full control of himself. He was seething, and killing in a fit of pique wasn't the image he needed to project. He hit Nareci hard across the face with the pistol. Then he turned to the crowd below, all watching in wide-eyed silence.

"That goes for all of you. I will not tolerate anarchy." Trescu raised his voice without actually shouting, an art that took some learning. "We're fighting for our existence and we have a common enemy with the COG. We need to do deals. Honorable death is all very fine, but the other word for that is *losing*. We have to *survive*."

He left Nareci on the platform between the water tanks and didn't look back to see if he'd managed to wipe the sneer off the bastard's face. The important thing now was to walk down the stairs and go about his business as if insects like Nareci were a mere annoyance, never a threat. Gorasni respected disdainful strength.

But Egar Trescu would have told his son he was soft and had shown his weakness by not executing Nareci on the spot.

Different times, Papa. But maybe, one day.

Yanik and Teo were loitering nearby, waiting for him. He didn't need looking after, whatever they thought.

"He *could* have killed you, sir," Yanik said. "You should gut him to encourage the others. Want me to do it?"

"I meant what I said." Trescu straightened his collar again. He didn't want to look as if he'd been in a bar brawl. "Not one more Gorasni dies while I'm in command. Not even him. And he wouldn't have killed me. He only gains if he humiliates me."

Teo didn't seem convinced. "People are getting very touchy about the fuel, sir."

"We'll get our share," Trescu said. "I trust Hoffman."

It was Prescott he didn't trust. He wondered for a moment if the COG leader would even think of backhanding his querulous councilman to put him in his place. He doubted it. But the man had pressed a button and wiped out every major city outside Ephyra, even his own countrymen. The personal thresholds of acceptable violence were curious things.

"Do you trust Old Misery-Guts even if that radio signal is still going?" Teo asked. That was what the COG sailors called Hoffman, albeit with some respect. "We picked it up again."

Trescu realized that he didn't want to think Hoffman was

capable of serious deceit. He wasn't sure if that was pride in his ability to read people or just that he had some regard for the colonel and didn't want to be disappointed.

"But who would they be contacting?" he said. "The Stranded? There's nobody else out there."

"Sir, I've spent too many years eavesdropping on COG radio traffic. This is different."

"Very well. I'll see what I can find out from Michaelson." Trescu's radio bleeped. He pulled his earpiece from his jacket pocket. "Trescu—go ahead."

"Everything all right, Commander?" It was Hoffman. "Couldn't help hearing some small arms fire."

"Just a little internal politics," Trescu said. "No casualties. Thank you for your concern, but everything is under control."

Hoffman paused for a breath as if he wasn't expecting that answer. "Goddamn it, don't get yourself killed," he snarled. "I don't have time to build a new understanding with your replacement."

Trescu decided he hadn't read Hoffman wrong at all. In a situation like this, it was a comfort.

"Nor do I, Colonel," he said. "Nor do I."

PELRUAN, NORTHERN VECTES: THREE DAYS LATER.

"Well, there goes our tidy plan." Rossi squinted into the sun, then checked something scribbled on his notepad. "It slowed down. Then it speeded up. Now it's slowed again."

Dom adjusted his binoculars. He could now see the relentless march of dead trees from the headland. "I'm going to plan for the worst. So will the old man."

"I still say it's going to miss the town," Rossi said.

"But it's going to cut it off from the rest of the island."

"Come on, it's just dead vegetation. Not a mountain range."

"Shit, what if they don't volunteer to leave?"

Rossi slapped him on the back. "Dom, they know the score. They can stay if they want, but we can't promise to defend them. Their call."

Dom wasn't sure that civvies under pressure could actually make that decision. That was what Gears were for, to decide how big the risk was and take it for them—however painful—for their own good. He'd watched shocked, scared civvies stream out of burning cities carrying fancy drapes but no water bottles or blankets. They needed to be told what to do.

But would I have been any different? How can I say what really matters to someone?

The short, spongy turf felt like carpet under Dom's boots and the sea air was so clean he could taste it at the back of his throat. A black-and-white COG standard billowed in the breeze and fell back against the flagpole in a lazy rhythm. This was the way the world should have been, not broken and crowded and filthy like Jacinto had been in its final years.

This would still have happened if we hadn't come to Vectes . . . wouldn't it? These folks wouldn't stand a chance without us.

He'd keep telling himself that. He didn't buy Baird's theory that the glowies followed the imulsion trail. The Stranded said they'd seen stalks on the mainland, so the things were spreading everywhere.

Rossi overtook him and walked into town with the air of a man who belonged here now and enjoyed it. His platoon was garrisoned in town and seemed perfectly happy to stay.

"So who are you seeing?" Dom asked, keeping a careful eye on the reactions of the locals. When Delta arrived, everyone knew they weren't on a day trip to buy postcards. "Because you've got that *look*, Drew."

"Ah, the math's on our side up here." Rossi winked. "More women than men. They love a uniform."

Dom found he could talk about other people's relationships now without becoming paralyzed by agonizing memories. Rossi's girlfriend had been killed in a grub attack five or six years ago, so he was proof that life could go on eventually if you wanted it to. Dom almost asked him how he managed it—if something had kicked him out of it, or if he'd forced himself to move on, or if he just reached the stage where his need for someone was harder to endure than remembering what he'd lost. But he didn't know Rossi well enough for that.

"You be careful of those jealous local lads," Dom said. "Remember they know how to castrate cattle."

He passed one of the small shops on the harbor road, not so much a store as a place where people bartered their surplus produce. The woman who'd once reminded him so much of Maria was outside stacking red plastic milk crates so old that they'd turned to powdery white on the edges.

But she didn't look like Maria at all. He had no idea why he'd ever thought she did. She nodded at him and he nodded back.

"I've got your cheese, Sergeant," she said to Rossi. "Hang on a minute."

She disappeared into the shop and came out with a parcel wrapped in very old, creased brown paper. Rossi accepted it with a big grin. "Why, thank you, Mrs. Daws."

"Services rendered?" Dom asked when she was out of earshot. "That's a lot of cheese."

"I just fixed the store's generator, that's all," Rossi said. "Her old man's built like a brick shithouse, and a bad-tempered brick shithouse at that. They're just clearing their stores."

Dom knew most folks here wouldn't be as relaxed as Mrs. Daws about being asked to abandon their homes on a maybe. Outside the town hall, Marcus and Anya stood by a Packhorse at the side of the road, talking to a group of townspeople. They looked cornered. Marcus was a hard man to corner.

"Can't say I blame them," Rossi said. "What if they evacuate and the brown stuff doesn't get here?"

"And who do you think they'll expect to save them if it does?"

"They didn't ask us to come here, Dom."

Yeah, Rossi was going native. It happened.

There was no chance of Marcus doing that. He could play the diplomat on the strength of his reputation for plain speaking and common sense, but he never looked comfortable about it. Dom could see his distinctive black do-rag above the heads of the crowd.

"Nobody's going to force you," he was saying. "We're just here to help you move out if you want to go."

"No, we just can't live in tents." One of the older women began walking away in evident disgust. "We just can't. We'll take our chances here, thanks."

Dom and Rossi ambled over and tried to look helpful and non-threatening.

"There's plenty of room down south, Miriam," Rossi said to the woman. He seemed to know her pretty well. "Len Parry thinks we can dismantle a lot of the buildings and move them. They're just wooden frames, right?"

"And how long is that going to take?" she asked. "If you've got enough time to do that, then why ask us to evacuate?"

Anya looked as if she'd been up all night, a little gray under the eyes. "Like I said, we're not going to force you. But we just don't know what this contamination is going to do next."

"Well, okay." Miriam started walking away too. "I'm staying put. That damn stuff might even reach the naval base before it touches us."

The impromptu meeting seemed to break up fast once a couple of people walked away. Anya watched them disperse with weary resignation, hands on hips and her Lancer slung across her back as if it had always been there. Maybe it was Dom's imagination, but she seemed to be putting on some muscle.

I remember Anya when she was this tiny little thing who wouldn't say boo to a goose. Now look at her.

"You can't save everybody," Dom said. "The CZ's slowed down again. They don't believe us."

"Well, four hundred people have said they want out, so I've got to get some trucks loaded." Anya strode away. She was even walking differently these days. Maybe it was the effect of wearing heavy armor.

Marcus opened the Packhorse's door. "Come on, Dom. Time to sweet-talk the farmers."

There were a couple of farms in the path of the CZ, a small chicken unit and a beef herd. Dom stared out the window, comforting himself with the idea that there was still an awful lot of island that was stalk-free. As the Packhorse headed inland, Dom picked up the odor of manure. The countryside didn't always smell fresh and invigorating.

"Where are we going to put the cattle?" he asked.

"Jonty's farm, for the time being."

"Poor bastard. I wish we'd got the Stranded assholes who did that to him."

"Yeah. Rotten way to go." Marcus turned off the gravel road and cut down a narrow strip of bare ground along the edge of a field. "Now let's see if this one's decided to leave. *Edlar.* Seb Edlar and his son, Howell."

They bounced down the rutted track and through a gate

that opened onto a farmyard full of outbuildings and machinery. Vegetable beds striped with tidy green rows like bristles on a brush stretched off to one side. A couple of guys were standing by the tail ramp of a cattle truck that didn't look as if it had moved in fifty years, trying to persuade a vast white pile of muscle with monstrous horns to walk up the slope.

"We should've brought Bernie," Dom said.

Marcus grunted. It was rueful rather than amused. "Her special skills are in demand."

"Yeah, like the engineers. Nobody needs soldiering."

"Don't tempt fate." Marcus stopped the Packhorse a cautious distance from the truck. Maybe he didn't like the look of those horns either. "I don't think we're going to be out of a job anytime soon."

The older man left the other to handle the loading and waded through the long grass toward the Packhorse.

"So you're leaving, then, Seb," Marcus said, stepping out of the cab.

The farmer shook his head. For a moment Dom thought he'd changed his mind about going. "I've spent thirty years building this herd," he said. "I can't lose these animals now. Look at 'em. Quality. Unique breed."

"Do you need any help?"

"They're pretty skittish today. God knows what they can sense out there. Can you cover the gate?"

Marcus shrugged. "How hard can it be?"

"They weigh up to a thousand kilos. That's how hard."

There were a lot of cattle milling around now, all cows. Damn, they must have been pretty well the same weight as the Packhorse. Some were lining up like impatient shoppers waiting for a store to open while others ambled around, ignoring a couple of dogs watching them from a safe distance.

One cow began wandering toward Marcus as if she wanted a word with him.

"I really miss Berserkers," he muttered, walking slowly across the cow's path. "Bernie said to move in just forward of their shoulders and they'll turn away."

"Yeah, she also told me to stroke them under the chin, but she must have left something out."

Marcus took a cautious step toward the cow, following Bernie's instructions, and the animal veered off just like she said it would. It ended up doing a U-turn. It was weirdly magical to see that stuff work.

"Awesome!" Dom said, caught up in the moment and forgetting just why they were doing this. "Damn, who'd have thought it?"

Then the cow threw up her head, wheeled around to Dom's right, and broke into an ungainly canter. The two guys loading the truck stopped. The other cows started backing away.

"Damn, what's got into them now?" Seb managed to dodge a cow as she changed her mind about climbing the ramp and shaved past him. "Whatever that stuff is, they can smell it."

Dom looked down at his boots. It was an instinct, just like the cow's. He did it before he even noticed what had grabbed his attention. It was a horribly familiar sensation from a world that was now an ocean away. The cattle scattered.

Oh God. I can feel it.

"Marcus . . ."

Marcus was looking down too. Every Gear did it. Everyone who'd spent years with grubs tunneling beneath them and bursting out of the ground was hypersensitive about vibrations. It was the first warning anyone got. Sometimes it ended up being their last.

"Everybody take it easy." Marcus checked his rifle and cast around. "Feel it?"

"Yeah," said Seb. The two dogs started barking their heads off. "What *is* that, a tremor?"

Marcus got on the radio. "Fenix to all callsigns—we're getting tremors five kilometers southeast of Pelruan. Nothing visible yet."

Click. Someone responded. "On our way to check it out, Marcus." It was Sorotki. "Eight minutes."

"Stroud to Fenix, we're getting it here too."

"We're going to do a search," Marcus said. "Too big for stalks. It feels like a quake."

A cow went careering past Dom but he forgot about being trampled by a tonne of beef because the vibrations underneath him were a lot scarier. He aimed his Lancer, looking down for ground deformation just as he'd done back on the mainland when he was trying to work out where an e-hole would rip the pavement apart and spew out grubs.

No grubs here. There can't be. But there is a dead volcano.

Things had been going from bad to worse, so an eruption wouldn't have surprised him that much. He forced himself to look up. It was such a powerful instinct now that he didn't trust the ground and it was all he could do to keep his eyes on the horizon. Even Marcus kept checking out the ground as he looked around for the source of the vibrations.

They were getting stronger. It was going on for a hell of a long time for a minor quake.

"Seb, get ready to run," Marcus called. "We'll worry about the herd later."

Dom couldn't see a damn thing happening. The cattle were still charging around in a panic on the far side of the field and the dogs were barking furiously. The vibration was building into a definite rolling shudder, like an engine misfire.

Then Marcus just said "Trees . . ."

Dom looked across the pasture at the woodland on the edge, about three hundred meters away. The trees were swaying wildly. It looked like they were being battered by a gale, but it was just a breezy day.

He started running. Polyps could climb now, the little assholes. They had to be in the trees. The mismatched scale of it didn't make sense, but he just saw trouble coming and tried to close the gap. The ground started shuddering.

Marcus overtook him. "Dom, what the hell do you—oh *shit!*"

Dom's legs kept going but his brain was already trying to slam on the brakes. He could see it, but it was too much to take in. The trees were pitching forward. They toppled over like an uprooted picket fence, root balls flinging soil into the air catapult-style, and behind them—

Rossi was wrong. It *was* a goddamn mountain range. And it wasn't polyps shaking the branches.

A row of stalks ripped up through the ground from one edge of Dom's horizon to the other, a dense forest of gray, twisted trunks taller than ever before. The landscape changed before his eyes in a matter of seconds.

"Now *that's* a fucking problem," Marcus said.

CHAPTER 10

*Of course we have a nickname for you too—we call you Cogs,
like you call yourselves. Why waste time inventing new words
when the old one is good? There is a Gorasni word that
sounds very similar, but it is probably better you don't learn
what it is. Yes, "Cogs" was a very good nickname.*

(Yanik Laas, partially explaining to Baird what
the Gorasni "Indies" called their old enemy)

**RAVEN KR-239, SOUTHEAST OF PELRUAN,
VECTES: PRESENT DAY, 15 A.E.**

"Fenix to all callsigns. We've got stalks. About twenty,
twenty-five—at least."

Baird leaned as far as he dared out of the crew bay but he
still couldn't see anything. The curve of the wooded hill
meant his line of sight was the north coast of Vectes. And
that looked just fine.

Then the Raven skimmed over the crest of the hill, and it
was pretty clear that everything was definitely as *un*-fine as it
could get.

"Man . . . just look at those motherfuckers." Cole
sounded stunned. "Baird, it's okay to piss your pants. Hell,
I'll join you."

An avenue of stalks now stretched right across the landscape. Trees lay at all angles around them like a tornado had zipped along in a near-straight line and torn them out by the roots. Baird scanned the line of trunks and his gut knotted. Even from this height, he could see the movement in the grass.

"Why is it all the big ugly assholes that turn glowie?" Cole asked. "I mean, why ain't we seen glowie mice? Glowie *butterflies*?"

"Maybe that's what polyps were," Mitchell said. "Count the legs."

Baird snorted. "Oh, good to see you're buying my mutagenic Lambency theory."

"If I knew what that meant, I'd only offer you a tenner for it."

"Come on, Mitchell. Cannon up. It's pop-a-polyp time." Sorotki reached the avenue of stalks and turned along their length at maximum speed. "Two-Three-Nine to Fenix, I see the stalks. Where are you?"

The radio was overwhelmed for a moment with the chatter of Lancer fire. "Two hundred meters the north side. Line up with the farm gate."

The Raven looped again. "Okay, we've got you. I just need to separate you from the psycho crabs."

Baird clipped two safety lines to his belt. "Better drop me and Cole down there. They're way too close for you to get clear shots."

"You can't outrun polyps, Baird."

"Look, I held the things off on a frigging *submarine*."

"Here we go again. My hero."

"I found 'em first. *Me*."

"We'll name them after you."

"Okay, if Lambency's an infection that causes mutations— one minute you're a nice, normal, psychotic leviathan, the next you're a piece of seagoing ordnance that's lit up like

Allfathers Day. So if we could work out what these things started life as, we could—"

"Corporal Baird?"

"Yes, Lieutenant Sorotki?"

"Shut the fuck up and *shoot*."

Baird squeezed off another clip as the Raven banked. When the horizon leveled again, he could see Marcus and Dom almost back to back, holding off what looked for a moment like an angry, gray-green, crescent-shaped hedge. Baird saw Marcus put his hand to his earpiece, firing one-handed. A line of explosions fountained up from the mass of polyps. Sorotki held the Raven at a hover directly above the seething wave pouring away from the stalks while Cole and Mitchell laid down fire from both doors.

"Two-Three-Nine, we can't stop 'em all," Marcus said. "They're spreading out into the field."

"Where are the other birds?" Sorotki asked. "Two-Three-Nine to Eight-Zero, One-Five—what's your ETA?"

"Eight-Zero here—two minutes, Mel."

"One-Five here, I have a visual on you." That was some pilot called Kenyon. Baird knew he didn't get out often, and there was probably a good reason for that. "I want to test my new polyp surprise."

"Oh, the flamethrower." Mitchell nodded and squeezed his trigger enthusiastically. "Yeah, that's going to make you lots of friends in the farming community."

"Burn some grass or lose some inbred yokels," Kenyon said. Wow, he was all charm, that one. "I'm easy."

"Okay, let's make some space for Marcus and Dom to get clear before we start toasting anything."

Sorotki headed for open ground just behind Marcus and brought the Raven down low enough for Cole and Baird to jump out. "Get them away from those things and then get clear."

Baird didn't need telling twice. He checked the potential escape routes as soon as his boots hit the ground. He didn't want an Embry Star. He just wanted his full complement of unperforated and unburned body parts at the end of the day. But Cole raced for the polyps with a degree of enthusiasm that Baird could only describe as worrying. That was Cole all over. He dealt with every bit of crap that life threw at him by running full-tilt at it and knocking it over before it got the chance to bite him in the ass.

"Whoo!" Cole started picking off polyps trying to flank him on the right, spraying short bursts. The earsplitting noise was like a chaotic artillery battle, sporadic bangs that occasionally turned into chains of firecrackers when an exploding polyp set some others off. "Remember that plastic bubble stuff you could pop for fun? Hell, these assholes are *way* better!"

"Yeah, let's market them." Baird felt that familiar chill flood his guts as the polyps started coming at him a bit faster than he could take them out. They were gaining ground. Two broke away and forced him to turn his back on the others to aim at them. "Like skeet shooting. Shit, when are these things going to stick to a plan? I tell you, they're getting smart."

"Yeah, come on, Kenyon!" Cole sounded like he was having fun. Baird suspected he wasn't but probably thought he had to keep everyone's morale up. "Save us some ammo!"

For a moment, the polyps looked as if they were thinning out. Baird got ready to sprint for it, but then another fresh wave boiled out of the churned soil around the stalks and headed his way. They were too smart now to rush in a nice orderly carpet. They swerved, jinked, and generally made it damn hard for him to target them. The assholes were definitely learning. They weren't going to get lured into traps and ambushes anymore. Baird found himself running further than he'd realized to chase one down, and suddenly three more were behind him.

Oh God, I'm going to die. Outsmarted by a frigging crab.

He whirled around. The difference between popping them and getting fragged by them was a matter of seconds. He caught a flash in the corner of his eye as he aimed and a polyp exploded close enough to splatter him. He recovered in time to let the other two have the full clip, then turned to see that it was Dom who'd saved his ass. Dom just did an angry, two-fingered look-where-you're-going gesture.

"*Fire!*" he yelled. The Raven was so close overhead that it was hard to even hear him over the radio. "Goddamn fire!"

"Y'know, I never thought of doing that."

Dom yelled again. "Fire! Shift your ass, Baird!"

"Look, dickwad, I—" Baird turned again and found he was looking southeast into an advancing wall of flame. "Oh, *that* fire."

Kenyon's Raven had finally shown up, advancing in a leisurely parallel line along the path of the stalks with its flamethrower. The closer it got, the louder the roaring and popping grew. Trees ignited. The stalks were enveloped in smoke and flame, and more polyps made a run for it. Kenyon peeled off to roast a bunch of them making a dash across the adjoining field. Baird couldn't see any polyps in front of him now.

"He's going to set the whole thing alight," Dom said.

The jet of flame licked down from the Raven's door and billowed across the field. Explosions in the grass went off like flashbulbs at a movie premiere. Baird bent over with his hands braced on his knees to catch his breath, wondering how long it would be before they ran out of ammo chasing every last frigging polyp, then realized he could hear someone yelling behind him.

Marcus was trying to calm the guy down. It looked like the farmer whose land was being turned to charcoal.

"It's okay, Seb," Marcus kept saying. "It won't spread. It's too damp."

"It's my damn wheat," Seb sobbed. "I've lost my bull. Now you're torching my wheat. For God's sake, you're doing more damage than the polyps."

So it wasn't grass. Baird added it to his list of interesting rural facts. Seb turned around, throwing up his arms in frustration, and called his dogs. They didn't come. He walked toward the trees on his left and stood there whistling and yelling their names.

Kenyon's voice came over the radio. "I think we got 'em all, Fenix. I'm heading back to VNB."

"Yeah, you got 'em all right," Marcus said. He went after Seb. "Okay, let's carry on and clear the farm."

But Seb wasn't going to leave until he had all his cattle. Baird could hear the argument going on.

"But there's six of them still out there, including one of the bulls. And the cows are in calf." Seb went to walk into the woods, but Marcus caught his arm. "And my dogs. They went after them."

"You're going into a contaminated zone." Marcus was all calm reason. "The dogs will come back. We'll find the cattle. But you've got to leave now. You've just seen how risky it is."

"You lose crops and animals—you starve," Seb said. "Do you get it? We keep you fed, and it's not easy."

Marcus dropped his voice a little. "I'll get Mataki to bring them back. She was a beef farmer. Let's leave it to her."

Baird gave Dom an impatient look and held out his wrist to indicate the watch. "Tell Farmer Giles to write off Daisy as barbecue. It's deductible."

"He's got a point," Dom said. "No farms, no food."

Seb walked away toward the farmhouse, shaking his head. The flames in the wheat were dying down but it was still a hell of a mess out there. The pall of smoke must have been visible from Pelruan.

"I thought it was grass," Baird said. "It *looked* like grass."

"Wheat." Marcus looked north-west in the direction of Pelruan and pressed his earpiece. "Ask Mataki to teach you crop recognition . . . Colonel? Fenix here. Have you had a sitrep from Sorotki?" Marcus got that defocused look as if he was waiting for a response. He grunted a few times, looked down at his boots, and nodded. "Okay. We'll finish up here. Fenix out."

"What did he say?" Dom asked.

"Compulsory evacuation," Marcus said, walking off. "He's decided to clear Pelruan whether they like it or not."

TWENTY KILOMETERS SOUTH OF PELRUAN, NORTHERN VECTES.

Isabel Hayman gazed out of the Packhorse's side window in silence, and that bothered Hoffman more than having her in full vitriolic flood.

In the past few weeks she'd only spoken to him when she absolutely had to. He knew why. She didn't forgive. She blamed Hoffman for letting Trescu shoot a wounded Stranded prisoner in her hospital. He couldn't really argue with that, but he wasn't going to apologize.

What he didn't know was why she'd asked to come to Pelruan with him. But he needed to mend some fences with her and he was ready to eat some humble pie if that was what it took. The last senior ER doctor left in the COG was a lot more use to him than the Chairman.

They'd be in Pelruan soon. He couldn't stand it any longer. "Did you have something to say to me, Doctor? Because you haven't come along for the pleasure of my company."

It was odd to see Hayman without her white lab coat. It was her armor, her uniform, her statement to the world. Without it she'd dissolved into a frail, wispy-haired, elderly woman—until she opened her mouth.

"You got that right." Hayman was pushing eighty, the former chief of ER at Jacinto's main teaching hospital, and her snarling exterior didn't veneer a grandmotherly heart of gold. She was an angry bitch to the core. "I was hoping for a private discussion. Can't get much more private than this."

"You want to unburden yourself, Doctor?"

"I want to know what the hell's going on. Why Prescott keeps bringing me his garden waste to analyze."

"Did you find anything?"

"Well, it isn't going to respond to antibiotics or bed rest, that's for sure." Hayman let out a long hoarse sigh and searched in her pocket for something. It was going to be her damned cheroots. He knew it. "Everyone thinks I'm omniscient. I'm an *emergency physician.*" She parked the unlit smoke in the corner of her mouth. "Not a veterinarian, and you can remind your lady friend about that. Or a fortune-teller. Or a damn microbiologist, or an analytical chemist, or whatever the hell Prescott thinks the word *doctor* means. Does he know *anything* about scientists?"

"Maybe he's forgotten what they look like. We lost all the grown-up ones."

"That's damned careless."

There was no harm showing dissent in front of Hayman. Any respect for authority was weak-mindedness as far as she was concerned. "Yeah. Isn't it."

She patted her pockets as if she was now looking for matches. Hoffman didn't volunteer to find a light for her.

"It was just dead leaf mold, soil, and imulsion," she said. "The stalks were interesting structures under magnification. A little like bone, but neither plant nor animal."

"Is that possible?"

She looked at him as if he was an idiot. "Fungi fall into that gray area. Nearer to animal, in fact."

"So you're not just a simple scab lifter."

"That's just high school science, Colonel, and my microbiology lab is a fifty-year-old microscope from the School of Dentistry."

"I didn't have a fancy education, Doctor."

"It shows." She was still rummaging in her pockets. "Anyway, I gave him the damn microscope in the end and told him to do it himself. He's got as good a chance of making sense of it as I have."

"So what do you want from me? Not my scientific opinion, obviously."

"Tell me what you're holding back."

"About the Lambent? Not a goddamn thing." He almost mentioned the disc. Damn, he was trying to justify himself to her. "Let's just say it's a contentious issue between me and His Highness."

"Cut the bullshit. Is it one of the biological weapons programs they used to have here?"

Hoffman hadn't put those two elements together before. Now he wondered why. He got that feeling—the tight scalp, dry mouth—that he'd had when Prescott had declassified the New Hope facility, and he *still* didn't know exactly what biological reasons the COG had gotten up to there.

You sat on that, you fucker. Now I bet you're sitting on this. Is that what's on your goddamn disc? Is this one of our own bioweapons that we let loose on the grubs and it's come back to bite us in the ass?

But something wasn't quite right. The grubs had been driven out of their tunnels by the Lambent. That was why they came to the surface. It had seemed like an interesting detail when Delta Squad had discovered it in the Locust records stored in their tunnels, but now it was a worrying anomaly.

If the Lambent were the result of a COG bioweapon, then it predated E-Day. And that meant someone knew they were down there, and that the Locust were coming.

"Dear God Almighty," Hoffman said to himself. "And this island was his choice of location. Not ours."

"You really are just a simple grunt, aren't you, Hoffman?"

He grappled with the thought that his own government, the flag he'd served all his life, might be responsible. But it wouldn't have been the first time that the COG had unleashed a weapon of mass destruction against an enemy and killed its own people instead.

No, I did. I killed millions. I turned the Hammer of Dawn command keys with Prescott and Bardry. For what? For this?

"If he knows what it is, he's hiding it well," Hoffman said, wondering why the Lambent had now dwindled in his mind to a monster less efficient than himself. "Maybe that's not an answer. He might know what it is, but not how to fix it."

"He'd know. But then you'd know if it had been deployed against the grubs. You used to be Director of Special Forces."

"Don't bank on it." Hoffman was rerunning old conversations and searching for clues he'd missed at the time. He couldn't pin it down, but if this was the COG's doing, there was something that didn't make sense. "He's still keeping stuff from me. I don't know any more than you do, and you can believe that or not as you see fit."

"Oh, I believe you," she said. "You wouldn't let your Gears go through this if you knew something."

No, not now. I kept my mouth shut once. Never again.

She went quiet. She seemed to have found her matches. It took her three attempts to light the cheroot, and Hoffman was about to ask her not to smoke in his damn Packhorse when he saw that her hands were shaking. He let her blow out a stream of pungent smoke and said nothing.

"When you get old, Colonel—*really* old, my kind of old—you'll find yourself looking at the way the world is going," she said at last. "And you comfort yourself with the thought that you'll be dead before any of the shit hits the fan. But I won't be, damn it. I think I'll still be here."

Hoffman could now see the smoke from the stalk fire on the skyline. It looked no more menacing than burning crop stubble. "Well, we do what we can. I've got to face a few thousand people who don't want to leave their homes."

"Your biggest problem is going to be famine, regardless of whether this thing is a pathogen that can cross the species barrier or not. The food chain's fragile."

"Well, we've got Lambent grubs. Lambent leviathans. Lambent eels."

"Doesn't necessarily follow that it'll show up in anything else. Worry about the vegetables first."

"Ever feel like you're pissing in the wind, Doc?"

"Every fucking day." Hayman let out another long breath of smoke, filling the vehicle. "And I still hold you responsible for letting that savage Trescu murder one of my patients."

"I can live with that, Doctor."

They'd reached a brutal kind of truce, an agreement to dislike but trust one another. Hoffman drove on in silence. The Packhorse passed a stand of dead stalks and Hayman swiveled in her seat to stare.

"Hell of a day out," she said.

As Hoffman drove down the approach road to Pelruan, he could already see some people loading up vehicles outside their houses. A lot of the locals didn't have transport, not even pushbikes. They relied on the farm trucks and utility vehicles if they wanted to venture out of town, something they hadn't needed to do in a long time. It was going to take COG vehicles to evacuate them all.

He slowed the Packhorse to acknowledge a middle-aged

couple cramming tools into the back of a pickup. There was a name painted on the driver's door, faded and flaking now but still legible: J.H. TILLO—PLUMBER. It might have just been someone else's truck. Hoffman stopped and leaned out.

"Are you a plumber, sir?"

The man looked startled, as if he hadn't seen the Packhorse coming. "I am."

"Report to Staff Sergeant Parry at the naval base. Ask for him when you get to the vehicle checkpoint."

"What about my—"

"Parry looks after his civvies, sir. You'll get accommodation in the barracks."

"Okay. Yeah. Sure."

Hoffman drove off. It was interesting how people who weren't used to following orders usually did what they were told if they were scared enough. He caught Hayman staring at him.

"What did I do wrong now?" he asked. "I didn't shoot him."

"No, you'd leave that to Trescu."

Anvil Gate became the here and now again. "I've shot civilians. Just like you've switched off life support machines, I'll bet. Everyone justifies their actions."

He wasn't sure if that had shut her up or if she'd just gone back to ignoring him. He found himself fuming and not sure who he was angry with, but it was probably Prescott.

Bioweapons. You bastard. Just tell me. We fucking fried Sera together, and you think I can't be trusted to know about this?

He had to find Baird and let him know. Or maybe he'd just go and punch it out of Prescott this time, or just punch him for the hell of it.

The pall of smoke that was drifting toward the town had

definitely focused everyone's attention. Hoffman got as far as
the town hall and had to park the Packhorse. Townspeople
were standing in the road outside and spilling onto the
green, clustered around the war memorial, and he could see
Anya and Rossi in the middle of the crowd. He rated the tension level at pissed off and scared but not dangerous. Even
so, he made a show of escorting Hayman into the center of
the mob to keep everyone calm. These were the kind of folks
who wouldn't start a ruck if a frail old lady was there.

"You cowardly *asshole*," she hissed. "You're using me as a
human shield."

"Diplomacy, Doc. Shut up and look sweet." Hoffman
steered her into the crowd and the focus started shifting to
her. "Mind your backs, people—medic coming through.
Anyone suffering ill effects from that goddamn smoke?"

Anya gave him a raised eyebrow that spoke volumes. "Sir,
we'll be ready to start moving vulnerable individuals in a
couple of hours along with the sector closest to the CZ. I'm
just explaining to the neighborhood delegates how we're
going to prioritize moving supplies and personal possessions."

"Two hours isn't enough," one of the men said.

"Then we'll come back for the baggage later," Hoffman
said, "as per Lieutenant Stroud's contingency plan." Was that
in there? He wasn't sure, but Anya knew what she was doing,
and he wasn't about to second-guess her in front of civvies.
"Lives first. Food next. Pianos last. That's the way we do
things. Go home and start packing according to that priority
list."

Hayman spoke up. "And if anyone thinks they've got
health issues, get yourselves into the town hall and I'll take a
look at you now."

Hoffman had no idea why she did that—to save face, or
help break up the crowd, or because it really needed doing.

He didn't care. The crowd began to disperse. Rossi did his gentleman act and escorted her toward the town hall.

"They're just cascading the information, sir," Anya said. "It's the easiest way to communicate with a couple of thousand people."

"We don't have accommodation ready at the other end yet. If any want to hang around, Sharle's going to be grateful for the breathing space."

"Have we got the time?"

"I'm still thinking in terms of a couple of weeks to complete this. Where's Delta?"

"With Lewis, talking to the fishermen."

"Better show my face," Hoffman said. Anya's honest efficiency just added to his guilt about not telling her about the disc. "It'll be good to have you back at VNB, anyway, Lieutenant. Might even cheer Fenix up a bit."

Anya looked down for a moment, charmingly embarrassed. "I missed the place. And the company."

Hoffman had to weave between obstacles—crates, dogs, kids, tractors—on the road down to the harbor. He could see the cluster of Gears on the slipway with the mayor, Lewis Gavriel, and Will Berenz, his deputy. There was some animated conversation going on with the trawler crews, some still on board their boats with their arms folded. As he parked the vehicle, Hoffman caught a glimpse of Baird's blond scrubby hair on deck of *Trilliant* as he tinkered with one of the trawler winches, clearly not taking part in the social stuff.

"How are we doing, gentlemen?" Hoffman asked, strolling up to the edge of the quay wall. It was a two-meter drop to the boats on this tide. "I'd hoped it wouldn't come to this."

The trawlermen were regulars at the naval base. They were used to having warship escorts and Gears on board for protection, and they knew better than anybody what the

Lambent could do—fishing boats had been sunk and crews killed. But there was a kid in his twenties standing outside the wheelhouse of a beam trawler. Hoffman caught the tail end of the conversation.

"It's my boat," the kid said. "My dad left it to me. I can do what the hell I like with it."

Marcus sounded calm but the set of his shoulders said otherwise. "Yeah, but how far are you going to get?"

"It's better than waiting here for those things to come and kill us."

"Come on, Simon," Gavriel said. "You won't even reach the nearest island. You owe the community. You can't take the boat when we need it so badly."

Simon stabbed his forefinger at Gavriel. "This isn't goddamn Emgazi—what's mine is *mine*, not the state's. Don't give me any of that Collectivist bullshit. I'm going. I'll take my chances."

Hoffman moved in almost without thinking. Losing a fishing boat took food out of everyone's mouth, but letting Simon leave meant others might follow. Fish was going to be key to their survival if the land was poisoned.

I've been here before. I know how far I'll go.

He strode up to the harbor wall and took his Lancer off his shoulder.

"I respect your ownership, son." He didn't take aim, but just unslinging his weapon made the threat for him. "But right now we can't afford to lose an asset like that. And you won't survive out there."

Simon looked up at him as if he was just some old bastard making idle threats. He obviously hadn't heard any of the gossip. "You reckon? The Stranded seem to manage okay."

For a moment, Hoffman thought it was just a protest, a natural reaction to fear and upheaval and the sheer damn unfairness of it all. The lad would calm down, take a few passengers and supplies on board, and head south to the naval base. But then Simon ducked into the wheelhouse and started the motor. The trawler puffed exhaust out of its stack and Simon came back onto the deck to reach for the line.

Marcus just stood with his arms folded and gave Hoffman a wary glance. "You don't want to do that, Simon."

"You stay and die if you want to, Sergeant."

Hoffman was aware of the rest of the trawlermen watching, and knew he had a few seconds to make his point or let the whole damn thing fall apart. It was a moment of absolute clarity. His authority here was just an afterthought. He aimed.

Simon looked back over his shoulder at Hoffman as he slipped the line and coiled the rope down onto the deck. "Go ahead," he said.

So Hoffman fired.

He put a single shot through the boat's radar housing as all the civvies ducked. Simon took a few steps back and almost went over the side. Hoffman could see everything around him in sharp focus, including Marcus moving toward him fast, and this time he aimed squarely at the kid.

"Simon, if I've got to shoot one guy to save a few extra lives, I'll do it," Hoffman said. *Is that me? Is that me talking? Goddamn it, so it is.* "You're not going anywhere. Dom? Get on that trawler and make sure it ends up in the naval base. *Now.*"

"You can lower your weapon, Colonel," Marcus said. He looked as if he was going to step in the way. "He gets the idea."

Dom scrambled down the ladder from the harbor wall and dropped onto the trawler's deck. The clarity of the moment suddenly evaporated and Hoffman realized Gavriel and Berenz were staring at him as if he was a stranger. But he didn't back off until he could see Dom in the wheel-house with his hand on the controls. Simon leaned on the rails and found his voice again, but it was breathless and indignant now.

"You were going to shoot me, you bastard!" he yelled. "You were, weren't you?"

"Only as a last resort." Hoffman slung his rifle, realizing that he hadn't changed at all, and that he still defaulted to black-and-white unemotional necessity in a crisis. He kept going, even though he wanted to apologize to Gavriel and especially to Marcus, who was looking at him as if he'd made a big mistake in ever forgiving him. "Baird, take a look at the radar and make sure I didn't hit anything critical."

It wasn't a good time to explain himself to Gavriel so he walked away. Marcus followed him for a few paces.

"Colonel, you want to leave this to us?"

"Don't worry, Fenix," Hoffman said. "I only needed to do that once. Everyone's going to behave from now on."

"Fishermen have got to put to sea. What are we going to do if they decide not to come back, send a gunboat after them?"

"We'll have Gears embarked with them again," Hoffman said. "We're still under martial law. Those trawlers will return to port for as long as we have people to feed, at gun-point if need be."

He kept walking and didn't turn around, to avoid having to decide if that look on Marcus's face was disappointment. He'd made his peace with the man and the only thing he regretted was that the painfully repaired relationship might now be damaged again.

At least I didn't lecture him on his duty.

But sometimes you've got to do some shitty things to save people from themselves. Or stop them from fucking things up for everyone else.

He climbed into the Packhorse and headed back down the road, feeling sick and shaky. Dr. Hayman was waiting for him outside the town hall, looking irritated with life. He got out to help her into the passenger seat.

"Did I hear a shot?" she asked. Pelruan was very quiet. Sound carried a long way. "What happened?"

"History repeated itself," Hoffman said. "It does that a lot."

He wondered how he'd ever coped when he didn't have Bernie to unburden himself to. He didn't like himself much right then, even if he wouldn't have done things any differently. Maybe that was how Prescott saw himself; not a good guy, but a necessary evil.

"So who's going to ask Prescott if we created the Lambent problem ourselves?" Hayman asked.

Hoffman couldn't get Marcus's expression out of his mind.

"That'd be me," he said.

BEAM TRAWLER *THRIFT*, EN ROUTE FOR VECTES NAVAL BASE.

Dom rested his hand on the trawler's wheel, keeping a wary eye on the coastline off the port side.

It wasn't the prospect of stalks or leviathans that worried him most. It was running aground.

"You sort of look as if you know what you're doing," Simon said. "But then again, you don't."

"I'm trained on rigid inflatables." Dom almost turned the wheel over to him, but wasn't sure he wouldn't veer off into deeper waters to make his point. "Commando."

"Oh, really?"

"Yeah." *I've docked a RIB in the cargo bay of a Sea Raven, at full throttle and under fire. I can handle this rust bucket.*

"And if I prang this, Chief Stoker Baird here can repair it with a piece of chewing gum."

"Haven't seen gum for years," Baird said wistfully, leaning against the door frame. He was picking the innards out of something electronic that Dom couldn't identify. "I'll just apply a thick layer of my awesomeness."

Simon had a look on his face that said no amount of humor and chumminess was going to smooth things over. Dom considered the prospect of armed enforcers embarked in every trawler and didn't like it much.

"That old sod wouldn't really have shot me, would he?" Simon asked, still sounding worried.

Baird nodded. "Sure he would. He's done it before."

"You're just winding me up."

"Seriously," Dom said. He decided not to use the Hammer of Dawn as an example. He wasn't sure if everyone in Pelruan realized Hoffman was partly responsible for that or not. "He's the guy who held Anvil Gate. He shot civvies for stealing food. You think he's going to just speak harshly if you guys decide to piss around?" For a moment Dom wasn't sure if he was making a point or wondering aloud how far his boss would actually go. He now knew how far he would go himself, and that had changed everything. "But he's not a psycho. You just don't realize how bad things are."

"I do. That's why I don't want to sit here like bait."

Simon went outside and leaned on the port-side rail, staring down into the water. Baird moved into the space he'd vacated and fired up the radar screen again.

"We should get them to train Gears to operate trawlers," he said. "Just in case we have to ground them all."

"Shut up, Baird."

"Just saying. Ooh, look. The radar's all better. Baird does it again. You can thank me later. Look, can you actually park this thing when we get into harbor?"

"Yes." He leaned over to tap the commando knife strapped to his calf. He'd been so proud of that when he passed his course. He'd shown it to Maria. "You know what this means, Baird? It means that despite not being a fucking rocket scientist like you, I can manage to stumble along and do quite difficult stuff."

Baird was about to retaliate but something interrupted him. Dom saw him shove his finger in his ear to receive a radio message.

So . . . it's private.

Baird made a noncommittal noise in his throat. "Well, if it's home brew, then let me ask my respected colleague here for his input." He turned to Dom. "Hey, Dom, you and Marcus rummaged through the vaults, didn't you?"

"You mean the underground storage?"

"The archives."

"Yeah. When we were gathering flammable stuff to burn in the polyp traps."

"Tell me you didn't burn any records."

"No, we didn't get around to it."

Baird pressed his earpiece again. "Might be worth a look, Colonel."

Dom gave him a look as he signed off. "What will?"

Baird tapped his chest plate and winked. He meant the data disc.

"What's that got to do with the archive store?"

"Doc Hayman thinks the glowies might be one of our bright ideas from the days when this was Toxin Town," Baird whispered.

Dom had heard that before. He didn't buy it. "Well, if it is, they wouldn't have left the formula in the files, would they? And, if it was the antidote, he'd use it, wouldn't he?"

"No, but the more we know, the more we have to shake down Prescott with."

"This is the Chairman we're talking about. He could look you in the eye and tell you your name wasn't Baird and you'd *believe* him. And who's *we*? The only one who's going to have the balls to shake Prescott down is Hoffman."

"Nyah nyah nyah." Baird mimicked Dom in a whiny voice. "Okay, if you've got a better idea, I'm all ears."

The trawler was coming up on the south-west headland now. Dom steered extra-wide because the coastline had changed from the old chart he was relying on. It had taken a Hammer strike to stop the last Lambent leviathan attack and the detonation had caused a massive landslide. Whatever had collapsed into the sea was sitting there waiting to put a hole in the hull.

Simon stuck his head through the door. "You want to hand over to a competent seaman, buddy? Someone who can use the fishing sonar?"

"Yeah, go ahead," Dom said, conceding defeat. The guy wasn't going to make a run for it now. When *Thrift* puttered into the naval base and came alongside in the small ships' basin, he actually seemed to relax. Dom suspected it was the big, solid walls and the reassuring shadow of the old gun emplacements that made it clear the place was heavily defended. Pelruan was just wooden cottages that a few polyps could burn down all on their own. The massive stone column with its cog and anchor naval emblem loomed over the base and reminded everyone that the COG was still in business and capable of looking after itself.

Or at least it felt that way. Dom tried not to think about the reality because it wouldn't help him get through the day.

"You still got people living on the ships?" Simon asked.

Dom turned to see what he was looking at. A bunch of civilians was leaning on the rails of a freighter, one of the ragtag fleet of NCOG and civilian vessels that had fled from the mainland. Laundry fluttered from cables strung along the upperworks.

"Yeah," Dom said. "We've got some way to go before we've built homes for everyone. The polyps burned down a whole section of tents last time they got ashore, too."

"I'll live on *Thrift*, then." Simon gave Dom a look. "You can disable her engines if you don't trust me. But I'm buggered if I'm going to sleep ten strangers to a room in some dorm."

"Yeah, but it's still safer here," Dom said. "If we thought we stood a better chance somewhere else, we'd go."

The small ships' basin was pretty crowded and maneuvering *Thrift* was probably a little more than Dom's rusty seamanship skills could handle. Simon seemed to be picky about berths. Dom would have tied up in the next available gap, but Simon took one look at the vessel alongside and grunted before moving on. It was a small Gorasni patrol boat.

"Didn't you like the color?" Baird asked.

"No," Simon said. "My granddad never came home from the POW camp at Ramascu."

Baird did his annoyed snort and went out onto the deck. Dom followed him.

"Terrific," Baird said. "Vectes is the fucking island that time forgot and the Gorasni are the least likely bunch we could ever run into, but somehow we manage to end up here with them *and* a bunch of locals with a grudge against them. Are we cursed or what?"

"The Pendulum Wars went on for three generations, at least. Lots of time for the whole world to work up some serious grievances."

"I bet he'll still fuel up with their imulsion."

"Whoa, when did you get to be an Indie lover?"

"Your war, Dom. Not mine." It just came out. But at least Baird had the decency to look guilty about it. "Sorry. I enlisted after the armistice. It isn't personal for me, you know?"

Simon rapped on the wheelhouse glass and gestured to them to move so he could see where he was steering. He'd found a berth next to an NCOG minehunter.

Dom stuck his head around the wheelhouse door. "You happy now?"

"Sergeant Mataki told us we wouldn't have to mix with the Gorasni," Simon grumbled. He came out and threw a line over a bollard on the jetty. "Seems we can't avoid the assholes."

"Yeah, well, she was being optimistic."

"You think the glowies are the worst thing that can happen to us, do you? All I can see is the government we've been loyal to commandeering our property and cozying up to a bunch of war criminals who murdered our troops just so it can get its hands on their imulsion."

Dom tried hard to put himself in Simon's position. He'd never even seen a grub in the flesh, and so far the glowies had been a sporadic terror that had had less impact on his town than the Stranded raiders. The bigger issue, the one that still hung over this community, was from another war.

But he was right. The COG had muscled in and treated it as its right to take over Vectes, and Gorasnaya had a long history of atrocities. Maybe Simon just needed to have the shit scared out of him by more Lambent to put things in perspective.

"Whatever," Dom said. "Look, you better go sign in at the reception office and get your ration card sorted out, or you won't get fed here."

"Very generous." Simon secured the line and climbed ashore. "I'll remember that when I unload my next catch."

He stalked off down the jetty. The rest of the trawlers were starting to arrive, but most of those used the naval base anyway and already had a designated berth. When Dom looked across the water at the parallel jetty, he realized there was a bunch of Gorasni leaning on the rail of *Amirale Enka*, just staring at the cabaret. Sound carried over water really well.

Dom recognized one of them. He wasn't a sailor. He was about Hoffman's age, a huge guy with a lot of scars, but he wasn't wearing the remnants of his army captain's uniform today. He just nodded at Dom and went on staring.

"Is that who I think it is?" Baird whispered. "One of the guys who got you and Marcus out of that Stranded ambush?"

"You're okay, Baird. The Gorasni love you. It's me who had a run-in with him."

Dom couldn't remember his name. It was something like Zaska or Sasku. But he did remember the guy had been held in the Learan prison camp in the last war and what the COG had done to him. Dom had made the mistake of telling him what a bunch of murdering shithouses Gorasni were before he found that out. It was getting harder to look the guy in the eye each time he saw him, but that was thankfully rare now.

Okay, both sides did terrible things. That's war. That's what humans do to one another, even the ones that are nice people if you put them in a normal situation. How do I even start to explain that to the Pelruan guys? How do I make myself feel it and not just accept it's true?

"Why do they keep saving our asses?" Dom asked. Baird knew them better than anybody. "Do you and Yanik ever talk about it?"

Baird shrugged. "I think they like having the moral high ground. They know we think they're thugs. They think they're superior because they had an empire when we were daubing our walls with horseshit for plaster. It's all about *dignity*."

"They seem pretty united. No whiny assholes."

"Ah, they have, but not in public," Baird said. "Trescu smacks the guys upside the head and tells them *da Gorasnayan people do not whine like cheeldren.*" He did a pretty good Gorasni accent, except he sounded more like Yanik than Trescu. "He hates them looking unruly. Lacks *deeseepleen.*"

Dom marveled, not only because Baird seemed to be chummy with a bunch of despised Indies, but that he'd made new friends at all outside the squad. Dom thought the only person that Baird could relate to on a daily basis was Cole. But then Cole was the most tolerant guy in the world. Even the endlessly patient Bernie had punched Baird out.

Every time Dom started liking the Gorasni a little bit, he reminded himself that they shot unarmed Stranded prisoners. They dumped the bodies of Stranded they'd shot in the widows' laps, even nice happy Yanik, a real charmer with a great sense of humor. It was an ongoing feud that had started when Stranded gangs committed their own atrocities in Gorasni villages. Gorasni didn't forget any more than the Tollen vets did.

The sane bit of him said that the Gorasni were just guys who'd seen their families and neighbors slaughtered by Stranded gangs and were settling scores, just as he was sure he would have done. The less logical bit of him said they were Indies, and Indies were all the same, and that Carlos would have been alive today if the UIR hadn't started the Pendulum Wars. He was pretty sure they had.

"You do make some weird friends," he said.

"It's not about who smiles at you," Baird said. "It's about who gets you out of the shit every time."

"You're not really used to this whole concept of friendship, are you?"

"I know who I give a shit about."

"How the hell did you ever get pally with a nice guy like Cole?"

Baird smirked to himself and started tinkering with *Thrift*'s winch mechanism.

"He pulled me out of some shit," he said.

CHAPTER 11

Where are we going to put all these people when we don't know where the next attack will be? How are we going to house, feed and clothe them when we're losing whole cities and the infrastructure around them? We're already splitting into two societies—those who've lost everything, and those desperate not to become like them.

(Natalya Vreland, Minister for Social Welfare,
Coalition of Ordered Governments, shortly after E-Day)

**KOSOLY BARRACKS, 4TH EPHYRA LIGHT
INFANTRY, CENTRAL TYRUS: ONE MONTH AFTER
E-DAY, FIFTEEN YEARS EARLIER.**

Cole knew the sound of a private fight when he heard one, and he could hear one now.

It was the lack of yelling and cussing that gave it away. Someone was getting the hell beaten out of them in one of the washrooms. All he could hear was the occasional metallic sound of a lightweight door being slammed against a wall a few times and some muffled grunts and thwacks, so someone was settling a grievance and didn't want an audience.

Most folks would have walked by, but Cole wasn't most people. He stopped and opened the door.

Yeah, it was a fight, all right. He couldn't see it at first, not until he walked to the end of the partition wall inside the locker room and peered around it.

A guy in fatigues was waiting outside a lavatory stall, catching his breath, and Cole caught a glimpse of another Gear in the open doorway, just a boot stepping back like the man was leaning over something. There had to be a third guy in there getting the worst of it.

There was. He burst out of the stall—blond scrubby hair, soaking wet—and head-butted his attacker.

He looked a hell of a lot more battered than the other two, but he didn't seem to know he was outnumbered. As he fell against a locker and his opponent started kicking him, he grabbed the guy's ankle—Cole gave him points for that— and brought his other fist up hard between the man's legs. The guy fell. They were both tangled on the floor now, gouging and punching. It was time to do something before the third guy joined in again.

Hell, it wasn't Cole's fight, but those odds weren't *sporting*.

"Yo, gentlemen!" Cole positioned himself squarely in the entrance, completely blocking it. That always worked. It demonstrated just how damn big he was and that there was no way past him. And he never had to prove he was as strong as he looked. "You wanna reconvene outside? I gotta take a dump, and I like my peace and quiet."

The two guys dishing it out whipped around. The blond guy taking the pounding seized the lull to lash out and punch one of them in the mouth. Cole stepped forward to haul the other one away by his collar in a single pull, and almost got a smack in the eye for his trouble until the guy looked him in the face.

Yeah, they recognized him. Being the Cole Train had some shock value.

Cole still had hold of the guy's collar. "Mind if I do my business now, baby?"

Whether they'd run out of steam or just didn't like the odds, they all stopped. The one who'd been doing the kicking dusted himself down and jabbed a warning finger in the blond guy's direction.

"Don't think it's the last of this, you prick," he said. "I'll see you again later."

The blond guy sneered. Damn, he just didn't know when to give in and shut up. "Yeah, asshole, that's what your mother always says to me after I pay her."

"Whoa, gentlemen—enough, okay?" Cole did his best to loom menacingly, arms at his side and fists not quite balled. "Ain't you all got some urgent embroidery to do?"

The two guys shot him a glance and walked off. Cole didn't know who they were, not with so many new Gears showing up at boot camp every day, and he hadn't looked at their name tabs. But he could read the name on the blond guy's fatigues: BAIRD D. S.

Baird braced his hands on one of the basins and leaned over to spit out some blood. His hair was soaking wet. Cole could see some white bits in it that looked a lot like bathroom tissue.

"You okay?" Cole asked. "Damn, did they shove your head down the toilet?"

"No, I *always* wash my frigging hair that way," Baird mumbled. He spat again. "Haven't you got a crap to take?"

Maybe it was too much to expect a thank-you. Boy, Baird looked a mess. They could at least have flushed the john first. "So what started all that?"

"My dad. Seems he handed out a sentence they didn't like. Well, that, and maybe something I said . . ."

"Your dad's a judge?"

"A magistrate. *Was.* He's dead." Baird looked up at the

mirror over the basin and his shoulders sagged. He didn't
seem cut up about his dad at all, so maybe it wasn't recent.
"Shit. I'm going to be on a charge again when old Iron Balls
sees this."

"You got a real way with charmin' people, then."

"Hey, is it my fault I'm an asshole magnet?" Baird paused
as if he realized that wasn't the smartest thing to say. "You're
Augustus Cole, aren't you?"

Cole tapped his name tab. "That's what it says on the
can, baby."

"I'm a Sharks fan myself."

"Well, I'll consider this missionary work, then, 'cause you
ignorant heathens don't know no better." Cole decided he'd
done his good deed for the day. "You take care of yourself,
Baird."

"Yeah." Baird turned on a faucet. "I intend to."

Cole went on his way. Folks were pretty strung out and
guys got into scraps for a lot less reason than someone's dad
pissing them off, so the incident was overtaken by harsh
reality. He'd had a month's basic training—just a month—
and he was deploying for real in two days. Part of him
couldn't wait to get out and start killing grubs, but part of
him had never taken a life before—*any* kind of life—and he
wasn't sure how he'd feel about it.

*I'm gonna be able to pull the trigger, ain't I? They're grubs.
They asked for it. It oughta be easy.*

As he passed the row of phone booths by the mess hall, he
had an urge to call home. Everyone else seemed to be doing
just that. There were long lines at each phone, with Gears
checking their watches and looking pissed off with whoever
was making the call at the time.

Goddamn . . . there ain't no home to call now.

Cole just kept on doing it. It was like he kept forgetting
what had happened and had to go through the bad news all

over again. Sometimes he really felt that if he picked up that phone and dialed, his momma would answer.

He wanted it to stop. His folks were gone. He knew that, but he didn't *feel* it yet, and maybe he never would. Now he understood why some people said it was a good idea to see the open casket and get the idea straight in your head. But he hadn't been able to do that. Grubs didn't leave much to look at.

So I won't have any trouble pulling that trigger. Will I?

He didn't see Baird around again until a few days later when his company deployed to Kinnerlake for real. The guy was standing on the far side of the airfield, and the only reason Cole spotted him was that damn blond hair. He was swinging his helmet idly in one hand by its chinstrap like it was a grocery basket, looking unimpressed with the world, while the rest of the Gears waiting for transport—all identical and anonymous in their helmets—stood huddled in groups.

Baird was conspicuously on his own. Cole guessed from the way he was standing that he didn't actually want to be but drew the line at walking over to join anyone.

Sergeant Iredell—Iron Balls to most Gears, at least when his back was turned—strode past Baird, said something short and sharp, and Baird put his helmet on like a sulky schoolboy. As soon as the sergeant was out of sight, Baird took it off again and replaced it with his goggles.

Damn, poor old Baird. Wants to have a war with every asshole he meets. Life don't need to be that hard.

It was easy being the Cole Train. Cole never needed to think twice about anything; he just opened up the throttle and did everything at full speed. Thrashball was easy, making friends with folks was easy, and living each day as it came was easy. When he ambled up to the rest of his company, they all stopped whatever they were doing.

"Hey, Cole Train!"

"You ready for the big day?"

"Cole! Where's your limo?"

Cole spread his arms. "I ain't lookin' forward to the helicopter ride, baby. Who's got my designer sick-bag?"

Everybody knew he got airsick now. Nobody jeered at him for it. If anything, they seemed to find it endearing. He glanced over his shoulder at Baird, still standing at a distance and looking sorry for himself.

Someone had to make the first move. "Hey, Baird?" Cole called. "You waitin' for your company or something?"

Alonzo, one of the combat medics, nudged Cole. "You *know* that asshole?"

"Yeah. Kinda."

"He's just been dumped on us from Bravo Company. Real obnoxious little shit."

"Oh, he's okay." Asshole or not, Baird was about to face grubs for the first time, and if nobody was looking out for him then he wouldn't be around tomorrow to do it again. He deserved a chance. "Baird, we gonna have the pleasure of your company for this day trip or not?"

Baird rolled his head a little and came over to join Cole, doing his best to look reluctant. "Well, that doubles the IQ of this squad, I suppose . . ."

Cole didn't take the bait. That was the secret, he reckoned—to let Baird cuss himself out and then see if there was anything real he had to say for himself. The regiment's Ravens were configured to take six Gears and two door gunners. It was just a matter of standing next to Baird and making sure the loadmaster didn't mind a change in her list.

"You're messing up my tidy chalk, Cole Train," she said, checking him off on her clipboard. "But because it's you . . . and put your bucket on, okay?"

Cole put his helmet on and tightened the chinstrap. "Thank you, ma'am."

Baird buckled in next to him and stared out of the open door, still helmetless, and the Raven lifted. It turned toward Kinnerlake with a stomach-churning roll. Cole lasted another five minutes before he had to take his helmet off and grab the safety line to puke.

Alonzo leaned across and tapped his knee. "You ought to take meds for that."

"Makes me drowsy," Cole said. "Better out than in, man."

This was the first time that Cole had flown over a live combat area. Nothing on the TV news or in training had really prepared him for what he could see through breaks in the smoke as the squadron of Ravens approached Kinnerlake. It *looked* like the news footage, but that was just movies; this was real, now, *happening*. There were huge smoking craters in the ground below and whole blocks of houses ground to rubble. A fractured gas pipe was shooting flames into the air. He could smell burning, and somehow that changed everything.

If I get this wrong . . . I ain't just gonna lose a game. I'm gonna die.

The rush of adrenaline that had been a thrill before a thrashball match had turned into something that almost paralyzed him. His heartbeat felt out of control. He was staring down a narrow tunnel. The weirdest thing was that the blood in his legs felt like it had frozen solid.

I'm scared. I'm really scared.

Cole had never been physically terrified before, not even as a kid. He had to get a grip. He took deep breaths and pressed the heels of his hands against his eyes for a few seconds. Way back, some coach had told him it did some shit to the nerves and calmed a guy down. The coach also swore blind that a winning streak was down to his goddamn lucky socks, so it might have been some psych-up bullshit, but Cole suddenly felt a whole lot better.

"Whoa, I'm back," he said to himself. "Yeah . . ."

Baird kept fiddling with his bayonet. "I think I'm just going to piss my pants, if that's okay with you."

Now Cole could see individual Gears down there. They were formed up by a line of tanks and APCs across a plaza in the center of what had once been Kinnerlake's main shopping mall. In a few minutes, that would be *him*. For real. He'd be that little dark gray toy down there on the ground.

I ain't gonna lose. I can't lose.

The radio crackled as the Raven descended behind the line of APCs. "Okay, people. We've still got grubs down there. Remember—they can come up anywhere."

"Come on, let's get this over with," Baird said to himself. "Hope you're happy now, *bitch*."

Cole couldn't work out who the bitch was and now wasn't the time to find out. Baird sure did have some issues going on there. But Cole forgot that and also everything he'd learned the minute his boots touched the ground. He didn't see where the rest of his company landed. He could only focus on what he could feel underneath him, the pavement shuddering beneath his boots. He'd come from Hanover: the grubs hadn't reached the city yet. It was like nothing else he'd ever experienced.

Grubs. That's them down there, for real. I can feel them. Oh shit . . .

"E-hole!" someone yelled. "Stand to!"

The pavement started buckling a hundred meters ahead. The tank guns swiveled, waiting for the road surface to crack and give them a target. Then another bulge started forming in the road, and another, and another.

"Multiples!"

It wasn't like thrashball at all. It wasn't easy and it wasn't natural. It felt weird and slow-motion. The tank nearest to Cole fired, sending smoke and chunks of debris raining down on the roadway, the line of Gears broke, and Cole didn't have any time left to think or worry. Something took over and it wasn't training, or at least not the training he'd had in the last month.

As soon as he saw movement in the clearing smoke, he charged at it without thinking. A couple of grubs were clambering out of another emergence hole in the middle of the street. They had two arms and two legs, but that was about all they had in common with people. They were real big *ugly* assholes with gray scaly skin, weird pale eyes and mouths like a knife-slash lined with shark's teeth.

They ain't human. They ain't even animals. And they killed my folks.

So you can die, you motherfuckers.

Cole should have been using short controlled bursts, but he just hosed them as he ran and couldn't stop. Any worries he'd had about not being able to pull the trigger were forgotten. So was the fact that firefights were going on all around him.

Something was driving him like a clockwork toy. He didn't know what it was, but it sure made sense to do what it wanted and keep firing.

The grubs fell back down the hole. He still had his finger tight on the trigger, but the rifle had stopped. *Shit. Reload. Yeah, reload.* As he reached for another clip, more ugly gray heads popped out of the hole and he saw the dull glint of metal.

"Goddamn—"

Cole managed to ram the clip home, but when he looked up to aim he found he was staring down a barrel with the ugliest bastard in the world behind it. The grub's head exploded in a plume of blood. Then he squeezed the trigger—so how the hell had he hit the thing?—but the rounds were striking grubs where he wasn't aiming. It was only when the things lay scattered across the road and he could hear his own ragged breathing that he realized someone was behind him. Someone else had been firing at the grubs too.

"Move it—they're coming up in the mall," Baird said. He was white as a sheet and really shaky, but there was nothing wrong with his aim. So that was who opened up on the grubs while he was fumbling the reload. "Shit, Cole, are you afraid of *anything*? Look, those things aren't rushing up to get your autograph. Kill the assholes at a nice safe distance, okay?"

"Thanks, Baird," Cole said. "Could have been a real short game for me."

Baird didn't seem to know how to take gratitude. "Yeah. Whatever. I need you around for the next time someone tries to flush my head."

The new drive inside Cole had kicked up a notch. He still didn't feel in control of it, but he was okay with that for the time being, and he knew that all he wanted to do right then was to carry on and kill more grubs. That was all he needed. He started jogging toward the mall, aware of other Gears around him for the first time in what seemed like forever. It was probably just minutes. Baird trotted alongside him, grumbling to himself like some cranky old lady.

"These fuckers ruined my life." Maybe he was joking. "I'm going to make them pay for that."

"Yeah, let's go pop some more of those bitches," Cole said. "You and me, I think we're gonna get *good* at this game."

"Hey, I'm just following you out of curiosity."

"Sure you are."

"Seriously. Don't you get afraid of *anything*?"

Cole knew Baird needed something reassuring right then, something he could believe in. And Cole was good at that, even if it meant lying just a little bit.

"Hell, no, I'm the Cole Train!" He whacked Baird playfully across the back. "Stick with me, baby, 'cause I *never* lose!"

"I'll do that," Baird said, following him into a mall full of grubs. "I've got nothing better to do."

HALVO BAY, SOUTHWESTERN BORDER OF TYRUS: THREE MONTHS AFTER E-DAY.

Dizzy had done this a dozen times in a dozen cities now, but it still didn't get any easier. He jumped down off the truck with his shovel and pickaxe and waited for orders while a thin, miserable drizzle of rain started to fall.

All he could hear was the sea in the distance and the rumble of truck engines idling. The dead city had nothing to say for itself, and neither did anyone else except the Gear in charge of the burial detachment.

"Okay, I don't want to see anyone without gloves or masks." He was an engineer, a corporal called Parry. "And listen for the whistle. Two hours on, fifteen minutes off. Get to it, people."

Halvo was mostly rubble. A week ago, it had still been a fancy seaside resort. Now the grubs had trashed it, the survivors had been evacuated, and it was time to clear the bodies and try to stop disease from spreading. Dizzy put on his rubber gloves. The white fabric mask didn't fit tight over his beard, but if he caught some shit and died then he didn't much care either way. Everything and everyone he cared about was gone—his wife, his stepson, and even the shipping line he'd worked for. He didn't know if any of his old shipmates were still alive, but the odds weren't good.

And I ain't alone. Look at those flags.

Someone had already worked through the rubble with sniffer dogs and stuck small red flags in the ruins to mark where there were bodies to clear. They'd run out of the thin metal poles at one point, and the red flags were knotted around bits of wood. And then the flags had run out as well, and there were just branches or long jagged splinters from planks with red paint daubed on them.

In the distance, Dizzy could hear the search team still moving through the city center. There was the weird tinkling sound of bricks and tiles sliding, and an occasional bark from one of the dogs. He looked up. He couldn't see them.

"We can't keep up with this." One of the firefighters was standing close enough for Dizzy to hear. "We're going to have to start bulldozing and burning."

Dizzy turned around, angry. "Well, I'm willin' to keep at it."

"Okay, buddy." The firefighter had probably lost family or friends too, and Dizzy felt bad for snapping at him. "No problem. You carry on."

The guy was right. It was a lot of time and effort wasted when the living needed their help a lot more. But torching the place still didn't feel like the decent thing to do.

Dizzy put on his mask and trudged down the path that had been cleared between the collapsed buildings, an area marked on his street plan as a road with pavement cafés and shops for the folks who used to come here on vacation. An emergence hole had punched up through it. If he marked the plan with whatever he found and where he found it, then there was more chance of working out what had happened in the final moments, although there were so many of those that he got the feeling the government would stop bothering pretty soon. Searching for ID was the thing he hated most. He could pretend the bodies weren't people at all until he put a name to them.

The recovery team today was a mix of city employees and refugee conscripts. He looked around the faces and found

there weren't many he recognized from the last time. It
wasn't the kind of work that drafted folks stuck with. Goddamn it, if he could stomach it, why couldn't they?

He pulled down his mask. "Hey, Chuck!" A guy he'd gotten to know in the last couple of weeks turned around
holding a pickaxe. "You seen that fella from Ilima?"

"Gray? No, he shot through." Chuck prodded around in
his pile of rubble. "Said he'd take his chances in the mountains. Crazy, if you ask me. The grubs could come up any
damn where. At least we got army protection here."

How many refugees would still be here tomorrow? Every
day, more folks vanished from the cities and camps and
headed for the wilds. Dizzy had thought about it, but he
decided that he probably wasn't that desperate to survive.

He put the idea out of his head again and started lifting
chunks of masonry. Rubber gloves didn't last long handling
razor-edged brick and broken glass, and he wished he still
had those leather rigger's gloves he'd had onboard ship, but
they were long gone now along with the *Star*.

The next obstacle in his way was a concrete slab with half
a shop sign still attached to it. It was too heavy to shift on his
own. He waved Chuck over in silence and they lifted
together.

Chuck grimaced at what they'd uncovered. "Goddamn."

"Y'know, I think that was probably a better way to go."

Dizzy saw it a lot. The grubs didn't get to slaughter everyone personally. Some people were killed when buildings
collapsed, like these poor folks had been. He was looking at
something that didn't much resemble human beings, something hit so hard and so fast by the falling debris that all that
was left was a pinkish mass, stained clothing, and hair.
There wasn't really anything left to recover for burial.

"Amen," Chuck said. "Now how are you gonna identify
that?"

Dizzy took what comfort he could from a quick end and hoped that was how Lena and Richie had gone. "I'll find something."

He rooted around in the debris for half an hour before he found a purse, but it might not have belonged to whoever he'd found. How many people kept their ID on them every second of the day? The charred card had half a number on it but he couldn't read the name. So he marked what he had on the street plan, put the card in a plastic bag, and carried on.

That was as lucky as he got that morning. The other bodies were in a state to be moved and bagged, and when he got a chance to dip out of sight for a moment, he switched himself off with a few gulps from the small screw-top bottle he always carried with him these days.

The only reason he'd ever had for staying sober was Lena and Richie.

The whistle went. It was time for the mandatory break. He walked back to the assembly area and went through the ritual of lining up at the mobile control vehicle to wash his hands and face in a bowl of antiseptic before going to the field canteen for a mug of coffee and a snack.

Corporal Parry came over and sat down beside him with his coffee. They kind of knew each other by now, or at least as much as a Gear and a refugee ever could.

"You're a volunteer, aren't you?" Parry said. "Don't get that many, not from the refugees."

"I was Merch," Dizzy said. "Imulsion tankers."

"That's not really an answer."

"Okay, maybe I didn't do enough to find my own family. So if I find someone else's like someone found mine, then I reckon I'm even with the world."

That was part of it. But it was an explanation he'd come up with after he'd been thinking about it for weeks. What was the word? *Rationalization.* He wasn't sure why he'd decided to do all this, although he worried that there was some crazy idea at the back of his head that if he kept looking, he'd find Lena and Richie even though he knew damn well they were already dead and that they couldn't possibly have been in the places he'd been sent to anyway.

Punishing myself? Maybe. Making myself look at death and accept that they ain't coming back? Yeah, maybe that too.

One thing he knew was that the work was so backbreaking and exhausting that he fell asleep as soon as his head touched the pillow and he didn't remember his dreams. It didn't let him think. In fact, it had taught him how to switch off because he couldn't avoid seeing those terrible damn things all day. He had to find a way of bringing down a big transparent shutter to stop himself from going crazy. It did what the hooch did, except it was free and a lot easier to get hold of.

"You could join the army, Dizzy," Parry said.

"You gonna tell me a man my age should be on the frontline and not hanging out with the old folks and medical rejects?"

"No." Parry shrugged and handed him half a sandwich. "You could be an engineer again."

"I just fix big marine engines."

"Can you drive heavy goods vehicles?"

"Probably."

"Well, then."

"I need to do this."

"Okay, buddy. I understand." Parry patted him on the shoulder and got up. "Nobody's going to draft you as an engineer all the time you're willing to do this."

Dizzy finished his coffee and went back into the rubble. The effort was killing him and that was what he wanted. Eventually the fatigue and the occasional slug of liquor ate up the hours and left no space for thinking. He was beginning to get that head-spinning, sick feeling—might have been the booze, might have been exhaustion—when he started hearing things.

Metal groaned. He knew that by now. When he lifted the weight off pipes and girders, some of them would make real scary sounds. He was surrounded by the dead. His brain made up shit to fill in the gaps and he tried hard not to listen to it.

That's not a voice.

Dizzy carried on hauling bricks and window frames away from a cluster of red flags. His boots crunched on glass.

Damn, there it is again.

He could definitely hear something moving and making noises. It wasn't rats. The next thought that went through his head almost made him crap himself.

Grubs.

Sometimes they came back after they'd finished trashing a place. They weren't heading anywhere in particular, just popping up and killing humans wherever they could.

Dizzy took a few steps back from the rubble. There was a big dark space down there. He could hear rock moving, like something was scrabbling to get out.

Oh God . . .

There were always a few combat Gears around. Dizzy pulled off his mask and took a lungful of air, stumbling backward, but before he could yell a warning he heard a voice.

"Help me!" It was faint, but it wasn't a grub, and he wasn't imagining it. It was a woman's voice. "Somebody help me! Get me out!"

"Everybody, quiet!" Dizzy yelled. "*Quiet,* goddamn it! Hey, ma'am, where are you?"

The voice drifted up from the hole. "In the basement. Who's that?"

"It's Dizzy," he said, which was dumb because that wouldn't have made any damn sense to a stranger. He started pulling at the rubble with an energy he hadn't known in a long time. "We got a live one! Someone give me a hand!"

Suddenly everyone seemed to converge on him—firefighters, Gears, the whole damn team. One of the firefighters dropped to his knees and peered down into the hole.

"Yeah, we got a void under this slab," he said, kneeling back on his heels. He called to his buddy. "Jerome, get a hydraulic prop over here. Come on, move it."

The firefighter lay flat and managed to get his arm into the gap to use his flashlight. Dizzy hung around, determined to stay until they got the woman out.

"I can see some movement," the firefighter said. "Can you hear me, sweetheart? Can you move? What's your name?"

The voice was faint, but she was definitely conscious and knew what was happening. "Rosalyn. My name's Rosalyn."

"Are you hurt?"

"No. I'm hungry."

"You got water down there?"

"Lots of it. The pipes burst."

"Do you know how long you've been buried?"

"No. Couple of days?"

"A week, sweetheart. You take it easy. We'll get you out."

"I locked myself in the storeroom. I couldn't get back up the stairs." She paused. "Dizzy, are the grubs gone?"

Poor woman. She probably thought he was a Gear. He knelt down and stuck his head next to the hole, ecstatically happy for no good reason. Part of him was thinking that if she could survive a grub attack then there was hope for others, but he knew damn well it was a trick his mind played on him. Nobody was going to find his family alive. They'd been found, all right, and they were dead.

"They're all gone, sweetie," he said. "It's safe to come out."

It took five firefighters and a hydraulic lift to pry open a wide enough gap for one of them to reach in and haul Rosalyn out. The damnedest thing was that she could walk. She put her hand to her eyes to shut out the light and she was a little unsteady, but she got to her feet and she *walked*.

There was no paramedic around because nobody was expecting to find survivors. Parry went to check her out, but she was too busy looking around at what was left of Halvo.

"Oh God . . ." She was maybe thirty or so, wearing a navy blue skirt and white blouse that might have been part of a work uniform. The street plan said the building had been a bank, so maybe she was a clerk there. And she wasn't wearing a wedding band. Dizzy began to build a picture of who Rosalyn might have been if her life hadn't been wrecked just like his had. "Oh God . . . it's all gone. Are they dead? Are they all dead?"

She said it to Dizzy. She didn't ask anyone else. So he answered her as best he could.

"Yeah, they're all gone," he said. "But don't you worry none. We'll take care of you." He paused. "*I'll* take care of you."

GALANGI, SOUTH ISLANDS: SIX MONTHS AFTER E-DAY.

Bernie had fallen into the habit of watching the TV as soon as she'd finished for the day and not moving until close-down at midnight.

It was all news now. There were endless reruns of old movies on the other channel, but Sera was shrinking a city at a time, and all the TV companies had shrunk along with it until all their resources seemed to be spent on news. The broadcasts were now coming direct from Kaia, the biggest island in the southern chain. She curled up on the sofa with Moss flopped across her lap and didn't dare take her eyes off the screen.

Neal appeared in the doorway. He'd changed into his best pants and decent shoes. "I'm going down the pub," he said. "And for God's sake stop watching that, Bern. You can't do a damn thing about it."

He didn't ask her to go with him. He'd finally given up trying a couple of months ago, and he didn't ask about 26 RTI, not that she saw much news about them lately. Somehow she thought she was slacking if she didn't keep her eyes open and live through this second by second, even at a distance. It was like falling asleep on guard duty. It was unforgivable. She'd be letting down her mates.

"There's a TV down the pub," she said, not taking her eyes off the screen. "You won't get away from it."

"Okay." His coat rustled as he zipped it up. "I might be really late. Don't wait up."

As the door closed, she wondered why even the end of the bloody world couldn't bring some people together. The problem with living apart from Neal for most of their married life was that they were now discovering what it was like to be married for real, twenty-six hours a day, and Neal didn't appear to like that any more than she did.

Naval marriage. That's what they say, isn't it? Terrific until the old man comes home from sea for good and you've got to get used to this stranger in your house when you've been used to running the whole show on your own.

Except the stranger's me.

Watching the endless misery on the screen stopped her feeling too sorry for herself. Every city looked the same. Every capital city was a similar pile of smoking rubble with few landmarks. Refugees all had that terrible stare. And all the Gears looked the same, which made it harder than ever not to worry about the mates she'd left behind.

She was doing her bit just like GH Noroa had asked her, though. She'd organized a militia, not that anyone seemed to treat it with the same urgency as keeping their farms running. She'd even acquired a radio transmitter. There wasn't much more she could do now.

Despite her best intentions, she nodded off into a light doze. The studio discussion about how long Sera could hold out and what Chairman Dalyell could do about it droned on in the background. It was only when the tone of the voices changed that she woke with a start and knocked her empty cup onto the floor.

". . . now ending this broadcast because we've been told to evacuate the studios. We don't have many details, but it seems we have . . . yes, we now have confirmation that there's been a Locust incursion just north of Autrin. That's ten kilometers away." Astonishingly, the news reader just kept going as if it was a traffic report. Bernie's heart was now hammering so hard she could feel it in her ears. "I'll repeat that—Locust forces have reached Kaia. I'm sorry, but we now have to stop broadcasting—"

The studio vanished abruptly and was replaced by a loud continuous tone and the emergency broadcast caption telling viewers to stay put, tune to their nearest radio station, and listen for instructions.

Oh God. Here it comes. Here it bloody well comes.

Bernie found she was clutching Moss. He looked up into her face, baffled, ears laid back. The grubs were finally here. Kaia was more than two thousand kilometers away, but that now felt like next door. She could have picked up the walkie-talkie and called Neal, but if he was in the pub he'd know anyway. Suddenly she needed to be with people—yes, with Neal—and she jumped up to grab her coat.

Under stress, she defaulted to drill. It never failed her. When the shit hit the fan, that training had to kick in regardless, and she found herself checking her weapons and revving up the quad bike. Most of the ride into town was lost in a haze of what she'd have to do to track the advance of the grubs, but she managed to walk into the pub with some semblance of calm.

The bar was crowded and absolutely silent except for a crackling radio. The TV behind the bar was still on, still showing that emergency caption telling everyone to stay indoors and listen for instructions. There was no point running if you didn't know where to run to.

Dan was leaning on the bar, frowning. He hardly turned his head but he'd obviously seen her come in.

"Well, who's next, Bernie?" he said quietly. "How long before they get here?"

"Maybe never." She couldn't see Neal. "Where is he? He said he'd be here."

Dan looked straight at her this time and didn't need to ask who she meant. "He's somewhere else, I think."

It took a couple of seconds to sink in. Actually, it took a bit longer than that. It was hard to process that many surprises in one night. She felt her scalp tighten and a wave of nausea rose in her throat.

"I'm sorry, love," Dan said. "I didn't know if you knew or not."

"This *somewhere else*—has she got a fucking name?"

Dan looked stricken in the way of all people who realized they'd said one word too many. "Bernie, I'm sorry, I—"

"Forget it." *Fuck you, Neal. Fuck you.* The world was going to hell one city at a time, and she didn't have time for this shit, and all men were the bloody same in the end. "I'm going to call GHN and see what the situation is. Meantime, we activate the lookout roster, okay? Because we don't know enough about those things to work out where they'll come up next."

"Bernie—"

"I said forget it, Dan. First things first. *Lookout roster.*"

Bernie turned around and left, trying not to meet the eyes of any of her neighbors in case they had that look that told her she really was the last to know about her old man's bit on the side. She couldn't cope with defending a community where nobody she knew had the balls to be straight with her. Deliberate ignorance was the only way she'd get through this. She rode back home, totally numb, and tried to radio GH Noroa. The receiving station was busy. So she passed the time moving her clothes into the spare room and making up the bed.

Fuck you, Neal.

But the world was ending. The grubs were getting closer by the day. She had to get her priorities straight.

Maybe Neal came in late, or maybe he didn't come back that night at all. But he was in the kitchen making breakfast when she got up the next morning, and he didn't try to explain or make excuses. He just looked at her.

"You want me to move out?" he asked at last. Dan had probably warned him. "I'll still work the farm."

"You do whatever you bloody want," Bernie said. The urge to just pack her grip and ask one of the trawler skippers to drop her on Noroa was close to overwhelming. She'd find a way back to Ephyra if it killed her. "Do you realize what's happening out there?"

"I do." He put a pile of bacon sandwiches in front of her, always his peace offering. It was probably just habit now, but if he was trying to placate her, it wasn't going to work. "But there's nowhere we can run and nothing we can do about it. Except get on with living until it finds us."

Neal moved out later that day. In the days that followed, it didn't feel as bad as she'd thought it would. Moss seemed to miss him more than she did, and lay down in the hall staring at the door until he worked out that Dad wasn't coming back each evening. Neal kept his word and turned up for work every day. But she found it hard being in that house alone, and she almost called Mick one night to say he could have his bloody inheritance.

She didn't. She could only do this one step at a time.

Three weeks after Kaia had stopped broadcasting, Galangi was blind and almost alone, just like her. The loss of visual contact with the rest of Sera was new and terrifying. If there was any of her pioneering colonial ancestors' blood left in her veins, it was hiding behind the sofa and praying for the monsters not to notice it. The indigenous warrior side of her bloodline wasn't doing so well either. She parked the utility vehicle on the headland facing west, turned on the radio, and spread her map over the steering wheel.

She'd been through this process a hundred times in the last few weeks, staring at that bloody sheet of paper as if it would change the future. Kaia was close to the shallow island chain branching north, so the grubs didn't have to dig much deeper to reach it. But they still hadn't breached the deep trenches or volcanic granite. The things probably just tunneled under the short stretches of shallow sea between the smaller islands. Bernie used her thumb to measure the relative distances to reassure herself—again—that they would have a much tougher job reaching Galangi. She traced the ocean contour lines with her fingernail, checking the depth of the trench between Port Slaughterhouse and the rest of the chain a few times to make sure. Yes, it could swallow the highest mountain ranges on Sera.

But have the bastards got ships?

Sooner or later, she'd have to find out. She fiddled with the radio tuner and strained to catch words in the crackle of static.

So . . . back on patrol again.

She'd make her daily call to GH Noroa in an hour, not that they had much more information than she did. They depended on the comms networks based on Kaia as well.

Maybe I'll see if I can get hold of Mick after all. But not yet.

She leaned back in the seat and accepted she was just wasting fuel patrolling the coastline. If the grubs came, the chances of seeing them in time to do anything about it was close to zero. She'd done all she could do: crunched numbers, worked out that there weren't enough ships and boats to evacuate the island in one go, and realized that there was nowhere to move fifteen hundred people except Noroa, and by the time Galangi was in trouble, then Noroa would already be charcoal.

There was one more thing she tried not to think about. If armored divisions on the mainland couldn't stop grubs, then a few shotguns and pitchforks weren't going to save Galangi.

But what else can I do? Give up?

The sun glittered on the water. She'd have to face up to that, too. Sooner or later the ferry would stop running and she'd need to get to Noroa, which meant climbing in a boat and heading out into open sea, a prospect she really didn't relish.

It's just like driving a pickup. It's—

The noise that suddenly jerked her out of her thoughts was one she hadn't heard since she was a kid. It was the air horn on the old lifeboat station. It wasn't the alarm signal she was expecting—a maroon—but nobody hit that thing for fun. She was already heading downhill to the gravel coast road by the time her walkie-talkie buzzed into life. It was Dan Barrett.

"Bernie, where the hell are you?"

She grabbed the walkie-talkie from the dashboard. "Okay, I'm heading for town. I heard it."

"It's a bloody boat," he said. "It's heading for the port."

"What kind of boat?" She was used to people who stuck to RT procedure and could accurately describe what they were seeing. He could have meant anything from a warship to a fishing smack. "Big gray one with guns? Little white one?"

"A yacht. Yeah. Sorry. Gabby was trawling whitefish when he spotted them."

"On my way. Have they got a radio? Radar?"

"If they have, they're not using it."

On the way into town, she found herself wargaming some awful scenarios. What if this was the start of some huge exodus from other islands? One thing she knew all too well from the last war was how fast disease could spread when bombed cities lost sanitation and the dead went unburied. After that, lawlessness set in. She never wanted to see that kind of thing again.

By the time she reached the port, there was a small crowd on the jetty with Dan at the center of it. Bernie fished out the binoculars from the back of the utility and took a look for herself. It was a big flashy motor yacht, a real gin palace, and it was following Gabby's puttering trawler with an escort of seabirds.

She took her Longshot from the cab and checked the chamber before slinging it over her shoulder. Dan gave her an odd look.

"What?" she asked.

"You bloody scare me sometimes, Bernie." The trawler came alongside and tied up. The yacht took its time mooring at the end of the jetty. "Come on, try and look welcoming."

They walked down the wooden pier, knowing that what was coming couldn't be good news. Gabby jumped ashore from the trawler and stopped them.

"They've come from Kaia," he said. "His name's Garyth. An accountant. He never takes it outside the marina usually, he says. And he hasn't got a bloody clue how to read a chart. It's a miracle they got this far."

Garyth had a straggly beard and an expression that said he couldn't go on much longer. He didn't step off the yacht. He just stood there, clinging to a rail. A woman and a couple of terrified-looking kids huddled together on the foredeck.

"This isn't Noroa, is it?" Garyth said.

"Galangi," Dan said. "You missed it by a long chalk, if that was where you were heading."

Bernie tried to be diplomatic. "What was it like when you left?"

"They trashed Autrin and Jasper," Garyth said. "Everybody was evacuated north by the army. But nowhere's safe from those things."

Bernie was aware of Dan staring hard at her as if she was going to say the wrong thing. But she had to know. "Anyone else trying to make it down here?"

Garyth shook his head. "No idea. We just got out and didn't look back. The army didn't stand a chance. I *saw* them. I saw them from my office window. These huge things like spiders burst out of the ground and just rolled right over the armored vehicles. They can't save us—we had to save ourselves."

Dan put his hand on her shoulder. She thought he was going to say something reassuring about dead Gears. But he didn't.

"It's okay, Bernie," he said. "We're not going to be overrun with refugees."

But it wasn't okay. It just confirmed what she dreaded. The COG army, the community she put her faith in, was collapsing. Somewhere far to the north, people she trusted with her life, in a way that she trusted nobody else, were almost certainly dead or wounded.

"Come on, Garyth," Dan said, holding out his hand to the bewildered weekend yachtie who'd somehow managed not to drown his family. If that amateur could do it, Bernie thought, she didn't have an excuse left. "Make yourselves at home. You're stranded here now, mate. *Stranded.*"

CHAPTER 12

All food supplies will be managed centrally while we establish
new crop production areas. Residents of New Jacinto are
already used to this system, but we know this will be
unfamiliar and even alarming for the Pelruan community. We
ask you to cooperate and hand over all stores to COG
Emergency Management to ensure fair distribution of food and
to deter hoarding or profiteering. The same has been asked of
the Gorasni enclave, so everyone is being treated equally.

(Notice to Pelruan Town Council from Royston Sharle,
Head of Emergency Management, New Jacinto: 15 A.E., present day)

**IMULSION DRILLING SITE, 18 KILOMETERS
SOUTH OF PELRUAN: ONE WEEK INTO THE
PELRUAN EVACUATION, GALE, 15 A.E.**

The rhythmic donkey-braying of a rusty hinge carried a long
way in the dead, silent woodland. Trescu parked the pickup
at the end of the trackway and looked at Yanik.

"You coming or not?"

"I need to keep an ear on the radio, sir," Yanik said, one
hand on the dashboard as if the receiver was going to make a
run for it. "The ghost. He's been transmitting on and off this
morning."

Trescu stepped down from the cab. Not knowing if the databurst source was the COG or the seagoing Stranded gangs was starting to eat at him, because he was now sitting on a commodity that was definitely worth killing for: an apparently limitless supply of fuel. He had no idea how many Stranded were holed up elsewhere on Sera, but if they had somehow all managed to unite, then they probably outnumbered the COG. It was an unhappy prospect. The Stranded had their own scores to settle, and they were . . . patient.

He followed the sound of the imulsion pumps, pausing to check the spread of the contamination on either side of the trackway. It looked as if it was slowing down. The engineers had hammered colored pegs into the ground every twenty-six hours to mark its progress, and the pattern of threads strung between the pegs now looked like the contour lines of a steep hill, closer together as they radiated further from the center of the site.

There was a time when Trescu might have thought that was a hopeful sign. But he knew this was just a temporary reprieve, buying time to extract as much imulsion as they could.

If I have to do the unthinkable, then I have to make my first move now. This is going to take preparation. I can't move the entire camp on a whim.

A row of primitive derricks was pumping crude imulsion into tanks. If the workers hadn't been wearing lightweight summer clothing, it could have been any small-scale imulsion facility in the cold north of Gorasnaya. Trescu walked between the derricks, nodding acknowledgment at the Gorasni workers.

A squad of Gears and a few COG staff from Royston Sharle's office were wandering around the site too. Everybody seemed to be quite *chummy*, as Michaelson liked to call it.

*Well, Papa, you wouldn't have believed it possible anyway.
You can take it up with me in the next life.*

"Good morning, Commander." Stefan sweated over a
wrench, trying to loosen a nut on one of the pumps. He said
it in Tyran rather than Gorasnayan, a rather diplomatic act.
There was nothing quite like hearing foreigners muttering in
their heathen languages to make the COG suspect they
were up to no good. "Just like the good old days. Imulsion
everywhere. It's a very rich field."

"A pleasant change to have some good news."

"What brings you here? Checking I'm not smoking near
hazardous materials?"

"Ah, I like to deliver my congratulations in person."
Trescu didn't trust the radio for anything remotely sensitive
these days. "Is everyone well? No ill effects?"

"I've been soaked in imulsion all my working life," Stefan
said. "Brushed my teeth in it, you might say. A little more
isn't going to make matters any worse. If it makes them
worse at all."

One of the nodding derricks was irritatingly noisy and set
Trescu's teeth on edge. "Are you going to oil that hinge?"

"Oh, that's a bearing. It's fine." He winked at Trescu.
"We'll *all* be just fine. The sound of full tanks is a wonderful
medicine. We won't go short, if you see what I mean."

For a moment, Trescu didn't get it. Then he looked
where Stefan was looking, and realized it was something to
do with the tangled nest of flexible piping feeding into the
storage tanks. So he'd found a way of diverting some of the
imulsion for their own cache. Trescu couldn't work out how,
but that didn't matter.

He didn't like being that underhanded, but there was no
guarantee that Prescott would be reasonable about sharing
fuel if the Gorasni fleet decided to leave on its own, even if
he depended on Trescu's team to extract and process the

imulsion. But there was plenty to go around. Nobody would suffer if Stefan put a little aside for a rainy day.

And it's Prescott I'm dealing with. I'm not betraying Hoffman's trust. There's no need to feel dishonorable about this.

He did, but that was soft sentimentality. Hoffman and Michaelson were pretty decent men, all things considered, but the policy decisions were Prescott's.

Including the Hammer of Dawn.

Trescu walked back to the pickup with the confident authority that his father had taught him to feign even when he was terrified, wondering where they would go next if they had to abandon Vectes without the COG. He had no idea. He didn't know what state the mainland was in—these stalks could take over an area in *days*—and he had no way of finding out fast. The COG controlled the air assets. It was a long flight back and that required a Raven with extra fuel tanks.

Which, in my case, I do not have . . .

It was a damn shame that he couldn't exploit the seafaring Stranded, but the scum couldn't be trusted for honest information anyway. He would have to find out for himself. Using *Zephyr* for coastal reconnaissance was a possibility, but even a submarine was a slow option, and everyone would notice eventually that she was missing.

Hoffman has to be thinking along the same lines. I should simply ask him. He's not a fool, and he won't waste time in a pissing contest.

When Trescu opened the driver's door, Yanik was cradling the portable radio in his lap. He didn't look up. A wire dangled from his ear and led to a jack-plug in the radio. Trescu leaned his folded arms on the roof of the pickup and waited. Yanik gave it a few more minutes and then unplugged.

"Nothing at the moment," he said. "But he'll start again soon."

Trescu started the pickup and set off across country to rejoin the paved road. "It has to be a reaction to what's going on here. But we know that. The range indicates the transmitter is local. So?"

"It's the COG. If it wasn't, Hoffman would try to find out if *you* knew anything about it."

"Not if he thinks it's us."

"Well, that *would* make him very unhappy."

Trescu reached the paved road and began pulling out when a blaring truck horn made him slam on the brakes.

Damn it, that was embarrassing. He just wasn't used to so many vehicles on this road. The evacuation of Pelruan was still in progress, an endless shuttle of small vehicles moving people, possessions, stores, food, and animals. It looked like the evacuations on the mainland after E-Day.

"I don't want an ironic death, sir," Yanik said. "Nobody should survive two wars to die in a car crash because their boss didn't yield at a junction."

"Point taken."

"When do we welcome our first COG guests?"

"Maybe never. Nobody's taken up our offer of hospitality yet."

"So what do we do next?"

"I think I might need to negotiate."

"With Prescott."

"With Hoffman and Michaelson. This is about transport. I want to see if they'll defy the Chairman if it's the pragmatic option."

"Bit risky, sir."

"If the worst happens, Yanik, we know how to get out fast, and we now have some fuel to do so."

"Changed your mind on standing with the COG?"

"No. Just recognizing that none of us can possibly predict how bad the situation might get."

"Good luck with getting out of the harbor, then. Michaelson's blockaded us before, remember."

"Ah, he's a sensible man. They have their imulsion now, and they can work out how to extract it without us, so why would they want to keep us here against our will?"

"Because we're good company and we do the dirty work that the COG's too squeamish to tackle?"

"I think they'll learn to shoot Stranded without us, Yanik."

Trescu kept an eye on the fields and woods to either side, working out where the north-south fissure would lie relative to the road. The approach road to the naval base and its surrounding shantytown was clogged with refugee traffic. Trescu could see Armadillo APCs and farm vehicles pulling off and parking on the grass while Gears tried to marshal the traffic. The line spilled back out of the main gates. The entrance to the Gorasni camp was the other side of the jam.

"So much for COG efficiency." Trescu wondered how the COG had ever managed to evacuate Jacinto when they sank it. They'd had just hours. Clearing Pelruan—a fraction of Jacinto's population—was taking weeks. "They're losing their touch."

But there was nothing he could do to bypass the jam. He used the idle time to work out how to confront Hoffman about oddly clandestine radio transmissions while begging him for a ride to the mainland in a Raven at the same time. He didn't have the leverage of an imulsion platform now, but then he probably never had. Once he'd placed his nation's fate in the hands of a much larger force, they could have taken what they wanted. He had no idea why they hadn't. They did seem to believe their word being their bond, at least most of the time.

"You can see the locals never had to run from grubs."

Yanik pointed out pickups in the vehicle tailback, heavily laden with furniture and ornaments. "So much useless *stuff*. No sense of priority."

Trescu glanced up at the side of a flatbed truck that had pulled off to the edge. He found himself looking into the face of an elderly man with that trident badge on his lapel, the Duke of Tollen's Regiment. The man didn't so much look at him with loathing as with indifference. Trescu had seen the veterans only once when the first Gorasni refugees landed at the naval base. Pelruan was an even more foreign country than the Jacinto shanties.

"Careful," Yanik murmured. "I've been spat at more than once."

"That won't kill you."

"It's still . . . disturbing."

"You're too sensitive." Trescu looked at his watch. "What the hell's going on up there?"

He jumped down from the pickup and started walking along the line of vehicles, catching a lungful of exhaust. Damn, couldn't these wasteful idiots even switch off their engines? He could feel eyes on him as he made his way to the head of the line and the source of the delay. It turned out to be inside the naval base gates.

A couple of Gears were arguing with a man driving a covered truck. It struck Trescu as one of those peculiar COG weaknesses; the island was being invaded and here they were, letting some civilian debate about his damned non-existent rights. It wasn't going to change a thing. He strode up to the Gears and intervened.

"What's the problem?" he demanded. "Get this line moving."

"I'm not going to give up my food." The Pelruan civilian jerked his thumb over his shoulder to indicate something in the back of the vehicle. "I damn well *worked* for that. We've already shared the town stores. I'm not giving up my larder as well."

The Gears didn't look like green recruits, so they should have known how to deal with this by now. Trescu had had enough. He wrenched open the door and pulled the driver out by his collar. The man pitched sideways and fell out, prompting murmurs and *aahs* from civilians watching the confrontation.

One of the Gears—a man in his forties—put his hand out as if to stop him.

"Whoa, sir, there's no need—"

Trescu hauled the driver to his feet and slammed him against the side of the truck. "I am part of the COG now, yes? I am an officer of the COG, then." The average Gear— even Baird—seemed to think he was an army officer, not a naval one, but it didn't matter. He still had the authority they'd accidentally given him. He turned it on the civilian. "*You*—you will do as you are *told*. We all face a crisis. There is no *me*. Only *us*."

"Who the hell do you think you are?" the man yelled. "You can't treat me like this! You're not even a Gear! You're a fucking *Indie*!"

The man didn't matter, so Trescu didn't bother to backhand him. One of the Gears put his hand on Trescu's shoulder.

"Sir, don't."

"If you can't deal with this, I will." Trescu shoved the protesting man aside and climbed into the cab to start the engine. "I shall park this in the compound, and then it will be unloaded. Do we understand?"

Suddenly it wasn't about being kept waiting but about teaching these people that they had to obey orders for the common good, and that there was no luxury of discussion about it. He could hear the commotion around him, but it was sullen muttering, nothing more. *See? Someone has to do it. They're soft. All of them. This community needs strength.* He drove into the base, looking for trucks being unloaded by Gears, and parked the vehicle at the first likely spot.

"Here!" He gestured to one of the engineers. Ironically, he knew more of them by sight than he did the combat troops. "No doubt an angry civilian will stop by later to protest about his rights. Feel free to shoot him."

"Right you are, sir," the engineer said, unmoved. "I'll mention that at my court-martial."

The line was moving much faster now. Trescu dodged past the steady flow of vehicles looking for Yanik who, he was sure, would have the sense to take the pickup and wait for him at the entrance to the Gorasni camp. He was about fifty meters from the gate on the far side of the parade ground when he saw Marcus Fenix bearing down on him from the right, looking even more grim than he usually did.

He was too busy watching Fenix to pay attention to what was happening on his left until movement caught his eye and a something smacked hard into his face. His ears rang; blood stung his lips. He didn't fall, but he couldn't see much for a few seconds. His fist balled instinctively as someone grabbed his wrist so hard that it hurt.

"You don't want to do that," Fenix said.

Trescu tried to clear his head. A punch in the face like that was enough to disorient anyone. When he recovered enough to look around, he realized he'd been punched by a very old man, one of the Tollen vets. People were starting to gather around them in that flashpoint kind of way.

"Okay, we stop this *now*. Everybody—beat it." Fenix had hold of Trescu's elbow and was trying to steer him away, one hand held out as if to fend off the old man. "We've all got enough to deal with. You too, sir."

Fenix wasn't talking to Trescu. He was addressing the
veteran. The old man, skin transparent and spotted with age,
nursed his hand while Trescu just stared at him, surprised at
the weight he'd put behind that punch. He looked as if it
had taken every scrap of strength he still had left.

*Very sensible, Fenix. Thank you. Hitting frail old men is
bad for diplomacy right now.*

"I've waited forty-five years to do that," the old man said.
"I just wanted to pay back one of you bastards before I died.
And I hope you rot in hell." Then he turned on Fenix. "And
you, Sergeant—your damn father should have finished them
all off with that Hammer of his when he had the chance."

There was nothing to be said at that moment that
wouldn't have made matters much worse. Someone stepped
forward to lead the veteran away. Fenix's gaze flickered for a
moment and he looked taken aback. So some things *did* get
under his skin—things about his father. Adam Fenix was a
war criminal, the creator of a weapon of mass destruction
that had forced the UIR to surrender in the Pendulum Wars
and was used again to sacrifice the rest of Sera to save the
COG heartland. Trescu was careful not to blame a son for
his father's sins.

"Welcome to the Monsters' Club," Trescu said. "It's very
exclusive."

"Do me a favor, Commander." Fenix had managed to
thin out a busy area in moments. Suddenly there was
nobody within ten meters of them. "People are cranky at the
moment. Leave us to handle the wayward ones."

"I have enough *cranky* ones of my own to occupy me,
Sergeant," Trescu said, wiping blood from his top lip. "And
you don't have to atone for your father, any more than I
need to atone for mine. Although he would think I was the
one in need of forgiveness for breaking a deathbed promise."

Fenix gave him a strange look, not the resentment he

expected but a searching expression, as if Trescu had come up with an answer that he'd been seeking for a long time.

"Yeah, I know neither side had the moral high ground," Fenix said. "And we all fail our fathers."

And if you and your comrades hadn't captured the Hammer technology from the UIR at Aspho . . . would we have used it on the COG eventually? Almost certainly. Then did you enable your father's crime? This is the problem with justifying outrage. It can't be done. Causality falls apart and we're back to our tribalism and excuses.

"I certainly failed mine," Trescu said, wondering what nerve he'd managed to hit. "But his life's mission was to preserve the Gorasni people, and I can't be inflexible about how we achieve that."

Fenix just met his eyes and nodded. The moment of revelation had vanished and he just looked tired and frayed. "Glad we've got our priorities straight," he said, and walked away.

Trescu's instinct was to head back to his own camp. But he could go anywhere on Vectes, and anywhere within this naval base. It was time to visit *Zephyr* and see how maintenance of the submarine was going.

And check what they've picked up on the radio.

Then he'd ask Victor Hoffman a few questions.

SUBTERRANEAN STORAGE AREA, VECTES NAVAL BASE.

"Goddamn it," Hoffman said. "We got through two wars without turning into a rabble, but ask some asshole to hand over their pickles and suddenly we're brawling like drunks."

Marcus walked down the tunnel ahead of Hoffman, switching on lights as he went. Old fluorescent strips and even older incandescent bulbs speckled with dead insects

flickered into life. "It probably popped the pressure valve
with the vets. That's something."

"How did Trescu take it?"

"The pickles or the vet?"

"The vet."

Marcus paused for a couple of beats as if he was trying to
pick the right word. "Calmly," he said.

The underground tunnels were usually silent but Hoffman could hear echoing voices. Sharle had taken over some
of the storage areas for accommodation. Hoffman was surprised that anyone was willing to sleep down here, but
perhaps it seemed safe to the folks from Pelruan. The dread
of tunnels and being underground was a legacy of fighting
grubs, and that was something they'd never had to face.

"Trescu's full of surprises," Hoffman said.

Marcus made a grunt that might have been agreement.
"Okay, it's down here. Turn left."

"Just as well we didn't burn this stuff."

"You've got Dom to thank for that."

Hoffman never expected to have a normal conversation
again with Marcus after the fall of Ephyra. What did you say
to a man you sent for court-martial, and then abandoned to
die in a prison overrun by grubs? Yet somehow they'd managed to grunt their way through a long drawn-out apology of
sorts over the last couple of years, and now things seemed to
be back to the level of mutual respect he'd had with Marcus
before the fall of Ephyra.

*He refused my orders. He punched me out. Damn it, I
could have forgiven the punch, but . . . I couldn't overlook the
rest. Could I? We lost Ephyra. He went to rescue his useless
know-it-all father instead.*

His father died anyway. Hoffman didn't have to be a mind
reader to know that Marcus was still beating himself up
about it.

Maybe he's got no room left to nurture a grudge against me. Yeah, we're both drowning in guilt. And I still say his father wasn't worth it.

Hoffman wished he hadn't said as much to Marcus, though. He'd earned that punch.

He made an attempt to keep the ragged conversation going. "You think I'm barking up the wrong tree, Fenix?"

"If you'd seen what we saw at New Hope," Marcus said, "you wouldn't ask me that."

Like all the COG naval bases Hoffman had ever seen, Vectes was built on top of an underground labyrinth of storerooms, shelters, armories, magazines, fuel tanks, and machinery spaces. It reminded him of a tree, as much of it below ground as above. And most of it looked exactly the same as the next bit if you didn't keep an eye on the rust-speckled metal signs at the intersection of each passage.

But Marcus seemed to know exactly where he was in the maze. He turned left and kept walking to the end of the tunnel. A pair of paneled doors reflected the dim light.

"Some light reading," he said, turning the handle.

As the door swung open, Hoffman found himself in a vaulted storeroom lined with wooden shelves and crammed with box folders. If all the boxes were full, there had to be hundreds of thousands of documents in here. He fought down a moment of daunted panic—how many months to read this stuff?—and reminded himself that the COG was tidy and methodical. The records would be in some kind of order.

"They're arranged by year," Marcus said. "Which doesn't help much."

Hoffman checked the files nearest to him. The date was three *centuries* ago. "Well, I can narrow things down to the last thirty years of the Pendulum Wars, I suppose."

"You realize they wouldn't file this shit under T for Top Secret."

"This is the only COG archive left on Sera. I'm just looking for a clue to other clues. Even a single name might shake Prescott down."

"That's what Baird said. Dream on." Hoffman expected Marcus to leave him to it, but he took a box and started examining its contents. "Prescott's like Trescu. Immune to the scheming of us lesser mortals."

Lesser mortals, my ass. The Fenix mansion probably had a library bigger than this archive. But Marcus had none of the habits of old money and privilege.

You're happy being a grunt, aren't you? Yeah. I was happy being a grunt too.

Marcus looked up from the folders as if Hoffman was thinking aloud. "There were definitely weird experimental programs. Like at New Hope. The Sires."

"But how do you get from that to stalks and polyps?"

"That luminous vapor in the Locust tunnels was moving around on its own. I don't believe in ghosts."

"But the only thing big enough to be worth keeping secret is a man-made biohazard," Hoffman said. "Why would he be so interested in getting specimens otherwise?"

Marcus shook his head. "He doesn't give a shit what we think. Whatever it is, he wants to find a way to stop it but he isn't letting us in on his plans."

The worst thing about trying to second-guess a devious asshole like Prescott was tying yourself in increasingly tight knots. Maybe it didn't matter a damn what was on that disc: so what if it had a formula for getting rid of grubs, or Lambent, or heartburn? There were no labs left to make the stuff.

Defeatist.

No, just coming to my fucking senses after all these years.

Marcus rustled paper and held out a large bound book to Hoffman. It smelled of old leather and mold. "Might as well show you this before it hikes your blood pressure. No, he never told me what he did here. But he wasn't a biologist."

Hoffman had to squint to see the page in the dim light. It was an old visitor security log. And there was Adam Fenix's handwriting, signed in to see some army major long before E-Day.

"I know," Hoffman said. "Lewis Gavriel said he met him here way back, remember? It's okay."

Poor bastard. Marcus sounded apologetic, as if he was saying that whatever else his dad had done, he wasn't responsible for the unwholesome bio-warfare shit the COG had worked on. He was a physicist. He designed bombs, delivery systems, the kind of weapons Hoffman thought of as clean and honest.

"He wasn't a monster," Marcus said quietly. It was an odd word to use, not like Marcus at all. "Just blinkered."

Hoffman had reached the age where he felt he had to say what was on his mind there and then, in case he died before he got his next chance. "Look, let's knock this on the head once and for all," he said. "Your dad built the Hammer of Dawn, and Prescott, Bardry, and me—we fired it. I don't know if mass slaughter is morally worse than killing one poor asshole with a bayonet, but either way, stop apologizing for him. We're still using the goddamn thing to defend ourselves."

Marcus just blinked slowly and did that slight tilt of the head that Hoffman always interpreted as disbelief. "Yeah. So we are."

Hoffman went back to sorting through the folders on the shelves, not even sure what he was looking for. But if there was anything on that disk that could have saved Vectes, Prescott would have been making use of it already. The sanctimonious bastard thought he'd been put on Sera to save humanity, and deluded or not, that narrowed down his motives. *Just blinkered.* Hoffman had to concentrate on the immediate threat.

He knew it all slotted together. He just couldn't work out how. The piles of checked boxes grew painfully slowly. He must have been working in complete silence for an hour or so before Marcus said something.

"This might be the last archive of any kind left on Sera," he said.

Hoffman could imagine Adam Fenix fretting about that too.

"The Stranded can't all be illiterate assholes." Hoffman went on scanning each folder, flicking through the papers, and wondering just how many engineering reports a naval base needed to file. "Someone's stashed a library away somewhere."

Eventually Hoffman lost track of the time. He didn't check his watch until he heard footsteps and glanced up at Marcus. Well, they didn't have to make excuses to anyone for being down here. If people weren't wondering if the base's shady history had anything to do with what was happening outside, then they didn't have much imagination.

Prescott? Yeah, walk right in. Let's have a chat.

Hoffman stared at the doors. They opened slowly. But it was only Anya.

She looked embarrassed. "Doing your own filing now, sir?"

"Desperation, Lieutenant." He wondered if Marcus had even hinted about the existence of the disc in his quiet moments with her. Even if he had, it was still time for Hoffman to come clean and tell her himself. "Is there a problem?"

"No, I just wanted to give you a sitrep on the evacuation. We've moved everyone. There's just livestock and food stores left to relocate. Oh, and Seb Edlar's still missing his prize bull and a few cows. Mataki's volunteered to retrieve them."

"Good work, Anya." Now he *had* to tell her. "Look, we're down here for a reason. Do you want to be burdened with information that might make it hard to look the Chairman in the eye, or remain in happy ignorance?"

He watched Anya shoot Marcus a cautious glance as if for a nod, but he couldn't tell if Marcus responded. She fixed Hoffman with that look of complete trust that was somehow harder to take than steely disapproval. She was utterly loyal to him. She deserved better.

"I function better when I've got all the facts, sir," she said.

"Okay . . . I stole an encrypted data disk from Prescott's desk a few weeks ago, and he knows I did it. But until he deigns to tell me what the hell's on it, I'm just playing guessing games." Hoffman took a breath and waited for her to look hurt. There was nothing he hadn't confided in that poor girl over the years—except this. "I'm sorry, Anya."

But she just picked up a folder and fanned through it. Maybe Marcus had told her after all. "So what are you looking for?"

"No damn idea. Maybe something that ties the stalks in with the research that used to go on here."

"Oh . . . God. Really?" She took that very well, all things considered. "I better help you, then."

It was another of those out-of-body moments when Hoffman saw how he might look and sound, and shuddered. *I'm off my damn head.* And now he'd have to tell Sam. Where would it end? Did it even matter now? Did it matter if every asshole on Vectes knew?

A voice in his earpiece distracted him from a promising-looking report on the installation of the base's computer system. "Control to Hoffman."

"Go ahead, Mathieson."

"Sir, message from Corporal Mitchell. He's finished the image analysis. He says all the CZs except the latest one south of Pelruan have shown no expansion for two days, and he felt you'd want to know right away."

"Good timing, Mathieson." *Please, please, please let it all be over. Or at least let it be doing what we expect it to.* "I needed some good news. Tell him I'll stand him a beer."

"Sir, one more thing—if you're passing CIC, I'd like a word."

Hoffman could guess what that meant. "On my way."

Marcus and Anya both stopped and looked up. "What good news, sir?"

"The CZs look like they've stopped spreading. Well, the oldest ones, anyway. I've got to go to CIC for a while. Don't feel obliged to finish this tonight."

Anya smiled. There was enough paperwork to keep them busy for weeks. Maybe she thought he was being gracious and leaving to give her some private time with Marcus after she'd been stuck at Pelruan for so long.

And he never told her about the disc? He never told his girlfriend? Dear God. Just like his dad never told him anything about the Hammer. What a family.

Hoffman climbed the last flight of stairs to ground level and found the naval base heaving with civilians who still hadn't worked out where they were supposed to be. It was early evening, an unexpectedly vivid sunset emerging from beneath the day's heavy cloud. Trescu stood outside the main doors of Admiralty House with Michaelson. They were chatting like old chums.

"Getting cozy," Hoffman said. "The extra bodies, I mean."

Michaelson did his diplomat act. "All trawlers present and correct, Victor. Life goes on, and I've taken delivery

of a rather fine batch of smoked snakefish if you're interested . . ."

"We're moving the smoking sheds down here, I hope."

"It's a priority."

Trescu was sporting a cut on the bridge of his nose and a
hint of a black eye on the left side. He was a fastidious man
and Hoffman had expected him to seem uncomfortable
with his wounds, but it only made him look harder and less
open to reason.

"Anything you want to share with me, Colonel?" he asked.

Hoffman wasn't sure if Michaelson had said anything,
but he couldn't see any harm in leveling with Trescu. If he
hadn't been asking himself the same questions, he would
pick up the buzz sooner or later. "I'm reduced to playing
long shots," he said. "Seeing as this place used to be BCD,
I'm going through the archive store to see if Lambency
might be one of our own little errors."

Trescu did his oh-really tilt of the head. "Even if it is,
there's apparently nothing the Chairman can do to stop it,
judging by his behavior."

"I'd still feel better knowing." Hoffman could have told
him about the disc now. He really could have. For the first
time, he felt that this wasn't just a former enemy that he had
a grudging respect for, but an ally—or as much an ally as a
man could be after nearly two million of his people had
been incinerated by the COG's weapons of mass destruction. "I'll let you know if I find anything."

Hoffman went into the building and stopped off at CIC.
Mathieson gave him an anxious look and held out a sheet of
paper. There was a battered jar of pickles of some kind on
Mathieson's desk, lots of unidentifiable layers swimming in a
dark liquid. It might have been cabbage. Hoffman suspected
it was another kindness from Yanik. The Gorasnayan had
really taken a shine to the young lieutenant.

"Our databurst friend's been busy overnight," Mathieson said. The paper was a meticulously written list of times, signal strength, and duration. "Different times, but the activity's definitely picking up. Oh, and Sergeant Mataki dropped by looking for you. I think you're in the doghouse, but not in the pat-on-the-head way that Mac is."

"Yeah, it's hard to compete with someone who drools and rolls on his back every time he sees her." He wondered if a tidbit for the dog and some of Michaelson's rum reserve for Bernie might save his ass, whatever it was he'd done or failed to do. "Okay, Lieutenant, I'd better do some penance later. Thanks for the radio records."

Hoffman checked his watch. The idea that there might be more Gorasni forces lurking out there didn't bother him half as much as he thought it would. It almost comforted him. Being the small, tattered remnant of a global civilization was a lonely and depressing thing.

And if the plague that was finally killing both the COG and the grubs was of their own stupid making, he didn't feel quite as bad about that as he did about a random piece of fatally bad luck. It was a perverse reaction, he knew.

He'd just had enough of mysteries and secrets.

BARRACKS, VECTES NAVAL BASE: 0600 NEXT MORNING.

The screaming worked its way slowly through to Dom's brain. He was vaguely aware of it for what might have been a second or an hour, then it became insistent and started shaking him furiously. Consciousness crashed down on him like a collapsing wall and he struggled to sit up.

It was the emergency siren.

"Dom, you in a coma or something? Come on, get up." Marcus was still shaking his shoulder, a looming dark shape.

Boots clattered down the hall outside. "We've got a levia-than."

"Where?"

"Just outside the five-klick limit. Come on."

Dom scrambled for his clothes and armor. Shit, how could he sleep through that damn siren? It was a terrible wailing noise, up and down the scale, probably picked by psychologists as the sound most likely to make humans crap their pants and run for cover. Marcus waited impatiently as Dom struggled into his boots.

"Lambent or regular ones?" Dom mumbled.

"Can't tell yet." Marcus grabbed Dom's ammo belt and shoved it at him. "Let's bet on the worst."

They headed for their stand-to position on top of the naval base walls. Cole was already there with a rocket launcher, patting it like a much-loved pet.

"No Baird?" Dom asked.

"He's been drafted for Hammer duties." Cole chuckled to himself. "Hang on to your valuables, baby. You know he can't even piss straight."

"Yeah, everyone's fed up redrawing maps each time he blows up a chunk of coastline."

"It's the Hammer. It's fucked. Gotta believe him."

Marcus grunted and sighted up. It was a shut-up-and-focus gesture. A Lancer couldn't hit anything at five kilometers. "If anyone's still interested in the leviathan, *Clement* picked it up on the hydrophones."

"Maybe it's coming to look for its buddies." Dom took the hint and looked up at the Ravens circling over the water. He hoped it wasn't Eight-Zero and Two-Three-Nine. Those two birds spent way too many hours in the air. "Some animals have long memories."

"Then it'll remember that we've killed three of the ass-holes. We can make that four if it needs a reminder."

Clement was out of torpedoes and limping along with temporary repairs after her last run-in with a leviathan. But in the dockyard below, every warship with a gun—big guns, deck-mounted machine guns, even the explosive harpoon that Michaelson had scammed off a pirate for a few cans of processed meat—had its weapons facing seaward. The old defensive cannons set on the fortlike walls of the base were trained southeast now.

But none of that stopped the leviathan last time. Did it?

Gears were spread out along the walls and in every defensive position on the docks and jetties. Dom couldn't see the leviathan until a sudden plume of white foam caught his eye and a tentacle crashed down into the water. It was hard to tell how big the thing was, but any leviathan was bad news. A relatively small one had crippled *Fenmont* and let hundreds of polyps loose ashore. They had to be kept far out to sea, preferably by blowing the shit out of them.

Anya came jogging along the wall. "We're going to try using the Hammer before it gets any closer," she said. "But there could be more than one out there, so everybody stay sharp."

"Has Garcia pinged another one?" Marcus asked.

"Maybe. There's something else out there, but it might just be a regular whale."

"Or another submarine."

"No, *Zephyr*'s close inshore, and Garcia knows her position." Anya looked along the walls in both directions, then headed for the steps. "I'm going to give Baird a hand. If the Hammer fails, then it's back to old-fashioned ballistics."

"Why don't the glowies go pick on the mainland?" Cole asked. "What are we doin' that's pissin' 'em off so much?"

Maybe the leviathan wasn't picking on them at all, just wandering by. But nobody in their right mind could pass up a chance to kill it. Dom watched a Marlin, one of the old rigid inflatables from his commando days, zip away from the docks and head out southeast trailing a wake of foam. He trained his binoculars.

"Place your bets," Marcus said. "Gorasni."

"Man, I ain't afraid of a healthy risk, but those guys got a death wish." Cole shook his head. "It's like they're always tryin' to prove they're crazier and tougher than us."

"It's not Gorasni," Dom said. He could see the crew now—CPO Muller and Commander Fyne. "It's the navy. Alisder Fyne and Franck Muller."

He'd forgotten all about Commander Fyne. Everybody seemed to. The poor asshole had kept what little was left of NCOG running for years until Michaelson was recalled, and then he just vanished back into the invisible task of keeping ships supplied and fueled. It wasn't much of a reward.

"They don't need *that* close a look at the thing, do they?" Dom asked.

Marcus didn't look happy. "Maybe they're going to use a hand laser for targeting. They should've asked us."

Dom was horrified to see the Marlin swing wide and circle the leviathan, coming dangerously close to getting slapped by a tentacle before heading back to the dockside. It was hard to get the scale of the animal, but Dom had seen enough of them by now to work it out. It was too easy to see the tentacles—five, ten meters long—and think that was the head end, and that it was all arms and almost no body, like a squid. But it wasn't. It had a long, scaly, snakelike body several times longer than the tentacles. The vast fanged maw could crunch through steel plate.

And if it was Lambent as well—then it wasn't just a big, dangerous bastard. It was a big, dangerous, highly explosive bastard as well, capable of generating enough energy to collapse cliffs and blow holes in bedrock. The infestation of polyps those things usually carried seemed to pale into insignificance.

Fyne's voice came over the radio. "Control to all callsigns, we have confirmation—it's Lambent. Stand by for Hammer deployment in *thirty seconds* . . ."

If it had been a regular leviathan, it was just something to be avoided instead of wasting ordnance on blowing it up. Now Anya and Baird—more Anya than Baird, Dom hoped—were going to detonate it out at sea like a stray mine. The leviathan was still on the surface, its undulating back breaking the waves as its huge fanged head lifted every few meters like someone doing the breaststroke.

"Stick your head between your ugly legs . . . ," Cole said.

"Fifteen seconds . . ."

". . . and kiss your ugly ass . . ."

"Ten seconds . . ."

". . . goodbye, motherfucker."

"Firing."

A beam of brilliant white light stabbed out of the sky and hit the water. But it struck twenty meters wide. The leviathan plunged beneath the surface and vanished for a few moments before popping up again, now on a different course. Dom watched it for a few seconds before he worked out that it was heading straight for the base.

"Control here, stand by—going again," Mathieson said.

Dom held his breath. "That better be you this time, Anya."

"Fifteen . . . ten . . . firing."

The beam hit the water even further off target. The leviathan picked up speed, trailing foam like a powerboat.

"Control to all callsigns—Hammer is now offline."

"Oh, terrific," Dom said. "What the hell happened?"

Marcus braced his elbow on the wall to sight up. "We've lost too many targeting sats. Can't aim the damn thing."

"Fine." Cole shouldered the Longspear. "I can aim *this* baby. Shit, least we're doing this in daylight for a change."

The ancient cannon mounted on the walls could still hit a target, too. Dom decided there was a lot to be said for old tech. One started firing its ranging shots, striking short of the leviathan and working toward it with a slow rhythmic *pom-pom-pom* noise. Everyone waited for the explosion. The arty guys didn't have a lot of time before the leviathan moved inside their minimum range, and they didn't have an infinite supply of ordnance.

One shell landed close enough to send a column of water crashing onto the thing, but it kept going. It didn't even slow down when the Ravens passed over—well out of tentacle reach—and strafed it.

And then it dived.

"The asshole's getting smart," Marcus said. "Okay, Cole—you stay up here. Dom—with me."

As Dom ran after Marcus, he could hear the confusion on the radio. Nobody could follow the thing visually now, not even the Ravens, but Garcia, *Clement*'s CO, had sonar and was calling ranges.

"Two thousand meters—bearing off gun emplacement, red thirty."

The gun battery lobbed another shell and raised a plume of water, but Garcia confirmed the worst.

"Fifteen hundred meters—holding its course."

Dom and Marcus running along the edge of the dock now, trying to work out where the leviathan was going to surface. But Mathieson had already plotted its course for them.

"Control to all callsigns, it's going for the oiling jetty. Everyone get clear. I said *get clear.*"

"Oh *shit.*" Dom broke into a sprint. The leviathan was going to smash into the fuel tanks. It was a giant pissed-off torpedo about to hit tens of thousands of liters of imulsion. "It'll take out the whole jetty."

Marcus sprinted ahead of him. "And half the docks. We've got to hold that asshole off somehow."

"*Six hundred meters*," said Garcia.

Nobody listened to Mathieson's sensible advice to get out of the blast area, least of all Dom and Marcus. They reached the pier opposite the jetty and aimed their Lancers across the water waiting for something to target. If the thing surfaced just *once*, if it got close enough to the surface for someone to see the movement and open fire to distract it, anything at all—

A small RIB suddenly roared around the end of the jetty in a cloud of spray, bouncing along the surface. The boat did a spectacular turn about three hundred meters out and Dom waited for it to capsize, but one of the two-man crew heaved something into the water and the boat zipped clear. A few seconds later a booming explosion threw a column of spray into the air.

The leviathan surfaced fifty meters off the pier and reared out of the water, bellowing.

"Depth charge," Marcus said, and opened fire. "Now it's pissed off."

The leviathan was going crazy. The explosion must have burst its eardrums or something, if it had any. It thrashed around, smashing splinters out of the wooden pillars jutting from the water, mouth gaping wide. *Yes, eardrums. Ouch.* Dom kept firing at the thing's head, watching the rounds do nothing more than send small puffs of spray into the air , but Marcus took a grenade off his belt and hefted it, ready to throw.

The RIB zipped around again, but closer. It was Yanik and Teodor. "What are you waiting for, COG?" Yanik yelled. "Do it!"

"Delicate job," Marcus muttered, unfazed. He lobbed the grenade into the leviathan's wide-open maw. The mouth snapped shut. It knew it had swallowed something. "Now *run*."

"Did you set the delay?"

"Thirty seconds."

The leviathan started panicking. It slapped down onto the water like a breaching whale. It might have been flailing randomly or it might have decided Yanik and Teodor were responsible for its pain, but either way it went after them and they shot off ahead of it at full throttle.

Then it dived again. The RIB looped back into the harbour. By now, other Gears had come running from across the docks to see if there was anything left to shoot.

"Fuck." Dom watched the water, helpless. Seconds passed. The frag should have blown by now. "Shit, if it's come in under the jetty again, we're screwed."

Whoomp.

The explosion was nearly a hundred meters away but it lifted the RIB clear of the water. Dom lost sight of the boat for a second or two as the sea rained down on the dock and drenched him. When everything settled, Dom could see Yanik and Teodor in the RIB, equally soaked and bailing out with a scoop. Bits of leviathan started floating to the surface along with a spreading carpet of stunned fish.

Marcus shook his head, getting his breath again. "There's risk taking," he said. "And then there's clinically insane."

"Like you wouldn't have done that."

"Depth charges." The idea seemed to fascinate Marcus. He stared at the bobbing raft of fish around the RIB with a distracted frown. "Ought to be easy to make some of those. They obviously can."

Yanik stood up unsteadily in the boat, looking like a drowned but optimistic rat. Teodor was now trying to rake in some of the fish floating helplessly on the surface. Well, food was food. Nobody forgot that starvation was a real possibility now.

"Bah, you are all *girls*! Whole army of *you* equals two poor Gorasni peasants!" Yanik taunted the watching Gears but it was all delivered with a big grin. "That was a nice *dropball* goal with the frag, Fenix. Is girls' game, yes?"

"Yeah," Marcus said. "I was the ladies' champion."

Bernie and Sam jogged up to take a look. Everyone was suddenly at that giggly relief stage that followed intense and bowel-loosening terror. Yanik and Teodor were serious about not letting the stunned fish go to waste, though. Teodor had found a net and was filling the RIB to the gunwales as if nothing had happened.

"Looks dead to me," Sam said. "Nice job, Marcus."

"With a little help from the psychiatric ward."

"This is just how Gorasni go fishing, *duchaska*," Yanik said, leering at her from the boat. "But the leviathan got in the way."

"You great big jessie." Sam had thawed a bit toward Yanik. He shot Stranded on sight and Dom didn't even want to know how he acquired his nickname, but it took some effort to dislike him. "Look at the state of you. You pissed your pants."

"Ah, this is just uncontrollable excitement at seeing *you*, my vision of loveliness!"

"Wanker."

Yanik laughed his head off, a bit too happy. Maybe he wasn't that relaxed about nearly getting spattered around the dock after all. A chunk of leviathan with a couple of tentacles still attached drifted like a raft toward the jetty on the current with a few polyps huddled on it, survivors from a shipwreck.

Bernie aimed her Longshot. She wasn't laughing now. "And you lot can fuck right off."

Her first shot hit one square in the mouth and detonated it. The watching Gorasni applauded. But it couldn't have had much juice in it because it didn't take the others with it, and just blew off one of the tentacles before sinking.

"Ah, sod it." Bernie reloaded the single cartridge and sighted up. "Okay . . . I'm channeling Blondie now . . ."

Bang.

The polyps blew up with the usual fountain of spray. Gears cheered. For a moment, everyone was hysterically happy just to have all their limbs and not find themselves staring at a fireball engulfing the docks. Dom found he came down to earth faster these days. When he reassured himself he wasn't dead, he remembered who already was and who might be this time tomorrow.

There were stalks slowly encroaching on the island and killing the crops. And there'd be other leviathans, and many, many more polyps. The number of attacks was increasing.

Sam caught his arm gently, cupping his elbow. "Come and have breakfast in the mess," she whispered in his ear, way too close for comfort. "You've got to see the tattoo I did for Rossi."

Dom turned and found Bernie looking his way. She was watching with that all-seeing, all-knowing expression that sergeants always had.

"Weird buggers, aren't they?" Bernie said. Ah, she wasn't thinking about Sam at all. "There's nobody I'd rather rely on than a Gorasni, except a Pesanga. They'll put their lives on the line for you and laugh their arses off about it. But then I think about what they did to our boys in the war, and I just can't square it."

Bernie shrugged and walked off, suddenly distracted by Teodor yelling something to her about salting the fish. Dom submitted to Sam and let her shepherd him toward the mess.

"I made sure I can make it more respectable later," she said, giggling. "Rossi's tattoo, I mean. He had too much of Dizzy's potato hooch."

Bernie was right. There were people you liked a hell of a lot and for all the right reasons, but something inside said that it was all wrong somehow. It didn't mean you could make yourself stop liking them. But you couldn't forget what the barriers were, either.

"Yeah, we all need something to numb the pain," Dom said. *Wrong world, wrong time. And wrong me.* "At least for a while."

CHAPTER 13

Everybody says they want answers. No, they don't. Most people just want reassurance that the world is the way they already think it is. Genuine revelation—the knowledge that changes minds—upsets them. And they'll hate you for doing it.

(COG Chairman Richard Prescott, in a rare conversation with Commander Miran Trescu)

GORASNI CAMP, NEW JACINTO.

"No, that won't lock out when he puts his weight on it," Baird said, peering at the lathe. "Are you sure you know what you're doing?"

Sandru went on grinding the metal pin and didn't say a word. The workshop was full of fascinating things, scented with unfamiliar lube oils and chemicals that the COG had probably banned on toxicity grounds years ago.

Yanik laughed. "Blondie-Baird, how many Gorasni do you see on crutches or in wheelchairs?"

"None, but that's probably because you kill and eat your wounded, right?"

That just made Yanik laugh louder. Even Sandru

managed a grin, the surly asshole. Baird wasn't used to getting laughs for his best lines and he rather liked it.

"This will work," Sandru said slowly, handing him the
joint. "I did this in hospitals. I made legs. Your friend will
need sticks maybe, but he will stand up again. Only one
knee joint missing. Much easier than *both* knees missing. I
show you why if you piss me off again . . ."

Baird found himself about to point out that Mathieson
wasn't actually his friend, but it sounded pathetically needy.
He examined the finished joint. It wasn't a state-of-the-art
modern prosthetic unit with electronics, but it was beauti-
fully made and it wouldn't need a team of experts to
maintain it.

"Okay, he'll think it's awesome." Now, what was the
magic word? "Thanks, Sandru."

"Hah, we like to show Cogs our technical superiority.
Now we have to make casts. This is a *slow* job, Corporal."

Yanik wandered over to the doorway and seemed to be
watching something outside. Baird kept an eye on him.
Yanik was part of Trescu's personal entourage and that
meant he wasn't to be trifled with. In a community where
everyone seemed to be a psychopath, that was some reputation. These guys didn't pull their punches.

"Ah, some excitement out there," Yanik said, ambling
outside. "Let's see what's happening."

Baird craned his neck to see where he was heading. The
dirt roads between the tents were dead straight, so Baird had
a clear view all the way to one of the communal areas that
housed the latrines and water pumps, the equivalent of a
town square in a place like this. There were an awful lot of
people gathering out there. Yanik started walking faster.
Then he broke into a jog.

Shit. I better call in.

Baird switched his radio on as discreetly as he could. He

usually kept the channel open even when he was off-duty, but he didn't fancy receiving a sensitive message on the subject of discs and data when he was surrounded by Gorasni. He liked them, but he wasn't stupid.

"Baird to Fenix," he said quietly. "Baird here, over."

"Go ahead, Baird."

"I'm in the Gorasni camp, getting Mathieson's legs made." *Suck on that, Marcus. See, I can be a good guy too.* "Is there some shit going on? I can see signs of collectively bunched panties here. I mean, it might be a coup or a lynching or some domestic Gorasni entertainment like that, but I thought I'd check in just in case."

"No idea, but Hoffman and Michaelson went into a huddle with Sharle a couple of hours ago and they haven't come out yet."

"Leviathan aftermath? No Trescu?"

"We'll find out soon enough."

Sandru looked up at Baird over spectacles that had been repaired with very delicate wirework. "Problem?"

"Everybody's getting edgy about the attacks."

Sandru let out a long sigh. "Yes, we're fucked," he said placidly, and went back to the lathe. "Pity. It's nice here."

Baird had to walk through the communal area to get back to the main gates. Idle curiosity made him want to find out what had sparked the gathering he could see ahead of him, but the Gorasni would be doing what any civilians did at a time like this—asking questions nobody had any answers to. Damn, he'd seen this so many times back on the mainland. It couldn't be any worse than the panic over the Hammer strike, that was for sure. He didn't know why he suddenly remembered that after all the shit had happened in the intervening years, but it was so vivid right then that he could smell the soot in the air and wished it would go away.

He hovered on the edge of the crowd for a moment. It was a mixed bunch of a couple of hundred, men and women of all ages but no kids, and they were scared. That much he could work out. His entire command of the Gorasni language consisted of *yes, no, shithouse, fuck off,* and a few numbers. If the meeting was a debate about identity and alienation in a post-apocalyptic world, then he was screwed.

And he could hear a familiar voice, although he couldn't see where it was coming from until he sidled up to Yanik. Then he saw Trescu standing on the flatbed of a junker to make himself heard.

He was laying down the law. Baird didn't understand a word of it, but Trescu was one of those guys who looked as if he was reining in a terrible temper—twitching jaw muscles and arms held carefully at his sides as if to hint that only superior aristocratic willpower stopped him from strangling his audience barehanded. It looked a lot more scary than red-faced cursing.

"What is it?" Baird whispered.

"They want a *ship,*" Yanik said sourly. "They want to leave."

"I bet the boss just loves the idea."

"Ungrateful bastards. After all he's done for us. We'd all be dead without him." Yanik looked like he was working up to a contemptuous spit. "Or worse—Stranded."

Watching Trescu was hypnotic. The shouts and arguments in the crowd were reaching a crescendo, and then Trescu snapped and punched his fist into his palm. He repeated something over and over, hitting his palm each time, and finally Baird recognized enough of the words to understand. *Numbers.* Trescu was repeating a number.

Four thousand.

Four thousand.

Combined with a sweeping gesture, it was suddenly obvious. He was reminding them there were just four thousand Gorasni left and that splitting up would finish them.

"So you don't have some secret navy out there, then," Baird whispered.

Yanik frowned. "What?"

"The weird radio transmissions. That's not you, then."

Yanik managed to look away from the crowd. "And it's not you?"

"Shit, no." Baird wished he'd kept his big mouth shut. God, what was he *thinking*? Hoffman would kill him. But it was too late now. "We thought it was *you*."

Ooooh, so we really trust each other. Great.

"Well, that's still a frigging mystery, then." Baird grabbed the chance to get out before he sank any deeper in the shit. "And if your guys are losing it, ours are probably descending into cannibalism right about now. I better go sweep up the debris."

Baird hurried off, chastened by seeing the Gorasni having internal spats. They always looked solid and unflappable, so couldn't-give-a-shit. He was a bit disappointed to realize they were as fucked up and scared as anyone else. He checked inside his armor to make sure the data disc was still there, like he did twenty times a day, and walked through the main gates. Well, if Hoffman yelled at him for mentioning the databursts, he could always defend himself with what he'd found out.

It wasn't the Gorasni transmitting them. He'd hold that nugget up in front of him like a riot shield.

He caught up with Cole on the walls and they leaned on the brickwork, watching the activity on the parade ground. A few weeks ago, it had been a model of military order, an open space despite the number of civilians who still had to live inside the base while the engineers built more housing. Now it looked like a Silver Era village, complete with farm animals, machinery that should have been in a museum, and eye-wateringly bad smells. There just weren't that many places left to put three thousand extra people, especially when everyone else had been pulled back inside the existing camp perimeters.

"Shit, is that a *goat*?" Baird asked, pointing.

Cole followed his finger. "No, that's just a freaky sheep. Some of them have horns too. Goats are skinny and got them crazy-looking eyes."

"Yeah, like that redhead who dishes up in the mess. Hey, since when did *you* become Farmer Giles?"

"Baby, we're slipping back in time every time we lose a piece of machinery. A guy's gotta know his sheep from his goats these days."

"This place is turning into a frigging zoo." Baird decided he'd rely on Bernie for all this frontiersman shit. "I even found one of them scratching around near my workshop."

"It's just a few chickens," Cole said. "And some dogs. Animals are real good early-warning systems for stalks."

"I meant the *civilians*," said Baird. "They always knew their place in Jacinto. They're even getting pissy in the Gorasni camp."

"And ol' Trescu the Terrible ain't smacked 'em around?"

"Not yet. There's a bunch of them that want to take a ship and make a run for it."

"Gonna be plenty more where *they* came from . . ."

"It's move to another island, or head home. Me, I call that frying pan or fire."

"Some of those pirate guys live at sea."

"Yeah, like you'd enjoy that."

"Didn't say I would. Just speculatin'."

Baird's radio interrupted the discussion. "Briefing from Hoffman in his old office, fifteen minutes," Marcus said.

"Must be a select gathering," Baird said. "It's not a big room."

"We're going to recon the mainland."

It had to be done, sooner or later. It was just the timing. Baird and Cole headed for Admiralty House, weaving between tractors. The place looked like a paramilitary county fair.

"Well, that's *really* going to stoke the rumor mill," Baird said.

"It's no big deal." Cole took it placidly like he always did. "We gotta know what's out there now."

When they reached the office, Hoffman was already there with Michaelson, Sharle, Marcus, Dom, and Gettner. *Gettner?* They must have performed surgery to get her out of that frigging cockpit, let alone lure her to an actual meeting. Everyone was crammed in, leaning against filing cabinets or standing with arms tightly folded. Hoffman wasn't a big-office kind of guy and seemed to feel safer in small spaces. The room smelled of barley coffee and floor polish.

"I hear there's some trouble in the Gorasni camp," Hoffman said. There was no sign of Prescott. "Someone else taking potshots at Trescu?"

"No, he's trying to hold his happy campers together." *Brazen it out. Don't act guilty.* "I don't speak the language, but a bunch of them want to leave Vectes and he's telling them it'll finish the Gorasni as a nation."

Hoffman gave him a dubious look. "For a man who doesn't speak the language, you pick up a lot."

"Well, Trescu's body language is pretty vivid," Baird said. He'd save the news about the databursts until Sharle was out of the way, but maybe he knew anyway. "Anyway, Yanik translated for me."

"We're going to recon a coastal strip from Corren to the

north," Hoffman said. "We've got enough fuel now, and we might get as far as Jacinto. We've got to start assessing what's out there or we can't make informed decisions about staying here."

"Who's *we?* Does Prescott know?"

"Of course he does," Michaelson said. "With the long-range fuel tanks, we'll have space for five in the Raven. We've got to have Royston on board, and I think we need Trescu for diplomatic reasons as much as anything, so I'll take a back seat. That leaves you, Victor, and two Gears for security."

"Volunteers?" Hoffman said. "Prescott isn't coming."

"Should we read anything into that?" Marcus asked.

"He said he'd only be going out of curiosity, and that it was more important to send personnel who could assess the situation professionally."

Baird found a space on the edge of the desk to perch his ass. "As in, the Raven might not make it back."

"It'll be back," Gettner said flatly. "He's just making sense again."

"Okay, me and Dom," Marcus said. "Baird and Cole can help the Captain here look after Prescott's richly varied needs."

"He's got Lowe and Rivera for that," Baird said.

"So you can keep an eye on them too," said Marcus.

"Done." Hoffman looked pointedly at Sharle. "Anything else you want done, Royston, now's the time to shout."

Sharle shrugged. "We could do with Parry along, but we can save him for the follow-up recon. Maybe sail to the mainland and fly the Raven off deck next time. It'll give us a better range."

"Okay, tomorrow morning, people—oh-eight-hundred on the landing pad." Hoffman stood back to let Sharle and Michaelson squeeze out of the room. He tapped Baird on the arm when they'd gone. "I'm going to go see Trescu now. What's the mood like over there?"

"It's just some asshole called Nareci whining—nothing Trescu can't slap down," Baird said. *Now's the time. Do it.* "And . . . well, you know that databurst shit? The Gorasni thought it was us. I told them we thought it was them." Baird blurted it out and braced for one of Hoffman's incandescent rages. "So it's Stranded, or else the polyps have worked out how to use a radio dial despite the lack of thumbs."

He's going to shoot me. Disc or no disc. I'm dead. So very, very dead.

Surprisingly, Hoffman didn't ignite. He just looked a little more battered and tired. "Well, at least that's one thing less to worry about."

"But we still don't know who it is," Cole said.

"It's not Trescu," Hoffman said. "And that means we've still got an ally who's playing straight with us."

Baird took the data disk out of his armor, relieved at escaping Hoffman's wrath. "Maybe it's time we let him have a go at this. He knows just about everything else that we do."

"When the time's right," Hoffman said. "And the priority is having a contingency plan."

KING RAVEN KR-80, EN ROUTE FOR THE MAINLAND: NEXT MORNING.

"You think we're going to keep this quiet?" Dom asked. "Once people find out we're flying recons, they'll think we're preparing to ship out."

"So we tell them," Hoffman said. "And we tell them we'll be doing it on a regular basis because that was the plan. Prescott's adamant about that."

"He can be most persuasive," Trescu murmured. He was wearing one of those old-fashioned UIR radio headsets, bulky things compared to the COG models. "The more open you are, the less people mistrust you, even if you're stealing their wallets."

Hoffman sat opposite Dom, arms folded, jammed up against Royston Sharle. Trescu gazed out of the other door while Marcus sat listening to the radio net with his hand to his ear. Barber was behind the door gun, messing around with the camera in his lap. From time to time he went and sat up front in the cockpit with Gettner. It wasn't exactly a high-spirited office outing.

Marcus leaned back in his seat. "Okay, we've lost the signal. We're definitely out of radio range. We can't rely on the global sats staying operational much longer."

"Better not get into difficulties, then," Trescu said. "Or let Baird use the Hammer again."

Gettner cut in on the radio, probably because she was fed up hearing them bitch, Dom decided. "Okay, here's the latest fuel calculation. We've got enough to cover a fifty-kilometer coastal strip to just north of Jacinto. Depending on the conditions we might get further inland, but I'm not taking any chances. If we see anything worth a closer look, we come back with a ship and fly a Raven off it. Okay?"

"Understood." Hoffman picked up his Lancer and hugged it as if he had plans for it. "I'm not expecting to find a beach resort and make a down payment. We're just assessing the degree of stalk infestation for now."

Trescu took a small monocular from his belt pouch. It was a satin-polished black tube with intricate gold-work at each end, very old, probably the same era as that antique wristwatch he always wore. Dom doubted it was a fashion thing or even the only device he had, because he could simply have used a detached rifle scope. No, this stuff was his father's, or maybe his grandfather's, a comforting link with a happier past. Dom understood that all too well. He put his hand to his collar and felt for his COG tag, intertwined with Maria's necklace.

Little cherished things like that made the difference in a world that was becoming more terrifying and alien by the day.

"If and when we leave Vectes," Trescu said, "I intend to resettle Gorasnaya. Even if it means living on board *Paryk* in Branascu harbor."

"I don't think we've got enough fuel to check it out, Commander," Gettner said. "Not on this trip, anyway."

"I know." Trescu peered through the monocular again. "I'm simply saying it to ensure that I do it."

Marcus got up and went to stand at the door gun. Nobody spoke. Dom looked at Hoffman and caught his eye. Hoffman shrugged.

"Anvil Gate," he said suddenly. "Anvegad. I ought to give it its proper name."

Gettner huffed. "Colonel, that's *way* out of range and you *know* it."

"I'm just saying that if I return to the mainland, I'd like to go back there one day."

If this had been a bunch of ordinary guys talking over a beer about moving house, it would have been idle conversation. But this was two men who'd decide the fate of the last organized human society on Sera. Dom felt his stomach knot. They were hard men who'd spent their entire adult lives in combat, and here they were talking nostalgically as if they were now looking for the best place to lay down and die. And Trescu was roughly Dom's age.

But if he thinks it's the endgame, he's right, isn't he? Because we're running out of everything. Time. Resources. Land. People. Hope.

Hoffman gazed up at the deckhead. He was still chewing it all over. "See, I can *defend* Anvegad, stalks or no fucking stalks," he said, almost to himself. "We could hold that place against *any* goddamn thing."

That was more like it. *That* was the Hoffman Dom knew and believed in. Dom decided not to point out that stalks could probably punch up through the fort as easily as they had on Vectes.

"Not a lot of room in there, though, sir," he said. "Five or six thousand people at most, Sam says. Not big enough for us."

"Yeah. Intimate. But with a water supply, and hydroelectricity, and a damned good view — nearly three-sixty degrees." Hoffman turned in his seat and stared out onto the sea below again. "But you're right. We need to find somewhere big enough to house a city."

"I keep telling you," Sharle said wearily. "We won't find anywhere with the kind of infrastructure we need. That's why we ended up on Vectes."

"We ended up on Vectes because it was warmer and Prescott suggested it," Hoffman said.

"We could try Port Farrall again if infrastructure is all we need, but it isn't. It's about being able to respond to threats."

Hoffman rubbed his forehead and said nothing. It seemed to be an argument they'd had before.

Nobody had any easy options, and Dom didn't need Sharle's qualifications to work it out. If there was anywhere habitable within easy reach left on the mainland, then Stranded would have found it. And if they'd found it, they'd either already stripped it of every usable plank of wood and scrap of metal, or they'd taken over the place. Nobody was in the mood for more fighting even if they'd had unlimited ammo.

"We've rebuilt once," Marcus said. Dom wasn't sure what had prompted him to say that. Maybe it was a thought from a conversation in his head that had just spilled out. "So we can do it again."

They still had a few hours before they hit the coast, so Dom shut his eyes and dozed. He'd spent two wars desperate for sleep, dreaming of a day when he could just ignore reveille or switch off the alarm, and now he had his chance. It was surprisingly easy to sleep in a helicopter. The vibration was blissfully numbing and after a while the engine just became white noise. He didn't surface until someone shook him—Trescu, of all people—and he woke with a start.

Barber gestured down and pointed out of the bay door. Dom leaned over to look, expecting to see the coastline of southern Tyrus.

He could see a coast, all right, but he could also see what looked like a mangrove delta stretching for kilometers.

It wasn't made up of trees. It was a forest of stalks.

"Oh God," he said. "The Stranded weren't kidding. They're here too."

"It's just the shallows," Barber said. "They're the first we've seen. There was nothing out in deeper water."

Dom almost pointed out that Barber had only covered a narrow strip in a vast ocean, so for all they knew the stalks were springing up like bristles everywhere else. But that was the kind of parade pissing that Baird did. Dom kept his mouth shut.

"We're coming up on Corren," Gettner said. Barber left the gun to grab recon images. "But when I say we turn back, we turn back, okay, Colonel? I'm not taking risks with fuel if we don't have radio contact with base."

"I'll man the gun," Marcus said. "I'm more worried about Stranded taking potshots. Last time we saw Corren they had a goddamn army."

"That's my kind of thinking, Fenix. They won't have forgotten how much they love us."

The stalks thinned out as they got closer to the city but when Gettner dropped lower, Dom could see some poking up through the buildings. The Raven circled over the center of town, but there were no signs of life at all.

"This used to be a really busy place," Gettner said. "Thousands of Stranded."

"Well, it's not busy now," Sharle said. "Stranded keep moving. It's how they've survived this long."

Sera looked like a wasteland, but over the years Dom had become attuned to the small detail that said a place was inhabited—smoke, attempts to tend crops, even sea-birds that hung around looking for garbage left by messy humans. The bigger settlements like Corren had sentries and observation posts you could see from the air. But there was nothing like that down there now.

Marcus unfolded a chart. "Okay, Major. Go east along the coastal highway. Look for the athletics track."

There were certain places that Stranded preferred. Every Gear knew they liked reservoirs, river estuaries, high outcrops or tall buildings that could be defended—and sports stadiums. Stadiums were ready-made forts.

"Okay," Gettner said. "I see it."

"And everybody keep an eye open for ground fire."

Dom rested his Lancer on his knee as the Raven descended. All that was left of the stadium was a skeleton of girders, but the lower half of the walls were intact enough to make the place defensible. Gettner circled cautiously as Dom kept an eye out for signs of habitation. There was nothing inside but a few ramshackle huts that were too dilapidated to be in use.

"Over there," Hoffman said wearily. "Stalks. Two of 'em."

Gettner skimmed close alongside. The stalks looked long dead. Dom strained to see any signs of the pods on the trunks, but there was no way of telling what had been a blister and what was just gnarling now that they were just gray husks.

"Hey, what's the one thing we *haven't* seen here yet?" Barber asked.

Marcus nodded. "Dead zones."

"Yeah, but we haven't covered any grassland so far," Dom said.

"That's next on the tour." Gettner turned north. "Reservoir at Hatton, Marcus?"

"Yeah. I'd be surprised if the Stranded abandoned that."

"It's like being the first explorers," Barber said. "We've got no idea what's down there now. Well, except we've got accurate maps. We know the geography and the shape of the coastline."

"Except Jacinto Bay." Marcus studied his chart. "I think we made that a *lot* bigger . . ."

Nobody asked the obvious. Were they going to take a look at Jacinto's submerged crater? Dom hadn't thought much about it since they'd escaped the flood, but now the prospect of having to look at it again seemed unbearable. Maria was down there in the tunnels somewhere with the drowned grubs and the Gears who'd died fighting them.

I couldn't even bury her. I couldn't even take her back to Mercy and let her rest alongside her folks. Maybe I can at least take her necklace back there one day.

"Absolutely not," Gettner said. They'd all been together so long that they all knew what the others were thinking. "I'm not diverting to Jacinto unless the Colonel's got a really pressing reason to see it."

Hoffman shifted in his seat. "Don't think I have, Major. Not yet, anyway."

Dom counted eleven stalks on the way to Hatton, all of them in built-up areas. On the way out of town, the concrete gave way to woodland and big gardens so overgrown that it was hard to make out the boundary fences.

"Stalk," Barber called. The Raven passed over a park. The

metal structure of a kids' climbing frame and a bandstand were still visible, poking above the ocean of unmown grass like icebergs, but the wooden planks had been stripped off. "Let's take a look."

"Well, most of the grass is still alive." Gettner headed for the stalk. As the Raven passed directly above it, Dom could see a pool of bare soil stretching for about twenty meters around it. "Oh, yeah, that's a dead zone. But at least we know it stops eventually."

"Actually, we don't, because we can't tell how recent that is," Barber said. "Colonel, how do you feel about trying to raise some Stranded on the radio?"

Hoffman glanced at Trescu but he didn't twitch at the mention of the word. Hoffman nodded.

"It's got to be done, Corporal. But let's see if we can eyeball any first."

The reservoir was visible for kilometers, a lovely lake from a distance. But the closer they got, the more they could pick out the shabby detail of a shantytown around its man-made shoreline. Smoke curled up from the rooftops. There were Stranded here, all right.

"Well, they can't miss a Raven, and we're the only guys flying these days," Gettner said. "You want me to flash them, Colonel, just to show manners? They usually hog the old emergency frequencies."

"Grit your teeth and be charming, Major."

"Charm offensive acquiring target . . . Stranded encampment, this is COG KR-Eight-Zero, the big black noisy thing heading your way, over."

Dom listened for the response, watching Marcus's reaction—completely blank, all emotion locked down—and then Hoffman's, which was a kind of glum resignation. There was a long delay. Gettner circled and tried again. "This is KR-Eight-Zero to—"

"This is the Reservoir, COG. We heard you." It was a woman's voice. "You've been out of town awhile. What do you want? Water? 'Cause we got plenty of that if you want to trade."

Hoffman cut in. "We want information."

"Who's that?"

"This is Colonel Victor Hoffman."

"Ooh, we got the brass coming to inspect us! Damn, we might even clear the dead dogs off the carpet for you. What's in it for us, COG?"

"Fuel."

Gettner snapped back at Hoffman on the Raven's internal circuit. "No, we haven't, Colonel."

"A five-liter can won't kill us."

"*Shit*, sir."

Hoffman ignored her protest. "Reservoir, we're planning to land. You tell us what you know about the state of the mainland, and I'll give you fuel. Deal?"

"Mainland? That's us, right? Sounds like you ran a *long* way away when you skipped town."

"I said—deal?"

"Why not? Just stay back from the houses, okay?"

Barber patted the door gun. "You bet," he muttered.

The Raven set down a cautious distance from the edge of the shanty and everyone checked their weapon. Even Sharle was carrying a pistol this time. Marcus and Hoffman got out first and Dom decided to stick close to Trescu in case the temptation to slot a few more despised Stranded got the better of him. A small crowd of armed Stranded, mainly men, gathered to block their way into the camp.

"The prodigals have come home, then." A woman aged about forty stepped forward, all tight-braided red hair and beads. When Dom looked more closely, he could see the beads were actually wedding bands, steel nuts, and coins—small barter currency. "Either you're nursing a delusion that it's safe to come home, or you're in the shit."

She'd got that right on both counts. It stung. Most of the Stranded leaders Dom had come across in the later years of his search for Maria were women, at least in the larger camps. They seemed better at holding a big community together than the male Stranded. He suspected it was less about the maternal wisdom thing than the fact they were more ruthless.

Marcus took a casual step forward next to Hoffman, cradling his Lancer, but said nothing.

"Just checking how far the stalks have got, ma'am," Hoffman said. "Have there been any polyp attacks?"

"Some." She looked Marcus over, then Dom, and then Trescu. He didn't seem to provoke a reaction in her, but then maybe Gorasnaya didn't mean much down here. "The bad news is we're seeing 'em more often. The good news is that we haven't seen a grub since the end of last summer, thank God. Why do *you* give a damn? You crapped your pants and ran away last year, didn't you? We hear you sank Jacinto."

"That's why you haven't seen any grubs," Marcus said, polite but pissed off. "We drowned them when they tried to tunnel under the city."

"My my, the COG's finally done something for us. Where did you go, then?"

"The Serano Ocean." Hoffman had obviously decided there was no harm telling them. The Stranded grapevine worked so well that they'd probably heard it from the pirates anyway. "There are islands out there."

"Very nice."

"Look, we're just trying to establish the extent of the stalks and if anywhere's habitable."

The woman laughed. "Why, you thinking of coming back?"

"One day, yes."

"Goddamn. You're serious."

"What happened to Corren?"

"Same as all the city camps. Stalks. There's something those things like about cities. You're talking on the radio to a camp one day, and the next—it's gone."

"Gerrenhalt?"

"Not a word for months."

"How about further afield—Bonbourg?"

"No. Ogari was broadcasting up to three weeks ago, though."

Hoffman took a breath. "How about Anvil Gate . . . or Branascu?"

"You're into the history books now, Colonel. Nobody went near Anvil Gate, *ever*. Too many kill-crazy savages up there in the hills. And too damn far." She paused. "And Branascu—never heard of it."

Dom wasn't sure if that was a relief to Hoffman or not. Trescu didn't say a word. He just stood there completely motionless, staring straight into the camp, not even blinking much. No, these folks didn't know what a Gorasni was, which was just as well.

"Are there any big camps other than yours?"

"You're racking up your fuel bill, soldier."

"Are there?"

"Not many."

The woman stared past him at the Raven. Dom turned slowly to see what she was looking at. Gettner was now on the door gun and Barber was hauling a couple of ten-liter fuel cans out of the Raven.

"You want my advice?" the woman asked. "Stay on your island. We've survived everything so far—your Hammer of Dawn, the grubs, the glowies—by being small." So everyone called them glowies. Dom decided that was proof they were in contact with the seagoing gangs. "We've got just enough people to keep a tribe going, but not too many when we need to move fast. So if you come back here and try to set up a big-ass city again, you're just going to be a sitting target for the stalks and the glowies with all the legs, and whatever else is coming." She lowered her voice. "'Cause it *is* coming. Now give me my fuel and run on back to your nice little island."

Hoffman seemed to give in pretty fast, almost as if he wanted to get out and something had made up his mind that this was a waste of time. He touched his cap politely. "Much obliged, ma'am. Here's your fuel. High-grade imulsion."

"Yeah, there's a river of the stuff at Descano Hill now," she said. "If you don't mind the glowies."

But she walked up and took the cans like bags of groceries when Barber put them down. Dom was impressed by a woman who could lift two heavy cans that easily. Only the toughest lasted long as Stranded.

Dom moved off cautiously, hoping that Gettner was as good a shot as Barber while they had their backs to the Stranded. But nobody put a round between their shoulder blades. They piled back into the Raven and lifted off.

"Glowies and imulsion again," Marcus said, looking down at the reservoir dwindling beneath them. "You know what Baird would say."

"What do you think, Royston?" Hoffman asked.

"You *know* what I think," Sharle said. "That woman nailed it. Stranded survive because they're small, mobile, hard-to-hit targets. Low resource use, low profile."

"What are you saying?"

"That moving a whole population out here is going to be a lot harder than relocating to Vectes was."

"Yeah. I know."

"We won't find an empty city capable of housing thousands ready for us to move into anyway. We could look at resettling Port Farrall, but that would mean preparing the place before we shifted the whole population, and that would take Gears and resources away from Vectes for months."

"Yeah, but we can't split up into groups of a few thousand," Marcus said. "People are used to a city with organization and specialist defense. They'd have a tough time fending for themselves. Defending a chain of villages would overstretch us."

Hoffman looked at Sharle, then Trescu. These were the guys who were going to make the call. It looked to Dom like they'd had this argument a lot in the last few weeks.

"Then we have to find a way of staying put," Hoffman said. "Because we can't split up and maintain any semblance of a goddamn society."

Trescu just nodded. As the Raven tracked north, Dom could see more stalks inland and some shattered cities that almost looked as if they'd been impaled on them.

The reality was dawning. They could either stay on Vectes and hope the stalks held off, or they could become like those desperate little camps struggling to eke out an existence here. Dom was suddenly scared that they were all talking themselves into it.

"Fuck that, sir," he said. "If we come back we'll end up like the Stranded, so what's it all been for? We could have done that years ago. We needn't have fought to defend anywhere. We could have just run and stayed out of the grubs' way. Maybe a lot more folks would still be alive now."

"I know, Dom." Hoffman took off his cap and rubbed his scalp one-handed. "You think I don't lie awake at night wondering if I've ballsed the whole thing up and wasted lives?"

"Sorry, sir. Yeah. Just frustrated."

The last thing Dom wanted was to make Hoffman feel bad about things that had never been under his control in the first place. He leaned across and patted the old bastard's knee.

If it was a choice between the COG and losing the last few people he cared about, the COG could go screw itself.

COLONEL HOFFMAN'S QUARTERS, VECTES NAVAL BASE: GALE, 15 A.E.

Mac was drinking from the toilet bowl again. Bernie watched him lapping for a while and decided it wouldn't do him any harm as long as Hoffman didn't catch him doing it.

"Where's your table manners?" She rubbed his ears when he came up for air. "Yeah, you're taking advantage of your old mum, aren't you? You're not an invalid anymore. Buck up, soldier."

He looked at her with pitifully sad brown eyes, but then that was how deerhound crosses always looked. It got him a handful of rabbit jerky every time. He chewed it as if he was humoring her and trotted across the room to flop onto Hoffman's bed as if his long legs had finally given way under him.

"I know the feeling, sweetie," she said. "Come on, you can't sleep there. You know Vic goes ballistic. Especially when he's had a bad week."

Mac just stretched out the full length of the mattress and shut his eyes. Bernie went back to the mirror over the washbasin and carried on braiding her hair into rows, but she was so engrossed in the fiddly job of tying them off that she didn't hear Hoffman coming this time, not until he let rip at Mac. He stood in the doorway like he was doing an unannounced kit inspection.

"Come on, *off*!" He snapped his fingers at Mac, but the

dog just opened one eye and decided he didn't really mean it. "Frigging dog hairs all over the place. Bernie, can't you keep this animal off the furniture?"

"He's convalescing."

"My ass. I could get over a heart bypass faster. What are you doing?"

"Plaiting my hair. Keeps it tidy."

"Not a problem I have to wrestle with." Hoffman reached across the basin to inspect his personal bar of soap, a precious commodity in a world without shops. Taken-for-granted groceries had become handmade luxuries. "Goddamn . . . there's dog hairs all over this."

"Sorry."

"And you've been using my razor again."

"Yeah. Sorry, love." It wasn't really about the razor. He'd been ranting ever since he came back from the mainland. He didn't normally hold anything back from her, so she was getting worried. "Do you want to talk about it?"

He picked the dog hairs off the soap with just a little too much concentration. "What, hair? I gave up that stuff a long time ago."

"Come on, Vic. We've both been through a lot worse than this. There's always a fix."

Hoffman put the soap back on the side of the basin and sat down on the bed, ignoring Mac's attempt to slobber over him.

"I like clarity," he said. "It's never been this hard before. Even the Hammer strikes. We were pretty sure what the options were."

"We'll know when to run. You can't make a decision yet. It's probably not even yours to make."

Hoffman smiled ruefully. "See, you always nail it."

"We've had a lot of practice at running, Vic."

"It's different this time."

"Yeah, we're stuck on an island."

"That wasn't what I meant." He braced his elbows on his knees, head bowed. "Sharle's right. If we have to evacuate, then our only chance on the mainland is dispersing in small groups. We'd be spread over a hell of a big area."

"Beats keeping all your eggs in one basket."

"But how do we defend the settlements? How do we stay organized as a state? Who gets the doctors, the Gears, the Ravens? Do we abandon the imulsion field here, or try to keep drilling and shipping the stuff back to the mainland?"

"That's routine stuff, Vic."

"We've always been concentrated in one defensible area before."

He didn't say the word *Stranded*. But that was probably what was getting to him. She understood his fears only too well because she'd been there too. It wasn't just the animosity between the COG and the Hammer strike survivors who felt betrayed and abandoned by it. It was about somehow becoming less than human.

"I survived the worst of it out there on my own," Bernie said. "All I had was a couple of rifles and a knife. A COG made up of villages can make it too."

Hoffman took off his armor and stacked it by the bed. Then he pulled something out of his shirt pocket and handed it to her.

"Sharle's drawn up a list of plans. Everything from staying put here to returning to Port Farrall, to breaking up into five groups or ten or fifty, to living at sea on the ships indefinitely. Lots of options, and none of them good."

Bernie took the folded sheets of paper, still trying to work out why this was hitting him harder than she expected. Perhaps it was cumulative—that he'd had to do so much shit, year upon year, crisis after crisis, and now it had finally reached critical mass and felled him.

"Doesn't that reassure you?" she asked. Her mind was now on the small detail that she understood all too well: food production. How would they divide up the livestock? How would they farm on the mainland?

And how are we going to deploy Gears if we're hundreds of kilometers apart and we don't have enough fuel?

It was starting to sink in. It wasn't the scale of the logistics that was getting to Hoffman. It was people. It was the possibility of a tight-knit family being broken up.

But that wouldn't affect us.

Bernie realized she'd assumed that the *important* people, the people she liked and cared about, would always be together at the heart of this. Delta Squad would always be there, as would Dizzy. Hoffman, Michaelson, Trescu . . . and even Prescott would still be running the show. It was just the civilians who would be affected.

But it wouldn't be that way, and now she knew it. The settlements would need to run themselves and that meant the command would need to be divided too.

"Got any places in mind?" She unfolded the handwritten papers and leafed through them. Sharle's neat draftsman's lettering listed names of places that meant little to her until she saw one out of alphabetical order.

Anvil Gate.

Bernie couldn't imagine many people who wanted to end up there. She wasn't sure if it was possible to know a man too well, but she could certainly think like Hoffman. He'd say it was a pragmatic choice, a place he didn't just know like the back of his hand but that he'd also held under siege, and he would have been right.

And he couldn't get the place out of his system.

She grabbed him in a playful headlock and rubbed her knuckles vigorously on his scalp. She could feel the slight drag of stubble. He didn't even protest.

"You daft old sod," she said. "This is the worst-scenario plan. We could still be here in ten years."

"I prefer to think the worst and get a nice surprise. But I'm still waiting for one of those."

"Well, there's me. You weren't expecting to see me alive again."

"That's true." He nodded, staring past her at nothing in particular. "You'd come to Anvil Gate with me, right? Even if it meant losing contact with your buddies?"

She hadn't really thought that through, but the answer was automatic. "Goes without saying."

"I thought it was best to check."

"But I keep the dog."

"Sure. I know where I fit in the pecking order." He was trying to make a joke of it all but he'd never been much good at that. He took off his holster belt, draped it over a chair, and vanished into the cramped bathroom to run the shower. "Shit. I'm sorry, Bernie. Just venting. It might never come to that, but you have to think the unthinkable."

She went on braiding her hair. Mac scrambled off the bed and sat by the door, looking at it expectantly. "I know. Look, I'm taking a patrol out to see if we can find Seb Edlar's animals. We're going to need them. Promise me you won't have hysterics if I'm late back."

She heard the soap drop on the shower tray, then nothing except for the hammering water.

"Vic?" The water stopped and he was so quiet that she wondered if he'd collapsed. He was a heart attack kind of bloke. "Vic? You okay?"

"Goddamn, just like the old days. Just remembering the last time I stood in a shower telling someone . . . telling Margaret that the world was going to rat-shit, that's all."

Bernie could gauge where he'd reached on the despair scale now—the final days before Prescott decided to deploy the Hammer. He hadn't even told his wife the strikes were coming until he was allowed to. She knew he despised himself for that.

"You can talk about her, Vic," Bernie said. "You can say her name. Don't shut out the dead, or else you erase them."

"Okay. I won't have hysterics." He was still sidestepping the issue. "Who are you taking?"

"Girls' day out," she said. "Anya and Sam. And Alex Brand. She says she's getting skills fade."

"Two sergeants on one patrol." Hoffman emerged, toweling his back. "Two women in a kitchen."

"Marcus and I manage it."

"Yeah. But he's Marcus." He tried to ruffle her hair, thwarted by the unfamiliar braids, and settled for a peck on the cheek instead. "See you later, babe. Don't take any stupid risks for a few cows."

She picked up her Longshot. "We're just doing girls' stuff. Bringing back the groceries."

Mac perked up and trotted after her. He wasn't terrific on steep stairs. Here was a dog that would fight polyps and take down armed Stranded, but needed a bit of encouragement to walk down flights of steps. No, that was unfair. He actually seemed to be limping this time. When they got to the ground floor, Bernie examined his paws. He flinched and whimpered.

"Okay, maybe you're not swinging the lead," she said. "You want to stay behind and take a nap? Vic won't mind. Then I'll get Doc Hayman to take a look at you when I get back."

She gestured up the stairs, but he sat gazing at her, looking a little martyred. He wanted to stick with his mum. She gave him a piece of rabbit and he trotted after her across the parade ground.

Sam was loading the Packhorse with Alex Brand while Anya sat on the tailgate, poring over recon images. Mac snuffled on the photographs and then squeezed past her to jump into the back.

"Ooh, like the hair, Sarge," Sam said. Alex looked up and frowned. "Very South Islands."

Bernie did a twirl. "Everybody ready for the roundup?"

"Shouldn't we take the farmer along? Don't cows recognize people?"

"They do. But I don't want to take a skittish civvie back into the contaminated zone." Bernie reached into the Packhorse and pulled out a small sack of cattle nuts. "This is doggie treats for cows. Shake this bag at them and you're their friend for life."

"I'm not going to pretend I'm confident about this. Goats—fine. Cows—scary. And there's a bull, too."

"We might just find chunks if they've run into polyps." Bernie opened the driver's door. "And don't forget we've got two missing dogs as well. Now, I've got to move one of the herd before we go, so let's familiarize ourselves with basic cow recognition. Everyone knows what a cow looks like, don't they?"

Alex climbed into the back seat with Sam. "I think so, Mataki," she said. She had a half-smoked cigar tucked in the rolled cuff of her sleeve and her hair was dyed a vivid red. Bernie wasn't sure what she used to keep it that color but it had to be a wild plant dye. If she'd found it herself, that was a survival skill of sorts. There was hope for the girl yet. "I'd better get a steak out of this."

Bernie didn't know Alex well, but she knew that Baird hated her guts, and that was enough to make her wary. For a moment, Bernie felt a pang of uneasiness at being among strangers. She was used to deploying with certain people, Gears she staked her life on, and all she could think about was how hard it would be to be separated from them even if Hoffman was with her.

For fuck's sake. After all this, after all I've survived, and I'm scared of change that'll save my life.

Bernie had survived two wars. She'd fought the grubs back in the Islands, she'd sailed halfway around Sera, she'd been raped, she'd nearly starved to death, and she'd killed Stranded out of revenge. It was hard to believe that there was anything left to scare her at this stage of her life, but she was back where she belonged and she didn't want to leave. Place had nothing to do with it. It was all about people.

The Packhorse wove through a crowded naval base that now reminded Bernie far too much of a Stranded encampment. An overwhelming need to rejoin the COG army had sent her on a terrible journey across Sera, and fear of descending into savagery like the Stranded she encountered along the way had kept her going, even when it would have been so easy to just lay down and die.

God. What's going to be left of us?

Anya tapped the back of her hand discreetly as it rested on the gear lever. "Are you okay, Bernie?"

"Just getting old, ma'am."

"Not you. You're indestructible. Mom always said so."

So was the COG. It had always felt permanent, embedded in history, the invincible world power. There'd been tough times, but the COG went on regardless and even a global war spanning generations couldn't bring it to its knees. Now it was cowering on a remote island, clinging to an old enemy for comfort. How long had it actually existed? A century, that was all. It was just a blink in the history of Sera.

Everything had its time.

"Yeah, I'm good at survival," Bernie said. "I've even got a badge to say so."

Every person on this island was a survivor. Everyone here

was alive despite the grubs or the Hammer strike or both. Bernie tried not to think about the vast majority of people across Sera, the billions who had simply done the ordinary, inevitable thing and died.

CHAPTER 14

Either we save who we can, what we can, and preserve humankind, or we do the equitable thing and let everyone share extinction. It's my call.

(Chairman Richard Prescott, informing Dr. Adam Fenix of
his intention to deploy the Hammer of Dawn
on Sera's cities, one year after E-Day)

**BRABAIO, SOUTHWEST INGAREZ: 30TH DAY OF
BLOOM, JUST OVER A YEAR AFTER E-DAY,
FOURTEEN YEARS EARLIER.**

"I don't wanna beg," Dizzy said. "I wanna work. I'm a marine engineer. I fix ships. Goddamn it, I got my *certification*."

The guy on the dock gates had the kind of clean shirt and neat haircut that only someone with a proper home could have. Dizzy had lived out of his kit bag for the last year, moving and being moved from one refugee center to the next. He knew he didn't look much like a skilled man with a trade.

"Look, nobody's hiring." The guy seemed embarrassed. "Half the merchant fleet's gone. The government's running what's left. I'm really sorry."

"Hell, I'll clean lavatories, then. Whatever you got."

Dizzy tried hard not to sound like a bum. "I got a pregnant wife to take care of."

Wife. Well, they weren't married, not all formal like, but Rosalyn was expecting, and whether Dizzy had planned that or not he had the same responsibilities as any father-to-be.

He owed Rosalyn. She'd stopped him feeling that sick dread when he woke up every morning and wished he hadn't because he had nothing left. He'd found a purpose again. She'd given it to him.

The guy rummaged in his pocket and pulled out a crumpled fifty. "I get a hundred people a day asking the same thing. Here, get yourself something to eat." He looked down at his shoes. "It's not charity, okay? Don't be offended."

Dizzy was pretty sure it *was* charity, but he took the bill anyway and mumbled his thanks before walking away. He wouldn't tell Rosalyn he'd scrounged it. A woman had to believe her man had some dignity left, even in a world where most every street or city was a wasteland.

I'm a COG citizen. We're Tyrans. We're not foreigners looking for handouts. What did I do wrong?

It was nobody's fault. The grubs had caused it. But that didn't make it any easier to bear.

Dizzy decided to leave it a while before going back to the squat and telling Rosalyn he hadn't found work yet. That was another taken-for-granted thing that he missed—knowing he had somewhere that he needed to be. He'd go to work, or come home, or wake up for his watch on board ship, but all of those things had vanished overnight. He was only one of millions of displaced people being shunted from one shelter to another. That was the government's word for it, *displaced:* now he understood how right that word was. There was no place for refugees, not just because nobody wanted them for neighbors—although the assholes didn't, he knew—but also because they didn't want to end up like them. Losing everything looked contagious.

He glanced across the road at a well-dressed man and a small boy who didn't look like they had anywhere special to go either. The man had a tight hold on the boy's hand, like he'd already lost someone he loved and was making damned sure he didn't lose his son. Dizzy could tell the locals from the displaced who'd been dumped on their doorstep, no matter how well-off they seemed. They all had that same look: guilt, awkwardness, and confusion.

He could see a bar now. Yeah, he knew there'd be one down here. He paused at the door for a couple of seconds before he went in, putting different thoughts in his head so he didn't automatically look like a reminder that the world was losing the war. The place was crowded. Bars always were lately. Folks clung together for comfort. Dizzy glanced at the big TV on the wall as he paid for a beer and a chaser with his small change—hell, not the fifty, that was for Rosalyn—and decided he didn't need to watch the news anymore. What was it going to tell him that he didn't already know? The COG wasn't winning. Nobody was. It was just a matter of which city had been hit today and how many more were dead.

A couple of drinkers glanced at him but looked away again, more interested in the bulletin. He found a quiet corner and started on his beer. There was an art to spinning it out so that the numbness settled on him gradually.

Yeah, he was getting pretty good at this. He let the sound of the TV and the burble of conversation wash over him for an hour until he reached the point of nodding off.

"Everybody, shut *up*!" The barman's voice shook him. "Listen! It's the Chairman! This is *important*!"

The bar went quieter than a funeral parlor. Dizzy half-listened, not that he was expecting any news that was going to matter a damn to him and Rosalyn. The last time he'd seen a bar hang on every word like this was when the TV showed the Grayson Cup final, Cougars versus Sharks, except people were excited about that. They sure weren't excited now. Dizzy wondered if the drink was messing with his ears.

"To ensure your safety and cooperation, we are reinstating the Fortification Act. All of Sera will be under martial law. No one is exempt. Survivors should immediately start evacuating to Ephyra—"

"What the fuck?" someone said.

"Shush! Quiet!" The barman turned the volume up full. "Just *listen!*"

Prescott was standing on some platform, all nice and neat in his suit with microphones lined up in front of him thicker than a fence. He'd only been doing the job for a couple of months since Dalyell died. Dizzy hoped he knew what he was doing.

"—therefore, in Jacinto, we are safe—for now. We won't let this rampage go further or surrender power. The Coalition will employ Sera's entire arsenal of orbital beam weapons to scorch all Locust-infested areas. For those citizens who cannot make it to Jacinto, the Coalition appreciates your sacrifice—"

Dizzy didn't hear the next bit. The bar erupted.

"What did he say? *What did he say?*"

"Bastards!"

"Is he fucking serious? He's going fry COG cities? *Us?*"

"No, they can't *do* that to us!"

People were yelling and swearing, the barman was trying to tune to another channel, and a couple of people just left their drinks and ran for the door. Two men got into an argument about who had gotten to the public phone first. Dizzy sat bewildered, wishing he hadn't had that drink and thinking he'd heard all wrong. He got up and grabbed the arm of the nearest person to him, a young woman in a neat business suit.

"Ma'am, what *was* that? What did he say?"

She was shaking her head like she was about to have some kind of fit. She looked straight through Dizzy, but she did answer him.

"They're going to burn the cities," she said. "They're going to burn us all. We've got three days to get to Jacinto. How the hell are we all going to fit into Jacinto? How the hell are we even going to *get* there in time?"

Dizzy found himself sober in a heartbeat, rushing from the bar and running hell for leather up the road back to the squat. All he could think about was grabbing Rosalyn and getting out. Jacinto? Three days? The government would lay on transport. They *had* to. The COG wouldn't do that to its own people, would it? Not after what the grubs had done to everyone. It *couldn't.*

For those citizens who cannot make it to Jacinto, the Coalition appreciates your sacrifice.

No, he was wrong. His own government *was* going to kill him, and Rosalyn, and everyone else outside Jacinto.

His lungs were screaming for air. But he couldn't stop. There was a terrible *uh-hah-uh-hah* noise following him like a dog, and then he realized it was coming from *him,* his own gasping breaths. There were people everywhere, but they blurred into a streak of color and sound that didn't matter anymore. He heard a car horn blare in his ear—hell, had he just run right across a road?—and reached the doors of the abandoned car dealership.

The refugees shouldn't have been in there, but nobody cared. Brabaio's refugee shelters were full. If people found their own place to sleep, that was fine by city hall. Dizzy's legs felt like rubber as he ran up the stairs at the back of the showroom and almost fell over the bedding left by two other families who'd camped on the floor. The whole place was weirdly silent. The high office windows were soundproofed. None of the noise from the panicking city got through.

"Rosalyn, grab your stuff." He could hardly get the words out. He gulped in air. Rosalyn was sitting on a box reading a single sheet of newspaper. "Sweetie, we gotta go. We gotta get out, right *now*."

"What's wrong?"

"They're going to use the Hammer of Dawn," he gasped. "We've got three days to get to Jacinto. We'll be safe there. Come on. Come *on*."

He could tell she didn't believe him. "Dizzy, that can't be right. Have you had a drink?"

"Damn it, sweetie, I'm not drunk. It's true." He grabbed the sleeping bag and began rolling it up. "They're gonna fry the place to stop the grubs. It's on the news. Look out the window."

Rosalyn grabbed the box and hauled it against the wall to step up and peer out.

"It's all traffic," she said. "Oh . . . the police are out there stopping the cars."

"Yeah, because everyone's going crazy."

"God. It's true, isn't it?"

"Just start packing. Come *on*."

Dizzy's pulse was pounding hard in his ears. Rosalyn kept trying to ask questions, but he grabbed her by the hand and they stumbled out into the street clutching all they owned: a merchant navy kit bag and a bright red hitchhiker's rucksack.

"Dizzy, *stop*!" She dug in her heels, nearly jerking his arm out of its socket. "How are we going to get to Tyrus, let alone Jacinto? We're a *thousand kilometers* away."

"I've got money," he said. *Fifty bucks.* That wasn't going to get them to the next city by bus, let alone cover a long train journey across the border. "We'll buy tickets."

"Everyone's going to be doing the same thing, Dizzy."

He pulled her arm harder than he intended to. She flinched. "Sweetie, you wanna stay here and wait to die? Do you? We got a baby on the way. I lost Lena and Richie, and I ain't gonna lose anyone else, *ever*."

It was a couple of kilometers to the nearest rail station. If they'd had a bus ticket or a car, it wouldn't have been any use to them now. The roads were gridlocked. The only way out was on foot.

When they got to the road to the station, there was a vehicle checkpoint in place manned by Gears and civil police. Dizzy tried to walk through—hell, he wasn't a damn car— but one of the police officers blocked his way, arms spread.

"Sorry, sir. You can't come through."

"We just wanna buy a train ticket," Dizzy said. He'd worry about how far fifty bucks was going to take them later. Maybe the Hammer wouldn't hit all the cities. It couldn't hit the whole world, could it? There'd still be somewhere safe. "My wife's expecting."

The officer glanced at Rosalyn. She definitely looked pregnant now. But it wasn't going to change a thing.

"They've shut the station, sir." The officer was a nice young man, no older than Richie, and he treated Dizzy with respect. But he still wasn't giving way. "IngaRail's not taking any bookings. Their switchboard's jammed and we've had to shut the concourse to clear the passengers already in there. I'm really sorry."

"When's it gonna be open again?"

"I don't know. Come back tomorrow, maybe, when everyone's calmed down."

Calm down? Shit, what was he talking about? Nobody was going to calm down after news like that. Dizzy turned around and steered Rosalyn away. They'd have to find somewhere to sit down and think of another way out.

"God, what are we going to do?" she asked, clinging to his arm. "How are we going to get to Jacinto?"

"We'll make it, sweetie." Dizzy squeezed her arm tight under his. "I won't let anything happen to you or the baby."

"Might be *babies*," she said. "Twins run in my family."

"Then I got even more reason to save you, ain't I?"

They walked down the road. It was getting harder with every block they crossed as the news sank in, and more people came onto the streets without any idea of how millions of COG citizens were going to cross mountains, oceans, and continents and cram into a small, safe part of a distant capital city.

A big bearded guy was sitting alone at a table in a deserted pavement cafe, ignoring the river of panic flowing around him. Dizzy decided it was a good place to stop and think.

"You're not trying to leave?" Rosalyn asked the man.

He smiled at her and sipped his coffee. "Crazy. They'll never use the Hammer. It's just to scare the grubs. Don't you worry about it, ma'am. Don't you worry at all."

EXCLUSION ZONE CHECKPOINT, NORTH OF JACINTO: TEN HOURS BEFORE THE HAMMER OF DAWN STRIKE.

"He's going to frigging *do* it." Baird stared across the park, squinting into the sun even though he had a pair of goggles parked on the top of his head. That guy was never going to wear a helmet, no matter how many charges Iron Balls stuck him on. "I mean, he's actually going to *do* it. *Wow.* If I ever meet the asshole, I'm going to ask him how long he'd been planning *that* shockeroo."

"Yeah, like Prescott's gonna drop by for a chat," Cole said. "Anyway, he's only been in office like *weeks*. Two months, tops."

"Yeah, Dalyell would never have had the balls to go the whole way. But he would have had the plan, right? That Hammer net cost us as much as Ostri's national debt, probably, so they didn't shoot *that* into orbit just to improve TV reception. Y'know, I've changed my mind. I'd like to meet that Adam Fenix instead. Now *there's* a clever guy. I mean, how many weapons engineers do the public actually know *by name*? He's the poster boy for intelligent people everywhere."

"Yeah, Baird. We'll add him to our dinner party guest list."

Cole liked Baird. Baird was his closest buddy now, a plain-talking guy who didn't suck up to him because he was a thrashball star or take pops at him because he was rich and famous. He just treated Cole like a regular human being. But sometimes Cole just wished he would shut the fuck up.

Like now. This was a dirty, nasty, rotten war, and Cole was fine with dirty and nasty as long as he was doing it to grubs. That was what he'd signed up for, to kill as many of the murdering assholes as he could. What he hadn't signed up to do was help humans fry other humans.

And that's gonna happen in about ten hours or so.

We're gonna kill our own kind.

Baird didn't mean any harm, Cole knew. He was just yapping because he was scared—hell, who wasn't?—and he couldn't take in all this Hammer shit, not even a smart guy like him. But Cole was unwilling to do his job, the first time he could remember *not* wanting to do something hard since his math homework.

It just wasn't right to close the border while there were people still out there trying to get to Jacinto. Hell, it wasn't even a *national* border. They were in Tyrus, part of the same damn state. It was just the Plateau district limits. What did a Tyran passport mean if folks couldn't move around in their own country?

Kilo Squad—Cole, Baird, Dickson, and Alonzo—were patrolling the off-ramp from the southbound highway. Traffic from Port Farrall was backed up as far as Cole could see and the city engineers said they couldn't handle any more traffic trying to join at this junction. Cole had thought this was just a traffic cops' job until he got his boots on the ground.

Scared, desperate people needed armed Gears to stop them doing something dumb. And Cole hated himself for being the one who had to do it.

He stood at the barrier with his Lancer, turning back cars and trucks. He'd even turned back a motorcycle because the engineers said *nothing*, no more traffic, not even a kid's push-bike. Shit, a motorcycle wasn't going to get in anyone's way. It could weave through the traffic jam. But if he let one through, then everyone else would want to get on the highway too, and they'd have a riot as well as a traffic jam.

I'm telling people they gotta die 'cause we got no more room. Me. Did someone stop my folks driving down a road to escape from the grubs?

The queue of vehicles for the on-ramp was gone now. Drivers had done U-turns and gone off to find another route into Jacinto, but there wasn't one. Cole tried not to look them in the eye because that was *real* personal. He knew he was turning them back just to get stuck somewhere else when the Hammer went off.

"Baird, this Hammer thing." Alonzo sidled over to Baird, chewing his lip like he always did when he was getting agitated. "Is it going to zap *everything*? Like, how far does it affect outside a city? Okay, you're going to be fucked sideways if you're in the center of town, but what about the suburbs? Or the countryside?"

Baird was staring south toward Jacinto, Lancer resting on his shoulder. "How the hell should I know? It's classified."

"Well, you're the technical guy. You're *intelligent.*"

"Thanks for noticing. But I still don't know. Better believe what Prescott says—if you value your ass, head for the Ephyran plateau." He shrugged. "Which is where we are, more or less. Hey, look at all those Ravens over the city. Never seen that many."

Cole knew that Baird wasn't fascinated by Ravens down in Jacinto. He had his back to the endless lanes of stationary traffic for a reason. He didn't want to look the drivers in the face either. They were a road-width away and at the wrong angle to make eye contact, but that was still too close for him.

"Dickson, did the engineers say anything about us closin' the highway?" Cole asked.

"No, and I hope they don't ask us. You want to go out there and put a DO NOT CROSS tape in front of some poor jerk's car now?"

"Yeah, that's why the cops fucked off and left it to the army," Baird muttered. "Because it's going to get ugly pretty fast when those guys down there work out that most of them have found their parking space for the Great Hereafter."

"What?"

"Do the math, Dick."

"Don't call me that, Baird."

"Okay, do the math, *Dick*son." Baird did an about-face and pointed north. "The engineers are giving us the traffic speeds, if you call one klick per hour *speed*. Unless those unlucky citizens over there start moving in the next four hours, then those back there—about where the radio mast is—are going to be barbecue. They might as well get out and walk. You think we should share that with them? 'Cause I think that'll be a *really* interesting social experiment."

That shut everybody up. There was one question nobody

had asked yet, and that was whether anybody had family still stuck outside the zone. Cole didn't, and he knew Baird didn't, but Dickson and Alonzo never said a word either way. And everybody was going to lose friends.

Hanover. Hanover's probably gonna take a hit. Where's Gaynor now? Where's Mortensen?

There was nothing Cole could do about it, so he tried to put it out of his head. He was staring down the on-ramp, trying to accept that there really was nothing anyone could do, when he saw a scruffy passenger van turn onto the ramp and edge slowly toward the checkpoint.

"Ah, shit," Baird said. "This isn't your lucky day, asshole."

He started to walk to the barrier but Cole slipped in front of him. As soon as the driver looked his way, Cole knew he was going to face the hardest decision of his life. It was just some guy in his thirties, balding and anxious, with a woman and a teenage boy. But he wasn't some faceless blur in passing traffic, or a number in a newspaper report that Cole knew was tragic but didn't grieve for. He was an individual, right here and right now.

The guy rolled down the driver's side window and looked at Cole as if he was his last hope in the world, which he actually was.

"Sir, the highway ain't goin' nowhere," Cole said.

Cole wanted him to give up the idea there and then, to look disappointed and reverse back down the ramp without being asked. That would have made it a bit easier to live with. But he didn't. The guy just slumped a little in his seat. Cole saw Baird moving in from the corner of his eye and held out his hand to stop him.

"We've driven for fifty-four hours," the driver said quietly. "I live in Jacinto and my wife's there. This is my sister and her boy. Is there another way into the city?"

It would have been easy to say there was, and to send the

guy down the ring road, but it would have been more honest to shoot him and save him what was coming. Cole knew he had to deal with this if he was ever going to get a night's sleep again.

"No, sir. It's all at a standstill."

The teenage kid leaned forward behind the driver and said something. Cole heard the whispered words *Cole Train*.

"Damn," the driver said, distracted for a moment. "You're the thrashball player, aren't you? Nice to meet you, Mr. Cole."

"Yeah, I'm Augustus Cole, sir."

The man looked embarrassed. Goddamn, he meant it. Cole wanted to disappear. How the hell could he turn this guy back? It wasn't anything to do with being recognized. It was a *human* thing, human to human, and if this war was about anything it was about stopping humans from getting killed.

"You wait a sec, sir," Cole said, and turned around.

Baird wouldn't look straight at the vehicle. He turned his head away and stood up close to Cole.

"Cole, no," he murmured. "No, no, *no*."

"So what you gonna do, Baird? You gonna do it by the book and send 'em back?"

"You going to pull back the barrier and start a *riot*?"

"I gotta live with myself, baby."

"We *all* have. Yeah, even me. But orders are there so we don't waste time and second-guess shit, and do things that look like a great idea but screw up other things we're not aware of. It's *not our call*."

"He's gonna die. And his sister, and his nephew."

Baird spread his hands. "Cole, this is like being a wildlife photographer. You have to stand back. You dive in and save the gazelle, but the lioness doesn't get her dinner and her cute little cubs starve to death."

"This ain't funny, Damon." Cole only called him that when he thought Baird was getting out of line. His momma called him Augustus when she was mad with him, never Gus, and the habit stuck. "That ain't funny at all."

"Okay, you let them through because they're the ones in front of you looking appealing and sad, and someone else further back in the frigging traffic queue *doesn't* make it. Only they're not in your face and you don't see them. You feel any better about that? Maybe they've got sweet cherubic little kiddies and nice sisters too."

"Yeah, but these folks *are* in front of me!" Cole knew Baird was right but it didn't help any. It still tore him up. "I seen 'em! They've talked to me and they've called me Mr. Cole. Goddamn it, how can I do all that common sense and logic shit to 'em when they've looked me in the eye?"

Baird just shrugged in defeat. Cole walked the few meters up to the main highway and looked down the line of traffic nearest to him. If that pickup moved right up to the next guy's fender, and the car behind reversed as far as he could, they could let that van in. Cole rapped on the pickup's side window.

"Sir, can I ask you to move forward? I'll tell you when to stop."

The driver looked surprised. He had that I-know-you-from-somewhere look. "Sure," he said. Cole watched him edge forward and knocked the hood when he was almost touching the vehicle in front. Then he waved the car behind back and created a van-sized gap, more or less. At least the nose would get in and make sure the family got into the line.

"You're off your head," Alonzo said. "We're going to get lynched."

"Yeah." Cole moved the barrier and beckoned the van forward. "You get your ass in there, sir, and don't tell anyone, hear?"

The pickup driver in front leaned out of his window and looked back. "How come he's allowed in?"

It was barefaced-lying time. *Okay, Momma, you know I gotta do this. Sorry. It's not like I'm lyin' to save my own ass.* Cole drew himself up to his full height. He was even bigger than most people realized when he was looming right over them.

"Medical personnel," he said flatly. "The hospitals are callin' in all off-duty nursin' staff. We're gonna be needin' 'em."

The pickup driver swallowed it whole and gave him a thumbs-up. Hell, who'd call the Cole Train a liar? It was hard to see what was going on in a line of traffic in a six-lane highway. The driver behind the van had seen the pickup guy approve of what Cole had done, and nobody else reacted.

"Let's put another barrier at the start of the ramp," Cole said. "'Cause I can't keep doin' that."

"Yeah, you said it." Baird trotted after him and they pushed a couple of abandoned cars sideways across the ramp so nobody was tempted to try to drive up it again. Then they walked back up to the barrier and stood looking south to Jacinto.

"How bad is it gonna be, Baird?" Cole asked. "The Hammer strikes, I mean."

"Really frigging terrible," Baird said quietly, and patted him on the back. "Terrible."

INGAREZ-TYRUS BORDER: ONE HOUR BEFORE THE HAMMER STRIKE.

It didn't matter. It just didn't matter anymore.

Dizzy and Rosalyn were hundreds of miles from Jacinto but even if it had been twenty, they'd run out of time along with hundreds of millions of others who never stood a chance from the moment Prescott made his goddamn announcement.

"That's it." Rosalyn had slowed to a walk again. Dizzy didn't have the heart to chivvy her along any further. "We're stranded here. We're not going to make it, Dizzy."

"We got an hour, sweetie." They were thirty kilometers from the nearest small town, walking along a country road lit by occasional sodium lights. "And we're gonna be okay. We ain't gonna get hit."

"Honey, don't humor me. Everyone's got their time. I should have died in Halvo."

"Don't talk crap, sweetie. You were meant to live and I was meant to find you. Keep going. We're gonna be alive tomorrow, I swear it."

Dizzy wished with every bone in his body that it would happen, but he was staring into a void. Even if they didn't get burned to death, what was the world going to be like with so many people dead and every big city destroyed?

He tried to imagine it. He couldn't. He knew what heavily bombed cities looked like, though, and how they burned. He'd seen stuff from the early Pendulum Wars. The Hammer of Dawn was a hell of a lot bigger than that; the Indies had finally surrendered because they'd seen what just one low-power Hammer strike did to their fleet. He caught hold of Rosalyn's hand again and carried on down the road.

From time to time he saw a car dumped at an angle, like a flood had carried it along and dropped it any old where. Folks had abandoned their vehicles in some crazy positions. Dizzy looked at every single one to see if any had keys left in them.

If they did, then he stopped to try the ignition, but so far they'd all run out of gas. He and Rosalyn weren't planning on going anywhere special now. They were just putting as much distance between them and the city that would probably be a fireball in just over an hour.

How far would the blast spread? Dizzy knew enough to

realize that fires like that meant ferocious firestorms, but he didn't know how far away was safe. So they kept going.

He tried another car. This time, it started.

"Okay, sweetie, let's see how far this gets us," he said, feeling his heart leap. *We'll make it.* "You feelin' okay?"

"Just hungry."

"I'll find something. Don't worry. And lock your door—I seen some bad stuff in some of the ports I've called at, and that ain't gonna happen to us, not now."

"People have been pretty good to each other so far," she said, pressing down the tab on the door with a clunk.

"That's gonna change if everything gets burned to charcoal, sweetie." Dizzy drove cautiously along the road, keeping an eye out for anywhere he might find some food and water. "Check what's in the back, will ya? We might be lucky again."

Rosalyn twisted in the seat and groped around on the back seat. "Empty water bottle," she said.

"Now that's gonna save our lives."

"Yeah? How?"

"Gotta carry water. That'll be harder than finding it."

The car kept going. Dizzy checked his watch, glad that he hadn't traded it for something, and saw they had twenty minutes left.

He could hardly bear to look at it because he didn't know if it meant he only had twenty minutes left to live. It made it hard to think straight. He had to forget about supplies now and concentrate on finding some shelter, some kind of protection for Rosalyn, because he didn't know if the Hammer strikes were going to scatter debris and shit around, or if the blast was going to blind folks if they saw it. There might even be shockwaves. They had to find somewhere solid to hide.

The last thing that crossed his mind was running into grubs. They scared him a lot less than his own government now.

How could they do it to us?

How could they just give us three days?

They know everyone's gonna die. The bastards are killing us off.

He'd been a hardworking, law-abiding fella all his life and paid his taxes. His stepson had served as a Gear and died doing it, died defending people the way the COG was supposed to. And all that ordinary folks got for their trouble was *this*. They'd been left to die while the folks in Jacinto, the rich capital, were going to be safe on their granite plateau behind their barriers.

Our government's doing more than abandoning us. They're killing more of us than the damn grubs have.

Now he had ten minutes, either ten minutes left with Rosalyn and his unborn child, or ten minutes left to find a way of surviving all this.

"There's a store," Rosalyn said. "It's shut. Looks like someone got there before us."

Dizzy screeched to a halt. Rosalyn saw a looted store, but he saw a bomb shelter and a source of stuff he could rip out and use to survive in the weeks and months to come. He hit the brakes and pulled up a safe distance from the front of the place. He didn't want to surprise anyone and get his head bashed in now.

The place looked deserted. A couple of strip lights flickered at the back above the refrigerators. There were empty boxes scattered outside, but he couldn't see any damage to the store.

"Maybe the owners cleared the place and ran," Rosalyn said.

"You stay in the car and keep the doors locked, sweetie."

Dizzy went to the trunk and took out the tire iron. He'd never broken into a building before or so much as taken candy from a store as a kid. But all goddamn bets were off now. The government had broken the rules of decent folk, so he would break the law with a clear conscience.

He had five minutes until the end of the world.

It took him a couple of practice swings to break in. The idea of glass shards flying around made him nervous, which suddenly made him start to laugh.

They're gonna fry every city on Sera in a few minutes, and I'm worried about goddamn broken glass?

He swung for real and the window cracked. It took a second swing to crack it again, and then a third brought the whole pane crashing down.

He ran back to the car and helped Rosalyn out, then took everything he could grab from it—a blanket and some tools in the trunk—before locking it again and bundling them both through the shattered window.

Three minutes. We're not gonna die, you assholes. We refuse to die.

"The power's on," Dizzy said. "Switch all the lights on as you go. No point falling over stuff in the dark." He steered her toward the back of the store and found a stockroom. "Wait there."

He had two minutes now. He raced around the shelves, looking for anything he could find, and scooped up candy bars and packets of cookies strewn around the floor. He found a couple of bottles of soda behind the cash desk with a bottle of liquor, both opened. That'd do. Hygiene was the least of their worries right then. He went back to the stockroom to give Rosalyn the looted stuff and found her in another back room next to it, filling the water bottle and a couple of buckets.

"The water's probably going to get cut off if the pumping stations get hit," she said.

"That's my smart girl," Dizzy said. "We got a minute. Come on, get on the floor and cover your head."

It was the dumbest advice he'd ever given anyone. He didn't know what the hell was going to happen. *I used to be an engineer. I used to keep imulsion tankers running. I can use my head.* He lay across Rosalyn to protect her from things he couldn't even imagine and shut his eyes.

"I love you, sweetie," he said. "And we're not gonna die."

He held his breath and counted. His watch must have been fast because there was nothing at all for another minute, and for a stupid moment or two he thought it had all been some stunt to fool the grubs. The government wasn't going to use the Hammer at all.

"Dizzy, if we—"

That was as far as Rosalyn got. Even with the door shut, Dizzy saw the pure white light flare through the cracks in the panel. A few seconds later, there was a distant booming roar that seemed to go on forever. He kept his head down and waited for a blast front to hit, but it never came.

The light was still there. When he raised his head a little, he could see it was coming from gaps around the door and from the dim overhead lighting. Somehow, the electricity supply was still working.

"Sweetie, you okay?"

"Is that it, Dizzy? Have they just started?"

"I don't know."

The roof didn't cave in. There were no flames and he couldn't smell smoke. He wasn't in pain. He could hear a train coming, though, but they were nowhere near a rail track. He knew, because he'd tried so damned hard to get them a ride out.

"It's a tornado," Rosalyn said. "It's coming this way."

"Can't be," Dizzy said.

She was almost right. It was a ferocious wind. It roared around the building and shook the doors and security grilles, and then it was gone as fast as it came.

They lay there for a while waiting for . . . what? Dizzy didn't know. He eased himself up on one arm and listened. He thought he could hear distant booming like artillery fire, but it didn't sound as if there was anything happening nearby.

Rosalyn sat up. "It's over."

"Can't bank on that."

Suddenly the lights went out and the background hum that Dizzy hadn't noticed before stopped dead. The power had finally failed. The hum had probably been the refrigeration or air-conditioning. Dizzy and Rosalyn sat there in the darkness, watching faint yellow light creeping under the door until he decided to get up and open it.

Even from the back of the small store, he could see that the skyline was a wall of red flame. He could smell smoke and something acrid like tar on the air.

"Let's stay put until it gets light," he said. "Too damn dangerous to wander around out there at the moment. Maybe there'll be army patrols around."

"What can you see?"

"Just fires. It's all a long way away. Don't you worry about it, sweetie. You feelin' okay?"

"Yes," she said. "I'm just scared."

He sat down again and Rosalyn put her head in his lap. She dozed off a long time before he did. But eventually he couldn't keep his eyes open any longer, and his head started to nod.

It was the light that woke him. It didn't seem to be coming from anywhere in particular this time. It was just very bright, almost like a sunny day but cool and white instead of golden. He shook Rosalyn awake and got to his feet.

"Must be a patrol," he said. "Leave 'em to me, sweetie, I'll explain."

"There's no cars out there," she said sleepily. "That's snow."

"What is?"

"That weird light. Haven't you ever woken up to snow-fall? It's all the reflected white light."

It was the end of Bloom, high summer. It wouldn't snow for months. Dizzy didn't want to see what he was going to find out there, but he had to know because they couldn't stay in here forever. He opened the door and found Rosalyn was right about a few things.

There wasn't any patrol vehicle, and the sky was overcast. It looked like winter. It even felt chilly.

He picked his way through the broken shelving and glass, realizing that the feast he thought he'd found last night was just a handful of candy bars and other junk. Even when he got to the front door, he still couldn't work out what he was seeing.

It was pale, but it wasn't snow.

It crunched under his boots as he walked down the deserted road, just a thin layer of the stuff, and it was whirl-ing in the air like a snowstorm was just starting, but it wasn't snow.

It was ash. He could taste it.

Even before he reached the ash-frosted trees and got a clear look at the landscape to the south, he could see the palls of smoke hanging like ladders up to the sky. Then he saw the horizon and a red glow that wasn't sunrise. He could pick out distant skylines now.

There were no buildings that he could identify, not a damn thing. He knew what should have been there, more or less, and it just wasn't there anymore.

Heels clattered on the road behind him, getting closer. Rosalyn trotted up behind him. He felt her hand search for his and grab it like she was afraid of falling.

The towns and cities had simply gone. What was left was burning. He couldn't hear any sound at all; not a bird, not a distant car, not even an emergency siren. Rosalyn took a deep gulping breath.

"Oh, God," she said. "What have they done? What the hell have they *done?*"

CHAPTER 15

SITREP #37D

Extent of contaminated zones and stalk ingress at 0001/G/12/15

NEW STALK INCURSIONS since 0001/G/11: 9

POLYPS: Not detected.

BEDROCK DISTRIBUTION: Sedimentary: 3. Metamorphic: 0. Igneous: 6

Current SOUTHERN extent of CZ: 12 km approx. northeast of New Jacinto, grids Delta 6/Echo 6. Other CZs by grid: see Appendix 5. Rate of spread: variable, slowing. Last 26 hours: 5cm approx. per hour.

Action: Four-hour monitoring to continue. Evacuation contingency team to remain on one-hour alert.

(Prepared by: Major G. Gettner and R. Sharle, 12th day of Gale, 15 A.E.)

NEW JACINTO, VECTES: PRESENT DAY—GALE, 15 A.E.

"Boomer Lady, what you doin'?" Cole asked.

"It's monster bait," Baird said. "She's been watching too many movies."

Bernie was hammering a big wooden post with a tethering ring into the patch of grass between the Gorasni camp and the walls of the naval base. She straightened up and shielded her eyes against the sun to look at Baird. A large brown cow was chewing thoughtfully, watching Bernie.

"We're going out to find Edlar's missing livestock," Bernie said. "We need every cow we can get. Can't let him go looking for them with polyps about."

A Packhorse was parked nearby. Mac the mutt had his head hanging over the tailgate, looking bored, and Alex Brand sat cross-legged on the hood, smoking. She waved to Baird with her free hand and slowly turned it to extend her middle finger.

"Yeah, *cows*, I can see that," Baird said, turning to drop his pants and bend over in Alex's direction.

Cole gave him a look as he straightened up. "Damon baby, you realize Anya's sittin' in the Pack, don't ya?"

"Oh fuck . . ."

"And Sam's there too."

"Why the hell didn't you tell me?"

Bernie was laughing her ass off. "Blondie, you're supposed to drop your boxers *as well*, you dickhead. Never mind. They're clean, and that's all that matters."

"Interesting choice of fabric for a boy," Sam called.

"Yeah, princess, very *individual*." Alex swung her legs off the hood and leered at him before stubbing out her smoke and getting back in the Packhorse.

"Ladies' only patrol, Bernie?" Cole asked. "Man, my momma warned me to stay away from girls in gangs."

"Don't worry, it's not a feminist statement." Bernie finished hammering in the stake and tied one end of the cow's tether to it. "This is Rose, by the way. She's a seismologist."

"Oh, I get it." Cole patted Rose warily. Baird kept well away from the animal's rear, which struck him as both lethal and messy. "She goes crazy when she feels stalks comin' up somewhere, yeah? A kind of early warning system with horns."

"I could make you a seismometer, Granny," Baird said. "All you had to do was ask."

"Well, yes, but cows don't need checking for readings." Bernie climbed into the Packhorse and started it. "And you can't milk a seismometer. Now you boys behave yourselves while we're gone, okay? No fighting."

"Yes, Granny. Interesting plaits, by the way. Looks classy with the dead cat boots."

Bernie winked and the Packhorse rumbled off down the track. Baird watched it go. Mac gazed at him from the back of the vehicle with a mute plea to be saved from the tyranny of harpies.

"Can't wait to see Bernie smack Alex frigging Brand into line," Baird said, looking around for the Gorasni fuel tanker. "She won't take any of that I'm-a-sergeant-too shit from *her*. Ah, here comes our ride."

The tanker rumbled out of the Gorasni compound and slowed to a halt beside Baird. Eugen stuck his head out the driver's door.

"Hey, Mr. Cole Train! You coming to teach our kids thrashball?"

Cole climbed up the metal ladder to the top of the tanker and gave Baird a hand up. "Yeah, lookin' forward to it. 'Bout time I got back in the groove."

"Trescu's boy's very excited. It's good of you."

"Hey, no problem, baby. I love doin' it. Long as the little ones don't show me up by runnin' rings 'round me . . ."

"I take good care not to drop you when we go over bumps, hey? Then you'll be fit to face them."

The tanker set off with Baird and Cole riding shotgun on the top. It was a great view. For a few kilometers they could still see the Packhorse ahead of them, but then the tanker peeled off to the right and followed the road to the imulsion field, where the view went from picturesque to grim brown death.

Maybe it'd stop. And maybe it wouldn't.

It was all about timing, Baird decided. If they were ever going to evacuate, they had to reach their destination in the summer to stand a chance of preparing for a shitty winter. Baird couldn't think of anywhere he particularly wanted to go as long as it wasn't as eye-wateringly cold as Port Farrall had been. If he had to starve to death, he'd do it somewhere warm.

"Ooh, that don't look good." Cole pointed left. The regular skyline of trees in full leaf was interrupted by a bald patch and the twisted shapes of new stalks. "Cole to Control . . . yeah, we're on the drill site road, 'bout seven klicks southwest of the site. I can see a couple of stalks west of here . . . No, they must be five klicks away. You might wanna get a Raven to take a look at that. Cole out." He hung on to the walkway rails as the tanker bounced a few times over ruts in the road. "Damn, all them stalks poppin' up, and only one imulsion site."

"Perverse bastards," Baird said. "And they're messing up my tidy theories."

The contamination had created its own weirdly alien landscape. If you drove far enough into it, there was no sign that there was a green and living world beyond. It looked like the entire island was dead and brown. The smell of imulsion and a flat, bitter scent that Baird couldn't identify just added to the feeling that this wasn't Sera. The only reassurance that he was still in the world he knew was the sound of the imulsion drilling machinery drifting on the air.

For a few minutes the tanker trundled along hard-packed soil interspersed with stretches of rubble and trackway. Sitting on top of the vehicle's walkway suddenly felt exposed and scary rather than bracing. Baird was relieved to see flashes of bright yellow through the dead trees before the tanker pulled into a clearing full of human beings and nodding derricks.

The site was operating twenty-six hours a day. The more imulsion they could extract, the more options they had. Without a stockpile, they'd be stuck here, and stuck on the ground.

Rossi and Lang passed Baird in their Packhorse as the patrols handed over. "It's all quiet," Rossi said. "Just a couple of glowies overnight. I hope you brought your knitting." Then they were gone, a pair of fading taillights in the shade of the dead branches.

Baird climbed down from the top of the vehicle and watched Eugen couple the pipe from the reservoir tank. Stefan wandered over.

"What's it like out here at night?" Baird asked. "Must be pretty scary."

"Ah, we have lights, and so do the polyps, which is very considerate of them," Stefan said dismissively. He took something out of his pocket and chewed on it. It looked like it was putting up a manly fight. "And we can run away when the polyps come back. Which was pretty damn hard to do on Emerald Spar, yes?"

"That was a great piece of engineering." Baird still felt depressed when he thought about the platform crashing into the sea. They'd never be able to build anything like that again. "Glowie assholes."

"You take care of our assholes for us, Baird. You are the champion asshole-slayer." Stefan rummaged in the pocket of his imulsion-smeared overall and held out a chunk of whatever the hell he was eating. "You want some?"

It looked like jerky. The one food on the island that was instantly available in large quantities was the local wildlife. Like Bernie, the Gorasni shot anything that moved and then ate it, and that worried Baird.

"Tell me it's not cat," he said. "I've only just come to terms with Bernie and her many uses for domestic pets."

Stefan roared with laughter. "It's only *seabird.*"

"Thanks," Baird said, appalled, and took it.

He did it because he didn't want to offend Stefan. It was a watershed in his life. He hadn't even been that bothered about offending Cole before he got to know him. Now he was about to eat something disgusting that would probably give him a tapeworm or liver flukes, just because he didn't want to hurt someone's feelings.

The Gorasni only knew him as the guy who could fix anything, the guy who'd been the first to fight off polyps and nearly got killed doing it. They didn't know him as Baird the mouthy asshole and social misfit. Even Baird wasn't sure which Baird he actually was these days.

He took a cautious bite out of the jerky. It was beyond awful. It tasted like a decomposing corpse that had been soaked in fish oil. Even as he chewed, he was keeping an eye out for somewhere he could hide and spit it out. Shit, he'd need to gargle with imulsion to get the taste of *this* out of his mouth. Stefan slapped him on the shoulder and went back to the derricks.

"What you eatin'?" Cole asked. "'Cause you look like you're gonna chuck it up any minute."

Baird tried to amble casually into the trees. His mouth was filling with saliva. "Don't ask."

I'm fucking insane. I'm poisoning myself to get approval. I never used to give a shit.

Baird managed to get about five trees deep in the woods before he was satisfied nobody could see him. For some reason he recalled the moment when the burning wreckage of Emerald Spar sank into the sea. That was when the war against the glowies *really* became personal for him. He'd thought it was all about the fantastic, impossible, *brilliant* structure lost to civilization forever, but now he accepted it was more about the men and women who'd lived a lonely and dangerous existence taking care of it.

Whoa, steady on. People? Me? Fuck that. No. Okay,
maybe. *Maybe I admire these guys. And that's why I volun-*
teered for the rig patrol here, then. Never realized that before.
What's happening to me?

Baird spat as quietly as he could. The lump of mummi-
fied seagull, barely changed by chewing, hit the trunk of a
dead tree and slid down it. He could still taste it. He spat a
few more times, but there wasn't enough spit in his whole
body to get rid of that and he found himself gagging. His
radio crackled.

"Baird, where are ya?"

Cole was on the far side of the drilling compound, pacing the perimeter with his back to the row of derricks.
Baird found himself doing a creep line search vertically,
looking up into the branches then running his eyes down
the trunks, scanning a section along the ground, then scanning up again. The one good thing about polyps, other
than the satisfying way the fuckers exploded when you shot
them, was their lights. In the gloom, they lit up like a fairground ride.

"I'm puking my ring," he said. "No cracks in front of the
Gorasni, okay? They mean well."

"Goddamn, you're growin' a heart. Better go see Doc
Hayman 'bout that."

"Yeah, that sounds malignant to me."

Baird bent over and braced his hands on his knees to try to
work up more spit without throwing up and getting the dry
heaves. He almost took a swig from his water bottle, but he
was convinced that the oily dead-fish taste on his lips would
contaminate it. Then movement caught his eye. He looked
up slowly.

"Cole?"

"You hear anything, Baird?" he whispered.

"I don't *feel* anything." Baird shifted his weight from one foot to the other a few times to test for tremors. No; nothing, nothing at all. "You see anything?"

Cole was level with him now, a few meters away. He held up his hand for silence as he walked slowly between the trees with his Lancer raised. The sawing rhythm of the derricks and the steady putter of the generators didn't stop, but the Gorasni chatter died away a voice at a time until nobody was talking. Baird followed Cole, going wide so they'd have overlapping arcs if they had to open fire.

Whatever it was, they'd have to take it down before it got near the drilling area. It was peppered with imulsion seeps, a bomb waiting to go off. They'd already had to fight a fire here once.

"I hear it," Cole said. "But it sounds a hell of a lot bigger than polyps . . ."

He was about fifty meters into the woods now. Baird could hear it. Something big was crushing twigs, moving at a lumbering pace.

"Baird, what is it?" Stefan called.

"No idea. But stay back."

"Eugen's going to move the tanker, just in case."

"Yeah. Great. Good idea. Do that."

It sounded like a single creature. Baird made sure he could still see Cole and kept walking, casting around for movement. What the hell would be that big, out here?

Oh great. If the stalks made it here, maybe the grubs did too. We've got a Berserker on a day trip. Or a Brumak.

"Left," Cole said suddenly. "Left, one hundred meters."

Baird looked around, lost for a moment, but then he saw it: a white shape moving slowly between the dark trunks, something big and heavy. It wasn't a Berserker.

"Okay, everybody relax," Baird called, almost giddy with relief. "It's the frigging prize bull that went AWOL when we evacuated the farm. He probably wants his dinner."

Cole was still stalking it carefully. "Baby, you saw the horns on that sucker, didn't ya? Well, I ain't relaxing just yet. He's a bad-tempered meat tank and he can stomp us into shit if we piss him off."

"Well then, we can shoot the thing and claim self-defense," Baird said. "I think we should do that anyway. I'll have the rib eye."

The animal wandered to the edge of the clearing. There was nothing for the bull to graze on, so maybe he'd heard humans and decided that they usually meant food was nearby. Baird could see the sweep of his horns now.

He was huge. *Scary* huge. He was panting like a steam engine.

"Baird, you know *anything* about cows and stuff?" Cole asked quietly.

"No, that'd be Bernie. Not me."

"I mean, do they usually look like that? Like they got rabies?"

Baird suddenly saw what Cole meant and almost shat himself. The bull was drooling. Animals always seemed to be leaking something messy from one orifice or another, but this just wasn't right. It had a faint yellow glow to it. The bull lowered his head and stared swinging it from side to side, making a mournful groaning sound.

"What's the luminous stuff?" Stefan said. He was right behind Baird now with his shotgun aimed at the bull. "What is it, Baird? Is it what I think it is?"

No, the bull didn't look well at all. He took a few steps forward. Now that he'd emerged from the trees, Baird could see his flanks heaving. There were reddish patches on his ass, suddenly conspicuous on that white hide.

"Oh, terrific." The realization hit Baird more slowly than he expected. "He's gone glowie. Look."

"Come on, Baird. Do we shoot it now?"

"Stefan—listen to me. It's fucking *Lambent*. I was right. I was goddamn *right*. This stuff is *catching*."

"Yeah, you get a gold star for that, baby," Cole said, circling around to the other side of the bull. "But we better persuade him to move along, 'cause if he's a glowie, he's a thousand-kilo *bomb*."

Bulls chased things. Baird knew that much. Stefan and the other rig workers started backing away and Baird saw some of them pick up buckets and firefighting equipment. He had to get this thing away from the imulsion before he shot it.

"Okay," Cole said. "I reckon I might be able to outrun him."

"You're insane. It's a bull."

"*Somebody's* gotta move him." Cole stepped in front of the bull and got his attention. Baird watched the animal's eyes follow Cole, white-rimmed and panicky. "C'mon, fella. Come and see what the Cole Train got for ya." Cole walked right across the bull's eyeline. "See, he ain't charging or anything. Polyps want to kill you as soon as they see you."

"Great," Baird said. "He's a big *friendly* thousand-kilo bomb."

The bull looked pretty sick, head down and panting, but as Cole walked into the trees and away from the clearing, he followed. Cole broke into a jog. The bull started to trot. Then Cole picked up speed. Yeah, bulls chased things. That much Baird knew.

"Whoo! Come on, let's play chase!" Cole waved his arms. "Baird, you better be right behind ready to shoot this asshole . . ."

If it had been an open field, Cole wouldn't have stood a chance. But he could zigzag between trunks and the huge bull wasn't so good at that. Baird sprinted after them, trying to pick the moment when they were both far enough from

the imulsion—and Cole had opened up enough of a gap—
for him to open fire.

"Somebody follow me with a bucket," Baird yelled.
"Because there'll be a fire to put out."

Baird couldn't keep an eye on everything. He was too
busy looking for his shot, the one chance he might get to kill
that thing before it got Cole. He heard people running
behind him and the metallic clank of buckets. The crazy
bull hunt was more than two hundred meters into the trees
now, maybe a safe distance to drop the animal without the
blast igniting the imulsion. He raised his Lancer.

Shit, either I stop and aim, or I spray the thing.

Cole was whooping but sounding less confident each
time.

"Baird, you ready?"

"Ready."

"I mean *seriously* ready?"

Baird had to fire *now*. He almost put a burst through the
animal, but the bull suddenly changed direction and Cole
was in Baird's line of fire. He couldn't do a damn thing.

"Do it, Baird!"

"Not yet—"

Then the bull wheeled right. Baird didn't know what had
distracted it, but it might have been the noise of the buckets.
Eugen was running along with a couple of tin pails. Baird saw
him hesitate and stumble a couple of paces over the tree
roots. The bull stopped, swung around, and started trotting
toward him.

"Shit, Eugen—get away!" Baird raised his rifle. "Just drop
the buckets."

Baird didn't think an animal that big could accelerate so
fast. It shaved past him and charged Eugen. Before Baird
could open fire, the bull rammed into the Gorasni, head
down, and caught him full in the chest.

The explosion wasn't the Brumak-sized detonation Baird had expected but it blew Eugen meters into the air like a land mine. Cole and Baird ran forward into a rain of debris. It was already too late but Baird's legs kept moving anyway. It was the dumbest thing; he could see the guy was fragged, *completely* fragged, but he still sprinted over to him and dropped onto his knees to try to stop the bleeding. Cole did, too. It took a couple of silent seconds before they looked at one another and the reality hit them. There was nowhere to even begin. Baird stared, trying to recognize what he was looking at. He'd seen this kind of shit a hundred times but now it felt like the first.

"Fuck, fuck, *fuck.*"

"Oh, man . . ." Cole said.

Suddenly Stefan was a few meters away and Baird got to his feet. He tried to stop Stefan going to Eugen's body but the man shoved him aside. Fire licked up one of the tree trunks.

"Oh God I'm *sorry.*" Baird couldn't put this right. It upended him. "I'm sorry."

"Somebody get a tarpaulin," Stefan said. "Do it."

They put out the fire with buckets of soil and then recovered Eugen. Baird's lasting memory of that day would be that they did it in total silence; no yelling, no crying, nothing. They just carried him away, stony-faced, and set him down in the clearing. Baird looked at Cole.

"Goddamn," Cole said. "Goddamn, that just ain't *fair.*"

"I fucked up. It's my fault."

"Baird, I didn't manage to get a shot in either. Nobody did."

Baird went over to Stefan. The derricks were still pumping but nobody was keeping an eye on them. The dozen or so Gorasni stared at Eugen, now covered by someone's coat, and still said nothing.

"We better shut down the pumps," Baird said. He could hear Cole on the radio to Control. "Let's move out."

Stefan finally looked away from his friend's body, tears streaming down his face. "I'll take him back to his wife. But we carry on, or else it's all for nothing."

"You can't. It's getting too dangerous."

"We will carry on." Stefan grabbed Baird's shoulder and almost shook him. "We carry on pumping imulsion because without it we will *all* die here."

Cole walked up and gave Stefan a crushing hug, because Cole could do that kind of thing as easily as breathing. But Baird had no idea what to say. He longed for that same effortless way with people in trouble. No, he wasn't a people person; he made damn sure he kept his distance from almost everyone. But he felt terrible about Eugen, and even worse watching the man's buddies go back to the derricks in tears to carry on working because a bunch of strangers—a bunch of old enemies—needed them to.

As he waited for the Raven, he tried to remember when he'd last used the word *Indies*. Whenever it was, he knew he'd never use it again.

FIVE KILOMETERS SOUTH OF EDLAR FARM, NORTHERN VECTES.

Alex Brand sat down on a stile and watched Mac sniffing around in the grass, evidently unimpressed by his detective skills.

"Does he know what he's looking for?" she asked.

Bernie stopped to inhale. On the other side of the pasture, Sam and Anya were kicking around in the grass, eyes down. At least those two seemed to be getting on well.

"Yeah," Bernie said. "Shit. Fresh shit."

"I hope he doesn't roll in it, not if he's coming back in the

Packhorse." Alex got up and ambled over to a cowpat. "This is the wrong vintage, is it?"

"It's an old one."

"So you had a ranch." Alex took the remains of her cigar out of her sleeve and rummaged for her lighter. "Must have been nice. Can't have been easy leaving that."

"Easier than you think." Bernie walked up and plucked the cigar out of Alex's mouth before she could light it. "Sweetheart, it's not just because I fucking *hate* seeing anyone smoking in uniform. It's because I need to use my sense of smell when I'm tracking. Save it for later."

She handed the stub back to Alex, who looked more surprised than annoyed. Bernie had always sworn she would never exploit the authority of age, but she did, and she also exploited all the stories that she knew had circulated about her since she'd rejoined the army. It just saved a lot of time. She was tired of explaining herself to strangers.

"Well, you learn something every day, Mataki," Alex said, and parked the cigar in her sleeve again.

Mac came loping back to Bernie, wagging his tail and wearing his I've-been-a-clever-boy face. "You found something, Mac?" she asked. "Come on. Show Mum. What is it?"

He trotted off, pausing every few meters to make sure she was still behind him. She wondered just how docile that bull would be now that he was on the loose with his cows and probably remembering what his natural role in life was— defending his females. It'd be embarrassing if she couldn't handle the animal when everyone expected her to work miracles with anything on four legs. The bag of cattle nuts rattled on her belt. Bribery would do the trick.

The radio interrupted her thoughts. "Baird to Mataki— you there, Grannie?"

"Mataki here." Baird didn't sound quite right. "Everything okay, my precious little ray of sunshine?"

"You need to watch your ass. We found the bull."

"In fragments?"

"Intact and psychotic. He turned Lambent."

It took a couple of seconds to sink in. "What do you mean, *turned Lambent?*"

"What does it sound like? He looked kind of rabid, his drool was luminous, and he exploded. Meets *my* criteria."

"So we could be tracking glowie cows." Bernie heard Alex sigh behind her. "Thanks for the heads-up. Now, what else is wrong?"

It came out in a small voice, not the cocky Baird at all. "Eugen's dead. It got him."

Baird was new to caring about people. He didn't have anything to fall back on for strength except his indifference, and he didn't sound as if it was working right then. She felt for him.

"I'm really sorry, Blondie. He was a good bloke. Are you and Cole okay?"

"No injuries."

"You come down to the sergeant's mess when I get back," she said. It was easier to tell him than ask him, given his social skills. "We'll have a beer. Talk it over. Mataki out." She changed channels. "Mataki to Stroud. Ma'am, they've found the bull. It was Lambent, so we better assume the cows are too. One Gorasni's been killed already."

The conversation was on the open network now. Anya took a few seconds to come back to her. "Any reason why we shouldn't go on?"

"None, ma'am. I'd rather kill every Lambent than take the risk of it spreading."

"Agreed. Stroud out."

Alex matched pace with Bernie, looking anxious. "Who bought it this time? Tell me it's not Cole."

"A Gorasni bloke," Bernie said. "One of Baird's mates."

"Goddamn. You really *are* chummy with the little princess, then."

Bernie bristled. She'd punched out Baird and said some pretty spiteful things to him in the past, but that was her privilege and they'd reached an understanding. Nobody outside the squad could say a word against him.

"I judge him by what he does, not what he says," Bernie said stiffly. "You leave my boy alone."

"No problem," said Alex. "You're more tolerant of dumb animals than I am."

There was no love lost between her and Baird, then. Fine: she didn't have to work with him these days. Bernie caught up with Mac next to a fine crop of cow dung still busy with flies. He looked up at her as if to swear blind that he wasn't even *thinking* of rolling in the stuff.

"You're a gentleman," she said, slipping him more rabbit jerky before putting the leash back on him. "Okay, find 'em. Seek."

Anya paused to peer at the dung before moving on. "Does that mean they're not Lambent?"

"No idea," Bernie said. "But Baird's theory that it jumps the species barrier looks more plausible every time we meet a new glowie variety."

"I'm not taking any chances, no matter how badly we need the meat and milk."

"Fair enough." Priorities had suddenly changed. It was more Lambent hunting than recovering livestock. "I still want to find out how cattle get infected. It can't be simple contact, or else Mac would be Lambent by now."

"And Prescott's going to want samples. He can't do a damn thing with them, but it's easier than arguing that point with him."

Bernie didn't want to get sucked into the guessing games of what Prescott was up to. It was bad enough waking up in the night to find Hoffman pacing around and fretting about that bloody data disc. But it was hard not to ask more questions each day and become consumed by them.

"Did anyone know Eugen?" Bernie asked, remembering something that actually mattered.

"Yeah," Sam said. "Was it him?"

"Sorry."

"His poor bloody wife."

No, the Gorasni really weren't the enemy now, no matter how much history said they were. They'd fallen into that broad, borderless, vague nation called Us. Mac dragged Bernie for a kilometer through lush grass and nobody spoke for a long time.

"Over there." Anya stopped and took out her field glasses. Bernie brought Mac to a halt. "Look."

A few sheep that had evaded the roundup were grazing on the short grass along the banks of a stream. But when Bernie looked harder, there was something else with them: a pure white cow. For a moment she was more worried about failing eyesight than Lambent.

"Please God, no exploding sheep," Alex said. "I don't want a surreal death."

"I'm not planning on *any* kind of death." Bernie found it revealing that Gears would happily take on grubs and glowies but were wary of farm animals. That was city kids for you. She thought again of a seventeen-year-old Dom and the look on his face when he had to kill a chicken in survival training. "Ma'am, I'll go and check them first. You wait here in case too many strange humans spook them. We don't want to end up chasing them all over the island."

"Isn't Mac going to scare them?" Sam asked.

"He's a local dog. He's used to livestock and they're probably used to him."

Anya tapped her on the arm. "Bernie, any risk—any doubt at all—and you get out of there, okay?"

"I've got plenty of practice at dodging cows, ma'am," she said, slipping the Longshot off her shoulder. "And two rifles. Don't worry."

Bernie took the bag of feed nuts off her belt and shook it as she walked toward the animals. The sheep raised their heads but didn't come rushing at her. Mac padded calmly beside her. The cow looked up and stared.

Cows were curious animals. They were used to humans, too, and humans meant feeding and milking to them, especially when the human was carrying a bag of recognizable food. Bernie expected the cow to amble over to check her out, and that was what it did.

"Don't let me down, Mac," Bernie said. "Not now I've told everyone what a good boy you are."

Bernie slowed to a stop, still shaking the bag, and waited for the cow. When the old girl got close enough and was busy with the cattle nuts, Bernie could put a rope on her. The animal definitely looked in calf.

But where were the others? They'd stay together as a herd, so it didn't bode well.

And where were the dogs?

If Mac was any guide, they'd have gone hunting polyps. They might not have been as smart or as lucky as him.

"Never mind, Mac," Bernie said. "Seb's got another bull. And we've got other herds. Beef's going to stay on the menu."

She was still watching the cow heading her way at a leisurely pace when something caught her eye. A streak of white shot behind some trees along the bank, moving faster than she expected. She dropped the bag and reached for her Longshot instinctively.

"Bernie?" Anya's voice in her earpiece sounded worried. "Bernie, what is it?"

"Another cow," she said. "Just being cautious."

The animal came cantering out of the tree cover. The

cow that had been ambling over to Bernie suddenly bolted, the sheep scattered, and Mac started barking. Both cows were now cantering toward her. She sighted up without a conscious thought and aimed at the first animal between its shoulder and throat.

The first shot dropped the cow on the spot. Bernie didn't have time to reload the Longshot. She dropped it and unslung her Lancer to open fire on the second animal. The cow swung wide and stumbled for a few meters before collapsing, bellowing loudly.

But they didn't detonate. *Neither cow had detonated.* The fact struck Bernie only after she'd dropped both of them. She'd shot two normal, healthy animals.

She ran over to the cow that was still bellowing and tried to get close enough to see how badly hurt it was. By now, Anya, Sam, and Alex had sprinted across the pasture to catch up with her. Mac kept barking. "Steady, girl. I'm sorry. I'm *sorry.*"

"They're not Lambent," Anya said, breathless.

The cow was still thrashing around, trying to stand up. "Yeah, I know that now, ma'am," Bernie snapped. She was appalled. Her first reaction had been a soldier's, not a farmer's. Drill kept you alive but it also meant that it rewired you to shoot without having a debate first. "Shit. *Shit.*"

A single Longshot round could stop a truck, but the Lancer needed a bit more effort. Bernie had just left the poor animal badly wounded. There was nothing she could do for it now except put it out of its misery. She rested the rifle's muzzle on the cross point between its eyes and horns and squeezed the trigger. The loud crack took a long time to die away on the air.

Bernie stood contemplating what she'd done. Anya put her hand on her back and said nothing.

"Well, they were coming at you, Bernie," Sam said. "I'd have done the same. What started them off?"

Mac's reaction should have clued them in. He was still barking, and Bernie finally got the message when she saw the trees a hundred meters away suddenly empty of birds.

"*Stalks!*" Anya yelled. "We've got stalks, people!"

"Where?" Alex swung around, rifle ready. "I can't feel any tremors."

Bernie started jogging toward the trees. Mac overtook her at full pelt. He stopped just short of the stream and began pawing at the grass.

"Mac, get away from there!" Bernie yelled. "We can see where it is. *Mac! Come back here.*"

"That's a handy trick," Alex said. Mac raced back to Bernie's side, still barking. "Now what are we going to do?"

"Kill whatever comes out," said Anya. "Spread out, people."

They stood back, staring at the spot Mac had picked. Bernie could feel a tremor, but nothing like as strong as the previous ones she'd experienced.

"It'll be a small one, Bernie," Sam said.

"God, we're getting blasé about these things."

Anya moved further right. "Everybody ready?"

"You haven't fought polyps up close yet, have you, Alex?" Bernie asked.

"Why, do I need a permit to kill the fuckers?"

"Just treat them like tickers. Only worse."

Mac started snarling. Everybody aimed at the imaginary point in the grass about thirty meters away where he'd been pawing. The taller grasses began shaking and the ground bulged slowly upward for a moment before a split cracked it open.

"Stay, Mac." Bernie gave his collar a jerk. "*Stay.*"

A single stalk erupted, punching four meters into the air.

Its trunk was dotted with pulsing blisters. Bernie held her breath, waiting for the polyps to surge out of the ground with it, but the blisters started to part along the cross-shaped indentations like seed pods struggling to open. Fluid sprayed out.

"Do they always do that?" Alex asked.

"It's a new one on me," said Sam.

Was that the stuff that killed the vegetation? Bernie had no idea until the blister she was aiming at burst open and something large, wet, and black was thrown out of it. It fell to the ground like a newborn calf and found its feet instantly.

"Now *that's* not a bloody polyp," Sam said.

It had four legs and a pointed snout. Then it parted its lips and snarled.

Bernie aimed. "Shit. It's a *dog.*"

The thing was dog-sized, dog-shaped, and when it ran at her it even *moved* like a dog. She put a burst of Lancer fire through it and it blew up in a sheet of flame, scattering debris that looked like burnt paper. Then the rest of the blisters split open. More dog-things spewed out and rushed at them, meeting a wall of automatic fire.

Nobody said a word. Bernie was in that familiar tunnel again, everything in her immediate path so clear and sharp that it looked luminous, the colors far brighter than anything she saw day-to-day, and everything outside it—her comrades, the muzzle flash—was a distant and muffled blur. It was one recurring second, the same shot at the same glowie and the same detonation over and over again. She ran out of ammo and only reloading snapped her out of the trance. She was just obeying her reflexes. The only conscious thought in her head was why this bunch of Lambent looked like dogs.

There seemed to be dozens of them. And being doglike, they had the anatomy to leap. One broke through the wall of fire while she was reloading and she raised her Lancer a fraction of a second too late. One moment the dog-thing was coming at her in midair and the next Mac cannoned into it and the two animals went cartwheeling across the grass to Bernie's left. The explosion sent charred fragments high in the air.

"Mac! *Mac!*" People did the weirdest things under fire. She'd hauled friends to safety, gone to retrieve weapons that could have managed just fine on their own, and now she was risking her life going after a dog. "Mac!"

Astonishingly, he was still alive. He staggered to his feet and shoved in front of her, snarling at the glowies and ready to tear into them again. She pulled him down by his collar and held him there, firing one-handed. Rounds zipped past her. Eventually the explosions thinned out and stopped.

The air stank of smoke and burned hair. "Well," Anya said, voice shaking. "There's something you don't see every day."

Bernie was suddenly back in the real world with a 360-degree awareness. Alex stood poking the debris with her boot. Sam came over and gave Bernie a hand up, and nobody asked why the fuck she'd risked her life for a dog.

"Is he okay?" Sam asked.

Bernie dusted Mac down and checked him for injuries. His fur was singed and he was trembling, but he looked up into her eyes and gave her a messy, wet lick across the face.

"Yeah, he's my little hero." Bernie cuddled him, all too aware how close she'd come to having a glowie detonate in her face. "Did you see that? Did those things come out of the pods?"

"That's what I saw," Anya said. "Anyone got a different theory?"

Sam joined Alex, who was searching through the grass. "Maybe it's connected to the two farm dogs. Although god knows how we get from two dogs being fragged by polyps to dozens of those things spawning from the pods."

"Whatever it is, the Lambent keep changing and they're doing it faster each time," Bernie said.

Alex picked up a few fragments of charred tissue that could have been anything. "We better find a recognizable lump. Nobody's going to believe us and I'm not in the mood to take any shit from Baird about it. That was damn *close.*"

Anya fiddled with a thick strand of hair that had fallen out of its pleat on one side. It was blackened at the ends. She tried to pin it back again and then sniffed her fingers.

"They've burned my goddamn *hair*," she said indignantly. "I'm going to have to cut it now." She sounded just like her mother at that moment, outraged by the insolence of a near miss rather than shaken by it. "I say we call off the search, Bernie. We've got a whole new problem."

"Permission to retrieve the cattle carcasses, ma'am?" *God, am I really asking that? Yes, I am.* " We just can't waste that much meat."

"I'll call in a Raven for that. Everybody—back in the Packhorse."

"Ma'am, I'm still looking for chunks," Alex said. "Wait one."

The dog-things had almost completely vaporized on detonation. The grass was scattered with thin, curled scraps that crumbled into soot when Bernie tried to pick them up, so maybe there was nothing left to prove what they'd just seen. But there was no point working with a dog if you didn't take advantage of his skills.

"Seek, Mac," she said. She held her ash-stained fingers under his nose so he knew what she was asking him to sniff out. "Find some dead glowies. Good boy."

"They can only do that in the movies," Alex said.

Bernie watched him limp away into the grass, head down. "You've never kept a working dog, have you?"

Mac sniffed around for a while and disappeared for a few minutes in the ruts of churned soil around the stalk. When his head bobbed up again, he had something in his mouth.

"That's my boy," Bernie said. "Clever Mac."

Mac trotted back and dropped a charred lump at her feet. It looked like a roast leg of lamb that had been left too long in the oven. The knee joint in the bone was visible and it was clearly a hind leg, a very doglike one.

"That'll do fine," Anya said. "Now let's go."

Mac wouldn't get in the back of the Packhorse on his own. Bernie managed to lift him in, but he whined pitifully when she tried to walk away. Anya got into the driving seat.

"You better sit with him," she said. "He's earned it."

Everything was starting to hurt now that the adrenaline had ebbed. Bernie could feel pulled muscles, bruises, and scraped skin. Mac didn't seem content to lie beside her in the back of the vehicle. He draped himself across her lap and shoved his head under her arm as if he was trying to hide. He smelled of singed fur.

"If Vic tries to kick you off the bed tonight," she whispered, "I'll bite him for you. Okay?"

Mac made a strange sobbing sound deep in his throat, distressingly like a child. Sometimes she was convinced he had a far better understanding of what she said than just a regular intelligent dog.

She just didn't understand his replies.

ADMIRALTY HOUSE, VECTES NAVAL BASE.

"Where's Prescott?" Hoffman demanded. "Does he know about this incident with the bull yet? Why the hell can't he wear a radio like everyone else?"

Rivera looked trapped and helpless like a kid caught

between two squabbling parents. Lowe wasn't around. Michaelson and Trescu stood back and let Hoffman handle it.

"Oh, he knows, sir," Rivera said. "He'll be back in a few minutes."

The door of Prescott's office was open. Hoffman motioned Michaelson and Trescu inside and didn't ask if Lowe had gone with Prescott.

"I'm not going to go through his desk again, Rivera." Hoffman was almost nose to nose with him. He'd been a solid frontline Gear, and it wasn't his fault that his boss was a secretive asshole. "But if you know where he is, tell him we need to talk right *now*."

Rivera nodded and disappeared down the stairs. Coming so soon after the mainland recon, the new Lambent form would only stoke speculation that evacuation was an imminent prospect. Hoffman wanted Prescott to get out there and do what he did best—reassure the civilians.

Hoffman also wanted to confront him. He'd had enough of the guessing game, and he needed to ask him a simple question and see his reaction. Was this a COG bioweapon gone haywire?

"I don't expect either of you to get involved in this," he said to Michaelson and Trescu. "But if I don't thrash it out right now with that bastard, I can't work alongside him another damn day. *Enough.*"

Michaelson gave him a slow pat on the back. "Come on. I'm involved, and I'm sure Miran is too."

Trescu stood staring out of the office window, one arm folded across his chest as he stroked his beard. Hoffman didn't know how close he'd been to Eugen, but the man always took every death personally, whether it was a friend or not. There just weren't that many Gorasni left for their leader not to care about individuals.

"Do you need to get to the site, Commander?" Hoffman asked. "I realize this is hard for you. You can go if you want."

"I'll go as soon as we hear what the Chairman has to say for himself." Trescu snapped his focus back to them. "But for the moment—I am, as you say, *in*."

They waited. Hoffman didn't want any more games. He especially didn't want to play them with Trescu.

"You had pretty good spies in the UIR," he said. "Did you ever investigate what kind of weapons we were working on?"

"Why ask me?"

"I'm the last asshole to get told *anything*," Hoffman said. "The COG's as secretive as any damn Indie state, believe me. I was Director of Special Forces but I got told sweet fuck all."

"We knew you had a chemical and biological weapons program. *Everyone* had one. As to what it was—your guess would be as good as mine."

The view from the window seemed to be distracting Trescu. Michaelson took a look, and Hoffman had no choice but to watch as well. He'd been used to an orderly scene in the basins and jetties, but the Pelruan evacuees had spilled over into the working areas. Some of them had to live on board the ships.

"It'll be easier when we get the work party rosters organized," Michaelson said. "They'll be working on the farms and the building sites. But for the time being, I do worry about the odd ship going AWOL."

"*Zephyr* will keep a watchful eye open if you wish, Quentin," Trescu said. "But do you want her to stop anyone leaving, or do you prefer to sink your own vessels?"

"We'll be happy to take tip-offs," Michaelson said. "We'd better do the beastly stuff ourselves. No Pendulum Wars reenactments."

Trescu seemed to take that sort of thing from Michaelson without turning a hair. They really did get along, personally and politically, but then Michaelson had always been a political animal. Hoffman felt further out of his depth with the situation every day and longed even more to be back fighting an honest war with a definable enemy.

"Control to Hoffman." It was Mathieson. "Sir, Lieutenant Stroud's on her way back with the patrol. Sergeant Mataki's got something weird to show you."

Hoffman marveled at Mathieson's deft touch. He knew exactly how to avoid hiking Hoffman's blood pressure. Something had obviously gone wrong, but Mathieson had managed to say in one breath that not only was it over, but also that Bernie was okay.

I have good people. That's everything.

"Did she say what it was, Mathieson?"

"A new kind of glowie, sir."

"Not the cows."

"No. A *really* new kind, sir. She's got a fragment."

"Have you told Prescott yet?"

"Oh, I can never get hold of him, sir. I'll leave that to you, if that's okay."

"Good man. Hoffman out."

Michaelson looked around. "More thrills?"

"Yeah." Hoffman sat down at the table. He could hear the distant sound of boots at the bottom of the stairs. "Mataki's bringing us a nasty surprise. Another new glowie."

"I don't like the way the pace of change is picking up," Michaelson said. "I really don't."

It was definitely Prescott coming up the stairs. Hoffman knew his footsteps too well by now. He watched the door and Prescott appeared.

The Chairman gave them a nod and wandered in, taking off his jacket. "Apologies, gentlemen. I've just taken a walk through the base to see how things are settling down."

"You've heard about the Lambent bull," Hoffman said.

"Well, we've been aware for a while that Lambency occurs in different species, so perhaps we're now closer to finding out how it happens."

It could have been a neutral and literal observation, but Hoffman heard it as a challenge. "People are going to assume the worst, though, Chairman, and right now we need order and discipline. I'm looking to you to say the right words to them."

"I think I can manage that. But you haven't come here just to ask me to make a speech, have you?"

Hoffman suddenly felt very alone. He ran on anger and indignation, and if he lost any of that momentum then he began to worry that he really was just the boorish, overpromoted infantry grunt that they'd once said he was, a man lucky to find himself in 26 RTI, a regiment with a long history of dominating army politics.

I should not be here. I should not be running this.

But he was, so he fronted up and earned it.

"Well go ahead, then, Colonel." Prescott glanced at Michaelson and Trescu. "What's the problem?"

It was still hard to say it. Even after fifteen years, with no UIR left to fear, Hoffman hesitated before talking about a classified facility. Habit was very hard to break. And damn it, he realized he was going to have to mention the data disc in front of Trescu without the courtesy of breaking it to the man privately. But that was just too bad.

"Lambency," Hoffman said at last. "Is that what the goddamn disc is all about?"

He was too focused on Prescott's face to watch how Trescu reacted. He was searching for any twitch or blink he could lean on and use. Prescott looked as if he'd taken a slow, discreet breath.

"You don't expect me to respond to such an open question, surely?" he said.

Prescott looked vaguely uncomfortable, but no more than any man would when faced with crisis after crisis. Hoffman wondered if he was looking too hard for reactions that just weren't there. The trouble with having others at the table was that he couldn't harangue him. Humiliating him—if Prescott *could* be humiliated, given his messianic detachment—wouldn't get any usable information out of him, not now and not later.

Trescu butted in. He wasn't used to answering to anybody. "If you have information, Chairman, then I expect you to share it with us." *Us* might have meant the three of them, but he might have meant only the Gorasni. "Sera is a wasteland and there's no harm we can do to you. If you have information that can help us survive, *give* it to us."

"I'm not sure that I do, gentlemen," Prescott said. He leaned forward as if he was going to stand up and leave again. "Right now, I'm as desperate to find a solution as you are, and just as afraid of what will happen if I don't."

Hoffman decided to drop the full payload. "Mataki's on her way back with another new glowie. You sure there's nothing you want to tell us?"

"What's she found?" Prescott was suddenly interested, totally focused on the news. "What is it?"

"I don't even know yet."

"I do need a sample, Victor."

Prescott wasn't dismissive, but definitely impatient, as if he had something much more important to do than listen to their petty concerns about his secrecy.

"Don't bullshit me," Hoffman snarled. "I'm immune. We've been doing this far too long."

Prescott didn't blink. "I should get on with addressing the civilians, gentlemen, and we can reschedule this."

"Why, Chairman? What's more pressing than why our last refuge is being overrun by this goddamn Lambent menagerie and our entire food supply *poisoned* by it?"

Prescott parted his lips a little as if he was about to say something but had thought better of it. He leaned back in his seat.

"I do think we should discuss this at another time, Victor."

"I'll ask you again. *Why won't you tell us?*"

Michaelson finally spoke, doing his soothing voice-of-reason act. "It's hard for us to understand what you could possibly want to withhold from your defense staff at this stage of the game, Chairman." He could make *fuck off and die* sound like a friendly greeting. "We really would function better if you leveled with us."

"Is this all about the disc?" Prescott asked.

"Well, that's for you to tell us, sir," Michaelson said. "What are we to think? More to the point, what are we to tell the civilians? And our Gears? There's only so long any of us can keep a lid on this, isn't there?"

Prescott frowned a little as if he was trying to work out what Michaelson meant. Hoffman could hear Margaret's voice in his head, as he sometimes did. Even dead, she put him on the spot like the trial lawyer she'd been. He never forgot her last words as she stormed out the door.

Fuck you, Victor. Fuck you and all your secret little cabals . . . and you kept it from me. How in the name of God did you think I'd react?

Hoffman struggled to shut her out. He focused on the Chairman and let rip. He had nothing more to lose. "For once in your goddamn two-faced fucking life, Prescott, *tell me the truth.* It's the Lambent, isn't it? You *knew.*"

Every drop of blood drained from Prescott's face. His voice was still very controlled, but Hoffman was shocked to see any reaction, let alone one like that. The man hadn't even broken a sweat when he deployed the Hammer. This was the closest Hoffman had ever come to cracking that facade.

"If I *had*," Prescott said carefully, "would it have made any difference? And if I had known, do you seriously think I'd have stood by and watch it consume us and not try to find a solution?"

That was pretty well what Hoffman had said to Margaret. He thought of her raging at him for not telling her the Hammer strikes were coming. *And what would you have done if I'd told you?* Yes, he'd said that to her. This was his punishment. He wasn't a man who believed in divine interference, but he accepted that fate and his own hypocrisy were forcing him to relive Margaret's viewpoint on that terrible day. Maybe there was such a thing as hell after all. Maybe this was it, and he was already dead.

But he clung to his anger and let it carry him along. He couldn't stop now.

"How the fuck could you *hide* it?" he demanded. "How you could *not* tell us that we did it to ourselves again? Was that it? Couldn't you face admitting that another of our god-almighty weapons came back to bite us in the ass?"

Prescott blinked a couple of times, staring into Hoffman's face. His focus flickered as if he suddenly didn't know what Hoffman was going on about. "I'm sorry?"

"*Lambency.* It's a COG bioweapon, am I right? We cooked it up right here during the Pendulum Wars, didn't we? And then we deployed it to kill the grubs, just like the Hammer, and now it's killing *us* too. Our own shit's killing us *again*. And that means you must have known the grubs were coming long before E-Day."

Hoffman felt his throat tightening as if his anger was finally going to choke the life out of him. His heart was racing. He felt as close to a stroke as he'd ever been, too drained and betrayed to summon up the energy to punch that bastard in the face.

But Prescott could always surprise him. For a moment, the man's expression became absolute despair before the mask snapped back into place and his real feelings were buried forever. It was so fleeting that Hoffman wondered if he'd imagined it out of sheer hope that he'd finally broken Prescott's silence.

"You have no idea," Prescott said softly. "Victor, you could *not* be more wrong. You really couldn't." He paused, stopped himself saying something—no, not an act, definitely *not* an act—and shook his head. "I'm sorry. It's not of our making. If it were, we might stand a better chance. And I had no warning whatsoever—no *idea* that the Locust were coming. No damn idea *at all*."

Prescott *was* telling some kind of truth. Hoffman felt devastated and angry. He'd wanted that truth so badly. Or at least he thought he did; what he wanted, he realized, was for Prescott to know what this thing was and reveal that he'd found a way to deal with it before the last humans on Sera were picked off. He really wanted the man to know best. He wanted a grown-up to put things right.

But Prescott didn't have a solution. That was clear. Hoffman's whole neat theory about Lambency, so plausible and such a perfect fit to events, was completely wrong. Hoffman was on his own again, orphaned.

"Goddamn," he said quietly, completely deflated. "I'll leave you to write your speech, then, Chairman. Good day."

Hoffman managed to get up and walk out. He didn't storm off. He couldn't manage it. Michaelson and Trescu followed him down the stairs in silence, already in the habit of waiting until they were out of earshot to react to events. They stood on the steps of Admiralty House, now an island refuge in its own right. The parade ground in front of them had become a crowded town square.

"I told you he was afraid of something," Trescu said at last.

"Well, well." Michaelson raised his eyebrows. "At least I lived long enough to see a miracle. Prescott, coming clean. The apocalypse must be due any minute."

Hoffman felt shaky now. He needed to see what Bernie had found. And he needed to lean on her for a little moral support.

"If I'd known what an honest Prescott reaction looked like," he said, "I might have saved myself a lot of time over the years."

"Have we ever actually caught him lying to us at all?" Michaelson asked. "No. He's just withheld information. Which is bad enough, but more confusing. I can't read him at all now."

"So what *is* on this disc you neglected to tell me about?" Trescu said quietly.

It was inevitable. Hoffman had to salvage the relationship. "I haven't even told most of my own men, so I didn't put you on the circulation list either. I *stole* it from the asshole. Other than that—it's as much goddamn use as a drinks coaster. We can't decrypt it."

"It's nothing personal, Miran," Michaelson said. "He didn't even tell me until a little while ago. Didn't want to drop me in the dwang."

"At the risk of sounding like an echo, is there anything you're withholding from *me*?" Trescu asked. He wasn't hard to read. He looked massively pissed off, a man who didn't feel any need to play diplomacy games with the COG. "Seeing as we're all being so trusting."

"No." Hoffman felt ashamed. "You've plumbed the depth of my ignorance now."

"Then you won't mind if we retain enough imulsion to enable us to leave independently if Prescott lets us down in any way."

Eugen was dead. It would have been churlish to respond any other way. "You're putting lives on the line for us," Hoffman said. "You've got a right to an insurance policy. Keep whatever you need, Commander."

Trescu nodded and looked down at his boots as if the comment embarrassed him. "I would prefer everyone to stick together, but the wild card, as you put it, is your Chairman. So we carry on. We plan for every eventuality, and we see what happens next."

"He obviously thinks he can find a solution faster on his own or else he'd be spending all his time demanding one from us," Michaelson said. "And that's starting to worry me."

They walked slowly across the parade ground, normally a good place to have unheard conversations, but it was too busy today.

"Maybe he just doesn't trust us," Hoffman said. "But that's a given. His kind trust nobody."

"Neither do I," Trescu said. "But I especially wouldn't trust a subordinate who stole information from me."

"Thanks for the vote of confidence, Commander."

"We're on our own, Hoffman. Actually, I *do* trust you. You're scared of lying. You blurt out the truth. That's why nobody tells you anything and you have to shake it out of them."

"I used to think it was a virtue."

"It may come to be one again. By the way—if you want encrypted COG data decoded, you had only to ask. We used to be *very* good at that. The offer stands."

Goddamn. What harm could it do now? "I'll probably take you up on that."

He left Trescu with Michaelson, knowing that any

damage he'd done would be smoothed over by Michaelson's wardroom charm. He was adrift again. He thought he'd been putting the pieces together in a logical way, and now he was back to square one.

His day couldn't get any worse. He was sure of it. Then he thought of Borusc Eugen's wife, and decided he'd gotten off lightly today.

CHAPTER 16

This isn't the first time that Lambency's contaminated another species. But I'd still like a tissue sample from the animal for storage in case we ever find a way of analyzing it. You're doing some very useful work, Corporal—I can always use someone technically minded on my personal staff. You might want to consider that.

(Chairman Prescott to Damon Baird)

CIC, VECTES NAVAL BASE.

"Hello, sir." Mathieson pointed to a clear desk in CIC. "If you park yourself there, you'll see the Pack as soon as it comes through the gates."

Hoffman steeled himself to stay calm when Bernie showed up looking the worse for the fight with the Lambent, which he knew she would. He sat down to go through the non-urgent signals while he waited. "Thanks, son. Any more databurst activity?"

"I couldn't monitor much this afternoon, sir. Sorry."

"That's okay. I realize it's been a shitty day all around."

"Everything all right, sir?"

"Oh, the usual. Frustrations boiling over."

Ten minutes later, the Packhorse rolled through the gates

into the vehicle compound and Anya got out of the driver's door followed by Sam and that red-headed sergeant that Baird couldn't stand. The first thing he noticed was the state of Anya's usually neat hair. Then Bernie climbed out of the back and spent a few moments extracting the dog and what looked like a large parcel in a battered canvas bag. Hoffman couldn't even begin to imagine what the hell she'd brought back.

Hoffman pressed his earpiece. "Hoffman to Mataki," he said. "Get your ass into CIC now, Sergeant."

The radio clicked. Only Bernie could somehow make that click sound pissed off. But her tone was completely neutral. "Yes, sir. On my way."

She walked into CIC covered in mud and reeking of smoke. Mac limped alongside her, looking equally bedraggled.

"The good news is that we've got a few steaks," she said, not doing a convincing job of humor. "The bad news is in here."

She held up the bag. Mac's eyes were fixed on it.

"Show me."

"It came out of the stalk—I mean actually out of the blister things. The pods. I wasn't imagining it, Vic. Ask Anya."

"Sir?" Mathieson called. It was a warning. "Sir, Chairman Prescott's coming . . ."

It was too late. Prescott filled the doorway. There was no way out of this now.

"I'm relieved you're back in one piece, Sergeant," Prescott said, putting paid to any examination of the sample without him. He went up to Mac and ruffled his fur, and Mac accepted it as if he and the Chairman were old buddies. "Is everyone else okay?"

"Fine, sir. I've got a sample."

"Good work. Let's look at this upstairs."

Bernie turned to Mac. "Stay, Mac. I won't be long." But he followed her, looking pathetic. She tried to get him to sit by pressing on his back but he wasn't having any of it. "Sorry. He saved me from a glowie today and he took a pounding. He's a bit clingy."

"Bring him along," Prescott said, all charm and understanding. He stepped back and ushered her up to his office like a perfect gentleman. Hoffman trailed behind him, seething.

Bernie laid the bag on Prescott's desk, scattering soil and ash across it. She reached in and tugged out a charred piece of meat, holding it up by a stump of bone. To Prescott's credit, he didn't flinch. He just reached into his desk drawer and took out a pair of old workshop gloves.

"Where did you find it, Sergeant?" He cleared the files off the desk and laid out some sheets of paper, then held out both hands for the remains. "Let's have the background."

He really did seem fascinated. He lowered the joint onto the paper and examined it like a pathologist. Hoffman caught Bernie's eye for a second. Like all familiar faces he saw, the slowly changing detail of aging was usually filtered out, but Bernie looked wrung dry and it scared him.

She shouldn't have to do this. Nobody should.

"There were lots of them." Bernie sounded hoarse. "They slipped straight out of the pods."

She reached across Prescott's desk and flipped the hunk of meat over to show a piece of exposed bone. When she took it in both hands by the charred ends and flexed it, the cooked meat pulled away from the bone in long strings. Now it was clear that one end of the lump was a joint, a small knee-like hinge.

"I heard about the bull, sir, but this one came as a shock," she said. "They looked pretty much like dogs. And I don't mean infected ones. Seb Edlar only lost two dogs, and it also doesn't explain why the Lambent ones actually came out of those pods. The blisters. Or whatever we're calling them now."

Prescott was riveted, hanging on Bernie's words. Hoffman could only watch. There was now no pattern to the Lambent, no logical progression, and the only consistent thing was that they exploded.

"Good God," Prescott said at last. He seemed genuinely taken aback. "Sergeant, would you put this in a freezer for the time being, please? If the cooks argue with you, tell them it's on my orders."

"Yes, sir." Whatever Bernie thought of Prescott, it didn't show on her face and she remained the dutiful sergeant. She rewrapped the charred leg. When she turned to go, she didn't even look at Hoffman. Mac followed her out of the office.

"Before you ask, Colonel," Prescott said, "I have no idea what that was." He gestured to the empty chair opposite his desk. "Sit down. We need to talk."

The office was exceptionally tidy. Prescott had always been the organized type, but he looked as if he'd been sorting out papers and cleaning shelves. In a normal world, the head of state wouldn't have had to dust his own office, but Prescott didn't seem to mind. There were things to admire about the man after all. They just weren't the qualities that Hoffman needed to put the lives of his Gears and the future of the COG in Prescott's hands without question.

He's never actually done anything crazy. He's never been incompetent. I'd have done what he did, every time. But he dicks me around. I can't stand that.

"Is this about the disc?"

"No, it's about what I've just seen. I'm as troubled as you are about the rate at which the Lambent are spreading."

There was none of that silky, calculating tone in Prescott's voice for once. "I realize that none of the senior staff think relocation to the mainland is viable yet."

It sounded like a perfectly normal discussion of the kind he was meant to have with Hoffman. They should have had a lot more of them.

"If we leave here, then we'll have to split up into small groups to survive," Hoffman said. "We don't have the resources to duplicate military or civic infrastructure across a dozen or more small settlements. It's going to finish us. We're stronger as a single entity."

Prescott didn't look as if he was resisting the pessimism. "That's a pretty stark assessment."

"It's the view of all of us. You know what the alternatives are, and they're much more tied to the seasons than to the level of threat here."

Prescott leaned back in his chair. "You know there are those who want to take their chances and leave anyway. I think we should let them go."

"No, absolutely *not*. We've been here before, Chairman. You let malcontents leave Port Farrall to fend for themselves, but they were only taking a few of their own private vehicles. Anyone who leaves Vectes takes a *vessel*—a boat that others are going to need one day. We can't replace ships."

Prescott nodded as if he was listening. "I see your point, but will you stop them trying?"

"I already have."

"It's not as simple as it looks, morally or practically. I worry about spending resources on corralling a minority."

"That's anarchy," Hoffman said. "Not on *my* watch."

"It might come to that, Victor." Prescott's tone softened even further, like a disappointed father who had to ask his son if it was true he'd had one beer too many and dented the car. "I want to ask a question, man to man. No games. A straight question, and I'll respect your straight answer. Well, that's the only kind you give, isn't it?"

This could have been going anywhere, but wherever it was heading, Hoffman knew he wouldn't like it. "You know it is."

"Why do you think you're now the senior commander, Victor?"

"Well, every other asshole died except me, sir." There'd been a lot of officers who just went missing over the years after E-Day. Sometimes that thought plagued him, but he filed them with the other missing billions of grub victims. Then he thought of General Bardry. "Or blew their own goddamn brains out in despair."

"Victor, you're here *because I chose you.* I chose you when I took office, actually. You do what needs to be done, however hard it is, when others are still consulting their rule books and wasting lives." Prescott leaned forward again. "I've read your service record. The one with the report *you* wrote about the siege of Anvil Gate, not the official bullshit that airbrushed out all the less savory parts. So I know what you're capable of."

"Would that be executing a civvie for stealing rationed food from my Gears, or shooting an honorable UIR officer who had taken my surrender?" *And who gave me water. And was prepared to treat my wounded. I know which one haunts me.* "I did a lot of unsavory shit, you see, sir. It's hard to keep up."

"I was thinking of the civilian," Prescott said softly. "But both showed that you had your priorities straight. And I knew that you would see the sense in using the Hammer of Dawn for asset denial."

Hoffman wanted to call a halt to this but it was like staring at a car crash. He couldn't drag himself away. "Yes, I kept it from my wife, and she ended up dead because I followed orders, while you even tipped off your goddamn *secretary* so she could get her family to safety. So we're both assholes in our own special way. Where's this going?"

Prescott's mask had started to peel away a little more. He really could control his facial reactions to things, the tiny giveaways that were involuntary in most people. Now he looked as if he was talking to Hoffman man to man.

But don't forget he's a terrific actor.

"I'm going to ask something of you very soon," Prescott said. "But I won't be able to explain why. All I can tell you is that there's something I have to do that can't wait any longer, and I need you to help me do it. What will you say?"

He's got to be winding me up for laughs. He has to be. How many times have we had fights over this secrecy shit? How many times does he think I'll bend over and take this up the ass?

Hoffman tried to give him a reasoned answer rather than just punch him in the face and have done with it. "If you'd asked me for blind obedience to an order ten years ago, Chairman, I'd have bitched but done it. But after the events of this last year—no, I would *not*, sir. I would not do your bidding unless you were prepared to tell me absolutely *everything.*"

"Thank you for your honesty, Victor." Prescott looked like he knew that was coming but thought it was worth a try anyway. "Unfortunately we're in a unique situation, one not dissimilar to your own at Anvil Gate. One requiring you and I to be bastards whose names will be cursed yet again. Still— I haven't given an order, so your refusal is hypothetical."

He meshed his hands on the desk. It was his your-call gesture, a challenge to cave in or walk out. Hoffman needed to make his getaway before he was seduced into agreeing to something he'd regret. He made an effort.

"If you don't need me anymore right now, Chairman, I need to catch up with debriefs."

"I'll ask you again, Victor."

"You'll get the same answer."

"The obviously decent and manly thing to do isn't always the thing that will save most lives."

"I know that, too," Hoffman said. For a moment something in him wanted to cooperate with Prescott, to justify this faith and flattery, this rare sense of personal connection, but he told himself that this was how politicians got the job done. They knew how to press those buttons. He had to resist. "But if I do something, I do it with full information at my disposal. Not on faith. Good day, sir."

Hoffman made his way down the stairs, disturbed rather than angry. He knew what Michaelson would say. *He can wind you up like a clockwork toy.* But what if he was wrong? He'd never actually caught Prescott out in a real, solid lie. It was all omission. He had no benchmark of dishonesty to work with.

He dropped by CIC on his way out. "Mathieson, I'm going to catch up with Delta." CIC was a different world, measurable and precise, where people told him the truth about anything he wanted to know. "What have I missed?"

Mathieson was looking more cheerful than Hoffman had seen him for a long time. The prospect of walking again, however hard it would be, had worked wonders. "Not much, sir. A couple more databursts while you were with the Chairman, but no more Lambent incursions. Mataki said she'd be in the sergeant's mess in half an hour if you wanted to discuss the dog polyp thing. Mac won't leave her so she had a bust-up with the cooks about taking a dog into a food area."

"God Almighty," Hoffman said. "We're worried about health and safety violations when we've got glowies up our asses?"

"You know how folks are, sir."

Hoffman was more baffled than ever by the databursts,

but it wasn't his biggest problem right then. Actually, he wasn't quite sure which one was. It was hard to tell.

The stalks were still contaminating more land, the Lambent were showing up in increasingly bizarre forms, and he was none the wiser about the contents of that frigging disc. What he did know, though, was that Prescott seemed as helpless and desperate as he was.

At least he had fuel at his disposal. Imulsion would be their lifeline.

CONSTRUCTION SITE, TWO DAYS LATER.

Baird accepted that he had a short fuse where idiots were concerned but he felt he'd lost a few more centimeters in the last fifty-two hours since Eugen got killed. His flash-to-bang time, as Bernie put it, was zero.

He really should have had that beer with her. Cole was his buddy and he could talk anything over with him, anything at all, but Bernie was somehow . . . well, more like a doctor, or a priest, or an agony aunt, close enough to feel comfortable with but distant enough for loss of face to be irrelevant. She'd seen and done it all. He didn't have to worry about looking like a dick in front of her.

He drove through the housing site, looking for Jace Stratton. The Packhorse creaked under the weight of timber and drums of bitumen. When he looked to either side at each crossroads—civvies just wandered around construction sites like suicidal chickens—he could see small knots of people huddled and talking to councilmen, not working.

The word was out. They'd heard about the bull. Had they heard about the dog-glowies yet? Every new act in the freak show started them fretting now. He thought they'd noticed that very few civvies were getting hurt and killed these days, a big improvement on the daily round of casualties back in old Jacinto, but no, some dick always had to whine about every damn thing.

It wasn't just Ingram and his one-asshole-one-vote brigade who were arguing the toss now. Other civvies, the regular kind who'd sucked up the pain just the same as Gears since E-Day, were starting to wobble too.

A man in his fifties flagged Baird down. He had a saw in his hand, so Baird thought he was going to beg some timber from him. Baird stopped the Packhorse and wound down the window.

"This is all spoken for," he said. "If you need materials, ask Parry."

"You found that bull, didn't you?"

Baird hadn't even realized that people recognized him, let alone knew what he did. He didn't take much interest in anyone outside his immediate circle so he assumed others couldn't give a shit about him. Wow, this felt weird.

"Yeah," he said, faintly disturbed. "What about it?"

"Are we all going to get infected?"

"What am I, a doctor?" Baird resented the man for worrying about his own ass when Eugen was dead. *Yeah, I know. My own finest quality.* "Look, I've been skewered by polyps and splattered with their guts, and I've not turned glowie. There's such a thing as hypochondria, you know."

Baird didn't wait for a reply and just drove off. The mood was changing. He didn't realize how quickly it was happening until he drove past Jace Stratton trying to hang a front door on one of the new houses—okay, *huts*—being built at the edge of the camp. The door hung from one hinge at a funny angle. Jace was surrounded by a gaggle of people, trying to explain something with the aid of a screwdriver. He looked like he was defending himself.

Okay . . . I'll do the decent thing. Got to learn by doing, Bernie says.

Baird parked up and ambled over to the discussion.

"What's the point wasting time on this?" one of the women was saying. *Typical. Never satisfied, women.* She took in the whole plot of new huts with a sweep of her arm. "We should be getting out of here while we can. We'll need all this for the mainland. That's what we should be doing, packing to go back to Tyrus."

"Look, lady," Jace said, "I don't make the decisions. Now, anyone want to give me a hand with this door? 'Cause it's real hard doing this single-handed."

"What about that *thing*? That leviathan? It came *right into the docks*. The Hammer of Dawn couldn't even kill it. We're just sitting here like those chickens, waiting to have our necks wrung."

Baird cleared his throat. "Hi folks. Not satisfied with the benevolence of the COG for some reason?"

The woman turned and stared at him. She could curdle milk with that face. "I don't call being exposed to unnecessary risk *benevolence*."

"You want to go back to the mainland?" Baird spread his hands. "Seriously? Have you got amnesia or something?"

The crowd was about fifteen people, mainly young mothers, kids, and a few older men who didn't look fit enough for work duties. Even now that a couple of thousand extra civvies had been squeezed into the camp, Baird didn't see much of these people and he didn't know them. Jace gave him an exasperated glare and pointed to the door. Baird got the message and went over to support its weight for him.

"You're not very respectful, young man," said one of the old men. "You know this is the worst place to be stuck when those Lambent are closing in on us. We could always move around on the mainland."

"Wow, there must have been a lot of head injuries around

here," Baird said. "Because I distinctly remember Jacinto being surrounded by grubs. Before we had to sink the whole city just to get away from them, that is."

"We could still run *somewhere*."

"This *is* that somewhere." Baird wished he hadn't started this. "Look, if you'd seen the recon postcards Hoffman brought back from his trip to Tyrus, you wouldn't be rushing to pack your bags. Trust me. Shit Central, people."

"Recon?" The old guy was so startled by the word that he didn't even bitch at Baird for bad language. "You mean someone's gone back already?"

"Nice one, Baird." Jace sighed. "Stoke 'em up some more, why doncha."

Baird didn't realize the civvies didn't know. It was just a recon. Everybody did recons. How else did they think anyone could plan ahead for a possible evacuation?

"They only took a look," Baird said defensively. "Prescott didn't put down a deposit on the place or anything. You want to sail thousands of kilometers without knowing what it's like first? Because it'll be a one-way trip."

"There's a *petition*," the woman said, as if that changed everything. "One of the other blocks did a *petition*. *Consultation*. We want a vote on whether we stay here or go now. If we're willing to take the risk, the Chairman should respect that."

Jace, who'd kept out of the debate to finish screwing in the hinges, swung the door shut. "Yeah. That's it. I'm done. Come on, Baird. We're just the hired help, remember?"

Baird started the Packhorse and drove east across the camp to the border between Little Gorasnaya and Civilization. That was what it said on the handwritten sign, anyway. He couldn't read enough Gorasnayan to translate what the Gorasni had scrawled in retaliation underneath.

"The civvies got a point," Jace said. "We gotta think

ahead. Can't just wait around to see if the stalks stop and things get better."

"That's what the management's paid to decide."

"But it's all guesswork."

"Hey, are you after my job as Resident Whiny Asshole?"

"Just sayin'."

"They ought to trust the brass. How many civvies have died since we got here? Other than natural causes, I mean. A handful. They were being slaughtered every day back home. They don't know they're born."

"Are you in love or something? 'Cause I ain't seen you this positive about them upstairs. *Ever.*"

"Facts, Jace. Just the facts."

Baird paused at a patch of open ground where Cole was teaching the camp kids the finer points of thrashball. Trescu's son was really into it, all grim concentration like his dad while he practiced throw-ins. The class was a mixed bag of youngsters—Gorasni, Tyran, Pelruan, even a couple of ex-Stranded—and they all looked mesmerized by Cole's moves. He always made it look so easy. He was also one hell of a showman. He scored, not really trying, and got all the kids lined up behind him pretending to be part of a locomotive chugging up to full speed.

"Whoo!" Cole pumped his arm like an engineer sounding a train's whistle. "Whoooo!"

Baird hadn't seen him do that since before E-Day. It was always his victory dance when he scored for the Cougars.

One of the kids chimed in. "Whoo-*whoo!*"

"The Cole Train don't go *whoo-whoo,*" Cole said, grinning. "The Cole Train goes *whoooo!*"

The train broke up and they went on playing again.

"Damn, he's still got the speed," Jace said.

"Yeah—he's the Cole Train." Baird didn't like the word *still.* "Why wouldn't he?"

"It's been fifteen years since he played, Baird. I mean, the man's a legend, but his career was *short*. Five years. And he's had a hard war."

Cole looked genuinely happy. He usually did, but *this* was what he was born for: thrashball. Baird rarely felt sorry for anybody but himself and he accepted that wasn't something to be proud of, but right then he felt terrible for Cole. Cole had been an international star. He'd been rich and adored, the biggest star of the biggest sport in the COG. He'd lost a lot more than Baird had. But he'd never once bitched about it, just joked at his own expense about how washed up he was and how all that money was just useful kindling now. Baird suspected the thrashball class was doing a lot more for Cole than it was doing even for the kids.

Good for you, buddy.

"Well, it keeps the little assholes out of trouble," Baird said, and drove on.

When he got back to the vehicle compound, a couple of the civilian support staff were arguing in the garage about their chances of surviving on the mainland. The debate was spreading like a dose of clap.

"Either we've got a pandemic or else formative causation really exists," Baird said.

"Well, they know Hoffman did the recon." Jace picked a splinter out of his finger, wincing. "Come on, I'm so damn hungry I could eat Bernie's cat curry. Hey, you know what she gave me?"

"A smack around the ear?"

"The Stranded left some feral moggies behind." Jace pulled a pair of beige suede gloves out of his belt and showed them off. The inside was glossy black fur, definitely feline. "She's the survival queen, Baird. And they do make damn fine gloves. Is it true they taste like rabbit?"

"I hope I never have to find out."

"Well, *rabbit* tastes like rabbit. They usually got some in the mess if you get in line early enough."

Baird wasn't in the mood, but he followed Jace into the mess anyway. When they walked through the doors, the rapidly spreading interest in glowie bulls suddenly made more sense. There was a TV program on the monitor with actual moving pictures for a change. It was Prescott. Every Gear at the tables was watching in silence, shoveling down food on autopilot.

"Holy shit," Jace said. "First time we see a show since we left Jacinto, and it's starring *him*. Is it too much to ask for a goddamn movie?"

There were very few TV monitors around the base, mainly because there was no TV service. Occasionally, there'd be broadcasts of dreary still pictures trying to spice up equally dreary public information shit recorded for the radio, but New Jacinto had slipped back centuries in more ways than one. A guy had to make his own entertainment. Baird found his eyes being drawn hypnotically to the moving images even though it was Richard frigging Prescott.

Y'know, he can't be so bad. He wanted me on his staff.

I never gave him an answer, though.

"Citizens," Prescott said, making that one word sound like a divine announcement booming through parting clouds. Yeah, the guy had a hell of a delivery, Baird had to admit it. "I realize the situation is difficult at the moment, and many of you are finding it challenging to adjust to such crowded conditions. Your willingness to endure this is appreciated. But life must become more restricted while we deal with the changing threat facing us. Those of you who come from Jacinto, Branascu, or any of the mainland cities know how to handle this. Those of you who have never experienced Locust emergence will have to learn. Gears will be conducting safety drills so that you know what to do in the event of a Lambent attack. The important thing to remember is that we've dealt with similar situations before, we have *survived*, and we will survive *again*."

Prescott paused for a moment. He looked down as if something was too painful to say—pure theater, because nothing ever was, not for that asshole—and then raised his eyes again, blinking a little.

"Our priorities are to secure the camp, deal with any polyp incursions, and to continue to salvage whatever we can of food crops and timber that falls within range of contamination," he said. "But we also have to plan for the future. We've always intended to regain our strength here and, eventually, to return to Tyrus and start rebuilding the Coalition. Now that we have imulsion supplies, we'll be carrying out regular reconnaissance missions to assess the changing situation on the mainland. That doesn't mean we're preparing to abandon this island. But it does mean that if the very worst were to happen, then we would be ready for it. I ask you to do what you do best—to remain calm and steadfast."

Jace stopped eating. "Holy shit, that's just gonna make the civvies want to leave sooner."

"He's covering his ass," said one of the gunners at the next table.

Baird sighed. "You're so cynical. That's the problem with folks these days."

The gunner burst out laughing and went on with his meal. Baird went through his hourly ritual of checking that the data disc was still safe in his pocket. Maybe that was why Prescott wanted him on his staff. The urgency of solving the mystery might have been overtaken by other events unfolding at a breakneck speed, but Baird still had a mission.

Everything that he imagined might be on it so far had been ruled out. It was infuriating, and it was also starting to worry him.

Okay . . . it can't be a recipe for Lambency. It can't be a police file on him whacking rivals, because what's a few assassinations when you've chargrilled billions of COG citizens? If it's blackmail photos of him doing the Locust Queen—nah, she'd have mentioned that when we had our little soirée in the tunnels, for sure. So what's left? Drink, drugs, hookers? No, a guy would want to brag about that these days. Well, I would, anyway.

It's got to be something we can't even imagine yet.

Baird put the disc to the back of his mind and fretted about the stalks spitting out glowie dogs. If the civvies wanted to shit their pants and run, that was fine by him. The COG army could survive on its own. It had all the skills a society needed.

"Nice touch to mention Branascu," Jace said, wolfing down his stew. "All one big happy family."

"Yeah," said Baird. "Shame about the abandon-ship bit, though."

"So what do you reckon? You ever want to go back to Tyrus? I kinda like it here."

It wasn't a case of *where* for Baird. It was a case of *who*. The realization that he was actually quite attached to individuals made him feel scared in ways he couldn't even pin down. It hurt. The more people he gave a damn about, the more anxious he felt.

"Put me down as a don't-care," he lied.

TEMPORARY HOUSING PLOT A5, NEW JACINTO.

"Have you heard?" Sam flipped through the sheets on her clipboard as the truck ground sedately through the dirt-track roads of the camp. "Mitchell says some of the dead zones have stopped spreading."

"Which means?" Dom asked.

"Well . . . there's got to be a maximum area they can kill off. They can't get everywhere, and the contamination only extends so far."

"You heard what Baird saw. And Bernie."

"Yeah, Lambent come in all shapes and sizes. So?"

"So what's going to turn glowie next?"

"Dom, are you channeling bloody Baird or something?"

"Sorry." Dom knew better than to get his hopes up. It was way too early for anyone to assume they had a handle on the Lambent. "It just feels like the last months in Jacinto again. Everyone crammed into smaller and smaller spaces. Driving around doling out food rations. You know."

Sam probably did. If she was half as tuned in to people as he thought she was, she'd understand that he was having one of his flashback days, when things didn't just remind him of old Jacinto. They reminded him of Maria and the kids.

"Got it," she said. And the subject was closed.

Engineers and off-duty Gears were still working around the clock to replace the wooden houses burned down by the first invasion of polyps, so the influx of refugees was creating an even bigger backlog. They were crowded into tents, a pretty miserable prospect after the comfortable fishing cottages they were used to. Dom braced for a sullen reception.

A line had already formed when they got to the distribution point, and it summed up the whole situation for him. He could tell the difference between the old Jacinto population and the Pelruan locals, even if they were all complete strangers, simply by the way they stood.

The Jacinto contingent had spent years queuing for everything, and their stances were relaxed as they took the opportunity to socialize. But the Pelruan folks had never needed to do it, and so they stood in awkward silence, facing the head of the queue as if they'd miss their turn if they dared turn around and chat with their neighbor. *Poor bastards*. Their lives had been wrecked in less than a year. If they were starting to hate their government and everyone who represented it, he couldn't actually blame them.

And then there were the former Stranded, and he didn't mean the decent and honest Dizzy variety. Some of the families of the gangs who'd accepted Prescott's amnesty hadn't left with Ollivar's pirate fleet. Dom had no idea why they stayed now, because they certainly weren't accepted by anyone, least of all the Gorasni. They were probably getting less to eat than the average Stranded gangster. They stayed in a tight, suspicious line of their own.

"So much for integration," Sam muttered, heaving the sacks off the truck. Dom had never done ration runs with her before and he suspected some well-meaning amateur matchmaker had deliberately paired them on the duty roster. "Come on. We've got four more stops and we've got to pick up supplies from Jonty's farm before lunch. Look, you drop the stuff down, vegetables and flour first, and I'll do the handovers and check them off the list."

"Sounds like a plan."

Sam had a natural talent for making people relax in what was a pretty degrading situation. She made it more of a street market than a grim soup kitchen, chatting and joking with people as if they were customers with a choice, not bums getting welfare. She patted their kids on the head and asked how the family was, even if she didn't have a clue who they were. At one point she found a misshapen carrot that Dom could only describe as *anatomically correct* and turned it into an impromptu stand-up routine.

"Oo-er, missus!" she said, laughing her head off as she brandished the thing like a grisly trophy. "Don't all rush at once, ladies! I might keep this one for myself. Perks of the job."

There was a lot of giggling and hooting from the women at the expense of the men in the line. "Ah, come on, you don't need it," one of the old women said. She grinned at Dom. "You've got this nice young man."

Dom felt himself blush to his roots. In a few short years he'd be forty, and here he was, embarrassed as hell by a bunch of housewives and unable to meet Sam's eye. But when he did, she wasn't really laughing. She had that odd, sad look as if she'd said something important to him but he hadn't been listening, and the moment had passed to repeat it.

But she seemed to shake it off and got the Pelruan people to join in the banter. They knew her better than the Jacinto crowd. Dom hoped the little kids didn't understand the carrot joke.

"Hello, Miss Byrne!" A small boy gazed up at her adoringly like she was a princess. "Where's your rat-bike? Have you killed any more crab glowies?"

"Ah, I'm putting blades on the wheels," Sam said, straight-faced. "It's going to cut right through them like *butter*. Legs everywhere. Splat!"

The boy laughed. Of course: she'd been the one up there fighting polyps with Anya and Bernie, so she was a heroine to them. They definitely looked at her differently from the way they looked at him. He was one of the bastards who made them leave the only home they'd ever known. She was the avenging angel who swooped in and blew the shit out of monsters.

This is why I hate doing civvie liaison. Find me a grub or a glowie to kill. Please. I can't do normal yet. Maybe I never will.

By the time the food packages had been handed out, the atmosphere—in that part of the camp, at least—was a lot happier and less tense than it had been when they drove in.

Dom headed to the next drop-off point, glancing at Sam occasionally as she went through her list ticking off names. He hated himself for looking. Every guy checked her out, because she had that dark Kashkuri glamour she'd inherited from her mom, but he found himself looking for something beyond that. He was caught in that painful, guilty place between wanting to feel at home with her and seeing Maria superimposed on every woman he glanced at.

"You're pretty good with the sales patter," Dom said.

"Oh, the market was a big social event in Anvegad. Real performance art." Sam looked up and kept her eyes straight ahead. "Besides, it makes it a lot easier for me than standing there throwing them scraps like we're some animal charity."

Dom decided not to ask why food handouts pissed her off so much. He watched her go through the same ferociously cheerful routine at every drop-off and realized that Anvegad must have been worse than a Stranded camp in the closing years of the Pendulum Wars.

Why did you have to be nice as well as good-looking? Couldn't you just be a total bitch and make it easier for me?

They reached the far end of the camp at the construction site, a no-man's-land of cleared fields and open countryside. There were as many Gears as civvies working on the site. Dom inhaled a pungent mix of sawdust, resin, and vehicle exhaust through the open window as he drove past the defended perimeter on the way to Merris Farm.

No, Jonty's farm. The name was changing. At least the poor asshole would be commemorated.

"I want rosebushes and an orchard," Sam said, sticking her head out the window to look back at the half-built new homes. "And a tank trap."

"Hopeless romantic, aren't you?"

"That's what they tell me."

Dom hadn't intended the conversation to go down that

route and he willed himself not to say anything else he'd
regret. A couple of Ravens passed north on patrol. He took
no notice until the radio net came to life a few kilometers
down the road.

"Control to any callsign north of the base," Mathieson
said. "We've got a possible polyp incursion near the old reservoir. Grid delta-seven."

Sam grabbed the handset from the dashboard. "We're
about ten klicks away, Control. We'll respond."

Gettner cut in on the circuit. "KR-Eight-Zero—on it."

Sam shook her head. "Does that woman ever land? She
must sleep hanging from the rafters like a bloody bat."

"She doesn't want time to think," Dom said. "You know
how it is."

Sanity was all about keeping busy and not allowing the
demons—or ghosts—any room to slip through, Dom
decided. He tried to visualize the map as he drove cross-
country, remembering where the big north-south fissure
stopped. The charts said thirty kilometers north of the naval
base.

"It can't be stalks." He headed off-road. The truck
bounced and shuddered with alarming metallic screeches,
complaining that it wasn't a 'Dill and that it really didn't
like this rough terrain. "The fissure doesn't come that far
south."

"What, then?"

"Either polyps move a lot further overground than we
thought, or the assholes have found something else to hitch
a ride on."

"It'd have to be the size of a leviathan. Those glowies are
a meter across."

"We'll know soon enough."

"Should've brought my bike." Sam gripped the dashboard as the truck threw her around. "*That's* how you fight

polyps. Okay . . . Byrne to Eight-Zero, can you see anything yet?"

"We're over the site, Byrne," Gettner said. "But it's thick tree cover. We need eyes on the ground."

"That's us, Eight-Zero. We'll use you for a marker."

Dom could see the Raven now, hovering above the woods. He headed for the edge of the trees.

Dom stopped the truck and they got out. "Listen. Hear that?"

Something was crashing around in the undergrowth. All they had to do now was wait, aim, and shoot. Dom climbed up on the flatbed to get a better view and gave Sam a hand up beside him.

"They must have heard us by now," he said. "They can't miss the Raven, either."

Dom stood still, just listening for a couple of minutes. Then he saw movement between the trees and the telltale flicker of yellow light in the dappled shade.

"Here they come," he said, taking aim. "Ready for you this time, bitches . . . yeah, come and get your rations."

The polyps broke from the trees and charged toward the truck.

There were more of them than he expected, a *lot* more. He opened up on them at fifty meters, detonating part of the first wave in a spray of greasy meat, but they kept coming. Even with two overlapping arcs of fire, a bunch of them dodged through and vanished under the truck before he could pop them. For a second, he and Sam stared at each other in horror. The little shits were right underneath them.

Shit. Fuel tank. Polyps. Truck bomb.

Sam grabbed his arm and dragged him to the edge of the flatbed. "Jump! Come on, Dom, bloody well *jump!*"

He fell more than leapt clear and rolled a couple of

meters. The truck rose a meter into the air on a cushion of smoke and flame as the explosion lifted it and sent it crashing back to the ground again. Dom didn't see the second explosion because he curled instinctively into a ball to shield himself. When he looked up, the truck was engulfed in flame.

"Where are they?" Sam was on her knees, groping for her Lancer. "Where the hell have the others gone?"

Dom could still hear the Raven overhead. He could see movement better on his hands and knees because he was at polyp eye level. For a moment, he expected to find himself nose to nose with them.

"Eight-Zero here, are you two okay? We heard that."

"Byrne here—no injuries." Sam got to her feet. "Except the truck. Can't you see the fire?"

Dom saw movement zip past his eyeline and knelt back on his heels in one movement to open fire. A small explosion shook the undergrowth, sending smoke and flame licking around the tree trunks before it died down.

"I can now," Gettner said. "We'll winch you up."

Sam looked down at the ground just as Dom felt something through his knees. It was like being on the deck of a ship pounded by heavy seas, a lurching sensation followed by a shock wave.

"Stalk," he said. There was another shudder. It was getting stronger. "Stalk . . . *stalk!*"

He was looking at the trees in front of him when they just tipped over. That was the only way he could describe it. He watched them part like fur on an animal as the ground heaved upward and two twisted columns dappled with red light punched out of the soil. For a moment he thought a crater was going to open up and swallow him. As he struggled to stand, he realized he'd lost sight of Sam.

"Sam! Sam, where are you?"

"Come on—*run!*"

Sam was behind him now, trying to haul him to his feet. When he stood, he tripped over the tangle of roots exposed by the subsidence. Run? They'd be frigging lucky if they could climb out of the debris. It was like a lumber yard that had taken a direct hit.

The last thing he saw before he turned and scrambled after Sam was those breathing, pulsing blisters on the trunks of the stalks opening like seed pods. He could have sworn he saw lumps spurt out of them, like the things were choking on food and coughing it up. He waited for glowie dogs to splash onto the ground and come after him.

"Santiago, get out! *Now!*" Gettner brought the Raven down so low that the few trees still standing swayed wildly, whipped by the downdraft. "Come on!"

Sam kept stopping to turn and drag Dom by the arm. He could see the Raven through the branches now. Leaves and twigs whipped around and peppered his face as he stumbled out of the undergrowth at Sam's heels and ran for the cable dangling from the crew bay. Training kicked in and he shoved the lifting strop over Sam's head and shoulders first before she could argue about it. Her boots were off the ground in seconds.

Dom turned around with his Lancer raised, ready for the wave of Lambent dogs he was expecting to boil out of the woods, but there was nothing behind him. He waited for the cable to pay out again, looped the strop under his armpits, and let Barber hoist him inboard and haul him across the deck on his ass as the Raven lifted clear.

"Get some images and plot those bastards, Nat," Gettner said. "Santiago, can you tell the difference between a vehicle and frigging ordnance? *Shit.* Another truck gone."

"Major, were you and Baird separated at birth or something?"

"Look, I'm glad you're okay, Santiago, but you can explain it to Len Parry. He'll be spitting nails about that truck."

"Okay, I'll go back and salvage what I can later."

"Let's make sure those things are dead first." Gettner held the Raven hovering at a cautious distance. "Nat, check my figures, will you? I make this well south of the end of the fissure line—about fifteen kilometers."

Barber secured the camera again and grabbed his chart. Dom knew damn well where the stalks had come up. He could read the truck's speedo. He knew how far he'd driven. But he still wanted to hear Barber tell him he was wrong, and when he looked at Sam he could see she wanted to hear it too.

"Nat?" Gettner said again.

"You're right, Gill." Barber marked a couple of crosses on the chart. "Fourteen-point-three klicks, actually."

It changed everything. The stalks had come up through solid granite bedrock, not the weaker sedimentary rock. All the plans about avoiding the softer bedrock areas and taking refuge on the granite had gone down the tubes. Nobody said a word for a while.

Shit, it really is Ephyra all over again. History repeats and repeats and repeats.

"That means those things can come up anywhere," Barber said at last, as if they hadn't worked it out for themselves. But someone had to say it.

A guy could stand his ground, or run, or die. The COG—especially 26 RTI—made a religion out of resilience. From childhood, everyone was taught to take pride in getting up each time they were knocked down, so much so that Dom used to wonder if folks had forgotten what they were bothering to get up for. Now he tried to find the line between noble refusal to accept defeat and just never learning to move on.

He could hardly bear to look back on the last fifteen years. It was starting to look like it had all been for nothing.

"There's nowhere safe on Vectes now," he said. "So it doesn't matter where the hell we go. Only what we do."

CHAPTER 17

We must plan on the basis that there's nobody else left out there. We can deduce that the Hammer of Dawn has been deployed from the reports received from ships and by the ash deposits, but we don't know why the decision was taken, or how many cities have been affected, or how many survivors there may be. All we can be sure of is that we will get no support from Ephyra for the foreseeable future, if Ephyra has survived at all. We're used to being cut off, and we are a self-reliant community. We will come through this. And, one day, we will not only discover what has happened to the rest of Sera, but we will rebuild, and we will thrive again.

(The Right Honorable Bryn Mackin, Governor of New Fortitude
Territory, in a radio broadcast to the people of Noroa and Galangi
shortly after the Hammer of Dawn strikes, one year after E-Day)

MATAKI FARM, GALANGI, SOUTH ISLANDS: TEN DAYS AFTER THE GLOBAL HAMMER OF DAWN STRIKE, FOURTEEN YEARS EARLIER.

The ash was everywhere today.

Bernie bent down to wipe it off the leaves of the laurel bush by the front door. She rubbed it between her fingers, wondering how far it had drifted, and realized that a percentage of it was probably incinerated bodies. She wiped her hands on her pants.

I enabled this. In a way, this happened because of something I did.

Connections were everywhere: loops had closed. She'd fought at Aspho Fields, part of C Company. They'd bought time for special forces to raid the UIR research station at Aspho Point, and grab the Indie research that gave the COG its Hammer technology. And now the people killed by that technology—and plenty of fucking grubs, she hoped—had finally come back to her on the jetstream in the form of ash from the burning cities. She was breathing them all in.

Why did they fire it? Must have been the last stand. At least we fought back. At least we put a dent in the bastards. Didn't we?

She didn't know. She might never find out. That got to her more than anything now.

Everything comes back to 26 RTI in the end. Major Fenix, 26 RTI, Marcus Fenix's dad—he designed the Hammer of Dawn. Shit. I wonder if Marcus is still alive? He was never the same after Carlos died.

The ash made a lovely sunrise, a vivid scarlet sky with a few wispy clouds across the fierce amber disk of the sun. The last time Bernie had seen anything like it was when the volcano on Soteroa had erupted when she was a kid.

But that was all that was lovely about it.

Ash was a pain in the arse for farmers. A good few days of rain, that was what she needed now. It'd wash the stuff off the grazing. If the ash built up on the pasture, she'd have to feed the livestock on hay and the last of the pellets. She couldn't keep that up for long.

"I'm a selfish cow, aren't I, Mossie?" The dog stopped sniffing around the corpse-coated grass and followed her up

the track to the calf shed. "All those people dead somewhere, and I'm worrying about stock I'm going to slaughter
anyway."

Neal was late. She could normally set her watch by him.
So this was how it was going to be for the rest of her life, a
daily routine of talking to animals and worrying about the
weather, without even the occasional glimpse of the rest of
the world on the TV.

*Home, my arse. What's so great about it? It's a building.
It's not people.*

The first task today was to get one of the calves to feed
from a bucket, but the poor little sod wasn't a quick
learner. Most got the idea in minutes; this one was on day
two. Bernie dipped her fingers in the milk and let him suck
on them, but every time she sneaked her hand lower to get
his muzzle into the bucket and hold his head down, he
panicked and jerked free. She now had more milk up her
sleeve and spattered over her face than she'd managed to
get inside the calf. He didn't care much that she was a sergeant who'd never had a baby Gear fail one of her training
courses.

"Okay, sweetheart, I'm going to put you back on your
mum," she said. He tottered away, mooing plaintively. He
was just a baby and he wanted his mother. "Sod the milk. I
can get it from Jim Kilikano."

Cows didn't forget a slight. This one had been calling for
her calf for days and she came at Bernie like an angry bull
when she opened the gate. Bernie let the calf loose and ran
for it. She slammed the gate behind her just in time and
stopped to watch the reunion for a few minutes.

*They're just like us. Emotional. Maybe that's how the
grubs see humans. Not an enemy, maybe, just another creature they can't afford to be sentimental about. How do the
cows see me?*

The sound of boots on the gravel track made her look up. She expected it to be Neal, but it was Dan.

"Morning, Bernie." He rummaged in his pockets for too long, as if he wasn't sure he wanted to find what he was looking for. "Shit. I don't know where to start."

"What's wrong?"

"Let's go into the house."

It had to be Neal—an accident, or something that would upset her or piss her off. "Just spit it out, mate. Is Neal okay or not?"

"It's not about him. Are you sure you want to talk here?"

"How do I know until you tell me what it is?"

"Okay." Dan took a breath. "It's your brother."

"What about him?" Bernie hadn't heard from Mick since he'd sent the photo of his new granddaughter a year ago. She really should have found a way of calling him on the radio. But even this war hadn't made them any closer. "We don't talk. You know that."

Dan had a crumpled piece of paper in his hand now. "He's dead, Bernie. I'm really sorry."

That took a few seconds to sink in. Her first thought was a heart attack. He'd spent his days either sitting on his arse driving a bus, or sitting on his arse watching the telly.

"How come *you* know?" It was such a pointless question that she knew she was shocked and going about this the wrong way. She didn't ask how Mick had died. "Who told you?"

"Some guy sailed in to Noroa last night. Took him months to get out of Kaia. He brought a list."

Dead. I never got on with Mick and now he's dead. And I feel terrible. I feel guilty. What the hell am I going to say to his wife, the snotty bitch?

"You've lost me, Dan," she said. "What's Kaia got to do with it? Was he taken to hospital?" If you needed cardiac surgery, you went to Kaia. That was it. It was all starting to make sense. "But the place was trashed by the grubs ages ago."

"I know," Dan said. "Forget the hospital thing. Mick was working in Jasper when the grubs came. The whole family was over there."

Dan stopped. Bernie had no idea that Mick had even left Noroa. Maybe that was why he sent the photo. She tried to make sense of the dates, and why he hadn't sent her a forwarding address, but all she could think of was that she'd been watching TV while the grubs were killing him. Drill kicked in and she made herself take control.

"Dan, are they *all* dead?"

"'Fraid so, love . . . look, I don't know what to say. Jasper was flattened. This guy's a paramedic and he ended up with a lot of IDs from the morgue." Dan held out the scrap of paper to her. She could see handwriting on it, a list like a grocery order. "You want to talk to him on the radio? He only made it because he hooked up with a couple of Gears and they took a boat."

The focus came back. *Gears.*

It felt like someone had plugged her back into reality, all bright color and sharp lines. "They pulled out of Kaia, then."

"I don't know." Dan's expression said it was a strange question to ask when he'd just told her that her brother and his family had been slaughtered. "Should I have asked?"

There were Gears on Noroa. That changed everything. "I'll ask them myself."

"I'm not quite following you. You sure you're okay, Bernie? You want someone to come and sit with you?"

"No, I can manage. Thanks, Dan."

Dan should have known her well enough by now. She wasn't callous. She was just defaulting to what she'd been trained to do. When Gears in her company got killed, she had to park it for later and get on with whatever had to be done.

And she'd been a lot closer to them than she'd ever been to Mick.

Bernie found herself back in the barn with no recollection of walking in there or of Dan leaving. Guilt at being a bad sister nagged at her until she made herself look at the piece of paper and saw all the names he'd scribbled on it— *her* name, her tribal name, Mataki: Michael J., wife, two sons, two grandsons, and one granddaughter, Philippa Jane, not a year old. Bernie had never even held the baby, but for some reason that death cut her up a lot more than any of the others.

There's no sense keeping things going here anymore. None of it. The line's broken. I'm the last Mataki. And Gears are back to Noroa. So that's where I need to be.

Neal wandered in at last. She didn't check the time.

"Sorry I'm late," he said. "Bloody ash clogged up the air filter and I broke down outside town. Had to clear it out."

"Mick's dead." She assumed the news was out and that everyone knew before she did anyway. Dan didn't mean to gossip. He just thought he was keeping people off her back. "They're all dead now."

"Yeah . . . I heard," Neal said. "I'm sorry, Bern. Sorry for what I said about him, too."

"You want to do me a favor?"

"Look, I said I was sorry—"

"No, I mean it like it sounds. I'm asking you to do something for me." As soon as she said it, the relief settled on her. She hadn't realized she was even thinking that decisively. "I want you to take over the farm."

Neal did his silent sigh, shutting his eyes and shaking his head. "You're upset, love. Give yourself some time."

"No, it's yours. Just take it." She really didn't need any

time. The longer she buggered around with the options, the less certain she'd be. "You made it what it is. Do what you want with it. I'm going to go to Noroa."

Neal sat down on the hay bale next to her. "You don't know anyone there. And you're the home guard, remember."

"The grubs don't even know Galangi's here. I can do more good on Noroa."

"Shit, Dan told you about the Gears, didn't he? Silly bastard. I told him not to."

If anything made her mind up, it was that. Neal thought she needed protecting from herself. Well, fuck that. She was leaving as soon as she could get transport. She took her house keys off the fob on her belt and shoved them into his hand.

"The farm's yours. I'll write it all down on a piece of paper, not that there's a land registry left to argue about it. Dan can witness it, like he witnessed the divorce. Clean break, okay?"

"God, Bern, you were always such a sensible woman. Why the hell are you doing this now? Galangi might end up being all there is left of Sera."

"And if I do this, maybe it won't be. Come on. You owe me that much."

"Okay," he said. She could see he was just humoring her. "Whatever you want, love."

Maybe she was more shocked and grieving than she wanted to admit, but when she started clearing out the farmhouse and deciding which things were really worth keeping, she felt better than she had for years. *This is me. This is who I am. I don't have to sit here and wait for death to come and find me.* She packed her rucksack and filled every spare space and belt pouch with ammunition for the two rifles.

As soon as she loaded herself up and tested the pack for balance, she felt fucking *terrific*—capable of anything, ready to go anywhere, and years younger again.

I shall remain vigilant and unyielding in my pursuit of the enemies of the Coalition. I will defend and maintain the Order of Life as it was proclaimed by the Allfathers of the Coalition in the Octus Canon. I will forsake the life I had before so that I may perform my duty as long as I am needed. Steadfast, I shall hold my place in the machine and acknowledge my place in the Coalition. I am a Gear.

That was the oath every Gear swore on recruitment, and she hadn't forgotten a word of it. *As long as I am needed.* Neal could take the piss out of her all he wanted, but she could still do the job, and that job needed doing more than ever before.

It took her three days to persuade Gabby to do some trawling off Noroa and take her along for the trip. He was a solid bloke. She'd known him all her life.

"You're afraid of the water," he said. "Always were. You sure you want to do this?"

"It's only four hundred klicks." He'd forgotten she'd taken part in amphibious landings during the war, shit-scared of water or not. She could make herself do anything if it needed doing. "Anyway, you've got to take me now. I already radioed GHN that I was coming."

"Okay. Just remember—wave once. Just once. And don't look back again. It's a lot less painful."

Bernie didn't ask him how he knew that, seeing as he'd lived here as long as she could remember. She just took the advice.

And he was right. It was.

OBLIVION CENTRAL SQUATTERS' CAMP, TYRUS: 182 DAYS AFTER THE HAMMER OF DAWN STRIKES.

One day, there'd be a world where assholes got what they deserved. Dizzy comforted himself with that thought, and made a silent pledge that he'd still be around to see it.

He had to be now, for his girls.

Twins. Goddamn. Can't say Rosalyn didn't warn me, but . . . goddamn.

He picked his way through Oblivion, looking for a gift. Folks brought things for the babies but they forgot that the new mom needed a little something *personal* to make her feel like a lady again, something . . . well, he didn't know exactly what, but he'd know it when he saw it.

He walked along the rows of people sitting around waiting to trade. One fella had a gilt brush and comb set on a little matching tray, a real nice thing if you had a dressing table to put it on. Dizzy squatted on his heels to look at the stuff laid out on the checkered cloth and turned over a leather-bound book. The back cover and some of the end pages were missing, and the edges of the leather were charred.

"Looking for anything in particular?" the man asked. "What have you got to trade?"

There were two things Dizzy did better than anyone else he knew. He could keep a big ship running, and he could brew great hooch. The two were connected. A good engineer knew how to build an efficient still. But nobody needed a ship's turbine fixing, and pretty well everybody needed to get away from the real world sometimes. Some careers just picked themselves.

"'Shine," Dizzy said. "I make pretty good 'shine."

The man perked up a little. "Ooh, yeah. I heard. Got any brewed now?"

"Just lettin' it rest a little. Acquirin' a bit o' *character*. Two days."

"You want to come back then?"

"Maybe. My need's kinda urgent today, though. I want something nice for my missus."

The man pushed forward the brush and comb set for closer inspection. There were still a few strands of hair in it, very fine, very blond. Dizzy put the thought out of his head and took a small wrench out of his pocket.

"Hate partin' with tools," he sighed, trying not to look too keen.

"Long as you come by with some of that hooch and give me first refusal, I'm willing to deal."

"Done."

Dizzy and the man shook on it and the brush set was his. He tucked it inside his coat just to be on the safe side. There were some nasty assholes crawling out of the woodwork these days. Most folks in the camps were decent human beings who were just unlucky—unlucky to have a shithouse government that didn't care if they burned alive so long as goddamn Jacinto was okay. They didn't know how to look after themselves in a place where there wasn't any law, so they were easy meat for the criminal types.

And the grubs. Most of the world's dead now, but the grubs are back. More of 'em than ever. What was it all for? What good did that goddamn Hammer do?

If anyone touched Dizzy or so much as looked at his wife and kids the wrong way—human or grub—he knew how to handle that. He felt in his pocket for the reassuring grip of heavy steel. A big industrial wrench was handy for more than fixing engines.

The barter market was at the end of what had been a rich folks' street full of trees and smart iron railings. Some of the trees were dead or just stumps, but one or two had survived

somehow and were trying to sprout new growth. All the
houses had been flattened. Kids squabbled over the bricks,
fighting to collect them. If they took them to the volunteers
building shelters on the other side of the camp, they got paid
in food. It was quite a business.

Dizzy waved to them. "Found anything 'cept bricks?"

One of the kids—nine, ten years old—stopped and
looked up at him suspiciously, hugging a red plastic bucket
that didn't have a handle.

"Nah, these were the nobs' houses," the kid said. "They
all got away and took their stuff with 'em." He kicked a few
bricks out of the way. "See?"

"We don't need their stuff, son. We're gonna do all right
on our own."

"Yeah!" The boy brightened up as if a really good idea
had occurred to him. "And when they come crawling to us
for help, we can tell 'em to piss off, just like they did to us!"

Dizzy didn't have the heart to tell him not to cuss. The
kid had a right. Jacinto had left them to die.

"I know it's hard not to hate 'em." Kids were impression-
able so Dizzy tried to pick his words carefully. "But we're
still alive, ain't we? The grubs couldn't kill us and neither
could the government. And we ain't got an army, but we get
by. We'll still be here when Jacinto's long gone."

The boy really looked as if he was taking it all in and feeling better about things.

"You're nuts, mister," he said, dropping more bricks into
his bucket. Then he straightened up. "Listen! *Listen!*"

Everyone stopped. For a moment, there was only thing
on Dizzy's mind: grubs. Kids had good hearing, better than
most adults, and definitely better than a guy who'd spent
years in a noisy engine room. The whole site held its breath,
waiting for a rumbling vibration to tell them the grubs were
coming.

But it was another kind of rumbling. An armored vehicle was coming down the road.

"Gears!" the kid yelled. "They're coming! *Gears!*"

Dizzy didn't want to be part of this. He took a few steps back as kids and grown-ups alike grabbed rubble from the debris and surged past him to stand on the edge of the road. He understood why they were angry but he just couldn't join in with all this stupid shit.

"Come on, fellas, they're just workin' men like us," Dizzy pleaded. *Could have been my Richie. They didn't want any of this.* "Ain't their choice what happened."

"Ah, you're a COG-lover," someone muttered behind him. "You'll learn."

The APC came into view. "Right, you bastards!" one of the men yelled. "Come on, let's see how frigging tough you are now!"

The APC barreled down the road, hatch open, not slowing down or preparing for trouble. Dizzy could see the Gear on top cover. When the vehicle was about twenty meters from the angry crowd, they let fly with a hail of bricks and stones, screaming abuse. The missiles bounced off the armor plate. The poor asshole on top cover ducked to shield himself but still got hit.

Dizzy thought the APC was just going to drive on like they always did, but this time it came to a halt and a Gear jumped out of the front hatch holding his rifle one-handed and looking like he meant business. He stormed right up to them and shoved one of the men in the chest. The rifle sobered folks up for a second and everybody dropped the bricks they were about to throw, but the storm of abuse carried on. Goddamn, some of it was even from the little kids.

"COG asshole!"

"Scum! Fuckin' scum!"

"Come to finish the job, have ya? Haven't killed enough of us yet?"

The Gear just waded through it. "Shut your mouth. *Now.*" No, it wasn't a fella. It was a *woman*, but it was hard to tell with the full-face helmet and bulky armor. "You want to live like animals—fine. But you stay out of our way. Understand?"

The guy she'd shoved squared up to her. "Or *what?*"

"Or I'll *clear* you out of the way. You impede my operation and you're aiding the enemy. Now either shut the fuck up or grow a pair and *enlist.*"

"Yeah, like we'd want to take orders from fucking Prescott after he fried us to save his frigging *oil paintings*. And we're *still* up to our asses in grubs."

The Gear rolled right over him, but then she'd probably heard it every damn day since the Hammer strike. "Oh, and another thing—if I catch you looting weapons from my boys' bodies, I'll make sure you join them."

"How else are we gonna defend ourselves?"

"Put on this uniform—that's how. Pull your weight and get fed like the rest of us." She prodded a warning finger at him. "You want to play Stranded martyr, go ahead, but touch my Gears—dead or alive—and I'll damn well have you. Got it?"

She jogged back to the APC and it rumbled off down the road. Dizzy could hear artillery in the distance. The Gears were probably on their way to an e-hole and fresh out of patience with anyone who wasn't one side of the line or the other. But that didn't change things. Nobody trusted the government now. The Stranded would take their chances out here in case the next official promise of safety ended the same way as the last.

Yeah, they *preferred* to be Stranded, even though it was a nice clean name for a dirty, terrible thing. The poor saps outside the wire were the betrayed. The COG was another enemy now, somehow even worse than the grubs. Grubs didn't kill their own.

The kids went around retrieving the thrown bricks. Business was business, after all. Dizzy decided it was high time he went back to Rosalyn. He headed for the corrugated iron hut that was now home—a pretty terrible come-down, but it beat sleeping in a burned-out car—to find Rosalyn curled up on the mattress with the babies all wrapped up and peaceful next to her.

The woman who'd done the midwifing gave him a disapproving glare. "Well, I'll leave you to it, then. The hero's returned. Been out celebrating?"

"Been out getting something special for my special girl." Dizzy didn't like to be rude to a lady but this was his home, and he didn't need any lectures from her. She flounced out, making him feel like some bum who put drinking above his family. "Hey sweetie, how's all my princesses?"

"Sleeping." Rosalyn took his hand. "Wow, I've never been this *tired*. Where did you go? I heard some ruckus going on."

"Usual foolery. Stonin' APCs. Just went out to see if I could get you somethin'." Dizzy could have stood there for hours just staring at the twins. "Hello, Teresa. Hello, Maralin."

He must have said their names a hundred times in the last ten hours. Every time he did, it gave him that same crazy thrill. *I have daughters*. Whatever else was going on out there, he had a family who relied on him, and that made him a man again.

"Anyway, just a little token of a new daddy's pride." He took out the brush set and put it on the chair beside the bed. "Sweetie, you don't know how grateful I am right now. I was a mess. You put me straight again."

"And you saved my life. More than once. Just in case you

forgot that." She tried out the brush as best she could without sitting up. "This is lovely. How did you find it?"

"Ah, I got my secrets. Ain't we a team?"

"We're going to do okay, Dizzy. We're going to make it."

The grubs couldn't touch him. He felt bulletproof at that moment, a whole world away from what was happening outside.

"Okay, time I got on with making some currency, sweetie." He peered at the fermentation lock on the plastic bucket of mash wrapped discreetly in blankets in the corner. The bubbles were still glopping through the water. "I'm a man in demand. My hooch don't make ya go blind. This is gonna keep all of us fed."

Rosalyn propped herself up on one elbow. "Long as you don't drink the profits."

"Just quality control, sweetie. You want anything?"

"No. Just a little nap."

Making moonshine was a nice way to spend a few hours. Dizzy got a kick out of all the tinkering to get the brew just right—smelling the mash, deciding when it was done fermenting, getting the still set up just right, and picking that crucial moment when the distilled liquor hit the right balance of fire and flavor and he could switch off the heat. This batch was apples. It was going to be goddamn *nectar*.

He eased the lid off the bucket to sniff for quality. *Appetizing*. That was the only way to describe it. The mash was a mucky-looking swamp that smelled of heaven. The surface shivered a little.

Mmm . . . mmm.

The shivering went on a bit longer than Dizzy expected. Then it turned into shaking. He stared at it, trying to work out what was vibrating nearby. The shaking became a rhythmic slopping.

Oh God . . .

"Sweetie, *get up!*" Dizzy dropped the plastic lid and went to grab the twins. Rosalyn struggled off the mattress and snatched the girls from him. "Get to the shelter! It's the grubs! Run!"

Outside, a car horn blared as someone sounded the alarm. Rosalyn stumbled out the door ahead of him but grabbed a kitchen knife from the table as she went.

"They're not getting my babies." The blade would give the average grub a nasty itch, nothing more. "I'll kill them if they lay a paw on my babies."

"You just get in the shelter, okay?" The grubs could pop up anywhere, even inside the makeshift bunker, but the alternative was to freeze like a dumb rabbit waiting to get torn to shreds. "Don't come out. Not for *anything*."

"Dizzy, you're coming with me, aren't you?"

"I'll be okay." He turned back in the direction the rest of the men were heading. Rosalyn was swept up in the rush with the other women and children. "Keep your head down!"

The camp dogs were barking their heads off. Dizzy was halfway down the road before he realized he might have seen his kids for the last time, but it was too late to run back now. Masonry tumbled into the street ahead, a sign of where the grubs were coming out. A bunch of men, all the ones who had weapons—hunting rifles, COG Lancers, even grub shotguns—formed a line in front of the shelter and opened up on the goddamn things.

"Where's your precious Gears now, Dizzy?" one guy yelled. His name was Nicklos and they said he'd been navy chief way back. "Where are they when we need 'em?"

The grubs charged down the street.

There weren't many of them, but holding them off with rifles was a tall order and Dizzy didn't even have a handgun.

I'm crazy. What am I doing? He took out his wrench and looked around for a chunk of pipe or a metal bar, a second weapon he could batter the assholes with. But the guy to his left fell backward with half his head shot away, and a rifle clattered to the ground.

"Pick it up!" someone yelled. "You know how to use it, don't ya?"

No, he didn't: he'd been drafted into the merchant navy, not the army. He knew how rifles worked, that was all. But he grabbed it, aimed at a gray shape heading his way, and fired. The recoil took him by surprise. He fired again, and kept firing even though he couldn't tell if he'd hit any of the grubs. It seemed like only a few seconds before the rifle stopped kicking his shoulder and just made dry clicks every time he squeezed the trigger. He didn't even know how to reload. Someone tossed him a clip and he was still fumbling for it on the ground and trying to work out where to slot it when the firing stopped and he could suddenly smell shit.

"I hate it when those bastards do that," Nicklos said. "Come on, we've got people bleeding out. Move it! Get 'em to first aid!"

Dizzy finally clicked the magazine in the right way and stood up to see what everyone was looking at. Dead grubs and men littered the road. One of the grubs was lying in a puddle of his own guts and a couple of the camp dogs were taking a keen interest in them. So that was the smell.

"I know you're new in town, buddy, but you're going to have to shape up fast," Nicklos said to him. "I want you frigging drill-perfect on that piece next time, okay?"

Dizzy clutched the rifle in his hands, an unfamiliar and amazing thing. Guns were for Gears. Civilians—and merchant navy—had never had a need for them before. He was going to have to get better at this.

He'd fought his first real battle and become a father, all on the same day. If that didn't call for a sip of 'shine, he didn't know what did.

"Who said keep going? 'Cause it wasn't me." Baird looked like he was being eaten by the engine compartment of the 'Dill, leaning into it with just his legs and ass visible outside the inspection hatch. "See, when the big engine thing starts making bad noises, *Dick*son, it's saying 'Ooh, I'm hurt.' It's not saying 'Hey, let's drive another five klicks and see if I can throw a con-rod!'"

"I got faith in ya, baby," Cole said, scanning the rubble for movement. *Assholes. They're out there.* "You can raise the dead. Engines, that is. Just do it *fast.*"

Cole, Alonzo, and Dickson covered Baird while he worked, sighting up on doorways and shadows on the look-out for grubs. Hammer or no Hammer, the things were back and stronger than ever.

And they were close. Cole could hear the rubble click-ing and tumbling every so often as they edged forward behind cover. They could have attacked by now, but they were probably waiting until Baird had fixed the 'Dill before they moved in. They scavenged every piece of COG kit they could get. They preferred their stuff in good running order.

But Cole had a new toy that they sure as shit weren't going to get their paws on. He hadn't used it on anything live yet, but he'd practiced on a frozen beef carcass in the cold store—man, the names that cook called him—and this baby felt like pure *essence.*

He admired the shark-tooth profile of his new Lancer's

chainsaw for the fiftieth time that day and carried on looking for grubs to ventilate with it. *Lots* of them.

This is the ish, baby. Hope you got a bonus for inventin' this, whoever you are.

"So how fucked *is* it?" Dickson was getting edgy about the sick 'Dill. "Abandon it, or call for roadside assistance?"

"It's wait-for-Corporal-Baird-to-finish-the-job. We're not leaving it."

"Oh, yeah, my bad. You got two new stripes. Can you remind us again?"

"Certainly, Private *Dick*son."

"Don't say my name like that. I've *told* you."

"Nyah nyah nyah . . . oh *shit.* Dropped a nut."

Cole could hear the rubble noises coming nearer. "Yeah, the grubs are gettin' impatient too. Busy-busy, Baird . . ."

"I say we crank up the cannon while we still can." Alonzo backed away in the direction of the 'Dill. "Just to show how much we frown on carjacking."

It was so quiet that Cole heard the nose hatch rasp open, then the whirr of the turret as Alonzo prepped to fire. Baird's wrench pinged and clanked against something.

Come on . . . come on . . .

This was just asking for it. Cole decided to move forward to flush the grubs out so they weren't close-in when the shooting started. Alonzo needed a little elbow room to do his stuff with the gun.

"Here, ugly . . . ," Cole murmured, tiptoeing through the rubble. "Come on out, 'cause I got some *real* pimped-out shit to show you . . ."

Alonzo's voice hissed in his earpiece. "Don't push your luck, Cole."

"I ain't waitin' for 'em anymore." Oh yeah, they were there, all right. He saw something out of the corner of his eye on the far side of the road, a flash of shiny metal, and he spun around to open fire.

Rounds struck and sent dust zipping in a line across the stump of a wall. Dickson squeezed off a burst too. Someone yelled.

"Hey, don't shoot! For fuck's sake, man, stop!"

A head popped up—human, civilian—and Cole nearly took it off by sheer reflex. "Yo, check fire, Dickson! *Stranded!*"

The guy came out from behind the wall at a crouch. "You could have *killed* me."

"Baby, you're damn lucky you still got a face. What the hell are you doin' here? You're in a live zone."

"*Recycling*, COG." The rubble rat was about Cole's age but half his size and only had a pellet rifle. Yeah, that would come in real handy if he ran into any angry flies. "In case you hadn't noticed, asshole, we *live* in a live zone."

Cole had been called *asshole* by Stranded so often that it sounded like *Private* to him now. He was more focused on the trickling noise he could still hear from the rubble. Judging by Dickson's reaction, he heard it too. It was either grubs or more Stranded. Dickson never took chances. He aimed.

"Get goin', buddy." Cole waved the rubble rat away. "Grubs are comin', and we don't brake for nobody."

Another guy surfaced a few meters away, gray-haired and clutching a Locust Boomshot. Then a couple more heads popped up further down the road. If the grubs came out now, this was going to get *messy.*

Then the debris in front of Cole flew up in the air and a Boomer rose out of it like a stripper from a cake.

"*Boom!*" it said. "*Hur—hur—hur!*" So the big ugly motherfucker thought it was funny, did it?

"Everybody—down!" Alonzo yelled.

Cole had already hit the ground before the turret gun opened up on the Boomer. Alonzo clipped it and Cole felt the wet lumps hit him, but the Boomer kept going. He rolled to get up. But the Boomer stepped across him, and for a moment Cole was looking right up between its legs. As it reached down to rip him apart, he flicked the chainsaw switch.

The chain's teeth were a screaming blur. Cole brought the Lancer up into the Boomer's crotch and it shrieked its head off. He'd expected to slice clean through it, but he hadn't. He wasn't sure what splashed on him, blood or piss, but it bought him a second to roll clear as another long burst from the 'Dill threw the Boomer backward.

"Yeah, you're singin' soprano now, bitch!" Cole jumped up to look around, not sure where the Boomer had fallen. Dickson opened fire on his left and the 'Dill's gun chattered behind him. Grubs burst out of the ruined storefronts. "Baird, you better pull your goddamn finger out *now*!"

Cole had three drones coming right at him. He knew the Stranded were still out there somewhere, but all he could do was keep firing or get shredded. He emptied a clip at the grubs and vaulted over a low wall to reload behind cover. Dickson was crouched there already, doing the same.

"Well, shit." Dickson shut his eyes for a second before he bobbed up again to fire. "You think that saw's going to catch on?"

"Everybody's gonna want one, baby."

"Cole, stay down! Just stay down!" That was Alonzo. "We're coming!"

Cole fired blind over the wall just as the 'Dill coughed and started up. Baird must have been driving because Alonzo was still on top cover, squeezing off short bursts at targets Cole couldn't see from ground level. The 'Dill bounced over the rubble like a toy and swung around hard left to come at the wall nose first. The hatch slid open.

"Look, I don't go south of the river, and the fare doesn't include tips," Baird said. "Let's go."

"Nice drivin'." Cole turned and grabbed Dickson's arm. "Mount up."

They scrambled over the wall and fell into the crew compartment. Baird backed up and swung the 'Dill around again as rounds pinged off the armor plating.

"Alonzo, get down and shut the damn hatch!" Baird yelled. He didn't seem to be driving in anything like a straight line. "Now *this* is what I signed up for. Yes!" *Bomp.* The 'Dill hit something and Cole realized that Baird was swerving to mow down as many grubs as he could. "Hey, mind my paintwork, asshole . . ." *Thud.* Another grub went under the wheels. "So, now we know a chainsaw doesn't slice right through a Boomer, but it *does* stop 'em breeding. What kind of girly-toy shit is Procurement sending us?"

Bomp.

Cole could see a porthole view of the street through a bulkhead vent. Baird brought the 'Dill to a halt. The hammering noise of rounds striking it had stopped, and there was just the steady burble of the engine idling. Cole got his breath back.

Damn, we had Stranded out there.

The poor assholes could have been lying out there wounded with all that stray fire spraying around. He had to check. He couldn't see much from the vent. 'Dills had a lot of blind spots when all the scuttles were shut, even with the driver's optics.

"Baird, you see anything?"

"Up scope!" He rotated the periscope like a sub commander, clearly having a ball. "Warship . . . tanker . . . no, sweet FA. I think there'll be some grub portions in the wheel arches, though."

"No Stranded?"

"Nope."

"I gotta check."

"They're not our problem, Cole."

"Okay, I'm goin' out the top hatch."

"Here's an IQ test. We're okay. The 'Dill's running. The grubs are dead. It's lunchtime. What's next in the sequence?"

"I gotta see for myself."

Cole unclipped the hatch and left it resting on the coaming for a moment while he balanced on the step. It was a tricky move—one hand to throw back the hatch, one hand full of shiny new Lancer. Baird didn't mean all that shit. He'd have driven off otherwise.

"Don't make me pull rank on you, Cole."

"Yeah, yeah . . . in three—two—*go*."

Cole punched the hatch open, expecting to be met by a burst of fire. But it was all quiet. He squeezed his shoulders out and listened to nothing but silence, his Lancer resting on the hull. If there was anybody still out there then they were either dead or unconscious.

He ducked his head to climb back down. But as he reached up to grab the handle and pull the hatch closed, a big gray head pushed through and knocked him down. A grub was right in his face, poking through the hatch like some ugly goddamn cork in a bottle. Something clanged on the 'Dill's hull and rattled down the side.

"Grenade!" Baird yelled. The 'Dill shuddered. Something exploded, but not in the vehicle. "No, no—he dropped it—it's outside!"

The grub landed on top of Cole then somehow sprang back onto its feet. Cole's reflex was to shove the Lancer in its chest and fire, but that was suicidal in a tight space so he swung the chainsaw into it instead. The moment was all screeching noise, spray, and confusion. His first swipe bit chunks out of the grub's face. The return swing skidded across its scalp. But the thing was kneeling on the deck now, bellowing and flailing, and Cole had the second he needed to push down past its left ear and slice into bone.

Eventually the grub stopped struggling and slumped on the deck. The seats and bulkheads looked like someone had thrown raw hamburger around. It was a lot harder to pull the saw free than Cole expected.

"Shit," Alonzo said quietly. "That's some respray, Cole."

Baird leaned out of the driver's seat to look at the Lancer. "Y'know, there's got to be a *technique* to that gizmo." He flicked some spatter off his armor. "But I don't think it should involve a mop and a bucket."

Cole still had to check outside. This time he opened the nose hatch with Dickson covering him and jogged around the last places he'd seen the Stranded, just a few meters from where the Boomer had emerged. The Boomer was still there, pretty well sliced in half by the gunfire. But ten meters away, Cole found the rubble rat and his pellet rifle. He wasn't going to be using that again.

"Goddamn." Maybe his buddies would come back and retrieve the body. Cole couldn't tell whose fire had killed the guy, but he assumed the worst. "Okay . . . let's move."

Alonzo took a look. "Come on, Cole, what else are we going to do, hold fire and let the grubs gut us? You told them to get clear."

"I know. Yeah, I did. I did it by the book."

Cole slammed the hatch and sat in silence all the way back to base, eyes shut. He was finding it harder each time to deal with the Stranded. Okay, so they had the choice of enlisting and living inside the wire like normal folks instead of looting and stoning patrols, but they were only out there because Prescott used the Hammer. Sure, he didn't set out to kill COG citizens. Cole hadn't set out to kill them either. They were just caught in the crossfire. But they were still dead, and blaming Stranded for being a pain in the ass was like stealing a guy's wallet and then complaining because he couldn't pay the rent.

"You okay, Cole?" Baird asked.

Cole sucked in a few deep breaths to steady himself and got a grip. "It's a fucked-up world, baby."

"I'll hose down the 'Dill."

"Yeah. Sorry about that."

"Hey, someone had to be the first in the squad to try it. It's got potential. Noisy, but promising."

They rolled through the gates of the vehicle compound rehearsing their excuses for bringing the 'Dill back with a screwed engine and grub guts baked onto the electrics. The duty mechanics were usually waiting for each returning 'Dill like a pit-stop team, but the vehicle bay was weirdly deserted today. Cole dismounted and looked around.

"Anybody home?" he yelled. "Guy needs a car wash here."

Baird sniffed the air theatrically. "Ooh, trouble. Smell it?"

Cole wandered into the workshop. The mechanics, all 3rd Ephyrans, were standing in a huddle and talking in hushed voices.

"Hey guys." Cole had to get their attention. "You open for business? My ashtray's full."

The staff sergeant turned around as if Cole had interrupted a funeral. "It's General Bardry," he said. "You been listening to your radio?"

Bardry was Chief of the Defense Staff. What the hell was *he* doing out popping grubs? Cole knew they were running low on officers, but that was weird. "What about him?"

"He's dead." The sergeant put two fingers to the roof of his mouth, pistol fashion. "Blew his brains out this morning.

Poor bastard. The Hammer strike really finished him off. Couldn't live with turning that key."

Baird made a puffing noise of disbelief. "Well, it doesn't seem to have traumatized Prescott much. So who's taking his place?"

"Hoffman."

"Fucking *Hoffman*?" Baird rolled his eyes. "Man, he even let his *wife* fry. Well, at least we won't get any angsty conscience shit from him."

"Is he even a full colonel?" Cole asked. "What about the Supply and Logistics boss?"

"You want the cooks running the war? Nah, it's the Two-Six RTI funny handshake again." The sergeant obviously didn't trust old regiments with lots of fancy silver in the mess. Everyone knew the Royal Tyrans got all the best posts and told the Defense Department how things were going to be. "And Hoff's Director of Special Forces. Who else could Prescott pick?"

"We haven't *got* any special forces," Baird said. "Just that commando ad-qual shit from the last war that Two-Six RTI wanted to take over—oh, yeah. I see your point."

"I still don't understand how we lost so many top brass." The sergeant was muttering to himself now, like that bothered him more than poor old Bardry eating a pistol. "Hoffman's the most senior officer left standing. What the hell happened?"

Cole chewed it over as he sat on the 'Dill's front scoop. Everyone was taking the same shit these days, even the senior officers. Generals got killed—or topped themselves. And the civvies, too—they'd lost a lot of the top scientists and professors. There was no goddamn tenure now. It was like the grubs had wiped out the best brains in COG society all at once.

Cole thought that was unusual bad luck, but maybe it

was a grub strategy to kill the elite. They were ugly, but they weren't dumb.

Hell, nothing in this war had made sense anyway, not from the moment the first emergence hole opened up. He pulled out his pay book and started writing a letter to his dead momma on the blank pages at the back. It always made him feel better.

Maybe even Prescott didn't know exactly what the hell was going on. Cole imagined him at his big polished desk, writing a letter that he'd never send to his long-dead daddy.

CHAPTER 18

VECTES NAVAL BASE, NEW JACINTO: ONE DAY AFTER THE STALK EMERGENCE AT THE RESERVOIR, GALE, 15 A.E.

The news was out, and Dom couldn't tell if the crowds on the parade ground were a loitering mob or just a bunch of people with nowhere else to go.

He followed Marcus as he shouldered his way through the crowd to reach Admiralty House. Rumors about the stalks' spread into the granite bedrock were doing the rounds, and that was the last thing people needed to hear when overcrowding was already making them short-tempered.

"I know a festering riot when I see one," Dom said.

"They handled it okay in Jacinto." Marcus sometimes had a lot more faith in people's common sense than Dom. "They'll handle it okay here."

A group of about fifteen men and women were standing in front of the entrance to Admiralty House. Dom recognized one of them as Ingram, but the others were people whose names he'd either forgotten or never known. He did know who they were, though. They were the neighborhood delegates, the nearest New Jacinto had to proper councilmen in a COG where there hadn't been elections of any kind since E-Day. Dom wondered why somebody hadn't already moved them on. Civvies usually did what they were told in old Jacinto.

Ingram turned and spotted Marcus. "Sergeant?" he called. "Sergeant Fenix, can I have a word?"

"Sure." Marcus ambled up to the delegates. "What can we do for you?"

"We're waiting to see Prescott. Is he going to make an announcement on the stalk situation?"

"I don't know," Marcus said. "The engineers are still out checking the bedrock. We'll go ask him."

The delegates were regular family types who didn't look like trouble. Dom found them the hardest to deal with. If he was facing a mob of big angry guys, he could go in hard to restore order, but it wasn't so easy dealing with women and anyone half his size and twice his age. All his upbringing and instincts told him it was wrong to strong-arm them.

Marcus didn't even try to go around the delegates to reach the door. He went to walk straight through them and they just stepped aside. It looked to Dom like a quick test of who had the upper hand, and as usual it was Marcus. He could get people to give in to him without making them feel they'd lost face. That was quite an art.

Dom climbed the stairs behind Marcus. "So what difference is an announcement going to make?"

"The more gaps you leave, the more folks fill them with their own nightmares," Marcus said. He reached the top floor and turned right toward the main meeting room, where the door was ajar and the burble of voices was drifting out. "He'll tell them everything that happened and we'll have extra safety drills. It won't stop a single damn stalk, but people will feel better."

Rivera was standing outside the door. Dom wondered what Prescott had said to him and Lowe to make them keep themselves to themselves, or why he'd selected them at all. Rivera wasn't a cheerful guy at the best of times but he looked even more subdued today.

"Hoffman called us," Marcus said. "Okay if we go in?"

Rivera nodded and held the door open. "It's a full house today."

Dom didn't know what he meant until he saw who was at Prescott's meeting, and that described the scale of the problem. It wasn't just Hoffman, Trescu, and Michaelson: Sharle, Parry, Baird, and even Bernie were sitting around the table too.

"Come in, gentlemen," Prescott said. "We're just scoping out a new worst case scenario. Carry on, Sergeant Mataki."

Bernie looked uncomfortable. She wasn't a meetings kind of woman. Dom automatically thought she was there because of her bushcraft and survival expertise, but it turned out to be a lot more grim than that.

"Okay, we select the breeding stock and animals for immediate food production," she said. "Pigs are the best option—they'll eat anything. Chickens—compact, but a big grain requirement, and we'll need that for human consumption. Sheep, goats, and cattle—big space requirements on board ship, plus feed issues, but we have to take a viable breeding population with us. So it's going to be mainly cattle and sheep that we cull, and that needs resources for preserving carcasses. Freezing's most palatable, but drying and salting will last a lot longer, and pemmican will keep for years. It's a big, messy job that's going to tie up a lot of people, sir. We're back to old technology now."

So she was there as a farmer, and one working out how to strip Vectes of food. It was depressing stuff. Dom reminded himself that this was all what-if planning, the very worst that could happen. But it was clear that Prescott was talking about an early evacuation. It was the first time he'd felt that sense of urgency about the man.

"But we've got to be able to sustain animals at sea indefinitely," Parry said. "There's no guarantee of finding grazing."

"The old navy took food animals on long deployments," Michaelson said. "And if we have to, so can we. But remember the Silver Era sailor didn't have quite the same attitude to hygiene that we do."

Sharle didn't look up from a pile of paper in front of him. "Like Bernie said earlier, we're probably looking at a big dietary change. Fish and grain, and quick-maturing container-grown vegetables initially. Which means that I want the Pelruan trawler crews to teach more people to fish."

"Are you getting some idea of the scale of the problem, Chairman?" Hoffman turned in his seat and fixed Prescott with one of his stares. "We escaped from Jacinto with almost nothing. We'd have been in big trouble if we hadn't come to an island with a decent food supply. Moving out with a comparable supply is a massive, long-term undertaking. By all means start it now, but I strongly advise against evacuation for at least a year."

There were a few nods and murmurs around the table. Baird caught Dom's eye and just raised an eyebrow, but it was hard to tell if he was bored shitless or appalled.

"We might not have a year," Prescott said at last.

"Then we do what we can," Hoffman said, "but we don't bolt until we absolutely have to. We're running out of human beings, Chairman. Let's not finish the job the grubs started."

"Yeah, what *is* the rush?" Baird was in full argumentative mode, chairman or no chairman. Nobody could accuse him of ever being awed by rank. "So the stalks can spread further than we thought. But most of the island still isn't covered in them, and most of the land still isn't dead."

Prescott paused. He always seemed to think longer before he spoke now. Dom wondered if he was just imagining it. In the silence, he could hear the background noise from the crowds in the parade ground like a distant rumble of traffic.

"The nature of the threat has *changed*," Prescott said. "We can't lock it out. And it appears to be able to do more than just spread between species. It's *generating* new life-forms."

"But how do we know if that means we should risk evacuating the whole island?" Marcus asked. "We don't know enough about the life cycles of these things."

Maybe it was that voice, or his service record, but Marcus could always silence a room on the rare occasions when he had something to say. He could certainly stop Prescott in his tracks. Dom watched the Chairman staring at his hands, carefully folded on the table in front of him.

"You're right," Prescott said. "We still don't know enough about the Lambent. But Colonel Hoffman rightly points out that we can't defend a string of villages on the mainland, so we need to re-establish a single settlement. Port Farrall is still the best option. We have to arrive during the summer months to prepare for the winter there, which means we go now, or we go this time next year. And we can't predict what this island will look like in a year's time."

Dom couldn't argue with that. He didn't think Prescott had an easy job, and he didn't have an opinion of his own because every option was a shitty one. He watched Marcus nod and fold his arms, leaning against the wall.

The door opened again and Rivera stuck his head in. "Sir, Sergeant Rossi says it's getting a bit tense out front."

"Yeah, Ingram and the delegates want to talk to you, Chairman," Marcus said.

Prescott pushed his chair back from the table and stood up. "Why not?"

He walked out. Hoffman stood up and indicated to Marcus and Dom to follow him. It was a real shame the building didn't have a balcony, because Prescott was going to get swamped in that crowd. But he was a big guy with quite a presence, so maybe all he needed was Lowe and Rivera making sure nobody threw a punch.

Why am I even thinking that? Things never got that bad in Jacinto. But then Prescott never had citizens living right next door to him.

By the time Dom and Marcus got down to the doors, Prescott was already on the steps with Rivera, facing the bunch of delegates with a general crowd growing behind them. There was no sign of Lowe. The noise that greeted Prescott was weird, a mix of murmurs, cheers, and even some folks chanting "Tell us the truth! Tell us the truth!"

"Dom, Baird, Bernie—get out front and stop anyone pushing his luck," Marcus said. "Prescott might not give a rat's ass if someone slugs him, but it won't help the general mood here."

Prescott didn't just stand there. He moved out into the crowd, the crazy bastard. Some people patted him on the back or reached out to shake his hand, and he stopped for every one of them. Dom once thought it was just politician's bullshit, but there was a real and necessary act of reassurance going on here, the man in charge knowing he had to give these people an answer.

"Just tell me what you want from me," Prescott said.

The silence spread outward from the people immediately in front of him and soon the crowd was listening intently. He didn't even need to shout or hold up his hand to get their attention. He was a lot taller than most of them anyway.

"Asshole," Hoffman muttered. Dom hadn't realized the colonel was standing next to him. "Goddamn *theater*."

"That's all we've got, sir," Dom whispered.

Everybody seemed to be looking at Keir Ingram to say something. Dom could have sworn one of the delegates shoved him in the back.

"We want you to give it to us straight, Chairman," he said. "How bad is this new threat, and is it true we'll be evacuated again?"

"The stalks could come up anywhere." Prescott didn't even try to dress it up in rhetoric. "It seems we can't rely on shutting them out. We're still deciding whether an immediate evacuation is advisable or not. There are risks in any option."

"Don't we get a say?" That was a woman lost somewhere in the crowd. "Don't we get a say in what happens to us? Okay, we didn't have time in Jacinto, but this is different."

"I say we get the hell out *now*!" a man yelled.

That started everyone off for a few moments, but it was just noise. Dom kept an eye on the body language. He could see Marcus checking it out too, just that little turn of the head and that slow sweep.

"Tell us what's happening on the mainland!"

"Yeah, what did you find on that recon? Why didn't you tell us about it?"

"We want a say in this! It's our asses!"

Prescott didn't even blink. Dom wondered what kind of Gear he'd been under fire, however short his time in the army had been.

"I've got an idea," Prescott said. Dom heard Hoffman groan. "I'll give everybody a vote on it. We'll show you the recon images and reports, just as we've seen them. They're not always easy to understand, but you can have free access to them. I'll tell you now that even Colonel Hoffman and I don't agree on the solution. But you can judge for yourselves, and we'll have a referendum."

"Fucking *idiot*," Hoffman whispered.

"Fucking *clever*, sir." Dom leaned closer to Hoffman. "He's always got a plan, remember."

Ingram didn't look overjoyed at the idea of instant unvarnished democracy. "But we don't have any electoral structure," he said.

"Ancient Pelles had a voting system five thousand years ago," Prescott said. "Pottery shards. In our case, neighborhood delegates can collate numbers in their areas. Not perfect, and open to rigging and error, but simple. I'm serious about this, ladies and gentlemen. There's nothing in the reconnaissance and situation reports to hold back. You'll know as much from them as I do. Do we have a deal?"

Dom caught Baird's eye and saw him mouth two words: *frigging awesome*. Yeah, it was pretty well done. Ingram didn't look so much defeated as overwhelmed, and the crowd fell into quiet mumbling.

"Has anyone else got a better idea?" Prescott asked. "And I do mean that. None of you survived the Locust by being fools. You're all capable of making your own decisions."

Someone started clapping, then someone else picked it up, and soon Prescott was getting another one of his ovations. Dom had seen it too many times now. Prescott could take a surly crowd or a defeated army and tell it that the sun shone out of its collective ass, and it would be transformed on the spot.

Marcus moved up beside Dom and nudged him. "Don't look into his eyes," he murmured. "Try to resist."

"What?"

"You're hanging on his every fucking word."

Dom bristled. "But he's not lying. Is he? He's laying it on the line. Okay . . . it's all PR somehow, but hell, it works."

It went quiet again. Prescott spread his arms, almost apologetic. "Thank you for your continuing courage, ladies and gentlemen," he said. "You know that I'll have to make hard decisions in the weeks to come, just as I've made them in the past. I don't expect to be loved for it. I just want you to know that whatever I do, however unfair it seems, however much you may feel I've let you down, I do it to keep as many of you alive as I possibly can. Please remember that when you think harshly of me."

Marcus grunted, probably still unimpressed. Dom was almost shocked to hear Prescott drop his warrior-emperor image and get personal. He felt a pang of guilt for being so cynical.

No, stop it. It's a line. It's just a clever politician's line.

Prescott went back into the building and the crowd didn't break up—it couldn't—but it did spread out and resemble a bunch of people at a loose end again. Hoffman and the rest of the meeting followed him back up the stairs to finish the meeting. Baird was just ahead of Dom, within conversation distance of Prescott.

"Nice move, Chairman," he said. He wasn't really ass-kissing as far as Dom could tell. "The delegates are going to be so busy debating what color the ballot form should be that they'll be off our backs for weeks."

Prescott didn't break his stride or look around. "I was serious, Corporal. I want them to vote on it."

"I note," Trescu said, "that you didn't actually say you'd be bound by the result. Will you?"

"There was a time when that would have been an astute political observation, Commander." Prescott reached the top of the stairs and stood back to let everyone take their seats again. "But I do want to know what they want."

"Very well, don't answer the question. So how will you vote?"

"I think we should go as soon as possible, of course," Prescott said.

Hoffman had that look on his face, the tight-lipped, unblinking glare that said he thought he'd been outmaneuvered again. "You realize this might backfire and mean the end of the COG."

"That," Prescott said, "may be a risk we have to take."

VECTES NAVAL BASE: TWO DAYS LATER.

"Shitty old day," Michaelson said, squinting against the driving rain. A gale was howling through the masts, rippling puddles and slapping the COG ensign at *Sovereign*'s stern like wet laundry. Out to sea, huge gray waves blurred with the sky. "On the other hand, perhaps a timely reminder to our citizens that sailing off into the unknown can be much worse than staying in harbor."

Hoffman ducked under the archway from the dock to the old magazine and shook off his cap. Trescu was already waiting for them, leaning against the brickwork and watching a bedraggled hen scratching around in the dirt.

"We could have met quite openly in the mess, Colonel,"

Trescu said irritably. "So . . . we prepare the battlefield before we see Prescott?"

Hoffman didn't mind a battle as long as he knew who he was fighting and what their objective was, but with Prescott he was guessing all the time. "Sharle just called me with the latest numbers," he said. "About seventy-five percent want to stay. You think Prescott's going to accept that, or carry on regardless?"

Michaelson grimaced. "I wouldn't like to bet on which way he'll jump. But he's set on going soon."

"Based on what? Goddamn it, how many times does Sharle have to tell him we're still not ready to go?"

"My people are unanimous," Trescu said. "We stay for the time being and assess the situation."

Michaelson winked at him. "No doubt quite a few fingers were broken and bottoms spanked to achieve that degree of harmony."

"I'm a most persuasive speaker. Perhaps I should speak to your malcontents too."

Hoffman checked his watch. *Fifteen minutes.* He'd known this day was coming sooner or later, but now it had leaped out at him from the shadows and demanded to know if he had the guts to do it right now, *today*, no dicking around.

I'm going to defy the Chairman. Refuse his orders. I hope Marcus Fenix enjoys irony.

Nobody was left to court martial him, or shoot him, or even block his promotion if he told Prescott to ram his plan up his ass. What scared him was that he was on the brink of refusing a lawful order, and one from the head of state. It was the anarchy he'd always feared, the end of order and decent behavior.

We're struggling to survive. And here I am worrying about integrity and the breakdown of command.

"I refuse to commit resources to it," Hoffman said. "We wait, and we prepare."

Hoffman was hoping for a murmur of support and assurance that they'd be right behind him when he did. Michaelson still seemed to be contemplating the chess game that Prescott might be playing.

"Perhaps he's overplayed his hand at last. He seems to have misjudged the mood of the community, although that's never influenced him before, so he's hoping we'll give him a way out of a tight spot." Michaelson stepped aside to let the chicken pass. "Remember what I told you, Victor. He can do nothing without your Gears, and go nowhere without my fleet . . . or without Miran's imulsion expertise. We run the COG, for all intents and purposes."

"And what happens when we want to run it differently from *him*? Is that called a mutiny or a military coup? I forget."

"It's called playing the rather strong hand you were dealt. We're not talking about lynching him and dancing around his severed head on a pole. Just politics."

Trescu applauded slowly. "Welcome to the real world, gentlemen. This is like watching my boy grow up."

"You got a better idea?" Hoffman asked. "Do share."

"You know what you have to do, as do I. My only concern is the Chairman's motive. It eludes me. I don't like that. He's a very calculating, rational man, and he does *not* blink when he faces an apocalypse."

"Well, the last couple of times we've faced one, he's had the Professor Adam Fenix handbook to back him up," Hoffman said. "He's on his own this time."

But Trescu was right. Prescott never panicked, and he wasn't about to start now. Hoffman just wanted to get it over with. For all he knew, Prescott would put a few more jigsaw pieces on the table in a few minutes.

"Let's do it," Hoffman said. "Just fucking *do* it."

The rain had sorted the purposeful from those killing time. The only people around the parade ground today were Gears and support staff in wet-weather gear doing essential work. The place had the air of a fairground hoping for the weather to improve before it could open, all dripping ropes and tarpaulins sagging under the weight of water. Hoffman climbed the staircase of Admiralty House and wondered where things would end. He tried not to let Anvil Gate shape everything he did, but he felt he was being made to relive that same decision-making process, being asked the question repeatedly until he got the right answer.

Isn't that what we all hate about the other guy? That his ends justify his means? I always do it by the book but it doesn't always work out. I hold Anvil Gate, but my wife's burned alive. Nothing tells me what I did right or wrong. The only compass I've got now is my gut.

"Morning, gentlemen." Prescott sat at the meeting table surrounded by piles of scruffy, much-used paper—the voting records. His jacket looked damp, as if he'd been soaked some time earlier and was slowly drying out. "I imagine you already have a good idea of the results. That's public ballots for you."

Hoffman hung up his cap and sat down. "We might not be up to speed," he said. "Better tell us."

"Only a quarter wish to leave."

Hoffman just looked at him. Maybe silence would force something out of him, because Hoffman knew he could never outfence him verbally. Trescu and Michaelson caught on fast and followed Hoffman's lead, or at least he assumed that was what they were doing. Trescu probably didn't give a shit and was just watching the show.

"I'd appreciate your views," Prescott said at last. "I know I said I would follow the vote, but I think it's insane."

"The majority want to wait it out," Michaelson said. "And so do we, so the issue's done and dusted. The only question is how we manage the twenty-five percent who've had their expectations of escape raised."

Hoffman hadn't expected the crafty old bugger to open the batting, and from the slight flicker in Prescott's gaze it looked as if he hadn't either.

"What he said." Hoffman looked at Trescu. "You too?"

Trescu nodded. "We stay. Mr. Sharle's made himself clear as well."

"I still think we should evacuate the island immediately," Prescott said. "How soon can we be ready?"

Hoffman took a breath. For a man who'd already decided to refuse an order, he was still surprised to hear Prescott fulfill his worst expectation.

"Chairman," Hoffman said. "We intend to remain here."

The first words of his mutiny slipped out, and suddenly it seemed so easy, so *done*, that the rest followed in a relieved stream as blissful and simple as pissing.

Prescott blinked a couple of times, but his voice was completely calm. "Have I understood you correctly, Colonel?"

"The situation's serious enough without actively seeking more risk," Hoffman said. "If we go, whether we go as a single community or disperse, we need a lot more preparation time to ensure that we can survive at the other end. And regardless of the changing situation with the stalks, we are *not* at that crisis level yet."

As soon as he said it, Hoffman knew he'd walked into an ambush. He could see it on Prescott's face. It wasn't an I-won-you-assholes smirk or anything triumphant like that, just a sense that the Chairman had finally led a difficult conversation where he needed it to go and wanted to let out a sigh of relief. Maybe it was the slight relaxation of the shoulders that gave it away. Whatever it was, it vanished before Hoffman could examine it.

"Captain Michaelson, Commander Trescu—is this a view you share?" Prescott pushed back a little from the table. "I assume it is."

"Yes," Michaelson said. "That's about the size of it. Just chalk it up to democracy. I doubt people will think less of you for it."

Trescu seemed to be scrutinizing Prescott as hard as Hoffman had. "I surrendered my nation and my assets to the COG after fifteen years of trying to survive on the mainland. It wasn't because of this island's bracing sea air."

Prescott looked down at his lap and nodded a few times.

"Very well," he said. "Then we stay put. I disagree with that, but the last thing we need now is a rift between military and state."

Oh, I get it. You want me to pull the trigger. Keep your hands clean. Hoffman bristled. "You haven't given me an order, Chairman."

"No point. You'd win. You three control the assets."

"I said—you have *not yet given me an order.*"

Prescott's lips set in a thin line for a moment. Hoffman never knew if those flickers of reaction were real or a brilliant act. "Very well, Colonel, I'm asking you to arrange the evacuation of all citizens."

"No, sir." Well, *damn.* It was done. Hoffman's mouth was dry and he had that heart attack feeling, or at least what he thought one might feel like. Even with the COG reduced to a town council, it was still an emotionally shocking moment for him. "I have to refuse that order."

He could see Michaelson and Trescu out of the corner of his eye. Now the meeting would move on, but he'd have to keep an eye on Prescott for the revenge that would inevitably come.

"Thank you for being frank, Victor," Prescott said. "It's clear I no longer have the confidence of any of you. So I'm going to do the only thing open to me, and resign my office. I'd have to refer to the constitution for the detail, but I believe that leaves you running the government until a time when elections can be held again, Colonel Hoffman."

Bastard. *Bastard, bastard, bastard.* Prescott had done it again. Hoffman found it hard to draw the next breath, but he found his voice somehow.

"Is this some frigging game of chicken, Chairman?" *How the hell did I walk into that?* "Is this to scare us dumb cannon fodder into changing our minds and begging you to carry on?"

"Oh, it's definitely not that," Prescott said. "But I've done all I can do, and my hanging around won't help you gentlemen deal with what we're facing here. It won't help anybody, in fact. Without your full support, I'm merely civilian liaison—which Major Reid does somewhat better than me, I might add. If you want to discuss how and when we tell the public, I'll be in my office."

Every word's there for a reason. Remember it. Remember every goddamn word he says.

Hoffman knew he needed to memorize every syllable that came out of Prescott's mouth now to analyze it later, but he was still too shocked. Prescott got up, gathered a few papers, and left with a polite nod.

It was a few long seconds before anyone spoke.

Michaelson twirled his pencil between his fingers. "We have, as young Baird might say, just been fucked into the middle of next week."

"Shit, he dug that trap and I fell right in." Hoffman caught himself running both hands over his scalp, a measure of how cornered he felt. "What the hell's wrong with me? I never damn well *learn.* So where are we now? Is he serious?"

"I don't know *what* you've fallen for," Trescu said. "Or *we* have fallen for, to be precise. But I do know it's not the excuse that came out of his mouth."

"Is it brinkmanship?" Michaelson asked.

"No." Trescu shook his head and stabbed his finger in the direction of the door. "*That* is a man looking for a way out. And he likes power too much to surrender it without a very pressing reason. No offense, Colonel, but I doubt that your defiance is enough to break him."

Hoffman's guts were in turmoil. What did he do now? "Okay, I'll take the asshole at his word, then. Reid can take his meetings, and we'll run the goddamn government ourselves."

"Apart from managing the brief communal shock when news gets out, I think things will run exactly as before," Michaelson said. "And he knows that, I suspect."

Trescu got up and opened the door. "I prefer my coups to end with a single shot to the head, but this has been *fascinating*. Now I must go and worry about Lambent killing my drilling teams."

Hoffman followed Michaelson down the stairs and stood outside on the steps of the building, confused and angry. The wind had dropped. The fine drizzly rain on his face actually felt soothing.

"Don't worry, I'll write you some nice words to read to the masses," Michaelson said, patting his back. "Ship's captains are used to being the lords of all they survey."

"You're in this shit too, Quentin. It's a joint office. Don't play the sidekick with me."

"Ah, I won't. And look how well Miran behaves when he's treated like an adult." Michaelson nudged him gently. "Good grief, we really *are* the Triumvirate. What are we going to do now?"

Hoffman realized he did in fact have a plan. He had his

inner circle based on trust and history, not rank—that didn't count for shit these days—or role.

"Well, I'm going to cry on Bernie's shoulder," he said. "Then I'm going to tell Delta Squad, and then I'm going to tell Parry and Sharle."

"All good people to watch your back," Michaelson said. "And we're both going to need to have eyes in our asses now that Prescott has time on his hands."

And Hoffman still didn't know what Prescott was up to. Chairman or ordinary citizen, he still had a plan of action he wasn't sharing with anyone else.

He always did.

CHAPTER 19

If we'd known the Locust were massing underground—if
we'd known they even existed—could we have destroyed
them before they had a chance to emerge? Perhaps. We
could probably have saved many more lives, at very least.
But the Lambent—I suspect even a warning would never
have prepared us fully to deal with them.

(Chairman Richard Prescott, from his unpublished memoirs)

SERGEANT'S MESS, VECTES NAVAL BASE:
LUNCHTIME.

Any minute now, the door would swing open. Bernie tried to
look as if she was paying attention to Rossi, but it was bloody
hard to act normally after what Hoffman had just told her.

". . . and then I take off the dressing, and I find *this* frigging thing." Rossi shoved his arm under Bernie's nose.
"Well, she damn well better tattoo over it. Okay, so I'd had a
few, and Muller says I asked her to do it, but I can't go
around with *this* on my arm, can I?"

On a regular day it would have been hilarious. Sam had
tattooed a comically cross-eyed death's-head emblem on
Rossi's arm. Actually, no . . . Bernie looked again. She'd

tattooed something *else* in the eye sockets, but you had to get up close to see what it was.

"You're lucky she didn't do a winged dick or something," Bernie said. "All she has to do is ink in the eyes."

"Ooh, you're acid today. What's up?"

"Sorry. Man trouble." Well, that was true, more or less. The door opened and Marcus stood there with his yeah-I-just-heard expression. "Got to go. Do me a favor, mate—look after Mac for me, will you?"

Rossi glanced down at the dog, sprawled on the floor by her stool and looking mournful. "Sure. Poor little guy seems a bit sorry for himself."

"That's why I'm asking you—I think he's getting arthritic. Keep him occupied so he doesn't come chasing after me and get soaked."

She ruffled Mac's fur and he flinched as if it hurt. *Poor old bugger. You and me both.* Marcus gave her an impatient jerk of the head and she followed him into the passage to find Dom waiting, wearing a matching frown.

"Hoffman just told me the news," Marcus said. "You got any special insight that I haven't?"

Bernie put her finger to her lips and gestured up the stairs to ground level. "Not in front of the children."

It was still raining. Nobody would think three Gears running across the parade ground to find shelter was anything to worry about. They raced for the vehicle compound and climbed into a 'Dill to guarantee some privacy.

"Look, all I know is that Vic refused to evacuate and Prescott quit." She shook her head, still amazed to hear the words coming out of her mouth like some bad joke. "So he's formed a junta with the two sailor boys, and now they've got to work out how to tell the voters."

"No, Prescott's just not that sensitive," Dom said. "The asshole's walked out for some other reason."

Marcus shook his head. "We'll cope with him or without him. I just want to know what he's doing *now*. Because I don't think he'll be writing his memoirs and offering Hoffman helpful advice on statesmanship."

"Vic said he was talking about having to do something—usual shit, wouldn't say what—and that he'd ask Vic to take it on faith. The next thing we know, Prescott throws in the towel."

Dom shook his head. "Come on, no guy who's launched a global Hammer strike and sunk a city would lose his nerve now."

"Maybe he's finally cracked," Bernie said. "Could happen to any of us. There's no rhyme or reason to it. Something random happens and it just tips you over the edge."

"Either way," Marcus said, "Hoffman made the right call."

"Is that a political opinion?" Bernie had never heard him express one. "That's a first for you."

"No, it's a strategic assessment. We're in no shape to go anywhere yet."

"Well, not much we can do here. Come on. We've still got glowies out there to worry about."

It wasn't a good day for observation duty on the walls, but even with the rain and low cloud they had a good all-around view of New Jacinto and the ship berths. Marcus settled in one of the sentry points built into the wall, elbows braced on the brickwork to steady his binoculars.

Bernie found it comforting to retreat to a high vantage point on an uncertain day. She'd reached that overload stage where one more shock or disaster wouldn't make things any worse. The stalks were getting everywhere and spawning things she didn't even have a name for, leviathans were cruising closer to shore, and now Prescott had handed back the keys. She tried to remember if she'd felt this overwhelmed when she only had grubs to worry about, but time had bleached the intensity out of the memory.

Come on, Vic. You can do it. You're not doing it alone, either. You've still got the same team.

"How do you think people are going to take the news, Bernie?" Dom asked. "You've seen Prescott out pressing the flesh. People have a lot of faith in him."

"Depends who gives them the news and how they do it," Bernie said. "Unfortunately, Vic's got the diplomacy skills of a house brick."

She didn't feel she was being disloyal. Bluntness was just the rough-cast underside of Hoffman's honesty. But she didn't know how civilians would view that now. Trescu was an Indie, which was going to take some selling to the Pelruan contingent even without his personal track record in slotting prisoners. Civvies didn't know Michaelson, but he was the one with the charm and silky voice who'd probably make the best front man.

Great timing. Just bloody wonderful.

"Hey, heads up," Marcus said. He rubbed the rain off his binoculars' lenses and adjusted the focus. "Trawler berths, halfway down the jetty."

Bernie strained to see what he was looking at. A Gear was carrying a box, heading toward the boats. She couldn't see who it was because he had his helmet on, but when he stopped alongside one of the small workboats that were moored with the trawlers, another Gear came out onto the deck and they manhandled the box down the ladder.

"What is it?" she asked. Gears did jobs around the docks all day. It was usually a busy place, especially since the Pelruan evacuation. She thought Marcus had seen something in the water. "Lambent?"

"No. The Gears. I think that's Rivera. And Lowe."

Dom took a look as well. "Yeah, are they still going to be holding Prescott's coat all day now that he's resigned?"

"What are they loading?" Marcus asked.

"*Whoa*," Dom said quietly. "Look who's coming."

Bernie could only see the back view of an oilskin jacket, but it was definitely Prescott. He walked down the jetty and stopped at the ladder down to the workboat to talk to the two Gears. Yes, it had to be his CP team. Rivera, the heavier-set of the two, stood next to Prescott talking on the radio, finger to his ear. Prescott half turned with his arms folded as if he was waiting for someone or for a reply. Then Rivera climbed down to the workboat and disappeared into the wheelhouse. Prescott turned fully to face the naval base and just waited, staring back up the jetty. If he'd spotted Marcus, he didn't show it.

"I don't like this." Marcus pressed his earpiece. "Fenix to Hoffman—Colonel, where are you? I'm watching Prescott and his CP guys loading a boat. You might want to find out why. They're at—"

"Hoffman here. I know. The bastard's just summoned me. Stand by."

Bernie looked at Marcus and Dom. "You think we ought to be down there?"

"Yeah," Marcus said, heading for the nearest steps. Bernie and Dom followed. "If only to haul Hoffman off him."

"Well, Prescott can't be skipping town," Dom said. "Not if he's called the old man down here."

Maybe this was it. Maybe this was the thing that Prescott said he would ask Hoffman to do but couldn't tell him why, the act of blind faith.

"He's going to meet someone," Bernie said. "That's why he's got Lowe and Rivera with him. Anyone want to place a bet on some deal with Lyle Ollivar? This resignation's got to be some scam."

"What the hell could he want from some pirate?" Dom asked.

Marcus shrugged. "Assistance. Protection. Who knows what the fuck goes through his mind."

No, a deal with the Stranded fleet didn't make sense either. But it might have explained the databursts. And how was he sending transmissions? Why would the pirates bother to do a deal when they were probably better off than the COG right now?

Hoffman was already on the jetty by the time they got there, walking briskly to the boat. Prescott must have seen them coming up behind Hoffman but he didn't seem to take any notice. Dom pressed his earpiece.

"We've got your back, Colonel."

Hoffman glanced back over his shoulder. "I don't think he's going to shoot me, Dom. But I might strangle the asshole."

Hoffman came to a halt in front of Prescott. Rivera and Lowe emerged from the boat and stood beside their boss, and Bernie found herself adopting the same defensive position with Marcus and Dom. It was a real study in body language, the state of the COG summed up in a few people unhappy facing each other down on a rain-lashed jetty.

Dom took a few steps back and turned away for a moment to radio someone. Bernie heard the word "Captain." Yes, Michaelson needed to be here too.

Prescott thrust his hands in his pockets. "Thank you for responding, Victor."

"What the hell *is* this?" Hoffman growled. "Where are you going?"

"I can't tell you." Prescott pulled his head back a little, almost looking down his nose. "But I have to go, and I have to go *now*. I can't tell you why, but if I did you'd understand the urgency."

"So how long are you going to be gone?"

"I won't be coming back. But if I left without telling you, you'd only waste scarce resources searching for me."

Bernie heard Marcus take a long breath. For some reason, the news didn't surprise her as much as it seemed to surprise him.

But Hoffman didn't seem to be taking it in. "This is some kind of joke, is it, Chairman?"

"No, Colonel. If only it were."

Bernie could only watch it in slow-motion horror. Everyone had their crazy moments, but Prescott had been the face of bureaucratic normality, the solid leader everyone accepted would always be there. And now he was leaving when there was nowhere much left to go.

"You are *shitting* me," Hoffman said. He started at a rumbling growl but crept up the register. "You are fucking *shitting* me. You're running away? You're fucking *running away* when your people need a leader more than ever? Where in the name of God are you running *to*?"

"I'm not running away, but I *have to leave*." Prescott said it slowly with that why-don't-you-understand look on his face, but this time one fist was clenched at his side as if he wanted to grab Hoffman and shake him. Lowe and Rivera were getting twitchy. Bernie could see Marcus shifting his weight from one leg to the other. "I told you I'd ask something of you, and you didn't want to listen, but I'm asking you again—come with me and help me do what I have to. I can't tell you more than that." He looked past Hoffman at Bernie for a moment. "You can bring Mataki. Damn it, bring Delta too. You'll understand when you see. Just trust me."

Shit, Hoffman was going to have a stroke any minute now. Bernie could see the color draining from his face. His voice dropped to a hoarse whisper. "Trust *you*?"

"You need to listen, Victor. And you'll still have to evacuate Vectes."

"Sir, you can ram it up your ass. Too goddamn *right* I won't listen." Hoffman was right in his face now, and if Lowe or Rivera didn't step in, then Bernie would. "I can't abandon thousands of civilians. Don't give me this bullshit about you can't tell me where you're going—I want you to tell my Gears and those poor assholes in the camp why you're *really* walking out on them."

Prescott seemed to have had enough. He took a firm step toward the boat, a final gesture. "Just tell them I ran away," he said quietly. "I'm sure you can make them believe it. And it'll make life much easier for you and Michaelson. It really will."

"Chairman, you could have run away any number of times over the years, but you never did." Hoffman's voice was hoarse. "Tell me. Tell me what the hell's going on. How can we survive if we don't know?"

"This isn't getting us anywhere, Victor." Prescott glanced at Marcus for a moment. Bernie wondered if he thought he was going to physically stop him. "And I really must go."

"Well, fuck off, then, you *traitor*." Hoffman turned his back on him for a moment and Bernie was certain he was ramping up to swing a punch. "Go on, get the hell out of here. At least I won't have to waste time keeping an eye on your goddamn games anymore."

Prescott had to turn to climb down the ladder bolted flat against the dock wall. It needed a careful maneuver to grip the high iron handrails while twisting to climb down backward. Bernie couldn't believe they were watching him go, but what was the alternative? To haul him back? To shoot him? His senior officers had mutinied. There was no Sovereign's Regulation to deal with what was happening now.

Then Marcus pushed forward.

"I abandoned my post once, and got men killed," he said. "I thought I had a damn good reason. So you better have a fucking *stunner*, Chairman."

Prescott looked up with one boot on the ladder. "I've done my duty all my adult life, Fenix, and I'm still doing it. I'm well aware of how many lives that's cost." He paused. Then his expression hardened as if he'd suddenly remembered something that disgusted him. "But I've never done it out of arrogance, and I never thought I always knew best."

It was a really odd thing to say, very specific, very *personal*. It sounded like it was aimed at Marcus, but nobody could possibly think that about him. Marcus's rigid self-control suddenly snapped. Bernie watched his fist ball, held tight against his leg. He had a bastard of a temper buried somewhere, she knew, but she'd never seen it this close to erupting. He looked like he was holding his breath.

"You're *accountable*, Chairman. You don't get to fuck with us like this. You *don't* get to fuck with what's left of us."

Prescott's expression changed instantly. He clenched his jaw. He was speechlessly angry for a second before he spat out his answer, and it didn't look like an act.

"Fenix, you have no idea. You have *no damn idea at all*. I've been a lot more accountable than your *father*."

Hoffman stepped in front of Marcus instantly and blocked him just as he drew his arm back. For a moment Bernie thought Marcus was still going to go for Prescott, but he got a grip of himself and stood down, looking murderous. That was his trigger—any insult to his dad. If you wanted a punch in the face, it was a good way to get one. Hoffman knew that from experience.

Hoffman jabbed his finger in the direction of the open sea. Bernie could have sworn he was shaking. "Okay, Prescott, get out. Go on. Run. Just get out of my fucking sight." He looked across at Rivera. "I'm not blaming you or

Lowe. Do what you feel you have to. But you should let the bastard drown."

Bernie could hear boots thudding now, someone walking very fast down the long jetty and almost breaking into a jog. It was Michaelson. He strode up behind Hoffman as Rivera slipped the mooring line and stepped down onto the boat. It puttered away.

"The bastard's taking one of my vessels?" Michaelson asked.

"Is that all you've got to say?" Hoffman snapped. "Nice of you to show up. Goddamn, Quentin, what's wrong with you?"

"Never mind, I can track him now." Michaelson looked indignant. "He'll have thought of that three moves earlier, but I'll ask Miran to get *Zephyr* on the case. The workboat's a lovely noisy little thing for a submarine to follow. Let's give him a head start and see what happens. He won't be going far in that without refueling."

Michaelson was a nice enough bloke, but Bernie was still wary of him. "Did you *know* he was going to do a runner, sir?" she asked pointedly. He relished these games. "What else do you know?"

"I didn't, Sergeant," Michaelson said. "But now that Prescott's on my turf, so to speak, I have the advantage."

Bernie wondered if the deal with the Stranded was as outlandish as she'd thought. Prescott might have been heading for a rendezvous. It explained the short-range vessel, anyway.

"Shame that *Clement's* out of torpedoes," Hoffman muttered. "But I need to know where that asshole's heading."

Michaelson patted his shoulder. "Think of Lowe and Rivera."

Wave once, and don't look back again. Bernie hung back to watch the boat for a few moments, then realized everyone else except Marcus had walked off, even Hoffman. The handful of civilians and Gears out on the jetties and on decks glanced up, apparently oblivious of what was happening. The rain started to hammer down in rods again.

Marcus stared after the boat with utter loathing. "I don't believe it."

Bernie wondered whether to ask him what Prescott had meant about Adam Fenix. She had a long history with Marcus. She'd been with him through some of the roughest moments of his adult life, so she could get away with it when others couldn't. But even she didn't dare, not right then.

"Well, we're really on our own now," she said.

"The hell we are." Marcus finally looked away from the shrinking boat. "*This* is still the COG. He's the one who's left it. We'll carry on without him."

Bernie decided to leave well enough alone. Hoffman needed her now. In a normal world he'd have been a couple of years into retirement, but now he was embarking on a new role that she knew scared him a lot more than grubs, glowies or even death.

He was the reluctant leader of the last remnant of the COG. He wasn't going to like that at all.

FORMER UIR SUBMARINE *ZEPHYR*, SOUTHWEST OF VECTES: TWO HOURS AFTER EX-CHAIRMAN PRESCOTT'S DEPARTURE.

"He's still there," said Teo. The workboat was heading southwest at a respectable speed. "What kind of range has that piss-pot got? Because it's not heading for the nearest land."

Trescu listened to its propellers on the headset, baffled. As far as he knew—and as far as Michaelson could tell him—the workboat had only the most basic radar and radio, just enough to do its job of moving men and material around a harbor. It had no sonar or advanced communications, because the NCOG fleet had been cannibalized. Everything useful but not essential had been stripped out to be used elsewhere—again, as far as Michaelson was aware. But Trescu didn't know if Prescott had managed to add some refinements that could detect a submarine tracking him.

When would he even get the chance to do that? Ah, maybe he has. The boat hasn't been used for months. It's small. And nobody was keeping a special eye on it.

Prescott would have to be an idiot if he didn't expect to be followed, though, and the man was anything but that. Did it matter if he knew where *Zephyr* was? He probably couldn't outrun her, but even if he did, even a small boat's props could be heard at a considerable distance in the current conditions. He couldn't just disappear.

And he was at sea now with a couple of infantry men. Trescu was a submarine officer. He was operating in his natural environment for a change, and he had the edge.

"Anything else?" Trescu asked. "Is there anything else out there?"

Teo shook his head. "All quiet. Everyone's betting that he'll rendezvous with Ollivar's fleet, because there's only leviathans, whales, and the occasional fishing boat for the next few thousand kilometers."

"What could the Stranded *garayaz* possibly have that Prescott wants?"

"Beats me, sir."

Trescu prided himself on understanding what drove people, especially his enemies. Whether it was tactical or emotional, he could read people's behavior. Not being able to guess what Prescott was up to worried him. It felt like losing one of his senses, like going deaf.

So what is he not *up to? He's not fleeing for his life, or else he would have run away years ago. He's not able to control whatever this is, or else he wouldn't be so driven by time—and he is. This is a man with deadlines not of his own making.*

And then there was the disc. A diversion to keep Hoffman busy, or sensitive data? Trescu had to hand it to Prescott. He was *good.*

Teo sat back. "Commander, the boat's stopped." He listened with his hands cupped over his headset. "If he's hooked up with anybody, I can't hear it. Do you want to risk active sonar? He *has* to know that Hoffman wouldn't just lose interest in where he was going. So it probably doesn't matter if we give away our position."

"Let's take a look first." Trescu turned to the helmsman. "Periscope depth."

Trescu fully expected the scope to break the surface and see a fishing vessel or Ollivar's powerboat. It took him a few moments to pick out the workboat at this range in the sea conditions, but when he did, it was on its own.

"So he's waiting," Teo said.

"We can wait awhile too. Let's get a little closer."

The helmsman brought *Zephyr* within five hundred meters of the workboat and Trescu took another look through the scope. There was still nothing happening. She wasn't under way, just riding on the swell.

"Might not be waiting for a surface vessel, sir," Teo said. "We managed to hide from the COG for years, after all."

Trescu kept the boat in his scope, occasionally looking away for a few moments to rest his eyes. The rest of the small crew sat in practiced silence. It was a damned long hour before Trescu decided to edge in a little closer.

The workboat was a small vessel with the kind of wheelhouse it was easy to look through at the right angle.

"There's nobody at the helm," Teo said.

That didn't necessarily mean anything. There was a small

engine space below decks, even if it was a very tight fit for three tall men, and there was nothing out here the boat might collide with. But the sea was rough. Someone should have been on watch, if only to keep a lookout for whoever might be meeting them. Someone should have been at the wheel to stop them drifting from their rendezvous point.

"Let's have a look," Trescu said. "Take us in."

Zephyr crept in closer. If anyone popped up on the deck now and spotted her scope and radio mast, it was just too bad. She was so close now that she risked a collision.

Trescu could see an orange polypropylene line trailing from the starboard rail into the water. It was just a rope hanging loose, but loose ropes fouled propellers, and nobody could ignore it on that tiny boat—not even men who weren't sailors.

There's nobody on board.

Damn it, there's nobody there.

How the hell did they manage that? Where did they go?

"The bastard's *gone.*" Trescu was more humiliated than angry. His mind raced through all the possibilities, all of them insane. "Take us up, helm."

"That's just not possible, sir," Teo said. "Seriously. We'd have heard another ship. Even a submarine."

It was a difficult maneuver to hold *Zephyr* alongside the workboat. For a few awful moments, Trescu wondered if he was wrong and that he'd now come face-to-face with Prescott. But that was fine. If he did, Prescott had only two Gears with him and Trescu had a crew of Gorasni seamen and much more liberal rules of engagement than the COG. He'd get answers out of him far more efficiently than Hoffman and Michaelson ever could.

But there was no Prescott, nor any sign of his Gears. Trescu stood on the casing of the submarine with Teo, not a reassuring place to be with waves slapping over it, while a couple of the crew got a line on the workboat. Even with safety harnesses and life jackets, boarding the boat was dangerous.

Teo managed to get on board. He didn't take long to go below and then come back up on deck.

"Yeah, the bastards are gone, sir," he said. "Nothing here. No men, no boxes, not even ash from a smoke. The helm's set on auto and the tanks are empty. It just ran out of fuel."

Trescu was stunned. *He* was the naval tactician, not that mollycoddled bureaucrat Prescott. "Where the hell could three men disembark without us knowing?"

Teo scrambled back to the submarine and nearly fell between the two hulls. Trescu grabbed his arm.

"I don't think it's some suicide pact," Teo said. "While we were dived, Prescott and his bodyguards were taken off that boat—somehow. Whatever it was didn't make enough noise for us to pick them up."

"A yacht?" Trescu could feel the wind biting at his face. It was Gale, always a stormy month, and the prevailing winds would have driven a yacht back to Vectes anyway. "No. Before we give up and look like pathetic schoolboys, let's do an active sweep." Trescu dogged the fin door shut behind him. "Even if that gets the attention of a leviathan."

If Prescott was relying on a small, silent yacht to escape, they'd pick him up now. Teo settled down to listen to the sonar returns while Trescu radioed Vectes. Ianu, one of the marine engineers, gave him a sympathetic look.

"I bet the databursts will stop now," he said. "Prescott's taxi arrived after all."

"You think that was what it was?"

"Damn sure, sir."

Eventually Teo took off his headset and spread his hands in defeat. "Nothing out there, sir. Nothing at all."

Trescu debated whether to tow the workboat back,

because every hull would count one day soon. It meant returning on the surface. And now he had to tell Hoffman and Michaelson that he'd lost Prescott. He'd lost the bastard despite a vast advantage. There was something that he was missing, something he hadn't factored in.

It was one of those situations that needed a diagram of who knew what and when. Trescu shut his eyes to concentrate and radioed Hoffman.

"I lost him, Colonel," he said. It paid to get it over with. "We followed an empty boat on autohelm. We found the workboat, but Prescott and his men have gone."

Hoffman sounded as if he'd taken a deep breath. "Goddamn it . . . *how*?"

"There are very few ways to leave a vessel at sea. You transfer to another vessel. You get winched off. Or you fall overboard. We detected nothing."

"I've ceased to believe in the omniscience of submarines, Commander. What can we rule out?"

"Nothing. But who else has submarines, or helicopters? Only you and I. Not easy assets to hide."

"You managed it . . ."

"We probably wouldn't have detected a sailing vessel on passive sonar. Not ideal for fast getaways, though."

"Well, I hope the asshole's enjoying a cocktail on Ollivar's goddamn luxury yacht. Maybe he'll choke on a lemon slice. Forget him. We've got Lambent to deal with."

"We'll tow the workboat back. It's out of fuel. I know Mathieson will monitor for databursts, but I suspect we've heard the last of those."

"One mystery down, maybe. An unknown number to go." Hoffman finally let out that deep breath. He sounded unusually resigned for a permanently angry man. "And nobody to kick it upstairs to now."

Trescu resisted tying himself in knots by peeling back the

layers of the disappearance. That would be playing Prescott's game. The man was no longer in command.

"You and I have been in this lonely place before, Colonel," he said. "And we beat the odds. We will beat them again."

He meant it. Gorasnaya would *not* die, not on his watch, and its future was now tangled inextricably with the COG's. Therefore the COG would have to survive—despite its best efforts to self-destruct.

He'd make sure it did.

HOFFMAN'S QUARTERS: A FEW HOURS LATER.

"I keep coming up with a different answer every time," Hoffman said. He stared out of the small window onto the docks, worried that part of him was hoping to see Prescott's boat heading back in the gloom of a wet late afternoon, and that it was all part of an elaborate ruse that a simple grunt like him couldn't begin to untangle. "All I know is that he played me. Whatever he did, it was so he could go wherever the hell he's gone. Was he even serious about evacuating? Or did he just pick that position because he knew the civvies would want to stay and he could treat it like a vote of no confidence?"

"Vic. *Vic.*" Bernie held a tin cup of Dizzy's finest under his nose. Mac muscled in between them and sniffed it warily. "You need a drink. Prescott's gone. It doesn't even matter why. What does matter is what happens here from now on in."

"I'll have it later," he said. "I've got to do the briefing. I'll make a statement to the civvies later. The sooner they hear it, the less uncertainty gets a chance to breed."

"I think it'll hit the public harder than us." Bernie took the mug away and started drinking it herself. "Hard to tell if

they'll turn on him, or cry for him like their long-lost mum.
But either way—the next stalk or polyp attack, and they'll
forget all about it."

"I wish."

"And you're not shouldering this alone. Make Michaelson and Trescu pull their weight."

"Okay." Hoffman couldn't put it off any longer. "Look,
I've got all the department heads and NCOs waiting in the
gymnasium. Let's go."

"You'll do fine, Vic."

"What would you have done?"

"About what?"

"Gone with Prescott, no questions asked."

Bernie stared into the mug. "I'd go with *you*, no questions
asked . . . probably. But him? Not if he wouldn't tell me
what was on that disc."

Hoffman had forgotten about that for a few hours. Maybe
it didn't matter now, but it would always eat at him. Then
his radio went off.

"Control here, sir."

"Okay, on my way, Mathieson."

"Just letting you know I haven't picked up any databursts
since yesterday."

"There's a surprise. Thanks, Lieutenant. I'll drop by
later."

Hoffman got up and checked himself in the bathroom
mirror again. He was sure he could see the fear on his face.
Bernie patted his back.

"Look, you got the Embry Star," she said. "And it wasn't
for your dressmaking skills. You're not in this job by accident, either. Even Prescott told you so."

The mention of the medal made him think of Bai Tak.
Like all the dead Hoffman missed, the man would be impossible to get out of his mind for a while, and then vanish

again. Bai would have cut the problem down to size in that clear-sighted, pragmatic Pesang way. But Bai was long gone, and maybe all his family too. Hoffman leaned on the basin and felt himself drowning in regret.

"What's wrong, love?" Bernie asked.

"Just thinking of Bai Tak." He couldn't remember how much he'd told her about his Pesang troops. "The one who died saving Dom at Aspho."

"I get the names mixed up." Bernie rubbed his scalp as if she was giving it a final polish. "You never even wear the ribbon. Does anybody even admit to having an Embry these days?"

"I sent mine to Bai's widow," Hoffman said. "He deserved it. I lost touch with her after E-Day."

He couldn't bear to think that all the Pesangas were gone, like most of the population of Sera. It hit him harder than ever at that moment. He gripped the edge of the basin, eyes shut, and when he looked up again Bernie was staring at him with tears in her eyes.

"*That,*" she said, "is why I'd go with you, no questions asked."

Her respect embarrassed him. "It was shame that made me do it as much as anything. Pesangas didn't qualify for the same awards because they weren't technically COG citizens. I wonder how the Indies would have played it." He felt a terrible need to change the subject and take refuge in a new crisis. "Come on. Let's do it. You too, Mac."

When they reached the gymnasium, the assembled Gears just stared at him. Michaelson was having a quiet chat with Major Reid, who looked crestfallen. So they knew. Well, that saved a few difficult lines.

"We heard, sir," Alex Brand said, studiously underwhelmed by the news. "Corporal Baird here wants to know if he can have his office."

"I could do with a workshop that doesn't flush," Baird said. "Just saying."

It was impossible to keep things quiet for long. The place was too small and there was, as Michaelson always reminded him, no such thing as a monopoly of information. It was hard for the senior commanders to have a bust-up with the Chairman on a public jetty and not get noticed.

"I hope we're not having a whip-round to buy him a going-away present, sir," Rossi said, heaving himself up to sit on an old vaulting horse with stuffing poking through a seam on its saddle. "I didn't even get to sign his card."

"He asked me to join his staff, you know," Baird said.

"And you accepted? So that's why the poor asshole ran away."

Hoffman hadn't expected his Gears to be sobbing in their handkerchiefs about Prescott's departure, but he made a note to keep a close eye on morale. The worse Gears felt, the more disinterested they acted and the more savagely they joked. The fight with Prescott was his alone, just internal political wrangling. The man had never let the army down or ignored military advice—until now—and most respected him even if they didn't like him.

"Okay, Gears, listen up." Hoffman plunged in. "I can see you're all totally devastated by the Chairman's departure. So it's business as usual—daily recons to map stalk distribution, perimeter patrols, everything we've been doing anyway. And the contingency plan will now be implemented."

"Which one, sir?"

"Readying all ships to accommodate personnel and supplies. Not because we're planning to cut and run, but so that we have somewhere else to house people if we have a stalk incursion near or within the perimeter. So there will be *no* chat or unhelpful speculation that might demoralize our citizens. Understood? It's just prudent planning."

Rossi raised his hand. "How's this command thing going to work, though? Sorry to be blunt, sir. *Sirs*, I mean."

"Captain Michaelson and Commander Trescu have a vote and so do I," Hoffman said. "And an order from them is as valid as an order from me. I am *not* the Chairman. Nobody is. This is an emergency arrangement, not a military dictatorship."

"Pity," Trescu said, smiling without a scrap of warmth. "They are *very* efficient."

He actually got a laugh. Most Gears had softened a lot toward the Gorasni, even if the Pelruan townsfolk still wanted nothing to do with them. Hoffman had another out-of-body moment and saw the COG's three reluctant leaders—an Indie who refused to surrender, a naval officer who got a kick out of ambushing pirates, and a colonel who wanted to be an NCO again—and wondered how the hell this was ever going to work.

Michaelson seemed to be finding it a lot easier than he did. "Major Reid and Mr. Sharle will handle Prescott's daily civilian liaison role," he said. "Of course, Mr. Ingram may be somewhat dismayed to see a military junta running the COG, but he'll have *lots* of homework to keep him busy. Seriously—none of us wants to be doing this job forever. Any questions?"

The catering corps sergeant raised a finger. "Sir, now that he's buggered off and left us, can we stop putting glowie body parts in the food freezers? I mean, someone did take them away yesterday, but it's not nice. And it's probably not *safe*."

"Ah, the specimens were just for the Chairman's benefit." Michaelson stopped mid-sentence, then recovered. "But I hear Sergeant Mataki has a recipe for them." Everyone laughed. "Yes, I'd like to know who removed them and what they did with them. We have to dispose of these things more carefully now."

The hell they did. There was diced polyp all over the island, not disposed of carefully at all. Hoffman looked at Michaelson, and Michaelson looked at him, and he didn't need to be telepathic to know they were both thinking of Prescott's fixation with keeping specimens.

So he took them. What the hell is he going to do with them?

"Good idea," Hoffman said. "Any other questions? Because this is an awful short briefing otherwise."

"When are you going to tell the civvies, sir?" Rossi asked. "Base patrols are going to get asked a lot of questions."

Hoffman checked his watch. "I'll do a radio broadcast as soon as we're finished here. Brace for a public outpouring of grief, or at least some anxiety. Prescott was good with the civilians. He wouldn't have lasted that long if he hadn't been able to reassure and inspire them, but now it's our job. So be goddamn inspirational, every last one of you, or you'll be on a charge. Dismissed."

He looked at Marcus, who just tilted his head back a fraction, the slightest hint of a nod. The gym cleared, leaving only Delta Squad, Bernie, Anya, Trescu, and Michaelson. Hoffman accepted that he relied on a small inner circle, and right then he was damned glad that he had one.

"I'm guessing that was what Rivera had in the boxes," Hoffman said. "The specimens."

"Sure as shit wasn't his picnic lunch," Marcus said.

"I'd prefer to think that Prescott just went quietly nuts and kept the bits like serial killers keep body parts, but that's not likely, is it?"

"If someone didn't just dump it all."

"*If* . . . then he's gone to show it to someone. Not our pirate buddies, though."

Marcus shrugged. "Some of them run drug operations." He said it like he'd reached a conclusion. "They'll have better labs than us. Maybe more know-how. And Ollivar's the one who said the COG was dead and that they'd be the new world order."

That sounded like Prescott, all right: opportunistic to the end. But for whose benefit? Whatever else was wrong with him, none of this seemed to be about saving his own skin. That was what made him so hard to fathom.

"I'd like to believe that," Hoffman said. "But it doesn't explain all the theatrics."

"Okay, but if he finally comes back with the pirate king," Dom said, "I'll shoot the asshole myself."

It was all too cheerful, that shaky relief after a near-miss. Anya didn't seem to be joining in the display of bravado, though.

"You okay, Lieutenant?" he asked.

"Oh, emotional girly stuff," she said, pushing her hair out of her eyes. She'd cut it to jaw length now, and it made her look even more like her mother. "I worked with the Chairman for years, and he leaves without a goodbye."

No, Prescott wasn't universally hated. Hoffman began to worry that he'd let his personal grievances cloud his judgment.

But there's the disc. There's all the things he never told me. There's all the things he still wouldn't tell me.

"I better get this broadcast sorted out before the gossip overtakes me," he said. "Come on, Bernie, it's stand-by-your-man time. Then I'll have that goddamn drink."

Who listened to the radio at this time of night? He'd have to get Major Reid to go see the delegates and make sure they all knew, just in case.

I didn't sign up for this. But I pushed Prescott, or at least I was such a gullible prick that I opened all the doors he wanted open.

And if I don't do it, who will?

The route to CIC from the gym was a maze of winding corridors lined with a mix of half-tiled walls and painted wooden paneling, all in the same utilitarian government green. Mac's claws tapped on the floorboards as he trotted behind them. Hoffman realized he would have been happier if every second of slack water in his life, every moment when he had too much time to think, could simply be erased. He hadn't learned the art of not thinking.

"Bernie, what if I've got this all wrong?" he asked. "What if Prescott really knew we were fucked but I wouldn't listen?"

"Trust your own judgment. It's kept us alive so far."

"But will I know when it's time to call it a day? Royal Tyrans never retreat. Will I realize when it's time to run?"

"Oh, you'll know," Bernie said. "Believe me. You'll *know.* And if you don't—I will."

CHAPTER 20

We're not Stranded. We just lost radio contact.

(Corporal Hugo Muir, 5th Kaian Grenadiers)

NOROA, SOUTH ISLANDS: SUMMER, 9 A.E.—
SIX YEARS EARLIER.

The grubs were on the move again, trying to push the wrecked truck down the road. It was a baker's delivery van, not a military vehicle, but they'd scavenge anything they could find after they'd finished slaughtering humans.

Bernie could hear them. She braced her back against the trunk of the tree and steadied herself with her boot jammed into the fork of the branch. They'd have to come back this way if they wanted to get that thing down into their tunnel.

City boys. You strayed too far off your home turf, didn't you, tossers? Bad call.

She looked around to check that Hugo and Darrel were in position. They were hard to spot in the foliage even for a sniper used to looking for people who didn't want to be seen, but she couldn't see Miku at all.

Bernie could wait all day if she had to. She had nothing better to do than kill grubs now. It was only a matter of time before humans had to abandon Noroa, but until that day came, she'd keep killing the bastards.

The first gray head presented itself about ten minutes later. She could see them below, six of them pushing the small truck, four at the back and one on each side trying to steady it. She couldn't see if there was one inside at the wheel, but if there was then he'd written his last letter home to his grub bitch of a mother.

Do they have mothers? Families? I hope so. I want them to suffer and grieve like we have.

She sighted up on the grub on the left side and waited until he passed her. The back of the truck was now level with Hugo's position, and that meant Darrel could take the one on the right. She didn't even need to signal them to coordinate the ambush now. Everybody knew the drill. All she had to do was squeeze the Longshot's trigger.

Steady . . .

Her optics framed the grub's face in profile. When she had a target in her scope, she wasn't worried about their wife and kids or if they didn't want to be fighting a war at all. They were just a threat to be eliminated before they could kill her mates.

Exhale . . .

It was even easier to detach when she saw that scaly gray skin and those weirdly inhuman eyes. She could look into the eyes of a cow or a dog and recognize the common thread of all life, but not these things. They didn't deserve to live.

Hold it . . .

The Longshot would take off the top of his head. His little gray chums would shit their pants and realize that humans wouldn't go down without a fight.

. . . and squeeze.

The grub's head snapped back as if he'd been punched, spraying blood right across the side of the truck. Bernie

shoved her Longshot over her shoulder and switched rifles.
The grubs at the back dropped for cover, looking around
frantically as fire started on three sides of them. One stood
up to return fire and took a chestful of rounds, but still
aimed up into the trees for a few seconds before he fell. Bernie made that two down and four to go, at least from what
she could see on this side. One rolled under the truck. He
stuck his head out too far and there was another rattle of fire.
The forest track fell silent.

She tried her radio. "Darrel, can you see them?"

"Yeah, three at the front."

"I've got 'em." That was Miku, at last. "When I take one
the others are going to bolt, so get ready. Both sides."

He must have moved all the way around through the tree
canopy. The kid was amazingly agile. Bernie felt the strain of
being in her mid-fifties but then remembered she wasn't up
for that kind of acrobatics even thirty years ago.

She aimed. "Go!"

A whiffling noise like an arrow broke the silence, followed by an agonized roar. A grub ran out in her direction
and she hit him in the chest before Hugo put a couple of
bursts into him. She didn't see where the third one went. A
couple of shots rang out.

"Clear," Hugo said. "That's all of them."

"I can still hear one moaning. He must be next to the
vehicle."

"I'll finish him."

"No, I'm heading down," Bernie said. "Then grab what
you can and get out."

It was harder coming down a tree than climbing it. Bernie had to drop the last two meters. She walked around to
the front of the truck to find a grub impaled against the
grille like an oversized radiator mascot. That explained the
whiffling noise; Miku had fired a crossbow quarrel on a

line like a harpoon, and the noise had been the line paying out.

The grub was still breathing, still struggling weakly as if he couldn't work out why he couldn't get away from the truck. She looked into his face for a moment, saw nothing there that she could pity or regret, and reloaded the Longshot.

Too good for the bastard. But it'll take me hours to saw through his fucking throat.

Bernie settled for making sure no grub medic could patch him up and send him back to kill more humans. She rarely used the Longshot at close range. It made a hell of a mess.

Miku walked up and pulled the quarrel out of the grub's chest with some effort. "I was trying to save you ammo, Sarge," he said. "And there you go wasting another round."

She picked up the grub's weapon and took the ammo from his belt. "It's not some cultural statement, then."

"You're taking the piss again."

"Come on, we're all Islanders here, son." Bernie tapped her arm to indicate her tribal tattoos. "Don't play the race card with me."

"You pass for white. You don't even have *bakuaia*." He indicated his own facial tattoos, intricate dark blue swirls like fractals. "You Galangi like tattoos you can cover up so the COG can pretend you're their own."

"Didn't make any difference in Two-Six RTI. And I *am* bloody part-white anyway." *Here we go again. Bit late for tribal differences now, kid.* "We had a couple of other Islanders with full-face ink. Pad Salton, for a start. And a guy from your neck of the woods. Tai Kaliso. Yeah, he was from Arohma too."

Actually, Pad *was* white, very white indeed with bright red hair and freckles. Bernie wondered where all her old mates were now. The thought crossed her mind at least once

a day and she wasn't sure if it kept her going or just pro-
longed a pointless nostalgia she'd be better off without. They
were probably dead.

"Hey, this wanker's got one of our radios." Hugo held up
a COG-issue receiver and earpiece. "A bloody *new* one. You
think we can get a signal out at last?"

"Look at it later," Bernie said. "Come on, we can't hang
around here."

They set off back to the camp, weaving through the trees.
As far as she knew there were just fifteen civilians left on
Noroa now, and if anyone else was still out there, they were
better at hiding than she was. The grubs came back a couple
of times a month to scavenge and sweep what used to be the
inhabited areas. Nobody tried to go back to the towns any
longer, not even the occasional Stranded who passed
through on their endless voyages around the islands. The
Noroa camp was hidden in the eastern cliffs overlooking the
ocean, its boats tucked in a narrow inlet waiting for the
moment they might have to put to sea for the last time. Even
Bernie knew they couldn't hold the place forever. It was
time to start packing up.

*We might even be the last Gears left on Sera. And Miku—
well, he's a Gear whether there's an adjutant here to stamp his
bloody papers or not.*

When the patrol reached the outskirts of the camp—an
invisible boundary, but there nonetheless—one of the sentries jumped out from the bushes with a Boomshot. He was
sixteen and very enthusiastic. Nobody could accuse the civvies of not getting stuck in.

"Glad to see you're alert, Jake." Darrel flinched and
turned the muzzle away with a careful hand. "Don't ask me
for a password, will you?"

"Did you kill any?"

Miku held up a couple of scavenged Locust weapons.

"Well, we didn't get this lot free with a box of cereal."

"Nice one." Jake let them pass. "We saw a boat earlier. We didn't radio you because it didn't look like an emergency."

"Where is it?" Bernie asked.

"Can't see it now. Passed by."

It could only be Stranded, so if they decided to come ashore they'd get a Boomshot welcome. Bernie wandered through the camouflaged huts and sat down by the observation post with the others to examine their haul. Every round counted.

"We've really got to think about going, Bernie," Hugo said. He peered at the radio he'd taken off the grub. "We've had a good innings. Eight years. I bet there were whole regiments that didn't hold out that long."

"It's got to be Galangi, then."

"It's too close to here. I mean go out and find a Stranded colony. Hook up with a bigger group."

"A bigger group of what? They're all shithouses."

"What do you think the civvies here are, if they're not Stranded?"

"You know what I mean." *Fucking Stranded.* She didn't have any time for them. The few that had landed on Noroa had just come to loot. "Look, the grubs don't have a navy. They're still tunneling after nine years. That means they can probably only move within the continental shelf because it's comparatively shallow. Galangi's on a volcanic ridge with a bloody great abyss in the way."

She sat cleaning her Indie sniper rifle, the semi-automatic that Major Stroud had given her way back when the CO was just a lieutenant. It grew more important to Bernie with each year that passed, although she wasn't actually sure of the date any longer. The rifle had come from a UIR sniper who had pinned down a company of 26 RTI in Shavad, and

Major Stroud had killed the sniper up close and personal herself. Stroud was that kind of officer.

It was a lovely piece. Bernie treasured it, not least because it was a personal gift from Stroud. The woman was a legend. And like all Stroud's Gears, Bernie had a strong personal loyalty to her.

But Helena Stroud was long dead. Bernie wondered if her daughter Anya was still alive somewhere.

Hugo shoved the radio under her nose, almost excited. "You know what this means."

"What?"

"It's definitely COG. See the letters on it? But this is recent. I mean it's a new model, and that means they're still manufacturing on the mainland somewhere."

That was a big assumption. She hated scraps of hope because they evaporated all too fast. But it got her attention, and Miku's and Darrel's too.

"It just means they were still making military radios after you left Kaia, that's all," she said. If Hugo could get it working, who would they call? Who was left to answer? "Even if it was last year, they could all be dead now."

"Well, either way, they're not going to pop down here to see if we're doing okay without them," Darrel said. "So that changes fuck all, doesn't it?"

Darrel was a practical man. Bernie had to agree with him. "Yeah. Better get the others used to the idea that we'll have to bang out of here soon."

Hugo fiddled with the radio and sighed. "It's not working anyway," he said. "See? Nothing changes with the bloody COG. We should have let the grub fix it before we killed him."

There seemed to be a communal relief about having to leave for Galangi, even if Bernie wasn't looking forward to seeing her neighbors again. She'd cut off mentally the moment she got on that trawler. But it was probably the safest place to be right now, and it had all the things that Noroa didn't—piped water, food, and somewhere you could sleep for the night without having to worry that every noise was a grub emergence hole forming under your bed.

It was a rough journey ahead at this time of year, but Bernie's definition of what was tolerable had changed an awful lot since she'd left Galangi. The last humans on Noroa began packing up what little they had left to load everything onto the largest fishing boat ready for the trip.

What the hell am I going to say to Neal? It's been a long time.

She was filling water cans a few days later when the small boat came back, the one that had passed by while she'd been out on patrol. Jake spotted it first. She grabbed her rifle and ran down to the headland.

Hugo was already there, lying prone with his rifle trained on the boat.

"Well, it's not a grub," he said. "What if it's someone looking for sanctuary? Another boat might be handy."

"We've got as many boats as we can sail. He can piss off."

The boat headed for the inlet, a little red and white thing with a mast and a motor. Bernie kept her Longshot trained on it all the way in and made sure she was the first down there to check it out, just in case Hugo was going soft out of desperation. It puttered into the inlet and slowed to a stop, bobbing on the water. Bernie and Hugo stood on the shore and aimed at the wheelhouse.

"We haven't got anything for you to take, so you can sling your hook," Bernie called. "Stranded aren't welcome here."

A bearded man in his thirties stepped out of the tiny wheelhouse. "Whoa, I'm not a pirate," he said. "I'm just looking for fresh water to top up my tanks."

"Well, you've got a choice of rivers inland," Hugo said.

"And grubs. Help yourself, but—ah, sod it. If your mates are all out there waiting to come ashore, you must be pretty dim even for Stranded. There's nothing left to steal."

"Are you Gears?" the man asked. "Shit, I thought you lot had all gone back to Ephyra when Prescott issued the recall."

Bernie wore salvaged chest plates and Hugo still had full armor and a Lancer rifle complete with bayonet. It was clear who they were. But Bernie heard the word *recall* and her stomach knotted.

"*What* fucking recall?" she asked.

"You've been out of the loop for a long time, haven't you? Three days before they launched the Hammer strikes. Prescott said everyone had to evacuate to Jacinto Plateau because the grubs couldn't tunnel there. Yeah, big frigging gesture, because most people couldn't even get within a hundred klicks of Jacinto before he pressed the button, even if there'd been room for us. So that's the COG for you, the murdering assholes."

Bernie hadn't known about the recall. Nobody down here had. She risked taking her eyes off the Stranded to look at Hugo for his reaction.

"They *recalled us*," she said. "Three days? *Three days?*"

"Don't think about it, Bernie."

"We were *recalled*."

"It was years ago. Doesn't matter a damn now."

But it did. It mattered to *her*. It meant that Jacinto might still be holding out. And if Jacinto was still functioning, then the Royal Tyran Infantry would be there.

"Any recent news?" she asked, trying not to look too interested. Stranded always wanted something in exchange for information. Her heart was pounding. She tried not to let that stupid hope take her over again, but there was no controlling it. "Who's still in Jacinto?"

The man shrugged. "Oh, it was a year ago now. Last I heard, Prescott was still holed up in his nice office, surrounded by his infantry in the middle of a damn wasteland. That might be really old news, of course. Can't remember the last time I met anybody dumb enough to go back and find out. All the smart folks stick to the islands."

Bernie didn't have an impulsive streak. She did things the army way, assessing information before making a decision. She didn't have much information this time but the decision had been made in a heartbeat. She'd already made it on E-Day.

She had to get to Jacinto now. She couldn't go back to Galangi or pretend there was nothing she could do about it.

"Okay. There's a river about ten kilometers from here." She pointed north. "Follow the coast to the next headland and you'll see the estuary. The grubs are everywhere, so you're on your own."

"You've changed your tune, lady."

"I'll change it again if you don't move."

The man stared at her for a moment as if he was waiting for her to relent and offer to fill his tanks for him. When she didn't, he shrugged, started the motor, and swung the boat around to head out.

Hugo gave her a disapproving frown. "Bernie, tell me you're not thinking stupid thoughts."

"You heard him. It's my regiment. It's got to be Two-Six RTI."

"Bernie, *no*. You'll never make it."

"If you heard that the Fifth Kaia was still operating somewhere, how would you react? Your mates. What would *you* do?"

"Oh, shit, is she starting that again?" Darrel said. "I thought she'd given up on that lost legion bollocks years ago."

"Look, you're a sensible woman." Hugo gripped her shoulder. He certainly wasn't the first man to tell her that. "I just don't know why you can't drop this. Things are hard here. Why go halfway around the world to find something worse? If you find it, that is. You probably won't make it to the next island, and I'm not going to divert a few thousand klicks to drop you off on Kaia, not with the fuel situation."

I'm getting old. I won't get another chance to do this. I'm going to die sooner rather than later anyway. So I'll die fighting with the regiment, or at least trying to get back to them. Not sitting here waiting for the grubs to come and get me.

"I don't need you to ferry me around," she said. "I'll take the day boat. It's got a sail, too."

"You can just about manage the coastal waters. You're not fucking navy."

"Then I'll have to learn on the way, won't I?"

"Bernie, we're a squad. We've done bloody well here. We protect what we can. We save who we can."

She felt something crack silently in her, like a joint popping. She shook his hand off her shoulder. "And I'm fucking Bernie Mataki, Two-Six RTI!" she yelled. "And I *will* rejoin my fucking regiment!"

Hugo spread his hands in defeat. She could have sworn his eyes looked glassy. "Okay, mate. Okay. Take it easy."

"Sorry." Her temper faded as fast as it had exploded. It was a stranger she didn't recognize. "I just have to try."

"Never known you lose your rag like that, Bernie."

"I think it's all that's kept me sane."

"Not us?"

"Well, you too, but—shit, you're a Gear. How can you not understand it?"

"Okay," Hugo said. She'd never seen him look hurt before, but he did now. "Okay."

Goodbyes were always difficult. She knew that she couldn't do them graciously, but now she realized she was afraid of them. It was the one thing in life that she didn't have the guts to face—that she might never see some people again, and so she had no idea of the right words that would turn it from a painful memory into knowing she'd taken leave of them well.

It was bloody hard to leave the squad, and even the civilians. But it was a lot harder to ignore the thought that ate at her daily, that her place was back with 26 RTI. She loaded as much food, water, and ammo into the day boat as she was due and left a note for Hugo and the others in the storage hut. It was 0400. A woman called Shula was on guard duty, a refugee from Kaia.

"We'll miss you, Bernadette," she said. "We wouldn't have survived without you."

"Oh, you'll see me around." Those kinds of lies were okay. They saved everyone a lot of pain. "And you'll all be fine on Galangi. They've even got a bar. Say hello to them for me."

When there was too much to think about, Bernie could make herself think about nothing but the immediate moment. She started the motor and steered the day boat out into an ocean that she had no idea how to navigate.

But she had a compass, a chart, and she was 26 RTI, the Unvanquished. She'd work it out as she went along.

STRANDED CAMP, ILIMA, TYRUS: 9 A.E.

There was just a road's width between life and death these days, a little bit of concrete, and Dizzy was on the wrong side of it.

He watched two COG army trucks and an APC grinding their way along the Ilima–Jacinto highway in the distance. It was a regular patrol at the moment, running every couple of hours. They were heading back to somewhere with medics and clean running water, invisible things he never thought much about until the day came when he needed them and they weren't there any longer.

He'd needed them when Rosalyn got sick but they hadn't been there. Life without her was going to be harder than he ever thought possible. He'd managed three days and he didn't know how he was going handle the next hour, let alone tomorrow.

With his back to the camp, all Dizzy could see was a row of pines along the road, clean craggy rocks, and not a cloud in the sky. Somehow that made matters feel a whole lot worse. Everything looked so bright and alive. He wanted the day to look the way things really were: hopeless, cold, and dead.

He took another gulp of 'shine and worked himself up to turning around to go back to the hut. It was hard facing Maralin and Teresa. He'd let them down. He hadn't been able to save their mom.

And God, he missed her. Folks told him he'd be numb for days and there'd be shock and anger and all that stuff, but he'd gone straight to pain and a full minute-by-minute awareness that she was gone. The only thing he was angry with was the COG—not even the grubs.

Dizzy turned and faced the jumble of corrugated iron huts. Maybe it would be safer in the city. It was hard to know what was for the best. A camp like this on open ground didn't have big solid buildings and power supplies that could be repaired, but you could get out of it fast if the grubs came. Those assholes liked prowling the cities. It was best to stay small and move fast these days. But then there was sickness, and when folks were all sharing a water pump and living packed together like this, diseases spread fast.

Folks were coughing as he passed them. Most would live through this epidemic. Some wouldn't.

He could hear the sound of a helicopter in the distance. There were a lot more reminders here that the COG was getting on with life inside the wire, because the Gears sent out patrols to keep the grubs away from Jacinto Plateau. They sure as hell weren't running relief missions and dropping off food.

The engine noise was getting louder by the second. The chopper was lined up with the main path through the camp and for a minute Dizzy had a crazy thought that it was going to open fire. Maybe that was the hooch thinking for him. It was just that big, black, scary-looking shape bearing down on him with the guns sticking out the sides. It came in pretty low, but then it lifted sharply and something flew out of the crew bay, breaking up into pieces.

No, not pieces: sheets of *paper*, for pity's sake, a load of garbage being dumped on his camp, his *home*. The stuff whirled everywhere as the chopper's draft kicked grit and garbage around. As it flew away, the mess of paper fluttered to the ground. Folks wandered out to see what it was.

One of the guys raised a middle finger in the direction of the helicopter. "Assholes! Go shit up your own town, why don't ya?"

Dizzy bent to pick up some of the stuff. It was a pile of leaflets, plain black print on dull white paper with a COG emblem on the top, nothing fancy. But if they had money and paper to waste on leaflets, things couldn't have been too bad in Jacinto, could they? Dizzy read one carefully.

OPERATION LIFEBOAT
STRANDED MEN AGED 18 to 50

You need not struggle to find food or medical care for your families. Enlist as a Gear, and you and your loved ones will receive the welfare and protection of the

COG. You can serve in combat or support roles,
including driver, mechanic, and construction trades.
Life in the camps will only get harder as the Locust
overrun more areas. Do your part to defeat the enemy
and provide for your family at the same time.

COG patrols will be visiting camps to recruit.
Recruits will also be accepted at the vehicle check-
point at Timgad Bridge, Jacinto.
THE COG'S WAR EFFORT IS YOUR WAR EFFORT

Some folks were scooping up as many leaflets as they
could. It wasn't because they were gung-ho about the goddamn government. It was because waste got mushed up,
bleached, and turned into new paper.

"They know we're dyin' out here," one woman said. "I
mean, how rotten is that? They know we got the sickness, so
they think we'll help 'em out just to get some medicine and
a few scraps to eat." She spat on the floor. "Assholes are
always comin' around tryin' it on, every time."

One guy picked up a leaflet and pretended to wipe his ass
with it. "That's about all it's good for," he said. "Just wish
they'd made it less rough and hard, that's all."

Dizzy shoved his leaflet in his pocket. He didn't have
anything to thank the COG for, so their war was their own
damn business now. Stranded looked out for themselves.
The idea of the COG timing their recruitment drive when
disease was killing Stranded made him wonder who the hell
the savages really were in this world, grubs or humans.

Goddamn, Rosalyn, it ain't fair. Sweetie, it just ain't fair.

He forgot the helicopter pretty fast. He had hooch to
brew and two kids to look after, and there was this sickness
still doing the rounds. Over the next couple of days, he did a
bit more drinking than he planned. It didn't change a damn
thing. He delivered a few bottles of 'shine to his regular

customers and came away with a few pieces of chicken—not a whole one, mind—and a box of six eggs. It was just what his girls needed.

When he got back to the hut, Maralin and Teresa were sitting at the table cutting up vegetables, really concentrating on slicing them up as if the world depended on it. There was a pot of something simmering on the burner. Maralin slid off the chair and went to him for a hug. They were real quiet today. Sometimes they didn't speak at all, and he didn't know if that was just the habit that Stranded kids got into so the grubs didn't hear them, or if it was because Rosalyn was dead and the girls really understood now that she was never coming back.

They knew what dead people looked like and that they didn't get up again. They'd seen too many.

Dizzy scooped Maralin up in his arms. "Hey sweetie," he said. "You makin' dinner?"

"Yes. We've got to take care of you now Mom's gone."

She was only eight years old. His heart broke. "Well, you be real careful with those knives, hear?"

"Yes, Daddy." She gave him a fierce hug and clung to his neck. "Daddy . . . you drinking that *stuff* again? It smells weird. You know Mom said it was bad for you."

Oh God. "I ain't gonna lie to you, sweetie. Sometimes I need it 'cause I miss your momma so much." He stopped short of saying that it eased the pain a bit. He didn't want his girls to grow up thinking liquor was the answer to life's problems, because he knew it wasn't, even if he couldn't do without it. "But I know it's bad. So I ain't gonna be a fool and have too much of it. Just trade it to folks who don't have two smart girls lookin' after 'em."

Teresa put down her knife and ran to him. She clung to his legs. "Daddy, you've got to stop drinking it. You'll die too."

"Okay, sweeties. Okay. I ain't gonna die. Come on, let's finish makin' dinner, shall we?" He put his hand on Maralin's forehead to check her temperature like he'd done a dozen times already today. She felt hot. He was sure of it. "You feelin' okay?"

She nodded. "Yeah. Just sad."

He checked Teresa too. Her forehead felt cooler, but he couldn't be sure. Maybe he was getting too worried and just imagining stuff, and the last thing his girls needed now was to be scared by a panicky dad. He put on his best we're-gonna-make-it face and sat down at the table with them to finish making the meal. Every scrap of peelings got saved for the hooch bucket. When he looked at the pile of stuff that most folks in Jacinto would have dumped as garbage or fed to pigs, and realized that was how he had to make a living to keep his daughters fed, it almost sank him.

Garbage. That was all Stranded were, garbage living on garbage. Not because they were worthless people—they damn well weren't—but because they'd been thrown away, not needed, no more damn use to the COG.

Until now.

He took the recruitment leaflet out of his pocket and wondered why the hell he picked it up in the first place, except to remind himself that the COG must have been in deep shit to want Stranded back inside the wire.

No, the COG could rot for all he cared. He spent the rest of the day making more hooch. Alcohol was pretty good for sterilizing stuff, not just wiping away bad memories for a while, so he made a second batch from the peelings that didn't taste so good. Nothing got wasted.

And every damn day's gonna be like this from now on.

That night he lay awake listening for trouble and misery. Maralin and Teresa slept on cots, one in each corner of the tiny room, while he bedded down on a few blankets right in front of the door with his rifle within reach. Nobody could get past him. And if the grubs came, he was right on the ground where he'd feel the tunnels being gouged out beneath the camp. Nobody would get his girls. *Nobody*.

He woke a couple of times in the night and grabbed his rifle before he even opened his eyes. The first time turned out to be some drunken assholes yelling and arguing somewhere outside. Damn, Dizzy knew he liked his drink too much, but at least he could hold it and not inconvenience other folks.

The second time he woke was because Maralin was whimpering in her sleep.

He went over to her and stroked her hair. Her head felt hot, *really* hot, and it wasn't his imagination. He knew he wasn't going back to sleep tonight.

"Sweetie, you okay?" He wound up the handle on the mechanical flashlight and shone it on her. "You want a cup of water?"

She tried to sit up. "I feel sick, Daddy. My head hurts. I'm sorry."

"Don't you be sorry. I'm here." He helped her sip from a cup and tried to make her comfortable. "I'm gonna sit with you until you feel better."

Teresa woke up and came across to sit on his lap. "Is Maralin going to die too, Daddy? Are we all going to die?"

It shocked the shit out of him. Kids got the damnedest ideas into their heads. But she'd just seen her mom take sick and die in a few days, and the illness was going around the camp. She was just working things out for herself.

"No, she ain't gonna die, and neither are you," Dizzy said. "She's gonna be fine in the morning. I'm gonna stay up and keep an eye on her."

Dizzy sat by the cot for the next two hours and Teresa fell

asleep on his lap. From time to time he reached out and stroked Maralin's hair, but after a while she stopped opening her eyes to look at him. He listened to her breathing. It was getting bad, real rough. He could hear a gargling, wet sound every time she took a breath.

"Okay, sweetie." He woke Teresa and carried her back to her cot. "I'm gonna get someone to take a look at your sister. You just wait here."

It was three in the morning. Mrs. Enszka, the old lady who knew a bit about nursing, wasn't too pleased to be woken up, but she came back to the hut with Dizzy to check on Maralin.

"Well, she's got what everyone else got," she said. Maralin seemed to wake up but she was just mumbling and not making sense. "And most kids come through it in a couple of days, 'cause they're tougher than us grown-ups, but some don't. All you can do is wait. Sorry, Mr. Wallin, but we ain't got the drugs, so it's nature takin' her course." She got up and patted his arm. "She'll probably be fine."

There was no point giving Mrs. Enszka a hard time, because she was right. There was no treating this, just waiting. There was no medicine and there were no doctors, not for Stranded.

Probably.

Probably wasn't good enough, not so damn soon after he'd lost Rosalyn the same way. He sat there thinking for another hour, looking for some change in Maralin. Teresa clung to him, watching as well. There was only one place he knew for sure had medicine and proper doctors, and that was Jacinto. And here he was, stuck outside Ilima.

No, he couldn't take the risk of waiting. There'd be a patrol along the highway in the next few hours like there'd been for the last ten weeks, and that was his best hope.

"Teresa, sweetie, pack the bag," he said. "You know how

to do that. Like we do when we have to run from the grubs, right?"

She did as she was told, like she always did. "Where are we going, Daddy?"

"We're going to find some Gears and get them to help Maralin," he said. "You come with me, and we'll see she's okay."

"But you hate the COG. *Everyone* hates them. They burned everybody."

"Maybe I don't hate 'em that much," he said. "Not as much as I love you and Maralin, anyway."

This was no way to bring up his kids. They had to have a better life than this. He didn't know if he was thinking straight so soon after Rosalyn's death, but he'd learned to trust his gut, and the only clear thought in his head right then was that there were patrols running that main highway, and he had a leaflet in his coat that said his family would be okay if he'd only sign up and join the COG army.

Operation Lifeboat. Yeah, he needed a lifeboat right now. He needed one more than ever. He'd lost his wife but he wasn't going to lose his girls. Whatever it cost, he'd pay that price, and leave behind what little he'd built up over the last few years.

Except my girls.

He carried Maralin through the camp with Teresa lugging the bag. It wasn't even daylight yet. They sat at the edge of the road in the gray dawn for more than an hour, waiting, wondering if he'd guessed wrong and the patrols weren't coming today. Then Teresa looked up.

"Daddy, it's coming! Listen!"

There was definitely a vehicle rolling down the road, probably an APC, judging by that distinctive whine. Engine sounds still spoke to him after all these years. This was his one chance. He stepped out into the middle of the road with Maralin in his arms, and planted his boots square across the center line.

"Teresa, wave the flashlight, sweetie. Stand at the side there and keep waving it. He's gotta see us."

A brilliant white headlamp wobbled in the gloom ahead. It was hard to stand in the path of an oncoming APC, but Dizzy had to. It sounded its horn.

He couldn't step aside now.

Okay, so they've seen me. They gotta stop or they gotta run me down, and my little girl with me.

The APC ground to a halt. It surprised him that the Gears stopped, but maybe a crazy man standing in the road with a little girl in his arms and another now clinging to his coat wasn't something they could pass by. The nose hatch opened and a Gear got out. He wasn't wearing a helmet like most of them did. Dizzy could look him in the eye.

"Whoa, fella, I nearly didn't see you there." He was about thirty or so, a regular-looking guy but very big. "What's wrong with the little girl? Has she had an accident?"

"She's sick," Dizzy said. "My Maralin's sick and I can't lose her, I just *can't*. Help me, buddy, will ya?"

Here he was, a Stranded bum asking a vehicle full of Gears to let him and his sick kid—maybe his *infectious* kid—sit among them. Dizzy braced himself for a brush-off and wondered what he'd do next. He didn't even know if it was already too late.

"Okay, get in," said the Gear. He had a corporal's stripes on his chest plate. "I don't know how I'm going to get the medic to see you, but I'll try."

So there *were* decent human beings still left in this world. Dizzy found himself sobbing. He squeezed into the crew compartment with Maralin on his lap and Teresa huddled wide-eyed and scared beside him, surrounded by six of the biggest guys he'd ever seen.

"Son," he said to the corporal, "you get my Maralin to the doctor and I'll do any damn thing you want. I'll sign up. I'll join your damn Lifeboat. Anything as long as my girls *live*."

The corporal closed the nose hatch and the APC did a U-turn on the highway. "Hey, it's a good life being a Gear. It's a family. You won't regret it. So what can you do?"

"I can fix big engines," Dizzy said. "And I can drive."

The corporal winked at one of the other Gears. "I think we got us a derrick driver, Vincenzo. Now let's get this little girl to a doctor."

TEMPORARY BARRACKS, WRIGHTMAN HOSPITAL, JACINTO: SUMMER, 9 A.E.

"Wow, things must be getting bad," Baird said, looking out the Packhorse's side window. "The rats are *joining* the sinking ship."

Another open truck full of Stranded recruits crawled past them into the barracks as Cole waited to drive out. They all had that same miserable look, more like prisoners of war than volunteers. Maybe that was how they saw themselves. Cole could understand that.

"They must be real hungry," he said.

Alonzo craned his neck to watch until the truck was out of sight. "You think we can we trust them?"

"Well, we've got their wives and kids in government shelters, all fed and cared for," Baird said. "They can do the math."

Dickson fidgeted in the back. "Better to have them inside the tent pissing out than outside pissing in, that's what I say."

"Ah, you did your business postgrad at La Croix University, I can tell," Baird said. "How *was* the module on managing the talent pipeline?"

Cole shut him up. "What, you think they're gonna

sabotage us? Why would they do that? They're gettin' killed out there too."

"Wouldn't you want some payback if you were them?" Alonzo asked.

"Not if I was up to my ass in grubs, baby. I'd save it for later."

"But you *would* save it."

Cole wasn't sure. He didn't bear grudges against people, just grubs. That was so easy that he couldn't imagine it being any other way. Grubs hadn't stood up and said what their problem was with humans, there didn't seem to be any damn point to them except killing, and until they came up with a real good excuse for slaughtering everybody, Cole wasn't inclined to wonder if there were two sides to the argument.

"Depends," he said.

Baird did his know-all head shake. "Don't be surprised if we find bulldozers going missing. Shit, we're giving them the keys to valuable assets. We should have locked them in the kitchens, not made them combat engineers."

"Yeah, well we ain't got much choice, seein' as we're sufferin' from *overstretch*."

"Herniated, more like."

"Someone's got to get out there and move the rubble."

Trouble was, the grubs came at you two ways: underground or on the surface. Ephyra was built on a plateau that was mostly granite. The grubs couldn't tunnel under the Jacinto district at all, but they *could* dig through most of Ephyra just fine. That was where most folks still lived and where the government buildings were. That was the real front of this war, right inside the city. Sometimes you held a street, sometimes you lost it, and sometimes you took it back again. Cole was surprised that more folks didn't just cut and run, but they didn't have much choice. There was nowhere else left to hide.

Smart folks—well, smart folks with money and buddies in high places, anyway—were trying to move back into Jacinto. Every other civilian had to take their chances.

Yeah, you Stranded ain't the only ones caught on the outside. There's always a safer place you can't get to. Just a matter of degree, baby.

Cole drove through the business district, noting that one of the bank buildings now had a lot of communications aerials, a COG Defense Department banner, and Gears guarding the doors. A Centaur tank was parked on the plaza in front.

"Damn, must be my investment account in there," Cole said.

"That's the divisional comms center now." Baird knew all this shit. He actually read the memos. "They're talking about taking over the Treasury, too. Lots of handy connecting tunnels and steel-lined vaults."

"Yeah, how long is *that* gonna stop the grubs?"

"Well, we're still here." That was a rare bit of sunny optimism, coming from Baird. "So we must be doing something right. Or else the grubs are busy trashing somewhere else."

The wire, the defensive cordon of razor wire, concrete barriers, and tank traps, looked pretty battered when Cole drove through the checkpoint each day. They couldn't stop the grubs digging e-holes inside the cordon, but they *could* try to stop the assholes moving across open ground, like forcing water through a narrower pipe to reduce the flow. Today they were looking for things the grubs had built overnight—bridges, rail tracks, anything that made it easier for them to move up stuff to dig in for a big assault on Ephyra.

And we know it's comin', baby. Sooner or later. The big one.

"You think they're trying to get a suntan?" Dickson asked. "They seem to be on the surface a lot more now."

"Maybe they've run out of air freshener down below. Man, those tunnels must stink."

The Packhorse moved out into no-man's-land, the outskirts where grubs came and went but where Stranded took their chances too. Cole passed a huddle of barricaded sheds with roofs made out of truck panels. A wisp of smoke curled up from behind the barricade, and a guy with a rifle was leaning on top of it. When he saw the Packhorse he just held up one hand, middle finger extended, and stared at them in total silence. It was creepier than getting pelted with stones or spat at.

"Yeah, thank you, citizen," Baird muttered. "I hope you get a Boomer up your ass."

Now that Cole was looking harder, he could see more wisps of smoke out there. Goddamn, the Stranded were all holed up in the ruins like gophers. He almost didn't see them.

"You ever been back to your old house, Baird?" Alonzo asked. "You were rich, right? Your folks were from one of the founding families or something."

"What, so I can watch a bunch of Stranded pissing in our swimming pool? No thanks." Baird tapped his chest. "*My* swimming pool. *My* inheritance. See, I wanted to be an engineer, but no, my bitch of a mother insisted—"

"Yeah, yeah, we heard that one," Dickson said wearily. "But you would have been drafted as an engineer anyway, and now you'd be working with the Operation Lifeboat bums."

"I feel so much better now. Thanks."

Cole spotted a likely structure in the distance. There was a rickety bridge across the river to the old power station, and it hadn't been there a couple of days ago.

"Heads up, people." He looked for a path through the rubble and swung east. "Anyone wanna knock down a bridge?"

"Every little helps," Dickson said. "But it'll be back in a couple of days."

"Okay, then we'll knock it down again."

Baird had the map on his lap, checking where they actually were. Maps usually didn't help much because the streets and landmarks were just rubble now. "Yeah, careful where you park, Cole. It's marshy down there. I don't want to have to dig the Pack out of the swamp, y'know?"

Cole reached the end of what had once been a road down to the waterfront. He could see the paving as he drove so he knew he was still on solid ground. The river wasn't quite in the same place shown on the map.

"I think some sluice gates failed somewhere," Baird said. "It's overflowed a bit."

Cole reached the end of the paved road by the shell of a building and put on the handbrake. It was about seventy-five meters to the bridge.

"Yeah, let's be sensible and park here." There was enough cover from the building if they ran into any trouble, and a lot of low walls and other obstructions they could use to move into position. "Okay, let's have some fireworks. I *like* fireworks."

They loaded up with charges from the back of the Packhorse and worked their way down to the water, moving from cover to cover. Baird was right about the marsh. By the time they reached the bridge, Cole's boots were soaked. It was only a shallow river, but a regular vehicle would have been bogged down here fast.

"Damn, my granny could build a better bridge than that," Alonzo said. It was a raft of wooden planks suspended from metal posts on the banks, not so much over the river as sitting on it. "Okay, who's going across to lay the charges on the other side?"

They all looked at Baird.

"Is this because I've got opposable thumbs?" he asked. "Because if not, I feel kind of victimized."

"You're lighter than us," Dickson said. "It's all the hot air."

"Fuck you," Baird huffed. "Okay. Watch and learn."

"Look, I'll go," Cole said.

"No, Private *Dick*son is right. I'm not a lard-ass like him so I won't sink this pile of cocktail sticks." Baird grabbed the charges and dets, looking up and down the river. The nearest cover on the other side was the power station. "And you better watch my back, because I'm not *swimming* across. That water's like the sewage outflow from a dysentery ward."

However much bitching and arguing Baird did, Cole knew he would always do the job. It was just noise to give himself a bit of courage. Baird tested the bridge with his boot and walked across, arms out for balance. The thing was vibrating with every step. When he got to the other bank he did a theatrical bow and started laying charges around the metal supports.

Cole began wiring up the supports on the nearside bank while Alonzo and Dickson kept watch around the waterfront. If the grubs were anywhere, they'd be holed up in the power station or further along the river.

"How you doin', Baird?" Cole was getting anxious. It was taking a bit longer than he'd hoped. "How many you got left?"

"Nearly done."

Cole looked up. Baird began edging his way back across the bridge, then stopped about five meters out from the bank and knelt down to peer underneath the structure.

"I missed some." Baird started unraveling wire. "They've sunk posts into the riverbed. Wow, they work fast. Maybe they'd like a job with the Ephyran Engineers."

"Come on, Baird. You're kind of exposed out there."

"You want this thing put out of action or not?"

"Just get a move on."

Cole watched Baird nervously. He laid a few more charges and was now about halfway across the bridge, lying flat with his head and arms over the side.

"Next time, why don't we just call in a Centaur and blow the bastard up?" he grumbled.

"That's probably gonna put it into orbit. Come on, get out of there, Baird."

"Just a few more."

"*Baird.*"

"Look, I'm—"

Cole didn't hear the rest of the sentence. The explosion felt like a nail being hammered through both eardrums. He found himself instinctively dropping flat as mud, twisted metal, and big wooden splinters the size of staves flew everywhere.

One of the charges had detonated prematurely. "Baird? Baird!" Cole scrambled to his feet. "Speak to me, baby!"

Oh shit. Oh shit. He's dead. Baird's dead.

"Well . . . *fuck.*" Alonzo already had his medical kit in his hand. "I can't see him."

The bridge was drifting loose from the posts on the far bank, or what was left of them. The planks were shredded like a shark had bitten a chunk out of it and a section had broken off and was floating away. Cole could see a pile of muddy armor.

"Oh, buddy, no . . ."

Then the mud moved. The armor unfolded into Baird. He knelt up, very shaky, blood all over his face.

"Whoa . . . okay, maybe I didn't check that . . . shit, Cole? Cole, what happened?"

"You're driftin', baby. Hang on. We're gonna get you." If there were grubs around, they'd be all over the place soon. Cole didn't have time to mess around. "Dickson, I'm gonna

bring the Packhorse down here and put a rope on the winch
to haul him in. That's the only way we're gonna reach him.
Just sit tight, okay?"

"You know he's still sitting on charges, don't you?"

"I do. So we're gonna be real careful."

Cole sprinted for the Packhorse, forgetting all that stuff
about progress behind cover. Baird was in deep shit. But
when he got to the vehicle, the hood was up, all the doors
were open, and even the tires were gone. There wasn't even
a rope or a tool left in the back. For a moment, Cole forgot
all his tolerance for the Stranded and their bad luck.

"You selfish motherfuckers!" he yelled. He clenched his
fists and looked around, ready to beat the shit out of them,
but they were long gone. He'd never felt that way about
another human being before. But damn it, this was Baird's
life on the line. "You thievin' no-good bums! Goddamn selfish *assholes*! Fuck you! I got a buddy out there and he's
gonna die thanks to you!"

How the hell was he going to get to Baird now? There
was only one option. He'd have to wade in and get him. He
didn't know how badly hurt he was, but he'd be dead if the
grubs were coming to see what all the noise was about. He
started running back down to the river, and then the firing
started.

Dickson got on the radio. "Cole, we got ten grubs on the
other bank. We're engaging."

Cole could hear Dickson yelling at Baird to stay down.
He had to call this in. "Foxtrot-Six to Control, we're at the
river opposite the old power station. I got a man down in the
river, no transport, and we're taking fire. We could do with
some help."

"Roger that, Foxtrot-Six. I'll free up a Raven when I can,
but we'll task the closest unit, okay?"

"Control, whatever you got is fine by me, baby."

The fire was coming horizontally across the river. Maybe the grubs hadn't seen Baird. Cole dived flat beside Alonzo and took aim.

"So where's the Packhorse?" Alonzo asked.

"Goddamn Stranded stripped it. Tires 'n' all."

"Assholes," Dickson said. "See, you can't trust 'em."

"I called in support." Cole could see that the section of bridge was drifting while Baird fumbled with his rifle. He was in no fit state to fire. Cole pressed his earpiece. "Baird, you hear me? They ain't seen you. Just lie low. 'Specially with all that explosive you're sittin' on, okay?"

Baird just waved back. Yeah, he'd got the message. All Cole and the others could do now was keep firing until the grubs were picked off or help arrived, and hope that Baird hadn't bled out by the time they got to him. Grub rounds were striking the broken wall right in front of Cole, sending puffs of brick dust into his face.

One grub fell backward in a spray of blood and Dickson whooped. Cole took out another, but the others were hunkered down behind a metal tank half sunk in the mud. Cole could hear the rounds striking it like a badly tuned gong.

Come on, Baird. Hang on.

Might just be concussed.

Might be skewered with a chunk of wood, too.

"Can you hear that noise?" Dickson asked.

Cole paused, trying to pick out something above the rattle of grub rifles. It was an engine, all right. The slope of the riverbank meant he couldn't see a damn thing coming.

"It's not a 'Dill, and it's not a Centaur," Alonzo said.

Cole could hear it really close now, a low grinding noise with a sort of burbling sound underneath, and the crack and crunch of rubble being crushed under tracks. He kept looking.

Dickson tried to look around. "What the hell *is* that?"

A shadow fell over Cole like someone had just dumped a skyscraper next to him. He stared up the incline at the biggest thing he'd ever seen, the underside of a chassis made up of huge, ugly metal pieces he didn't even have names for, but he was damned sure they did the job.

It was a Mammoth, a bridge-laying tank. He could see a dozer blade on the front.

Okay, not a Raven, but . . .

A voice he didn't know came over his radio. "Now, you know how women drivers are, honey, so I suggest you boys move aside. Let Ailsa solve your problem."

"We hear you, Ailsa. And we're movin'."

Cole had no idea what the tank was going to do. Rounds were pinging off it from across the river like flies hitting a bug zapper, so Foxtrot's new friend was probably going to move in and give them cover while they tried to reach Baird. The Mammoth groaned over the incline and thudded down the bank. It took out the intact section of the grub bridge right away, setting off the charges and just ignoring the explosion like it was an annoying fart.

Man, that was *impressive*. Cole gaped for a moment.

"Holy shit on a bike," Dickson said. "But I bet she can't park that thing."

"She's going to sink," said Alonzo.

"It's a bridge layer. It does rivers."

The Mammoth had definitely distracted the grubs. Cole took the opportunity to move down the bank and get level with Baird's raft of splinters and high explosives. The Mammoth suddenly paid out a couple of sections of its bridge and spanned the river right opposite the grubs, then crossed and just kept going. The grubs, dumb assholes, maintained fire and tried to fall back, but the tank was on the far bank now and moving a lot faster than they expected. It rolled right over them.

"Man . . . that's messy," Dickson said.

Ailsa seemed to be backing up a bit to make sure she'd got them all. "Can you see any more grubs, boys?" she asked.

"In one piece? No, ma'am."

"Good. I'm goin' to come back now. You got someone in the water?"

"See the raft?"

"I'm relyin' on cameras, honey. You're goin' to have to help me out."

It took a while to maneuver, but the Mammoth returned to the bank, headed downstream, and bridged the river again to trap the raft with Baird still on it. Cole and Alonzo managed to get onto the raft and manhandle him up onto the Mammoth's hull.

"Hey, what *is* this?" he mumbled. His hair was sticky with blood. "Ooh—this is interesting . . ."

"He's concussed," Alonzo said. "At last. We finally found a way to stop him bitching."

Ailsa opened up the tank's main hatch and watched Alonzo checking Baird over. She was—just as she sounded— a Stranded lady with an Operation Lifeboat badge on her overalls, maybe late thirties, all blue-black hair she probably wasn't born with and a real nice smile. Baird had just had his ass saved by a Stranded bum, and a female one at that. Cole wished Baird had been alert enough to savor the irony. He was none too keen on having ladies in the army.

"You boys need a ride home?" she asked.

"Yeah," Dickson said, obviously not thinking too carefully. "The Stranded stripped our Packhorse, the assholes."

"Well," said Ailsa, "we better go pick up what's left before the *assholes* take the rest, right?"

Cole elbowed him. "No offense, ma'am. We're just kinda strung out."

"Time's gonna come," Ailsa said, "when you folks are gonna be just like us, except we'll have a head start on you."

Cole didn't spend much time talking to Stranded beyond yelling at them to get clear of this place or that, but when he did they made an awful lot of sense. Somehow they'd survived everything the COG and the grubs could throw at them without an army or any fancy technology, and they just seemed to be getting tougher and smarter by the day.

"That's a thought, ma'am," he said.

"Survival of the fittest." Ailsa hummed happily to herself. "Hell, we'll still be here long after you've gone."

"Where are we?" Baird asked.

"Eatin' humble pie, baby," Cole murmured, knowing he'd remember that. "Eatin' humble pie."

CHAPTER 21

SITREP #475B

Extent of contaminated zones and stalk ingress at 0001/ BL/10/15

CURRENT BOUNDARY OF CZ: 22 km approx. north of VNB, 30km west.

RATE OF SPREAD: Currently no activity. Irregular in shape and rate.

FORECAST: suspended. Action: Daily monitoring to continue. Evacuation contingency team to remain on one-hour alert.

WEEKLY RECON TASKING: KR-239 to East Tyran seaboard; KR-15 to SW Pelles; KR-80 to Central Massif.

(Prepared by: Major G. Gettner and R. Sharle)

KR-239 ON RECONNAISSANCE SORTIE TO PORT FARRALL: APPROXIMATELY THREE MONTHS AFTER PRESCOTT'S DEPARTURE, BLOOM, 15 A.E.

"Well, there's still somewhere left to park the dinghies," Sorotki said. "But that's about it. Do you even want to land, sir?"

"We can see enough from here." Hoffman leaned out of the Raven's door. He didn't look like a man who'd just been vindicated. "At least I called that one right. Goddamn. What's left?"

Trescu took no pleasure in watching the man's hopes dashed. Merrenat Naval Base and Port Farrall, one single sprawl fanning out from the docks, was now a forest of stalks. Its ship basins and jetties were crumbling where the huge growths had broken up the concrete. Hoffman sat back in his seat and studied his map with Marcus Fenix, shaking his head occasionally.

This place had been the COG's best hope for relocating as a single community. They'd have to think again. Sharle and Parry consulted their own chart.

"It was fine last month," Sorotki said. "Which just goes to show. Plan B, anyone?"

"Look, we're back to the dispersal scenario." Sharle was right, but nobody wanted him to be. "I've scoped out every variation on it for you, so it's your call. Just remember that if you disperse across more than fifteen settlements, we won't have enough core skills to share between them. The tough decisions are going to be who gets told to go where. You're going to have to break up a lot of teams."

Hoffman passed the map to Trescu. "And the command team."

"Well, we have to return to Gorasnaya. Whatever state it's in." Trescu couldn't imagine going anywhere else. It was a lottery. Any place on Sera probably stood the same chance of coming under Lambent attack. "And if any of your people wish to come too, it would be ungrateful of me not to extend the same welcome to them as you did to us."

"I'll assume that's not sarcasm."

"Absolutely not."

Everyone had a depressingly accurate picture of the evacuation sites, pieced together sortie by sortie over the weeks. The map on Trescu's lap was covered with pencil marks that told the story of dwindling options. Towns had been circled and then crossed out: too far from the sea, too far from rivers, too hot and arid for crops, too cold in winter for humans, no infrastructure left, already occupied by Stranded—or already infested by stalks. Those that remained possibilities were either spread along the Tyran coast or hundreds of kilometers inland, isolated and hard to reach.

But it would always have been this way. Even without the Lambent. The entire world has to be rebuilt. Technology has to be reinvented. Whatever happens, none of us will live to see a Sera anything like the one we've lost.

"You're going to need a decent warship to replace *Nezark*, then," Hoffman said. "We'd better talk to Quentin when we get back. Sorotki, how are we doing for fuel?"

"We can swing past Gerrenhalt and Vonner Bay before we need to refuel."

"Top of my list," Sharle said.

Fenix turned his head slowly and looked at Hoffman. Trescu didn't recognize either name. Who noticed or cared what happened to COG cities when Gorasnaya's were being laid waste? They seemed to have some significance for those two, though.

"Good idea," Hoffman said quietly.

The Raven hugged the coastline heading south. Trescu simply watched with interest, thinking of Branascu. It was only when Sergeant Parry began to look uneasy, gaze darting between his chart and the terrain below, that it occurred to Trescu where the flight path would take them.

They'd pass over Jacinto, or whatever was left of it.

Mitchell stuck his head into the crew bay. "Okay, gents, we're ten klicks from Jacinto," he said. "What do you want to do?"

"Just grab some images, Mitchell," Hoffman said. "We know there's no infrastructure left."

There was a time when Trescu would have cracked open a fine vintage to celebrate seeing the COG capital destroyed. His father's ambition was to roll through the streets with an armored division and pull down the COG flag from the House of Sovereigns. *But you didn't need to, Papa. They did it themselves.* The coast below was dotted with town after town of buildings that looked as if they'd been cut off at the foundations with a scythe. Where their walls had survived, not one seemed to have a roof left. From time to time Trescu saw the occasional gray husk of a stalk, sometimes in the deserted streets, sometimes on the shore or a little way out to sea. He leaned out as the Raven banked, and saw a long spit of land curved around a huge natural harbor, almost on the scale of a volcanic caldera.

He was a navy man. He knew his charts. He knew what was coming, but it still made his stomach knot.

"Dear God Almighty," Hoffman said. He put his hand to his mouth as he looked down. "Dear *God.*"

The vast harbor was Jacinto. The city was gone. It was absolutely *gone.* Nothing broke the surface of the water. Along the new shoreline, rail tracks dangled in midair and bridges went nowhere. A fine old spire leaned at a precarious angle over the water, a roost for red-beaked gulls that scattered like confetti when the Raven passed.

"Yeah, that did the job," Fenix muttered. He was a hard man to read, but Trescu was betting on dismay. "One Lambent Brumak."

Trescu had to ask. "You detonated it."

"It was all we had left."

"I mean *you* detonated it." Trescu needed to know for his own peace of mind. "Personally."

Fenix gave him that slow stare. "Yeah. With the Hammer."

"Actually," Sorotki said, "it was me, Mitchell, Baird, and

Dom too. Plus Stroud doing the backroom work. Just for the record. In case Marcus gets pilloried in years to come as the guy who took Jacinto off the map."

"Maybe that's my inheritance," Fenix said, and went back to studying his chart.

Trescu assumed it was a reference to his father. For such a private man, Fenix sometimes provided surprisingly raw glimpses of his mind. Hoffman frowned briefly to himself as if it were a coded message only he understood.

There was a whole history between them that Trescu knew he might never unpick, but one thing was clear: when events changed the course of the war, that same small group was usually involved somehow. The key decisions that shaped the future of the COG, and with it the fate of Sera, had long been in the hands of a very small and powerful patrician clique such as the Fenixes and the Prescotts, aided by a few loyal foot soldiers. Trescu came from a clique too, generations of senior commanders. There was an odd sense of inevitability about finding himself in this circle.

Mitchell, braced against the edge of the open door, showed no emotion as he took photographs. The COG could not only think the unthinkable. It was also willing to do it, even to itself. And then it recorded it.

Trescu felt a pang of something that wasn't quite fear, or even mistrust, but a reflex reminding him that his new allies would have finished off Gorasnaya without a second thought, and that he should never forget that.

And I would have finished them off, too. I promised my father I would. But here I am, thinking only in terms of individuals I would rather see survive than die.

The harbor that had been Jacinto vanished behind them. There were still stretches of unspoiled coastline between the ruined towns, which Trescu noted as somewhere to consider retreating with tents if things went from bad to worse. After half an hour, he began to see the cracked remains of paved roads again. It was hard to tell how much damage had been done by the Locust and how much by the Hammer of Dawn.

"Vonner Bay," Sorotki said.

Sharle pointed. "And there's Corren."

"I'm going to set down. Eyes peeled, folks. Might be a popular Stranded beach resort by now."

Trescu couldn't see any smoke or other signs of habitation. When the Raven set down on the coast road, Mitchell took up position on the door gun and Fenix jumped down first. It was fascinating to watch Hoffman and Parry suddenly turn into frontline Gears again, scanning for sniper positions with their Lancers ready.

Sharle checked his handgun casually. "I think I still remember how to use this." He winked at Trescu. "Navy."

Trescu checked the magazine on his assault rifle and nodded. "Navy."

Vonner Bay was a small town that looked as if it had escaped a direct Hammer of Dawn strike, but had been caught by the firestorm. Trescu was all too familiar with the aftermath. The intense heat turned paved areas into something that looked like badly fired ceramics, and there was always a vast crater left at the point where the lasers converged on the ground. Vonner Bay looked as if it had simply burned, and the buildings were mostly intact shells whose windows and doors had vanished. Parry walked down the center of the road, casting around on the ground for something. He stopped and took out his knife.

"Give me a hand." He'd found a manhole cover. He raised it a fraction with the blade to get his fingers underneath and lifted it with Fenix. "Let's see what's left."

He peered down the hole. Hoffman was looking out across the water at the remains of a city that hadn't fared

quite as well. The tower blocks were just jagged stumps and
the few tall buildings that hadn't been leveled stood at
impossible angles, as if the ground beneath them had tipped
up at 45 degrees. The colonel stared at it for a long time.

Sharle did a little embarrassed nod. "Corren," he whispered. "He lost his wife and sister-in-law there during the
Hammer assault. Or somewhere on the way back from
there. I can't remember if they ever found their car or not,
but it's not the kind of thing I'd want to ask him."

Even to themselves. Trescu marveled at the COG sometimes, but for all the wrong reasons. *Could I have done that
to Ilina, even for my nation's survival? For Sera's? What are
you left with in the end?*

Hoffman looked down at his boots for a moment and
then wandered back toward Sharle.

"I wonder what happened to Pad Salton," he said, more
to himself than to Sharle. It didn't look as if Sharle knew
who he was referring to or why the view of Corren had trig-
gered the memory. "Well, what's down there, Staff?"

Parry straightened up. "Plenty of cabling, sir. Even if it's
not connected to anything, it'll come in handy."

"Takes a lot of people to strip every town, Royston," Hoffman said, looking almost satisfied. "Sera ran out of people
fast. We'll keep finding all kinds of useful shit, wherever we
go."

"A larger crude carrier," Trescu said. "*That* would be useful. Even if every blade of grass on Vectes is poisoned, we
might still be able to extract imulsion."

Hoffman turned, frowning. "You're not seriously suggest-
ing anyone would stay there, even for short periods."

"It's in the contingency plan," Sharle muttered. "It's *all* in
the plan."

"It would be very much like living on a deep-sea drilling
platform," Trescu said. And it would be worth some

sacrifice. "If we were forced to leave, we might still be able to continue extracting fuel for some time."

A flock of gulls rose suddenly above the roof of a derelict store. Fenix spun around. Trescu's immediate thought was of stalks, but he couldn't hear anything or feel any tremors, and there were still birds sitting on the road sign at the other end of the street.

Stranded, maybe. They can't miss us. They spot one Raven, and they pass on the word.

"I'll check that out," Fenix said. "Sorotki, you see anything?"

"Negative, Marcus."

Fenix moved to the end of the road, rifle raised, and edged around the corner. Hoffman motioned Sharle and Parry to wait while he followed him. Trescu decided that didn't apply to him. But before he could reach the corner, Fenix lowered his rifle, stepped out slowly into the road, and stood staring at something. He held his hand up to Hoffman in a take-it-easy gesture. The colonel joined him. The two of them just stood there, looking up the road.

Whatever it was had riveted them. Trescu crept up to the end of the building and peered around the shattered brick wall.

It was a stag in full antler. The animal stared back at them for a while, then lowered its head and went on grazing along the overgrown grass verges, moving back up the road toward the hills.

"Goddamn," Hoffman said. "Doesn't look like he's been bothered by humans before."

Fenix stood watching the stag for some time after Hoffman had walked away. If that had been Sergeant Mataki, she would have been sizing up the animal for meat and hide. There was no telling what Fenix was thinking. He looked almost wistful.

"You coming, Fenix?" Hoffman called. "We've got some ground to cover."

Fenix turned and walked after him. "Sera's still alive," he said as he passed Trescu. Trescu wasn't sure if it was a conversation or just thinking aloud. "So we can still save it."

"Perhaps we can," Trescu said, but the conversation ended there.

They spent the next hour wandering from street to street, identifying buildings for immediate occupation and checking for connected plumbing and other utilities. It was going to be a more primitive existence than Vectes, but the Stranded thrived in far worse conditions elsewhere.

"We could house a couple of thousand people here," Sharle said. "What do you think, Len?"

Parry nodded. "Works for me."

Trescu almost offered an opinion, but checked himself. *This isn't my concern. I have to focus on Gorasnaya. And if we disperse—when we disperse—I'll probably never see any of these people again.*

He hadn't realized what a depressing thought that would be.

Sorotki did a couple of circuits over the town for Mitchell to grab more images before turning for Gerrenhalt. Trescu checked his watch and estimated they had about two hours left before they'd need to return to the ship to refuel. Perhaps there'd be time to visit Branascu tomorrow after all.

"*Fort Andius* to KR-Two-Three-Nine."

"Two-Three-Nine receiving, Commander," Sorotki said.

"KR-Eight-Zero has a message for Hoffman."

Hoffman perked up. "Go ahead."

"Major Gettner says you're not to blow a gasket, but she pushed her reserve tank and made it to Anvegad. She's on her way back with the recon images. She managed to land Rossi inside Anvil Gate."

Hoffman shut his eyes for a second. "And?"

"Deserted, sir, and in one piece. And he says the river's still flowing into the cisterns."

Trescu knew little detail about Anvegad except that it had an underground river that provided its power and water. Even when the river had been dammed by the UIR during the siege, the garrison at the heavily armed mountain fort had still been able to hold out for months. But he knew far more about the COG lieutenant who'd not only held it but had ambushed a UIR regiment that had come to take his surrender. He watched Hoffman's face carefully.

"Well, damn," Hoffman said, as if someone had told him they'd met an old friend who'd asked after him. "We could use a place like that."

CNV *SOVEREIGN*, VECTES NAVAL BASE: ONE WEEK LATER.

"Peas," Sam said. She had a bag of them stashed in her belt and kept sneaking out a pod to pop it and devour the contents. "I never thought I'd crave peas. You know when you just *have* to eat something sweet? Well, *peas*. Hits the spot."

"Do you remember chocolate?" Dom found himself thinking of luxuries he'd never been fond of when he could buy them. "I mean really remember what it used to taste like."

"Like coffee. That barley stuff is okay, but I know if I tasted the real thing again I'd get a shock."

They were building bunks in one of the weapon sections on board *Sovereign*, hammering nails into wooden frames. The old Raven's Nest carrier was becoming more of an ark than flagship. Michaelson seemed pretty relaxed about seeing his warship turned into a cruise liner, but Dom suspected it couldn't have been easy for him.

No missiles left. Not even a full squadron of Ravens. What else are we going to use all this space for?

"There." Dom stood back to admire the precision of their carpentry. Actually, it was pretty rough, but it wouldn't collapse, and that was all that mattered. "It's amazing what a Gear can do. Look how many skills we've had to learn."

"Well, the next one to learn is making wooden joints instead of using nails," Sam said. "Because we're going to be running out of those, too."

"They're rehearsing us."

"What?"

"How many people sleep ashore now? You tell me. They're getting us used to the idea of moving out."

Sam picked up the tool bag and gave him a look. *"They?* You're talking about Hoffman and Michaelson, Dom. Not some dickhead politician. They're our own. They've always been straight with us."

"Sorry. I just—ah, I'm finding it hard to think about how we'll have to live if we leave here."

"Oh God, not the Stranded thing again. Please."

"It's not about being like the Stranded, Sam. It's about why we bothered to fight for so long when we could have just called it a day fifteen years ago."

Sam slung the bag over one shoulder and her Lancer over the other. Even below decks, every Gear kept their rifle with them. She took hold of the handrails on the ladder and looked back at him.

"You've heard the saying about throwing good money after bad, haven't you? Well, fighting's like that too."

"Yeah. I know."

"You know what worries me?"

"What?"

"If we go, we have to split up into smaller groups one way or another. Groups of a few thousand, at most. There'll be people we won't be seeing again. The Gorasni, for a start. The Pelruan people. The Gears who end up as shore garrisons."

Dom knew that, but he also took it for granted that in Michaelson's emergency plan, he'd still be with the people he'd always lived alongside—Marcus, Anya, Cole, Baird, Hoffman, Bernie, Rossi, and Jace. It was the old gang. That was all he cared about.

Am I being selfish? It's going to hit the Jacinto civvies really hard.

"We'll be okay," he said. "We've still got a lot of Gears. Hell, there are Gears here I hardly know, even after a lifetime in the army. People stick to the little tribes they've always been part of. That's what people do, COG or Indie."

"And what if those people have jobs that mean they have to go somewhere else? Every settlement needs a medic, and an engineer, and so on. You can't do that without splitting people up."

It was too much for Dom to think about. People would be upset, but that was life. It beat being dead—well, generally.

"Radio," he said. "We'll talk on the radio. Seriously. It's not like we're going to be cut off from everyone forever."

Sam gave him that sad, exasperated look. She was probably asking in a roundabout way whether he wanted to be with her, not whether he cared about the trauma of separation for civvies he didn't have much contact with anyway. Dom was on the brink of answering the unasked question at last when he hit that glass barrier again. *Damn, damn, damn.* It wasn't as if she was some woman he didn't care about who was sweet on him. That would have been easy. He just couldn't move on, even though he knew it was a really great idea.

So I can't ever nag Marcus again about Anya. At least they've got a relationship, however distant it looks. They're an item. Even Baird's got more of a life than I have these days, God help me. Frigging Baird's turning into a social animal.

"Come on," Dom said. "The planks won't walk themselves down here."

Up on the flight deck, *Sovereign* looked like any warship undergoing a refit. There were huts and tents everywhere, and seamen working with civvies.

But these weren't temporary workshops. They were here to stay—they were greenhouses, storage tanks, and sheds. There were even raised vegetable beds being built.

"The Aleksander Reid Tomato Sanctuary," Dom said, desperately trying to lift the mood. "I'm going to name a variety after him."

"Cometh the hour, cometh the man." Sam rubbed a leaf between her fingers, releasing the pungent green scent of tomato. "Yeah, you were right. If he hadn't kept on about it, we'd be in trouble now."

"Simple plan. Grow everything in containers. Even trees. Always stay one step ahead of the stalks."

The timber was stacked on the jetty but there was no such thing as a stevedore these days. They had to shift their own materials. Sam selected some lengths of two-by-four and began tying them at both ends. There wasn't much room to maneuver with all the activity going on around them.

"We could be here for years," Dom said. "Or we might just move up the coast. Yeah, Hoff and Captain Charisma are right. Stay flexible."

"And Trescu," Sam said, but she was cut short by the rising note of the warning siren. Everyone froze. "Oh shit, what's that?"

Everyone who had a personal radio seemed to press RECEIVE at once. Most civvies didn't have one. They stood watching anyone in uniform for a clue. Out here in the docks, they couldn't tell what was going on inside the base itself or in the camp.

Dom listened to his radio, staring at Sam. It was like looking in a mirror. She had her finger to her ear too, and probably the same expression of dread that he knew was on his face as well.

"Control to all callsigns," Mathieson said. "Tremors detected close to the north perimeter. Stand to."

Sam dumped the tool bag on the timber to lay claim to it and ran after Dom. It was a well-practiced routine, but not because of drills. They did it for real too often. Every Gear dropped what he or she was doing and ran for the positions they would defend in an attack, leaving the civilians to report to muster points and get to shelters.

That was the plan, anyway. Dom knew—as everyone did—that there was no way of predicting where the stalks would come up, and so nowhere was a safe shelter, and nowhere was the right place to be to deal with an attack. The plan had to be there. It just wasn't meant to be followed that closely.

"That's got to be a record," Sam said, pointing up.

There was a Raven in the air already, hovering over the south wall. They'd got off the ground inside two minutes. It had to be Gettner.

"She's obsessed," Dom said. Sam would know who he meant. "She must just sit in the cockpit all day, waiting."

"She does. I've seen her."

"What about poor old Barber?"

"Him too." Sam peeled off to go to her stand-to point on the gun battery. The caged chickens placed around the base were squawking and flapping. "That's why you can't beat them at cards."

Marcus was already at the gate with a flatbed Packhorse

idling and its machine gun loaded. Dom could feel the tremors under his boots now.

"So much for the early warning chickens," Dom said. "They're *all* going nuts. It would help if they were a bit more specific."

"Okay, either it's close, or it's a lot of them," Marcus said. "What do you want to do, drive or shoot?"

"Shoot," Dom said.

He climbed on the back of the Packhorse and checked the ammo belt. Now it was just the awful waiting for things to come up or for Gettner to call it. He could still feel the tremors.

The Raven circled, and then a second bird joined it.

Come on . . . come on . . .

"Switch that damn siren off," Marcus muttered. "We heard it already."

Come on . . .

"Two-Three-Nine to all callsigns, it's in the camp—it's coming up inside the wire." Sorotki had spotted it. "Block H for Hotel. *Inside the wire.* Two stalks—no, three."

"Hang on tight, Dom." Marcus hit the gas and the Packhorse shot off through the gates and down the main track through the camp.

Civilians were standing around, panicked and confused. They knew the drill. When they heard the siren, they turned on their broadcast radios, if they had them. The rest was word of mouth. In a fast-moving incident there was no way of making sure everyone had the right information anyway. Chaos unfolded despite Sharle's meticulous planning.

Dom could only yell at them. "It's in the camp—get inside!" Inside where? There was nowhere safe to send anybody. At least he could tell them where *not* to go. "It's in block H. Get off the roads."

The crowded camp seemed a lot bigger when he needed

to get somewhere fast. He hung on to the rail one-handed as Marcus careered down the narrow tracks and took a sharp right, nearly throwing him out. But now he could see the stalks above the single-story homes, three twisted gray things with pulsing blisters on them. More pushed up out of nowhere while he watched, another six in a matter of seconds. This was going to be bad.

"Eight-Zero here, we've got polyps—lots of polyps. I can't engage. Too many civvies. Ah, shit—" Gettner went off-mike. The next thing Dom heard was the bullhorn on the Raven echoing over the roofs. "Go right! Get to the main track! Go right! Run!"

Gettner was doing her best to herd the people out of the way. "Get me in there, Marcus," Dom said. "Come on." He could hear the screams and the grenade-like explosions. "It's all kicked off."

Marcus slammed on the brakes at the end of one of the tracks. Dom could hear other Packhorses heading their way and the sound of boots running everywhere, but once he saw the view down that path he couldn't focus on anything else.

All he could see was a tidal wave of people running toward him in blind panic, some carrying kids or trying to drag old folks, others stumbling and unable to keep up. He could only guess what was happening behind them. It looked like a rank of machine guns was mowing people down from behind. A mass of polyps was racing after them.

Marcus was out of the Packhorse and charging through the center of the crowd by the time Dom pulled the machine gun off its mount and ran after him. Civvies parted around him like a river hitting a rock midstream. A matter of meters above the buildings, a Raven hovered with its door gunner loosing off short bursts straight down at the ground behind the civvies.

"Come on, *come on*, get out!" Marcus was pushing

people past him with one arm, Lancer held clear of the stampede with the other. "Just run! *Run!*"

The explosions behind the crowd got louder. "Eight-Zero here — there's hundreds of them, Marcus." That was Barber, manning the Raven's door gun. "They've scattered everywhere. It's not all polyps. We've got fuck knows what coming out of the pods, too."

"We've got it, Barber," Marcus yelled. "Move on. Stop the rest."

The Raven banked away. Dom was right behind Marcus as they pressed through to the rear of the crowd and suddenly the civvies were gone. Dom felt like he was falling off a cliff. For a second he was staring at a scuttling mass of gray legs and things with fangs that reminded him of grotesquely deformed cats, trampling over a carpet of bodies that he couldn't bear to look at. Marcus ran on and opened fire. Dom had to run over them too. They charged into the mass of glowies and hosed everything that moved. Dom dropped the machine gun when he ran out of ammo and switched to his Lancer.

The things were exploding so close to him that he felt the spatter like drops of boiling water hitting his face. If there was anybody on the ground who was just wounded, they didn't stand a chance. There was nothing he or Marcus could do to stop and check. They were knee deep in Lambent, and they had to keep firing. Once Dom got into this rhythm, it was unconscious and almost impossible to stop. He was still firing and reloading when Marcus grabbed his arm and he realized he was yelling at him.

"I said *stop*, Dom!" Marcus's face was all shock and sweat. "Come on, next road — can't you hear it?"

The screaming and explosions suddenly hit Dom like the sound being turned back on. He ran toward it. Rossi, Jace, and Anya were already there alongside a couple of civilians with shotguns. A 'Dill behind them was blasting away at the seething mass. Some of the huts were already on fire. It was chaos; nobody could hold a line like this when the polyps were swarming everywhere. The most anyone could do was surround them and work into the mass from the outside. But they were fast and small, and whatever the hell the cat things were could move even faster. Dom was firing on reflex.

Suddenly it seemed like every Gear in the base was packed into these few roads, shooting anything that moved. The explosions become less of a continuous firecracker of sound and then sporadic ones and twos, and then stopped completely.

All Dom could hear now was sobbing, shouting, and Ravens overhead. Marcus was clearing a space at an intersection of the paths for one of the birds to land. Anya grabbed Dom's arm.

"Come on, Dom." She squeezed his biceps. Maybe he looked in a bad way. "We've got a lot of casualties. Help me do some triage."

One battle was over but the next one had started. As firefighting crews moved in to douse the fires, the task of getting the wounded to the infirmary began.

Adrenaline and drill formed a powerful anesthetic. Dom switched off for the duration and found himself making terrible choices, deciding who was too badly hurt to save and who might make it, worrying about the silent ones more than those screaming, following the procedure he'd been taught and that he'd gone through so many times on the battlefield over the years. There were burns and missing limbs, and abdominal injuries so bad that he couldn't recognize what he was looking at as a live human being.

But he was coping. He worked through the mass of casualties on the ground with Anya and the other Gears. He was coping right up to the moment he saw a small boy; the kid's eyes were wide and he was shaking uncontrollably in complete silence, huddled against a woman who was obviously dead. Dom was paralyzed for a moment.

Is that how Benedicto spent his last moments? Is that what happened to my Bennie?

Marcus stepped out of nowhere into Dom's path and scooped up the kid. "It's okay, Dom," he said. "I've got him. Move on."

Somehow Marcus was always there when Dom reached the brink, and always knew how to pull him clear of it. Dom snapped back into the moment and carried on.

Yeah, as long as Marcus was around, everything would be okay in the end.

INFIRMARY, VECTES NAVAL BASE.

Doc Hayman was the last person Hoffman wanted to cross and the first he wanted around when casualties really overwhelm them.

He found her in one of the two tiny operating theaters, just well-lit rooms with a little more kit than the first-aid stations, standing in blood while she closed.

He was no stranger to blood, but seeing it pooling on a hospital floor was another thing entirely. One of the orderlies moved about the room cleaning as best he could, swabbing the floor around Hayman's shoes with a mop. After a few minutes she stepped back and handed over to Tom Mathieu, a combat medic who'd had to get very good at trauma surgery very fast.

Hoffman had reached a watershed. He tried to work out whether he'd just lost his nerve on a bad day, or if he'd really reached a point where the decision to abandon the island was inevitable.

All on my watch. All these people dead on my watch. What am I doing to these poor bastards?

"I've been operating for six hours. Now I'm going to have a smoke, Colonel." Hayman looked him in the eye, gloved hands held away from her makeshift apron. "If you want to talk, prepare to inhale my fumes."

"Can I do anything?" he asked.

"Yes. Stop bringing me dying people."

Outside in the corridor, wounded civilians and Gears were still waiting for treatment. Michaelson was walking around being comforting and charming to them. They were the least badly injured—nothing minor, mostly severe burns and shrapnel wounds. Anyone with less serious injuries would have gone home and fixed themselves up somehow. Hoffman wandered over to a couple of the Gears and sat with them, unable to say much.

"It's over, isn't it, sir?" one of them said.

"We regroup and move on." Hoffman patted his back. The man's hands were completely black and blistered. "The bastards won't beat us, son."

Hayman came out of the washroom in her white lab coat, an image much more reassuring than her bloodstained scrubs. She went outside into the rear courtyard and stood among the shoulder-high waste bins to roll her smoke.

"Twenty years ago, Colonel, most of the patients who came here alive would have survived," she said. "Ten years ago, I could have saved half. Today, I've lost sixty percent of the traumatic amputations on the table. I've got no safe anesthetics, I started with nowhere near enough plasma, and when the infections start setting in, as they surely will, I've got no decent antibiotics. The death toll *will* rise. I just want you to be aware of that."

She was disturbingly adept at rolling her smokes. It was a smooth, automatic ritual, from licking the edge of the paper to cramming the tobacco inside and somehow, with just a quick roll of the fingers of one hand, turning it into a tightly packed cylinder. She lit it, took a long drag on it, and closed her eyes.

She'd had her say. She was a lot less angry than Hoffman had expected, but she was exhausted and she knew Hoffman couldn't magic up resources for her. There was no point tearing strips off him.

"We've got two hundred and thirty-one dead, including ten Gears," he said.

"Is that including the ones who've died here?"

"Up to an hour ago, yes."

"How did we lose so many? Confined space?"

"That's about the size of it. Large influx of assorted Lambent. People unable to get clear fast enough. We're too overcrowded now."

Hayman just inhaled again and Hoffman didn't see any smoke curl back down her nose for a long time. She smoked the thing halfway down without pausing.

"You sure you wouldn't rather have a coffee?" he asked.

"I know what keeps me going, thanks," she said. "So are you moving people onto the ships? Not just those who don't have homes."

"As many as we can."

"I can't see many wanting to sit tight here now. Not now that they've seen what a random incursion really means. Grubs—well, there was a kind of logic to them. They had a plan. The Lambent are just animals and plants. It's as if Sera itself has turned on us now."

Hayman had a talent for cutting to the chase. No, it wasn't like the grubs bursting out of e-holes back in Ephyra, something they'd gotten the measure of; the Lambent couldn't be kept out by anything, not even granite bedrock, and they were constantly changing into something that seemed worse with each outing. Grubs didn't poison the land, either. There was an invisibility about the Lambent, something that struck a nerve deep in the human psyche.

And the grubs have been through this as well. They ran from the Lambent too. That's why they came out from underground and wanted us out of the way. We can't hold off the glowies now any more than they could.

Vectes suddenly felt very small and isolated. Hoffman hadn't even felt this cornered and hopeless at Anvil Gate.

"I can't take the risk that this is an isolated incursion," he said. "It's never going to stop. And we just can't afford to lose this many people each time."

"Well, a couple more incursions on this scale, and we'll run out of every medical consumable and drug anyway, Colonel. You'll have to shoot people to put them out of their misery. Now if you'll excuse me, I've got an abattoir to attend to."

Hayman stubbed out her smoke on the wall and put the dog-end carefully in her pocket. Hoffman had never been a man to resort to meetings in a crisis, but he had to make a decision now because waiting and seeing how things panned out wasn't going to be an option. He went back into the corridor.

"Come on, Quentin." He beckoned to Michaelson as he pressed his earpiece and gave Control plenty of time to respond. "Time to look at the contingency plan . . . Mathieson? Roundup time. Get Trescu, Sharle, Parry, Reid, Ingram and Gavriel. Main meeting room, thirty minutes."

Walking from the infirmary to Admiralty House meant crossing the parade ground, running the gauntlet of a community that could now see in detail exactly what kind of threat they faced. It had always been at a distance before, experienced via third-hand stories from the handful who'd fought glowies at close quarters. Hoffman and Michaelson

got just fifteen meters from the infirmary doors before someone pounced on them with questions.

"Colonel, we can't stay here now. Are you going to evacuate?" The man was one of the Raven maintenance crew, a
guy called Daventry. "I know it's going to be tough on the
mainland, but at least we can run away from these things
there."

"We'll make a decision soon," Hoffman said, hearing
Prescott's smarmy tone as he said it. *What have I become? Is
that what happens to everyone in power?* Some people
caught themselves sounding like their fathers, but he was
doomed to hear echoes of the Chairman, taunting him that
this government thing wasn't as simple as it looked. "Just
hang in there."

"We're still a few recons short, Victor," Michaelson said,
taking his seat in the meeting room. "This is going to be a
literal leap of faith."

"You've got a vote." The naval base was a strange and
depressing sight from the meeting room window. On the seaward side, the activity in the docks carried on, busier than
ever. On the camp side to the north, smoke hung over the huts
as Parry's engineers cleared burned buildings. "If you think we
should stay put, say so."

"Actually, I don't think we could hold it together here for
more than a few more months, even if there wasn't another
attack like this one," Michaelson said. "People are going to
try to take ships and leave, and Gears are going to have to
stop them. That's the point where everything falls apart."

"But I know we're not ready to go. Not by a long chalk.
We'll fragment anyway."

"But as long as we maintain some cohesion between the
Gears and the civilians, even if the COG collapses, people
can survive."

"And if the COG collapses, what have we got?"

"What have we got *now*? This is basically Jacinto City Council, Victor, with a couple of parishes nailed on—Pelruan and Gorasnaya. And I'm not so sure about Gorasnaya."

How could Michaelson say that, after all he'd been through in the last war? "We're talking about shrugging our shoulders and effectively dissolving a state that's existed for—"

"Just under a century. That's all."

"Why does time matter? Too many people fought and died for it for us to shut it down like it's some thrashball club that's gone bust. I believe in the Octus Canon. I believe it's how we should live as a society."

"Then stick to the Octus Canon. But the Allfathers were just an alliance of imulsion-rich states looking after their own interests during a fuel crisis. In the end, the labels don't matter. Human society does."

"Well, you had the fancy education. I just know it's my flag."

"Come on, Victor. You're smarter and bigger than that."

The argument was cut short as Major Reid walked in with Ingram and Gavriel. The last thing they needed to see was two buddies going at each other at a time like this. Trescu, Parry, and Sharle were just behind them. They all took their seats and looked at one another in silence for a while.

"This is it, then?" Sharle said. They'd had this kind of meeting every week, even back in old Jacinto. For fifteen years there'd always been some crisis or other. "Are you declaring an emergency?"

"What do *you* think?" Hoffman asked. "That's not rhetorical, by the way. I want opinions."

"Let's start with yours."

"We're in pretty deep shit. I think we've run out of road, gentlemen. If we call this wrong and wait, we might not be able to leave at all."

"Well, it got pretty deep in Jacinto, too, but we still stayed. On the other hand, the Locust equivalent of what the Lambent can do forced us to sink the city."

"Is that a yes?"

"Loading the ships and getting everyone embarked is going to take a week or two. I don't want to try doing that when half the naval base is overrun."

Michaelson didn't look up. He was reading something on the table in front of him. "Count me as a let's-go."

"Commander?" Hoffman said, looking at Trescu.

"We go."

"Put it another way." Hoffman glanced around the table. Lewis Gavriel looked heartbroken. Everyone else had evacuated from places before, but not him. "Does anyone think we should sit this out?"

The silence said it all. The Tyran stand-your-ground stoicism did have its limits.

"So the next step is to agree where we go," Hoffman said. For a moment he wondered how Prescott would have handled this. "I'd have wanted to send advance parties to prepare sites for habitation, but that's not going to happen. We have ten locations identified, eight coastal, two inland."

Sharle shuffled through his papers. "And I've got a scenario for that, too. We stay together as a fleet for a while and live on the ships offshore until we're ready to disembark. We just retain a rapid response force in *Sovereign* to provide support for the coastal settlements until they can look after themselves. I mean a defensive force of Gears, medical facilities, and so on."

"And what about the inland sites?"

"They'll be on their own. Especially Anvil Gate. But it's the largest single defensible settlement, so we need to use it."

Hoffman didn't look at Michaelson. He'd muddled along pretending there was some permanence to the command structure, and his instinct was to stay based in *Sovereign*. Damn it, he *liked* Michaelson. The man was his friend.

"If everyone from Pelruan went to Anvil Gate," Gavriel said, "we wouldn't have to split up our community. It could accommodate us all."

That pressed Hoffman's guilt button. "I can't imagine what a trauma this has been for your town, Lewis. I'm truly sorry."

"Can we go there?"

"You're fishermen and farmers. It's a goddamn mountain fort."

"*You* survived there, I seem to recall."

This time, Michaelson caught Hoffman's eye. He seemed to think Hoffman *wanted* to return, that he had something to prove to himself. Hoffman was pretty sure that Anvegad didn't matter to him half as much as staying with the core team in *Sovereign*, but the moment he accepted that people would have to try to live there, he also knew that he was their best hope for survival.

I don't know why I'm drawn to it. But I do know what the chances are of anyone from Vectes making a go of it without me.

"Would you go, Colonel?" Trescu asked.

"If all the defense expertise is in *Sovereign*, that's as bad as abandoning civvies to their fate and going off with Prescott on his jaunt," Hoffman said, ignoring his own instinct. "Wherever the hell he wanted me to follow him."

"Let's work out the detail later," Michaelson said, ever the diplomat. "The bottom line is that we have to use all the identified sites, and we have to clear Vectes and embark. We need to start on that now, and we need to start dividing the population according to where they'll end up. You have yet another variation on the contingency plan, I expect, Royston?"

Sharle never looked beaten, not even now. "Yeah, I have the nightmares so you don't have to. Of course I have a plan. We *always* have a plan."

"One last thing," Hoffman said. "Which has nothing to do with immediate needs, but which matters to *me*. When we leave here, the COG no longer has a capital. It no longer has a structure. It isn't centered in any one location. We may have to accept the fact that it will cease to exist."

The look on Major Reid's face was fascinating. It was almost pity. Hoffman got the feeling he was the last man in the room who thought the COG still existed anyway.

Jacinto City Council. That's about right.

"Do we have a decision, then, gentlemen?" he asked. "We begin evacuation procedures immediately, based on dispersing across ten settlements each with their own garrison of Gears, and head for the southeast Tyran coast in convoy. Are we all agreed?"

Everyone mumbled "yes" except Trescu.

"I think this is where I say it's been a pleasure," Trescu said. "But we'll wait to sail with you. In the meantime, I'd better ensure that we keep pumping imulsion until the last moment."

Like his mutiny against Prescott, Hoffman found the decision almost a blissful relief. He stood looking out of the window, his back to the room as everyone left, and leaned on the wall. Michaelson stayed behind and put his hand on his shoulder.

"I'm not pressuring you," Michaelson said. "But this is a naval operation now. The Gears embarked in *Sovereign* will be marines, effectively. If you want to go to Anvil Gate, you won't be abandoning me."

Hoffman tried to imagine himself based on the helicopter carrier and what would worry him, and then reversed the picture and tried to visualize what might preoccupy him at Anvil Gate. *Pelruan. No experience of grubs. We fucked their little island and ruined their lives in a matter of months. They won't last on their own at Anvegad. So what do we do, split them up and destroy the last thing they have left, their community? It's one thing I know I can do. One bunch of people I can save. Because I've screwed up everything else.*

He just had to be sure that he wasn't seduced by his own pride, the belief that only Victor Hoffman could hold Anvil Gate.

"I'd keep Delta, of course," Michaelson said. "The rapid reaction force has to have priority."

"Sure." Hoffman tried not to show how much that stung. Delta was his right arm. "I'll find volunteers for the Anvegad garrison."

"And I do think we should let Miran have *Timgad* and let him rename her. As you said, he really does need a frigate if he's going to hold Branascu."

"You're the boss once we weigh anchor or whatever you sailors call it."

"I prefer the Gorasni alive and amenable rather than nursing a grudge. The world runs on the trust between individual men, not on regulations and treaties."

"Mind if I take the Hammer equipment? I know it's screwed, but I'd feel safer stowing it where no other assholes can take it from us and misuse it."

"Be my guest."

"Damn. Maybe this government shit *is* easier than I thought."

Michaelson had always been the smart one, the political animal, and his time had come. Hoffman's had, too, but he could see that it would be elsewhere now. The Lambent could come up anywhere, so no place was any more secure from them than another. But he knew he could defend Anvil Gate from other threats like the Stranded who were still out there in their thousands.

What is it Bernie always says? Don't look back.

"I'll expect a weekly sitrep from you, at the very least," Hoffman said. If he didn't break this up now, he'd find himself tearing up. It was old age, he was sure of it. His life had been one long round of sudden, brutal endings, and they'd never caught him short like this. "Did I fail, Quentin? Did I fuck up after all? Have I made all the wrong decisions?"

"Well, we're still alive despite everything, so I'd say you made all the *right* calls," Michaelson said. "Damn, I'm going to miss you, you old bastard. I insist you help me finish that reserve of rum before we go."

"Count on it," Hoffman said.

He waited until he heard Michaelson's footsteps fade on the stairs and took a few deep breaths before he went down to CIC. He could hear a noise, as if someone was already moving heavy furniture out of the building, clonking it down on the floor. When he went into CIC, he only found Mathieson there, but it was a walking, *mobile* Mathieson.

Hoffman stared for a few moments. He'd had no idea that Baird's project had been so successful.

"Well, what do you think, sir?" Mathieson clunked across the floorboards on a pair of forearm crutches and flopped into his chair. "Isn't this something?"

He was walking again. It looked like it was damn near killing him, but he *was* walking, after a fashion.

"You in much pain, son?" Hoffman asked.

Mathieson grinned. "Oh yeah. Like you wouldn't believe. But I'm walking, aren't I? Baird and his Gorasni buddies really did it."

"Yeah, they did." Hoffman patted him on the back. "Goddamn it, Donneld, you've just given an old bastard some hope."

"So we're going, then, sir."

"We are. I'm not going to pretend that it's going to be a

happy relocation, but those assholes aren't going to finish us off."

"Just as well I'm walking, then."

Mathieson adjusted his position and smiled to himself, just a flicker while he was distracted from the events outside. It had been a terrible day of high casualties and agonizing decisions. But here was a man who'd reached a personal milestone that Hoffman had thought was impossible, and it had happened because of a strange friendship between the most unlikely allies.

Just seeing the look on that kid's face rescued Hoffman on the spot. Everyone could adapt.

And everyone could survive, with or without him—and with or without the COG.

CHAPTER 22

*It's funny how differently we see people. Hoffman couldn't
stand Adam Fenix. Still can't. He thinks he was an arrogant,
ivory-tower boffin who should have stuck to his laboratory
and stayed out of military matters. But Major Stroud served
alongside him and she told me he was as hard-arsed a Gear
as she'd ever seen. And he did manage to stop the
Pendulum Wars, didn't he? If we hadn't threatened to wipe
them out with the Hammer of Dawn, the Indies would never
have surrendered.*

(Bernie Mataki, discussing perspectives with Drew Rossi in the
sergeants' mess, VNB)

CNV *SOVEREIGN*, VECTES NAVAL BASE: LATE BLOOM, 15 A.E.

Where there had once been rows of helicopters, rotors folded
and wheels chained, there was now a canyon of stacked
crates. It ran all the way to the deck lift, long walls of random
bricks that somehow managed to look orderly. Bernie picked
her way through a gap, praying that the securing strops held
and that she didn't end her combat career crushed to death
by a bloody grocery larder.

She paused to check the contents stenciled on the sides:

fermented cabbage, salt pork, dried beef, pemmican, dried fruit and vegetables, pickles, and hard tack. The COG's menu had suddenly rolled back centuries to what Michaelson liked to call "the wooden navy."

And Captain Charisma just loves this seat-of-the-pants stuff. It's the end of the world, and he's up on the foredeck or whatever the fuck they call it, laughing in the face of the gale and telling the glowies to bring it on.

No wonder Michaelson's crews would follow him anywhere. He had a bit of Major Stroud in him, that visible, luminous certainty of victory however bad the odds. Bernie wished some of it would rub off on Hoffman.

"Boomer Lady," said a voice from the end of the passage of crates. "You know I ain't the complainin' kind, but you wanna tell me what the hell I'm supposed to do with *this?*"

Cole, silhouetted by a bulkhead light, held up some rectangular objects about the size of a deck of cards.

"It's a ship's biscuit," Bernie said. "Hardtack. Lasts forever."

"Am I supposed to eat it or repair the goddamn hull with it?"

"Soak it in water and make a porridge out of it. Crumble it in a stew to thicken it. Beat vermin to death with it. Dead handy stuff. If you're lucky, you'll get some weevils in it eventually."

Cole handed it to her. The civilians had been working around the clock to make thousands of them. The whole base had been turned into a massive food processing plant, and some wag had pressed the words FUCK YOU PRESCOTT onto this particular batch.

"Yeah, I think I'll wait for them weevils to break it up a bit first," Cole said. He didn't look his usual chirpy self. "Or get Dizzy to drive Betty over it."

"You okay?"

"No. To tell you the truth, I ain't."

"Want to tell your old mum why?"

"I heard about Anvil Gate. All the Pelruan folk sayin' how much better they feel knowin' Hoffman's gonna be lookin' after 'em up there."

Bernie kidded herself that she hadn't made up her mind to go and so she didn't have to tell anyone in Delta yet, but she knew it was a bad case of denial. Of course she was going with Hoffman. How could she not?

It still broke her heart. She wondered whether to tell Cole that she'd had the chance to veto it, but it was all too complicated, too close to making her change her mind.

"He could cope without me," she said. "But I want him to have a better existence than just coping."

"We're gonna miss you." Cole draped his arm around her shoulder and walked her up the deck. "Yeah, that's kinda obvious, ain't it? You're just gonna have to call us on the radio and make sure we've washed behind our ears."

"I will."

Lady, you got a handshake like a Boomer. I like that in a woman. It was the first thing Cole had said to her when they met. The Boomer Lady nickname had stuck. She could leave Delta, but that small stuff would be embedded in her forever. In hindsight, it had been a lot easier to leave Galangi.

"Come on," she said. "I've got to get up to the farm now. I'm not looking forward to this."

"Baird and me, we thought we oughta give you a hand."

"It'll be pretty grim up there, Cole."

"That's why we gotta be there."

They climbed the ladder to the next deck. Baird was waiting on the brow, a small glass jar clutched in one hand while Mac sat at his feet and stared up at him as if he was the most fascinating person in the world.

"Yeah, you'd eat this, wouldn't you?" Baird was telling him. "But you lick your own ass, so what do *you* know?"

"Are you tormenting my child?" Bernie asked.

Baird shoved the jar under her nose. "This is your recipe, right?"

"Pemmican. It's just dried meat preserved in fat."

"Granny, I've flushed things down the crapper that had more taste appeal than this."

"Look, I'll show you how to use it," she said. "When you're starving to death somewhere, you'll thank me."

"Not if he's gotta spread it on that ship's biscuit, he won't," Cole said.

Baird scraped a chunk out of the jar with his knife and plopped it on the deck at Mac's feet. The dog pounced on it and looked up expectantly for more. It wasn't like Baird to make a fuss of Mac, so Bernie braced for a bad reaction to the news that she was going to Anvil Gate instead of staying with the main rapid reaction force in *Sovereign*. It would come, one way or another.

Well, I asked for it. Can't build a bond with people and then just walk away and expect them not to feel let down.

Maybe Rossi could cope with command of Anvegad. Maybe . . .

It was all too seductive. And she was still thinking in terms of command structures and governance, when she knew damn well that the COG was done and dusted the moment they left Vectes. It had to be. Settlements needed to realize they were on their own in a loose alliance of mutual aid, just like the rest of the Stranded out there.

She hadn't escaped her worst nightmare in the end. The thing she despised most, the thing she dreaded, was becoming Stranded—uncivilized, undisciplined, savage. But COG or no COG, she was going to carry on at Anvil Gate as if everything was still in place

"Come on," Baird said. "Haven't we got some cows to practice head shots on?"

Cole sighed and cuffed him playfully across the back of the head as they walked down the brow and onto the jetty. Yes, that was exactly what they had to do. Bernie saw no point in sugarcoating it. The cull had been going on for a couple of weeks and it was getting to her. She couldn't leave it to the poor bloody farmers. There was nothing worse than having to kill your own healthy stock.

She comforted herself with the excuse that if they just abandoned the animals they couldn't take with them, then they'd end up turning Lambent or blown to pieces by polyps. Or they'd starve to death when all the grazing was finally killed off by whatever the stalks were spreading. She was just saving them from a slow death.

And us. We're not going to die. Not now.

Before she reached the main gate, another open truck rumbled slowly past, laden with cow and sheep carcasses and even a couple of deer. It reminded her of TV news footage that had worried her father when she was a small kid, black-and-white images of Kaia's mass culls when a livestock epidemic swept through the island. The sight of dead animals piled high and pathetic legs sticking out at angles took her back to a time when she'd felt scared for reasons she didn't understand. All she'd known was that the grown-ups were afraid because they couldn't make it go away, so she was afraid too, because grown-ups were supposed to be able to make everything all right.

Yeah. And they still can't. I'm a sixty-year-old scared kid now, that's all.

Vectes had a lot more livestock than its population needed. It was good news when Jacinto's refugees had arrived, but now it was a problem that had to be solved the hard way.

"What about the pigs?" Baird asked, climbing into the Packhorse and starting the engine. Mac got in the back seat with Cole and rested his chin on Baird's shoulder, devoted to his new best mate.

"Pigs earn their keep better," Bernie said. "You can pet them if you like. They're really intelligent."

"They're *breakfast*."

"Ah, that's the callous Blondie I know and love."

"Hey, Clayton Carmine stands there murmuring 'bacon' at them. Go lecture *him* about callous." Baird's mouth was set on maximum crassness today, a sure sign that he was upset. "Okay, how hard can this be? What do we do, sit on the fence and just pick them off?"

"They'll panic, Blondie. So we walk them into a barn one at a time, put some food down to distract them, then pop them about *here* at point-blank range." She indicated the point on her own forehead. "If I had horns, it'd be on the diagonal with my eyes."

"If you had eyes at the side of your head."

"Yeah. You get the idea."

Baird went quiet for a while. Cole was talking to Mac about a racing career and seemed to be achieving some level of conversation. They were heading for Merris Farm—Jonty's farm—where most of the stock that hadn't been selected for live transport was being brought. At least poor old Jonty had been spared the sight of his herd being put down. The Packhorse was a kilometer away and she could already hear sporadic single gunshots.

"So," Baird said, not looking at her. "You'll be able to blow the brains out of all kinds of unsuspecting wildlife up in the Kashkuri mountains, won't you? You still got that sniper hat I found for you in Port Farrall?"

"Of course. And the grub cleaver." That was the real Baird she'd come to know, the basically decent human being who gave friends things they really needed. "I'd never part with them. It means a lot to me."

It was probably the wrong thing to say to him, too open and too emotional.

"Yeah, I understand," he said, all bravado. "If Hoffman's going to go, then you've got to go with him. I mean, you're not going to find another guy willing to hump you at your time of life, are you? And you've got him pretty well house-trained now. No point starting over."

"Damon baby, you're gonna get a smacked ass . . . ," Cole muttered.

Sod it, Bernie had to say what was on her mind. She wasn't going to get many more chances. Things left unsaid were the ones that would eat at her for the rest of her life.

"It's okay, Cole." It came out a lot more easily than she'd imagined. "Blondie, I'm leaving my *family*. I'm leaving people I love. Yeah, even you. I know I'm going to miss everyone and how much that's going to hurt, but I know how much I'd miss Vic, too. Besides . . . I don't want him not going to Anvil Gate because of me and killing himself with guilt. I just want him to understand that sometimes you have to say 'You know what? I did my best and I gave it all I've got. And now I'm done.' Maybe all this shit is someone else's fault and maybe it's nobody's, but it's not his."

Baird's knuckles were clenched white on the steering wheel. "Y'know, I was fine when I didn't care. This is what happens when you make a pet of an animal like me instead of leaving me in the barnyard. You just turn me into something that can feel hurt."

It was the raw core of him, sudden and unashamed. Bernie felt terrible, not just because he was right but because he'd taken the risk of dropping his total-bastard act.

"I'm sorry," she said. *And I'm not going to be there to keep an eye on Anya, either. Sorry, Major. But she's definitely capable of looking after herself now.* "But it'll only be for a while, until everyone gets on their feet. A year, maybe."

It might have been true. She had no idea. It wasn't an unreasonable thought.

"And we'll be in radio contact," Baird said, as if it had really made him feel better. "Because you're going to need someone to bitch to about Hoffman leaving the toilet seat up."

"Count on it," she said.

Seb Edlar was standing outside one of the livestock sheds, shotgun broken under one arm while he took a breather. Bernie got out of the Packhorse. As she walked toward him, another shot rang out. It made her flinch. Even twenty-odd years on the front line hadn't managed to make her do that.

"We'll take over, Seb," she said.

"Thanks. I could do with a break."

He looked at the pens of cattle on the other side of the field. Bernie could see some of his big-boned white Pelruans and someone else's dairy herd, pretty little light brown animals with dark muzzles, and a small herd of black bullocks. It all looked so unnecessary until she took in the skyline behind them and noticed the stalks among the trees in the distance—not the far distance, either—and then the reality crashed back in on her.

"Okay, off you go," she said, and patted him on the back.

Baird and Cole opened the shed doors a little and peered in. Bernie looked between them. There was a truck backed up to the doors on the other side, and Seb's son Howell was hoisting a carcass onto its flatbed with Crabfat, the kid who used to crew one of the trawlers sunk by a Lambent.

"Let me get rid of this one before we bring the next one in," Howell said. He looked at Baird, who he'd obviously pegged as an ignorant townie. "Abattoir regulations. So they don't get upset."

Baird turned to Bernie. "Shit, they know what's going to happen to them?"

"Of course they know," she said irritably. *Just like us. Now I know how they feel.* "Species that can't sense danger don't survive."

"No wonder this is taking so long if we've got to do them one at a time."

"Look, just keep them calm and then they never know what's hit them."

She checked her ammo and went to get the next animal. *It's healthy. This is a terrible waste.* Her thoughts must have shown on her face, because she led it as far as the shed and Baird stopped her.

"I can do this," he said. "You just lead 'em in, walk away, and get the next job candidate."

Cole blocked the doors. "Yeah. Leadin' 'em is the hard bit. They *kick.* I ain't doin' that."

"I'm not going to have hysterics," Bernie said. "I was a bloody beef farmer, remember."

"Yeah," said Baird, "which is why a city boy who doesn't give a shit and doesn't understand can do it without losing sleep. You'll just be worrying about losing bloodlines and yields and all that agricultural shit."

Baird and Cole really did care. They were good boys. Only a Gear would have understood why offering to shoot a cow for a lady was a gentlemanly and considerate act.

"He won't screw it up," Cole said.

Baird put on his I'm-a-bastard face, which had stopped convincing her a long time ago. "Well, not as long as I get that rib eye, okay?" He indicated a five-centimeter gap between thumb and forefinger. "About so thick."

In a way, it was worse being the traitor who led the animal into the shed and made it think it was having a nice feed. Mac lay with his head on his paws, staring accusingly at her.

After the first ten, Baird's expression had become fixed as if he'd made up his mind not to let her see any reaction, and then Cole took over for a while. It took four miserable hours. Eventually Baird came out of the shed and fumbled in his pockets. He tossed Mac a ship's biscuit.

"I think I'll skip the steak for a few days, Granny," he said. He looked a bit distant. "No wonder you made a good sniper."

"You're not hungry enough," she said. "Come on, Mac."

Mac had wandered a few meters away and was standing with his head down, flanks heaving. She walked over to him. "You all right, sweetie? What is it?"

He didn't turn around. She only saw the drool at first. *Oh God, no. Not Mac. Please, not Mac. Not him as well.* Her hand went to her pistol as she looked for the telltale luminescence, wondering if she could actually pull the trigger.

"Boomer Lady, what you doin'?"

"Oh *shit*," Baird said. "Bernie, you might want to step back. Like *now*."

Then Mac's shoulders convulsed and he hacked up a cough like a fifty-a-day smoker. A big chunk of biscuit plopped at her feet.

"Greedy little sod," she said, cuddling him with relief. "I nearly slotted you. Don't bolt your food."

Baird grimaced. "Gross."

But Mac wasn't giving up on the biscuit. He picked up the chunk again and insisted on getting into the passenger seat of the Packhorse with it, crunching noisily.

"You better drive," Cole said. "We'll sit in the back. I know what's gonna happen next."

They were halfway back to the naval base before Mac decided he didn't like the hardtack after all. He spat it out again, dropping it in Bernie's lap almost intact.

"I love you, Mac, but you're disgusting sometimes," she

said. "You want me to pass on your complaint to the catering manager?"

The biscuit still had an imprint on it, although dog spit had softened it a lot. The civvies co-opted into making the hard tack obviously had some serious grievances if they were prepared to spend time scrawling angry protests into the dough.

This one just read: PRESCOTT = COWARD.

Bernie decided she would have faced the future with a bit more confidence if he *had* been. Instead, she wondered what the hell a courageous if totally unlovable man would abandon his desperate people to pursue.

GRINDLIFT RIG BETTY, FIVE KILOMETERS SOUTH OF THE IMULSION SITE: ONE WEEK LATER.

Sam hugged her Lancer and stared out of Betty's side window. "I hear Rossi's squad's volunteered for Anvil Gate. *All* of them."

"Well, they got real friendly with the folks at Pelruan," Dizzy said, winking. He didn't plan on going into any juicy detail, not with the girls sitting in the back. "Kinda nice, if you ask me."

"All these people I've got used to. Now they'll be gone in a few days."

They hadn't been here a year yet. People made friends real fast and held on to them harder than they ever had before. "Better gone than dead, Sam."

"Where are we going to go, Daddy?" Maralin leaned forward from the small space behind the driver's seat. "Everyone's got their location. We haven't."

Sam looked at Dizzy. He concentrated on the road. "Depends, sweetie," he said. "You two keep changing your minds."

"How can we tell if we want to go somewhere until we get there?" Teresa asked.

"Now ain't that a woman's logic."

Dizzy knew where he wanted to go. He still didn't think the Pelruan folk saw him as anything but a Stranded asshole, but one thing he'd learned in those god-awful years outside the wire was how to sniff out his best chance of survival. He had the girls to think of. Since the stalks had come up inside the camp, he'd kept them with him twenty-six hours a day even when he was driving through pretty hairy country.

Anvil goddamn Gate. Where the hell is Kashkur, anyway?

Dizzy had complete faith in the Colonel. Hoffman was harder to kill than a cockroach with a machine gun. If anyone could keep a bunch of people safe, it'd be that old buzzard holed up in his mountain fort.

He wondered why nobody else had laid claim to it if it was as safe as folks said, but the world was a real big place and there weren't many people left to fill it.

"KR-One-Five to all callsigns off-camp."

Sam stirred. "Byrne here, One-Five. We're on our way back to base with a mixed cargo."

"Byrne, if that mix includes imulsion, watch out for polyps south of you."

"Thanks, One-Five. Byrne out."

Dizzy patted Betty's dashboard. "Don't you worry none, sweeties, Betty ain't gonna stop for 'em this time."

Sam rolled down the passenger side window and rested her Lancer on the rail, ready to open fire. "Have you seen Barber's recon images of Anvegad?"

"Not yet."

"It's changed. I hardly recognized it."

"Is Kashkur nice? I mean, you're the local expert."

"Bits of it are. Or were." Sam shrugged. "But Anvegad's a long way from any of them."

Dizzy didn't press her. He asked himself if he'd go back to Mattino Junction, but he knew he'd never be able to face it. Sometimes you had to move on. But he wasn't going anywhere unless Hoffman said he could. He was tied to Betty, and Betty was a *resource*, not his personal transport. Len Parry might want her elsewhere.

But someone else could learn to drive her. Couldn't they?

Sam leaned forward and narrowed her eyes. "Roadkill," she said, squeezing her upper body out of the window to aim her Lancer. "Up ahead."

The polyps were cropping up everywhere now, roaming the dead areas in small packs. Dizzy didn't give a damn about them as long as he was in Betty. They'd done their worst to her and she'd survived. It was payback time.

"Save your ammo, Sam," he said. "Roll up that damn window, too. Everybody just sit back and enjoy the ride."

Dizzy hit the gas. Betty could withstand mines, so as long as she didn't stop and let the polyps climb aboard, the little assholes wouldn't do more than make a mess on her paintwork. They weren't as dumb as they used to be, but they still didn't get out of the way when a vehicle approached. About nine or ten were spread across the road. He could see their lights.

It was only ten out of hundreds, thousands, maybe even millions out there somewhere, but it sure did feel satisfying to splat them.

Betty hit them head-on. The explosions shook her as she rolled right over them, but she shrugged them off and carried on. When Dizzy checked in the rearview mirror, there was just a little smoke hanging in the air, dwindling in the distance. For a second it felt like he could solve the world's problems if they'd just let him keep driving over all these damn freaks, but then he caught sight of stalks among the dead, brown trees. It wasn't something anyone could fight.

"Do you ever wonder where Prescott is now?" Sam asked.

"I try not to, sweetie." Dizzy could see an open truck up ahead loaded with sheep carcasses. He slowed right down because he really didn't want the girls to have to look at that for the next couple of kilometers. "It just makes me mad."

"We just don't ask enough questions," she said. "We're so busy staying alive that we just *give up asking questions*. Right after E-Day, people kept asking where the grubs could have come from, but they just seemed to forget how much it mattered after a few months."

"Yeah, well, I did . . ."

"Why? Seriously."

"Because it didn't make a speck o' difference either way. They were there. That was all there was to it."

"I want to live long enough to find out," Sam said. "I really do." She looked over her shoulder at the girls, like she'd forgotten they were there and wished she hadn't started on about Prescott. "But we will, I promise you. It's all going to sort itself out."

She settled back in the seat and stared out the window again. She was a good influence on the girls. Dizzy was going to miss her.

"Control to all callsigns," Mathieson said. "Anyone out there who can call in at Pelruan? We still haven't recovered the war memorial plaque. The vets are still going on about it. We can't leave it behind."

Sam leaned forward to grab the handset but Marcus cut in immediately. "Fenix to Control—Dom and I can get it now. Tell them not to worry."

"Thanks, Sergeant. Control out."

"That's Marcus for you," Sam said. She squeezed her hand inside her armor and took something out, a locket or something. She looked at it for a moment before putting it away again. "Which reminds me. I need to ask Hoffman to do something for me."

It was as good a time as any. "I got to ask him a favor, too," Dizzy said. "Let's go find him together."

Dizzy drove into a ghost town. The camp outside the naval base walls was almost deserted now, with just a few of Parry's guys pulling up cable runs. Most of the huts had been dismantled and the wood reclaimed. He could still see the outline of the paths between the huts, and the stones some people had laid out carefully to mark boundaries. But New Jacinto had packed up and got ready to go, and folks were already on the ships. Some had been on board so long that they were getting fed up with it, Sharle had told him. Well, at least that put them in the right frame of mind for getting where they were going.

Betty rolled through the gates of the base and the parade ground was almost back to its old state, with just folks in uniforms and overalls going about their business, and the only townspeople around were the ones unloading the sheep carcasses from the farm truck outside one of the workshops. The sheep looked like they'd all been sheared recently. Nothing got wasted, that was for sure.

"It's mutton on the menu for the next week, then," Sam said. "Make the most of it."

They looked at each other. "Okay, girls," Dizzy said. "You wait here until we get back. We're just gonna talk to the Colonel. Someone's gonna come along and unload Betty, but you still stay here."

"Does that mean you're going to Anvil Gate?" Sam asked.

"If he lets us."

Teresa groaned. "It's all the Pelruan people. They don't like us."

Sam turned around to look at her. "Then they'll bloody well have to *learn*," she said. "You're as good as them. *Better.*"

"Can we say *bloody*?" Maralin asked.

"No you can't, sweetie," Dizzy said. "We won't be long. Don't go wandering off, hear?"

Sam jumped down and radioed Control. The whole place felt empty and echoing, just like it did when Dizzy first arrived. Goddamn, it could have been nice here. Now it was just one more place he had to forget.

"Come on, Diz," Sam said. "Mathieson says he's up on the walls."

Dizzy followed her across the parade ground to the brick steps that led up to the fortifications. "I thought he'd be in some meeting again."

"He's with Anya," she said. "I don't know what they're doing up there."

Hoffman was leaning on the top of the wall, looking out over the docks with Anya beside him. They didn't look like they were talking, just looking. Dizzy didn't know if he was interrupting anything personal so he hung back and waited until Anya turned her head and noticed him and Sam.

"It's okay," she said. "We were just reminiscing." She patted Hoffman's arm. "I'll catch up with you later, sir."

Poor kid. As she passed them, she smiled like she always did, but Dizzy could see she was trying real hard to look cheerful. Hoffman wasn't. He half turned, and leaned one elbow on the brickwork.

"I'm being a sentimental old bastard at the moment," he said. "What can I do for you?"

Sam looked at Dizzy, a bit embarrassed, but she took a breath and got her request in first. It was all kind of personal now. But nobody had any secrets left.

"I need to give you something, sir. Seeing as you're going to Anvegad." She reached inside her armor again and Hoffman held out his hand. Sam pressed something into his palm. Dizzy could see it was the locket, silver and engraved, no chain, almost worn smooth. "If you find Dad's grave or something, would you put this on it?"

Hoffman had a way of pressing his lips into a line when he was about to get angry or upset. He was definitely upset this time. Dizzy found it hard to stand and watch.

"You got it, Sam." He closed his fingers around the locket. "Count on it."

"Are we going to see you later?" she asked. "Before *Sovereign* slips?"

"Yeah," he said. "Damn, there's so many people I should have spoken to by now. I'm going to have to catch up with most of them during the voyage. Everyone's done a fine job. I want them to know that."

"I think they do, sir." Sam nudged Dizzy and turned to climb back down the stairs. "Go on, Diz. I'll go see to the girls."

"So, Colonel, you got room for an engineer?" Dizzy asked.

Hoffman looked kind of relieved. "You want to come to Anvegad?"

"Well, it's your decision where Betty goes. You'll need Betty more than the others will. 'Course, I know how the Pelruan folks feel about Stranded and Indies. I'll understand."

"Goddamn it, Diz, you're not Stranded," Hoffman growled. "But even if you were, I'd still be damned happy to have you there."

"I do brew good hooch, sir."

"True, but you know how to survive out there in small communities, too. I'm going to rely on you a lot." Maybe he was just being a good officer and saying one of those morale-boosting things that he was supposed to. But Dizzy got the feeling he meant it. Hoffman had never been one for bullshit. "Go see Michaelson and tell him he's got to keep a slot for her. She'll have to be loaded in the right order so you can drive her off first."

"Thank you, sir. I sure appreciate it. I gotta give my girls the best chance, you see."

Hoffman patted Dizzy's shoulder in silence, then looked at his watch and frowned. They were facing away from the sea now, looking north over the base and out across the countryside. Dizzy could see just how close the contamination had come. It looked like someone had dumped a consignment of brown carpet a few klicks outside the camp. The skyline was jagged with the twisted branches of stalks.

"Those damn Gorasni guys are still drilling," Hoffman said. "I better go get them recalled. Come on, Diz. We need to start switching off the lights, figuratively speaking."

Dizzy followed him down the steps. "Includin' the COG, sir?"

"Yeah," Hoffman said. "We're shutting up shop for good."

MAIN GATE, VECTES NAVAL BASE: TWO DAYS LATER.

"You sure you don't want a ride?" Sorotki asked over the radio. The Raven was hovering overhead, its downdraft parting Dom's hair as he waited by the Packhorse. "No trouble."

"Haven't you got loading to do?"

"It won't take long."

Marcus helped Frederic Benten into the passenger seat and closed the door before responding to Sorotki. "Thanks, Lieutenant, but we'll drive. I don't want to rush Mr. Benten."

"Mind your asses, then. Pelruan's Stalk Central now. Two-Three-Nine out."

The Raven peeled off in the direction of the naval convoy assembling one ship at a time at the one-kilometer anchorage. Dom should have been on cargo duties too, but sometimes there were higher priorities. If he was going to uproot a bunch of veteran Gears, he owed them the courtesy of doing whatever might make leaving a little easier.

Benten wanted to collect the plaque from the war memorial himself. Dom understood that completely. The guy needed one last careful look at his home, too, if only to let it sink in that there was no chance now of staying and toughing it out.

Marcus swung into the driver's seat. "Okay, let's go."

Dom settled in the back of the Packhorse with his arm over the rear seat so he could keep watch through the open tailgate. Benten said nothing as the Packhorse bounced over ruts. From time to time, Marcus swerved off and bumped along the grass verge for a while before steering back onto the pavement. The road was cratered and broken where polyps had detonated or stalks had erupted.

Benten gazed out of the window at a horizon that had changed from the gently curved crowns of trees to a barbed-wire wall of stalks.

His voice was almost a sigh. "God, what a mess."

"Soon be there," Dom said. "One day, we'll come back and clear all this."

Benten was pushing eighty. There wasn't going to be a *one day* for him.

From half a kilometer out, Pelruan itself looked untouched. The grass was still lush and the roofs were dotted with seabirds basking on the tiles, not a single sign yet that the Lambent had ever existed. It was an oasis in a brown, silent desert.

Marcus brought the Packhorse to a halt fifty meters from the town hall and got out to look around. Dom climbed out and stood beside him.

"Well, we ended up cutting this fine," Dom said. He

thought of the Gears they'd had to bury on Vectes, like Andresen, and DeMars, and Lester. If he even mentioned it to Marcus it would make him feel obliged to exhume them. There was nothing anyone could do. One day, when life was some way back to normal, they'd come back and bring them home. "It was easier leaving Jacinto."

"Goddamn shame," Marcus muttered. "But third time's a charm."

They could see the war memorial on the green, a tapered square granite pillar with the Coalition cog and eagle emblem on the top and the names of the fallen engraved on two bronze plaques set into the pillar. The grass around it— still green—had grown thirty centimeters without the sheep to graze it down, but everything looked quiet and peaceful.

"I just wish it had looked wrecked," Dom said. "But it looks as nice as ever. And just as hard to leave."

"Okay, let's do it," Marcus said. He turned and went back to the Packhorse. "Mr. Benten, you want me to drive you over there?"

Benten got out, looking mildly indignant. He had his best blazer on and his full set of medals. "I can still walk, Sergeant," he said. "Just not twenty klicks, that's all. Lead on."

The three of them wandered down the deserted street. Dom could smell that bitter, flat, burnt scent on the sea air, and the lack of noise struck him. There were still the rhythmic sounds of the ocean and the occasional cries of gulls, but everything else—the birdsong, the hum of generators and tractor engines, the hum of voices, all the layers of sound that he'd never consciously noticed—had fallen silent. He stopped in front of the memorial, not sure if three men should have formed up in a rank or not, and read the names on the bronze plaques.

They were mainly Gears from the Duke of Tollen's Regiment, the Andius Fuseliers, and the NCOG Corps of

Marines. There were a couple of names from support regiments, but nobody from 26 RTI. It seemed to be the one place that his regiment hadn't made its overwhelming presence felt.

"This is like decommissioning a warship," he said. "There ought to be a ceremony for this."

Marcus straightened up. "There is now. Atten-*shun*."

They all snapped to attention and saluted, eyes forward. Dom found himself following his lead automatically. They stood frozen for a few moments before Marcus lowered his hand—longest way up, shortest way down, a reflex ingrained in every Gear from day one of boot camp—and turned to Benten.

"Anything you want to say, sir?"

Benten stared at the plaques for a while. "Can I have a few minutes, Sergeant Fenix?"

Marcus nodded. "Sure. Take whatever time you need."

Dom walked back to the Packhorse with him and rummaged around in the toolbox for a screwdriver. The plaques were only held in place by screws. Nobody would have dared steal the bronze for scrap, not here.

"What did they do with the flag?" Marcus asked. There'd once been a COG flag flying on the town hall. "We need something to wrap the plaques in. I should have brought one."

The bronze had withstood the weather for years and didn't need protecting. This was the formal, sentimental Marcus that only Dom and a handful of others knew. "Hoffman took it back to the naval base," Dom said. "You know how he is about ceremonial. Let's see if there's anything in here."

Dom was searching under the seats when he heard Marcus call out to Benten. "You okay, sir?"

When he stuck his head up, he could see the old guy

looking a little unsteady, still standing in front of the monument but with one arm out a little to his side as if he was
afraid of falling.

"Just getting old, I think," he said. "I'll be fine."

"Come on. Let's take those plaques off."

Marcus took the screwdriver and a hammer, and strode
off toward Benten. The screws weren't giving up without a
fight: they were a different metal that hadn't stood up so well
to the salt air, and the heads were caked with corrosion.
Marcus tapped the end of the screwdriver like a chisel to
loosen the threads. Flakes fell away and he started easing the
screws out.

"There's a space behind this one," he said.

Benten and Dom moved forward to support the plaque
while Marcus took out the last screw. As it slipped down,
Dom could see a small square hole cut into the stone
behind it. Marcus reached in to feel around in the void,
then took something out and peered at it. He handed it to
Benten.

"Sovereign's Medal," Benten said, looking into his palm.
"Well, I'll be damned. I never knew that was there. Let me
see whose it is." He held it at arms' length and squinted at
the inscription, struggling to read the small letters. The ribbon was faded and stained. "Sergeant, give me the
screwdriver. I'll do the other plaque. I'll call you if I need
you."

Marcus handed over the tools and walked away with
Dom to stand at a discreet distance.

"Goddamn," he murmured. Dom knew exactly what was
going on in Marcus's mind now. "I should have done this for
Carlos. The Tomb of the Unknowns. Before we abandoned
Jacinto. I should have gone back."

Carlos had been buried with full military honors in the
COG's memorial cemetery to its fallen. Dom remembered

it all too well, standing over Marcus as he buried his newly awarded Embry Star in the gravel chippings covering Carlos's grave.

"Come on, it was a granite headstone," Dom said. Had *anyone* kept their Embry Star? The highest decoration the COG could award, and Marcus had buried his, and Dom had sold his to pay for a legal appeal against Marcus's sentence. He'd never seen Hoffman wear his. These things could mean everything and nothing. "There wasn't a plaque. You couldn't walk off with a slab of granite."

"But his name *was* on a plaque," Marcus said. "They were all on a plaque in the mausoleum."

"We were pretty busy not getting drowned. He'd understand."

Marcus looked at him with an expression of utter loss. "I've got nothing left of him, Dom."

Dom still found facets of Marcus that surprised him even after nearly thirty years. They'd grown up together, the awkward rich kid and the two Santiago brothers, so close since childhood that Marcus was family. But sometimes he gave Dom a glimpse of a troubled, emotional man held tightly under control.

Yeah, you miss him as much as I do.

Dom reached inside his chest plate and fished out his pack of precious photographs, wrapped carefully in a plastic bag. He leafed through them—God, all those loved faces, nearly all dead now—and took out the one with Carlos, Marcus, and himself on a rare night out, long before the grubs came. They were laughing at the camera, thumbs up. They were all somebody else back then.

"Here you go," Dom said, handing it to him. "Maria took it. Can't remember which bar it was."

Marcus stared at it. His brow creased for a few seconds. "So we knew to laugh."

For a moment he looked as if he was going to hand it back and say he couldn't possibly take it, but he slid it carefully between his chest plate and his shirt. Benten was still engrossed in the medal. Dom was anxious to get out, if only to shake off the ghosts, but it seemed damn rude to rush the old man. He took a step forward.

Shit . . .

For a moment he thought he'd had a giddy turn, like standing on the rolling deck of a ship. It passed instantly. He was a couple of strides from Benten when it hit him again and he saw Benten totter as well. That was when Marcus rushed forward and grabbed the veteran.

"Get clear!" Marcus yelled. *"Run!"*

Every Gear was alert to tremors. But this felt nothing like an emergence hole forming or a stalk pushing its way out of the ground. The solid earth beneath them had turned into something soft and springy like a deep mattress.

The three of them ran for the Packhorse, but it was like running through sand—wet sand—and then mud. The pungent fuel smell hit Dom as his boots sank into it.

"Shit, it's imulsion—"

Suddenly Dom was half a meter shorter, knee-deep in a soup of grass and mud and looking up at Marcus as he shoved Benten to safety.

"Hang on, Dom."

Dom made a grab for the crumbling edge of the concrete road. "I'm sinking. What the hell is this—"

Marcus reached out to grab his arm and pulled: Dom's boots were on something firmer than the mud but he could still feel himself going down. He pitched forward and got a faceful of oily, pungent mud. For a moment he couldn't see a damn thing and his eyes burned, then he gasped for air and sucked in a mouthful of the stuff. He could hear the Packhorse revving. Marcus was yelling "Back up! *Back up!*" right above him but it might as well have been a world away. Then something hard and cold hit him full in the face.

"Come on, Dom, grab it!"

He couldn't see, but he could feel a rope now. He grabbed it and wound it around his arm. For a moment he couldn't work out where Marcus was, and then he felt the rope jerk as the slack was taken up and he was yanked roughly over a sharp edge that skinned his arm. He hit the concrete chest-first.

The Packhorse engine was still running. "Goddamn, will you look at that?" Benten said.

Dom scrambled onto all fours and coughed his guts up. It took him a few moments to stand up even with Marcus trying to lift him. When he rubbed his eyes clear of the stinging imulsion mix, he still couldn't work out what had happened to the landscape. He had a clear view of the ocean, but the walls of the cottages had vanished. He could just about see their roofs.

"Great," Marcus said quietly. The quieter he got, the worst things were. "I should've taken Sorotki up on his offer. Control? Control, this is Fenix at Pelruan. We're going to need extraction . . . soon as you can, please."

Dom, still coughing, had to stare at the horizon for a full minute before he worked out what had happened. The land in front of them had swallowed the houses, the whole town for as far as he could see. There was a thick, glossy, light brown mud up to windowsill level. He could see whirlpools in it.

"What the fuck *is* that?" he asked. It was the best he could manage.

"Liquefaction," Marcus said wearily. "Where a quake churns the soil and groundwater into wet cement. It can't be more than a few meters deep, though. It's just topsoil on the granite bedrock. You okay, Mr. Benten?"

Dom turned just to check where Benten was. The old guy was standing by the Packhorse's open door, two bronze plaques clutched tight to his chest, staring blankly at the sinking town.

It just kept happening. It was Jacinto again, the sea rushing in, the buildings toppling into the fissures, vehicles and bodies swept down into whirlpools like garbage flushing down a drain.

And then Dom looked past Benten, south toward Vectes Naval Base, and realized the town hall had also sunk halfway into the imulsion cement. They were standing on a small island of solid land, surrounded by deep mud.

Dom sighed, turning back to Marcus. "Is *anything* ever going to go right for us?"

Marcus was looking right past him. He checked his Lancer as if he'd seen something. "Sure it will."

Dom scraped the mud off his rifle and turned to see what had distracted Marcus. He was staring out over the sea of mud. The air was thick with imulsion fumes.

"What's that out there?" Benten said. "Looks like air bubbles."

Dom had to strain to see the slight rippling movement on the surface. The only thing that broke the silence now was the distant crash of waves and the creaking and groaning as the currents in the mud tugged at the wooden houses.

Then his radio popped. "Eight-Zero to Fenix—on our way."

"Thanks, Major," Marcus said. "And watch out for imulsion vapor. We're stuck in a seep as big as the town."

KR-80, EN ROUTE TO PELRUAN.

"Are those Gorasni lunatics still drilling, Nat?" Gettner took the Raven low over the stalk forest that was creeping meter by meter across the western side of Vectes. Baird was about to tell her to shut her yap and put her foot down, or whatever it was that pilots did. "Holy shit, they *are*. Look."

The helicopter passed over the drilling site and got a wave from the crew. "We're going to be out of here within a week," Barber said. "Isn't it time they packed their bags?"

"Isn't it time we pulled our frigging fingers out and got to Pelruan?" Baird asked.

Cole nudged him. "I think the lady's going flat out, baby. Gonna be in town in a few minutes."

"Yeah, no stick, no vote, Baird," Gettner said. "Shut it."

"I never did get around to takin' up fishin'." Cole had a talent for changing the subject whenever he felt things were getting too tense. He crouched down to help Barber lay out the lifting strops on the crew bay deck. "Bernie was gonna teach me. She made all them fly things out of feathers for me, remember? Damn. Ain't gonna happen now."

Baird hung onto the safety rail and looked out over what was left of Vectes. A lot of things weren't going to happen now and he didn't see any point thinking about them. He longed for the days when he felt that everyone in the world had crapped on him and so all he was obliged to care about was the welfare of Baird, D. S.

Just stay alive. Look out for Cole, too. That's all you can do.

"I wonder where Prescott is now," he said.

Gettner snorted. "I couldn't give a damn as long as he's not out there screwing things up for us."

"Oh, you think this shit could get shittier, Major? Do tell."

Gettner didn't bite back with her usual stream of creative vitriol. She went quiet on the radio for a few moments.

"Hoffman's been around as long as I can remember," she said. "And Prescott, for what it's worth. I just wonder how long we can hold anything together without them. However good Michaelson is."

Cole jumped in right away, which told Baird all he needed to know. "The Colonel's just gonna be a radio call away, ma'am. Like he's always been. We'll be fine."

Baird resumed his position at the open door, hanging on to the safety rail. He'd done the run to Pelruan so often that he thought he knew every meter of the terrain by now, stalks or no stalks, but he found himself struggling to work out where he was. He called Marcus on the radio.

"Baird to Marcus. Are you going to be easy to spot?"

The channel popped loudly in his earpiece. "Yeah, I'll be wearing a fucking red carnation."

"Whoa, pardon me for asking."

"Baird, we're on a sixteen square meter chunk of concrete in a mud-field. I've got Benten with me. The Indies couldn't kill him so I'll be damned if a flood of shit is going to get him."

That explained it. Marcus was being Saint Marcus. He'd never have snarled at Baird just because he was worried about his own ass.

"Okay, but I'll want to see some ID. Baird out."

Cole joined Baird at the door, slapping the bright orange lifting strop against his thigh like a fly-whisk. Only a big guy with huge hands like Cole could do that. "Okay, good try, but I gotta start givin' you lessons on morale-boostin' chit-chat. See, what you gotta remember is—goddamn, take a look at *that.*"

Cole gestured with the strop and Baird's eyes followed it. They'd been closer to Pelruan than he'd thought. It took him a couple of seconds to orientate himself because the landscape wasn't the one he was used to. The terrain was shiny and light brown, like simmering chocolate sauce, and only the top third of the houses were visible above it. The stalks

looked about the same height as before and so did some of
the trees. Things had sunk rather than been engulfed by rising mud. A COG eagle emblem, wings outstretched as if it
was waving to be saved from drowning, poked out of the
slime at an angle, the last part of the war memorial left
above the liquefied ground.

"And that's all imulsion soup," he said. "Wow. We didn't
even bring a spare fuel can."

Barber interrupted. "Got a visual on them. Marcus and
the old guy look okay. Dom's covered in shit or something.
And they've still got the Packhorse."

"Underslung," Gettner said. "We're not leaving that
behind. Plan A, ladies. Winch the guys inboard, then drop
Barber and Baird to put some strops on the Pack."

"Gee, thanks, Major."

"I know how emotional you get about nuts and bolts,
Baird." She made a noise that might have been amusement.
"Eight-Zero to Fenix. We see you. Get ready. Benten first."

The Raven settled in a hover above the patch of solid
ground. The more Baird looked at the imulsion-sodden
ground, the more he thought it looked like it was cooking.
Okay, if the imulsion was coming up through fissures in the
rock, then there'd be air pockets glopping to the surface. *And
vapor. Flammable gas. Shit.* Vectes was on one of Sera's
major fault lines, part of a volcanic ridge, so that was probably the layer at which the imulsion circulated. It was that
simple. That was why they were awash with it. It was all
making more sense.

But why now?

He didn't have an answer. He watched Barber lower the
lifting strop and waited while Marcus slipped it under Bent-
en's armpits to winch him inboard. Dom was squinting out
across what was left of the town, frowning. He was caked in
mud.

Baird blipped his radio. "So you fell in."

"No, it gave way under me." Dom looked more interested in something that Baird couldn't see. "I don't like the look of those bubbles. You know what methane does to a chopper. Well, that's going to be—*shit!* Polyps! Look—they're coming right up out of the mud."

"Come on, people," Gettner said. "Chop chop. All aboard. Forget the Pack."

Barber reached out and grabbed Benten's blazer to haul him across the deck. The old guy was clutching a couple of metal plaques. "If we shoot one of those little assholes, we might ignite the gas," Barber said. "Marcus, can you hear me?"

"Yeah, Barber. I know. I *know*. Move it."

"Okay, winch *out*."

Baird and Cole went over to the opposite door and leaned out as far as they could. There were a couple of polyps thrashing their way through the mud. Baird knew from his first encounter with them on *Clement*'s hull that they weren't champion swimmers, but they seemed to be able to handle themselves better in something viscous. It was slowing them down, though.

"They're struggling, Marcus," Baird said. "No rush."

"On deck . . . disconnected," Barber said. Dom thudded into the crew bay. "You reckon."

"Hey, I'll go down and put a sling on the Pack—*that's* how much I reckon."

"The hell you will," Gettner said. "Nat, get a move on. Gas, hot engine parts, kaboom. If I go down, I want to go down fighting, not fucked by chemistry."

"Winch *out*," Barber said. "Ten meters."

Baird trod on Dom on his way back to the other door to take a look at Marcus's progress. He was dangling from the strop about ten meters below and looking none too happy about it. The winch motor chuntered away to itself, reeling him in at a steady rate.

"Baby, we got a bubble bath startin' down there," Cole called. "And more polyps."

Baird did a quick bit of guesswork about gas volumes in the open air. *Nah, not a clue. No idea.* "I'm still up for grabbing the Pack," he said.

Barber didn't blink. "Five meters—four—three—two—one—on the deck." Marcus scrambled to his feet and unclipped the strop. Barber gave him a that's-*my*-job look. "Disconnected, then. Okay, good to go, Gill."

The Raven lifted. Cole was still staring down at the mud. "Y'know, that ain't gas, baby," he said.

"I know." Gettner circled as if she was sizing up whether to go back for the Packhorse. "We're still in one piece."

The whole area for as far as Baird could see was shivering like a pan of oatmeal. Pelruan was sinking. The Packhorse sat like a lonely toy in the middle of it.

"It's *polyps*," Gettner said quietly, so matter of fact that Baird almost didn't take it in. Then he saw spiked front legs poke out of the mud here and there, and within seconds the whole area came alive with the things, hundreds of them.

No, thousands. Hundreds of thousands.

The ground was a seething carpet of polyps, so many of them that they were clambering over each other and running across the backs of their unluckier buddies to reach solid ground. In seconds, it became a tidal wave. They reached the paved road and began to merge into a river of dark gray-green crablike backs. It happened so fast that Baird could only gape. They just kept coming up from the mud as if this was Polyp HQ and someone had opened the gates and told them they had a five-day pass.

Gettner hung on for ten more seconds. "I think we've got

at least half a million of them. God almighty. Where did they all come from? More to the point—how far do you think they're going to get?"

Marcus moved from one door to the other, then back again. "We've got to detonate them. If only ten percent make it south, then we've got trouble."

"They'd have to leg it for seventy klicks, Marcus," Baird said. "They'd probably all be smoke and shit before they reached the base."

"You want to take that chance? Most of our defenses are stowed in the goddamn ships now."

"Fair point."

Marcus pushed past Dom and Benten to grab the Long-spear grenade launcher. "Major, get us ahead of their column and stand by to bang out fast. I'm going to try to get a chain reaction going."

Baird suddenly got the idea. It was an awfully long shot in every sense of the word. "You're going to use the little shits for a *fuse?*"

"It's all we've got, Baird. They set each other off. You've seen it. Cole—stand by to reload for me."

Gettner sighed over the radio. "You better hope they all stay scrunched up close, then."

Baird found himself reaching for a frag. He wasn't sure if he could lob one far enough, but raw terror stopped him just standing there to watch the wall of polyps surging south. The Raven banked and he had to pull back into the crew bay, and then he lost sight of the polyps as Gettner put some distance between the helicopter and the front of the column. She swung the Raven to port at the last moment and held it side-ways on to the road. Marcus had a head-on shot and an open door behind him to vent the backblast. Even so, Baird pressed himself as close to the bulkhead as he could. Everyone took what cover they could find.

"Do it, Marcus," she said. "Give the man some space, people."

Marcus aimed the Longspear and fired. The round streaked out, filling the crew bay with vapor for a moment, and then hit the polyps about three ranks back from the front. The explosion wasn't as big as Baird had expected. Cole had already stepped in to reload the Longspear and a second round was away before the firecracker effect began.

It seemed incredibly slow at first. Maybe that was just the adrenaline doing its thing, Baird decided. The Raven turned away in apparent slow motion just as the whole mass of polyps turned into flashbulbs. The bird seemed to crank up to maximum speed in a split second, and then the whole bay was flooded with brilliant yellow light. Dom flung himself across Benten and Baird ducked, neither of which needed doing, but all their hardwired reactions kicked in. The deafening explosion followed seconds later.

And then it didn't stop. The explosions were so close together that it sounded like a drum roll. The Raven kept going flat out.

"Eight-Zero to Control," Gettner said. "Control, we've detonated an imulsion seep at Pelruan. Hundreds of thousands of polyps on the move. I'm going to evac the drill site just in case. It's only eighteen klicks away."

Mathieson answered. "Control to Eight-Zero, we just heard it. *How* many?"

"Call it a million. A carpet of them across a kilometer of land, at least."

"What's your ETA for the drill site? I'll warn them."

"Three minutes."

Baird tried to look back at the town. Another massive explosion, the biggest by far, sent a fireball climbing high into the air. The last time he'd seen anything like it was when the Hammer of Dawn had taken out the cities. Black, roiling smoke rose up in a twisted column that looked close enough to touch.

"Yeah, that worked," Baird said, feeling shaky. "Holy shit, Marcus."

"Lucky," Marcus said. "In one way, at least."

Mathieson came back on the radio almost instantly. "Scrub the evac," he said. "The Gorasni are driving out."

That brought it home to Baird better than anything. The Gorasni rig workers had hung on to Emerald Spar until the drilling platform was glowing red hot and about to sink into the ocean. They had to be dragged away to the lifeboat. The fact that these crazies were ready to run for it now told him just how big that explosion had been, and how scared everyone was—even Stefan and his people.

Gettner followed the road as far as the drill site. Baird could taste smoke and fuel on the air now. The wind was carrying the debris from the explosion across the whole island.

"Just making sure," she said. "In case one of their wrecks breaks down on the way back."

The Raven moved off parallel with the road and Baird looked down. A fuel bowser and two trucks were speeding south down the rutted concrete, the lead vehicle belching blue smoke from its exhaust. *I could have fixed that for them. They only had to ask.* In the back of the open truck, Amelie the flamethrower woman seemed to be leading the other workers in a spirited sing-song that Baird could see but not hear. She looked up at the Raven and gave them a thumbs-up. She yelled something, too, but it was impossible to hear her. Baird just waved back.

"Hoffman to Delta." Getting an earful of Hoffman always made Baird jump. "Have we got some kind of goddamn polyp uprising or something?"

Marcus took a slow look at the vehicles below as the

Raven matched speed with them. He pressed his earpiece casually as if nothing much had happened that day. "They're coming out of nowhere, Colonel. Something's got them on the move. Had to stop them."

"Understood."

"I don't think they were chasing us," Marcus said. "I think they were trying to get away out of the imulsion."

"Well, that's academic now." There was a pause as if Hoffman had gone to the window or something. He sounded subdued when he spoke again, a different man in an instant. "We can't predict the next incident, so we sail on the next high tide. That's tomorrow morning. Anything that's not stowed by then—too bad." He paused again. "I hoped I'd never see that kind of thing again. Hoffman out."

Marcus scratched his ear thoughtfully, then looked back at the smoke that seemed to be forming a cloud layer across the sky. Baird couldn't take his eyes off it. He was back in Jacinto again, one year after E-Day, emerging from the temporary shelter of a storm culvert with Cole, Dickson and Alonzo to stare at a sky from hell while Sera burned from horizon to horizon.

"Yeah, Colonel," Baird murmured to himself. "I kind of hoped that, too."

CHAPTER 23

I told the COG our time would come, and it has. The new world order isn't about who's got the Hammer of Dawn or the army or the imulsion or the warships, but about who's fit to survive. And that's us. So the COG's finally had the good grace to die, has it? Well, let's see how they cope with being Stranded. There's a lot more of us than there are of them. It's a new world order, and they can't say we didn't warn them.

(Lyle Ollivar, head of the Lesser Islands Free Trade Association,
a seagoing Stranded community sometimes
referred to as pirates, on hearing of the evacuation)

DEEPWATER BERTH, VECTES NAVAL BASE: 0725, NEXT MORNING—THE FINAL DAY OF THE COALITION OF ORDERED GOVERNMENTS, 15 A.E.

Hoffman could taste the soot as he inhaled the early morning air.

A fine layer of gray dust had settled on the jetty. He scuffed his boot in it and hoped it hadn't clogged up vents and filters on board the ships. It was another good reason to get out sooner rather than later.

And it was as good a day as any for the past to repeat itself and remind him of the moment he'd walked out of CIC with Prescott and Bardry to look at what the three of them had done to Sera fourteen years ago. He forced himself to look north to Pelruan. A mountain range of smoke still hung in the air. It merged into a layer of black cloud made up of the smoke and debris from the burning imulsion field that in a week or two would travel around Sera. There might even be some spectacular sunsets in the days ahead.

I'm good at finality. Real good. End of an era, yet again.

"You ready, Victor?" Michaelson asked.

"Just about," he said.

Hoffman had a long and uneasy relationship with ceremonial. It was, for the most part, to give closure—upon death, withdrawal, or commemoration. Today was probably all three. He decided that the simple ritual of a lone bugler or a silently folded flag sealed an event in the mind far more effectively than hours of speeches. But nobody had ever shut down a country and switched off the lights before. There was no regulation to cover it. He decided to treat the ceremonial like decommissioning a ship. Vectes was a naval base, a shore establishment, and that was good enough.

And if any asshole disagrees on protocol, they can write to Prescott. Good luck with that. Come on, Bernie. Where are you?

There was nobody on the quayside now except Michaelson, Trescu, Lewis Gavriel, Anya, and Delta Squad. The last COG standard flying anywhere on Sera hung from a flagstaff on the quay, rippling occasionally in the breeze.

CNV *Timgad* now had a Gorasnayan pennant code painted on her hull and GENERALE EGAR TRESCU stenciled on her stack. If anything said that this was the end of an era, then maybe it was that, not the lowering of a flag.

Hoffman studied the last remaining ships and boats assembled around the docks and realized he was looking at

rank upon rank of people standing on the decks, superstruc-
ture, and every possible vantage point on every vessel.
Damn, he should have asked Mitchell or Barber to take an
official photograph for the record. Dissolving a government—a country—was definitely something a man needed
to keep a receipt for.

But someone would take a picture from the decks. And
he wasn't doing this for the history books.

Michaelson nodded at him. "Here she comes. Hope it's
the right color. Remember Miran's got some big guns now."

Hoffman looked around to see Bernie coming up the
steps from the basin below, clutching something in one
hand as if it was ordnance in need of urgent disposal.

"This is the best they could do," she said, handing him a
piece of folded fabric the size of a brick. He could always tell
when she'd been crying. "I checked. The Tollen boys have
vivid memories."

Hoffman studied the flag in his hand and hoped the
woman who'd made it in a hurry had got it right.

"You can still change your mind, Bernie," he said. "Just
say the word."

"Don't be so bloody daft. It's done."

She gave him a quick salute and walked off to stand with
Delta. It was 0730 by his watch. The moment that he'd been
dreading couldn't be put off any longer and he turned to
Lewis Gavriel.

"Mr. Gavriel, lower the standard."

It was all the more poignant for being silent. If anyone
had the right to shut down this base, it was the poor bastard
who'd kept the island going for fifteen years while it was cut
off from the rest of the COG. Everyone saluted. And that
was the moment when Hoffman truly felt that the COG was
dead.

Gavriel lowered the standard and fumbled a little while

he detached it and folded it. Then he handed it to Michaelson, all very formal and naval.

*What the hell do I say? Does it matter? Will anyone
remember?*

He glanced at his watch. "As of oh-seven-thirty-two this
morning, the Coalition of Ordered Governments is dissolved." Then he walked up to Trescu, saluted, and
presented him with the Gorasni flag he'd had made. "Commander Trescu, as an independent state, you'll be needing
this."

Trescu didn't seem to be expecting it. He returned the
salute a little awkwardly and opened the flag fold by fold, as
if he couldn't believe what it was. He probably had flags
every damn where, but for what it was worth this mattered.
He actually looked upset.

"You may always call on us," Trescu said at last. "Remember that."

"Well, Gorasnaya outlasted the COG. So you kept your
promise to your father."

Trescu gave him a formal bow of the head. "We have
long memories, we Gorasni, and not only for grudges. Safe
journey, Colonel."

Hoffman didn't dare look at Michaelson. It was just too
fragile and difficult a moment for three grown men. They'd
see one another when they were cross decking supplies and
vehicles in a few days' time, and they'd talk on the radio
for a long time to come, but this was the moment when
everything ended.

But some things began, too. "Let's move, Delta," said
Anya. In full armor and with a Lancer on her shoulder, she
looked like she'd never been anything else but a frontline
Gear. "We've got a ship to run."

Hoffman looked up, praying that the Tollen veterans
weren't watching and expecting to find they were. But there

was no sign of them. His gut began to unknot. He hadn't expected to be so relieved that this was over.

But the Lambent aren't. We're just catching our breath.

Michaelson caught up with him on the brow. "That was nicely done, Victor. Very naval. With a little bit of emergency physician thrown in."

"May Sergeant Samuel Byrne forgive me, and his poor damn daughter who never knew him."

"She's definitely not going with you, then."

"No. Her life's here now." It really was time to change the subject. He nudged Bernie in the back. *You're still here, woman. Thank God for that.* "Quentin, is it my imagination, or is this floating casino even more crowded than it was when we first came out here?"

"You know it is. Especially with a zoo embarked."

"Goddamn. I'm going to sleep on the flight deck."

Baird chipped in, right behind him. "It's only a short cruise, but I'll be filing a complaint with the tour company the minute I get ashore, Purser."

This was always the way; after the painful and terrifying moments, the necessary black humor kicked in. Everyone tried too hard. Hoffman went up to the bridge to watch the motley fleet leave Vectes for the last time. It was going to be a straggling convoy. By the time *Sovereign* and *Paryk* had offloaded all the people, animals, and vehicles that Hoffman needed for the overland convoy to Anvegad, the smaller vessels would still be catching up along with their frigate and destroyer escorts.

"Where are *Clement* and *Zephyr* now?" he asked.

"*Zephyr's* tailing us." Michaelson tinkered with his radio console. "*Clement's* sniffing around up ahead. I think it'll have to be her last patrol. Ah well. Her spare parts will live on in us. And razor blades."

Hoffman thought the next few days would be full of the

awkwardness and tearful sentimentality he found hard to handle. But there was a lot of work to do before they went ashore, and it ate the hours mercifully fast. When he finished checking the vehicles on the packed hangar deck that night, he went up to the observation platform next to Flight Control for some fresh air. He could see navigation lights dotted across the ocean as the distance between *Sovereign* and the other ships gradually increased.

Looking out over the ship's wake, he could have sworn it was glowing. He couldn't take his eyes off it.

"It's just bacteria, Colonel." The voice came out of the darkness and made him start. "Bioluminescent bacteria."

Marcus was sitting on an ammo crate at the other end of the platform, Lancer resting on the rail.

"Damn it, Fenix, you nearly gave me a heart attack."

"Baird's looking for you."

It had to be the data disc. Hoffman hadn't forgotten about it, but it had taken second place to the main business of evacuation. "Has he cracked that disc?"

"No."

"I'll go find him later."

Marcus didn't say anything else. Hoffman listened in to the comms traffic on his earpiece for a while, realizing it was probably one of the last chances he'd have for a personal conversation with Marcus but not sure what use to make of it.

And he was going to lose Delta. He couldn't imagine life without them.

Hoffman had a conscience like a life raft. Everything he found floating got piled onto it, weighing it down more every time. He had to jettison something before it was too late.

"I'm sorry," he said at last. Marcus would know what he was sorry for. *I left you to die in prison. Nothing's going to change that.* "Not the first time I've said it, but I'm still sorry."

"No problem, Colonel." Marcus's voice was almost a whisper. "But it's only the guys who didn't make it out of Ephyra who can forgive me."

And your father. But you don't owe him anything, Marcus. You really don't.

Knowing that someone you'd wronged had their own burden of guilt sometimes made it easier to live with. Honest men did dumb, crazy, awful things. It didn't make them bad people. Hoffman knew he'd have to learn to judge himself by the standards he set for others, but it was going to be hard this late in life.

"You listening in on *Clement*?" Marcus asked.

Hoffman changed channels to find the submarine frequency. "I am now."

Michaelson was talking to Commander Garcia. He'd picked up some obstructions on sonar that might have been stalks, and whatever it was lay close to their course. Hoffman and Marcus stood in silence, watching the port side. About half an hour later Hoffman thought he could see land very close even in the darkness, and then shapes picked up what little light there was and he realized what he was looking at. Damn, didn't he know these things well enough by now?

The glowing wash of the ship flowed into a sparse forest of dead stalks jutting above the surface of the water, swirling around their trunks and giving them an odd, illuminated look. *Sovereign* slowed. Crew came onto the flight deck to watch. The ghostly blue display lasted for twenty minutes as the ship moved carefully past the stalks, and then vanished astern as she picked up speed again.

"We're going to see a lot more of those," Marcus said.

Over the next few days, though, they didn't see any. Hoffman found himself still hoping that the stalks would reach a limit and become a nuisance they could avoid but never eradicate, like icebergs and venomous snakes. But he'd seen

Vectes devoured in months. There was nothing special about the place. It was just an early warning for Sera as a whole.

He just didn't know how early.

Michaelson took *Sovereign* a long way north of Port Farrall into an inlet that would cut a few days off the drive to Anvegad. Port Caval still had a deepwater jetty, but very little else. Every scrap of building material and metal had been stripped out, leaving just a slab-sided dock.

"Much easier to offload cargo this way, Victor," Michaelson said to Hoffman. He stood leaning on the bridge console, watching the steady flow of vehicles, people, and animals coming down a ramp straight off the hangar deck. "We'll be done in a couple of hours." He paused. "I suppose you're going to mutter something gruff and stride off through the mountain passes and into the pages of history."

"Actually, I'm going to take a leak and then go round shaking folks' hands."

"After you've washed yours, I trust."

Hoffman laughed, not something he did much, and it caught him by surprise. "Don't make me miss you, you bastard."

"Oh, we'll cross paths again. Give it six months to a year. We'll be on our feet again by then."

Everybody said that. They said it knowing it was anything from fairly likely to impossible. Few people had the balls to say that this was final and they wished they'd spent the time leading up to it in a more fitting way. The final hour evaporated. Hoffman watched the last pickup come off the ramp and steeled himself to go.

"I'm scared, Quentin," he said at last. "I am *so* fucking *scared*."

"So am I, Victor."

"Take care of yourself. You've got Delta, so that shouldn't

be too hard." He gave Michaelson a fierce hug and slapped his back. "If you ever find Prescott, give him a kick in the nuts from me."

"Ditto, but delete Delta, insert Bernie, old friend."

Bernie had told Hoffman that he had to walk away and not look back. He followed the advice. He managed to get down to the brow without making a sentimental asshole of himself, but then he had to run the gauntlet of Delta, and the only way to do that was fast. He worked out who he could hug—Anya, Sam, Cole, Dom—and who got a handshake.

Baird fumbled in his pocket and pulled out Prescott's data disc. He handed it back to Hoffman. "I worked on it right up to this morning, Colonel. I even got a Gorasni ex-spook to come up with some ideas, and he was *paid* to spy on us. But—ah shit, it's beaten me. The Gorasni think it might even need a physical key—maybe another disk run simultaneously, or even a fingerprint."

"Damn," Hoffman said. "I knew I should have chopped something off that asshole before he ran out on me."

It was the best he could do in an unfunny situation. He confined himself to a handshake, but he was now at the stage where he wanted to hug everybody. He looked at Marcus, last in the line waiting by the brow, felt unbearably bad about all the shit between them, and simply shook his hand.

Marcus just nodded. But that was a lot for Marcus.

Hoffman didn't look back. He had a long walk to the front of the convoy, but by the time he couldn't bear to *not* look back and had to turn around, the curve of the line meant he could see nothing but tankers, trucks, junkers, trailers, and the huge bulk of Betty. There were even boats on trailers. Kashkur had rivers and lakes, and fishermen still needed to fish.

It was a whole new existence. It sure as shit wasn't the

army any longer. "Well, fuck you, Chairman," he muttered. "I'm not done yet."

Bernie was sitting in the passenger seat of the Packhorse fussing with Mac when Hoffman got in and turned the key. He didn't look at her, and she didn't look at him.

"You got yours over with, then," he said.

"Yeah. I'm an old hand at this." She cleared her throat. Mac stuck his head between the seats and slurped at Hoffman's ear. "Rossi's taken a rat-bike and gone on ahead with one of the engineers."

"Is this damn dog going to dribble on me all the way?"

"Probably."

"This is your revenge on me for dumping you all those years ago, isn't it?"

"You bet."

"Fine by me," Hoffman said, and drove off.

NORTHERN EDGE OF ANVEGAD PLAIN, KASHKUR: FOUR DAYS LATER.

Bernie got out of the Packhorse and stood staring at a fort straight out Silver Era history. The tiny walled city of Anvegad clung to a rock overlooking a mountain pass, daring all-comers to take a shot at it and see how much good it did them.

"This isn't anything like the brochure, Vic," she said. "Can we get our money back?"

Hoffman had a roll of paper in his hands. He unfurled it like an architect checking a building against a blueprint. "I was shipped out on a medevac thirty-odd years ago, babe. Things might have changed a bit."

He handed her the paper. She'd seen it before. It was a watercolor of Anvil Gate fort, one of dozens painted by his old captain. The man had been killed at the start of the UIR siege, leaving Hoffman to step up and hold the garrison. The watercolor showed a starkly beautiful, barren terrain with an old fort clinging to the rocks, its guns pointing south. Now the landscape was covered with conifers and birch. It was hard to see the fort at all from some angles.

But the twin guns were still there.

"Colonel, you said this place was the pimply ass-end of Sera," Dizzy said, tipping his battered straw hat back on his head to look up at the crags. "Don't look too bad to me. Kinda scenic."

"Well, at least the trees made a comeback." Hoffman looked around, frowning. "Nobody out here now to deforest the slopes. No goddamn goats grazing it to death, either."

"And rainfall," Bernie said. "It's wetter than it was thirty years ago." She pulled out her field glasses and took a look. She could hear a fox barking. Predators meant a healthy food supply. "Goat. Delicious. I'll take a hike up there soon and see what's for eating."

Hoffman studied the fort thoughtfully. "That wasn't there before," he said at last. "The earthworks. That was a steep drop. There's another entrance now. Yeah, it was always a bastard to get vehicles in and out."

Like all old battlefields where nature had healed the land, it was hard to imagine the siege that Hoffman described taking place here. This couldn't be the Anvegad that kept him awake at nights. It was a new place, a *nice* place, all forest slopes and birdsong. A lovely sunrise was shaping up behind the trees.

Rossi walked out of the ancient gates with Ormond, one of Parry's engineers. "Still all clear, sir," he called. "Check-in time."

"Okay—wait one." Hoffman walked back a little way along the row of trucks, adjusting his cap, and stopped at Lewis Gavriel's pickup. "Lewis? Come with me, please."

Bernie thought Hoffman was going to do a hearts-and-minds offensive and let Gavriel be the first to enter the town. Sometimes, just sometimes, he was capable of real diplomacy. Gavriel climbed down from the driver's cab and followed Hoffman to the head of the convoy with that permanent oh-shit-what-now expression that had grown on him in the last year. Hoffman stopped just in front of the gates, came to attention to face Gavriel, and saluted.

"Mr. Gavriel," he said. "I am now handing over Anvegad to civilian control. As commanding officer of Anvil Gate garrison, I am at your disposal."

Nobody was expecting that, least of all Bernie. Gavriel didn't manage to say anything for a moment. She couldn't tell if the look on his face was horror or surprise. He stood with his hands thrust in his jacket pockets, looking as if he was trying to work out if it was a joke. Everyone in earshot was now watching intently.

Eventually, Gavriel found his voice. "But this is your city, Colonel," he said. "I'm just a dockyard clerk who ended up being mayor of a fishing village by accident."

"Well, sir, now you're the mayor of Anvegad. Permission to proceed with the resettlement? I'll carry on as planned until you tell me to do otherwise."

"You don't have to do this, Victor."

"Yes, I do. I said there wouldn't be a military administration for a second longer than was needed. I'll do my job so you can get on with yours."

Bernie had to hand it to Hoffman. He always kept his word. If anyone thought he wanted to be the warlord of Anvil Gate, they just didn't understand what drove him. It certainly wasn't power. He stood back and gestured at Gavriel to enter the ancient gates.

"Oh . . . very well, Colonel," Gavriel said, taking a few hesitant steps inside. "I'm sure we'll work something out."

"Okay, let's move, people." Hoffman waved the trucks forward. "Don't take the peace and quiet for granted. The Stranded at Corren said there were still crazy assholes up in the mountains."

Rossi grinned. "That'll be us from now on."

Bernie checked her Lancer's charge and got back into the Packhorse to wait for Hoffman. He jumped into the driver's seat and said nothing as he started the engine.

"You okay, Vic?"

"Yeah." He didn't look okay. "You want to do the tour? I've got ghosts to visit."

"No worries. Take your time." She patted his hand on the steering wheel. "You know Gavriel's still going to be running to you for permission every time he wants to have a pee, don't you?"

"That's not the point," he growled. "The army carries out the will of the elected government. And he's the nearest thing to an elected leader that we've had for fifteen years."

It was still Hoffman's show, though. Bernie put the same amount of faith in him as everyone else did. He'd drawn up a recovery plan so that everyone knew roughly what they had to do and what had to be stored where. There'd be some changes inside, but he knew the turf.

"Shit, it's tiny." She stared ahead into an empty courtyard like a Silver Era museum tableau. It looked like they were the first people to enter Anvegad in years. "Won't get lost in here, will I?"

"Come on, park up and let's walk." Hoffman put his finger to his earpiece. "Hoffman here, people. Watch out for the usual surprises. Booby traps in particular."

"You're jumpy."

"Well, that's what *I* did, remember."

They left the Packhorse by the south wall and walked along the narrow street, keeping close to the gutter. Vehicles streamed past them, each driver with some kind of street plan pressed against the steering wheel by a thumb or stuck to the inside of the windshield. Hoffman appeared to be heading for the center of the town.

"Garrison buildings are that way," he said, jerking his thumb. "Lots of storage inside the gun emplacement." He stopped to point up at the metal gantries that connected the emplacements to other buildings and walkways. "Even if some asshole gets in here, you can take them out from the top."

Mac sniffed around but didn't stray far. "Where are we going, Vic?" Bernie asked.

"Just got to pay my respects." He took off his cap and shook his head. She suddenly saw him as he was thirty-two years ago, a newly commissioned officer making the hard transition after years in the ranks. That was how their lives had diverged. An officer had to have an officer's lady, not an enlisted Gear. "We burned a lot of the place to the ground and they had to rebuild. Goddamn, it's even smaller than I remember."

It was hard to tell where the fort ended and the town itself began. Some of it was still firmly Silver Era, all narrow alleys and picturesque arches, but now Bernie could see the uglier modern reconstruction. Urban fighting was hard and dirty. She didn't envy anyone trying to take this place—or defend it.

"Ah, I'm not senile yet, then." Hoffman's voice changed. "Well. This is it."

It was just a concrete plinth at the intersection of some narrow cobbled streets. Hoffman stared at it for some time.

"Samuel Byrne," he said. Bernie only vaguely recalled him, but she knew the story almost too well by now. "We had a Stomper position here. He was still sitting on the gun like he was taking a breather. But he wasn't."

The only sign Bernie could see that a Stomper had ever been mounted there was a rust stain in the concrete. History had happened here, a man's history, a man with a name who lived and then stopped living right there on that very spot. Hoffman looked as if he expected the concrete to show more respect. He squatted to touch it.

"Hi Sam. Your girl's doing fine." Hoffman could be a callous and unthinking bastard, but when he spilled his guts, he didn't hold back. He took out the locket that Sam— Samantha—had given him and held it out as if Samuel Byrne could see it. "She's called Sam too, you know that? She wanted you to have this. I don't know exactly where you're buried, but I'll find you, buddy. She's a good Gear. Steady under fire. She's got Sheraya's looks, too." Hoffman straightened up, eyes brimming, and put the locket back in his shirt. "Stand easy, Sam."

Bernie found that kind of raw connection hard to handle. She had to look away for a moment. But this was Hoffman's pilgrimage. He just needed quiet support.

"Am I embarrassing you?" he asked.

"Not at all."

"You're crying, Bernie."

"So are you."

"Well, I'd better get a grip before the evacuees see me, then, or they'll think I'm senile after all." A pickup crawled along the road toward them, unused to the narrow streets. Hoffman pointed at the plinth and flagged down the driver. "Off-limits. Get this plinth cordoned."

Hoffman walked back toward the gun battery, pointing out other landmarks from the siege. That was the gun floor where he'd seen Captain Sander killed by an RPG; this was the council building where he executed a civilian for stealing food, and shot a UIR officer who'd given him water. That alley down there was where the Pesanga detachment sorted out the Indies their own way. Bernie wasn't sure who found it more harrowing, her or him.

"Everyone's got a defining moment in their life if they do anything worth a damn," he said. "Something good or bad that shapes every day of your existence from then on. Mine was here."

Hoffman always rolled up his sleeves and unloaded trucks with the laborers, but today he just sat down on the carved edge of a dry fountain and watched the activity. Bernie wasn't sure if he was just tired from days on the road or feeling his age. But when Dizzy came striding up to him with a big grin, he perked up.

"Just testing the generators, Colonel." Anvegad sat on top of a fast-flowing underground river, giving the city unlimited power and water unless someone decided to blow up the cliffs again and divert the river. "Good choice, sir."

"Yeah, we're going be right at home here, Diz." Hoffman waited for him to walk away and lowered his voice. "Am I still entitled to call myself a goddamn colonel, Bernie? We're all Stranded now. No COG, no army, no rank."

"Vic, everyone needs you to be Colonel Hoffman," she said. "You did the impossible here thirty years ago and people feel safer knowing that. Nobody gives a shit about the technicalities."

"Is that my pep talk for the day?"

"Yes. Everyone who set out from Vectes got here in one piece. Now go find your office while I take a look around."

Bernie worked out that she couldn't get lost in Anvil Gate. It was too small. Wherever she went, she could just look up and navigate by the gun emplacement. The place was crowded and noisy, but by the end of the day they had everyone in some kind of shelter and fed, and Dizzy had mustered a gang of workmen to get the lighting and water pumps working. It was all going to plan, going so well that

Bernie didn't have time to think about people she might never see again.

She decided not to risk walking on the gantries before they'd been checked for corrosion. So she climbed the stairs inside the gun emplacement and looked out over the plain. Mac joined her to contemplate the view, chin resting on the brickwork. There were no stalks, no dead brown areas, and no devastated cities out there, just trees and bushes. The grubs hadn't ever bothered to come this far. It was Sera as it used to be, when the only creatures kicking the shit out of each other were humans.

"Lots to eat out there, Mac," she said, rubbing his ears. "When we've got the place straight, we'll go exploring. Okay? Let's go see Dad. Come on."

She found Hoffman in a small room at the top of the barracks block, staring out at the view through a small window next to a washbasin so old that the ceramic had turned a faint yellowish gray.

"Makes you want to look at it all day, doesn't it?" she said. "So this is home."

"It's going to work," he said, more to himself than her. "I know it is."

Home was a bedroll on the bare floorboards but she'd had a lot worse. There was water, and plenty of it. That made all the difference. By the next evening, Lewis Gavriel had got the communal kitchens set up and Will Berenz had started supervising the conversion of derelict buildings. By the end of the week, it felt like a construction site rather than a ghost town. Bernie had to keep moving Mac out of the way of busy boots.

"Come on." She was still a Gear and her duties hadn't changed that much. "You want to do some work with Mum? Yeah? Good boy."

Bernie made good use of the guns, even if they'd never

fire again. The staircase inside the gun emplacement was broken in places and she didn't risk climbing right to the top, but she could see plenty from the gun floor. The metal tracks were still set in the flagstones, polished by centuries of movement. She paused for a minute, trying to remember where Captain Sander had been killed.

It really was one hell of a view.

It wasn't just beautiful unspoilt scenery. It was designed to be a perfect overwatch position. The road was visible despite the trees' best efforts, and it was the kind of road you couldn't drive off easily with steep embankments and thick forest to either side, so if anyone wanted to play silly buggers she could pin them down with a few careful shots.

This was the whole point of Anvegad. It was here because no invading army could approach unseen, and if anyone was stupid enough to try then they had to run the gauntlet of the guns. She felt powerfully safe. Something about this place made her want to dig in and defend it.

And there's lots of life out there. Goats. Deer. Good hunting. Even fishing.

I think I could get used to this.

She spent half an hour scoping through, more out of habit than anything, until movement on the road caught her eye. Mac pricked up his ears. Five trucks were making their way to the fort. She counted them as they passed between the gaps in the trees, then got on the radio.

Shit, trouble already? She'd just found something to be grateful for and now some wanker was going to muscle in and ruin it.

"Vic, this is Bernie," she said, as if he needed to be told. "We've got visitors. Looks like Stranded inbound. Five vehicles."

"Assume they're hostile until proven otherwise." Hoffman paused. "Where are you?"

"Gun floor."

"Okay. Stand by."

The warning siren blipped a couple of times to alert everyone, a noise that could probably be heard twenty klicks away. Bernie settled down with the Longshot resting on the sill of one of the windows and laid out a dozen high-velocity rounds within grabbing range. A round through the engine block of the lead truck would stop the whole convoy.

Mac stared into the distance, frozen. Bernie couldn't see the machine gun positions to either side of her because she didn't dare look away, but she heard the shouts and orders as Gears rushed to man them. The lead truck slowed and stopped a hundred meters back from the gates.

She sighted up. She could see the driver in her optics now, or at least the fact that it was a man with a rough brown tunic and very old military webbing.

Stranded looted any COG facility they found. They robbed bodies. Who had he taken that webbing from?

Bastard.

The man opened the door slowly and stepped down from the cab. All she saw at first was a shock of white hair, but then she saw his face. It was the tattoos that made her hold her breath for a moment. His cheeks and chin were covered in intricate Islander tattoos, but he was white—very white indeed. She hit her radio.

"*Vic!* Hold fire." She could hardly get her breath. "For fuck's sake *don't shoot.* You're not going to believe who it is. I'm coming down."

Bernie grabbed the ammo and ran down the stairs as fast as she could, Mac scrabbling behind her. It was a long sprint from the bottom of the steps to the main entrance and by the time she got there, the gates were wide open and Hoffman was walking slowly toward the trucks. He had his rifle raised.

She caught up with him just as the driver held both hands out to the sides to show he was unarmed.

"Dear God." Hoffman's voice cracked. He stared at him. "Dear God . . . *Pad?* Padrick Salton?"

"Yes, sir." The driver walked up to him and started a salute, but then stopped as if he'd remembered he didn't have a cap on. He held out his hand instead. "Shit, sir, you haven't changed much, have you? Haven't grown any hair, either."

Hoffman grabbed his hand for a moment and then just hugged him. "Damn! *Damn!* Where the hell have you been, Pad? What *happened* to you?"

Padrick Salton—Private Salton, 26th Royal Tyran Infantry, a sniper just like Bernie—jerked his thumb over his shoulder at the line of trucks behind.

"I've been with the Pesangas, sir. Nobody messes with them." Pad suddenly noticed Bernie. "Mataki? Oh God, I thought you were dead. *Everyone's* here. It's a bloody Two-Six RTI reunion."

"Pad, did you bring Pesangas with you?" Hoffman asked.

"Yes, sir. We heard you moved back into the fort. You don't mind, do you? We just thought you might need some backup. They're no trouble. Well, not to us, anyway."

Hoffman's voice shook. "*Mind?* The whole damn Pesang nation's welcome here. Get 'em inside. We're still fixing the place up, but there's room for them. You bet there is."

"Their leader wants a word with you first."

Hoffman glanced at Bernie, looking stunned. Seeing Pad walk back from the dead was enough of a shock, but to have a load of Pesang hillmen show up too must have winded him completely. He loved those little buggers. It brought it all back for her, too. Yes, this was a 26 RTI moment. The refugees watching this unfold wouldn't have had a clue just how bittersweet this was for them all.

The past never leaves you alone. But maybe that's for the best.

"Fine by me," Hoffman said. "My Pesan's a bit rusty, so I hope he speaks some Tyran."

"You'll manage," Pad said. "And she does."

"She?"

Pad walked back up the line of trucks and helped someone down from the cab. A tiny Pesang woman in a traditional knee-length tunic and scarf walked up to Hoffman and gave him a polite bow of the head. He returned it. Bernie watched, transfixed. Hoffman seemed baffled, though. He really didn't know her.

"Ma'am," he said. "I've had the honor of serving with your people. Welcome to Anvil Gate."

The woman smiled at him. "You do not know me, Hoffman sah?"

Something she said seemed to startle him. Bernie saw his lips twitch.

"Apologies, ma'am," he said. "But I don't think so."

"We never met. Until now. But I know *you.*"

She took a small blue cloth from her pocket and unfolded it. Bernie couldn't see what she was unwrapping at first, not until she held it up by a striped ribbon. It was a medal. It was the Embry Star.

"Oh God," Hoffman said. "Oh . . . *God.* Harua? You're Harua? You're Bai's wife?"

He put his hand slowly to his mouth, completely stunned. The woman took his other hand and placed the medal in his palm, gently folding his fingers closed around it.

"I could not sell it," she said. "It had to come home to you. Bai would want that."

"Damn . . ." More Pesangas had climbed down from the truck. They walked up and stood with her, grinning at

Hoffman like he was a movie star they'd wanted to meet for years. "I'm so sorry. I am *so sorry*."

"No *sorry*, Hoffman sah. These are Bai's sons and grand-children. Your money—it kept us alive. We do pretty good, lots of cattle and land. Now we look after *you*."

For a moment Bernie thought Hoffman was going to collapse. She took a step forward but he seemed to pull himself together and straighten up to become the Colonel again. He helped Harua back into the truck and beckoned Ormond to take care of the convoy.

Pad just stood there, arms folded, smiling. He winked at Bernie.

"Job done, mate," he said.

"Can't wait to hear where you've been all these bloody years."

"Are Dom and Marcus still around?"

"Yes, but they're at sea now." She patted Pad on the back, completely lost for what to say. "This has to call for a drink. I'll come and find you later when I've jump-started Vic's heart."

Pad laughed. "You don't give up on anything, do you?"

He got back into the truck and started the engine, still grinning like an idiot. Hoffman stepped back and watched the convoy roll through the gates.

Bernie held out her hand. "Can I see it?"

Hoffman fished the medal out his pocket and gave it to her. The inscription around the edge read: MAJOR VICTOR HOFFMAN 26 RTI—FOR COURAGE. It was a very plain medal. The more you did, the less it needed commentary.

"So you didn't just send her this," she said.

Hoffman found his voice at last. "It was damn *shabby*, babe. No medals and no pension. I told Chairman Dalyell exactly what I thought of it. It's a hard life out there. The Pesangas live on next to nothing."

Hoffman still had his secrets, then. She was so proud of him that it hurt. If he'd done nothing else in his life, if all he'd ever done was save Bai's family from starving, then he was worth his salt.

"You're a good man for a bad-tempered, callous, bald old bastard, Vic," she said. "I might let you have a share of Mac's dinner tonight."

He smiled. She hadn't seen that kind of smile for bloody *years*. Only a few days ago he'd been fretting about being Stranded, dreading a purposeless existence, and battling with ghosts again. Now he wasn't Stranded at all, and he wasn't a refugee. This was where he was meant to be.

He sidestepped Mac and didn't even gripe about dogs getting under his feet for a change.

"Come on, woman," he said. "Let's go home. I've got a garrison to run."

CNV *SOVEREIGN*, OFF THE COAST OF SOUTHERN TYRUS: EIGHT DAYS AFTER THE EVACUATION OF VECTES.

"Now, who's the last person you'd expect to hear from?" Anya peered around the greenhouse door. "Dom? Are you there?"

Dom stood up from behind the rows of tomato plants. For a split second, stupid reflex optimism bypassed his memory and made him think the impossible: *Maria*. Shit, he should have been past that stage by now. He must have been really engrossed in the plants to have zoned out that much.

"Is this good news?" he asked.

Anya looked put out. "Well, Marcus seemed pretty pleased."

"Who, then?"

"Padrick Salton. You remember Pad, don't you? The

sniper?" Anya did a circle around her face with her fingertip. "Ginger-haired Islander with face tattoos?"

Damn, how could anyone forget Pad? Now that *was* news. Dom tried to remember the last time he'd seen him. It must have been twelve or thirteen years, not long after the Hammer strike. Miracles happened. He'd been sure Pad was dead.

"So . . . where is he?"

"He showed up at Anvil Gate with a convoy of Pesangas. We just received Hoffman's latest sitrep."

"Goddamn." But Anvil Gate might as well have been the other end of the world. Dom really wanted to see Pad. "Are we going to get any radio time? Man, I'd love to talk to him again."

Anya winked. "I'll see what I can do."

She seemed at ease living in this crowded ship, or maybe the novelty hadn't worn off yet. Perhaps it was suddenly having Marcus around all the time. Some people thrived when they were cooped up like this, and some didn't. Dom was already hearing reports of people on some ships asking to be put ashore whether it was safe or not because they couldn't stand the confinement. And they weren't even two weeks out of Vectes.

It took some getting used to, he had to admit. It was often the little things that grated. He had to remember to sweep up the dirt he'd spilled in the greenhouse and scatter it back in the pots. Every scrap of soil had to be brought on board now. All the animal waste was recycled for fertilizer, and even some of the human variety. If he'd thought life ashore was tough, living on a self-sustaining ship was a whole new world of frugality.

And this crew's not going ashore. Not for years, maybe.

He picked up his Lancer and went on watch. Marcus was walking up and down the port side of the flight deck, keeping a lookout. *Sovereign* was ten kilometers offshore but the coast was busier than Dom had expected, with Stranded fishing boats passing close every day to check them out. An NCOG warship was a real novelty here. If anyone got ideas about going after the small boats in the fleet, the sight of the massive carrier towering over everything was a sobering warning. Even with her flight deck covered in huts, storage tanks, and vegetable beds, *Sovereign* still looked like a heavily armed steel island.

"Here we go again," Dom said, pointing northeast at a beam trawler heading their way. "We should charge a fee."

Marcus was watching the trawler through his binoculars. It was chugging closer, almost on a collision course.

"When did they last see a Raven's Nest?" he asked. "You can't blame them."

"Well, as long as they remember we can't swerve to avoid them."

The trawler held its course. It was moving so fast that Dom got ready to fire a warning shot to get the skipper's attention, but the trawler gradually slowed and swung around to come up alongside *Sovereign*.

They looked down over the side. The skipper came out on the deck and craned his neck to look up at the skyscraper towering above him.

"Hey, are you navy?" he yelled. "We ain't seen the COG at sea for years."

There was no easy answer to that now. "There's no COG anymore," Dom yelled back. "No Chairman Prescott, either."

"Ha! You're Stranded too! Goddamn. That's a fancy tub for Stranded, fella. So what are you doing here?"

"Just looking after our fleet."

"You got anything to trade? Couldn't help noticing the fuel tanker passin' through with you. The bright green one."

He meant the Gorasni tanker from the Emerald Spar. Dom could imagine what kind of welcome the trawlerman would get if he caught up with them.

"You better avoid that guy. He's Gorasnayan. They use Stranded for target practice." Dom looked up and wondered automatically where *Zephyr* might be lurking. The last thing everyone needed now was another Stranded boat getting a torpedo up the ass like last time and starting another turf war. "So what fishing towns are active around here?"

"Right now? Port Lorrence."

"See many stalks?"

"Ah, don't worry about them. You can just steer around them."

"Yeah, right," Marcus muttered. "If we want to trade sometime, where do we go?"

"Well, there's me . . ."

"What if you're tied up in a meeting?"

"Just go ashore anywhere you see a camp and ask around. Or signal a boat. How come you don't know that?"

"We've been away for a bit," Marcus said.

The trawler skipper looked at him sideways for a moment, then waved and chugged away. Word was getting around the Stranded network. But this was the way the evacuees were going to have to live, reaching some kind of understanding with every Stranded tribe out here, whether ashore or at sea.

"You heard about Pad Salton, then."

"Damn . . . yeah." Marcus shook his head. "After all these years."

"I always thought he'd kill himself. Remember how weird he used to get after Baz died? Proves one thing. Stranded survive."

"That's us," Marcus said.

Dom was trying to get used to the idea. It wasn't going to be easy to stop thinking in terms of the COG. It was a

whole culture, not just an administration. It was like trying
not to be Tyran. It took time. For the next hour or two he
wandered up and down the deck, an area big enough for a
few games of thrashball if every available space hadn't been
taken up with the business of survival. There were even
pigs penned topside, rooting around in a trough of food
waste.

Is this really so bad? We'll adapt. We always do.

But he was missing Hoffman and Bernie already. It wasn't
right to split up the last of the regiment.

A sound from the ship's broadcast system made him
look around. It was just loud enough to get his attention,
but it was snatched by the breeze. "Hey, Marcus, was that
the collision alarm?" Dom was still getting used to the variety of signals and pipes on board ship. He didn't respond to
them by reflex yet. "Damn, you can't hear anything out
here."

"Control to Delta Squad." It was Anya on the radio, not
Mathieson for a change. "Report to the command bridge."

Marcus responded. "On our way. Was that an alarm? We
can't hear."

"We've got a visitor," Anya said. "He showed up on the
radar, and now he's on the radio. Lyle Ollivar."

"Well . . . imagine that." Marcus began working his way
through the maze of huts and crops that covered the flight
deck. Dom followed. "He's a hell of a long way off his turf."

"He's talking to Michaelson now. Says he's got something
we want."

Dom could think of one really good reason why Ollivar
had come all this way. "Looks like the Prescott pirate deal
theory isn't so off the wall, huh?"

"Well, Ollivar isn't the welcome wagon, that's for sure."

The Stranded bush telegraph was pretty impressive. Dom
wasn't sure exactly how they did it, but a combination of

ground relays and archaic signaling systems seemed to give them almost a global network. It was slow and uncertain, but right now it was doing a hell of a lot better than the failing satellite technology of the COG. In a world that was sliding backward, the Stranded way of life was coming into its own, just as Ollivar had warned them.

And they probably outnumber us. We're trying to be like them now, just to stay alive. The whole damn world's turned upside down.

They reached the ship's island, the huge control tower that made *Sovereign* look in danger of tipping over, and headed for the bridge. Michaelson was standing at the console, binoculars trained on the horizon. Cole, Baird, and Anya were watching the radar over Mathieson's shoulder.

"He must be missing us," Marcus said.

"Oh, we parted on quite civilized terms, remember," Michaelson said. "And he can still count. He's not going to be a silly boy and start a ruck."

"Has he said what he's got that he thinks we want?"

"No, but the speculation is entertaining." Michaelson lowered the binoculars. Dom peered out of the window and saw Ollivar's big white powerboat roaring toward them. "And he's putting himself in our hands, so he must think there's a deal worth doing."

Baird snorted. "Can't wait to see his face when he asks for a ransom and we say he can keep the asshole."

"I see everyone's betting on our beloved Chairman being returned to us," Michaelson said. "Fascinating."

So Prescott had hooked up with Ollivar. Well, maybe Trescu wouldn't feel so bad about losing the Chairman—ex-Chairman—when he heard about that. But Prescott had a reason for risking that meeting, and all the unanswered questions surfaced again.

Now we'll get some answers.

Dom looked at Marcus and nodded. Yeah, he was thinking the same. The pieces were coming together.

They met Ollivar as he climbed up a long ladder and a
scrambling net from the boat below. It was the only way to
transfer, but Dom thought it was a nice psychological
bonus to remind the guy that COG or no COG, he'd be
taking on a fucking *warship* if he got any pirate-shit ideas
this time.

Ollivar stepped onto the flight deck and looked around.

"I bet your Raven pilots *love* all the debris from this," he
said. "Well, good morning, Captain. And how nice to see
you again, Sergeant Fenix. Oh, wait . . . no, it's just Quentin
and Marcus now, isn't it? I'm glad you dropped that COG
delusion at last."

Ollivar was a well-spoken guy in his thirties, a long way
from the blue-collar, moonshine-drinking Stranded image.
This was organized crime. He'd organized his pretty efficiently. Dom didn't underestimate his gang's abilities.

"What can we do for you, Mr. Ollivar?" Michaelson
asked. He'd run anti-piracy patrols for years and it was clear
that he still relished the sport of tormenting them. "Lovely
boat, by the way. I'm *so* glad she's still running."

"Oh, I think you know why I'm here."

"Welcoming us to the Stranded family?"

"Exactly." Ollivar strolled a few paces and looked at a
raised bed of bean plants with its scruffy but effective irriga-
tion system. "I'm *really* impressed with all this."

"Major Reid's brainchild. You'd like to trade vegetables?"

"In a way."

Ah, here we go. Dom glanced at Baird, who had that
smug look of a man who'd bet on the Prescott option. *But
why does Ollivar think we want him back? Maybe he doesn't
understand us as well as he thinks. Or he's got half a solution,
and needs our other half . . .*

"I'm all ears," Michaelson said. "I haven't forgotten what you did to help us deal with the Lambent, by the way. As you can see, it didn't hold them back for long, but it did buy us a little time."

Ollivar looked at him as if he was trying to work out if this was another one of his elegantly worded and smiling threats. "You've found another source of imulsion, haven't you?"

"Possibly."

"You got a fairly substantial fleet up here from Vectes and made enough noise doing it, so I'd say it's more than *possibly*."

Michaelson's expression changed a little, a kind of oh-dear slow revelation. "You do realize that we left Vectes because the stalks overran the place, don't you?"

Now it was Ollivar's turn to look caught off guard. "I hadn't realized things had gotten quite *that* bad."

"Ah. I see." Michaelson changed tack. "Look, we're not trying to muscle in on your various territories. Please don't worry about it. Just pretend this fleet isn't here. Especially the big gray vessels with the guns. They're not here at all."

Crafty old bastard. Dom loved watching him psych someone out, and it was obvious that Michaelson loved doing it. *And he's put him off sniffing around Vectes by telling him it's infested with Lambent.* But when the hell was Ollivar going to play his card?

"I wondered if we might reach an agreement like gentlemen, then," Ollivar said at last.

"Let's try."

"This imulsion . . . and our global connections . . ."

"I know what *I* have that *you* might want, Lyle—you don't mind if I call you Lyle, do you?—but I'm still not sure what *you* have that *I* might want."

"Well, for a start, you probably want to reestablish a presence ashore, I think. That's where I can come in handy."

"Oh."

"What were you expecting?"

"Don't you want to tell me about your guest? Rather aristocratic chap in an oilskin jacket? Couple of Gears with him? No?"

Ollivar looked at Michaelson as if he was nuts. He wasn't putting it on, either. "I'm not sure we're on the same page."

Marcus looked at Dom and murmured to himself. "Shit . . ."

"Prescott," Michaelson said. "I'm not sure he's worth a ransom, but we do want to ask him—and you—a few questions, so perhaps we could reach an agreement."

"I haven't a clue what you're talking about," Ollivar said. He looked as if he was repeating it to himself. "Are you serious? You've lost your *chairman?*"

"It's a little more complicated than that, but he certainly left in a hurry with a box of interesting *things.*"

Ollivar started laughing, that embarrassed, surprised kind of laugh that said he'd played this all wrong. "Damn, you think we kidnapped him? Kidnapped *Prescott?*"

"I rather hoped he might have made contact with you and offered some cooperation in exchange for information."

"You've lost your fucking chairman. *You've lost your fucking chairman!*" Ollivar stopped laughing. He seemed to realize his bargaining chip wasn't quite what he thought it was. "Well, that's a bit careless of you. Why do you want him back so badly, anyway?"

"Ah, if we knew that, we wouldn't be asking," Michaelson said.

Dom hoped Ollivar couldn't gauge the expressions of the squad watching him. He avoided meeting anyone else's eye because the let-down was crushing. Okay, everyone was busy just trying to survive, but now that the specter of Prescott had been raised again, getting answers seemed urgent.

"If I see him, I'll be sure to give him a ride and bring the poor lost soul straight back to you," Ollivar said. "In the meantime, have a think about that imulsion source you've stashed away, and how we might cooperate in future. You're all Stranded now, remember. New world order and all that. We do things a little differently."

Dom finally got it. Ollivar had heard the COG had broken up. Now he saw the fleet as a rival pirate force with a new set of agendas, and he wanted to get things on a business footing rather than shoot it out with a bunch of warships.

"I'll definitely consider it," Michaelson said. "I have the power to do that now that my poor dear Chairman is no longer with us. I'll get back to you very soon."

Ollivar still looked a bit bemused as he did the long, scary climb back down the side of the carrier and dropped onto the deck of his gin palace. It roared away in a spray of white foam and Michaelson let out a long sigh.

"Interesting," Marcus said.

Baird was really pissed off. "Asshole. Prescott, I mean. He can't even do a dirty deal right."

"It's a disappointment, I admit," Michaelson said. He folded his arms and seemed to be contemplating the beans. "Because I have no idea at all now who Prescott rendezvoused with. And he did, I'm sure of it. But our primary goal now is to survive, and all previous bets are off. We have to think differently now."

"Yeah." Marcus sounded unconvinced, but then nodded. "We've still got Lambent out there. And a lot of civilians to find safe homes for."

"Exactly. And who better to help us do that than Mr. Ollivar?"

"So we're doing deals with pirates again."

"Try to think of it another way," Michaelson said, starting

a slow walk back to the bridge. The world had changed again in the space of a few minutes. "They're just seagoing Stranded in an unfriendly world. And like the man says— we're all Stranded now."

EPILOGUE

NCOG RADIO LOG
VESSEL: CNV SOVEREIGN CALLSIGN CNV27
DATE/TIME: 20/BY/15 0455
STATION TO: ANVIL GATE/ANVEGAD
FREQ/CH/SAT: H5
OPERATOR REMARKS: ROUTINE SITREP CONTACT
FAILED. AERIALS CHECKED SAT H5 STILL
UNRESPONSIVE. RADIO CONTACT PRESUMED LOST.
ACTION: ALL WATCHES TO AUTO-REPEAT CONTACT
ATTEMPT DAILY UNTIL FURTHER NOTICE.
OPERATOR: LT. MATHIESON D.